IN MAREMMA

VALANCOURT CLASSICS

IN MAREMMA

A STORY

by

Ouida

Edited with a new introduction and notes by
Natalie Schroeder

VALANCOURT BOOKS
CHICAGO

In Maremma by Ouida
Originally published in 1882
First Valancourt Books edition, December 2006

Introduction and notes © 2006 Natalie Schroeder
This edition © 2006 Valancourt Books
"Valancourt Classics", "Valancourt Books", and the Valancourt Books
logo are trademarks of Valancourt Books.

ISBN 0-9777841-7-7

Published by Valancourt Books
Chicago, Illinois
http://www.valancourtbooks.com
Cover design by Ryan Cagle
Cover illustration: Adriano Bonafazi, *Peasant Girl from Capri* (1877)

Ouida, 1839-1908
 In Maremma. A story / by Ouida [pseud.]; edited with a new introduction
and notes by Natalie Schroeder.-- 1st Valancourt Books ed.
    p. cm. — (Valancourt classics)
Includes bibliographical references.
 ISBN 0-9777841-7-7
 1. Italy—Fiction. 2. Tuscany (Italy)—Fiction. 3. Maremma (Italy)—
Fiction. I. Schroeder, Natalie, 1941- II. Title. III. Valancourt classics
(Series).
PR 4527.I53 2006
823 D374i

10 9 8 7 6 5 4 3 2 1

CONTENTS

CONTENTS

INTRODUCTION

OUIDA (penname for Marie Louise Ramé) was a nineteenth-century literary phenomenon. During a career spanning almost forty years, she wrote twenty-four novels, two volumes of essays, as well as short stories and numerous articles on animal rights, politics, women's suffrage, and the arts. Her bestselling novels testify to her versatility and were read by a remarkably diverse audience: males and females, youths and adults, working girls and elevator boys, canonical novelists and European statesmen. Beginning with the high society novel (for which she is best known), she also wrote romances, political adventure stories, and caustic social satires, establishing a lucrative career as an openly acknowledged female author in a male-dominated profession.

Her flamboyant personality and peculiar, fiercely independent lifestyle also brought her considerable fame. Legendary for her audacity, eccentricity, and extravagance, Ouida, in both her fiction and her life, embodied the contradictory ideologies of the Victorian age. Her vehement antifeminist professions found striking contradiction in her own unconventional, often scandalous behavior. And while she gloried in her independence, she openly avowed a deep-seated longing for romance and marriage that frequently prompted her to ridiculous adolescent behavior based on naïve romantic fantasies. What's more, despite the vehement critiques of Victorian materialism that dominated her work, she lived with a public ostentation far beyond the means of even her conspicuous income.

Ouida's Life[1]

Ouida was born 1 January 1839, in Bury St. Edmunds, Suffolk. The name "Ouida" was derived from an infant attempt to pronounce "Louisa." Her mother Susan Sutton was the daughter of a wine merchant, and her elusive father Louis Ramé may or may not have been the son of a tailor and a secret agent for the then-exiled Louis Na-

---

[1] The materials in this biographical section were taken from Ouida's two most recent biographies: Monica Stirling's *The Fine and the Wicked* and Eileen Bigland's *Ouida: The Passionate Victorian*. See also Natalie Schroeder, "Introduction." *Moths* by Ouida. Peterborough, Ont.: Broadview Press, 2005.

poleon. While he never totally abandoned his wife and child until his final disappearance in 1871, Ramé did not often live with them. In 1857, when Ouida was 18, she moved to London with her mother, her 85-year-old maternal grandmother, and her dog Beausire. Inspired by her new surroundings, Ouida determined to support her mother and grandmother by writing short stories. Their family doctor and neighbor, Francis Ainsworth, introduced Ouida to his cousin, William Harrison Ainsworth, the editor of *Bentley's Miscellany*. When Ouida sent him her stories, Ainsworth promptly published *Dashwood Drag; or The Derby and What Came of It* in the April and May 1859 issues of the *Miscellany*. For the next few years he continued to publish her "society stories," peopled with rich aristocrats and set in foreign places such as Bohemia, Vienna, Germany, and France.

When Ouida was twenty-two, Ainsworth serialized her first full-length novel, *Granville de Vigne: A Tale of the Day*. When her novel was published in three volumes in 1863, she changed the title to *Held in Bondage*. Her first novel was immediately followed by *Strathmore* in 1865 and *Chandos* in 1866. Fueled by Ouida's unorthodox behavior, rumors spread about the "mysterious" new bestselling author.

After mourning the deaths of her grandmother and beloved dog, the young author moved to the luxurious Langham Hotel in London where she spent money recklessly, behaved outrageously, and hosted elaborate dinner parties and evening receptions, often smoking cigars with the men. *Under Two Flags* (1867), featuring the unconventional heroine Cigarette, mascot of the French Foreign Legion, became Ouida's greatest success to date. In 1871, Ouida and her mother traveled to the Continent, and she fell in love with Italy, which became her home for the next twenty-three years. Within a few months she met the Marchese Lotteria Lotharingo della Stufa, a gentleman in waiting to the King of Italy, who "aroused in Ouida the greatest passion of her life" (Stirling 89). They shared a love for animals, politics, and nature, and for several years he showered her with attention. Ouida was unaware, however, of Stufa's long-term love affair with Mrs. Janet Ross, and her friends didn't want to disturb her happiness by enlightening her.

During those "blissful" years, Ouida continued to pen novels, the heroes of which she modeled on Stufa: *Idalia* (1867), *Tricotrin* (1869), *Puck* (1870), and *Folle-Farine* (1871). Her popular children's tale, *A Dog of Flanders*, was published in 1872, followed by *Pascarel* (1873), *Two Little Wooden Shoes* (1874), *Signa* (1875), *In A Winter City* (1876), and *Ariadne* (1877).

After a ten-year relationship with Stufa, Ouida learned about his ongoing affair with Mrs. Ross. Although Ouida was suffering from severe depression, she wrote a scandalous *roman à clef* which exposed the affair. Stufa's lover became the model for Ouida's fictional adulteress Lady Joan, while Ouida cast Stufa as Prince Ioris, and herself as Étoile in *Friendship* (1878). The main characters were compromisingly recognizable. What's more, Ouida declared that except for setting the novel in Rome rather than Florence, everything in the novel was true.

Despite the sensation she aroused by exposing Stufa's affair in print, Ouida still aggressively pursued him, following him twice to Rome until he finally "looked straight through her when she addressed him, and walked on" (Bigland 143). But regardless of her romantic disappointments (or perhaps in part because of them), she continued penning stories. *Moths*, her greatest success both financially and artistically, was published in 1880. *A Village Commune* (1881) and *In Maremma* (1882) (Italian peasant novels like *Pascorel* and *Signa*) were followed by more high society novels: *Wanda* (1883), *Princess Napraxine* (1884), *Othmar* (1885), *Guilderoy* (1889), *Syrlin* (1890), *The Massarines* (1897). In the 1890s, she also published assorted short fiction and her critical essays in *Views and Opinions* (1895) and *Critical Studies* (1900).

Even with her productivity and success, however, Ouida lived far beyond her means and spent money recklessly (on clothes, dogs, flowers, bric-a-brac, and so forth). Repeatedly she found herself in difficult financial straits, which reached a crisis in 1893. When her mother died later that year, Ouida kept the body in the villa for ten days because she was ashamed to have her buried in a pauper's grave. Ouida spent her final years in penury, living alone with her dogs and her faithful peasant maid as her eyesight and health drastically declined. She died of pneumonia in 1908, at the age of sixty-nine.

Ouida's Female Gothic Novel: *In Maremma*[1]

As Talia Schaffer has argued in *The Forgotten Female Aesthetes*, "in her novels of the 1880s, Ouida "explores the female victim of the

---

[1] Parts of this section come from a paper presented at the Eighteenth and Nineteenth Century British Writers Conference, April 14-17, 2005 in Lafayette, Louisiana, and were co-authored by my colleague, Shari Hodges Holt.

Gothic tradition. . . . The Gothic was a useful genre for Ouida, because built into the structure of the Gothic itself is a profound ambivalence about female behavior" (127). In *In Maremma* (1882), Ouida significantly revises the Gothic tradition to reflect a fantasy of female empowerment.

She uses traditional Gothic motifs—the oppressive landscape of secret passages and subterranean terrains, jagged mountains and wild scenery, the dashing bandit and ghostly apparitions, the persecuted heroine and evil aristocrat, imprisonment, madness, and doubling—in unique ways to signify the heroine's ultimately futile renunciation of conventional female roles.

The orphaned heroine Musa is brought up in Maremma, a wild, nocuous Gothic setting, which is, for the most part, a malevolent presence. Pestilential vapors rise from the marshes, killing those who are too weak or too poor to escape to the mountains during the summertime. The towns are isolated, particularly on the ravaged seashore. This desolation, alienation, and gloom, as well as the heroine's ambiguous relationship with her father, are also prime ingredients of the Gothic.

Musa's father, the popular bandit Saturnino, with "gleaming eyes and flashing firelocks" is a romantic hero and martyr to the people. When the bandit is apprehended for murder, to repay a favor Saturnino did for her years ago, Joconda Romanelli agrees to raise his abandoned child. After a difficult climb up a mountain, the hard-working widow finds the bandit's den, with the toddler sleeping amidst loose coins, jewels, and pools of blood—"a scene of carnage." Pitying the two year old "who was left a heritage of crime and woe," Joconda takes the sobbing child back to Maremma. Musa never learns her father's identity, but she grows up on tales about the mythic folk hero.

The town where Joconda lives is "full of miasma and fever in the hot season." Her oppressed neighbors are illiterate and despondent. Both the infectious air and the heavens, which hang over the sea, suffocate the listless, indifferent, God-forsaken peasants. Thus, her hostile environment confines the Gothic heroine from childhood.

Joconda raises Saturnino's daughter as a Christian, hoping that when she dies Musa will find safety and refuge with the nuns. Finding the four walls of the church confining, however, Musa rejects Joconda's plan. The church anticipates several other enclosed spaces that will confine the heroine. Musa's rejection of the nun's life, one of the few roles considered socially acceptable for orphaned peasant girls, is the first in a series of deliberate rejections of the restrictive roles imposed upon women.

Driven by a "restlessness which tormented her like a fever," Musa cares only for things in nature. Although sickness and death are all around her, as if she were enchanted, Musa thrives in the unhealthy atmosphere. She virtually grows up in the sea and from it she gains strength and vitality. Her boat allows her to explore the picturesque, sublime Gothic vistas in the Maremma. From a solitary beach, she wanders farther inland on solitary moors, which conceal buried Etruscan tombs.

Like conventional eighteenth-century Gothic heroines, who discover ruins and secret passages, Musa stumbles upon a buried staircase that leads to labyrinthine tombs. It is there that she first confronts fear and death. When she notices the decayed corpse of a dead warrior-king: "she was afraid, but her fear had the sublimity of awe in it, and nothing of the feebleness of terror. . . . She was afraid, but she was enthralled: the horror that was upon her had beauty and tyranny in it." The womblike tombs are an ambivalent, androgynous shelter. They offer the womb-like comfort of the matriarchy and the confinement of the patriarchy.

When Musa explores the tomb, she discovers "secret passages," and as it grows darker, her terror turns to horror: "a heavy impenetrable" darkness seems to fall upon her, and she falls under its spell:

> For the ghastly dread of the unknown and of the unseen was for the first time upon her. She tried to call aloud, but she was dumb. . . . "This is death!". . . Death had been here so long alone and in peace, and she had broken in upon his rest, and he in wrath had claimed her. So she thought, dully and feebly, as the darkness seemed to bend her under it . . . and she lost all knowledge and all sight.

Imprisoned in the darkness with the corpse—the patriarchal father-figure—like the stereotypical Gothic heroine, Musa faints. When she awakens, she believes that she is free–that the dead are gone, and she recovers from her initial terror of the tombs. Musa's freedom, however, is illusory. While the Etruscan king's corpse has disintegrated with exposure to air and light, his memory fascinates Musa and she returns to the tombs repeatedly, obsessed with knowing where "he" has gone—to penetrate the mystery of death.

For two years Musa continues to visit the womb-like tombs. She prefers the dead to the living. The tombs are a living force, ironically both nurturing, caressing, and imprisoning her. The tombs then become an alternative to an oppressive life of conventional domesticity. The requisite imprisonment of the Gothic heroine is thus transformed as Musa voluntarily makes the tomb her own, not knowing that the tombs have actually claimed her as their own. She disregards the gold and precious pottery, but instead she objectifies the dead, creating her own alternative domestic world in which the dead become her family and lover. However, symbolized in the many intrusions of males into the tombs throughout the remainder of the novel, the power of the patriarchy invades and destroys Musa's illusion of a separate space.

First, as if she had summoned his presence, Musa's actual threatening father, an ancestor of the Etruscan dead, returns. Alone on the moors, she spots a drowning man who has escaped from the penal island, and she swims out to rescue him. Unaware of who he is, she resuscitates him and offers him shelter in the tombs. Jane Jordan's interpretation of this scene is enlightening: "This compensatory control over the father (which suppresses the fact of his neglect in empowering the daughter to give back life to *him*) is important in the novel, which also offers us a symbolic castration, Saturnino having lost his precious dagger in the sea" (95). Musa's reaction to her father, the man who was taken from her when she was two-and-a half years old, in the midst of the Oedipal or Electra stage of psychological development, suggests that her early repressed erotic feelings for her father have subconsciously resurfaced: "the heat of the night was around them like steam: it seemed to her startled fancy as if his eyes and his mouth gave out fire. She was rooted to the ground as by some spell; a fascination that she was powerless to resist held her there, by this young man, though she knew he could turn and rend her as the wild boar tore the young dogs."

However, when Musa leaves the convict alone in the tomb to bring him food, drink, and a knife, he steals the Etruscan gold and flees. Returning to find the tombs ravished, Musa feels violated. Saturnino's betrayal, his pillaging the property of the dead, is a metaphorical rape. Jordan notes the significant sexual symbolism of the bandit's act and states: "The novel . . . plays on the reader's fear of a sexual conjunction between father and daughter. It is not difficult to see the tombs as womb-like, and the entry as vaginal . . . (95). While Musa's first interaction with her father enacts a fantasy of female domination, the "rape" results in the female's anxiety about the pervasive power of the patriarchy.

Significantly, on the night of her father's return, Musa's adopted mother Joconda dies. Despite her fascination with death, the fifteen-year-old girl is unprepared for her loss, and grief-stricken in her isolation, she decides to retrieve Joconda's coffin from the graveyard. Grave robbing is traditionally considered an illegal, sacrilegious, masculine crime, but in Ouida's inverted Gothic tale, the heroine defies church, state, and patriarchy. She digs up the coffin and transports it to the tombs where she places it in one of the inner chambers. There it becomes a magically protective female image.

Like the characteristic Gothic heroine, Musa is persecuted by men, but her harassment takes an atypical form. The goal of Musa's first two pursuers is not the heroine's violation, but to protect and domesticate her—to tamp down her independence. As early as childhood she had shunned marriage, and the offers of two well-meaning men are detestable to her. She is "married" to death. But like protective supernatural presences watching over her, both men reappear various times in the novel and aid her when she is threatened.

However, while Musa resists domestication, she becomes the center of a Gothic perversion of the nineteenth-century domestic ideal. Her life drastically changes one day when a convict who had escaped with her father and who becomes his double, seeks refuge in the tomb. Like the others, he violates her sanctuary, but, unlike them, he is a privileged aristocrat. After he melodramatically kisses her skirt and faints from a gunshot wound, Musa becomes immediately preoccupied with helping. She nurses him to health and taxes all her stamina and ingenuity to find food that will give him strength. She becomes both the feminine ideal of the homemaker and nurse and the masculine ideal of breadwinner and protector. For a while they live together naively unconscious of one another's gender: brooding over his captivity, Este is often oblivious of Musa's beauty and the sacrificial care she offers him. Thus her androgynous life of autonomy remains undisturbed, until she falls in love with her patient. Este, in turn, becomes aware of her sexuality. As soon as he forces her to confess her love for him, he takes on the role of the threatening male who is intent on seducing the heroine. Bored with his captivity, he seeks the "only one joy near him possible to him" and begins to harangue her with his sexual advances.

For a while Joconda's spirit/ghost protects Musa. She denies Este because she had promised her guardian that she wouldn't allow a man touch her unless he married her. Musa quells her own increasing desire by keeping Joconda alive in her mind. Every time Este makes a sexual advance, she retreats into Joconda's inner tomb—a room Este dares not enter. Like a traditional Gothic villain, however, Este becomes unrelenting in his persecution. "[H]e bruised her, wounded her, stung her, bewildered her, tortured her," trying to convince her to submit. Musa only yields when Este appears on the beach like a preternatural presence. Concerned about her absence during a violent storm, Este leaves the security of the tombs, finds her body washed upon the beach, and carries her back to shelter. Because he risked his life for hers, in response to Este's kiss she submits. As a result, Este becomes empowered and Musa transforms into the submissive Gothic heroine: "He loved her; at least he loved her enough to have that power over her which steals all the strength away from the woman it rules, and closes her eyes in a trance."

Predictably, once Este possesses the "one joy" he had sought for so long, he wearies of Musa. She has a prophetic dream that foreshadows his departure and her abandonment. Alone again in the tombs, her love for Este then becomes her religion, and her only hope is that he will return. She assumes a parodic version of the dedicated domestic widow.

Because I hate introductions that give away the whole plot and spoil the suspense for the reader, I will stop here with the deserted heroine, who still has to face death, sexual abuse, imprisonment, madness, vengeance and patricide. I have shown, however, that by reversing many of the motifs associated with the traditional Gothic heroine, Ouida's *In Maremma* provides a critique of patriarchal culture's oppressive gender roles that places the novel in the female Gothic tradition.

Contemporary Reviews

In its 1882 review of *In Maremma*, *The Athenæum* objected to the sexuality in the novel and to Ouida's showing the dark, immoral side of her characters. The reviewer said that *In Maremma* would leave most readers with an:

> unpleasant taste in their mouths. There are cruelty and lust enough in it to satisfy one of Juvenal's ladies. It is ridiculous to pretend that this kind of thing is what is called holding up the mirror to vice; rather is it a picture of the world seen through the distorting medium of a distempered imagination, which either has ceased, or affects to have ceased, to believe in an essential difference between right and wrong, or in the ultimate ascendance of the better side of human nature. (410)

On the other hand, *The Times* said that "*In Maremma* is the most powerful novel that 'Ouida' has lately written; nor is there anything in it to which the fastidious moralist need take exception, although an unsophisticated maiden whose innocence is childlike is betrayed into a connexion unsanctified by the Church." *The Chicago Daily Tribune* gave it even more praise:

> We doubt much whether "Ouida's" prolific pen has ever given to the world a better proof of its unrivalled facility in the delineation of Italian life and Italian character than in this volume, . . . "In Maremma" is a thrilling, heart-moving story, comparatively free from the faults so conspicuous in many of this writers other works, and not devoted to a wholesale uncovering of vice in order to contrast it with virtue. If it is not a book fitted for the shelves of a Sunday-school library, neither is it a volume devoted to insulting morality. . . . "Ouida" is a brilliant novelist. She understands thoroughly how to play upon the chords of the human heart." (9)

Four years later, in her essay on Ouida's fiction published in *The Atlantic Monthly* (1886), Harriet Waters Preston is especially complementary of Ouida's Italian novels:

> I believe the love which this queer genius bears to Italy to be an entirely genuine and disinterested sentiment,—as much so, perhaps, as any of which she is capable. Those books of hers which like, Pascarel, Signa, and In Maremma, may be classed under the head of Italian idyls do really teem with something resembling the large, lawless, unkempt, and yet impassioned beauty of the land itself, while the chronic and patiently borne misery of a large proportion of the Ital-

ian population fires her with a sort of wrathful pity, which in its turn moves her reader to honest sympathy with herself. Moreover, she feels the *picturesque* of Italy in every fibre;...(51)

Finally, in a lengthy 1890 essay praising Ouida, Marie Corelli extolled *In Maremma* as "a perfect Love-Poem" in prose: "Ouida deals with a beautiful *fact* . . . the pitiful love of poor 'Musa' . . . is to the full as touching and pathetic as any of Bocaccio's [*sic*] far-famed stories, and as probable in all points as any of the legends of poetic love and passion in all ages, while the style in which it is written is exquisite, delicate and scholarly to a degree, unsurpassed by any modern *male* or female writer of to-day's fiction" (367).

Natalie Schroeder
Oxford, Mississippi

August 20, 2006

ABOUT THE EDITOR

Natalie Schroeder is Professor of English at the University of Mississippi, where she teaches courses in Victorian literature, Dickens, women's literature, and the Gothic. She recently completed a book-length study of Ouida's fiction and is working on a forthcoming edition of Ouida's *Under Two Flags* for Valancourt Books. She has also edited Regina Maria Roche's *Clermont* for Valancourt Books.

Works Cited

Bigland, Eileen. *Ouida: The Passionate Victorian*. New York: Duell, Sloan and Pearce, 1951.

Corelli, Marie. "A Word About 'Ouida.'" *Belgravia* 71 (March 1890): 362-71.

Jordan, Jane. "Ouida: the Enigma of a Literary Identity." *Princeton University Library Chronicle* 57 (Autumn 1995): 75-105.

Preston, Harriet Waters. "Ouida." *The Atlantic Monthly* 58 (July 1886): 47-58.

Rev. of *In Maremma*. By Ouida. *The Athenæum* 1 April 1882: 410.

Rev. of *In Maremma*. By Ouida. "Recent Novels," *The Times*. 14 April 1882: 3.

Rev. of *"In Maremma"* By the Author of "Moths." *The Chicago Daily Tribune* 29 April 1882: 9.

Schaffer, Talia. *The Forgotten Female Aesthetes: Literary Culture in Late-Victorian England*. Charlottesville: University Press of Virginia, 2000.

Stirling, Monica. *The Fine and the Wicked: The Life and Times of Ouida*. New York: Coward-McCann, Inc., 1958.

A Note on the Text

The Valancourt Books edition of *In Maremma* is based on the first American edition of 1882, published by J. B. Lippincott & Co. (Philadelphia). The first edition was published at London by Chatto & Windus in 1882.

As many of Ouida's contemporary reviewers noted, her novels were filled with grammatical errors. I have retained the original spelling, punctuation, and word usage. Ouida was also criticized for padding her novels with obscure allusions and foreign words. I have made every effort to translate and to identify her allusions. Unfortunately, some of them proved to be too obscure and remain a mystery.

I want to thank James D. Jenkins for his help with the translations and for suggesting that I use a nineteenth century Italian dictionary with the dialect of Tuscany: Pietro Fanfani's *Vocabulario della Pronunzia Toscana*. (Firenze: Successori Le Monnier, 1879.)

IN MAREMMA.

A STORY.

"AMOR CH' A NULLO AMATO AMAR PERDONA."[1]

CHAPTER I.

THERE was a very busy crowd gathered in the cathedral square of garden-girdled Grosseto.

It was the end of October, and the town and all the country round it were awakening from the summer desolation and sickness that reign throughout Maremma from spring-time till autumn, whilst all the land is sunburnt and storm-harassed and fever-stricken, and no human beings are left in it, save the tired sentinels at their posts along the shore, and a few villagers too poor to get away, sickening amidst the salt and the sea-weed.

With late October the forests begin to glow with a golden tinge or a scarlet flush, the fever abates and slackens its hold, the ague-trembling limbs grow stronger, the north winds come, and the swamps are healthy with the smell of the sea or the scent of the woods; the land that has been baked and cracked till it looks like dried lava, or is soaked by torrential rains till it is one vast smoking morass, becomes ready for cultivation.

Then the real life of Maremma begins: down from the mountains

---

[1] "Love, that exempts no loved one from loving." From the "Paolo and Francesca" episode of Dante's *Inferno* (Canto V).

[2] The Etruscan civilization flourished to the north of Rome from the 9th to the 1st century B.C. In Tuscany, Umbria, and Northern Latium, many Etruscan tombs have been excavated, bringing to light innumerable works of art manufactured by this highly-skilled people: carved stone sarcophagi, wall-paintings, bronze reliefs, ceramic vases, golden jewelry, and other objects dating from well over 2000 years ago.

of the Lucchese and Pistoiese districts laborers troop by the thousands; shepherds come from the hills with long lines of flocks; herds of horses and cattle go daily by the roads; hunters chase the boar and buck, and charcoal-burners and ploughmen pour themselves in busy legions over the plains and the woods.

The country then is full of the men come down from the hills, from far and near, *"il montanino con scarpe grosse e cervello fine,"*[1] whom the Maremmano employs, envies, and detests; brown, erect, healthy, smiling, stalwart; looking beside the pale, swollen, ague-shaken creatures who live there all the year through, like life beside death. They are all mountain-born, and chiefly from the chestnut woods of the northern spurs of the Apennines, where the snow has fallen already; here, down in the green Maremma, they will, year after year, arrive all their lives through, to plough and harrow and sow, to hew and saw and burn wood for timber and charcoal, all the winter long; and then, after waiting perhaps for the first hay-stacking or wheat harvest, will go back, with the money in their pockets, to reap and plough and gather the nuts and prune the olive on their own hills; a half-nomadic, half-home life, that is rough and healthy, changeful and pleasant, and makes them half vagrant and half husbandman; bitter foes and hot lovers; faithless ones, too; for when the Maremma girl sings of her lover he is always some Pistoiese or Lucchese *damo* from the Apennines, and the burden of her song is always one of absence, of doubt, and of inconstancy.

When he goes away with the rich loads of summer grass or grain, he goes to his own hamlet up high in the chestnut forests of a healthier land, and it is seldom indeed that he will cast any backward look of regret to misty Maremma steaming beneath its sickly suns. And when he comes back another year there,—then he finds some one else.

This day in Grosseto there were many hundreds of them come there for the hiring by owners and stewards of this perilous yet fruitful Maremmano soil; the same men came for the most part year after year, and were well known; the market-day was the day to find masters and make terms for their winter labors; and from here they would all scatter themselves far and wide, north and south, east and west, on their several roads; some to the swamps and the thickets; some to the

---

[1] Literally, "The mountain man with large shoes and a fine brain." "*Cervello fine*" could also suggest a "shrewd mind."

pine and oak woods; some to the seashore towns for the industries of the coast; some to the vast level fields that stretch level and dreary as moorland and bring forth the finest grain in all Italy.

There were gathered together hundreds and even thousands of them; but this morning they had other thoughts besides those of their hire and wages; they were standing under the broad, blue, autumnal sky, patient, and yet eager to see a great sight,—no less a sight than the passing through Grosseto of the brigand-chief of Santa Fiora,—Saturnino Mastarna.

The news of his capture had startled the town at midnight when the carabineers had ridden in, thirty strong, with a man bound hard and fast in the midst of them; and the Grosseto citizens, for the most part in their beds, had lit their lanterns hurriedly and thrown open their casemates as the tramp of the horses and the clatter of the weapons had awakened them from sleep.

"He was a man!" the good folks had said, with a sigh of sympathy and regret, and had murmured to each other mournfully, "*È il nostro Saturnino!*"[1]

As the troop of guards went past under the dull brown walls of their dull little city, a torch here and there flickering on their naked sabres and the barrels of their short carbines, and a moonbeam here and there glistening on the whiteness of their cross-belts and the foam on the manes of their horses, there were few in Grosseto who did not pity the captive in their midst, with his arms tied tightly by cords behind his back,—few who did not for his sake wish the troopers a sudden death and a bad one.

When the trot of the chargers and the clash of the steel had passed into silence, and the town had lapsed into its wonted quietude, the burghers of Grosseto, putting out their lanterns, had sighed, "*Quel povero Saturnino, Aie! Chè peccato!*"[2] For Maremma had always adored her Saturnino, and it regretted his capture very greatly; he had never done any harm, he had only robbed the rich and killed a foreigner now and then; he had been a holy man, and the priests had always been the better for anything he had done; and he had been so precious as a theme for talk in the long, dreary, wintry nights, in the still longer, still drearier, summer days.

---

[1] He's our Saturnino.
[2] That poor Saturnino. What a shame!

Without Saturnino Mastarna the Maremma would be more than ever desolate.

The province had always been full of sympathy with its great robber, whose popular boast it was that he never had wronged any poor man. All the creatures of the law, soldiers, guards, coast-guards, and carabineers, were hated and shunned throughout the province, got help from none, and were again and again baffled and laughed at by the shrewd finesse of the people in the woods and on the shores. To cheat a *sbirro*[1] was a loyal task that brought praise and honor to whosoever had accomplished it.

Therefore for years the seizing of Saturnino had been impossible, and scarcely even desired by the authorities, so great an unpopularity was his capture certain to produce.

But at the last the brigand had grown too audacious: he had seized foreigners of note, and foreign governments had bestirred themselves, and it had been thought needful to show some vigor and vigilance against a mocker of the law who would stride about in the towns of the Maremma in festal bravery, secure of immunity, and boasting that no ruler of them all would dare to touch him. Troops were put in motion; municipalities were arraigned by ministers, and at last it was felt that the great days of Saturnino Mastarna must be numbered.

All men in Grosseto this autumn day were talking of that one theme: Saturnino of Santa Fiora—il gran' Saturnino!

So they murmured with one accord, leaving business and bargains to crowd together and tell the tale over a thousand times and in a thousand different ways, and agree among each other, cordially and with many an oath, that to have captured Saturnino and slung him across a horse's back, with heels tied together like any sheep's, was a sin and shame in the executive.

For Saturnino had been their hero, looming as large as gods loom in the mist of myths. "He was a man!" they muttered one to another; and then the natives of the little city seized the strangers who came down for the first time from the Lucchese hills, and told them wondrous tales in passionate high vibrating voices, and cried a hundred times,—

"Do your mountains breed the like? Nay, not they. There is but

---

[1] Unkind name for a policeman (cop).

one Saturnino. Never would he hurt the poor. Nay, not a poor soul in the land but had him for a friend. And a dutiful man too has he always been. When he came down into the towns, straightway would he go to the church and be shriven, and to the Madonna he would send always half the jewels that he might light upon: a good man and a great! And now, see you,—oh, the pity of it!—they have trapped him and taken him, like any greenfinch in a net. Well, he will not be forgotten. We will tell our children's children."

Then, as talk is always thirsty work, they would go in and drink a good rough red wine, with the Lucchese and Pistoiese strangers, wherever some green bough hung out over a doorway, and over the wine tell how a wagon full of barrels of Neapolitan Lacrima had been stopped but last week by Saturnino on the Orbitello road, and the wagoner, because a crusty and unpersuadable obstinate, had been left in the dust with his feet cut off, Saturnino being intolerant of obstinacy.

Meanwhile, the yellow autumnal sun shone on the gray stones of Grosseto, and bells clanged, mules brayed, horses champed, swords clattered, and towards the doors of the prison a fresh *péloton* of carabineers, come to replace the jaded escort of Saturnino, rode slowly across the square amidst the muttering of the hostile people. What mattered the wine-carrier? He had been only a Romagnolo.[1]

Besides, all Maremma knew that it was not for the wine-carrier at all that their demigod had been hunted down, but for a *straniero*,[2] that no one cared about except the government,—a traveller that Saturnino had shot in a paroxysm of jealous rage, and who had been a person of distinction enough for the nation to which he belonged to demand that justice should be done on his assassin. The stranger had been waiting for a ransom to be sent, and had looked at the beautiful Serapia who dwelt with Saturnino too long or too boldly, and Saturnino without waste of words had blown his brains out,—a rash act of violence which had become his own undoing.

The government had been told by foreign nations that it behooved its own honor not to leave him at large any longer. So strenuous efforts had been made all summer through, and the hill-sides had swarmed

---

[1] *Romagnolo*: From Romagna, now part of Emilio-Romagna, a northern Italian region bordering Tuscany.
[2] Foreigner.

with scouts and sharpshooters, and at last on one misty October night the State had been one too many for its wary and ferocious son, and Saturnino, asleep and heavy with wine, had been surprised, and, after bitter and murderous resistance, been vanquished, and dragged from where he dwelt among the clouds of the mountain's top, where Monte Labbro reared its silver summit to the whiteness of the moon.

All men of the Maremma had been proud that their province boasted so dread a name as Saturnino's,—a name sweeping clear, like a scythe, all the country-side of travellers, and resounding even down to the very walls of Rome.

That terrible shape and rumor up there in the Maremma labyrinths above the stormy Fiora water had lent mystery and majesty to the land,—had hung a dread tale to every wayside bush along the lone sea-roads and haunted every thicket of mastic and laurel that grew above the old ways of Porsenna's[1] kingdoms. They had been proud of Saturnino, the great Saturnino, at the lifting of whose voice all the wet grass upon a summer's night would grow suddenly alive with gleaming eyes and flashing firelocks, as though he called men up from the very stones to do his bidding.

And now Saturnino had been taken,—taken just like any common thief who robbed an old dame of a copper coin,—taken by those general foes, the soldiery, and brought down into the lower lands with his feet tied under a horse's belly, as helpless as though he were a kid in a butcher's hands. They were restless, curious, passionately eager to see and hear; but there was only one emotion among them,—regret,—a regret which was full of resentment and sympathy and indignation; and which would have burned fiercer and higher and become revolt and rescue had not the military force been strong and the mounted guards many.

All the multitude was awed and chilled. A heavy sense of the power of the law—of a law which they had no sympathy for, and which they feared with the angry fear of impatient resentment—was weighty upon them, like a sheet of lead.

Many of them were sensible of more or less close abetting of the hill thieves, more or less passive or active interest in the lawless acts of the band of Santa Fiora. Many a tradesman there had never sought

---

[1] Lars Porsenna was an Etruscan king known for his war against the city of Rome.

too curiously to know how the black-browed seller of rich brocades or costly jewelry had come by them, or how foreign gold had found its way to sunburnt, powder-blackened hands.

Even those to whom the great Saturnino was but a name, the youngsters come down for work from the high villages of the Carrarese and Lucchese ranges, were dumfounded and regretful. Saturnino had always been the friend of the forester and the ploughman and the shepherd; the lads felt that when no more tales could be told of the king of Maremma, savor would be gone out of the goat's flesh roasted in the charcoal in the woods, and the wine-flask passed round when the last of the long furrows had been turned across the plains.

In a gloomy silence, broken only by gloomier mutterings of the crowd, the carabineers drew rein before the prison.

The closely-packed, loudly-chattering groups of men, few women among them, but many in the doorways of houses and churches, stood gathered together to see him brought out and taken on his next stage to the tribunal of Massa, where his trial was to take place. They were all sorrowful. None blamed him. None thought him a criminal. *Poveretto!*[1] he had lived a bold, vigorous, manful life up yonder on the snow-capped hills above the foaming Fiora, and down in the deep, dark ravines where the Fiora water rolls, and in the rich vale of the Albeyna, and on the treeless lands that stretch away to Ostia far down in the south. He had been a fierce fellow, indeed, and a terror to all travellers, and many a tale of his ferocity to captives was told from mouth to mouth along the marshy shores of the Maremma and in the huts of the shepherds on its moors; but the travellers were all strangers, and the captives all rich men, for from the poor he had never been known to levy a crust or a coin, and the sympathy of the crowds was wholly with him as they hung about the cathedral walls and outside the wine-house doors, waiting until the prisoners should come out with the strong guard that was to march them to their resting-place on the little island that was then glancing to amethyst and gold in the glory of the sunset light, away there to the west on the seas they could not see.

They had not to wait very long. As the time grew near, the people became very quiet in the hush of expectation.

---

[1] Poor thing.

For many and many a year to come the imagination of the Italian people will be always captivated and blinded by the bastard heroism of the brigand; he is born of the soil and fast rooted in it; he has the hearts of the populace with him; and his most precious stronghold is in their sympathy, from which no laws and no logic of their rulers can dislodge him yet.

Saturnino Mastarna was to all the Maremma shore a hero still.

A few quiet citizens of Grosseto apart, the people looking on were all for him, and muttered menaces of the guards. The mountaineers and wood-cutters and rough laborers of all kinds that had come down into the town were most of them men to whom "to take to the hills" seemed a bold and bright thing to do; most of them would have been not unwilling to try it themselves; many of them had been often in secret league and complicity with the terrorism which was no terror to them, because it only struck the rich and never harmed the poor. They would have all been willing to rescue the doomed man, but they paused doubtfully, no one taking the lead.

"*Poveretto! Poveretto!*" they all muttered in regret for him; and had there been an adventurous spirit amidst them to advise his rescue, those gathered laborers of the forests and the plains might have been formidable in their resistance to the law.

But the Italian loves to talk; he loves not equally to act. And so they stood there, sullen, sympathetic, but inert, as the prison-gates opened and the carabineers rode out with Saturnino in their midst.

The autumnal floods had for the time rendered the railway that runs through Grosseto from north to south impassable, and the carabineers had had their orders to ride with him through the twenty-odd miles that were under water. It was thought well that the folk of Grosseto, whose traders were suspected of collusion with the brigand by the purchase of many of his stolen treasures, should see the famous marauder in this sorry plight in their streets. Farther south, such a spectacle would have provoked a rescue, or at least a riot; but, in Grosseto, blood ran more quietly and more soberly, and the multitude waiting there only muttered a curse or two as the little troop of horsemen passed out of the court of the prison and came in sight.

With his legs tied beneath his horse, Grosseto saw its fallen hero.

He was in his own mountaineer's dress, a sheepskin jacket, breeches of untanned leather, a sash of brilliant crimson, weather-stained, a broad-leafed hat with golden tassels, and in its band a little gold image of Our Lady. At his throat, too, was a Madonnina. His pistols, his knife, his ear-rings, they had taken away from him; but these little images his captors had left him, from a charitable feeling that it was as well to leave the man, in such a strait as this, all such aid as he could have from heaven.

His great black eyes were sombre and terrible; his dark locks hung to his throat, slightly curling, for he had been vain of his good looks; his lips were rich and red, his features straight and handsome; his brow was low, his chest and his limbs were massive. He was the true robber-chief of romance.

Who could say what blood ran in his veins? His name was the old Etruscan name that had once been that of Servius Tullius; he had been the son of wild mountain-hunters; who could say what blood of omnipotent Lucumo,[1] of augur weighted with the secrets of the stars, of languid and luxurious Lydian, of lustful lord of Sardis, might not be in him, hot and cruel and lascivious? The Etruscan name had been his forefathers' for hundreds of years counted on the hills.

Grosseto knew him well. He had loved to ruffle it, in all his finery, on feast days, in its wine-shops and on its public ways, in open bravado and scorn of the power of the law to touch him.

"Is that truly Saturnino who is taken?" asked an old woman on the edge of the piazza, a tall gaunt woman with blue eyes and snow-white hair, who had a different accent and look from those of the crowd.

"Ay, mother, that it is," the man nearest to her answered, sorrowfully.

"Dear God!" she muttered, "how are the mighty fallen! Only the other day and his name was a terror that made the very dead quake in their graves."

And she pushed a little nearer, to see better.

"It is verily he!" said the crowds now wistfully gazing up at this fallen majesty, bound there on his horse's saddle, with the muzzle of a trooper's carbine resting on either side of him, as the little band

---

[1] Lucumo (Tarquis Priscus) migrated from Etruria to Rome and eventually became the legendary fifth king of Rome. Servius Tullius was his successor, the sixth legendary king of ancient Rome and the second king of the Etruscan dynasty. Another legend represented Tullius as an Etruscan soldier of fortune named Mastarna.

halted for a moment in the midst of the cathedral square while the captain bade farewell to the syndic of the town. "It is verily he!" they sighed, and were full of regret. What would Maremma be without its Saturnino?

"Ay, it is he!" said the old woman, bending her piercing eyes upon the face of Mastarna. She was a plain-featured, clear-skinned woman, much beaten about by sea-winds and scorched by poisonous suns; but she had a frank, straight, and even noble regard. She dwelt on the low shores of Maremma; but in her youth she had come from the Alpine ranges of Savoy.

She looked at Saturnino as she stood on the edge of the crowd, and said, "Ay, ay, it is he!"

"You have seen him before, mother?" said an eager youth, who had come from the Apennines to go and make charcoal in the Ciminian woods away yonder to the southeast.

"Ay, ay," she said, briefly, and said no more, being a woman of few words, who, though she had dwelt here fifty years, was always called the "woman of Savoy" and deemed an alien and a stranger.

She was standing near the troop of horsemen, clad in a russet gown, with a yellow handkerchief tied about her white hair. The brigand was sitting in his saddle, sullen, sombre, ashamed,—ashamed to be brought thus amidst the people, like a netted calf, like a yoked bull.

The old woman with the keen blue eyes and the face that had once been fair stood and looked with the rest, and, though she was an honest woman, law-abiding, God-fearing, her heart also was heavy for this hawk of the hills that forever was caged.

She had been a woman of many sorrows, to whom death had been unkind, and a little son of her dead daughter's had been all that had been left to her of the children of her blood. And one day the little lad had been lost, going with his goats on the high passes above the Albegna valley, and there had been found by the dread Saturnino, asleep, and frozen, where the snows were deep, and Saturnino, who never hurt the poor, had taken him up in his arms and carried him to his own lair miles away, and there fed and tended him, and next day sent him down by one of his own men into his native village safe and sound and with twenty broad gold pieces in his little woollen breeches.

She, being a brave woman and a holy one, no sooner found her one lost lamb thus than she took the most precious thing she had, an image of Our Lady, that had been blessed by God's Vicegerent, and slipped that and the gold coins in her pouch, and said to the mountaineer who had brought her boy, "Lead me to your chief, that I may thank him."

The man demurred and was afraid, but finally she prevailed, and he took her back with him, a long and toilsome tramp up into the hills, staying one night at a cabin on the way, and when they started on the morrow blindfolding her eyes that she should not see whither she went.

When the handkerchief was lifted, she was in the presence of Saturnino, whose eyes, according to the people's tales, could send out flame and burn up those on whom his rage lighted.

But she was not afraid. She took out of her pouch the holy image and the gold pieces, and she held them both out to him.

"Saturnino," she said to him, "I have come up hither to bless you with my own voice, for you have restored to me the only little living thing I have to love, and night and day I will pray to the saints to have you in their holy keeping. And I have brought you the only bit of value that I own—a Madonna that our Holy Father blessed; and do you put it by a string about your throat, and it will keep the thoughts and hopes of heaven with you. But this gold that you gave to my boy I bring you back, because I know too well, alas! alas! how all your gold is gained."

The men standing around thought that he would cut her down with a stroke of his sword straight through skull and throat. But he did not harm her. He took the image meekly like a chidden child, and the gold pieces he dashed in the snow.

"A brave soul!" he said of her, and she blessed him once more, and kissed his hand that had sent many a one to an untimely death, and took her homeward way again, praying silently that the holy hosts of heaven might be about his steps and win him from his sin.

Since that time, when she had gone up into his very lair, she had not seen Saturnino. Twenty years had gone by. The little boy that he had saved had died of fever,—the ghastly fever that walks these shores all summer through, like the ghost of dead Etruria.

Twenty years had gone by, and Saturnino, from a young and generous man who, although fierce and terrible, could be merciful and just, had grown year by year a deeper terror, a dreader name; not to Maremma still, for still he spared the poor, but to the law and the State. More murders lay upon his soul than he had time to count; his will, which was unchecked by those around, and unbridled by any fear of consequence or qualm of conscience, had grown overbearing, intolerant, exacting, and capricious almost to madness.

Among his many loves he had conceived a violent passion for the woman whom he had carried off and taken up into his mountain by force,—that most beautiful Serapia, of whom the stranger waiting for his ransom had been too amorous. Serapia had died, and after her loss all that there had been of any softness in the nature of the man had been burnt out under the fires of his hatred of fate and rebellion against his misery; he had become a monster of cruelty, having in him the same temper as of old made the tyrants of Padova and Verona and Brescia the scourges of their generation. Even his men had begun to grow disloyal under the iron heel of his unendurable despotism, and the treachery of one of these had delivered him over into the chains of the State at which he had laughed in secure defiance for so long.

Yet the hearts of the men in Grosseto were sad for his fate, and the old woman with the Northern eyes said to her neighbors, "Nay, I am sorry he has been taken. You remember how he saved my Carlino. Always I have hoped that with time and my prayers Saturnino would some day turn to an honest life."

"Nay, mother," said a Pistoiese, "of a fox never can you make a house-dog. The pity is that such a man had not luck to the end to die of a shot or a sword-thrust out on his own hill."

The people murmured assent: that would have been fitting enough, certainly. But the galleys! For Saturnino to be chained and numbered, set to work with an axe or a spade in dock-yard or on high-way, cowed with the whip of the overseer, and pointed out like a wild beast to strangers, that seemed hard.

The thought of it made the blood curdle and grow cold in their veins with the fear of that law which could work this miracle.

"If one may not kill the man who covets our *ganza*,[1] of what use are powder and shot?" said the men of Grosseto.

Suddenly the old woman of the North put her hand into her pocket, drew out a piece of money, pushed her way to a wine-shop a

---

[1] Wild goose.

few yards behind her, bought a stoup of the best wine, and came out with it. She went straight up to the carabineers, and said to them,—

"Yon man did me a good turn once. Will you let me give him this to wet his lips? A good man he is not; but he was good once."

The guards hesitated. They were not churlish; they had a lingering sympathy themselves for their prisoner, who had been taken in a snare at the last, after having been the hero of all Maremma twenty-five years and more; for he had been a mere lad when he had first captured a great English milord, and had let him go with only the loss of one ear cut off, in consideration of a ransom of thirty thousand scudi.

Saturnino, sitting with his head erect, and his great black eyes blazing in a scorn he strove to assume, that he might hide the bitter shame at his heart, heard the voice of the woman, and glanced at her.

The carabineer on his right side, relenting, held the wine towards his mouth. The brigand's hands were tied behind his back, or he would have dashed the pewter cup down. As it was, he would not drink; but his sombre eyes dwelt on the woman.

"Let her speak to me," he said.

The carabineers were ill disposed to obey, but they saw that the crowd was eager and full of pity for Saturnino. They were afraid to irritate, since they had not gagged him; and, after all, a woman could do no harm.

One of them moved, so as to let her in between his horse and that of the captive's. He kept the muzzle of the cocked carbine pointed against her; but she was a brave woman; she did not heed that.

"Drink my wine, Mastarna," she said to him, and lifted the cup herself.

"Is it you, Joconda?" he said.

But he did not drink.

"It is Joconda," she said, curtly. "How came you in this plight?"

"I was betrayed," said the brigand, while his great despairing eyes flashed as a knife that is raised to kill flashes in the light, and he said it more truthfully than many greater conquered conquerors who excuse their own feebleness and lack of forecast by the plea of treachery. He had been betrayed and seized as he had sat drinking at sunset at the door of his hut in the hills.

"Joconda, I saved your lamb," he said, after a pause.

"You did. You are a butcher, but you saved my lamb. That is why I am sorry to-day."

"Save my lamb, then."

"Have you one?"

"I have one that I love. She is Serapia's child. I loved her mother, and her mother is dead. Go and save her."

"Where is she?"

"Up yonder," he answered, with a backward gesture of his head to where, in the haze of the far distance, the snowy hills of his own lair lay. "Any one will tell you on the hills. Ask for the Rocca del Giulio. They seized me; my men fought, but they killed them. She was with women; but they may have fled. Will you find her, and bring her up in your house?"

The face of the old woman grew weary and perplexed.

"It will be a burden, Mastarna."

"Ay, it will. Do as you choose. But she is little and alone."

The woman paused and mused.

"I will take her if I can find her," she said, at length.

Across the bold, sombre, fierce face of the fettered man a strong emotion swept.

"Lift your wine to my mouth," he said, "I will drink it now."

And he drank.

"Loosen the image from my hat. She has the same about her throat; her mother hung them both. I have your Madonnina still at mine," he muttered, when he had drained the cup.

She put one foot on the stirrup,—for she was strong and active, though old,—loosened the golden image, and detached it from its place. At that moment the officer in charge of the escort, arriving in haste, reproved his men in fury, and the horses started so suddenly that she could scarcely save herself from falling between their legs and being trampled to pieces on the stones.

By good fortune she escaped injury, and only fell on her knees, and rose again unhurt. The troop of carabineers were trotting out of the square, their carbines pointed at the head of Saturnino.

They soon vanished in the golden haze of the rising sun.

A hundred hands were stretched to touch her; a hundred questions rained on her ear.

"What did Saturnino tell you, mother?" cried the Grosseto folk, jealously, for they had been so kept at musket's length by the guards that no one had heard a syllable of what had been said.

"I knew him years agone," she answered, "and he bade me hang this image in some chapel, that Our Lady may have grace to him. Nay, hands off: it shall go where he told me. And he whom you call your Saturnino needs heaven's mercy sorely; for he was a murderer many times,—many times."

For these were her foolish notions, she being a woman from the North.

More they could not get out of her. She carried the empty wine-cup back to the wine-shop, and then made her way quietly out of the square by a narrow lane.

The people stood about in a silent, sad, sullen mob, discomfited and dissatisfied with themselves that they had not struck a blow for their hero.

Saturnino Mastarna had been a robber, and, as she had justly said, a murderer many times. He had swooped down on the lonely mountain paths above the mountain-born Fiora, and along the once consular and imperial highway that runs through Orbitello and Civita Vecchia to Rome, even as the eagle of these hills swoops down from his cliff-nest made of oak-leaves and olive-boughs on to the water-fowls of the pools, until the daring and the frequency of his captures had made his name a household word that had rung far and wide beyond the confines of Maremma.

Therefore Maremma had been proud of him,—proud in a fierce, defiant way that had given him many a nameless ally amidst the scattered gentry of all that wild and lonesome country; and even here in old grave Grosseto, a score of miles away from the foaming waters of the Fiora, people had felt the same pride in him, and now as the trot of the horses and the clangor of weapons died away into silence, there were regret and a smothered rage in the populace to think that their hero should have been brought through their streets with his feet tied under the belly of his horse, to go to the galleys of Gorgona or the salt-mines of Sardinia, and be no more seen of men, although for years and years to come the story of his exploits would be told from mouth to mouth wherever a group of woodmen sat about the forest fires at night, or a couple of fishermen whiled the becalmed day away with talk, or in the winter evenings in farm-houses far away on the

Lucchese hills men and maidens munched the chestnuts with white teeth.

A great stillness and gloom fell on the populace, and the tongues of the people for once ceased to buzz and scream, and were only heard in a few rebellious mutterings against the State, which took a frank freebooter like a rat in a trap and dealt with him as it dealt with any paltry thief of the cities. Saturnino was gone,—a dead man, or worse than a dead man,—and never more would his native Maremma thrill with the Homeric tales of his acts; never more would this town of Grosseto see him stride through their public places with his pistols and knife in his broad red sash, and his bold black eyes full of challenge and scorn.

It was all over, like wine spilt on the ground: henceforth the Maremma would speak of him only with bated breath, and memories half glorious, half sad, like the memories of dead heroes. Saturnino Mastarna was gone,—seized by the impalpable, far-reaching, spectral arm of the law, which to a rustic and simple people is so vaguely terrible, so unjust, so incomprehensible, coming out, as it seems to them to do, from the infinite and the unknown to seize them for their secret sins.

He was gone, and there was little mirth in Grosseto that day, though usually the October weeks are full of merriment and business, of song and dance, of bargains made, and of wine drunk, and of gladness at the coming winter, and of sportive love offered and returned. But this day the crowds were dull and vexed, and looking in each other's faces read one unspoken thought there, common to all,—

"We should have rescued him!"

CHAPTER II.

MEANWHILE, Joconda Romanelli, the woman who had had the courage to speak a bold word for his sake, left the town to itself and prepared to return on her homeward way to her village of Santa Tarsilla, a long way off upon the coast, a low-lying, sickly, sea-shore place.

Twice a year regularly she yoked her mule to her cart and drove into Grosseto, making a two days' journey on the road each way, on purpose to sell the homespun linen she had woven from thread she had spun in the six months' time. She knew a hosier in Grosseto who only sold "*nostrali*"[1] linen, and who gave her a fair price for hers at spring and autumn. She thought him honester than Orbitellano folk, so made the longer drive across the wild and lonely country.

She went now to the tavern where she had slept, and where her mule was put up, harnessed him with her own hands, and drove out of the city gates with her hardly-earned gains in a bag among the hay and straw at her feet.

She went over the flat desolate lands that lie cheerlessly and barrenly about Grosseto, past the lime-quarries of Alberese, over the narrow ill-made roads that traverse the marshes, over the rivers by ford or ferry or bridge, and underneath hills dark with forest where the buck and the boar roamed at liberty. She drove as long as it was light, then reached a miserable little inn, but a friendly one, and slept there; then at dawn resumed her homeward way.

She drove on and on, the old mule ambling slowly, for he only had long journeys twice a year, and resented them mournfully: the moss and the marshes, the wide fields lying red and bare for the plough, and the little knots of pale dust-colored houses that made the villages of the hill-sides, were passed in succession, until she got across country and down to the level of the sea, and saw little else save stunted aloes and sand, though the distance was dark with the outskirts of the retreating Apennines, and the woods upon the Giglio island rose up in sight.

When she could see the isle she had reached her home, an old house of stone and oak timber standing near the wharf of the small township of Santa Tarsilla, on a little bay, that scholars affirmed had once been, like its neighbors Telamone and Populonia, a port of those sea-kings, the Etruscans.

In this little bay some small traffic in fish, and in the stone and charcoal from inland, kept the little place from absolute stagnation and death; but in the summer nearly all its few souls fled away, and in summer no coasting-smack cared to lie by its little quay.

For it was full of miasma and fever in the hot season, like all these places on the low Maremma coast; even now in the late days of October the fever-mists still hung about it, the pools and the beach still

---

[1] Literally "our"; that is, linen that is locally made.

sent out noxious vapors, the scanty population sat about listless and
shivering, the children lay on the sand too weak to care to play, and
there were but two or three of them in all the place; a few fishermen
were out upon the shore, a coast-guardsman paced to and fro, a little
vessel was shipping grain, anchored among the mud-choked shoals:
that was all.

It was a dreary place at the best of times; antiquaries said that the
sea had receded nearly a mile since the days when the Etruscan pirates
had sailed from that bay, and Etruscan lucomonies had had their fortresses and their tombs away yonder where the shore-line grew dusky
with thickets of bay and rosemary and the prickly *marucca*, or holy
thorn, so common here.

"You are safe home, mother?" said the pallid women, as the mule
of Joconda picked his way amidst the stones and sand to his own
house door.

"Ay, the saints be praised," said Joconda, and said no more.

They knew the woman of Savoy never chattered, and that it was
useless to ask from her gossip of Grosseto until she had stabled her
beast and broken her fast, and not very much use after that. Joconda
went on to her own dwelling; it was all of stone, with a roof of red
tiles; it was old and spacious, and had pointed casements and a massive
oak door; her living-room and her bedchamber were all the rooms she
used: the next room she had given to her mule and her poultry and
a fine black pig. The floors were of stone, and the ceilings too; there
was an open hearth that served her for cooking; the hearth now was
cold.

She first put her money into a secret place, stabled her mule,
counted her fowls, to be sure none were stolen, and then lit a little fire
and put on a pot of vegetable soup. Then she sat down and thought,
while her frugal supper was simmering.

She did not tell any one of what she had seen and heard and
promised in Grosseto. She was not a sociable woman, and she had
only neighbors, no friends.

Joconda Romanelli had been taciturn and grave for forty years,—
ever since one summer day, when her man had gone down in a white
squall, like that which wrecked Shelley. She had loved the man, and
had been sternly faithful to him and to the offspring he had left her.
She had always got her own living by carrying cargo to the coasters for her husband's comrades, and taking her linen into Grosseto;

in bad weather she sat at home and span, or made fishing-nets and sewed sails. She was active and very hardy; she lived honestly, and in a stern, cleanly fashion that made her village people think her odd and be a little afraid of her. Her sons had died of the marsh fever, and her daughter had left her a motherless grandson, a bold fair boy, the lamb that Saturnino had saved ten years before when the boy had gone up with his goats into the mountains; for which mercy Joconda and her lad had blessed him every day and night they told their beads.

But, though Saturnino had spared the boy, the fever had not done so; and ever since his death Joconda had dwelt alone with her dead memories. She was a sad woman always since then, but she was a strong one. She worked for her living, and owed nobody a bronze piece, and was half respected and half feared, which she liked better than being loved.

Fifty years before, she had been brought here from her mountain-home fronting the noble chain of the Grand Paradis by her husband after a fishing-cruise to the seaboard of Savoy, and the tradition of her Northern birth made her still "a stranger" to the people of Santa Tarsilla and all the low-lying shore. She had never seen Savoy for nigh fifty years, but she was "the woman of Savoy" to them all.

It had been a fatal day for her when her mother's sister, a farmer's wife near St. Martin Lantosque, had lost her cows one by one by disease, and sent to beg that her niece, who was so skilled in dairy-matters, would go and spend a summer with her; and in the course of that summer, up at Lantosque to visit mountain-neighbors, there had come some seafaring men from Villafranca, away on the seaboard, and among them had been a man of Maremma, Sostegno Romanelli, the owner of a tartana then lying off the shores of Savoy. He had been a handsome young man, and at that time well-to-do as a coaster; he had persuaded the blue-eyed maiden from the green alps above the Val de Cogne to give a favorable answer to his wooing. She and he had been wedded that same summer at the little church of St. Martin, and she had gone to live with him at his native Maremmana town.

Things had done very well with them awhile, then turned and went as ill. The tartana had to be sold, and its owner had to become a deep-water fisherman, working for the gain of others. His wife, ashamed of their troubles, which her own people had predicted, ceased to write to the chalet under the glaciers of Grandcrate.

They were homely people there on the fir-clad heights above

Cogne, but there was always a homely plenty, and no penury touched them. They were good-hearted, but hard of mind and scanty in sympathy. She could never bring herself to tell them that she had married into poverty and was sick to death of this fatal shore to which her Maremmano had brought her.

So silence fell between her and her own family, and up on the mountain-slopes that faced the Grand Paradis her brothers and sisters ceased to remember and ceased to regret her.

She slept a little now over her supper, being weary; she was woke by neighbors' voices; women were looking in at her window and tapping at it, being unable any longer to subdue their eagerness for news.

"Is it true that Giulianino has been taken, good mother?" they asked her.

"Ay, ay: why not?" she answered, crossly. "He has been taken."

"Did you see him in Grosseto?"

"Yes, the poor soul! with his legs tied under the horse's belly."

"Oh, the hard pity of it!" mourned the gossips, with a wail.

"He has got his deserts," said Joconda. "A fine long time he has been loose on these hills. Luck always changes."

"It was that foreign man that made the fuss," the women muttered. "He must have been some great prince, else never would they have captured Saturnino for his misfortune."

"Misfortune" was their fine way of speaking: they knew well that the traveller had been foully murdered.

"He killed the foreigner," said Joconda, curtly. "He had killed scores. That one was the one too much. That was all."

The women at the window muttered that this was just the caprice and injustice of the government and the soldiers; a murder more or less (if it were a murder), did it matter so much? Saturnino was a fine bold man, and never had harmed the poor.

"Why, he had good about him," assented Joconda. "But murder is not a good thing; I wish he had had other ways of living. Alas! poor soul! upon that rock of Gorgona his crimes will be cold comfort to him."

"And that is true," said the gossips, crossing themselves. "Did you speak to him, mother? Was there any chance to say a word?"

"Yes; I spoke to him."

"What did he say to you?"

"He reminded me of my dead lamb, and I told him I had not forgot my debt."

"Was that all?"

"Yes. Get you to your beds: I want to get to mine."

And she nodded to them, and shut her latticed casement behind its wire grating, and shut out the sight of the moonlit sea, and the shining sands that hid her dead. She heard them under her house-wall on the edge of the beach, for the night was still young, talking of the hero of the hills and of his fate. She heard the deeper tones of a man's voice strike across theirs and say,—

"No bolder soul ever lived than Saturnino Mastarna. They have taken him, and they will cage him out on Gorgona yonder, or send him to the king's mines. If man could free him, I would free him. What did he do ever? Did he steal from the poor? No. Did he rob the church? No. Did ever a peasant miss his sheep, or a woodman his wallet? or a laborer that had got his wages in his waist-band, was he ever lightened of them by Saturnino? Nay, never. That we know. We have come and gone on his mountains and never were we the worse. When old Montino was lost in the snow on Santa Fiora, what did Mastarna do when he found him? Took him to his own hut, and warmed and fed him, and gave him of the best, and when he saw that old Montino had a bag of gold pieces with him he said to him, "Fear nothing; neither I nor my men will touch your gold, because you are an old man and a steward, and the loss would get you blamed by your masters, maybe thrown in prison." And when full day came, he himself took Montino down the mountain as far as the first ford that crosses the Fiora. Five hundred times, if once, have I heard the history from Montino himself. Nay, Saturnino was a brave man, and a generous, and because he aided this stranger to escape from the burden of life they have caged him in a trap as you catch a *dondola*.[1] It is vile. The stranger was a rich man in his own country, a great prince, they say: what did he do here in Italy? why not stay where he was? It was always the rich that Mastarna made war on; the poor were sacred to him. That we know. Yet he will lie in chains amidst the waves on Gorgona, or waste his strength in the mines in the bowels of the earth. It is unjust. It is unjust."

---

[1] Ouida may mean "donnola", a weasel.

Then an assenting and approving murmur rose up from the listening people and joined with the murmur of the sea.

Joconda heard them as she lay on her hard straw bed.

"And there is a grain of truth in what they say," she thought. "Yet his sins were many and deep, poor soul! and they will be heavier about his neck than the chains he will wear on Gorgona. May Christ lighten them!"

Then she slept.

She was a woman who usually enjoyed the dreamless, heavy sleep of the hard worker; but all through this night she dreamed, and saw the bold form of Saturnino chained, and with his crimes written on his breast for any who chose to read, even as he would be henceforth in all his years to come on the sunburnt, wave-beaten rock: the eagle of the mountains fettered to a stone in the sea.

At daybreak her mind was made up; she took a stout staff in her hand, slung her wallet about her, with some bread in it and some goat's ham cured Savoy fashion, and went out towards the mountains.

She was a strong woman, though old, and she walked briskly. The pasture-lands and marshes were desolate, and she met scarce any one,—here and there a furze-cutter or a ploughman with his oxen, that was all. She soon quitted the sight of the sea, and bore inland by the course of the Albegna River through solitary untracked thickets, and over rough rocky ground.

After some hours she came to cross-roads, and there sat down on a stone, and waited for the public wagon running from Orbitello to Monte Murano to come by. When it jolted near her, its miserable horses straining at their rope harness, she stopped it, and got into it: it lumbered on under a volley of blows and oaths rained on the patient, sinking beasts.

At Monte Murano she descended, and was forced to sleep; with daybreak she left the place, and thence had to make her way as best she might up to what had been the brigand's favorite lair, although he had others in the fastnesses of the Ciminian mountains, which he frequented when it pleased him to descend upon the southward road nearer Rome, where more than once he had even stopped the mail-train itself as it had rolled over the marshes and beneath the sombre gloom of the maritime pines, and had swerved off the line as it encountered the timber and stones that Saturnino's men had placed there in its path.

He had been always called Saturnino of the Santa Fiora, though his range had extended so much farther than these peaks, and towards Santa Fiora she made her way through the dense underwood and luxuriant vegetation that here cover the soil, where the roads are mere mule-tracks, often effaced, and the amphitheatre of the mountains encloses a solitude and a silence scarcely ever broken save by sound of sheep-bell, or cry of bittern, or the browsing murmur of the teeth of wild cattle chewing the luscious grass.

Here on the wooded cliffs was once Saturnia, whose giant walls still remain, overgrown with laurestinus and mountain-box and butcher's broom, and in the hovels that occupy its site, and take its name, where Saturnino forty-five years before had seen the light, there is a filthy little drinking-house, whose only customers are the shepherds and the wood-cutters and the muleteers.

There Mastarna, as the hero and martyr of the soil, was being lamented by a knot of ill-looking foresters as Joconda passed the open door by which they were sitting together playing at dominoes. Being a brave woman, and not caring for their ill looks, she gathered from them what direction to take so as to reach the mountain-crest without sinking miserably in a quagmire, or wandering till dead of hunger in the intricacy of the pathless jungle.

She asked for Santa Fiora, and they pointed it to her,—far, very far away, where the autumn snows lay on the highest lines of the hills. She took her staff and wallet and set out again.

"You cannot reach it to-night, mother," the men said to her.

She said to them, "Very well. No one will hurt me. I am old and ugly, and I have not a coin to steal."

They laughed, and asked her why she went; she told them "to get a child to nurse," and, with the prudence of her country, appended to the fact a fiction of a daughter whose infant was dead, and she needed one to suckle.

"A little lie is always useful," thought Joconda, though she was not a false or a faithless woman.

Then she lost sight of the foaming, turbulent Fiora, and began her climb towards the mountain-summits. The ways were very steep and very long; night overtook her. She took shelter in an empty hut of a shepherd, and ate and drank out of her wallet, and slept not ill, for she was tired and not timorous.

The great lonely mountain-side, with the water freshets of au-

tumn tearing down it to swell the Fiora water, was about her when
she awoke. She could not see the rock she wanted above her, a gray
speck under the snows. She was stiff, and felt as if she were frozen
from sleeping out of her bed on the damp leaves; but she resumed
her upward way. It was again noon when she passed the last robur-oak
and cork-trees and came up amidst wind-wasted pines and boulders
of granite and slate, tossed about on a wild mountain-scarp, as if in
the horse-play of giants.

She saw scarce any one; the scattered folk of the hills were most
of them in hiding, stricken with terror at the seizure of Saturnino,
with whom they were all in habits of greater or less complicity.

One old man was met with, very old and bent. He was looking
for simples in the many herbs that clothed the hillside. He told her at
last where the Rocca del Giulio was, pointing, as he spoke, to a spot
far away amidst the snow that had fallen on the heights.

"That was Saturnino's nest," he said. "Poor soul! They have taken
him, and killed most of his men. He never did me any harm."

He was very old, and not curious: being so, he let her go on upward without question.

Here the snow had fallen heavily. It had ceased to fall, but there
was a sharp frost on these heights, and the ground was white and
hard. The stunted trees looked black. It was very desolate. The clouds
were low upon the mountain-side, and their mists were all around
her. She could see the white crests of the Labbro and the Santa Fiora
loom close on her, it seemed, in the steel-hued fog. She had never
been so high up on the mountains since her girlhood, sixty and more
years before, in the alps about the feet of the Becca di Hona. The sight
of the great cones of snow so near beside her, the feeling of the crisp
clear air and the icy freshness of it, gave her a strange sensation,—the
sickness of nostalgia coming on her in old age, after a long life in the
swamps and on the shore.

A thirst of longing made her heart ache for her old home, set on
a granite ledge of rock, with the valley of Cogne stretching below it,
and the white summit of Mont Blanc in sight, and nearer at hand the
peaks and glaciers of the Grand Paradis; her old home, with its girdle
of deep green forest, and its ceaseless sound of rushing water, and its
alpine winds, that are known no more to the dwellers of the plains
than what the condor of the Andes beholds in its flight is known to the
hedge-sparrow in the thorn-bush by the road.

It was sixty long years since she had felt that wind upon her fore-head, and heard that rush of ice-fed waters as they leaped from rock to rock; since she had lifted her voice in the jödel of the hills, and rested her eyes on that fresh flowering grass, those deep cool shadows of the pines. Yet now and then it all came back upon her, as it did now, clear as a dream of the night, and then the sea would fade away, and the sands recede, and the misty scorching dust-gray shores grow dim to her, and her eyes would only be dry because she had grown too old to weep. And when she slept it was of these she dreamed almost always,—above all, in the stifling midnights of the terrible canicular heat, when the air was like steam, and the soil was like brass, and there was no freshness or peace in the darkness, and with its fall no dews.

She felt for the brigand's image in her bosom, and drew it out and looked at it, then walked to the first house that lay in her way.

They seemed all empty. There was not a sound, except the sough-ing of wind in the tops of the pines. She called, and no one answered. She shouted again and again, but her voice died on the mountain-still-ness unanswered. Then she pushed open a door and looked inside. The houses were little more than stone huts, and they were all deserted; hastily deserted, it seemed to her, for there were things strewn about them, and here and there pools of blood, and broken arms upon the frozen snow. She could have guessed how it had been, even had she known nothing of the capture of Saturnino,—guessed that there had been a struggle here, and the women had left after hurried flight.

"How shall I find his lamb?" she thought, with a sigh half of re-gret, half of relief; and she stood still and looked.

The few people who had dwelt there had fled, that was plain to her; most likely out of fear of the soldiery.

"Poor souls!" she said, and crossed herself, seeing the scarcely dried blood on the stones.

A dog's bark startled her.

It was a bark of anger and of appeal both in one. She rose and went in the direction of the sound. It came from the last of the stone huts. She pushed open the door as she had done that of the other. A great dog, snow-white, stood in the centre of the clay floor; under his body was a child asleep.

"The child of Serapia!" she thought, as she looked down on the sleeping infant. Serapia had been but a name—a legend—to the dwell-ers of the shore and plains.

Wild tales were always told of how Saturnino had ravished her from her people,—people beggared though of noble blood, who dwelt on a wind-swept spur of the Sabine hills, by whom she was cursed and looked upon as one dead.

A beautiful, ignorant, mindless thing she had ever been, foolish and passionate from the hour that she had been borne away, a second Proserpine, to the night of oblivion, peril, and crime in which her brute-lover dwelt. One short year only she had been carried, half a captive, half a willing mistress, to that topmost haunt of the hills where all that Saturnino knew as home was made. There she had died; some said of fever, some said of a blow from Saturnino; anyway, she had died, and had been buried where the tall stone pines rose up like columns of a temple against the marble of the porches. And her child was here, asleep amidst a scene of carnage made more horrible by the dreaming smile of a baby's rest.

In the cabin there were loose coins, gold and jewels, dropped and stamped on as they had been caught up in the haste of flight; a rich shawl was thrown aside upon the beaten earth of the ground, a length of gold brocade was tossed against a rough-hewn table, overturned; close to the child's bed there was a carved ivory toy such as are made in India. In the child's hand was a dry half-eaten crust.

Joconda looked neither to the gold nor stuffs. Her soul was sick at the sight of the pools of blood still wet, and at the sight of the dreaming creature who was left a heritage of crime and woe.

"The blood of Saturnino!" she thought; it seemed to her that it must be as a stream of lava and of poison in the veins of a female child.

"This must be the child," said Joconda to herself, and stood looking; she was afraid of the white Molossus dog.

The child was two years of age, or two and a half, she thought; not more. It had been forsaken, no doubt, when the mistresses and wives of the band had run for their lives after the men's struggle with the carabineers.

Joconda stood wavering, on account of the dog. At length she spoke to him, and he looked at her. Then he ceased to growl, and smelt her. Then, apparently satisfied, he let her draw near the child, who was sleeping; a lovely creature, half naked, with long black lashes lying on cheeks like mountain rose-leaves, and loose thick curls like rings of amber.

"It is a woman child; so much the worse," said Joconda, looking down on it.

If it had been a male, it would have been much easier for her; a boy could soon have run about and done something for his daily bread in the boats, or with the mules, or in the fire-woods. However, she remembered that, be it what it would, she had promised Mastarna. She looked timorously at the dog, and raised the child without waking it; he looked at her in return watchfully, but comprehending that she meant it no injury. She saw at the baby's throat a little golden image; then she wrapped her shawl about it, and said to the dog, "Come."

For the dog was alone, and Joconda was a woman of hard aspect but good heart.

The dog was of the same race as Ulysses' faithful friend, perhaps the purest and most ancient canine race of all in the world, and one of the boldest and most beautiful; he was fierce and powerful, but full of sympathy and wisdom; he bent his head, sniffed at her feet, gazed sorrowfully in her eyes, put his nose to the child's cheek, then went with her down the path by which she had climbed to what had been, until the night before, the brigand's home.

She began to descend the mountain, but night drew nigh, and the child, who still slept, was a heavy weight. She stopped at the first cabin she came to, and asked for shelter. The charcoal-burners, who dwelt there, knew the look of the child and the dog, and would not take her in; they were afraid Saturnino's daughter might bring them trouble with the police. Joconda cursed them heartily for cowards.

She made her way with great fatigue, and with strong effort managed to reach the inn where she had slept the first night. Here they did not know the child or the dog, or did not say that they did.

"Ah! thou hast got the baby for thy step-daughter," was all the woman of the house said to her; and Joconda answered,—

"Ay; but it has ceased to suck; that is a pity."

Long before this the child had wakened more than once, and had cried and sobbed and become very troublesome. The dog was quiet and sad.

They gave her goat's milk and black bread, and let her and the child and the dog sleep all together in a room fall of hay and straw. She and the baby slept well; the dog but little.

The following morning she resumed her journey, and returned

as she had come, only that she had the burden of the infant and the companionship of the animal.

The child was now wakeful, impatient, tyrannous; the dog, as he got farther and farther from his old home, was melancholy, and footsore, and anxious.

"You are like a white lion," she said to him, and named him Leone: what names either he or the child had borne before she could not tell.

It was still fresh, fine weather, happily for her, for she had to walk much, and it took her several days to return on foot, and the diligence only ran once a week, and she missed it at Monte Murano. She was an old woman, and she became very weary.

It was evening once more when she drew nigh her own village.

The pale sands, the tufa rocks, the background of marshes and stagnant water, looked very dreary even to her who had been used to them all her life; there was a sickly haze upon the sea, and a fog upon the horizon.

Two or three of her neighbors, wasted and wan-looking folks, gave her good-evening, and glanced at the child and the dog.

"Is that child of thy kin, mother?" they asked, curiously.

"Nay; I have no kin here. It is a dead friend's child," she answered them, wearily, for she was very tired.

"And the dog?"

"He was my dead friend's dog: he followed me. I could not turn him adrift."

"They will be hungry mouths, mother?"

"Ay; but I will not ask you to feed them."

Then they laughed, and stared, and wondered, but dared not ask more, and let her be.

She made her way to her own house, and drew the great key from her girdle, and unlocked her door and opened it, and entered, leading the child by the hand, and followed by the dog.

It was cold and dark and cheerless. The child was awed, and the dog dulled, by the stillness and solitude, the grayness and gloom. The sound of the sea breaking on the sands below was more mournful than perfect silence.

Joconda kneeled down by the crucifix that hung on the wall, and made the little limbs of the baby kneel too.

"See me, good saints, and bear ye testimony that I have kept my word. Be this young thing blessing or curse, I have kept my word. Be ye good to us both."

Then she rose, and fetched from her closets water and milk, salted fish and bread, and broke her fast, and gave food and drink to both the child and the beast.

When she went to rest, the rosy and fresh warmth of the child was on her rough couch, and the white Molossus was stretched before her door. She could not tell whether she were sorry or content. She was at least no longer alone.

"But the blood of Saturnino?" she said doubtfully to herself. Anyway, she had kept her word.

As she had stumbled down along the stony mountain-road, the weight of the two-year-old child heavy on her shoulder, she, being a religious woman, had bethought her that surely it had never been baptized, and pondered on what holy name to give to this offspring of sinners.

She knew her calendar by heart, and called to mind that this autumnal day, with the deep white snow on the heights, and the red and gold of the ash foliage in the woods, was the twenty-ninth of October, the day dedicated by the Latin Church to that sad and little remembered Eastern saint, Mary the Penitent.

Joconda was not a book-learned woman. She could spell out her missal, that was all; but she vaguely remembered that Santa Maria Penitente had had the grace of heaven given her after sorrow and shame, and that in her story there was a dragon who devoured a dove, and out of the body of the monster the beautiful white bird had come forth unharmed and spread its wings and shot upward to the sun. And for sure this is a dove come forth from a dragon, she had said to herself, looking at the sleeping child, and so had resolved that when she should get down back to her own little town the child should be received into the Church by the name of Maria Penitente and no other.

CHAPTER III.

SANTA TARSILLA was a dreary place midway between Telamone and Orbitello, lying low upon a shore half sand, half swamp, with aloes and sea-fennel and the prickly samphire for all its vegetation, and blocks of stone and marble strewn about, some Roman, some Etruscan. There was beauty, indeed, on its horizon,—in the luminous distance where the distant snow-peaks of Corsica and the near crags of iron-bound Elba could be seen, with Capraja and far Monte Christo, and many another island nameless to the world. But to see these it was needful to go a good way out upon the open water; from the little crooked landlocked bay there was little to be discerned save the low pale coast and low red tufa hills that locked in the harbor, but where the waters were shallow, almost stagnant, choked with weed and sand, though beyond the Ligurian sea, blue as turquoise in some lights, blue as lapis-lazuli in others, sometimes rose in fretted turbulence, and sometimes rolled in a sullen swell.

A little way inland the moors began, in grand level stretches of gorse and brushwood, covering many a buried tomb and buried town, with the lentiscus and the rosemary waving above them. Nigh at hand were dark lines of pine forests, although their balsamic scent and res-inous breath could not purify the miasma of the coast, and eastward were the still wild and scarce-trodden woodlands, stretching away to the mountain-ranges where the robber had made his lair. But wood and hill were all too far away to alter the weary monotony of the scene at Santa Tarsilla. It seemed all shore,—pale barren shore; and shallow sea,—sea which yet drowned so many that it seemed to the people like a graveyard.

On a narrow tongue of sandy land there was a little fort; sickly soldiers came there, and guards to watch the coast. There was also a furnace-house to make the salt that was raked upon the beach; but smoke seldom issued from its chimney, though wood was to be had for the getting, and salt for the taking of it. The people had little strength and less spirit. In winter-time their lives were very hard, and with the summer came the pestilence, and then ague and fever fed on them and drained their bodies, and left them scanty force to do more than sit in the shade of their boats or their walls and push out for moonlit fishing when night fell. It was the strong people who came down from the mountains of Pistoja and the hills of Lucca that did their work and reaped the harvest on moor and in forest when autumn came round.

The people of the shore were nearly all dropsical, and the few soldiers and coast-guardsmen sent on duty along the shores suffered more than the native population at most times. But the Pistoiese and the Lucchese and the armies of winter-workers did not come into San-ta Tarsilla itself except at rare odd times, when some of them brought

from the interior grain or timber or charcoal to load the little coasters
that were the only vessels insignificant enough to deign to remember
this secluded little bay; and even to these the port-dues were so heavy
as to be wellnigh ruinous, and the skippers, poor men of Livorno
and Genoa for the most part, were scarcely able to scrape a profit
from their cargoes. The port-dues and shipping-taxes have crippled
and nearly destroyed all the commerce of the minor merchantmen of
Italy, and they have struck a death-blow to the humble industries of
the little Maremmano sea-towns.

Before the independence, of which the Maremma heard much
but understood little, Santa Tarsilla had been very feeble, but able to
get its own living; since then it had become paralyzed, and was perish-
ing off the face of the earth.

The waters teemed with fish; only looking down from the side
of the boat you could see fish by the thousand gleaming like gold and
silver in those bright transparent depths with the feathery weeds and
the branches of coral. There was always fish indeed; but fish, though
it will serve to fill your own mouth and the mouths of your children,
is of very little further use unless there be buyers for it. The waters
teemed, the nets ran over, but as often as not the living spoils of the
sea were thrown down and left to rot in noisome heaps upon the
sands, because there was no one to purchase it and no means to carry
it to other towns. Now and then they took it on mules to Grosseto
or other places on the line of rail, but there was little sale for it; and
before it could be passed through the gates of any town there was so
heavy a tax on it that it paid no one to load a felucca's deck or a beast's
panniers with so perishable a thing.

So Santa Tarsilla was sad and solitary, and usually sickly enough
always; there was never any mirth or joviality in it; the young men
grew impatient of its loneliness and poverty, and always went away
as soon as they reached years enough to be their own masters. There
were only a few old men, and some women and children; all the
stronger folk who had been born in it were elsewhere, coral-fishing in
the south, doing forest-work on the hills, or gone to live at Follonica
where the foundries are.

Only the feeble, the old, and the very poor stayed in the little bay
that had once been a great port for the galleys of Porsenna, as Joconda did, who had neither means nor strength to move away to a
cooler land. An almost absolute silence reigned here, only broken by

the booming of millions of mosquitoes and the tinkling now and then of the one feeble church-bell. The many peddlers that travel through Maremma did not very often give an hour to Santa Tarsilla, unless their way lay most directly over the Tonaboro or sandy shore. Now and then one came with needles and pins, the tapes and the kerchiefs, and a hundred other small articles of merchandise, packed in the wooden or leathern case upon his back; and when he did come, there was much gossip but few pence for him, for every one was poor in the forlorn forgotten town, which would have been no more than a village had it not been for its coast-guard and its church. By June, when the harvest was reaped, the laborers fled; a few fisher-folk remained, sallow and lean with weakness, or swollen with the dropsy common to the coast. Its very priests were sent to Santa Tarsilla as a penitence, and its soldiers were stationed as a chastisement: of late years, even the little garrison of soldiers had been withdrawn by the government, and there were none nearer than Orbitello. The little fort was falling to decay, and even the coast-guardsmen dwelt not at Santa Tarsilla itself, but in a tower on the coast a mile away.

Nothing could be sadder than this place, or seem more forgotten of God and man.

Joconda sometimes, sitting at her door in the heavy parching summer heats, thought with a dull agony of remembrance of the mountain-home of her birth.

In these unhealthy places of Maremma, where no one ever stays who can get away, and nearly all who remain are ague-stricken and fever-worn, young children not seldom thrive well enough. The poisoned air, so hot, so damp, so laden with seeds of disease, seems to have mercy sometimes on these young open lips and bare, soft, uncertain limbs, and in six years' time from the capture of the brigand of Santa Fiora there was the little figure of a beautiful child, bright as a rose, erect as a palm, on the pallid sands under the sultry skies.

The child that was Saturnino's throve, and grew without ailment, without accident, without a flaw anywhere, in feature, or limb, or body.

When Joconda had come down the hills with the weight of Saturnino's legacy in her arms, she had pondered long and anxiously as to whether she would tell the people of Santa Tarsilla that it was the daughter of their hero whom she was about to take beneath her roof. She had turned the matter over long and anxiously in her thoughts, and as the public wagon rumbled on its way down the long stony roads, and at length had decided with herself not to let them know it. Joconda was a woman more truthful than the rest; that is to say, she saw no harm whatever in an untruth if it were necessary and injured nobody, a distinction that in Italy is rarely drawn, but she did not think a lie the natural answer to, and legitimate offspring of, a question, as most of her neighbors did, and she preferred to tell the simple truth when she could, which is esteemed in the country generally as but poor dull work, showing great lack of invention in whosoever is content with it.

At last, as she had lain the night through wide awake, disturbed by the presence and the thought of Saturnino's offspring, she had resolved that it would be best not to tell the truth here. The people would make an idol of their hero's offspring, and the child, as she grew older, would be restless and perturbed if she heard that her father was a galley-slave on Gorgona.

Joconda feared no scorn and unkindness on the score of her birth for the child, if that birth were known; on the contrary, she feared the vanity and the evil passions that, with the knowledge of the blood of the Mastarna in her veins, might by public sentiment be engendered in her.

She would be the child of a hero, almost of a martyr, in the esteem of Maremma. She would hear no account made of his crimes; she would only hear of his valor; and if she lived she would grow up to think of her father as a sufferer by the law's injustice.

To the cooler, sturdier, Northern sense of right and wrong which abode in the mountain-born spirit of the woman of Savoy, this prospect carried a fatal future to give to any child; and she resolved within herself to keep the secret of the baby's paternity from all, save, of course, her confessor. To him she told the truth.

To the rest of the shore-people she said merely that it was a friend's child come from over the other side of Monte Labbro, and she, being a close and resolute woman, was impenetrable to the curiosity of her neighbors.

They were not very curious, either.

A child was no rare treasure, and there was nothing strange in a lone one being placed with a lone woman who was known to have a little money secured and hidden somewhere. Plenty of people along the coast would have been willing and glad to let Joconda adopt their children, would she have taken them. So without more comment or inquiry the child and the dog were domiciled at the old stone house by the pier in Santa Tarsilla, and there grew and throve, as they best might, in an air that to many was death.

Joconda's first care was to have her friend and director, the priest, baptize the infant and wash away in holy water the sins of its fathers from its soul. She knew not what it had ever been called, or if it had ever been called anything, but the name of the saint on whose day she had found it she gave to it, as on the mountain-side she had resolved to do. By the sad recluse of Syria the little large-eyed rose-cheeked child of Saturnino and Serapia was named, and Joconda saw a storm-swallow fly beyond the grated casement of the church, and said to herself that it was a dove. She was not a superstitious woman, but still, if such things once had been, why not again?

"She is a love child?" said the priest, as he gave her back to Joconda's arms, weighted henceforward with the name of the Syrian Magdalene. "A child of crime," said Joconda; for she had not the indulgence to the sins of Saturnino Mastarna that the Maremma had. She was a Northern woman.

The old priest died a short time after that, and Joconda did not tell his successor of the child's parentage.

"They are good as good can be, the holy men," she said to herself, "and of course they never tell anything out of confessional,—no; but still, when their housekeeper gets gossiping over a nice bit of fried liver, or their cappellano[1] comes in with some new wine, they are but human, and they may mix up a little that they hear in the street with what they hear in the chapel. Why not? A man must talk, even when he is a holy one: that stands to reason."

So she, who did not feel the necessity to talk, kept her own counsel.

She said to herself that it would be better the child should never have known that her father dwelt on that stony face of Medusa. What good could it do? As the child would grow older the thought would torment and fester in her, and lead her to evil, so she thought; and, being a woman with a strong power of silence, the silence of one who has long lived alone with God, she never breathed the secret to any living soul.

---

[1] *Cappellano*: Chaplain.

Slowly the memory of Saturnino would die away, she knew, when he should be no more a living wonder on the hills, to feed their fancies with fresh legends of violence and romance. Saturnino was caged up in that isle whose strange shape lies on the blue waves, carved like a woman's head, with hair outfloating on the deep, and blank eyes staring up at heaven. Costa has painted it so, and its name of Gorgon is old as the rocks are old.

There galley-slaves (keeping their old name also) are mewed in a bitter company, and every now and then one escapes, and most likely is drowned, or shot, as he struggles in the waves; and every now and then strangers, curious and indifferent, come over the water to see these caged gallows-birds and stare at them blankly.

There are Italian children who look as though they had stepped down from a predella or a tryptich; they are like the singing children of Angelico, the light-bearing angels of Filippino, the pages of Vittorio Carpaccio, the winged boys of the Siennese masters. The old type is there still in all its purity,—the oval face, the level brows, the curling hair, the spiritual eyes, the rose-like, smiling, yet serious mouth, which the painters of those happier times saw around them in the streets and in the fields.

There are so many Italian children still, looking on whom one thinks at once of dim rich altars, of gold-starred vaulted niches, of lunettes glowing in the dusk like jewels, of vaulted roofs that are borne up by the wings of sculptured angels.

This child, born from a mountain-robber and named from the anointed penitent, was like one of these children who, in the works of the early masters, stand, with chalice or lyre or dove of the Holy Spirit, about the feet of martyrs or around the throne of Mary. Only in the eyes of this creature, who was called a penitent ere she had sinned any sin, there was a rebellious light, and in the arched mouth there was a resolute scorn that the masters did not put into their young servitors of God.

In feature she was strangely like the Angel of Annunciation of Carlo Dolce. It is the mode nowadays to deride Carlo Dolce, as it is the mode to deride melody in music; but let them chatter as they will, none can take away the lovely living light on his Gesù's infant face, or deny the exquisite beauty of that angel who has all the yearning of humanity and all the grandeur of heaven in that perfect face which bends beneath its cloud of nimbussed hair.

I pity those who can look unmoved on that angel where the painting hangs in the forsaken bedchamber of the Pitti, whilst beyond there is the sweet still sunshine and the sounds of the falling waters of the gardens. Who can do so may have the jargon of art on his tongue; he has not its secret in his soul. I would almost give up even the divine visions of Raffaelle to have that herald of Christ forever before my eyes.

There was a bad feeble copy of this seraphic thing in the church of Santa Tarsilla, but a copy of Carlo Dolce's own time, and therefore one made with reverence and tenderness; and Joconda would look at it where it hung above a side-altar, and would think to herself, "If it were not profane, how like the child of Saturnino!"

This likeness grew more and more strongly visible as she grew up to girlhood, and when her hair blew in the sea-wind of autumn, and the sun found the gold in its bronze, then had she an aureole too, and she had the light, the strength, the power, the mystery that are in Carlo's angel face.

"Almost one looks to see wings spread from your shoulders!" said old Andreino to her, meaning only that she was like the sea-swallow in her swiftness and her faith in the sea; but Joconda, hearing him, thought, "Have you too seen that likeness in her to Carlo's angel?"

But he had not: his eyes were always on the fish and the nets.

Fed on black bread and dried fish, with rarely anything else, for milk there was none, and fruit there was none, and meat was ever scarce, except when a lamb or kid was killed from some shepherd's passing flock, she grew erect, strong, bold, bright, handsome, with a clear, colorless skin, and brown, lustrous, astonished eyes, and bright bronze-hued hair that Joconda brushed back from her brow in rippling masses and cut short at the throat.

In summer she was clothed in the blue homespun linen that Joconda made, and in winter she was clad in blue woollen stuff instead; both short straight little garments, very like in form to those of the Florentine choristers of Luca della Robbia.

In all weathers it was her delight to cast this off, and plunge into the sea and float there, indifferent to wind or sun; and this passion for the water got for her in her fourth year a popular name in Santa Tarsilla, which quite displaced and effaced the saintly one she had been baptized by; she was always called by the people—the few sickly suffering people, to whom the sea was but a breeding-bed for fish—the velia, or sea-gull, that *larus marinus*, with plumage white as his native snows, which came from the northern ocean as soon as the north wind blew.

"*C'è una velia!*"[1] an old man had said once, seeing the child in the sea on a stormy day, when she looked no bigger than a sea-bird on the crest of foam; and from that time she was known by that word and by no other; also as the Musoncella.

It troubled Joconda to have that good name of Maria Penitente so utterly put aside and abandoned. It seemed as if the saints rejected the child of Saturnino, she thought. But when a popular tide of feeling rises high, no one can change it, even when it only sets towards a trick of speech in a fishing-village, and Velia Musoncella the child was called by one and all, even by Joconda, who could not get out of the contagion of the nicknames.

"Musoncella!" the other children cried after her; for in the songs that are sung in the Maremma round the charcoal-burners' fires in the forest, and on the decks of the fishing feluccas on the sea, and behind the driven buffaloes in the reedy swampy plains, the girl that turns her face away is always twitted with this epithet.

Far il muso is to be scornful of, and sullen to, your kind,—to have the black dog on your back, as Northerns phrase it.

She would not play with them; she played with the sails, with the surf, with the crystals of the salt, with anything rather than with the children, who, compared with her, were very timid, and were afraid of her, they could not have well told why. Except that once, when one of them, twice her age, had worried Leone, she had darted into the hut and rushed out of it with a burning brand, which she would have hurled into the face of the boy who had hurt the dog if the women had not flung themselves on her.

When Joconda, who was absent that day, returned and heard, she trembled again. "She is of Saturnino's blood," she thought with fear. She was herself so old; she felt unequal to the task of training this lion-cub to lie down amidst the folded lambs.

The child certainly was not tender, and could be very fierce.

She liked best to be alone and to be always in movement; she never cared to be still, except in the church when there was a requiem or a

---

[1] "She is a sea gull."

choral mass, and the sounds went floating away into the dark dimly-lit place and mingled with the sounds of the seas and the winds without. Then she would sit motionless, and sometimes her voice would come out of her and rise far above her ken and hover in the air like a bird, and then the people would hold their breath to listen and mutter to one another, "There must be a saint that thinks about her, after all."

For herself, she did not want any saint. The religion of Santa Tarsilla went past her; it never reached her, still less did it ever enter into her. They had taught her the usual formula, and she had had the priestly benison on her dusky head like other children; but it all went by her as the wind did; it never took hold upon her. "And yet Saturnino was a true believer," said the good Priore of Santa Tarsilla, to whom alone Joconda had told the truth. Yes, the murderer and robber had believed devoutly, and had been a true Christian, so far as faith and fear could make him so, but this child was a heathen.

"I do not care for them;" that was all she answered to the priest when he strove to make her love Christ and the saints.

She cared more for a fish with jewel-like eyes, when she could steal it away from the overflowing net and let it glide back into the sea, and watch its fins stir and its languid life quicken, till with a rush and a dash it vanished into the lustrous silent depths where it had its being. The child's desire to set all things free gave often a sharp pang to Joconda's heart.

"What would she say if she knew of her father on those rocks up yonder?" she would mutter now and then to the Priore, who would answer, "There is no reason that she should ever know of him. It could do no good. She would think him a hero, as Maremma has done."

"She would try to set him free, too, if she swam all night and all day to reach him," said Joconda.

And as she grew older, and age with its many infirmities made her weaker both in brain and body, she began to be afraid, nervously afraid,—calm, strong woman though she was,—that any one or anything should ever tell the child of that galley-slave at Gorgona.

No one did, and the child but rarely wondered whence she came; she took existence as a matter of course, like all ignorant creatures; it was no stranger that she should be alive than that the fish should be so in the water and the birds in the air. Culture alone sets before the baffled brain the cruel problem, *why are we?*

Musa was absolutely ignorant. But ignorance is not always stupidity; and she was full of a restless, though dormant, intelligence which was always groping about blindly for knowledge. Of the arts she knew nothing, not so much as their names, but she had an instinct towards the love of them; the lore of books was unknown to her, but she caught eagerly at all fragments of legend and tradition that came to her from the mouths of the old men and women around her; that earth and sky were lovely no one had ever told her, but their beauty was full of vague delight to her. "A strange child," said the people of Santa Tarsilla always, because she would sit for hours quite still, with her dreamy eyes fastened on the stars of a summer night or the sea of an autumn day.

Once a fisher-lad, thinking to please her, had given her a branch of coral. Musa had taken it in silence. "You can sell it," said another girl of her age. "It is a brave piece and of rare color." "When you grow bigger, and go in with the mule to the town," said another, "you can have it cut into beads to wear; it is a brave piece."

Musa said nothing, but she got old Faullo's boat that day and rowed out to where the water was deep, and purple in color, yet transparent as glass in its great depth, and there, being all alone, leaned over the boat's side and dropped the coral into the water, and watched it sink down, down, down, and join the coral that grew there, far, far down below.

"It will be happier," she said to herself: "it is not where it came from, I dare say, but it is the best I can do."

It seemed to her that the coral would be so glad to be once more in those calm, cool, and shadowy deeps where never burned the sun and never sound was heard.

When she reached land afterwards and met all the other children, and the giver of the coral among them, and they asked her for it, and she answered, "I have put it back into the sea," they screamed at her; and the fisher-lad swore at her and tried to give her a blow; there was all her gratitude, they cried, in offence and wrath.

Questioned, she could not very well have told why she had done it. Only she pitied everything that was taken out of that fresh free life of the deep sea, and not seldom when she got a chance slipped back from the net into the waves the shining silver of the struggling fish, caught when the moon was high. For which not seldom she had got a blow too. For men and women do not like pity that interferes with their livelihood.

"Thou art a strange one!" said Joconda many a time, for the splendid, abundant, daring health and strength of the child seemed strange
there in those pale fever-mists, amidst that pallid, inert population.
She was good to the child, but she was afraid of her. The crimes of
Saturnino seemed to her fancies to hover like a cloud of guilt above
this innocent head. The blood that coursed so buoyantly in those blue
veins was the blood of an assassin and a robber. Joconda could not
forget.

When she looked at the form of the child leaping naked in the
blue waters, she could not but look over to the north where the islands blent with the golden sky, and cross herself as she thought, "The
father is there in chains!" She was not even sure that the child cared
for her; the child seemed to love nothing except Leone the dog, and
the sea. She had a passion for the winds and the waters, for the open
moor, for the free air, and was no more to be kept within doors than a
mountain-beast or sea-bird would have been; but for human creatures
she did not care, and she had none of the caressing, clinging ways of
childhood. The thought of her weighed heavily on Joconda; it was a
burden to her, night and day.

"Does one suffer for doing good?" she muttered, with a sigh, to
her priest.

"If one did not, where would be the merit of it?" said he.

But Joconda shook her head: the ways of the saints were hard.
Her old age had been already joyless and laborious and bare and mea-
gre. But it had been tranquil, with no heavier care than to get proven-
der for her mule, and bread for her own soup-pot. But now a weary
apprehension, an anxious trouble, were with her always.

If the child, like the father, should offend God and man?

She knew nothing of transmitted taint and hereditary influence,
but her experience told her that what is bred in the bone comes out in
the flesh; and her fears made her see forever behind the proud, bright,
noble figure of the child the scarlet spectres of carnage and crime, the
shadow of Saturnino's sins.

"And I am old," she would think, "I may die,—die soon; and what
then?"

Once she terrified Joconda and the village. A man threw a stone
at Leone and hit the dog in the eye; the child flew on the man and
stabbed him with the knife with which she was cleaning a gourd.

The knife only made a skin-wound, and the man was appeased

with wine and a little money; but the terrible fury and convulsive rage of the child scared the people of Santa Tarsilla, though they were used to dagger-thrusts and long feuds.

Joconda reasoned with her, and punished her, and threatened her; but nothing that she could do could convince the little girl that she had been wrong.

"Leone bites those who hurt me," was all that she would say.

The child grew to eight years old without ever seeming to think of accounting for her own existence.

Then, abruptly one day she said to Joconda,—

"Are you my mother?"

Joconda's weather-beaten hard face broke into a laugh.

"Lord, baby! why, I am seventy years old!"

"Where is my mother, then?"

"In heaven," said Joconda; and thought, "poor soul, more like in hell!"

The child was silent, pondering.

"Where is my father, then?"

"Why do you ask such things?"

"Because the others, they have a father and a mother apiece: where are mine?"

Joconda had often dreaded the question that sooner or later was sure to come.

"Your father is dead," she answered.

"Dead in the sea?" said the child.

People were so often killed by the sea in Santa Tarsilla.

"Yes," said Joconda, and she looked over to the north where she knew that the isle of Gorgona rose from the waves.

"Did he go to fish?" asked the child.

"No, dear," said Joconda, with a pang at her heart. "No, dear; he was a mountaineer, he lived up yonder,—in the hills. Do not vex your soul over that, child: it is of no use."

The child did not understand, nor did she give much heed; her grave straight brows were drawn together in thought, and her curved rosy lips were shut fast.

"I think I do remember him," she said, at last, very slowly. "I remember him kissing me, and he had something cold and bright that hurt me, and he put it away, and then there was smoke, and screaming, and shots, and I crept under Leone's stomach and hid. I do remember."

"You dreamt that, baby," said Joconda, harshly, because she was pained; "the cold bright thing" that had hurt her must have been the dagger red with so much blood! But the child shook her head, and persisted,—

"No: I do remember."

And she sat down on the earthen floor, and put her arms round Leone, and leaned her head on his, and asked him, did he not remember too?

"Bless the good God that made the beasts dumb!" thought Joconda.

She hoped the child would not tell it to the neighbors. The child did not. She was never talkative, but held herself aloof,—not out of shyness, nor yet out of temper, because she was a bold child, and, except for rare fits of untamable passion, was of serene temper, but out of a seriousness and indifference that seemed strange in one so young.

There was no one to give her counsel in Santa Tarsilla.

The priest Dom Piero was a homely, ignorant man, son of a fisherman, one of themselves in both his ways and thoughts, and the rest were all poor creatures in her estimation, shrunken and sickened with fever, swollen with dropsy, or palsied with the ague of the coast, as they so often were, and living quite away from the world of men, hardly knowing when revolution was running riot in the cities, hardly hearing when ships were sinking and squadrons were falling in war upon sea or land.

There is perhaps no isolation more complete, no ignorance more absolute, than that of a little obscure town on the "accursed Maremma," as the people call this rich and fruitful land, because the greed and the folly of men have cursed it.

No one comes nigh it; nothing is done for it; now and then, with years between each, travellers may wander to the sites of Etruscan cities, or hunters come to kill the wild, soft creatures of the marsh and moor; that is all. The only thing known of government is the tax wrung out of the empty pocket; the fine, for which the cupboard must go breadless; no one can write, scarce any one can read; submission and weakness beget indifference to all things; if any great tidings is brought, no one cares; it will make no difference to the people. They creep about in the sun, and the slow boats go out, and the sultry heavens hang over the torpid sea, and when the bell rings they all wend their listless way to the old church and pray to Something which they believe in, but which does not help them, and so their lives go on and end: and no one cares.

It is the sea-shore, indeed.

But all the health and vigor and strong activity and pungent fresh odors and buoyant winds of the sea elsewhere are too often missing here. No one knows how hateful the blessed and beautiful sea can be who has not seen it, oily, and glassy, and motionless, stretching under a gray sky parched with mists of intense heat, and with the fever-fog of the poisonous summer hovering about the glaring sands.

It is no sin of the sea's: the sin is man's alone.

Centuries upon centuries of carnage and destruction and fatal waste have laid the land bare, and brought disease and desolation in their train. Perhaps one day the whole earth will be like this wasted Maremma shore; it is very possible. This land was healthful and lovely enough in the days when the legions of Fabius coveted its wealth; and even in the later age, when Rutilius dropped anchor at Populonia, it was still for the most part busy, crowded, prosperous.

The sickliness of the shore, however, seems little to affect children, and it hurt not at all the buoyant health and elastic strength of the young child they called Velia. For one thing, she was forever in the water when she was not scampering, fleet of foot as the hill-goats, along the sands, or farther out to the moorlands, where the fresher air was. Hardy men came from the mountains, and fell sick, and even died; strong soldiers came on guard from hot cities, and there grew wasted, and languid, and ill; but Velia throve there with a splendid vitality and vigor that was the pride of Joconda and her shame; her shame, because it recalled to her the face and form she had seen for the last time by the red autumn light in the market-place at Grosseto.

"She is his image," she would say, scanning the pure, oval face, the arched, proud lips, the eyes like the eyes of the Braschi Antinoüs, the whole face that had the color and the beauty of a flower with the firm lines of a classic bronze.

Of beauty she was no great judge, herself, but she knew that this child was beautiful with the terrible beauty of Saturnino.

The law, with its curious one-sided chastisement which it calls justice, had taken to itself the guilty man and left the innocent offspring alone to perish as it might; and the heart of Joconda was heavy because she herself was old and the child was so young, and was not a child to put away in peace within convent-walls, nor yet grow up to dwell contentedly in a fisherman's hut.

"Blood will out," said Joconda.

Meanwhile, the child for the time was content enough; she fared hardly, for Joconda could do no better for her; she bit black bread and salt fish with her pearl-like teeth and often was hungry; she raked in the glass-wrack and the ribbon-weed for fuel, and wore rough home-spun clothes about her supple loins, but she was content enough; she had the freedom of the shore and the sea, and if any maltreated her it was the worse for them. And she knew nothing of that wild life which had been caught like a wild beast, and caged like one, on that island which lay far off upon the waters like a little light golden cloud.

When she grew old enough to listen to what people said, the story of Saturnino had grown old and few even gave a thought to it. There had been wars and other heroes since then; he was at the galleys at Gorgona, but the Maremma had ceased to talk of him except when now and then, round a fire, in the forests or becalmed out at sea, a charcoal-burner or a coral-fisher would say, "Aie! he *was* a man!—that was in the good time; we have no such men now; we are all afraid."

For as the monotonous years rolled on all alike, exactly alike, bringing the drouth of summer and the storms of winter over the low sea-shore, twelve years had drifted away like twelve hours, and the child was fourteen years old before Joconda could have counted twelve on her fingers,—so she said one day, looking up at the lithe figure between her and the sunshine.

"Holy Mary, you will be a woman before one knows it!" she cried, with a pang at her heart, for she was now very old herself, and when she was gone—who could tell?

"A woman!" repeated the girl: it did not seem a word that suited her.

"Yes; you are not a boy," said Joconda, testily. "So a woman you will be, worse luck. If one could only see a little way ahead!—woe's me!"

"Does it vex you I am not a boy?" said the girl. "Why should it vex you? I can do all that they can. I can row better than many, and sail and steer; I can dive too, and I know what to do with the nets: if I had a boat of my own you would see what I could do."

"All that is very well," said Joconda, with a little nod. "I do not say it is not. But you have not the boat of your own, that is just it; that is what women always suffer from: they have to steer, but the craft is some one else's, and the haul too."

The child looked at her from under bent brows. She did not understand the words; she took them literally.

"For me," she said, "I do not care whose it is, not at all; I care for the fishing, but what does it matter who has what it brings?"

"It matters when one starves," said Joconda.

"But we do not starve."

"No, we do not."

She spoke with curtness, but there was a dimness in her eyes that was not merely from old age. They did not, while she was here, with her right to the old house, and her prudent savings; but when she was gone?——

The people were very poor; they could seldom get food enough for themselves; who would cherish a nameless child? She herself, though she had neighbors, had no friends; she was always the "woman of Savoy" to all the folks of Santa Tarsilla.

It made her very anxious, for she was a good woman, and the creature that lay on her bed and ate at her board she loved, though she said but little.

"Do you ever think that I shall die?" she said abruptly to the child, who looked at her in some surprise.

"Die?" she echoed. "That is going away into the earth, you mean, as everything does, and then it goes upward and lives with God, they say; would you wish that?"

"I will have to do it whether I wish or not, and about living with God I do not know. I am a sinful soul, though not worse than most. But you do not understand. When I am dead, under the earth as you say, what will you do?"

"I do not know."

She did not; she had never thought of the matter; her mind was blank, though her body was vigorous. Then she added, after a little thought,—

"I will give myself to the sea: that is the way I will die."

"You! I speak of myself."

"I will die if you do."

Joconda looked at her amazed and keenly touched.

"Do you love me so much, then?" she cried, suddenly.

"Is that love?" said the child. "I should not like to live if you were not here. I do not know if you call that love."

"It is love," said Joconda.

She felt her eyes full of the slow tears of age, tears salt as the crystals the sea left on the shore. "Ah, my dear, my dear," she muttered, "it is not myself that will cause you to die for love, but it may be some other,—when I am gone and cannot keep you! Ah, child, why were you born?"

Musa did not hear; she was standing with her brown hand on the white head of her dog, looking out seaward: the words that had been spoken had not saddened her because they were vague to her. Joconda had always been there: why should she go away to earth or sky?

It was an April day; at this season the sea had no vapor and the shore no miasm; there was enough breeze to curl the little waves and send the foam in ripples; the boats were out, and the low pale beach was alive with life as the women shook and tossed the sea-weed and raked up the crystals of the salt in the morning light.

"If I had only a boat!" she said, with a sigh.

It seemed to her the one supreme glory of life,—a boat.

A boat altogether one's own, to go out with in wild weather when all others were afraid; to lie in, all still and alone, on tranquil waters gazing down into the blue depths where the coral-branches were, and the starry flowers of the sea, and the gem-like eyes of the fishes; to steer all by one's self through tossing roaring breakers, through wind and tempest, under inky skies and beating rocks, with the fierce hurricane in front and the thundering waters behind; a boat all one's own; that was the one triumph of life.

But she had no boat; Joconda could not give her one; and when it was stormy weather the men put her back and would not let her go with them because she was a child, because she would be a woman. Yes; she understood as she thought of the boat; she understood that it was very bad to be a woman.

Joconda broke in on her thoughts.

"Wild bird of sea and cloud," she said, more tenderly than she had ever spoken, "you are a stormy petrel, but there may come a storm too many; and I am old. I have done my best, but that is little. If you were a lad, one would not be so uneasy. I suppose the good God knows best,—if one could be sure of that. I am a hard-working woman, and I have done no great sin that I know of, but up in heaven they never take any thought of me. When I was young I asked them at my marriage-altar to help me, and when my boys were born I did the same, but they never noticed; my man was drowned, and my beautiful boys got the fever and sickened one by one and died: that was all I got. Priests say it is best: priests are not mothers."

She was silent awhile, her thoughts travelling backward many a year to the time when she had been young and had known both the joys and the travails begotten of love. She had been a hard-working woman, toiling for the bare bread of life, until she had grown old; but she had been faithful and she had not forgotten.

Only heaven had forgotten her.

She was one among so many, she thought: it was not wonderful.

Then she roused herself and went on with her speech to the child.

"I am old, and you are young. Soon I must leave you, dear: down in the earth, up in the sky, one way or another I must go. I am anxious. There is the little money in the jug under the bricks, and the linen, and the mule, that is all: the house goes back to the master. I cannot tell what you will do: may the saints spare me just a little! If you were a woman grown, one would not be so anxious. To please me will you go and learn of the Sisters?"

"No," said the child, resolutely. There was a bare, dreary place near at hand, where a few good women dwelt, who nursed the fever-stricken and taught the children. They would have taught this child, too, but she would never go to them.

"Within four walls I am stupid as a stone," she said, and said aright.

"But the Sisters would help you to learn things useful for all your life."

The child shook her head.

"I can sail a boat and cast a net; they cannot."

"Some fisher-lad must take you in a year or two."

"They will not take me," said the child, not understanding the sense that was meant. "They are jealous because I am strong. The old men take me; they are kind, sometimes; old Andreino most of all."

Joconda said no more: she would not disturb the innocence and ignorance of the child by saying what she herself had meant.

"These thoughts come soon enough," she said to herself, and added aloud,—

"Dom Piero says you sing like all the angels. That is better than even to sail a boat, for it pleases those in heaven."

"I sing for myself," said the child, "and it is on the sea that I sing the best. In the church my throat gets full of dust; there is no air, and I hate it."

"Hush, hush! The church is a holy place, and the sea may drown you some day."

"It is a good death," said the child, carelessly.

Joconda shuddered; she remembered the night of fifty years before, when her husband's boat had gone down, heeling over into the white, boiling surf, on the very edge of the shore.

"There are such beautiful things to see down, down, deep down, in the sea," added the child.

"What good is that to them? Dead men are blind," said Joconda, wearily. "Whether you lie in the sand or the sea it matters nothing once you are dead, but it matters to those that are left. Child, do not talk of such things; death is no toy, and the sea is greedy always."

"The sea is good," said the child, jealously, as if some creature she loved were aspersed. "The sea is better than the land. You wish me a boy. It is a sea-gull that I wish I were; I would be if I could."

"A sea-gull cannot sing."

"I would sooner fly than sing. It is something that sings in my throat, not me; but when I swim, when I dive, that is *all* me."

Joconda, for her part, did not understand.

"You are a strange creature," she said, impatiently. "It would have been better if you had been ugly and quiet and without that devil in you that will never let you be still. But it is no fault of yours. There are sea-gulls and there are barn-door fowls, and the good Lord made them both. Well, go rake some sea-weed together or any other rack of your precious sea that one can burn; we are very poor; we shall be poorer, for I get too old and you are too young."

Joconda looked after her as the lithe erect figure stood out in the light against the turquoise blue of the sky and sea and the primrose color of the low sunlit clouds.

"She would never be a housekeeping, heaven-fearing thing," she thought, with a sigh. "All one can hope for is that she may please some

fishing-lad and be an honest mother of young sea-dogs. There is fierce
blood in her: it will out."

And she felt sorrowful, and as though she herself had done some
sin, sitting on the stone archway of her house door with the heavy
brown sail dropped across her knees.

Meanwhile the child went out to her task. She was always willing to labor in the open air. It was only against four walls that she
rebelled.

She had taken a creel and a fork, and went down to the black and
purple masses of algæ that a rough sea of the night before had cast on
the shore. Her feet were bare; her blue linen garment clung close to
her graceful and strong limbs; her hair was cut so that it only touched
her throat, and was as brilliant in the sunshine as that bronze of emperors which has gold ungrudged in its formation; her noble eyes,
grave, lustrous, wide opened, gazed over the sunlight, beyond the bay,
to the open sea.

She was not unhappy, because Joconda was good to her, because
she had perfect health and strength, because she had no sorrow and
took no thought, living a simple unconscious existence like any one of
the Northern birds that she was called after; but she was always restless; she always wanted something, but she never knew what; sometimes she would dive head-foremost into the deep water and fancy she
might find it there; sometimes she would get away into the moors in
the great summer silence, and sit there alone and wonder; but nothing
was very clear to her.

Without culture, neither wonder nor wishes are very intelligible,
and Velia, though she had been forced to put letters together till she
could read the names of the boats and the saints and other familiar
things, was very ignorant. Her mind was a blank,—as her soul was;
all that was alive and strong in her was physical life,—life abundant,
vigorous, untiring, beautiful, like the life of a forest animal.

The few fishing-cobles that Santa Tarsilla owned were out at sea;
there was only one man left on the beach, who was tinkering up his
own old boat and humming to himself that song of the coast,—

"Chi va in Maremma, saluti il bel giglio
    Che sta sulle montagne di Solia!"

He was called Andreino, or Little Andrew, perhaps for no other reason than that he was a very tall, lean, angular man; bent, and yellow, and very old,—so old that his age was lost even to himself in the fog of some irrevocable and inconceivable past.

"Avante 'l regno dei Francesi,"[1] he would say, with a vague sense of unlimited ancientness. When a boy he had been very nearly shot by a squadron of French lancers, and this had impressed the epoch of invasion on him; and most things with him were referred to that time.

He was a garrulous man, and had many stories, mythical and fantastical, in which he believed,—things that he had seen and done in real truth, but which had become distorted or transfigured, according to their kind, through the lapse of his many years. To these tales Santa Tarsilla always listened in the long hot evenings of the weary summer, when scarcely a hand had strength to twang a string of a chitarra,[2] and only the tongues wagged on as their owners lay full length on stone or sand. Among his listeners there was none so attentive as the wild bird Velia. She would stand or sit with parted lips and wondering eyes and listen to all he said without a word, mute and awed, and charmed to stillness. For that homage of attention, which she had rendered to him ever since she was old enough to know the meaning of words, old Andreino favored her.

Santa Tarsilla did not. She was stronger, brighter, bolder, than its sickly children, and moreover it was jealous because it was always thought the woman of Savoy had hidden treasure, and of course what there was the Velia would have when in due course the silent life of the Savoyard should sink into the intenser silence of the tomb.

"They say he sang too well, and that was why they burnt him," said Andreino to her to-day, after telling her for the hundredth time of what he had seen once on the Ligurian shore far away yonder northward, when he, who knew nothing of Adonais or Prometheus, had been called, a stout seafaring man in that time, among other peasants of the country-side, to help bring in the wood for a funeral pyre by the sea.[3]

---

[1] "Before the reign of the French."
[2] A guitar.
[3] The allusions here are to the poet Percy Bysshe Shelley (1792-1822), author of the poems mentioned here, *Adonais* and *Prometheus Unbound*. Shelley drowned July 8, 1822 in a sudden storm while sailing from Livorno to Lerici in his schooner.

He had known naught of the songs or the singer, but he loved to tell the tale he had heard then, and say how he had seen, he himself, with his own eyes, the drowned poet burn, far away yonder where the pines stood by the sea, and how the flames had curled around the heart that men had done their best to break, and how it had remained unburned in the midst, whilst all the rest drifted in lashes down the wind. He knew naught of the Skylark's ode,[1] and naught of the Cor Cordium;[2] but the scene by the sea-shore had burned itself as though with flame into his mind, and he spoke of it a thousand times if once, sitting by the edge of the sea that had killed the singer.

"Will they burn me if I sing too well?" the child asked him this day, the words of Joconda being with her.

"Oh, that is sure," said Andreino, half in jest and half in earnest. "They burnt him because he sang better than all of them. So they said. I do not know. I know the resin ran out of the pine wood all golden and hissing, and his heart would not burn, all we could do. You are a female thing, Musa: your heart will be the first to burn, the first of all!"

"Will it?" said Musa seriously, but not in any way alarmed, for the thought of that flaming pile by the sea-shore by night was a familiar image to her.

"Ay, for sure; you will be a woman!" said Andreino, hammering into his boat.

She knitted her brows in angry meditation, and went slowly away from him.

Andreino looked after her as Joconda had done.

"She grows fast," he said, as he took his pipe from his mouth. His wife was sitting near him on a block of stone, a feeble, ague-stricken, wasted creature.

"She grows fast," he repeated. "I wish we could get her for little Nando: she has a rare courage, and is as handsome as an almond-tree in flower."

"She is a child," said the wife: "how you talk!"

"In a year she will not be a child. The almond-tree is first to flower, but it is soon off blossom," said Andreino, hammering at the crazy

---

[1] "To a Skylark" (1820), an ode by Shelley.
[2] *Cor Cordium*: Latin for "heart of hearts", this phrase is inscribed on Shelley's tombstone at Rome. It is also the title of a later poem by Algernon Charles Swinburne.

timbers of his old boat. "The woman of Savoy should look out for a stout and honest lad. She is too much alone. She ponders too much. That is not good. Were she my girl I would get a good lad."

"There are no lads here."

"But some come ashore from the coasters: a child as handsome as that one, with the pretty penny the woman of Savoy has got under the hearth-stone, need never go a begging. If she were like Dina, yonder, she would soon leave off thinking about dead singers and their hearts."

He pointed with his pipe-stem to his granddaughter, a young woman, who, with one child on her breast and another on her back, was mending nets on the mole wall.

"She is a baby herself," said his wife, "and it is you who tell her all those tales. Why did you tell her, if it was anything wrong?"

"It is nothing wrong," said Andreino, offended. "Is it likely I would tell a child a wrong thing? All the others listen and gape; it is only she who takes the tale to heart in that fashion. Things one says are like waters: it is the pitcher they are poured into that colors them."

"The pitcher is as it is made," said the old wife, who was a sensible and positive woman.

"I never said it was not," said Andreino.

She worked steadily at her task, carrying load after load of marram grass, cudweed, and sea-hay into the house, which stood at the edge of the little mole of Santa Tarsilla between the quay and the beach.

When she had reached her last load, and Joconda, looking up from her own work at the sail, called out from the distance, "Enough!" she stood a moment with her hands lightly resting on her hips, and looked over the pale sands, the white stones, the blue waves.

Then she pursued her task of carrying in the weed, as other women were doing also. The morning was young still; there was an opal-hued light on land and sky and sea; the low, flat beach was wet with recent showers; the air was cool and fragrant; even the stagnant salt-pools and the dreary marsh-lands took the sweet hues of the spring-time and the morning.

When she had taken in a good provision of the algæ and salt-water plants and stacked it in the mule's stable, it was still early. Joconda was baking her black loaves of bread, and the house was full of gray smoke.

"Run out again," she said to the child. "You are like a goat: you stay ill at ease in stall."

Musa wanted no other word; she was out and away along the shore almost as soon as it was spoken, the dog Leone with her: though he grew old, he seldom left her side.

"May I have the boat?" she asked of her friend Andreino, and he nodded assent: he had to stay at home and mend his nets. He had his legs stiff and helpless with rheumatism. He adored his boat, but he could trust her with it. She was as good a sailor as himself, and knew no fear.

She ran down to the place where the boat was drawn up on the low sands, and pushed it to the water; she sprang in, and bade the dog stay and mind Joconda. She set the sail. There was a fair wind blowing from the south; the little boat went with it. Now and then she gave it the aid of the oars, but seldom. She could sit at rest with the tiller-rope round her foot, and let the boat go along the shore.

The land had no loveliness on that bay, but the sea had much in that radiant and tranquil morning, and from the water even the land looked almost lovely, with the dark masses of the mountains at the back still keeping the clouds and the mists about them. They were far away, but they looked almost near, those blue and sombre hills that had held so many secrets and so many sins of the father of whom she knew nothing.

When she had left Santa Tarsilla behind her by a mile, the water was rougher, the wind was brisker, the boat flew faster, the child grew gayer. She was all alone on the sea as far as her eyes could reach, except for a few large vessels away on the horizon, merchant-ships bearing grain or spice to the old harbors of the classic world.

The voice that according to her own fancy was not herself, but some bird singing in her, rose unconsciously to her lips as she felt happy,—happy in the sense of liberty, of movement, of space, and air, and light. She sang aloud,—all that sweet, wild, unwritten music of the people which they sang at marriage-feasts and in threshing-yards, about the forest fires, and behind the oxen's yoke; natural song, pastoral and amorous, that might thrill the world with its sweetness; only no Theocritus[1] has arisen among these singers to make fair in

---

[1] Theocritus was an ancient Greek poet.

fame this sad Maremma land, and to string strophes that would echo through two thousand years, telling stories of their sorrows of the sea and their loves and lives on land. Centuries come and go, and every winter the people sing around their fires, and every summer the fever wastes them and they die, and the living still sing because they still love; but the world does not hear the song. Shelley and Theocritus are dead.

Musa sang as the birds do, scarce knowing that she did so, and the clear, tender notes, with all the flute-like melody of extreme youth in them, echoed over the waters and startled the rock-martins working at their conical houses.

The child was happy without any reasoning or any consciousness that she was so, like any other young animal. The sense of motion, of fresh wind, of wide sea, of being able to go wherever she chose and guide the boat as she liked, appeased the restlessness which tormented her like a fever when she was in the house of Joconda, or in the church with the other singing children, or wherever, as she said, there were four walls imprisoning her. The other children thought her fierce and sullen, the women thought her dull and intractable, the priests thought her heathenish; but she was none of these things: she was only a young creature of splendid health and vigor, with sentiments in her that had no name and found no home in the world that was around her: she was the child of Saturnino.

The boat went through the waters swiftly, as the wind blew more strongly; the sandy shore with its scrub of low-growing rock-rose[1] and prickly Christ's-thorn did not change its landscape, but what she looked at always was the sea,—the sea that in the light had the smiling azure of a young child's eyes, and, when the clouds cast shadows on it, had the intense impenetrable brilliancy of a jewel.

In the distance were puffs of white and gray, like smoke or mist; those mists were Corsica and Capraja.

Elba towered close at hand. Gorgona lay beyond, with all the other little isles that seem made to shelter Miranda and Ariel;[2] but of Gorgona she knew nothing; she was steering straight towards it, but it was many a league distant on the northerly water.

When she at last stopped her boat in its course, it was at the Sasso

---

[1] *Cistus helianthemum.* [Ouida's note.]
[2] Characters in Shakespeare's *The Tempest.*

Scritto—a favorite resting-place with her, where on feast-days, when Joconda let her have liberty from house-work and rush-plaiting and spinning of flax, she always came.

Northward, there was a long smooth level beach of sand, and beyond that a lagoon where all the water-birds that love both the sea and the marsh came in large flocks and spread their wings over the broad estuary in which the salt water and the fresh were mingled. Beyond this there were cliffs of the humid red tufa, and the myrtle and the holy thorn grew down their sides and met the fragrant hesperis of the shore.

These cliffs were fine bold bluffs, and one of them had been called from time immemorial the Sasso Scritto,—why, no one knew; and the only writing on it was done by the hand of Nature. It was steep and lofty; on its summit were the ruins of an old fortress of the Middle Ages; its sides were clothed with myrtle, aloe, and rosemary; and at its foot were boulders of marble, rose and white in the sun, rock pools, with exquisite net-work of sunbeams crossing their rippling surface, and filled with green ribbon-grasses and red sea-foliage and shining gleams of broken porphyry, and pieces of agate and cornelian.

The yellow sands hereabouts were bright just now with the sea-daffodil, and the sea-stocks, which would blossom later, were pushing upward to the Lenten light; great clusters of southernwood waved in the wind, and the pungent sea-rush grew in long lines along the shore, where the sand-piper was dropping her eggs, and the blue-rock was carrying dry twigs and grass to his home in the ruins above or the caverns beneath, and the stock-doves in large companies were winging their way over sea towards the Alps.

This was a place that Musa loved, and she would come here and sit for hours and watch the roseate cloud of the returning flamingoes winging their way from Sardinia, and the martins busy at their masonry in the cliffs, and the Arctic natatores[1] going away northward as the weather opened, and the stream swallows hunting early gnats and frogs on the water, and the kingfisher digging his tortuous underground home in the sand. Here she would lie for hours among the rosemary and make silent friendships with the populations of the air,

---

[1] *Natatores*: Swimming birds.

while the sweet blue sky was above her head, and the sea, as blue, stretched away till it was lost in light.

Once up above on these cliffs the eye could sweep over the sea north and south, and the soil was more than ever scented with that fragrant and humble gray shrub of which the English madrigals and glees of the Stuart and Hanoverian poets so often smell. Behind the cliffs stretched moorland, marshes, woodland, intermingled, crossed by many streams, holding many pools blue-fringed in May with iris and osier beds, and vast fields of reeds, and breadths of forest with dense thorny underwood, where all wild birds came in their season, and where all was quiet save for a bittern's cry, a boar's snort, a snipe's scream, on the lands once crowded with the multitudes that gave the eagle of Persia and the brazen trumpets of Lydia to the legions of Rome. Under their thickets of the prickly sloe-tree and the sweet-smelling bay lay the winding ways of buried cities; their runlets of water rippled where kings and warriors slept beneath the soil, and the yellow marsh-lily, and the purple and the rose of the wind-flowers and the pasque-flower, and the bright red of the Lenten tulips, and the white and the gold of the asphodels, and the colors of a thousand other rarer and less home-like blossoms, spread their innocent glory in their turn to the sky and the breeze, above the sunken stones of courts and gates and palaces and prisons.

These moors were almost as solitary as the deserts are.

Now and then against the blue of the sky and the brown of the wood there rose the shapes of shepherds and their flocks; now and then herds of young horses went by, fleet and unconscious of their doom; now and then the sound of a rifle cracked the silence of the windless air; but these came but seldom. Maremma is wide, and its people are scattered.

In autumn and in winter hunters, shepherds, swineherds, sportsmen, bird-catchers, might spoil the solemn peace of these moors, but in spring and summer no human soul was seen upon them. The boar and the buffalo, the flamingo and the roebuck and the woodcock, reigned alone.

The child loved them and came to them. Tireless, she would wander over the grass and moss and thyme for hours and hours; even when the sun was so strong that the very cicalas themselves were silent against their wont, she felt no harm from it, and the fevers that lurked in bush and brake never touched her; in these great calm solitary places where she was alone with the great powerful creatures, four-footed or winged, that slept beside her in the drowsy, sultry noons, she was at ease and happy. Even in the sickly drouth, when the turf was like sheets of brass, and the very trees seemed to faint and pant, she was well here.

Musa tied her boat to a tough shrub growing on the edge of the shore, and began to go inland; a slender figure for her age, tall, brown, and lithe, with a proud dauntless carriage of her head and body, and eyes that seemed made like the eagle's to dart their light into the light of the sun.

The road she took now lay over the cliffs and across the moorland; although so much nobler and more beautiful than the marshy ground that stretched so drearily around Santa Tarsilla, it was not much healthier, for heavy vapors hung over it, and stagnant waters intersected it; but it had much more character, and a luxuriant vegetation, though both were sombre and mournful from the utter loneliness that prevailed there. Musa went onward, happy though solitary, watching with grave eyes the flight of feathered things and the movements of animal life. She knew their ways better than those of the human people around her at Santa Tarsilla; the turtledove and the common coot, the fox and the hare, the mole and the porcupine, and a hundred other tribes that lived their life in the dull waste once peopled by the nation of Pelasgic and Etrurian,—all were dear to her and familiar; and even of the savage boar, the monarch of the marshes, she was never afraid when he passed her with gleaming tusks and fierce eyes, crushing boughs and branches in his ponderous haste and pushing his shaggy crest through the reeds.

She used to wish that she were he, great, strong, bold, ruler of the swamps living his hardy life under the oak shadows, and dying, when he did die, with his front to the foe and his fangs red with vengeance.

"Why cannot they let him alone?" she said to herself once, when she saw hunters pursuing him with their hounds through the hot dank solitudes that were his rightful kingdom. She had sympathy with the hunted, not with the hunters.

The boar, let alone, did no living thing harm; he ate the green leaves, the wet grass, the red reeds, the wild fruits; he only wanted the air to breathe, the moor to roam over, the pool to bathe in. Where was the sin of such a simple need? She did not reason, she only felt, and the fate of the hunted and innocent brutes seemed a wrong to her, a cruel and wanton wrong.

To-day she saw a herd of them a little distance in peace, pushing through the reedy thickets, happy in their own rough clumsy way, lifting their bristling manes above the flower-foam of the spring snow-flakes and the Lenten lilies.

She was glad to see them so, and went on, content.

The sun shone, the birds sang, the roots of the nuphar lutea were beginning to spread their broad leaves on the waters, the primroses and daffodils were making the sombre earth bright in many a nook by the shallows and pools. It was in Maremma, accursed Maremma, but it was spring-time, and even here the world was once more young. Musa passed singing,—like the poet's Pippa.[1]

She was accursed for no fault of her own, like her native Marem-ma, but it was spring-time with her also, for it was youth. Suddenly, as her light feet went over hills and hillocks that here were of yellow sandstone, not of tufa, and were clothed and covered up in greenery, she felt the earth give way beneath her; she sank through the creep-ing moss and maiden-hair up to her hips; she thought it was one of the innumerable spots where stagnant water was hidden under foliage and flowers, but her feet were not wet; it was not even mud. She had caught hold of some tangled juniper as she felt herself sink, and by these raised herself on to safer standing ground. Looking down to see why it was the earth had given way, since there was no water and no swamp, she saw a hole in the ground like a fox's earth. It was into this hole her feet had gone. Thinking always of the creatures of the moorland, she leaned down to see which of them might have made his lair there.

The woodland grew very thickly everywhere, arbutus and bilber-ry and laurel, butcher's broom and mountain-bog and the ever-prevail-ing marucca; they grew more thickly still above these mounds. She stooped nearer and cleared the grasses away; there was an orifice large enough for all her body to enter, and she saw a step of stone down in the dusk of the opening. Musa did not know fear, and enterprise was strong in her. With some difficulty she thrust herself downward into the aperture, and, groping with head bent and shoulders bowed, got

---

[1] A reference to Robert Browning's *Pippa Passes*.

her feet upon the stone. It was the first step of a staircase,—such a staircase as was hewn roughly and laid together in the old house of Joconda to lead down into the cellar. The descent was difficult, the passage very narrow; the sunbeams slanting in showed her the outline of the stairs, and she thrust herself down them, bruising herself at every step.

There was at the end of this stairs a large stone slab or door; she had torn and pushed the shrubs away from about the entrance, and the light from the cloudless skies above shone down steadily. She pushed with her hands against the stone with the innocent unreasoning curiosity of a child; it yielded to the touch; it moved slowly and turned inward; the girl stood on the threshold of a narrow chamber hewn in the dark gray rock; on either side couched a stone lion. Musa entered, timid for the first time in her bold brief life.

Around the walls ran benches of stone; on them stood vases and jars in black ware, and others in white painted pottery, bronze lamps, and amber ornaments, and strange little vessels whose like she had never seen. A niche like a dog's kennel held a little gray dust. There was nothing else. An archway, however, in the end wall showed beyond another and larger chamber. Curiosity and wonder mastering fear, the child passed through the first room and entered the second.

On its threshold she paused, entranced and appalled.

Upon the walls of this spacious place were painted figures seated at a banquet, dancing before an altar, leading strange forest beasts, playing on lyres, riding on many-colored steeds: around them and above them were pictured lotus-flowers. But these she scarcely saw in the dim shadowy atmosphere: what her gaze was fastened on, what made her tremble in every limb, was the recumbent figure, stretched upon a bier of stone, of a man in armor and casque of gold; a gold cup stood beside him on the ground, and a shield of gold was on the bier, and a golden lamp was near, of which the light was spent. About his helmet was a wreath of oak-leaves in gold, and on his breast was an ivory sceptre tipped with wings of gold.

Beyond this chamber in which the Lucumo and his treasures had lain, an open arch led to another room of the same dimensions, and from that again, beyond other doors of stone, two others, divided by a wall of the natural rock. In all these three there were, as she saw, not then but in after-days, stone benches and stone chairs, dust-covered. The dust had been human bones when the air from the outer cham-

bers had reached them, and in a brief while had changed them to ashes, having for the most part little injured the ornaments and the armor
that alone would have told the student, had such been there, of the sex
of these dead occupants. Here, too, there were painted jars and bowls,
bronze candelabra and utensils of beautiful workmanship and exquisite form, ivory and enamel toys, glass and gold necklaces and clasps
and brooches, amber amulets, and jewelry and rings. The walls and
the roof also of these tombs were painted. In one, Mantus and Mania
held dread court of judgment; on another the twelve gods sat in council; here the lotus and the bulrush sprang to life, and Etruscan boys
danced and leaped and strung the lyre; there Cupa and Harta sported
amidst flowers, and Vertumnus was crowned with fruit. These tombs
had been undiscovered alike by Roman or Gothic greed of gold, and
modern science had not dreamed of their existence, even whilst busied in the excavations of Cyclopean Cosa, near at hand, southward, on
the same sea-shore. Doubtless other sepulchres adjoined these, made
under the same low swell of friable sandstone cliffs and hillocks, but
any others were grown over by brushwood and engulfed in earth disturbed by volcanic action: no trace of them, or of any opening that
might have led to them, was ever found, even though in after-days
Musa searched diligently and often.

The graves had doubtless all belonged to the family of the great
Lucumo, whose skeleton and armor had melted and vanished at the
first touch of air. Possibly he had been one of the forgotten kings
of the Tyrrhene people; certainly he had been some mighty warrior-
prince, since he had the *corona Etrurio*[1] about his casque, and the wings
upon his ivory sceptre. The shape and sentiment of Greek art were
visible on all the ornaments of his burial-chamber; the painted vases
were all of Greek taste, polychrome and decorated with divine figures
or groups of fruits or flowers,—such vases as are oftener found in Athens than in Etruria. Probably this Lucumo had been contemporary
with or somewhat earlier than Alexander of Macedon.[2]

When the vast, desolate, lonely lands stretching towards the
south had borne on their breast the towers and walls and palaces and
sepulchres of Vitulonia and Cosa, of Rusella and Tarquinii, of Aidea

---

[1] Etruscan crown.
[2] *Alexander of Macedon*: Alexander the Great (356 B.C. – 323 B.C.), a military com-
mander who conquered most of the known world before his death.

and Norchia, this man had been a magnate of the land; his women, his children, his servitors, his descendants for many a generation, had doubtless been laid in costly state here, where the mastic-tree and the mountain-bay now flourished and built a green wall between them and the world. Youth laughed and kissed; ships went and came over the sunny sea; street-crowds still met for sale and barter, and marble walls still towered up to heaven in man's pretence of majesty and mockery of the imperishable; in cities and ports human life was still the same as in the days of pride of Telamon and Populonia, but little changed in substance and in temper, if altered in mere outward form. Yet, though all living mankind were his brethren like unto him, as one white bean of the fields is like another, unimproved, unpurified,—nay, in some senses far more ignorant and unlovely than he,—the Etrurian noble had no friend or remembrance among modern multitudes, and all his pomp and elegance in death, and all his tenderness for those he loved, had failed to keep him a place upon the earth; and the weeds and the wild shrubs had covered him, even as they covered the empty hole of a dead snake.

The child, who knew nothing of the great Lydian nation that had once reigned in her Maremma, stood silent and immovable in great awe. For a few moments her eyes beheld the form of the dead warrior; then, all in an instant, it crumbled away before her very sight, riveted in amaze upon it.

The air and the light entering with her, after exclusion for two thousand years or more, reached the oxidized armor, the recumbent corpse, and melted them back to dust. Soon, where the warrior, who looked to her but sleeping, had been stretched on his cold bed, there was nothing but a few gray ashes. She stood motionless as though she were changed to marble; a sort of trance had fallen upon her as the golden king had faded into that heap of pallid ashes. A cloud had obscured the sun, and the feeble light that had reached the subterranean chamber had ceased to come there; the painted figures on the walls faded away in the gloom; it seemed to be already night.

She was afraid, but her fear had the sublimity of awe in it, and nothing of the feebleness of terror. Was it death? was it life? was it a god? was it a devil that was near her now?

All the words that she heard in the church of Santa Tarsilla, and which had no real meaning for her, thronged on her memory now.

She was afraid, but she was enthralled: the horror that was upon her had beauty and tyranny in it.

This king was dust. All his gold had availed him nothing; when the air or the light had touched him, he and it had dissolved and perished. He had been there one moment before, and now was gone forever.

An immense wonder and an infinite pity began to drive the terror from her soul and take its place. There was his place of rest, there was his bed of stone, and he was gone, taking his treasures with him. Had they melted into the rays of the sun and gone on the wings of the wind? Why had he not taken her too? She would have been so glad to go.

The place grew darker and darker; for up above, in the world of the living, the sun was sinking to its setting into the deep-blue sea.

Absolute night enshrouded her here; the great cold of the tomb began to chill her veins and freeze her heart; for the first time in all her fearless young years she was afraid; she longed for some human voice, some touch of warm and moving life, some friendliness of animal or bird. For the ghastly dread of the unknown and of the unseen was for the first time upon her. She tried to call aloud, but she was dumb.

A heavy impenetrable darkness seemed to fall on her, and she thought, as it smote her, "This is death!"—that death which Joconda had spoken of that day, which then to her had been unintelligible and without dread. Death had been here so long alone and in peace, and she had broken in upon his rest, and he in wrath had claimed her. So she thought, dully and feebly, as the darkness seemed to bend her under it as under some falling mountain, and she lost all knowledge and all sight.

When she regained her consciousness, a slender thread of light was shining on the rocky floor. It was a ray of the risen moon. Day was quite gone, and night had come to bear death company.

She raised herself slowly upon her feet, and, though her heart beat with the force of hammers, and every limb quivered with a ghostly fear, the courage inborn in her roused itself, and moved her to struggle for life and liberty. The gray dust lay behind her, the dust which was the only thing left of a human corpse and a golden treasure. But the dust to her was neither warrior nor gold; to her the dead man had arisen at the touch of the sunbeams, and had gone out away into the light, and had left her alone in his place.

The great fear was still upon her, like frost upon a flower.

She could not understand what she had seen. She could not comprehend what place this was in which she stood. But the instinct of reviving life made her long to rise and flee, it put strength into her limbs and courage into her veins; she dragged herself towards the entrance, thrust herself through the aperture, and forced herself once more up into the air, under the open sky.

When she saw the bushes around her, and the stars above, she gave a cry of joy: they were familiar, they were friends.

She breathed again.

She felt no fear of the fresh night of the lonely moors, of the silence and the solitude of these marshes that stretched around. She knew them all. When the bats flew by her, and the owls, she stretched out her arms to them and laughed aloud.

After that awful silence, that intense cold, that terrible nameless burial-place, the moles burrowing in the black earth, the water-beetle blundering through the shadows, the stealthy polecat hunting rats through the prickly *pungente*,[1] the common snipe foraging for slugs and snails among the sharp spines of the water-soldier, the woodcock winging his way against the wind as he likes best to do, the great plover trotting to the marsh to drink, these were all dear companions, welcome as the air.

She made her way quickly over the solitary moor down to the beach. Some far-off bell from a church far inland on the waste was tolling for vespers; the night was clear and cold. She found her boat safe, and unmoored it and rowed backward. There was no wind, and the way seemed very long. For the first time in her life she felt terrified and feeble. The sea looked so wide and the heavens so vast.

The moon was full and of a deep gold color: she wondered was it the dead man's golden shield that lay in the tomb all day and at night was held up there by unseen hands? A golden shooting-star flashed down the west: she thought it was the dead man's vanished spear.

The dead had risen and fled.

Was he there in the lustre of the sky?

The great fear went with her like a pursuing shadow, yet an immense longing, an intense eagerness, were with her too: if only she could go where he was gone, if only she could know that mystery!

But she could only bend over her oars and send her boat through

---

[1] *Scarpiurus muricata* [Ouida's note].

the phosphorescent calm of tranquil water. Neither sea nor sky answered her.

When she reached Santa Tarsilla, the village was all dark. It was midnight. The fishing-smacks were still out, far away by many a mile, and the men with them. The women and children slept. She fastened the boat to its iron ring in the stone landing, and went slowly ashore.

On the edge of the little water-worn low pier an old woman stood and a white dog; the dog rushed to her, the woman cried angrily, "Why give us this fright? I bid you always be in at moonrise. I have been here hours, looking, looking, looking, while Leone howled——"

"It was not my fault," said the child, in a low tone. "I have seen strange things."

"Pray God you have not seen your father!" thought Joconda, as she said, aloud, "Come to the house; you must be hungry."

"No," said Musa; but she went with Joconda homeward, and when she got there drank thirstily; she could not eat. Joconda waited for her to speak in vain.

"What have you seen?" she asked, at last.

"I have seen Death, and it is beautiful," the child answered, wearily.

"Beautiful?" said Joconda. "Child, you have not yet seen what you love die! Do not speak in riddles. What have you seen?"

Musa told her what she had seen,—speaking in a hushed strange voice and with pain.

"Is that all?" said Joconda, when she had ended. "That is nothing. You stumbled on a grave. I know those people. They are underneath the soil everywhere hereabouts. We call them *buche delle fate*. They were great people once, I have heard tell, who had cities and palaces and the like, and all is covered with thistles and thorns now; they buried their gold with them, but it did them no good. There are plenty of their graves all over the country, and treasure is dug out of them. But it is not well to rob the dead. For me, I would not do so. You took nothing?"

"I? It all went away with him,—went away into the air."

"That is folly," said Joconda, "and if you talk of it so, none will believe you: they will say you have robbed the tomb, and there will be bad work, and I am not sure whom that waste land belongs to. Say nothing. That will be best. You have seen something, surely, for you look scared; but to say the gold and the dead went into the air is folly."

"I say the truth," said the child.

"You slept and dreamed, and I am tired. Get you to bed. It is midnight."

"But who were those dead people?"

"That I do not know; and what does it matter? Poor souls, their day is done."

"But the earth,—is it all a grave?"

"Ay, and we shall be in it; no fear of our not having our turn. I almost wish you had brought a bit of the gold, if you really did see it; not that it would have been right."

"Did God make men and women?" she asked, meeting the eyes of Joconda, who answered, testily,—

"For sure; and he might have made them better when he was after it."

"He must have been more glad when he made the coral in the deep sea and set the lilies in the pools," said the child.

Joconda sighed and stared. "Ay, there is nothing to make him glad in any of us. The wicked never cease from troubling, and the whitest souls are but grayish and spotted, like a fungus in a wood. Sometimes I have thought myself he must repent. But I talk wickedly. Have you lain in moonlight, child, that you say such odd things?"

Musa was silent. "I think those people are my kindred," she said under her breath to Joconda, who replied,—

"Well, they may be; no one knows whence you come," and said to herself to excuse the lie to her conscience, "and no one does, for I never heard tell who Serapia's people were: some said one thing and some another."

"But how did I come to you?" said Musa, with that direct question which Joconda had always dreaded.

"I picked you upon the hills in chestnut-time," said Joconda; and said to herself, "and that certainly is true."

Musa asked no more. Her thoughts were with all those dead people under the ground, whose gold outlived them.

Her great eyes looked up through the unglazed window to red Arcturus shining in the constellation of Boötes.

"Do the dead sleep all day in the dark in the earth and at night shine in there?" she asked, gazing at silvery Spica hanging above the sea.

Joconda pushed her to her bed. "Leave the dead alone. You have just begun to live. Get you to bed, for it is late and oil is dear. If you had brought a little bit of the gold, now—God forbid I should tell you to steal, but the dead are dead, and it could not have harmed them."

The child lay down and turned her face to the wall: her cheeks were wet with tears.

CHAPTER IV.

THE child never after that night spoke of what she had seen in the tomb. She shut it in her thoughts with many another thing, and did not share it. But her mind was constantly busy with these dead people, who all slept on their beds of rock and when the air touched them fled. She longed to see them, know of them, go with them.

There was no one to tell her anything. In this ancient land of theirs no one knew of the Etruscans. Strangers came and dug indeed about the Maremma, and rifled the graves that they found, that they knew; but there were no graves known of at Santa Tarsilla, and the subject had no interest for them, and was not even intelligible. In other parts the scattered peasantry here and there made a little money as custodians of the opened tombs, and wondered to see travellers ford bridgeless streams and force a difficult way through the prickles merely to see painted caves with coffins of stone.

But there were none of these near at hand, and Santa Tarsilla knew nothing but of its own fever, its own fishing, and its own smuggling, carried on under the very eyes of the sickly coast-guard in a small way, but successfully; Santa Tarsilla within a few miles of Cosa and Vitulonia knew nothing of Etruria.

That Joconda knew anything was because she was a Northern woman, and so had keen use of both her eyes and ears, and coming and going to and from Grosseto through fifty long years had gathered many a quaint random scrap of information, and remembered it even when she could make but little of it.

Musa had a strong visionary fancy, though no poet read or history studied had fed it. All she had ever had to nourish it were the songs and improvisations of the foresters and mountaineers, when with autumn and spring-time they came into Santa Tarsilla on their way to and from the woods and hills; rough men and wild, but often eloquent, making their lutes sound by the side of the moonlit sea, or rolling out strophe and antistrophe, unconscious of their harmonies, as the wave broke upon the sand.

Her fancy, untrained but strong, like the wild "mother of the woods"[1] that brought forth its blossoms unseen over the waste around, made of the dead Etruscans her own nation, and of their subterranean graves her temple.

"You live too much with these dead people, child," said Joconda to her.

"They do me no harm," said Musa. "The living make me angry often, and I strike them sometimes; the dead make me ashamed that I am ever wicked."

"They were wicked enough themselves, most like," grumbled Joconda. "I will be bound men and women have never differed much."

"They do me good," said Musa; and she said no more.

They were sacred to her. She could not have put into words what she felt, but it was very strong in her, this sense of tenderness, of kinship, of reverence, with which the lonely tombs moved her.

Musa, in her utter ignorance, would not for her life have robbed of an ounce of gold or a vase of clay these dead sleepers of a sleep of three thousand years.

She was jealous over them, she worshipped them, they were her idols; let others have their saints as they would, she had never cared for the saints; she cared for these ghostly hosts who filled the under chambers of the earth and waited so calmly, so patiently, with the oak and the thorn and the myrtle growing above their heads.

On all the earth there is, in truth, nothing so intensely sad, so intensely solemn, as the thought of the buried cities that lie with their buried millions under the hurrying feet of living multitudes, or lost in the green silences where orchids bloom, and the thorn of Christ puts forth its golden flowers, and the dragon-flies spread gossamer wings above the fritillaria and fraxinella. As scholars know, she knew nothing of them; but as poets feel for them, she felt.

Whenever Musa had a day of freedom, fascinated by her very fear, she went to the spot on the moor where she had found the sleeping warrior. The place had awe and seduction for her stronger than

---

[1] A beech tree.

anything else, even stronger than the sea. She felt that the earth held a mystery, a whole inner world of mute motionless creatures.

Of death she had never thought except on that one day when Joconda had spoken of dying. She had seen the dull black bier go by borne by the beccamorti;[1] she had seen the torches flare as the dead went home, and knew that they were put away under ground, and wondered that they were not thrown into the sea. Children who had been at play on the shore beside her one week, the next were dead of fever, and were buried; that she knew very well, but she had never thought about it. These skeletons on their beds of rock were the first creatures that made her think of the fate that waits for every living thing.

Was he dead indeed, that hero robed in golden beauty who had passed out under the stars and been seen no more? Then death could not be terrible, she thought; to lie still undisturbed till you went out to the stars and the clouds, that was so sweet and grand, no one need fear it.

She conquered her first terror and went again and again to the tomb. There was the couch of rock, the floor, the walls, the faintly-colored banquet, but the hero returned no more. When the day was bright and noon was high, she would go down out of its heat and light into the gloom of that cold chamber, and sit upon the bed that the dead had left, and watch, always vaguely and wistfully, hoping he would return to tell her all the secrets of the grave, all the glories of the skies.

Another year went by, and the girl grew taller and stronger, and had Santa Tarsilla counted young men amidst its population, they would have looked full well and often at that dark yet luminous face that was by old Joconda's side in the morning mist and the troubled sunlight of the dull church at time of mass. Joconda kept her close, and encouraged her to be silent. Joconda was not loquacious, like those chatterers of the seaboard, and she always thought that no harm could come from holding your tongue, though much might come from wagging it.

At fifteen, Musa, as she was now oftenest called, and would be called in Santa Tarsilla if she lived in it a century, was a noble-looking and beautiful creature, with pride in her glance, and more still of

---

[1] Men (literally vultures) who carry the dead away for burial.

shyness, with a bearing royal in its calmness and its freedom, and an untamed and sombre spirit in her blood.

When old Andreino saw her at his tiller, or from his boat's side looked down at her as she lifted her bronze-hued, loose-curled head, like a young god's, out of the waters, he would say to himself, "That suits her better than distaff and missal: there is the courage of sea-lions in her."

But going to mass by Joconda's side, with her cross on her breast and her palm-branch in her hand, before Easter, she looked but a girl, simple, silent, docile, wise in some things beyond her age; yet she seemed out of keeping with the place and with the people; and the old woman would glance at her, and think, "Would not one know there was wild blood there?" and feel her own heart heavy as she looked.

She had been brought up in the best ways Joconda knew,—had been taught cleanliness, truthfulness, and industry, and could spin well, and be useful in the house, though she hated confinement under a roof, and the moment she was set free rushed to the air like a bird loosed from a cage.

Whether she had affection in her or not, Joconda could not tell: the only creature she ever caressed was the Molossus dog.

As for learning, she had little. She could read slowly, and she could write very badly; that was all that she had been forced to do. But she could, as she said, steer and row like the best of them; she could take the helm of a felucca and bring it safely in over the algæ-heaps and dangerous shallows of the choked harbor; she could fling a net with force and skill, though when it was full of shining, struggling little fish, she often liked to loose it and let them all slide back whence they came; and, furthermore, she could sing all the *rispetti* and *stornelli*[1] of the Maremmano shore to the throbbing strings of an old lute, which Joconda's sons in their short lives had loved to make music with, when they came home from the coral-fishing. The chords of that lute and the clear voice from her young throat made the only melody that ever enlivened the damp hot nights, when the sirocco was filling the sorry houses with sand and the haze on the sea hid the green Giglio isle.

Even her singing took its character from the melancholy and abandonment that characterized the land and the water, and it was

---

[1] Popular Tuscan peasant songs.

rarely that she chose other themes than the passionate laments of the provincial canzoni, for those who go far out to sea at risk of life, or for the faithless mountaineer who leaves *amara Maremma* without a sigh or a backward look, or, more tragic and more terrible still, that tale of Pia Polonia, whose despair has echoed through so many centuries, and whose history still often makes the theme of their song to the mariners and the marsh-laborers of the Orbitellano, of Massa Maritima, and of the Patrimony of St. Peter.

But when she sang of love and all its sorrows, she knew nothing of the meaning of the words; and she liked better songs of war and death. When she sang,—

> "Tartarella c'ha perso la compagna
> Di giorno e notte va melanconesca,"—[1]

she did not understand why any one should grieve to be alone; when she sang,—

> "Come volete faccia che non pianga
> Sapendo che da voi devo partire?
> E tu, bello, in Maremma, e io 'n montagna
> Questa partenza mi fara morire,"—[2]

it seemed to her but poor and feeble nonsense. And yet her voice gave intensest passion and longing to the words; and when she sang,—

> "Andai a bere alla fonte d'Amare,"—[3]

Joconda shook her head, and thought, with wistful pain,—"Ah, you will drink indeed, one day,—drink so deep that you will drown!"

Joconda was always anxious and troubled lest anyhow she had missed the way and done less than she might in the fulfilling of Saturnino's trust. The man was but a galley-slave, a thief, a murderer; but Joconda was faithful to him as though he had been a king.

---

[1] Tartarella, who has lost her companion,/Is melancholy day and night.

[2] How do you expect me not to cry/Knowing that I must leave you/And you, beautiful, will be in Maremma and I in the mountains/This departure will make me die.

[3] I went to drink from the fountain of love.

She was always anxious. The Mastarna, of whom there were none living save this child and the galley-slave, had all died by violent deaths, the deaths of hunters, of smugglers, or of brigands; of Serapia's people she knew nothing, but report had spoken of that dead woman as of a beautiful light voluptuous fool. From both sides Musa had dangerous heritage, dark precedent. The old woman, with her tender conscience and her upright soul, was always harassed with fear.

Musa had a great skill at such improvisations. Silent at other times, with a silence that was in strong contrast with the loquacity of those around her, she would at times, when the fit fell on her, recite, in the *terza rima* or the more difficult *ottava*, poems of her own on every theme that came before her eye,—poems that the next hour she forgot as utterly as the nightingale forgets no doubt the trills that he sets rippling through the night under the myrtle- and the bay-leaves. In country places where the dreary levelling parrot-learning of the towns has not touched and destroyed the natural original powers of the people, this gift of musical language, of words that burn and paint their pictures with fire of passionate and just recital, still refreshes and adorns the life of the laborer of the cornlands and the fishing villages and the old gray farm-houses, set high on a ledge of Carrara or Sabine hills and the fragrant orange thickets, and the sombre calm woods of Sardinia or Apulia. Where the Italian has not been dulled, stiffened, corroded, debased, by the levelling and impoverishing influences of modern civilization, there is he always classic, eloquent, ardent, graceful in body and mind; there he is still half a Greek and wholly a sylvan creature.

Musa, with her old mandoline with its ivory keys across her knee, and her brown hand every now and then calling the sleeping music from its strings, had moments of inspiration like any pythoness of old, and at such times her eyes flashed, her lips grew eloquent, her color came and went, her voice rose in cadence that stirred the sluggish sickly souls around her with joy and with terror. All the fire and the force that were in her blood came out of prison in those recitations, and, listening to her, Joconda thought, with a shudder, "That is Saturnino who speaks so of love and hate and war and death!"

A thousand memories that were not of her life, yet seemed of her remembrance, thronged on the child at such hours. She seemed to hear the clash of arms, the roll of artillery, the shrieks of slaugh-

tered children, the hiss of the hot blood pouring out as the cold steel
plunged in through flesh and sinew; strife, combat, violence, fierce
courage, ghastly death, all seemed familiar to her, and she sang of
them as Tasso[1] sang of the strife before Jerusalem that never his eyes
looked on. Higher and higher, stronger and stronger, her voice would
rise as the rhyme rushed from her lips, and the lute under her fingers
would scream and sob like a suffering thing, and a great fear would
come over all her listeners; and when, all suddenly, she stopped, pale,
breathless, with dilated eyes,—the eyes of those who see what is not
upon the earth,—the neighbors would steal away alarmed, and yet
entranced, and Joconda would cross herself, and think, "All the dead
that her father slew seem to cry out to her."

It was not very often that she could be induced to take up the
mandoline, or show this power to others; but song and narrative flavor
the daily bread of all households of the South, like the onion or the
melon; and even in these languid, naked, fever-haunted shores there
was always some knot of tired seamen, of weary women, to gather in
the shade of a wall, or under the hulk of a stranded boat, and beguile
the time with *rispetti* and recitative.

Such as these would coax her or bribe her with some carnation
flower or some nautilus-shell to come among them and conjure up,
to thrill their sluggish veins, some tragedy of sea or land, some vision
of love or death. So she sang of things she knew not, and in the sultry
evenings, when the skies were livid and seemed hard as metal, and
the sea swayed heavily under the heat like a flood of molten lead, the
drought and the shivering sickness and the parched poisonous land
were all forgotten as they listened to that voice of hers which seemed,
even as the nightingales' voices do when many of them sing together,
to be like the sound of silver cymbals smiting one another.

Joconda discouraged and disliked this power of improvisation,
this inborn melody. "Who knows where it may lead her one day?" she
thought; "and if she become one of those singing-women who give
their throats for gold, and show themselves half stripped upon the
stage of the world, then had I better have left her to be eaten by the
rats under the pine-trees of her father's lair."

For Joconda was a Puritan at heart, having in her the Walden-

---

[1] Tasso was a sixteenth-century Italian poet who wrote the epic *Jerusalem Delivered*.

sian[1] blood; and she did her best to discourage the gifts of voice in Saturnino's child. But nature is stronger than counsel, and Musa rhymed and sang. Knowing nothing of the metrical laws that govern the sonnet, she yet imitated these so well that she strung many a sonnet like a row of pearls, only never hardly could she keep the text unchanged; her fancy varied, and her spoken poems varied also as the quail's call varies, when he cries across the waving grass to his mate.

"Sing the same as yesterday," her neighbors sometimes would say to her; and she would answer, "Can you call yesterday's wind back, or the clouds of last night? Can you gather them together this morning? I can only sing what comes to me."

Under other influences it would have become genius, this facile power of stirring the brains and hearts of others with sound; but here it remained only a gift of verse, as many had, though fresher and more eloquent than most. There was no food for it, except a strophe of the "Gerusalemme Liberata," a story from the "Furioso," or the "Morgante Maggiore," passed from mouth to mouth of the people. Once she found in a drawer a torn and yellow transcript of the sonnets of Petrarca,[2] copied in a crabbed hand by some poor scholar of the past century: it was the dearest treasure that she had; it was her only book. She read with trouble and slowly at the best of times; but by degrees she learned these sonnets all by heart through dint of going over them so often, and the stained rough yellow leaves were sacred to her as the Holy Grail to a knight. She knew nothing of who Petrarca had been, nothing of Vaucluse, or of the entry into Rome; but she loved those "liquid numbers" with all her soul, and in her thoughts he was vaguely blended with the dead hero of the tomb.

So she dreamed the hours away, whilst her bodily strength labored at the crank of the water wheel, at the mounds of sea-weed, at the sickle with which she cut the wild oats for the mule, at the heavy sails which she dragged over the sands for Joconda to mend. So she never saw the lads who came with the coasters, and who would fain have had play or flattery with her in the evening-time, when the

---

[1] A Christian denomination believing in poverty and austerity, founded around 1173, promoting true poverty, public preaching and the literal interpretation of the scriptures.

[2] Francesco Petrarca (or Petrarch) was a fourteenth-century Italian poet. Many of his poems were addressed to Laura, an idealized beloved who died young.

tarred ropes lay idle over the sea-wall, and their tartanas anchored in the weed-choked, sand-filled bay; and they grew angry, and hooted after her, "Musoncella!" and turned their thoughts to Giano the pilot's daughter, who had yellow hair and red-brown eyes, and was esteemed a beauty, and kept her pink-and-white skin safe by going up out of the heat every summer to the house of an aunt who lived high on the Valterian hills, although Giano's daughter at her best was, beside the lustrous color of Musa's beauty, as a pale aster in September's sun is beside the glow of the autumnal rose.

But Giano's daughter, Mariannina, smiled and listened and flirted, and had a merry word and a bashful blush for each of them; and Musa they found a restive, silent, scornful creature; for what do young sailors, or landsmen either, want with a girl who only sees Laura's dead lover and has no eyes at all for them and their *festa*[1] bravery?

Joconda had reared the child well, if with some severity, and throughout Maremma, where love plays fast and loose, and the sower of the corn is seldom the reaper of it, and the hunter of one autumn is rarely the same as another,—in Maremma, where the passions are lava and the faith is thistledown,—the boldest and the lightest would never have dared an amorous word to the Musoncella.

There was a straight, far-away look in her great blue eyes, and a curve on her red lips, that would have scared them, even had any of those passers-by had time to tarry and see what a rare and strange flower was growing up in the stony, reedy sands of the dreary, world-forgotten place. And, besides, there was Joconda, who always banged the door with scant ceremony or grumbled a morose good-morrow if she saw any human being looking twice at the child whom she had called after Mary the Penitent.

Joconda was always afraid for the future. There was the galley-slave on Gorgona, and there was the wild blood in the storm-bird. The only good, she thought, she could wish for the daughter of Saturnino was to live without sin in this desolate spot, unseen, unknown, with little more soul in her than was in the stout shore thistle, that neither sands nor sea could swamp.

"So, the saints will pluck her to themselves at last," thought Joconda; and the dreariness, the lovelessness, the hopelessness of such

---

[1] Festive.

an existence did not occur to her, because age, which has learned the solace and sweetness of peace, never remembers that to youth peace seems only stagnation, inanition, death.

The exhausted swimmer, reaching the land, falls prone on it, and blesses it; but the outgoing swimmer, full of strength, spurns the land, and loves only the high-crested wave, the abyss of the deep sea.

There were sixty-five years between the souls of Joconda and the child who slept in her bed, sat at her board, and knelt before her cross. They were too many for sympathy to bridge them, and, though she loved the child, behind the love was always fear,—the human fear of the tiger's cub.

Meanwhile, Andreino, who was a shrewd and sagacious person, had other schemes for her future; he liked the child, and he liked still better the thought of the good store of gold and silver pieces that rumor assigned to the woman of Savoy. He had a rickety, ague-shaking little great-grandson of eighteen, with a pretty, sickly face, who lived with his father at a wine-shop in a little sea town in Apulia. "Why not get the girl for the lad?" he thought.

"And they could live with me," mused this disinterested old man; "and she is stronger than many a boy, and loves steering and rowing, and would go out to the night fishing like any man among them. It would be but kind to speak of it to Joconda."

And he went and spoke of it, with his pipe in his mouth, one day that Joconda was sitting in the shade of her house-wall mending a sail, for she was never idle. Joconda gave him few words in answer.

"One does not mate a trailing weed with a young oak," she said, with calm contempt, having well in her mind's eye Andreino's sickly and shaking descendant; and, though he talked his best for the chief part of two hours, he did not come any nearer towards changing her convictions.

"She is a crafty, crabbed soul," thought her neighbor. "Maybe she has some one in Savoy——"

At that moment Musa came in sight.

"We were talking of marriage for you," said Andreino, with a grim smile, as she drew near them.

Musa looked at him a little perplexedly under her straight brows, then her grave face laughed.

"Marriage! I know what that is: it is for the woman to stay at home and spin while the man is at sea, and to go out and rake wood and salt while he is drinking at the wine-shop. That is what it is. It is not for me."

The old fisherman laughed.

"It is not only that. There are——"

"Hold your tongue, Andreino," said Joconda. "It is oftenest only that or worse. The child need not think of it for many a day."

"Men will think of it," said the old sailor, "and you have a pretty penny, and it would be well to find a decent lad."

"When I show the penny the lads will come like flies to wine, never fear," said Joconda, grimly. "The child has no such thoughts. Let her be."

Andreino went away grumbling. He liked to act the part of the *padrone d'amore*,[1] though the sickly and scant population of the coast gave him little scope for the taste, and he had thought to taunt and tease the woman of Savoy into proving to him how many of those pretty *amorini*, good solid coins, were in the pitcher under the hearth, or in the bucket sunk at the bottom of the well, or in the hole in the brick wall behind the mule's manger, or wherever it might be that the savings of her long life were kept.

Joconda, left alone with the girl, looked at her a little wistfully.

"Child, you are handsome," she said, at last. "That old cracked chatterer said true. Some one may want to marry you."

"Yes," said Musa, indifferently.

"Though there is not a soul here, still sometimes they come,— Lucchese, Pistoiese, what not: they come as they go; they are a faithless lot; they love all winter, and while the corn is in the ear it goes well, but after harvest—phew!—they put their gains in their pockets and they are off and away back to their mountains. There are broken hearts at Maremma when the threshing is done."

"Yes," said Musa, again.

It was nothing to her, and she heeded but little.

"Yes, because men speak too lightly and women hearken too quickly: that is how the mischief is born. With the autumn the mountaineers come. They are strong and bold; they are ruddy and brown; they work all day, but in the long nights they dance and they sing; then the girl listens. She thinks it is all true, though it has all been

---

[1] Matchmaker.

said before in his own hills to other ears. The winter nights are long, and the devil is always near; when the corn goes down and the heat is come there is another sad soul the more, another burden to carry, and he—he goes back to the mountains. What does he care? Only when he comes down into the plains again he goes to another place to work, because men do not love women's tears. That is how it goes in Maremma."

"Yes," said Musa, for a third time.

"Child, do not let a man touch you till you have had the blessing of Church upon you. Remember that. Whilst I am here, if a man come, it will be the worse for him if he come not honestly. I am tough still. But when I am gone there will be no one, for Andreino is but a gawky gossip full of tales. Promise me that: let no man touch you till the Church has blessed you. Promise that."

Musa at last was astonished and startled. A warmth of blood came over the delicate brown of her face and throat.

"I promise," she said, quickly. "But I do not see any men: I do not want them."

"Some one will come," muttered Joconda. "Some one always comes. Swear me that by the image you wear."

The child kissed the silver Madonnina that hung about her throat, and said, "I swear it; but a promise is the same."

"With me I think it is," said Joconda. "But, Lord, what are you yet? A bird not out of nest,—a bud all folded up. You do not know what you will be in a year or two. And now that you have sworn you will remember."

"I will remember," said Musa.

Joconda was silent, reflecting, as she twirled her flax, on what the Maremma had always said of Saturnino,—that he was true to a plighted word through good and ill, and when he swore on his Madonnina abode by his oath, whether it were for blood guiltiness or for the sparing of blood.

"She is Saturnino's own child," thought Joconda. To the mind of Joconda that one fact made this calm young life seem like a fair garden outspread on a volcano's side. There were the budding lilies indeed, and the half-shut roses, but there was the lava-stream beneath them that any day might rise in fire.

"If only I could be always here," she thought, poor soul, fancying that she would find some force to stay the lava with the uplifted crucifix. But she knew she could not be always here; she was eighty-six years old this brilliant day of San Zenone, when the light and the fragrance of spring were beautiful, even in cursed Maremma.

When Musa was asleep that night, and all the little place was still, Joconda, behind her barred shutters and bolted doors, by the light of her lantern looked at her little hoard, which was kept under a stone in the paved floor of her kitchen. She counted it. It was but little, though the fancy of Santa Tarsilla made it much. Fortunes are not made by weaving hemp and mending sails.

There were some score of gold grand ducal coins and some hand-fuls of Papal silver ones; that was all. Before the child had come to her she had thought the money would do to bury her and buy some masses for her soul. Now the child was there she said to herself, "My soul can do well enough without masses: she must have it all;" and caused to be scrawled in Grosseto, by a friend, on a scrap of stamped paper to make it good, these words of formal bequest:—

"All this is for the child Maria Penitente, whom they call Musa or the Musoncella, and the parish may bury my body, and my soul will be with God, who will do what he likes with it. *Deus exaudit nos.*"[1]

This, which had been written at her own dictation, she wrapped carefully round the money, and with a sigh replaced it in the hole, and set the stone down over it. It was but little to be the only plank between a girl and hunger and thirst and homelessness and shame.

Yet over the face of Joconda a grim smile fluttered as she put out her lantern. "Andreino thinks I have a pretty penny," she thought; "and he would like to sell me his rickety grandson, that shakes with ague like a jellyfish in a lobster-pot!"

The smile faded as she laid herself down to sleep: she knew all the niggardly self-seeking ways of the people, and had diverted herself with them through all the silent years of her life on these shores; but they were sorry neighbors to whom to leave a solitary child for care and for mercy.

"Well, the good God will be with her," sighed Joconda, in the for-mula of her faith. But she was a woman whom a formula could but half console.

Deity at his best was very far away, and always silent.

---

[1] Lord God, hear us.

She would gladly have had those pieces under the pavement more by a hundredfold. She glanced wistfully at the figure of the girl ere she put out her light, as Musa lay on the rough bed scarcely covered, with her slender straight round limbs glistening like some golden-hued marble, and her head hung downward in deep rest, as a flower hangs when full of dew.

She thought once of her own people, but she knew nothing about them. More than sixty years had gone by since she had come down the mountain-paths out of the mist, and said farewell to the great snow-peaks, the forests of pine, the green glacier-waters tumbling through the ravine. She had never seen them since, nor any of her kindred. Letters had come once now and then in two or three years' time, but that was long ago, long ago; she had had but two brothers, and they had forgotten her when once she was married and far away over the Southern sea.

It was of no use to think of them.

"Never hearken to the voice of a man that bears you away," she would say to the unconscious child, as her memories drifted to that time, so long ago, when she had left her Alps for her lover's shores. He had been a true lover, indeed, that dark-eyed Maremmano, but he had perished before her eyes, and his boat had come in on the surf keel upward, and all the widow's jointure he had left her had been sorrow and disease and barren years dry from grief as the shores were dry with the sand-bearing sirocco. If she had never known him, she would no doubt have lived and died amidst the peace and plenty of those Alpine farms.

"Love is a cruel thing," she thought: and the next day she brought out their few scant letters, of which the latest was thirty years old, and bade Musa read them aloud to her.

The child read them with some difficulty; they were short and grave, such letters as busy farmers would write on a winter's night when the chalet was blocked in snow and their mountain side seemed severed by a wall of ice from all the world. Joconda listened, and said never a word. Her heart was full. Herself, she could not read, but she looked at the signatures, Anton Sanctis, Joachim Sanctis, and it seemed once more as though she were fifteen years old, and her brothers were breasting the face of the rocks and calling to her where she stood above, with the red-and-white cow Dorothea. She had never spoken of her youth to the child before. She spoke now in a few words, but tenderly.

Musa, with the old, faded, yellow, ill-writ letters lying on her knee, sat in the sultry pestilential mists of a summer day in Maremma, and heard of that land of coolness, of rest, of forest stillness, of glacier solitude. It seemed strange to her, and very wonderful.

"Are they all dead, do you think?" she said, sharing Joconda's vague anxiety.

"Ay, for sure they are all dead," said Joconda, with a smothered sigh; and in the dust, in the glare, in the furnace-blast of the sirocco that is like a curse from the mouth of a fever-stricken man, she told her beads and muttered to herself.

"Dear heaven! for the feel of the snow in the air, for the smile of the great pine woods in the wind, what I would give, what I would give! But I have nothing to give; I am old and a fool; and they are dead, my brothers."

To be sure they were dead,—dead many a year, no doubt, with the cross set at their headstones, about the little chapel under the crest of the mountain,—the little chapel that she remembered so well, lying so high that the clouds bathed it and the snow scarce melted till June. And she would herself lie here in the sand and the sun.

During this hot summer season the thought of them, her two only brothers, grew stronger and stronger upon her; and as she went one day into Grosseto the remembrance grew so vivid that she went to a scrivener and said to him,—

"Write me a long letter and a good one, and word for word as I tell it you; and write it so that it can go over the sea and the hills without harm; and when it is written address it clearly and in a bold hand to Anton and Joachim Sanctis, above the Val de Cogne, in the kingdom of Savoy."

As she dictated, so the scrivener wrote, and with her own hand Joconda dropped the letter into the bag of the post as it went out of Grosseto that evening time at sunset.

Anton and Joachim, if alive, would be very old men, for they had been older than she by some years; but that scarcely occurred to her. She always saw them as she had seen them last, bold mountaineers and farmers, stalwart and handsome, angry at her wedding with the Italian from over the seas, and bidding her and him a reluctant and sullen God-speed as the mules jolted down the steep ways into the valley, and the glaciers of Grandcou and Monei and the peak of the beautiful Grivola were lost forever to her sight.

"Ay, I had better have stayed there," she thought, with a wistful sigh, as she dropped her letter in the post and made her way through the pale dusty haze of a summer twilight in sickly Grosseto.

The memories of the mountain-winds, the deep still woods, the crystal clearness of the cold bright air, the forest silence on those heights where the sole visitants were the eagle and the vulture, came back upon her mind amidst the heat, the dust, the heaviness, the nauseousness of the atmosphere of the seashore in Maremma.

"Surely I am near my end," she thought, knowing that when the thoughts of youth return fresh as the scent of new-gathered blossoms to the tired old age which has so long forgotten them, the coming of death is seldom very distant; and she jolted home behind the mule, falling asleep at intervals, while the beast took his homeward course unerringly, and when she awoke with a start and saw the level and mournful plains around her, she did not for the moment understand, and began to call Rosa, and Nix, and Dorothea, the cows that she had had at pasture on the Alps when she had been some fifteen summers old!

"Lord! their bones lie bleaching fifty years!" she said to herself, knowing her own folly; yet she could see them all,—the dun, the black, the pretty red-and-white, thrusting their noses through the lush Alpine grass, and lowing their welcome to her through the Alpine mists of morning. "When one leaves one's cradle-land one does ill," she thought, wearily, as the sea gleamed in her sight, pale, smooth, ghastly, in the light of the moon,—the bottomless grave that held her dead.

Each day after that she began wistfully to hope that she might hear some thing from Savoy. The postman came over the plains and along the shores very irregularly to Santa Tarsilla. If it were not the soldiers or the priest who had a letter, no one else ever saw such a thing, save once, when Andreino had been known to have one announcing the death of a son of his, who kept a wine shop far up the Riviera, where the orange and the lemon and the fragrant olive grow together by the edge of the sea. Joconda began to look wistfully for the dusty jaded figure of the tired *postino*[1] coming across the sand, but she looked in vain. The weeks came and went; the drought became greater; the plain grew yellower and the sky grayer; the air was like a furnace, and over the water there hung always a livid fog of heat. But she got no answer. "No doubt they are dead," she thought, and felt the sadder and the lonelier for the thought.

CHAPTER V.

MEANWHILE, for sympathy Musa went elsewhere. She turned to those who had been dead three thousand years if one.

She had never spoken of her dead; the secret was sacred to her, and sweet; she loved the moors and the city of the dead that was beneath them. All the leisure that she had she spent there. With the help of Andreino she had made herself a rough little boat out of drift timbers lying about, and she rowed herself hither and thither in it: it was not very sea-worthy, but that had no terrors for her: she could swim like a fish. She visited her Etruscan burial-place with each fast-day that came round, when the crisp snow of December made the marsh ice and the world white, or when the suns of August sucked up the venom from the emerald soaking swamp.

She found the other spacious chambers connected with the first grave,—tombs with stone biers around the walls, and the same strange fantastic paintings on the wall, and many earthenware cups and trays, and some lamps and goblets of gold. These last had not been oxidized as the first that she had seen, and therefore did not vanish at her touch, no doubt because, though she could see no ray of light into these inner chambers, some air had always come, for the dead were not there, not even their bones and ashes: these had long ago gone forth on the breath of the wind, as her warrior king had done.

To any scholar, or even to a traveller unscholarly, these tombs would have seemed capable enough of simple explanation; but to her they were as an enchanted city, as a world apart, as a thing given to himself from some unseen power that set the planets rolling and made the storm arise and sweep bare the sea.

---

[1] Postman.

When the bare cold rocks blocked her passage, she felt very sure that beyond it, though she might not behold farther, were all the other kingdoms of the dead, all the hosts over whom the king who had vanished in the light of the stars once had reigned.

The upper world, that bore the oaks and the grain, the honeysuckle and the holy-thorn, became almost nothing to her: it was but as a mere crust above the true world, the world where the dead in their millions slept and awaited—what? She did not know, but she felt she would wish to wait with them forever, rather than be one in that sordid, sickly little living world she knew, with its greed over a haul of fish, its savage quarrels over a copper piece, its worry, its weariness, its wailing, its beds of sickness, and its hearts of stone.

To whosoever dwells in an ideal world the world of men and women seems but a poor thing; and Musa began to dwell in one,—she, whose father had seen no beauty save in a scarlet lip, a narrow poniard, a sack of gold, a pool of blood.

The little that Joconda had said of the nation of dead, instead of allaying the fever of her fancy, inflamed it.

"Do they tell of these dead people in books?" she asked Joconda, once, who answered,—

"Ay; all lies come out of books, I believe, and some truth too, they say. For my part, a book was always a thing I thought best put in the priest's hands and left there."

Musa grew diligent in her endeavors to read well and rapidly. But nothing did she find of the dead people. All that she had to read in were stories of the saints, and the proclamations about taxes and other annoyances that were posted up on the piers of Santa Tarsilla.

"Who has got books?" she wondered.

No one at all in her world.

She went back to the world of the dead, and imagined all that she would have liked to find in the books. Imagination without culture is crippled and moves slowly; but it can be pure imagination, and rich also, as folk-lore will tell the vainest.

There was that in the silence, the solitude, and the sense of ownership which made the subterranean sepulchres beautiful and beloved to the child: if any other had broken in on them, their spell would have been weakened: she grew familiar with the strange dancers on the walls, the strange creatures, and flowers, and symbols; she found ornaments on the floors and on the stone biers, but she only looked at them reverently; everything was only waiting: the dead people would come back.

The gray shadows of these chambers grew dearer to her than the light of spring or summer in the thickets or on the sea. Their intense stillness seemed sweeter than even the sound of the waves she had so well loved. She returned to her home with sorrow; there were the jar of shrill voices, the hissing of oil in frying-pans, the cry of hurt animals, the rattle of copper vessels, the babble of sickly women.

An Italian village is never lovely.

There is always so much dust, so much dirt; there is too much stink of oil and sickly smell of silkworms; the dogs and cats and the fowls and mules look hungry and scared. The children play in mud or sand with some live thing they torture; even amidst the hills or beside the pastures they are always marring the beauty of the country thus. By the palsied shores of the Maremma this squalor, this cruelty, this unloveliness, were a thousandfold more painful.

When she went back to them from the silence and solemnity of the Etruscan moorlands they hurt Musa with a sudden sense of their unfitness and their hatefulness.

"It is better with the dead," she thought, when she went reluctantly back to the low-lying shore when the flat roofs of Santa Tarsilla were white and blank under the moon.

When a certain Etruscan tomb was broken open in Italy, and one of those necklaces of fine gold that no known work can surpass for skill was found in the stone grave, a duchess, still living, put the dead woman's ornament on her own throat and danced in it on that night. Musa never so offended the dead. She would as soon have rifled the Madonna's altar as have touched their jewels.

She let all the gold and the earthenware lie or stand where she had found it, where the mourners had placed it when the dead had been laid there; and although in one of the empty biers there were golden chains and golden fringes, and a girdle of gold such as might well tempt a girl to put above her linen bodice and about her woollen kirtle, she let them lie,—she whose father had snatched gold wherever he saw it.

She spent many an hour in loneliness, sitting in the twilight of the tombs, studying the figures on the walls till they seemed alive to her, and thinking, not clearly, but dreamily,—as the ox thinks in the meadow-heats of noon, as the deer thinks, and the dog, and the great eagle when he sways on an oak bough, and looks down through ten fathom deep of azure air and mist of sunbeam in the gorge below.

The summer grew very hot and full of mist and of disease, as summer on those shores is always; the moorland grew full of dangerous gases, the broad oak foliage sicklied and looked parched; the sea was gray and hazy with the horrible haze of heat; pestilential vapors rose in steam from the marshes; clouds hung on the windless air, that were clouds not of rain but of mosquitoes; all animal life grew feeble, languid, and inert; the time was come for the curse of Maremma, the midsummer that elsewhere is the year's crown of rejoicing. In this oppressive weather, when the heavens looked a vault of copper, and the sea a breathless noxious oily plain, and all the marshes and the moors were as though a destroying wind of fire had passed over and scorched them brown, Musa, all by herself, still sought the shadow and the shelter of that tomb whose secret was known only to her.

She was never afraid; she was always watching, watching for the dead to arise or to return. The intense silence did not appall her; the intense solitude there underneath the soil, all alone in that vault of sandstone, with the bones strewn on the beds of rock, had no terrors for her. These dead were like her people.

She was afraid lest any one should come to share their secret with her.

The moor was very lonely; far off, now and then, the figure of a shepherd, satyr-like and clad in goatskin, would loom black against the orange of the sunset sky; and she would watch him angrily and suspiciously lest he should bring his flocks to crop too near the mouth of the tombs, and learn their existence and rob her of their solitude. But no one disturbed her. The herds of buffaloes tramped by, snorting and bellowing as the gnats stung them and the flies fastened in their flesh; the wild boars would come too, seeking roots in the cracked dry ground, and thrusting their snouts amidst the saw-grass.

These were the only visitants that she had, except the frogs that croaked on the stagnant mud of the steaming pools, and all the feathered tribe of summer-singers, that were mute under the burden of the windless weather, and sat dull and gasping in the carob boughs.

One day at early morning, going there, she saw for the first time a human being amidst the maidenhair and the vetches about the opening of the warrior's tomb. She saw him with displeasure and fear. Yet he was only a young goatherd, about ten years of age, whose goats were all about him, cropping the herbage,—gray, and black, and white, wise-looking, bright-eyed creatures, half beast, half faun, as all goats are, always looking as though they had strayed from Hymettus or from Tempe.

He was a pretty brown boy, a mountain and moorland boy, half naked and playing with his reed pipe, like a true son of Pan.

"Who are you?" she said, angrily; for she felt that the moor was her own.

He laughed.

"I am Zeffirino; they call me Zirlo. I know you. You are the girl they call Musoncella and the Velia down in Santa Tarsilla."

"What if they do? Either is as good a name as Zirlo. Why do they call you Zirlo?"

"Because I sing!"[1]

"Who does not sing? That is nothing. Why do you bring your goats here?"

"Why not here? The moor and the marsh are free. It is hot, but there was no grass on the mountain: so I came. I live in a hut on this moor in winter. I have not been down here since Pasqua."[2]

Musa was silent. She knew that it was true the land was free.

"Do you live far off?" she asked.

"Up there," he said, and pointed vaguely across the plain.

"What do they call it, where you live?"

"San Lionardo. It is over there."

He pointed again across to where the red sullen haze of the heat overhung the inland moors, where they swelled upward and met the first spurs of the mountains.

Musa stood and looked; he was close by the aperture of the tombs, which she had carefully covered with stones and dead branches; he, Zirlo, was lying on his back, with his reed-pipe in his half open hand; he had a lovely, dusky, innocent face.

"Why do you mind my being here?" he said, good-humoredly. "It is all so dry; my poor goats have had scarcely a mouthful all the week; just here it is a little better, because there is so much water. Why do you mind?"

"I like to be alone."

"Ah, yes, you are the Musoncella. But it is not good to be alone. I

---

[1] Zirlo means the song of the thrush. [Ouida's note].

[2] Easter.

never am, because I have the goats. I have heard say you are wicked. Are you wicked?"

"I do not know."

"They say you strike people."

"Sometimes."

Zirlo raised himself, a little in apprehension.

"Why do you strike them?"

"Only if they make me angry."

"You are angry now. I will take the goats away."

Musa's eyes shone; then she relented. He was afraid of her, so he disarmed her.

"I do not want to hurt you. Let the goats feed," she said. She said it as a princess might have done, giving them leave to crop the roses of a palace garden.

Though she was like a young dryad, and he like a little faun, they were but children, after all. The childhood in them had its affinity and its attraction.

It was early in the day, a burning day in August,—August, the most cruel month of the Southern year, when even the red of the rosebud seems pale with heat, and even the gold of the sunflower wanes and rusts; when the birds are silent everywhere, and the grass looks like the sand of a desert, and even the deep still hours of midnight are stifling and without air, and the cloudless heavens are as a furnace of brass.

There was a broad ilex-oak here, and the boy was in the shelter of its shade, and the goats too. Musa sat down beside them. She had some black bread and a flask of water; he had the same. They ate and drank as two children might have done on the slopes of the Sicilian hills when Theocritus was shepherd there.

The boy was timid and yet attracted; she was displeased, and yet did not wish to be unkind. The great heat was around them and above them, like a sea of hot vapor; there seemed no hues anywhere that were not either gray or yellow; it looked as though dull sinking fires were burning on the horizon all around in a ring of flame; it was always so every morning and every evening while the sun was passing through the sign of Leo.

Musa sat and thought, How could she descend to her refuge without this lad learning the secret of it? As for him, he had taken his pipe, and was playing on it those melodious, carolling, tender little lays

which had earned him his name from the people of the little moun-
tain-hamlet where he lived.

Musa, while she pondered, on her own thoughts intent, lifted her
voice and sang; Zirlo sang too. The clear voices burst over the silence
of the songless moor, and floated away over the silence of the buried
tombs. Pan might have listened with joy, had not Christ killed him.

When their voices were tired of leaping and falling and piercing with sweet sound the drowsy heaviness of the atmosphere, they
drank the water of their flasks and ate of their black crusts, the ilex
leaves, black and gray against the yellow sunshine, drooping above
their heads, unstirred by any breeze.

Suddenly the grazing goats stopped browsing and began to bleat
uneasily, standing with their heads seaward.

"There will be a storm," said Zeffirino. "We cannot see it coming,
but they can."

"If I were out at sea, I should know," said Musa. She was not so
familiar with the portents of the land.

In less than ten minutes the storm broke, sudden, violent, terrible
as only a rainless storm can be. The sky was a sheet of lightning; the
wind rose in fury; the thunder pealed as if heaven and earth were
meeting; clouds of dust were driven before the wind over the moor;
and herds of buffaloes, with their horns sloped downward, rushed like
a whirlwind over the ground towards the shelter of the thickets.

The goats massed together, with stern outward, resisted the force
of the hurricane as best they could, trembling and staggering as the
wind struck them like a scourge. Musa, who stood erect, though she
was shaken like a young tree, seized the boy, who had fallen upon his
face.

"Get up; bring the beasts into shelter, or they will perish!" she
cried to him, as she grasped him by his shirt of goatskin and plucked
him from the ground.

"Shelter! There is no shelter for leagues round!" he screamed, and
strove to cast himself again upon his face.

She dragged him up by sheer superior strength.

"There is shelter," she said. "Follow me, and make the flock follow you."

Deafened and blinded by the hurricane and the dust-storm, she
managed to keep her feet and reach the aperture that she had covered;
she tore away the brambles and boughs till the stone steps were laid

bare; then by force of will and force of limb together she dragged the little shepherd down with her, whilst she called his beasts. More sagacious than he, with a headlong rush the goats descended into the refuge, while the storm which for one instant had lulled broke out afresh with increased violence. Musa, with the goats around her, stood in the warrior's tomb. Zeffirino was trembling and white with terror: he had fallen on his knees.

"Oh, you coward!" she said, with boundless scorn: she, the daughter of Saturnino, had no fear in her.

Zirlo did not hear: he was so aghast at his own plight that he was scarcely sensible. Overhead the tempest was pealing with awful fury; the echoes of the thunder pealed through the hollowed rocks; but the tomb was a safe shelter, the goats gathered themselves together against the bed of the vanished king, and were no more afraid: they bleated gently, that was all.

"They say their prayers," said Musa. "Say yours, if you are so afraid."

Zirlo began to murmur words that he had been taught to say at mass.

Musa stood and looked at him in the semi-darkness, with pity and contempt.

"What would you do on the sea?" she said. "That is a storm. There are fifty every summer."

"I was not frightened when I was on my face," whispered Zirlo, trembling. "But this place, this dark cold place,—where am I? And your eyes blaze so: you frighten me more."

"Do my eyes blaze?" said Musa, who was pleased to hear it. "If they do, it is because you are such a coward. Zirlo they call you? A thrush would have more sense. This is mine, mine,—do you hear?— this place, and you must never speak of it."

Zirlo stared at her in the twilight.

"Yours?" he said, wonderingly.

"Mine, because I found it," said Musa, and added, under her breath, "Of course it is theirs."

"It is a cave," said Zirlo, as his eyes wandered over the vault and the walls.

"It is a tomb," said Musa.

The boy shuddered.

"You say that to frighten me. There is never a tomb made like this.

A little hole in the earth, and a wooden box pushed in,—that is what they call a tomb. I know, for they buried my mother last year."

"You have no mother?"

"No."

"I too have none."

The common misfortune drew them together a little nearer: Zirlo's eyes filled with tears; Musa stood grave and absorbed: he knew all he lost; she could only imagine it. The storm still beat above ground; they could hear the breaking of boughs, the rushing of winds, the scampering hoofs of terrified animals running hither and thither.

"If it would only rain," said the boy, listening.

"It will not rain," said Musa. "It will not rain for a month,—perhaps not then; the fishermen said so this morning."

There is something awful and weird in a rainless storm, that seems unnatural, and is more deadly far to vegetation than the storms that drench and flood the land. When they are past they leave a benison behind them, in all the freshened soil, the deepened streams, the brimming rivers. But a rainless storm is like a loveless life: it brings and gains no blessing.

The children in the hollowed tufa stood and listened to the sounds in the earth above. If it would only have rained, how welcome it would have been to hear the sweet cool fall of the big rain-drops! But it scarcely ever rains in August in Maremma, and, besides, "There is a red moon," said Zirlo, in the common superstition of all husbandry.

To the red moon the vine-dresser and the tiller of the fields ascribe half their ills. When the red pestilent dew is over leaf and soil, no peasant will ever believe that it is not the moon that causes it.

It grew darker and darker; the roll of the thunder was continuous; the blaze of the lightning lit up now and again all the shadows of the Etruscan sepulchres.

"I am afraid!" cried Zirlo, and hid his face, as the electric glare shone on the painted banquet of the walls.

"There is nothing that will hurt you," said Musa, more gently, remembering the great awe that had fallen even upon her in this place.

"But who are those?" said Zirlo, trembling, pointing to the figures of the frescos.

"They are pictures of the dead,—the dead of long ago," said Musa, with a wistful sadness and reverence in her voice. "They used to reign here,—here,—and they must have been happy, I think; and they had flowers; see, there are the roses like our roses now, and the dog like my own white dog, and the pipe like that pipe you have cut from a reed. And yet it is all long, long ago, Joconda says,—so long that the earth has had time to pile rocks and grow trees above their graves, and men have quite forgotten who they were."

Zirlo was silent: this was a thing he could in no way grasp, and of time he had no notion. If he had been asked how long he had lived, he would have said that he could not remember; he had been always on the moor, always with the goats; he knew what to do for them, and that was all he did know. His fathers before him had been shepherds, and he had been born in a hut made of reeds and bramble amidst the goats, and he had sucked them as the kids did, and grown up from a baby to a child amidst them, and then had had a goatskin garment girded about his loins and a staff put in his small hand, and had been told to take the kids to pasture. That was all so long, long ago to him: he did not think these dead people that she spoke of could be so far away as that.

Nothing is so impossible for the uneducated mind to grasp as the idea of time. Musa only understood it with her imagination: her fancy enabled her to conjecture what her knowledge left a blank. But Zirlo had not this fatal gift; his mind had never got beyond the marsh and moor, the flock and fold. The bare bold scarp that was called San Lionardo was the outmost boundary of his world. As he thought that the ivy and the honeysuckle only grew for his goats, so he thought that the sun and the rain were only made for them.

It is this narrowness of the peasant mind which philosophers never fairly understand and demagogues understand but too well and warp to their own selfish purpose and profits.

When the hurricane had lulled and they could leave their refuge, Musa bade him good-day, and took her own way to the Sasso Scritto, three miles off: the storm had quite passed, but it had only left the earth more arid and more desolate. Broken branches strewed the ground, and the earth had yawned open in many places as if by an earthquake; the lizards swarmed, making the dry grass crack and rustle as they kissed or fought; here and there out of a hole a snake thrust his black or leaden-colored head. The intense heat lay like a fog on all the country,—a heat breathless, scorching, cruel, in which all hues were blanched and all animal movement seemed suspended.

It was near the close of day; the sun almost touched the horizon; it was dully red, and rayless.

When she reached the edge of the waves the red globe seemed to rest upon the water; a cone of luminous white light replaced it in the heavens; and on each side of it there glowed another crimson sun.

It was but the optical effect well known to astronomers, due to the refraction and reflection of light. But it terrified philosophers and astrologists and conquerors in days of old, and startled her now.

The long straight shores, the sea still as "a painted ocean,"[1] the gray skies with their pallid mists, the black heaps of putrefying weed upon the beach, the fierce sickly heat that had a pressure on the brain like the heavy hand of an invisible god,—these were all too familiar to her to seem strange; but the white iridescent intense light of this atmospheric phenomenon she had never seen, for in these latitudes it is rare.

She stood still and looked at it as Antoninus and Pliny and Constantine looked before her; herself, and the boat, black as figures on a camera against the yellow haze of sea and sky.

As she gazed in some vague awe, beholding the sun thus multiplied, she saw the head of a man in the sea. He seemed not to swim, but to be at the pleasure of the water to float him where it would. He never moved, or struggled, or seemed to exert himself at all. Musa, looking intensely, used to all the ways of the water and those who trusted themselves to it, saw that the swimmer could not make any way, that he was cramped and paralyzed. A mere black-looking log, he lay on the glassy surface with the vertical transparent gleam of the luminous column behind him. Then, as she looked, slowly, quite slowly, he sank.

He was drowning, peacefully, unresistingly, as the sun seemed itself to sink into the sea, tranquilly and of its own will.

Musa wasted not one moment, nor thought again of the apparition on the heavens, but waded in, and struck out towards him.

The water was still warm from the heat of the day; it felt oily and unwholesome; the storm had left a heavy turbulent movement in it that was like a tide and was hard to breast. But she had lived in the sea for hours most days of her life, and was a strong swimmer, capable of

---

[1] From Samuel Taylor Coleridge's *The Rime of the Ancient Mariner*.

long exertion. The body rose up, and once again sank, as she neared it; she knew it would rise yet again; if only she could be certain where it would rise it would be possible she thought to herself to save him yet. She made her way steadily and swiftly, cleaving the Mediterranean with her brown supple arms and keeping her head and throat well above water. It would have been better if she had had the boat, she knew; but it was ten yards off her, moored under the Sasso Scritto, and it would have wasted many minutes to unloose and launch it.

She rested on the waves a moment and watched for the man, who might be drowned and dead by now, to appear again: it was very dark upon the sea; the brief light of the parhelions[1] had faded; the sun and its phantoms had alike gone from sight; there was only a dull red spent color far away in the west, and the moon had not yet risen.

At last something came in sight; it would have been hard to tell what it might be in the dusk, and with the sea churned to white foam from the storm as it was.

But she swam to and seized it; she felt the round shape of a human head in her hand, and, being close to it, she saw the dusky bulk of a human body. The skull was close shaven, and there was nothing on the body to hold by except a trouser-belt about the loins, which she could dimly see as the foam broke over it and the motion of the water rocked it. She grasped the belt with one hand, and, swimming with the other, turned now flat upon her breast instead of on her back, she towed the body before her towards the land, as she might have towed a piece of drift-wood.

She thought he was dead, but, having thus reached him, she could not abandon him; and there might be breath in him still. She had seen drowned men restored to life.

Happily for her and him, she was but a little way from shore, or she could not have continued to push and drag the inert mass that lay so heavily upon the water. The sea upon that portion of the beach was shallow; she soon stood upon her feet and waded up to her middle, always dragging the senseless swimmer with her till she gained the pebbles and the sand, and let him drop on them.

It was now very dark.

She bent over him and breathed into his nostrils, and tried to make

---

[1] A bright spot sometimes appearing on either side of the sun, often appearing as a halo.

him vomit the water from his lungs, and did what she had seen the fishermen of Santa Tarsilla do for any one of their number overcome with such exhaustion. The fishermen's were rude ways, not founded on any scientific reasons, but often tried in actual experience; they sometimes succeeded, and they succeeded now: the heart of the man began to beat feebly, the sea-water poured from his mouth, a shiver ran through all his frame; he awoke to life. He was a large, sinewy, supple-limbed man; he wore canvas drawers and a belt of leather; he was burnt almost black by the sun from the forehead to the waist. He was about fifty years old or more. He raised himself into a sitting posture on the sands, and stared into the dusk with wild, fierce, suspicious eyes, not knowing where he was, not seeing the girl in the deep shadows, not understanding what had come to him.

"Do not give me up," he muttered; and his hands felt at his ankles and his wrists, as if seeking something familiar that was not there. He lifted his head and glared around, trying to pierce the gloom. He was confused and stupefied, but his eyes had ferocity and fear like those of a captured wild beast.

"If I had only a knife!" he muttered. "If I had only a knife!"
Musa listened and was sorry for him. He was afraid, this strong, rough, savage creature; afraid of something,—perhaps of capture. She did not think that he might be dangerous to her. She touched him on the shoulder.

"Why do you want a knife? And what is it you dread?"

He looked at her, and realized in a dim way that it was only a girl, whose figure loomed dark between him and the gray sea-sand.

"How came I here?" he asked her, confused still. There was scarce any light; but the little there was, reflected from the skies, showed her a face so sullen in its despair, so brutal in its ferocity, that, bold child though she was, she trembled as she saw.

"You were drowning," she said simply. "I saved you. That was all."

"You saved me!"

He looked at her and laughed, a hard, grinding, joyless laugh, that grated on her ears.

"*You?*" he echoed: "you are a baby. It is a lie. There are men hidden——"

"There is no one. I am strong. I swam and saved you. I was foolish to do it."

He was still sitting on the sand, his soaked canvas clinging to him, his breast and back bare and looking like the torso of a bronze Hercules; his head was shaved close, his shoulder had a brand.

Musa felt the bright brave blood in her veins run cold. She had heard of galley-slaves; she knew now that she was facing one, alone on the lonely shore.

"I understand," she said, very low. "You have escaped—?"

He moved his head in assent.

"You will not betray me?" he said, quickly. "If you do, though I have no knife, I will kill you. You are young. One could crush you to death."

"You could," said the child, and stood looking down on him, wondering why she had seen him this hot, silent night,—why she had saved him.

Another of her age would have fled in terror; Musa did not leave him. His very ferocity and wretchedness rooted her there and kept her wondering, and forgetful, or indifferent, of personal pity.

"How did you escape? By swimming?" she asked, breathlessly; the longing for the bold, strange tale that he must have to tell overcame every other feeling in her.

"Are you alone?" he said, disregarding. "If you lie, I will tear you with my teeth, and kill you so."

"Why should I lie?"

"To hunt me down."

"I would not help them to hunt you; not more than I would to hunt the boar."

He stared at her with brooding, blood-shot eyes that glowed in the gloom like a jackal's.

"Was I drowning, do you say?"

"Yes, you were drowning: who are you?"

He ground his teeth that flashed white like an angry dog's.

"Who? Who? I am nothing. I have no name; I am numbered, like a beast of burden. I am dead and buried. But if I had a knife!—if I had a knife!——"

"What would you do?"

"I should be a man once more. To have a knife and a gun, that is to be a man."

His head sank on his chest; he was stupid, and his mind began to wander a little; he had been in the water for hours; he was numb and felt strange. He stared at her with reddened eyes that were black and sombre save for the flame that could light up in them.

"You are a strange wench. Perhaps you mean well. If you did save me——"

"I did save you."

"You are strong and bold, then. Yes, I swam. I have lain hid on the rocks at night and crept along the coast by day; we had sighted a boat; we sculled along in her, but in the storm just now she heeled over: we swam for our lives; he who was with me is drowned, I think. Just now I grew blind and numb, and I could not make way any more. I suppose it was being so long in the sea. I am thirsty. Give me to drink."

She had had the half-emptied gourd slung at her side, and had set it down on the beach when she plunged into the water. She held it to him, and he drank it dry.

"Were it but wine!" he said, with an oath. "Give me a knife now."

"I have no knife."

"You can get one."

"Not here. This is all wild coast."

He sat up and stared still sullenly into the gloom; he was bewildered, but he remained suspicious and ferocious like the tiger chased by night and dazzled by torches and fire.

"I was Saturnino," he said, low in his teeth.

She understood. She had heard of Saturnino.

"If I had only a knife!" he repeated; "only a knife or a gun!"——

His bronze-like shoulders glistened with the salt of the sea; he sat erect on the beach, regaining strength and consciousness with each breath; the heat of the night was around them like steam: it seemed to her startled fancy as if his eyes and his mouth gave out fire. She was rooted to the ground as by some spell; a fascination that she was powerless to resist held her there, by this man, though she knew he could turn and rend her as the wild boar tore the young dogs.

"Tell me how you got away," she said, very low, at last, spurred on to rashness by an unquenchable longing to hear and know. "Tell me, tell me; I will tell no one else; never, never will I tell."

The hunted creature that had once been the superb chieftain of the hills did not heed. He was looking down the long, low, level shore that shone ashen and white in the strong moonlight.

"Is there no place to hide in?" he muttered; "is there not a rock, not a stone? Is it all bare,—bare and accursed? They will come hunting at daybreak."

"Do they know you are away?"

"Know? Every day I balk them and beat them. I lie hid, and I hear their feet on the stones above me. I see the shine of their steel through the gaps. Where can I hide? You are of the coast?"

"Yes."

"Where can I hide? Hide me. If you betray me I will kill you,—somehow."

Musa did not answer. She was thinking.

"I know of one place," she said slowly.

"On the shore?"

"No. Inland; a little way."

He rose with difficulty,—a tall, gaunt, terrible form, black and weird against the shining sea and the starry skies.

"Lead me there. Remember, I need no knife to kill you. You are young, and to me are little."

"I am not afraid that you should kill me."

She spoke the truth; she was not afraid. An immense pity, and what was that stronger sister of pity,—sympathy, were in her for the hunted, houseless man, and the strength of that emotion absorbed into itself all weaker, slighter feelings, and made selfish dread impossible.

She was awed, but she was not afraid. She wished to help him as she had wished to help the driven boar at bay.

Her lustrous, unfathomable, star-like eyes looked up into his wild and sombre ones; they did not know one another, but each trusted the other after that one long look.

"Come," she said, simply, and struck inland.

The light was clear almost as the day; the pale, sad shores looked wan; the brown and shadowy moors had a mysterious, unearthly calm; the heat brooded on sea and earth like a cloud of pestilence slowly gathering its forces to destroy. From far off down the shore in the intense stillness there came a sound. It was the sound of the horses' feet of the carabineers: they were seeking the galley-slave.

He listened with pricked ears, and crouched, like the hunted fox; then he followed the child, their two shadows falling one on another in sable blackness on the pallor of the sand. Musa led him to the tomb of the Lucumo.

CHAPTER VI.

He followed her mutely, and asked her nothing. He did not doubt her. He did not question her. The sound of the horses' hoofs in pursuit had gone from off the stillness of the night. His quick and apprehensive glance told him of the excellence against discovery of the tangled scrub and thorny brake through which she led him. When they descended into the tomb he asked nothing still; to others it might be a tomb, to him it was only a hollow in the ground, as is his earth to the fox.

"It is good," he said, as he looked around him in the chamber of stone.

She drew the lamp forth and lighted it. His glance glistened; he saw gold.

"What place is this?" he muttered, the sight of the gold stinging his senses to life.

"It is a grave," said Musa, in a hushed and tender voice. "And these are sacred things,—sacred to the dead, and to the gods."

He laughed; his laugh was hard and low, and hurt her.

"The place is good," he said, once more. "Is there food in it?"

"There is no food. But I will bring you some at morning,—some bread at least."

"And a knife. Bring me a knife."

She hesitated.

"I will bring you bread and wine."

"Bring me a knife."

"But you will kill some one?"

"What of that? I will not kill you if you keep faith."

"I did not mean that. I am not afraid."

"Bring me a knife, if you are not afraid."

"I am not."

"Who knows of this place?"

"Not any one; only I know and a little goatherd."

"That is well. Go get me the bread: I am sick with hunger."

"I cannot: it is miles off that I live; but at daybreak I will be here."

A gleam of sullen, suspicious wonder flared like a dull flame in his eyes.

"Why should you do this? You cannot care."

"You are hunted," she answered, simply.

That was the truth: he was hunted, and so she aided him.

"You can sleep there," she said to him, and pointed to the couch of stone on which the golden warrior had rested. "I am sorry that I have no food. I will try and be quick. But I am tired, and it is far."

His eyes gazed at her sullenly, wonderingly, yet with a gleam of gratitude, like the gleam in the eyes of a fierce dog which, after being lashed and chained through years, is loosened by a tender hand, and wonders, distrusts, and yet is thankful.

"If you do come back you will be brave as men are rarely," he said, with a gloom deep as night upon his darkening face.

"I will come," she said, simply; then she looked up once in his face, put the lamp down on the stone, and went.

"Perhaps I should have killed her," thought Saturnino. "It would have been safer, and it would have been easy,—that small throat."

His fingers closed instinctively as though they were closing upon the slender neck.

But Musa was away, running fleet through the pallid moonlight.

When she reached the edge of the sea, there was no sound; her boat was rocking on the surf; the moon had climbed into the zenith; far away upon the white expanse of the sands she saw four dark specks no bigger than four stalks of grass: they were the carabineers riding on southward towards Santa Tarsilla.

"They are fools!" said the child, with scorn. Had she been in pursuit of any creature, she would have noticed the signs on the sands disturbed where she had dragged the swimmer ashore; she would not have ridden by unheeding as they did, and passed on, as they were doing, to Santa Tarsilla unsuspecting.

"They are fools!" she said to herself, with that pleasure in the defeat of authority and that contempt for its narrow means and narrow sight which had been born in her with her blood. Then she loosened her boat and rowed backward to the little town.

The carabineers were always in sight,—little dark specks in the white space of the sandy shore.

She was very tired. Strong and young though she was, she was exhausted by the efforts she had made and by the long hours in which all her muscles had been strained to unusual effort. The heat was still intense, for in midsummer in this country the heat in darkness is often more oppressive than in the hours when the sun is shining. At midnight and for a little after midnight it will at times be chill, but before midnight it is sultry still. The heat, the sullen, heavy air, the singular drowsiness which comes with the moon's rays after these burning days, united with the fatigue that she had borne, made her eyes grow weary and slumber steal upon her ere she was aware. The oars lay motionless in the row-locks, her head dropped, her arms relaxed their tension, and she fell asleep.

The sea was calm as glass; her boat floated on it with hardly any movement; the great white flood of moonlight fell upon it and her: together they made but a small, dark, motionless thing in the midst of that silvery field of light. How long she slept she never knew: when she awoke with a start the cool of the midnight had come that comes with the descent of the dews.

Used to the look of the sky, she knew that it was midnight by the stars. She awoke refreshed, but conscience-stricken. Every moment she delayed was a pang of hunger and of fear more to the hunted man. She owed him no service, but she pitied him; she had promised him; these were bonds that knit her to him strongly, and that it never occurred to her to break.

But how to get him food and wine and the weapon that he had prayed for?—the weapon that she could understand would be sweeter to him than any drink to his thirst, any bread to his famine? She did not know how to find them. The houses of Santa Tarsilla would be all shut and the people all slumbering by the time she reached there, and money she had none, even had there been any place upon the coast nearer than the fishing-town that was her home. There was nothing for it but to ask Joconda.

She bent her back to the oars once more and rowed on steadily; the carabineers had passed out of sight long before: whilst she had been asleep they had ridden down into Santa Tarsilla and had revived long-dormant memories with the old forgotten cry of Saturnino.

She rowed on, and in somewhat less than two hours she saw the low, gray line of the stone piers of the little harbor, and the masts of the few old useless boats that were left at home, and the round white towers of the soldiery and coast-guard. All was quite quiet.

She steered herself carefully within the shallow water, and fastened the boat to the ring. Where the moonlight is so brilliant the shadows are proportionately black. She could keep out of sight in these shadows and did so, for she heard voices and a sort of stir in the narrow lanes that parted the houses one from another. Some people were awake, loitering languidly on the stones, or hanging from the open windows. The passage of the mounted carabineers through the town had roused them, but only roused them slightly. To men and women shaking with ague, feeble with fever, ill always through brain and bone with the deadly air, it mattered very little whether the law had its rights or not.

For the most part they would have hindered the law rather than have helped it; but even to hinder it they would have had but scant energy.

She went by under the shade cast by the projecting roofs unseen by any of them. She gathered from their talk that the carabineers had searched through the place, then ridden on; men were saying to one another that they remembered Saturnino Mastarna, remembered the day the guards had brought him down from the hills with his feet tied under his horse's belly for the market crowd to gaze at in dull Grosseto.

"He was a brave man," they said, with a reverence in their voices that they never gave to the guardians of the law.

"He was brave," thought Musa, as she heard. "Then it must be right to save him."

She went to her own home.

All was locked and barred; but she pushed herself through the stable-windows by withdrawing the wooden shutter on the outside.

Leone did not give tongue; he came to her in silence, only moving his tail with welcome. Joconda lay in a sound slumber, so sound that she might have been murdered in her sleep without awaking. A gleam from the moon came in and fell on her hard, toil-worn, withered face, and her knotted hands, and her rough white hair, and the sheaf of bleached palm blessed at Easter that hung above her bed to keep away evil spirits and to please the saints.

Musa looked at her with a great tenderness gleaming in her own eyes.

"I am going to rob her," she thought, wistfully. "But I will tell her in the morning, and if she be angry then I will sell my gold Madonnina and pay her. That will be just."

Without arousing the sleeper, she took a brown loaf, a flask of wine, and a knife.

Then she soothed Leone with a caress, and went as she had come,

softly and unseen, drawing the stable-shutter behind her carefully
when she had gone forth again into the air. She was now very tired.
But her spirit was strong and her will resolute. She never thought of
not returning to the tomb. Not to keep faith with that friendless creature would have seemed to her most vile. She could not have told why,
but when he had every man's hand against him it would have seemed
to her vile and mean to desert him or betray him. To spare herself did
not occur to her. She would go on, she said to herself,—go on till she
dropped down, perhaps, as the women did sometimes from sunstroke
when they were raking in the salt.

It was now day-dawn; the pale gleam of morning was beginning
to show over the dusk of the marshes and mountains far away inland.
Another long, dreary, scorching, cloudless day was about to be born
on Maremma.

She stepped once more into the boat, and once more retraced her
path across the waters.

The gossipers had all gone within to sleep a little; a few early-risen
toilers, too aged or ill to be away with the coral-fleet, were getting out
tackle and nets to go and try for fish close in to shore, or going with
their sickles to cut the maritime rush that grew in long lines here and
there between the beach and marsh.

No one noticed her, because they were so used to see her out at
daybreak by, or on, the sea.

She got away safely, and rowed on along the coast. She was so
fatigued that she could barely grasp the oars and move them, and she
made slow headway against the inert water. There were fish rising
all around her; before going deep down in the heat of the noon they
passed the early morning on the surface, catching insects and infuso-
ria. The sun was not yet up, and it was cool; yet all the landscape was
pale, gray, and weary-looking, as if the night had brought little repose
and little freshness.

It was a toilsome journey: it seemed to her to be endless. Midway
in it the sun rose, and the touch of its rays on her bare arms felt like
fire. In the great heats even sunrise loses its charm, and seems but a
trouble the more to the tired eyes that wake from startled sleep and
wasting sweats.

With pain and effort she dragged herself ashore at last, three
hours after she had left the pier of Santa Tarsilla, and began her toilsome walk through the close-growing timber and thorny thickets up

to the tomb. Her head swam, her sight began to fail, her limbs felt heavy as lead; but the thought of the faith that she kept, of the succor she went to give, sustained her.

"He will not doubt now," she thought. "He will be glad."

She had brought away with her, as well as the knife, three silver coins that had been given her once by a traveller whom she had guided across the marshes: they were all she had; she meant to give them to Saturnino.

She pushed her way through the cistus, and bearberry, and rosemary; now and then a partridge flew up before her feet, but there were no birds singing; the season of song was past. There were hundreds of lizards rushing to and fro, and the big wood rat, and the fox, and the snipe, and the plover, were still astir, going home after their night's foray; that was all.

She pushed the bushes aside and ran down the steps, and entered the cave without fear, thinking only of the help that she brought. The tomb was empty.

In answer to her shouts there was only a dull echo thrown back from the roof of sandstone.

Suspicion and distrust, the seeds sown by captivity, and sure to bring forth fruit in sullen sins of hatred and of fear, had been too strong for the nature of the galley-slave to resist their influence and their instinct. How could he tell that she would not sell her secret for a price, and only return to bring his capturers with her? How could he tell?

Alone there in the bowels of the earth, cowardice and mistrust had mastered him. He had left his shelter and fled.

Looking round, she saw that the golden lamp and the golden helm and all the toys of gold were gone.

Saturnino had robbed the dead.

CHAPTER VII.

WHEN late in the hot day Musa returned to Santa Tarsilla, after long dreamless sleep of intense fatigue which had lasted many hours, she was very pale, and her face had a look of sullen pain. For the first time in her young life she had been deceived. Where he had gone in those wild swamps and barren moors she knew not, but he had deceived her: that was enough to know.

He had robbed the dead and their gods. He became abhorrent to her.

Of the thanklessness to herself she thought little, but of that theft of the sacred things she had no forgiveness. She had never felt even tempted to take them; they had been hallowed to her; they had been the armor, the arms, the jewels, the possessions, of the golden king whom the first ray of light had set free to ascend to the stars. She would sooner have stolen the chalice off the church altar, the jewels off the saint's shrine, than have touched those treasures of the Etruscan dead.

The flight and the theft of the man she had saved weighed on her with a sense of shame; a burning indignation consumed her. She was silent by nature; she crushed the pain in silence into her heart, and said to herself that she would never speak of that traitor,—never tell any living being of her rescue of him and of her betrayal by him,—never; not even Joconda.

She came home to the stone pier of Santa Tarsilla and fastened up the boat in silence, and took her way through the little town, steeped in the drowsy calm of a sultry and late afternoon.

Here and there in an open court, or upon a stone bench, or under the deep eaves of a roof, some figure was lying asleep: that was all. The stillness of heat and of exhaustion had fallen on all the place, and the very dogs lay motionless and stupid in what little shade there was to be found anywhere.

Where was he, the hunted man, in this intolerable glare of day?

She thought of him fleeing always over the brown burnt moors, the pallid wastes of sand, with the stolen gold that he would be able neither to eat nor drink, and would not dare to barter. Let the guards have him if they would, she thought: he was vile.

Nothing is so cruel as youth in its scorn: she was full of scorn, and cruel. She would have seen the guards take him now, and would not have lifted her hand or opened her lips. He was a traitor and a thief.

Yet it hurt her to remember what he had done. The betrayal weighed upon her with a heavy hand. She had given him sanctuary, and he had robbed her.

A girl she knew, Fulvia, daughter of Gianno, was sitting in an open door, sunning her rich gold tresses in the old Venetian way.

"Where have you been?" the girl called to her. "There was a stir last night. Some carabineers came hunting for a man that had got away off Gorgona. They said he was Saturnino. Saturnino used to rule all the mountains over there, so my father says: have you heard tell of it?"

"I have been away on the sea," said Musa, and passed on. The girl called after her,—

"He is loose on the country, so they say; he has got away somewhere: I thought you might know. But you have never a word for any one, you graceless, sullen thing."

Musa passed on along the line of burning stone-faced houses with their middens stinking in front of them, and beyond the middens the rotten sea-weeds, the salt and clammy beach.

She reached her home in a few moments: the house was closed as it had been at midnight, and was quite as still. She was not frightened at that, since often Joconda went far afield with the old mule, and shut her dwelling closely in her absence. Perhaps Joconda had gone to seek for her, herself, alarmed at her being away so long upon the water: so she thought.

She tried the house door: the dog was howling low within. She could not stir the door, which fastened within with ancient iron bolts and locks. She unslipped the stable shutter, as before, and by the stable entered the house as in the night. The mule was in his place, munching straw and the withered leaves of cane.

She went thence into the room of Joconda: Leone did not cease to howl, although he saw her.

Joconda still lay sleeping.

"She must be ill," thought Musa, with a sudden pang, and the chillness of a new vague terror falling on her.

She sprang to the bedside where the dog lay moaning. Joconda had not moved since the night: only on her face there was shining, instead of the silvery moonlight, the yellowish, sickly glare of the setting sun.

She had died in her sleep.

A terrible cry rang through the empty house out to the seashore.

Musa was left alone.

CHAPTER VIII.

WHILST in the midnight hours the carabineers had searched Santa Tar-silla, and the people had spoken of Saturnino and recalled the old days of his prowess and fame, this long, toil-worn, rough, enduring life had come to an end,—decently, silently, without complaint and without companionship, as it had been spent.

When the neighbors, apathetic but not brutal,—though, being a foreign woman, they had let her live alone,—came running in at the sound of that terrible, desolate cry, they found Musa lying senseless by the white dog, and the blanched blest palm hanging above a body already cold in the stiffness of death.

Joconda must have died somewhere about midnight, so the apoth-ecary told them when he came. He said that death had come from sheer old age; the life had ceased, that was all,—as an old tree falls, as an old clock refuses to move and grows dumb. There was nothing strange in it. She had been eighty-five years old, if one. No one had noticed her house being closed all day, because it was so often shut up in that way when she was absent.

When Musa regained consciousness, she saw the brown, with-ered, labor-bent body lying still upon the mattress, as an old broken bough will lie on the cold ground.

"I robbed her last night!" she said, suddenly, with a piteous self-reproach. Her great eyes had a grievous despair and shame in them.

Happily for her, in the clamor of tongues around her no one heard or heeded. No one thought of her, or troubled about her. Jo-conda must be buried before another day broke, that was what they thought of, and talked of who would have the little she had saved, and the mule. It was a strong beast and useful, although old; they began to ask each other what they would give for it, and to wonder who had the right to see to the burial and pay for the mass. She was known to have had a little money hidden somewhere, but perhaps she had people that belonged to her over seas there in far Savoy. None of them thought of Musa, who, when that first bitter cry of self-reproach had burst from her, had sat mute and still beside the dead, with the white dog between her knees. When they fetched the priest from vespers, he spoke to her. She stared; his words went by her without awaking in her any sense of them; she was dumb as the dog was; her sorrow had neither tears nor speech, yet it was very great.

Between Joconda and herself there had been seldom tenderness, but there had been always love. An immense void had suddenly yawned in her path; an immense loss, that she could ill measure, had fallen on her. She had not been very happy, for life at Santa Tarsilla does not contain many of the elements of happiness; she had always vaguely suffered from the narrowness and stupor of it, from the languor and disease that were around her, and her whole nature and intelligence had always needed a richer soil, a finer air. But Joconda had been good to her always. She had been all that the girl had known of mother-like care and watchfulness; she had been always just, and in her own rough way indulgent. What she knew of the wild, fierce strain that was in Musa's veins had made her very patient of her wanderings on sea and land, and of her sudden passions. Joconda had always said to herself, "It is the blood of the Mastarna," and so had made excuse.

It had been a part of her life to see Joconda always near her; she had never had to take thought for herself; the bread and the broth were always on the board; her linen in summer, her goat's-wool clothes in winter, were always ready; as she had dropped asleep she had always heard the voice of Joconda muttering her aves in that faith in some answer coming some time, from somewhere, which had never left her; though an answer she never had got, unless this death which had come to her all unawares in the stillness of the night could be called one.

CHAPTER IX.

THEY buried Joconda at midnight, with the horrible, selfish haste of the country's habits and laws in death.

The day before she had been alive,—a shrewd, brave, wise, and faithful woman in her own rude way, boiling the soup in her pot, cutting the canes for her mule, looking at the sea and the sun, giving good-day to her neighbors from her house-door; and now she was thrown into a hole of the earth, and the earth was cast in upon her, and she was nothing,—nothing,—less than the fish that died in the nets on the shore, for they could be sold, and so were of value. To the living, human beings are cruel very often; but to the dead they are always brutal, be the dead pauper or king.

Only one torch burned for her: old Andreino, the fisherman, bore

it. It burnt steadily in the hot, heavy night. Musa and the white dog
stood by the grave. She moved as if she were walking in her sleep, and
never a sound came from her lips. The dog hung his head, but was
quiet, pressing close to her side. Once he threw his muzzle in the air
and howled. It was when the first shovelful of sand and clay fell on the
dead body.

The priest spoke some commonplace words of consolation and
of hope: he was a simple, honest man, the son of seafaring people,
and born fifty years earlier in Santa Tarsilla. Musa did not hear what
he spoke.

She went home in unbroken silence; the night was oppressive, the
sea was still, the heavens were covered with mist. There was one more
grave on the low sandy shore; that was all.

She went home to the house and barred herself in and threw herself on the bed where Joconda had died. No one had the heart to disturb her that night.

"Let her sleep if she can," said the priest and old Andreino. But for
them the women would have dragged her out and made her understand that she was homeless.

All the day following she kept her door and her shutters barred,
and would see no living creature. Towards evening the priest of the
parish came: he was an old man, a little bibulous and garrulous, not
clever or wise, but simple of spirit, and honest and cheerful. She would
not open to him until he said that he brought her a message from the
dead. Then she let him enter, shutting the door again on the peering
faces of Andreino and some women gathered out there in the hot
air.

The priest spoke kindly to her, a little frightened at her looks; she
was quite silent, and her eyes were dry, though their lids were swollen
and very weary.

He told her that the dead woman had left with him the knowledge of the precise spot where her little treasure was hidden, and he
counted the stones of the paved floor from right to left, and found
the one beneath which was the pitcher containing the coins in it, and
he raised it up and took the pitcher out, and read to her the words of
bequest leaving to her the money, the furniture, the hardware, the
mule,—all, in a word, that Joconda had possessed,—on the bit of yellow paper folded across the jug.

Musa listened and saw; she said nothing; she did not even notice that on that paper she had herself no name save the baptismal one from the Egyptian saint. She only thought all the while,—

"She was all I had on earth, and she is gone."

The priest tried to speak a few phrases in season of counsel, to hazard a few questions, but he made no way. Musa was still and mute; she seemed to him like a statue; she said only, as she looked at the pitcher,—

"This is mine?"

"Surely," said the priest. "At least there are none that I know of nearer of kin to dispute, and, even if there were, the bequest, I think, would hold good. I am not sure, but so I believe."

Musa lifted the pavement and replaced the pitcher with its coins in its hole. Then, with a sound that was half sob, half sigh, she sat down on the edge of the low bed and said to the good man,—

"Father, will you go? I am best alone."

"But you cannot remain alone,—you, a girl so young—"

She did not answer. There was something in her look and in her attitude that awed him: he was used to the vehement outbursts and the evanescent passions of a passionate but quickly-consoled people; he did not understand her; he thought hastily that in the morning he must take counsel with the Sisters up at the convent, and muttered his blessing feebly and went away. She barred the door behind him.

The good man went home and ate his little supper of small fish and oil, and drank a sweet pale wine, and gossiped with his *capellano*, telling him that the woman of Savoy had, after all, died worth a pretty penny,—a whole jugful of gold pieces under the stones and left to the girl. Who was the girl? What would she do?

The *capellano* in turn went out and gossiped with the few dwellers in Santa Tarsilla, all loitering or lying about by the edge of the sea this hot night, gasping for a breath of air, and, in default of the air, grateful to hear some news.

They grumbled much one to another; for they were dissatisfied, and their curiosity had no food for its appetites.

"One would have thought to know who that wench is now," they grumbled to one another, and some of the women said,—

"She has got no name. That is odd. Do you mind of the time when Saturnino was taken up in the hills yonder? Some did think then the girl was Saturnino's daughter. But Joconda was always so close."

Musa herself did not notice that she had no name in that little wrinkled bit of paper which gave her the money and the mule.

Alone she passed the long oppressive sultry hours.

She heard the voices of the people outside as the sun dropped and the night came; but she would not open, even to old Andreino, who rapped at the door with a stick and called to her more than once. She lay awake all the night long; towards dawn she fell into what was rather stupor than sleep. In her sleep she was always trying to loosen the weight of the sand and the earth that lay on the body of her lost friend, and to lift up Joconda from that close and cruel prison. She thought she could have borne her loss if the dead woman had been laid gently down upon those rocky biers in the Etruscan tomb, there to wait till the moonlight should touch her and take her to itself, as it had touched and taken the Etruscan king. But how could she ever rise from that narrow bed, from that stifling sand, from that ghastly crowded place where the dead lay like mounds of putrid fish, thrown down and forsaken?

It was late in the day when the child awoke from this heavy troubled sleep, which left her dazed and fatigued, as she had been at night,—awoke with the burning sun on her aching eyes, to hear impatient hands knocking at the shutters and the house-door.

"Art thou dead too?" the shrill voices of women were calling.

Musa shuddered, and in the scorching heat of the morning felt cold.

Was Joconda in truth lost forever? Had this death which had been so long in the mist of a vague dread and foreboding become a fact? Would she never come back? The girl felt numb and frozen.

The neighbors knocked louder and louder. She rose, clothed herself, and opened to them.

"What do you want?" she asked of them.

They burst into the room, the five or six women who were all that Santa Tarsilla held in summer-time; a little sickly child or two between them, old Andreino a little way behind.

"My dear one," he said, with a hand to his eyes, "if any love can be of use to you I and my Serafina too——"

"You can have nothing ready in the house. Come and break your fast with us, Musa mine," said the foremost woman, ruthlessly drowning the rest of his phrases with her own shrill tones, to be in turn swamped in a neighbor's fuller voice, that cried,——

"Not a wink of sleep have I had this night, thinking of the good soul gone to her rest; neither have you closed your eyes, my dear; that one sees without asking. I have brought a fresh egg——"

"Addle your eggs!" cried a third, elbowing her way with scorn; though, indeed, eggs were rare as roses on the sad sea-shore. "Let the girl come and take bit and sup with those who can be as a mother to her. How should she dwell alone and fare and cook for herself? My man has just brought in some fine fresh crayfish——"

"Get out," said old Andreino, fiercely: "who should she come to, if not to her oldest friends? My Serefina is in bed with the ague, or she would have been here all night. My house is Musa's, and that I promised long ago to the good dead soul sitting out by the threshold there. I said to Joconda,—I said,——"

He continued to talk for ten full minutes, but no one heard a syllable more that he said, by reason of the superior strength of screaming that the women's lungs possessed.

Amidst the hubbub and outcries the girl stood quite still; she scarcely seemed even to see that the people were there. When they found her silence continue so long, and that neither by look nor by word was she moved to respond to their hospitable and fond entreaties, they began to grow angry, all save Andreino; and one of them said, tartly and hotly,——

"We come in charity and good will, but we may go in wrath. Musa, there is money here, and there are debts that should be paid with it."

"Debts!"

It was the first word she spoke. She had heard of debt; she knew that it was a great calamity. Joconda had always spoken of it as a great shame; she had seen the man of the law going into the wretched cabins of the neighbors more than once, and seizing and selling the very chattels of the cupboard, the very mattress of the bed; and at such time Joconda had always said, "They have burned their candle at both ends; they have eaten their Paschal lamb at Ognissanti; poor fools, poor knaves!"

She knew that debt had no more clung about Joconda's honest name than ill-got gold had clung about her honest fingers.

"You have got all the money she left," said one. "You are a brave and honest girl, Maria Penitente: you will pay that *quintale*[1] of hay for the mule——"

"And my little bill for the coffee and the beans and the cheese," said another, who kept the small *pizzicheria*[2] shop by the church. "It has run and run, goodness can tell how long, but I was never one to press; and we all knew that the old soul was safe and warm though she was niggard."

"And there are the three pair of boots owing to my husband," said the cobbler's wife, who had come on his errand because he was such a poor weak white-livered thing himself: "Joconda wore out a many boots; tramp, tramp, trot, trot, forever as she did, and too proud-stomached ever to go to *à scalza*——"[3]

"There is a trifle of oil, a quarter-barrel; I let her have it last Night of the Kings as I had fetched it in from the country, thinking it only neighborliness," said a fourth, who had a year-old baby at her breast.

"And there were little sums I lent, on and off,—not much; she put her cross for them; she was a lone creature; one could not be hard. I have got them all fair writ out, and her cross is at home in the book," said the woman who lived next door, whose husband owned three of the fishing-smacks and was a *strozzino*[4] in a little hungry way,—*i.e.*, a usurer who lent out small sums at large interest, and kept his gains in a deep well in the court of his old house, and could never sleep at night for thinking of them, and who was in a fair way to grace a madhouse before long: a man who Santa Tarsilla had cursed as it never had cursed Saturnino.

Musa was still and mute; she heard them; she stood erect in the centre of the floor, whence the sunlight made a golden glory all about her.

Old Andreino sidled through the vociferating knot of women, and came close to her and put his mouth to her ear.

"Never listen to them: her debts were her own if she had any; let them take their scores to her grave. Come home with me, my dear, and bring the pitcher with you, and we will count it out fair and straight, and think what best to do with it: you might put it in my

---

[1] A unit of weight equal to 100 kilograms.
[2] A shop that sells cheese and cold cuts.
[3] Barefoot (without shoes).
[4] Pawn broker.

son's wine-shop, and he would give you a good profit out of it, and
so——"

Musa shook him off; she stood like one slowly awaking out of a
hideous dream; she looked from his face to the faces of the women,
and a darkness of scorn and of rage gathered over her own.

"You all lie! You all lie!" she said, sternly. "She never owed man or
woman a handful of leaves, or a hank of wool, or a copper coin, in all
the days of her life. Never, never! She robbed herself to give to me.
She robbed no other. Oh, tongues false and accursed!—have you no
fear when you lie of the dead?"

For a moment they were silenced before the intensity of scorn,
the solemnity of rebuke. For a moment their falsehood and their
greed shrivelled up as dry leaves shrivel before a flame. But only for
a moment, for they had so lied one to another that their lie almost
seemed a truth to them; almost they had persuaded even themselves
that they had a claim to the gold of the woman of Savoy.

"Would we come with false claims?" they shrieked aloud, in chorus of wounded honor, and cried one against another, "This is what
comes of too great goodness! We trusted a foreign woman, and we
left her alone because she was old, and then, when her end comes,
we are despoiled! This is our reward! This is the justice we get from
aliens!"——

"Be quiet! be quiet, my dear friends, my good sweet neighbors,"
murmured the old man, running from one to another, and thinking to
himself, "Whether she owed them or not, not a stiver of that good money shall go in the maw of these pigs. No, no; my grandson and I will do
justice by her; and if she love not the wine-shop we might buy a share
in a boat, or in the salt-working, or purchase a *pineto*[1] and clear it——"

For as yet he did not know how much was in the pitcher; but he
was quite sure the amount must be large.

The women began to shriek more and more loudly; they screamed
one against the other. Conscious that proofs were wanting, they made
up for lack of evidence with storm of noise; they howled aloud that
they were honest as the day, and were robbed; they reviled the dead in
her grave.

"Proof! She wants proof!" they yelled. "If we have no proof, or

---

[1] A *pineta* is a pine forest.

but little, it is because we were too good. We trusted an old lone creature. We let her take our substance and never asked her a quittance.
We were too good, too simple, too long suffering; and now we are
cheated at last."

Musa stood and looked at them; her face was pale and cold as
marble, only in her eyes a passion of hatred and of scorn shone as the
lightnings would shine at night in the purple skies of the summer.

She bore in silence for a while that hissing steam of angry breath,
that harsh shrill uproar of abusive voices, their menacing hands that
dashed about her in the air, their glittering eyes that seemed to dart
at her like snakes' tongues in the sun-rays. Then, all of a sudden, she
stooped, lifted the loosened stone, and took up the pitcher from the
hole. She raised it above her head one instant, high above her head
and their reach, as she had held a pitcher of water a thousand times
if one.

"You are false and accursed," she said to them, and her voice was
deep and clear, and smote them as if it were a sword. "You are false
and accursed; and she owed no man or woman a thread in her garments, a crust in her mouth. She was honest and faithful and true, and
cheated not a dog nor a mule of his rights. But all she has left—take!
Take and scramble for it, like the thieves you are; and may the bread
and the wine that you buy with it blister your mouths and consume
your bodies."

Then with a single gesture of magnificent rage she dashed the
pitcher down through the sunlight on to the floor amidst them; it fell
shattered in a score of pieces on the stones, and the coins rolled hither and thither, and their metal gleamed in the sunlight. The women
threw themselves on them. The old man screamed.

Musa called Leone to her side, took the linen and the summer and
winter clothing that belonged to her, took the lute and the distaff, and
the trifles that were her own, passed into the adjacent chamber where
the mule was stabled, bridled him and led him out into the open air,
first having bound upon his back her own mattress, with its hempen
sheeting and its coarse but warm blankets.

The women were yelling and quarrelling over the scattered coin;
the old man was trying to snatch his share, and was buffeted and beat-
en between them. In their haste and their greed and their struggle
they did not notice or know what she did.

Without looking back once, she passed out of the old home of her childhood, and went out between the blocks of stone and the stunted aloes, leading the mule and followed by the dog.

She went straight across the tufa mounds, and the narrow paths crossing the reedy, moist soil, the rank grass-lands, and the wild undergrowth that stretched around Santa Tarsilla, and walked slowly on and on, on and on, for eight miles, plunging into the deep woodland and entering the vast virgin meadows, until she came within sight of those cliffs of sandstone where the tombs of the Tyrrhenes were hidden away behind the fence of thorny ruscus and the dense walls of bay.

"They will not be angered against me, nor will they speak ill of her," she thought, and led the mule straight onward to the place she loved, where the leafless, blasted cork-tree rose up from the thickets, and the white-flowered cistus bushes, and the hawthorns, and the myrtles, and the yellow-blossoming Christ's-thorn covered the burial-place of the Etruscan dead.

Intense heat still brooded over all the land, but she was used to it; it did not harm her.

For miles around there was nothing visible; not a sail in the distant sea, not a bird in the air, not a boar in the brakes, not a snake in the sand.

She led the old mule, and paced beside him; her heart was like a stone, her feet felt like lead: all at once she realized all that the faithful, kindly, fostering love of Joconda had been to her, and knew that it was gone from her forever.

She went on with the animal through the hot white light, their shadows black behind them on the scorched grass and the gray sand. An immense sorrow had entered into her, and an immense regret. She thought, "I was never thankful!"

She had not been thankful because she had not understood. As the child does not comprehend his cost to the mother who bore the burden of him, so she had never understood what she owed to the woman who had sheltered her nameless life.

She had taken all that was about her, as children do, unthinkingly; they do not ask why the sun shines, why the bread is there, why the roof is between their heads and the winter storm; these things are so: they accept them, and do not question or wonder. She had not been thankless; she had only been a child. Now she was a child no more. She had looked on death, and it had left her desolate.

She had made her mind up to go and dwell with those whom she had called her own people, in the twilight of the earth, underneath the grass and canes. She was sure that they would not repulse her.

She preferred their mute mercy to the clamoring greed of the living. What appalled her was not that she was penniless, but that she was alone.

She went across the moor in the strong unchanging sunlight, that, as day grew apace, ceased to have the relief of any shade of leaf or blade of reed. She met no living thing. She uncovered the entrance of the tomb and descended the steps into it; and the mule, used to the stone stairs that led to his stable, was with little trouble induced to follow. She unloaded the things off his back and laid them down; she took her sickle and went up into the air and cut for him thistles and dry grass, and filled a stoup of water at the half-dry pool, and stabled him there in as much comfort as she could. Then she gathered sticks together and lit a fire on the stones of the entrance-place, and set a little soup-pot on to boil with some herbs and beans and fish in it that she had brought, with some rough bread, to make her mid-day meal.

The food seemed to choke her, but she ate, being young and in health, so that hunger came to her despite her sorrow.

When she had eaten she laid her bed-clothes down on the stone couch that had served for the last sleep of the Etruscan Lucumo, and sat down in the soft gray gloom of the twilit place, sheltered from the glare and scorch of day, and said to herself, "My home is here."

Santa Tarsilla was no more her home. It was full of liars and of thieves. She abhorred it. Though its sands were to become of silver ore, as the soil of Populonia once had been, she said to herself that never again should her feet tread them.

Let them keep the money and kill each other fighting over it! She almost smiled as she sat there in the gloom and thought of old Andreino beaten to and fro by the struggling women, and clutching at the coins and shrieking in his feeble treble.

"One would think gold were God!" she thought; remembering how but three days before the galley-slave had robbed her,—robbed the tomb that was sacred, the dead that were defenceless.

The terror of her own lonely and hapless fate looked at her from the awful eyes of the sculptured Chimera and the frowning brows of the painted Typhon; yet so consoled was she to be in this silent sanctuary that she began to think of her future maintenance and her future liberty here with a sense of deliverance rather than of danger. There would be no means of gaining any livelihood here. She could spin well, indeed, but so could every one else in the province, and she could make nets with skill, but so could every fisherman on the seaboard; and there was nothing beyond that to do.

Work!—it is the political economist's one advice and panacea; but there are many places in the world where it is not possible to work, and the Maremma in summer-time is one of them. There is nothing to labor at; all has been done by the army of laborers that stream down from the mountains. The few that are left lie in the sun and think themselves blessed if they do not sicken or starve; many do both.

But of sickness she had no fear, and she was not even afraid of famine.

She thought if she could manage to make her bread from the *saggina*[1] or wild oats that grew all around, she could live here well enough. She scarcely, indeed, took more thought of what might be her bodily privation than the nightingales coming back, whilst the days are still short and the woodlands still brown with their first budding, take heed of the wild weather that may come to still their song and stay their courting.

She had never known any kind of indulgence or fastidious appetite. She had always eaten sparingly of the simplest food; the idea that she might have only a bit of oaten bread for weeks together did not frighten her. She was very well aware that she would have to depend on what her own hands could gather.

The old mule was lying down on the litter of dry grasses; the dog was asleep, for he was old and soon drowsy; the twilight of the tomb was like the soft shadows that herald the dawn; the painted shapes upon the walls played on their pipes and wreathed their garlands and danced in the border of lotus flower; outside the burning day was fierce and white, the animal life of the moors was all hidden and still, there was only the rustle of the snake through the tall stalks of the flowering-shot, the hoot of the cicala swinging high on the carob boughs; the sound of the insects' odd singing came faintly into the stillness of the tombs. "If only she were here!" thought Musa. Who had been those vanished people who had known so well how to cher-

---

[1] Sorghum, a tall grass cultivated for use as grain.

ish their dead and lay them gently away in their painted chambers with the toys of their infancy or the weapons of their manhood and the jewels of their virginal or matronly pride tenderly placed beside them? Who had they been, those forgotten peoples who robbed death of half its terrors, and laid the dog beside his master, the toy beside the child, in cool, fresh, sacred chambers where the dead seemed not dead but waiting?

Ah! why was she not here!—she, thrust into that hole in the sand in that box of pitch-pine, thrust out with unseemly haste, with a brutal eagerness to be rid of her and forget that ever she had been. Musa could not have reasoned out the thing she felt; but the ghastly rites, the hideous selfishness, the vulgar hurrying cruelty, that mark out the Christian treatment of the dead weighed on her with their harshness and their horror as she sat in the grave of the Etruscans,—made ere men had heard of Christ.

Then for the first time some great tears rushed into her eyes, and she wept bitterly, and, thus weeping, fell at the last asleep,—a merciful sleep, that lasted through several hours, while the hot day throbbed itself away without, and the rays of the sun beat in vain upon her resting-place and could not enter.

When she awoke, it was dark; the night-herons flying over the marshes sent forth their loud harsh croak. She mounted the stairs and looked upward, and guessed the hour by the stars. She went down again and ate a little and drank some water, fed the dog and the mule, shut them both in the chamber, and went out into the open air.

She had an errand to do, which undone, it seemed to her she could not sleep. A strange fancy had come to her, and the fancy assumed the shape of duty to her,—a duty of gratitude so imperative that it would have been a guilt in her sight to evade its execution.

The uneducated are perhaps unjustly judged sometimes. To the ignorant mind right and wrong are only instincts; when one studies their piteous and innocent confusion of ideas, the twilight of dim comprehension in which they dwell, one feels that oftentimes the laws of cultured men are too hard on them, and that in a better sense than that of injustice and reproach there ought indeed to be two laws for rich and poor. Musa walked through the still sultry night. There was a haze of heat over the heavens that obscured the stars, and there was no moon.

When she reached the entrance of Santa Tarsilla it was midnight and quite dark. There were no lights in any of the houses; far down the coast there was the gleam of the pharos of Orbitello: all else on sea and earth was in impenetrable gloom.

She, who had known the ways of the place from infancy, made no error in her going. She took her way straight to that field of death where they had laid Joconda.

The walls of the cemetery were low and white; one of them was washed by the sea. Her eyes, grown accustomed to the blackness of the moonless air, discerned the outline of the walls, and over the inland one nearest her she leaped with the agility of her strong youth, and slowly took her road over the rough clods and the rough grass of the enclosure.

Then she lit a lantern she had brought with her, and by its light found her way to the freshest grave that was there, hard by the sea-wall.

The earth lay all broken up into hard clods and heavy lumps as the earth, sun-baked by a scorching midsummer, always lies, beat it as spade and hoe may. She stood by it, looking down on it timidly and tenderly with yearning eyes awhile; then she lifted her lantern and went to the little white-washed shed which served as a funeral chapel. There was a tool-house close by it, the door of which was never shut; she went in and got a pickaxe and other tools and returned with them to the grave of Joconda. She began to loosen the earth,—that brutal earth which lay so heavily on the breast of her old best friend. Southward on the sea there were a crowd of lights burning yellow against the deep blue of the summer night; the men of the Orbitellano were spearing the fish frightened and blinded by the blaze of lanterns. But there was no sound in all the place except the ripple of the water against the low mortared wall. Once a dog, far away in the fields, barked.

She labored on undisturbed.

The earth loosened when so dry does not readily adhere together again, and the clods were all easy to remove. In an hour's time she had uncovered the rough deal box that they had called Joconda's coffin.

She took breath and leaned against the wall and gazed down into the chasm. Before womanhood had fully opened for her she knew the doom that comes with age. She lived with the lost dead instead of with the living.

A deep-toned clock in the house nearest struck faintly the thirteenth hour: the old way of counting time still prevails in Maremma. The fear of interruption gave her fresh strength and energy. She knew that to raise the coffin would be more difficult than to uncover it; but she descended into the pit, tied cords about it, and, after another hour's hard and patient toil, raised it up on to the ground above.

Then she trembled; the great dews rolled off her forehead; in the hot night she grew cold.

The only human soul that had ever loved her was there at her feet, helpless and senseless as the clods of clay,—no more a human creature, but a thing thrust out of sight and forgotten of all.

She shivered as she looked on it; then she took up her spade and shovelled in the earth; dry as it had been and loose, she knew that in the morning would bear no sign of disturbance to careless eyes, and most likely there would not be even a careless glance cast on that waste corner by the old sea-wall.

When it was all filled in, the earth was lower than it had been, but that would seem no more than the natural in-sinking of the soil. She rested once again a moment from her labor, and drew breath again for her heaviest trial of strength, the lifting of the coffin over the wall and into the boat beneath. She had great strength in her symmetrical limbs; she was shaped as nobly as a Greek statue, and in her beautiful arms, her straight limbs, her superb hips there was no less force than grace. All her childhood upward the sea had bathed, the wind had fed, the sweetness of sound sleep and the tonic of athletic exercise had nourished her. Beside the sun-starved, room-cooped prisoner of the factory and of the school-room she would have been as Atalanta beside the dried and shrivelled atomy of a specimen-jar. With all her strength now she raised the coffin by the cords she had knotted about it, lifted it up on to the wall beside her, which was of breadth enough to afford safe footing, and thence by degrees lowered it into the old wooden craft, half boat, half tub, belonging to Andreino, in which she had spent her happiest hours.

She descended into the punt, laid the coffin reverently at her feet, loosened the chain from the staple, and, taking up her oars, bent over them and began to row back to the place on the sea-shore where she had rescued the galley-slave Mastarna.

She was drenched with the sweat of exertion, she was cold with a nameless terror, she was aching in every muscle with the strain of her overwrought labor. But she was content. She had done her duty as she saw it. When her eyes rested on the deal surface of the oblong thing at her feet, she thought, tenderly,—

"Surely she knows; surely she is glad I take her to them?"

It had seemed to her so brutal, so vile, so thankless, to thrust the dead, only because it was dead, into the earth, in a waste hole of ground, and leave it alone to the growth of the rank grass and the thistle, to the companionship of the newt and the worm.

The sea was perfectly placid; the air was still without wind; the moon had now risen, and seemed like a friend in the sky. In Santa Tarsilla no one had awakened; all was still. She was safe, and her errand was done.

When at length the boat reached the place on the sands where the low myrtles and rosemary grew wellnigh to the edge of the sea,—the place where Saturnino had sat on the sand and cursed mankind and his own soul,—the lovely pomegranate hue of early daybreak in the Maremma was slowly spreading over the heavens.

She sprang into the water, and with infinite tenderness and solemn care drew the boat with its freight upon the shore, amidst the sea-stocks and the samphire. Then she dragged her weary feet over the three miles of heath that lay between her and the Etruscan tomb. She went down into the grave, stirred the old mule from his slumber, and placed his pack-saddle on his back; then, followed by Leone, she led him by the bridle to the shore. She was now so fatigued that her limbs shook under her, and her head swam. But she pursued her way.

Reaching the edge of the waves, she drew out the coffin from its shelter beneath the shrubs, raised it with great difficulty on to the saddle of the mule and fastened it there; then once more, with her hand on the mule's bridle, and with the dog beside her silent and subdued, she went back, now not alone, to the grave of the kings. As she went,—the mule patiently bearing the burden of the dead mistress who had fed and tended him for twenty years, rendering his owner this last service ere he, too, should fall away into that uselessness of age, into the darkness of death,—Musa looked back once at the open sea. The rose of dawn was all above her head, the waters lay wide and peaceful in the sweet mysterious light.

Her heart was full.

"Surely she must be glad," she thought; "she will be with them, and she will know that I did not forget."

CHAPTER X.

THE removal of Joconda's body from its grave was never noticed by the sacristan of Santa Tarsilla, or by any one of her neighbors. No one ever went nigh that rough space of ground under the sea-wall. They had done with her when they had buried her. When the torch of Andreino had flared itself out, the last rite of remembrance had been finished forever.

Santa Tarsilla was like the greater world that lay around outside its desolate plains and swamps.

"That girl is a base one," said the neighbors: "never so much as a wooden cross set above the grave, or a two-soldo print of a saint hung above it!"

They knew she had gone to live away on the moors; where, they were not sure; it was a matter of indifference. They had got the money, and had torn each other wellnigh to pieces over it: they were readier to forget her than to recall her. If she had come back, she might have demanded some clear account of their alleged claims, and to satisfy her would have been awkward. The landlord, or rather his steward,— for the landlord was a gay noble, far away,—came and looked about the house, and affirmed that he had a title to a year's rental, and sold the sticks of furniture, and the pots and pans,—the mattress on which Joconda had lain every night till she had slept on it her last sleep, and the porridge-pot from which she had given the child of Serapia her first bit and sup. The landlord was far away; the steward pocketed the proceeds of the sale, though Joconda had paid her rent beforehand, as every tenant does in Italy; and he took credit to himself, as he conversed with people, that he did not find the girl out and make her render him up the mule. So an honest life went out under the smirch of calumny, as a sweet-smelling pine cone goes out in smoke when it is thrown on a coke fire.

In Santa Tarsilla the August weather was hot with the cruel, unchanging, misty heat that breeds all manner of disease from the waters and the earth, and which is only good for the lecherous vine that strangles the maples and lives on to steal the soul out of man by and by.

After the momentary excitation following on Joconda's death and legacy, the few inhabitants returned to the dull, dropsical apathy in which they were wont to pass their lives. The girl was somewhere on the moors, and her old boat was missing from its mooring by the mole; but it was no concern of theirs. Curiosity consents to close its unwinking eyes when interest sings its lullaby. Old Andreino had, indeed, spasms of the pain of conscience, for in his way he had been fond of Musa, and had a regard for the woman of Savoy. But he never sought for her. Nay, if he had not been ashamed to put up such a prayer to his saint, he would have entreated San Andrea to grant him never to see her face again, for he felt that the rebuke and the reproach of those magnificent jewel-like eyes would be very hard to bear, and he remembered how strong her wrist was, and if it should please her to belabor him with one of his own oars he would be as a rush in the grasp of the reed-cutter. And when his conscience pricked him, he felt that he had behaved not nobly; and he was sorry for his conduct; for, after all, the women had hustled him so that he had not been able to get one single coin that had rolled out of the pitcher.

"I might just as well have stood up for her," he thought, wofully; "and, after all, she might in time have come to think of Daniellino. I was too quick with her, that is the truth; and then those hags came between us with their screeching—well, the saints grant me not to see her face!"

He was terribly afraid lest he should see her. When he sat on the mole smoking his pipe as the shadows lengthened, he scanned anxiously the open sea and the low shore in fear lest he should behold the figure of Musa coming between him and the evening sky.

But the days and the weeks and the months went by, and she never came back to Santa Tarsilla. One night Santa Tarsilla, which never hardly heard any news at all (the only news-sheet in the place being the priest's copy of the *Voce della Verità*)[1], was a little stirred out of its feeble, feverish drowsiness by hearing that the escaped galley-slave Saturnino had been captured afresh,—taken by the carabineers after a fierce fight, having been discovered as he was hiding in a wine-shop, whose owner, a widow woman, went into Orbitello to sell some Etruscan ornaments and an Etruscan lamp to a goldsmith. The woman's poverty, and her halting story to the goldsmith, had roused the suspicions of the police, and the carabineers, entering her house by force, had shot down Saturnino through the keyhole of a door, and

---

[1] "Voice of Truth."

had seized him, after being crushed by his arms and rent with his teeth when he lay shot on the ground, as though he were a beast of prey they were driving out of his lair. Wounded and disabled, but not so greatly as to be thought in peril of his life, the once famous brigand had been borne to the casemates of Orbitello, and thence back to his doom on Gorgona. So the pale, emaciated, fever-shaken soldiers said one night, standing about on the mole, and smoking their rank tobacco.

More than fourteen years had gone since the name of Saturnino had been at once the pride and the terror of Maremma, and the legends of him had faded off the minds of the people, as the frescos of their churches faded in the damp of ages. Yet when they heard his name again,—that name which had been as a trumpet-call, as an incantation, as the bellowing of the king-stag in the forest to his herd,— even the sickly women lifted their heads, even the palsied men took their pipes from their mouths: "He *was* a man!" they said, softly, under their breath.

The mountain-robber always bewitches the fancy of the multitude, and the robbery which only strikes at the rich always seems a sort of rough justice to the poor. Beneath their subjugation by the witchery of adventure and of defiance, which allure the imagination of the populace, there is always also the resentful thought, "He is condemned, this bold marauder who carries his life in his hand, whilst the sleek poltroons, the thieves in broadcloth and fine linen, the Barabbi of commerce, stalk abroad, through the tens of thousands they have duped or ruined, untouched by law, undenounced by any wrath of earth or wrath of heaven." The preference of the multitude may be unsound morality, but it has a wild justice and a rude logic at its base.

Santa Tarsilla once more lamented for Saturnino. It was of the same mind with the mob of Orbitello,—which, could it have got at the woman whose stupidity had cost him his liberty, would have made her rue that ever she had been born.

In like manner all the villages and the towns in Maremma mourned for him, feeling for the old hero of their rocks who had broken loose from his cage only to be trapped afresh. He had once been the hero of Maremma; the country was hurt in its own pride to think their hero was dealt with like any mean cut-purse of the cities.

Even to little San Lionardo the tidings of his sad fate travelled,—

travelled by the mouth of a *sensale*,—that is, a go-between, who nego-tiates with the farmers or shepherds who sell cattle, and the butchers or breeders who buy them.

Owners and buyers would be much better served if they did their own negotiations without the middleman; but Italy is the land of go-betweens, in commerce as in love, and these men swarm over the land and fill their money-bags not ill nor slowly.

This man, riding about the moors in the evening time, viewing herds and flocks, had business which took him to San Lionardo,—a little whitewashed place lying on the amethyst and pearl-gray of the hills like a little, clean, humble sea-shell on a grand table of *pietra dura*[1] and mosaic.

These little white hamlets and towns of Italy glisten all over her long, low, mountain-sides, their church-towers red-roofed with tiles or brown with wooden belfry, or pointed with the air-perched statue of a saint in their midst, and not seldom around them the circle of bro-ken walls which tells the tale of their ancientness and of their bygone wars. Oftentimes they are old as Rome itself; classic as Tusculum; full of memories as the foundations of Troy; but no one comes to them. They are little, lonely, humble places now, far out of the highways of men; and, save their spinning-women and their hinds and herdsmen and their priest, they shelter no living thing. When winter comes they are severed by unbridged torrents even from other villages that lie along the same line of hills; and up to their heights in the snow, or in the heat, no traveller ever wanders.

There is something quaint, pathetic, touching, in the lives that begin and end in these solitary places; the hamlet is the nation of its people, and the church-tower to them is the centre of the world. The great plains lie beneath them, and often from their walls the sea is visible, but the cities and the seas of the world are nought to them: their history lies in Tippa's plaiting, in Sandro's bridal, in the birth of children, in the huckster's price for wool and linen. They are peaceful lives; simple, archaic, close-clinging about tradition, more innocent than most lives are; when they are no more on the face of the moun-tains men will be sadder, and earth will be the poorer.

Into little San Lionardo the *sensale* came this day, and, drinking his

---

[1] Hard rock.

thin red wine at the inn door, told the few people of the hamlet how the brigand had been captured, away there in Orbitello. There was a little fellow there who heard, while his goats and he were lying in the shade of the house wall, he having come up with them from the moors below by his father's mill because of the middleman's visit.

The little fellow was Zirlo, who had taken his goats up out of the heat of August, and he listened as he lay in the shade on the stones.

When he could take his flock again on to the lower lands in the grayness of dawn, which is the freshest hour at this season, he lost no time in descending the mountain-side and making for the moor, until he came to broad pools, yellow with golden and white lilies, and cliffs of sandstone clothed with broom and rose cistus.

San Lionardo never knew anything unless by some rare stray visit of a peddler or of a dealer; it had very few dwellers in it, and had not even a church or a priest. When any were wedded or buried in San Lionardo they had to go up miles above, along the road that wound over the bare face of the stone mountain, where every tree and shrub had been felled, and the sun scorched the rock, that had not the shade of even a leaf or a blade of grass.

There he whistled like the thrush.

"*Via!*"[1] cried the voice of Musa from beneath his feet, and presently the face and throat of her raised themselves from out of the wild plants that grew about the entrance of the tomb. She lifted him up a little brown earthenware can; he took it and milked one of his goats, and handed the can back to her full of milk. She had been up an hour; her brilliant face was like a flower in its freshness, for she bathed herself in the sea every daybreak; her hair was brushed back in its massive undulations and just touched her throat, as Joconda had always kept it; her clothes were still of the linen cloth Joconda had spun. She took the milk and gave him a little copper coin, and came up with a piece of black bread in her hand, and ate the bread and drank the milk sitting on a stone among the wild clematis, and sharing her meal with Leone.

She had made friends with Zirlo; there was a certain distance between them always, because he was a little afraid of her, and she was a little suspicious of him. He had been forced to swear to her that he

---

[1] "Shoo!" or "Go away!"

would tell no one how or where she dwelt, and, having sworn that, he shared her confidence. One thing alone she never told him,—that she had brought the coffin of Joconda there, and had laid it in an inner chamber of the painted tombs.

He was of use to her. She cut the rushes and wove them into rude matting and into frail baskets, and he sold these to San Lion-ardo folk for a few centimes. She had learned many uses of edible roots and cryptogams from Joconda, and gathered those, and he sold them also; he brought her flax and she spun it; he brought her straw and she plaited it; his goats were on the hills and his smaller brother minded them, and he ran to and fro on her errands. Busy and fond of money, which his father never let him handle, he was glad to go between moorland and mountain on these missions, and could cheat her comfortably with a childish glee that was united with a shrewd self-interest.

He was only a little fellow, living, with his goats and his reed pipe and his naked feet, the most sylvan and pastoral life in the world; but he knew the worth of money as well as the *fattore*[1] adding up figures in his fat note-book, or the inn-keeper selling watered draughts to thirsty wayfarers.

Zirlo was a pretty little curly-headed boy, with a sweet voice, a sunny smile, and limbs like a child Bacchus; he was affectionate and he was very innocent, but all the same he knew how to lie and he knew how to cheat, his round laughing eyes open and candid all the while, and his mouth smiling.

Why not? Had he not seen the wine-carriers bore the hole in the cask and suck the wine out with a straw, and sell such a drink to anybody on the road? Had he not always heard his father, bartering with the *sensale*, say, "And what will that be as *mancia*[2] for me?" which meant, "How much will you let me rob my master if I get him to sell you this thing?"

So he himself robbed this strange maiden, of whom he was half frightened always, and yet loved her and admired her in his way and kept her secret for her, because he thought if others knew that she lived here down in the ground they might do what she wanted, and so he would lose all these loose centimes that got him bread and polenta

---

[1] Bailiff.
[2] A tip.

and baccala and rude sweetmeats, such as old Deianeira sold in San
Lionardo, sitting at her stall under the battered Madonna that, in her
iron cage, against the old watch-tower wall, looked down from the
hills on moor and sea.

"Are you happy here?" he asked her now, sitting with his legs
drawn up among the purple loosestrife, all dry with the summer heat;
watching her as she ate, while his goats strayed about cropping what
they would,—the four-footed Huns that ravage the mountains and
the forests and lay them bare as with fire, so that nothing will ever
spring again where their little hoofs have trodden and their little teeth
have browsed.

"Happy!" echoed Musa; the word sounded strange. "I do not
know. I am alone: that is always good."

She had never heard of Chateaubriand, who wrote above his
house in the depth of the Breton country *"A l'abri des hommes."*[1] But
the spirit that moved him to write it was in her.

Zirlo tilted himself over on his back.

He was a child, so he let the reply he had had go by without com-
pliment. He said instead,—

"I forgot to tell you Saturnino is taken."

"Taken!" She left off eating and stared at him, with a light in her
gaze and a flush on her cheek.

"Yes. On the coast. He was selling gold things, and they shot him
down in the Orbitellano."

She leaped to her feet, her eyes flashed, her whole face lit up with
exultation.

"Selling my gold,—*their* gold! They took him so? I am glad! I am
glad!"

"It was not yours?" said Zeffirino, who knew from her what the
galley-slave had done.

"No. It was *theirs*. It was sacred. He stole it; he is well served. If it
had been my own I would not have minded; but a thing that belonged
to the dead!—oh, it was vile, vile! And I wronged Joconda that I might
feed him; I left her alone to return to him, and she died! I am glad
indeed that they have got him. Are you certain it is true, Zeffirino?"

"Oh, yes," said the little lad; "they shot him down as they shoot

---

[1] A haven for men. The quotation appears in René Chateaubriand's *Memoirs d'Outre
Tombe.* He was considered the founder of Romanticism in French Literature.

the roebucks here, and took him; he was alive, though badly hurt. He fought like a devil, but there was the whole troop of the carabineers all there. They do say that another one who got away from Gorgona with him is loose still, hiding somewhere in the hills; but about that I do not know much. But there is a reward for any one who sees him, and I mean to look about: I might get the money as well as another."

"I am glad he is taken," said Musa, unheeding; "I am glad. He robbed them, and he was false to me."

Zirlo shuddered. Had he not himself cheated her to go and nibble at mother Deianeira's stall?

"You are savage," he said, with a little whimper and tremor. "That poor soul was a brave man, they say, and never did any sin except lightening rich men's purses; he used to live upon the mountains right away there, as high as the stars are, and never touched a poor man; they all say so,—only the rich——"

"And is not the gold of the rich their own as well as the crust of the poor?" said Musa, with scorn in her low tones. "He was a thief; a thief and a traitor. I sheltered him, and he robbed the dead. He was a thief and a traitor."

Zirlo rolled over and hid his face in the sand, pretending to catch a lizard. He had gone back into the tombs that very day after the galley-slave had robbed them, conquering his abject fear of the place for sake of the gold chain and the gold lamps that he too would have taken if he could have found them.

"And I should not have been a thief," thought Zirlo, with national sophistry instinctive in him. "I should not have been a thief; they belonged to nobody; they were as much mine as hers."

Yet not for worlds would he have had her know that he had ever crept into the graves on any such errand.

"He was a thief and a traitor. And he was taken as he sold the gold? I am glad," she said once more; and her face was exultant, sombre, almost cruel.

The fate of the robber of the tombs seemed to her so just; it was almost beautiful in its inexorable and instant justice.

"You are savage," said Zirlo.

"Why not?" she answered; to be savage was right enough: it was what they called the boar, when he fought for his own poor life and for his own lair in the thickets.

Zirlo said nothing. He was frightened. If ever she knew, he thought, of those centimes?

Musa rose, leaving the rest of her bread uneaten, and dropping it between the paws of the dog.

"He wronged my shelter and betrayed me," she said once more. "He has met a right fate. Zirlo, drive your goats farther on: my mule needs this forage."

Zirlo rose and mutely obeyed.

His heart was beating. He wished all the polenta and baccala that had tempted him, and all old Deianeira's luscious muscat wine that was like the honey of thyme-fed bees, had been down the throats of the people of San Lionardo instead of down his own.

"If ever she knows, she will beat me black and blue, or throw me with one hand into the sea," thought the little sinner, miserably.

She went down into the tomb, and brought the mule up to pasture while there was still some coolness and shade; then she again descended, lit her little fire and put on her pot with fish and herbs to stew by noontide, and took up her distaff and went and sat in the open air once more.

She was oppressed and absorbed by the tidings of the galley-slave's capture. She was glad; yes, she was glad; but the gladness began to glow less hotly in her: she thought of the wretched homeless fugitive as he had sat on the sands after her rescue of him: for what had she rescued him?—only for fresh torture.

All was still around her in the hush of early day: the only sound was the insect life that is never still on those moors and marshes night and day. The heavy rains of September had fallen, and the refreshed earth was growing once more green, and the fainted leaves arose and stood out in the clear air. The snakes were sorry the drought was gone, but all other living things were glad.

Zirlo, who had sent his goats farther away, strayed back and stood looking at old Cecco, the mule.

"He is of no use to you?" he said, timidly.

"No use; no."

"Would you not sell him?" he said, more timidly too, thinking of the *sensale.*

"I would not sell him."

"You would get money for him,—much money———"

"I do not want money."

"But you want to eat."

"I get enough to do that."

"He is old———"

"The more reason to keep him by me: old things fare ill with strangers."

Zirlo eyed the mule wistfully, and went away a little sulky and a good deal afraid.

"What will you do in the winter?" he said, fretfully. "I cannot leave the goats to run your errands in the winter. Sometimes it snows, too, and I am always very busy. You must go up and live in San Lionardo: that is what you must do."

"I shall not do that," said Musa: "I shall live where I am. You will do my errands in winter and in summer both when you want a bowlful of soup or a handful of mushrooms."

Then Zeffirino cried.

He did not like her to fancy him selfish.

"For if she once think me so," he thought, "she will begin to doubt, and to count the centimes."

But Musa did not count the centimes.

When the heat of noon came, she took the mule down into the painted chambers of the dead, and sat there herself. Zirlo came too,—a pretty little quaint figure, a childish Faunas,—and asked her for a bowl of soup. Then together they ate, using the black earthenware cups and platters that had been strewn on the floor of the tombs,—cups and platters made two thousand years before, made for the banquets of the dead, and perhaps profaned by their young lips, yet innocently so.

So the days passed by, and the weeks, and the months, and the life was always the same there.

The death of Joconda had left an awful blank of silence and loneliness around her. In its desolation she realized all that the dead woman had been to, and had done for, her, and a great remorse entered into her. She had been too thankless, she had been indifferent, unthinking, hard of heart, so she thought; and she would have given her life to have those brown, wrinkled, rough hands in hers for one hour.

Apart from this great sorrow she was happy in her wild, lonely life on the moor. She had no one to say her yea or nay. She was as free as the wild boar himself; and the wholesome winds of the west blew against her face, and nigh at hand was the green winter of Maremma.

So she took up her domicile in earnest there, and ceased to feel quite desolate.

The jewelry was all that Saturnino had robbed from the tombs, and the utensils of bronze and of pottery served all her daily needs. Untroubled by any knowledge of their history and antiquity, yet vaguely moved to reverent use of them because they belonged to these dead owners of the place, whom she revered, she took the bronze *oinochoë* with her to the water-spring, she set her herb-soup on the embers in the bronze *situla*, she made her oaten bread in the embossed *phiale*, she drank the broth out of the painted *depas*,[1] shaped like that cup of the sun in which the Python Slayer once passed across the sea. She used all these things reverently, washed them with careful hands, and never thought they were dishonored thus.

The Typhon frowned at her from the ceiling of the tomb, and the Dii Involuti[2] turned their impassive faces on her every time she passed out of the stone doors or climbed the steep stair passage to the open air; but she knew nothing of their dread attributes, and though they awed her they did not fill her with any painful fear. She did not understand them; there was no one to explain to her the meanings of the paintings and carvings and the letters on the walls; but she grew into a great and tender sympathy with them which was in itself a sort of comprehension.

Even of the terrible shapes she had no fear; the dread winged boy with hoary locks of age, that the Etruscans feared as higher than the gods, had no terror in his frown for her; and the veiled divinities who sat beside the inner door of the warrior's tomb, who for the dead had been tyrants of fate, mystic, inscrutable, omnipotent, grew to be to her as playmates and as friends. The very twilight and hush and solemn sadness of this place were but so much added sweetness to her. And in her there seemed to have been always that melancholy, and that obedience to destiny, which were the characteristics of the Etruscan religion, even when most they loved the lyre and the lotus garland and the brimming rhyton.

Here was her refuge, her palace, her place of sanctity and dreams;

---

[1] An oinochoë is a one-handled jug; a situla is a sacred water vessel; a phiale is a flat drinking cup; a depas is a bowl.

[2] In Greek mythology the Typhon is a monster with a hundred horrible heads; the Dii Involuti were superior Etruscan gods who were enveloped in mystery.

here the native unconscious poetry and passion in her found a likeness to themselves, a consolation for the unlovely life that seemed to
pollute the sea and shore in the only group of human habitations that
she knew, and which hurt her without her ever tracing the why or
wherefore.

She managed to live very well; her wants were few, and the moors
supplied all save one or two of her needs, such as oil to burn, and flax
to spin, and hens to keep for eggs, and these Zeffirino brought to her,
being paid for them with scrupulous punctuality out of the two silver
pieces that she possessed.

She could cut the wild oats in plenty for the old mule, which was
all she needed. She could live on the bread she so made. She could
take fish enough any day in the year for herself and the dog.

It is wonderful how few are the actual wants of a human life that
is far away from all artificial stimulus and necessities.

She was up as soon as the white gleam of dawn showed above the
barren mountains of the eastern sky-line, and, long before the heavens
there grew warm with that sunrise flush which is as bright and deep a
rose as any oleander-flower, she said her Latin prayer at daybreak beside the coffin of Joconda, as she had been used to do by her side, and
then tended the mule and the dog, baked her rude loaves, and swept
over and burnished her stone chambers and her bronze utensils with
those Northern habits of cleanliness and order in which the woman
of Savoy had reared her. Then she was free to roam all the day long,
and go out upon the sea as she might choose: every day she dipped
and dived and swam like any gannet. She bathed twice daily, either in
fresh water or salt water, with as much zest as her winged comrades;
and she kept her thick hair, that clustered like the bronze curls of a
Greek bust, and all her simple apparel, clean and in order, obeying all
that the dead Joconda had enjoined on her as her daily habits, with as
implicit an obedience as ever on that soil the Etruscans had shown to
the commands of Tages.[1]

That was her fashion of repentance for many a moment of petulance and many an hour of wilful indifference, which were to her
memory as the sting of the spine of the yucca is to the flesh.

Now and then, faintly from a distance, the bells of some hamlet

---

[1] The Etruscan god of wisdom.

or of some monastery would ring over the plains, and be wafted by
the wind to her ear; now and then some shot would sound from some
little lagoon, or some thicket of box, elder, and wild olive, where the
strangers were slaying the natives of the marsh and the moor: this was
all she heard of the living world, and she desired to learn no more. She
lived with the dead; and something of their cold repose, their ineffable
indifference, their passionless defiance of mankind, had come upon
her and entered her soul.

She had quite forgotten she was young. She had never known that
she was beautiful.

She was not afraid of anything; she had the courage of Saturnino
in her blood, and with it the superb innocence of a child's soul that has
never been dimmed by the breath of folly.

Whilst it was summer weather even shepherds and herdsmen
were never seen; the flocks were on the mountain, the harvests had
been reaped at mid-summer, the chase was forbidden by the law: all
Maremma was as silent as the heart of the Sahara. Sometimes, against
the law, which is utterly defied in this respect all over the country,
men would come over the scorching moor at eventide to set their fell
net, the square *paratoio* with its fettered call-bird, and would watch
all night at peril of their lives from the swamp-gases, and at daybreak
would carry away their poor fluttering struggling prey. But even these
were few and far between, because the fever and ague of the marshes
had terrors enough to daunt and conquer greed.

In summer she and Zeffirino had these moors to themselves, and
even Zeffirino was more afraid of the heat and the fever than she,
and would stay for days together upon the wooded spur of his native
mountain, where the miasma seldom reached.

So the long days went by, one by one, and were not long to her;
and at noontide she slept soundly and dreamlessly within the cool
solitude of the tombs, safe as a mole in his castle, refreshed as a coot
on the breast of the pool. In the short nights, above all when they
were moonlit, she did not care to sleep; she sat at the entrance of the
graves with the white dog like a carved marble thing at her feet, and
watched the sylvan life that stirs at dark flit over the face of the sky or
the shadows of the earth. She could not see the sea, the growth of the
low woodland was too thick, but she could hear the surf breaking on
the shore, and often when a steamer was passing, or a brig coasting, or
a fishing-barque standing in under the wind, she could hear the beat

of paddles or the rattling of halyards or the voices of fishermen calling to each other.

The sea was near enough to give the sweet sense of its strong
companionship, and if she climbed the sandstone only a little way and
overlooked the darksome stretch of myrtle and oak shrub, she could,
at any moonlit hour, see it sparkling underneath the stars, flowing
away into the infinite space of the clouds and the night, phosphorescent, radiant, hushed,—the black fantastic crags of Elba borne upon
its waters like a barque.

So the summer passed with her untroubled except by that sense
of ingratitude towards her lost friend which lay like a stone on her
heart. Whenever she knelt by the poor bare deal coffin she said at the
close of her prayers always, "Dear and good one, forgive me. I was
blind!"

The need of companionship never weighed on her. She was unconsciously happy in the air, in the liberty, in the delightful sense of
healthful and untrammelled life.

Her mind busied itself with its own vague imaginations, and her
mode of life was filled with that sombre mystery which she loved as
the Etruscan race had loved it. If she had been shut in the garret or the
factory room of a city, this temper would have become morbid and
dangerous in her; but, braced by the daily physical labors of her life,
and by the abundant and vigorous exercise of all her bodily powers,
it only served to give a solace, and a sort of sublimity, to a fate which
would have seemed to many hard and friendless. The moorlands and
the moorland sepulchres were made for her, and she for them.

The visits of little Zeffirino kept her from that absolute solitude
which in time hurts the mind and distorts it. He was a very human
little thing,—greedy, playful, timid, kindly when it cost him nothing,
most kindly when he gained most by it; a complete little epitome of
humanity clothed in shaggy goat's hair.

She grew fond of the child, and was indulgent to him with that
indulgence of the strong to the weak which is often misunderstood,
abused, and preyed upon by the feeble. She knew that he told lies by
the hundred, and pilfered when he could, and had no more real heart
in him than the red-and-white pumpkin that keeps the beauty of its
quaint shell whilst the summer sun has sucked up all its pulp inside it.
Yet he was loving and lovable in his own way and Musa, who thought

he loved her, was glad to see him always, as she was glad to see the birds and flowers.

They were more truly her companions, however, than he. She was always in the air, except when the sudden and frequent storms of the Maremma drove her perforce into the shelter of the sepulchre. The "bolt-hurling gods" of the tempests had no terror for her, as they had had for the Tyrrhenian multitude who had seen divine wrath in every electric flash, and heard imprecation and prophecy in every roll of thunder that echoed from the Apennine to the Ciminian hills.

The white straight rain, the slanting wind-blown showers, the blackness of hurrying storm-charged cloud, the strange yellow light that made the leaves look like foliage cast in copper and the skies like a vault of brass, the ominous hiss and shriek of the wind that made the slow buffaloes gallop fast with fear and filled the air with the hurrying wings of frightened birds, all these were to her only as the sound of trumpet and the smell of powder to the war-horse. The storms were fierce and swift, and rent like a veil the drowsy languor and heat of the usual atmosphere. She would see them coming over the sea from the west at sunset, or gathering above the southern horizon, where the Roman Campagna and the Pontine marshes were steaming with vapor.

When the autumn arrived, she was undismayed by the prospect of winter there, although she felt afraid that it would be more difficult to keep out of sight of men in the season when the waterfoul and the roebuck and the boar were hunted from dawn to twilight in their native haunts.

At this time of the year, too, the flocks came down from the mountains, footsore, travel-tired, with the shepherd and his woman and children behind them footsore also, and the white dogs that were kin to Leone running among the bleating sheep. She saw these travelling tribes more than once,—little dusty, jaded crowds, moving slowly over the marsh and moor. The shepherds are solitary and sullen people for the most part, and instead of a crook they have a carbine. She avoided them, and let them pass on southward to the rich low pastures, afraid that if they knew of her retreat they might rob her of it. As little did she like the hunters who harried the boar in his brake and shot the wild-foul in the marshes. What harm did those wild boars do, living on the roots of the earth and the acorns, or the lovely green-throated drake of the swamp, floating his little day away among the weeds and lilies?

Except these, there were not many new-comers to fear. Her own immediate portion in the Etruscan kingdom was so overgrown with thickets and low timber and matted parasites that walking was almost impracticable, and a bill-hook was needed at almost every step, and the quagmires and swamps that separated it from the vast grain-fields to the north deterred all save the boldest and the hardiest from adventuring there.

It never occurred to her that her life would alter. Of love she knew nothing, and marriage, when she thought about it, seemed to her, as she had said to Andreino, an unequal and unjust division of toil.

Her only fear of men was lest, if they knew of her beloved tombs, they might drive her out and rifle them of the bronze and the pottery as the galley-slave had done of the gold. It was for that reason alone that she scanned the horizon with the keenness of the roebuck, and fled at any sound of steps into the shelter of the thorny covets with the self-preserving instinct of the mountain-hare.

The chill season was at hand, but she was not much in awe of it; she was only afraid lest those sportsmen whose guns echoed over the lonely wastes, or the laborers from the north who passed by on their way to level some remnant of sacred wood or of historic forest, should see her and wonder and talk.

She grew learned in all the ways of nature, and, could she have told or written all she saw, would have lent much to the world's knowledge of fauna and of flora. In proportion as she fled from man so she grew familiar with and endeared to the beasts and birds that filled the moorland with innocent life, and with as deep an interest as ever the Etruscan priests had watched them, to forecast from them augury of the future, did she watch in awe and ecstasy that miracle—perhaps of all the greatest miracle—of nature, the migration of the winged nations of the air.

She did not know what these flights meant, but she observed and pondered on them with intense curiosity and interest as the winged tribes changed their feeding-grounds, and came, and went,—the Northern birds arriving as the songsters of the South fled.

A triangle of silvery gray would float slowly down the yellow light of closing day: it was the phalanx of the storks passing over the country without resting there, wisely distrusting the land beyond all others fatal to all birds. Less wise, though usually so cautious in his ways, there flew here in large bands the bright and gracious lapwing from the frozen canals of the Low Countries and the German forests covered deep in snow.

In a waving line, graceful against the sky as the sway of a reed against the water, a band of the glossy ibis would go by on their aërial voyage to Egypt or to India. The crows sailed over her head from Switzerland or Sweden, not pausing, or, if pausing at all, dropping on the moor for a few days of rest only, and going straight towards the Soudan or the Blue Nile. The ever-wandering quails fell, in autumn as in spring, panting and exhausted, in millions on the beach and turf, so strangely ill fitted by nature for the long, almost perpetual, flight that nature impelled them to undertake. There would break upon the silence of the moors at night a sound as of flames crackling and hissing over dry turf and through dry wood: it was but the noise of a mile-long troop of wild ducks coming from the Polar seas to the Tuscan lagoons.

The kittiwake and the tarn and the storm-swallow forsook their Finnish fjords and Greenland rocks to come and fish in the blue Ligurian waves. The graceful and vivacious actodroma, and the trustful sanderling, alighted here in simple good faith to escape the death-grip of the Arctic ice; the cheery godwits settled upon sea or sand, and looked like clouds of silvery smoke touched by red rays of flame. The shore was peopled with the feathered exiles of the North, whilst, inland, the common buzzards arrived with the first gold of autumn to wage war on rats and snakes in honest open combat; the superb merganser spread his bright plumage to the sun and surf of this unfamiliar shore, and the sea-mew less confidently trusted himself to the southwest sands, where the aloe, and the hesperis, and many an unknown thing growing there, startled him as he made for the inland pools and streams. The laughing-mew and the stream-swallow sought the shelter of the rushes and the reeds, and most of the family of the gulls were to be seen upon the wing above the shallows where sea and river blended. More rarely, and alone, might perchance be seen the Northern oyster-catcher (misnamed), hunting his worms and tiny fish in the shallows of the shore, meeting perchance the merry turnstone bent on the same quest, but never wetting his slender feet more than by contact with wet pebbles he was compelled to do. Whilst, by the side of the polar *piscatricides*, with their plumage of snow-white or gray, there were along the line of the breaking waves, and oftener beside the shallows of the swamps, slender and lofty shapes of radiant rose color, bending their slim long necks, lithe as wands of willow, or standing motionless and dreaming in the wintry sunshine on the sands: they were the flamingoes.

Some of them live all the year round here, as in Sicily or Sardinia, but these are not numerous: in large numbers they only arrive in the cold weather to depart on the wings of the first March wind.

Though they are so shy of human eyes, she had seen them ever since she had been old enough to come here, and she had always fancied that they were half flower half bird: no heart of a June rose or cluster of rose-laurel blossoms has ever more lovely crimsons, more delicate flush of color, than the *phœnicopterus roseus* of Egypt and of Asia. Flying, the flamingoes are like a sunset cloud; walking, they are like slender spirals of flame traversing the curling foam. When one looks on them across black lines of storm-blown reeds on a November morning in the marshes, as their long throats twist in the air with the flexile motion of the snake, the grace of a lily blown by the wind, one thinks of Thebes, of Babylon, of the gorgeous Persia of Xerxes, of the lascivious Egypt of the Ptolemies.

The world has grown gray and joyless in the twilight of age and fatigue, but these birds keep the color of its morning. Eos has kissed them.

Farther inland yet, the jays came, saddened and stupid as all birds are when they first arrive in a strange country, missing their dark pine forests of Scandinavia, of Lithuania, of Thuringia. With them there came the redwings, the redstarts, the redbreasts from the mountains and from farther afield, the little English and French robin,—dearest, cheeriest, brightest, kindest of little birds; and even he too was sorrowful and timid at the first, though soon, plucking up his gallant little spirit, he sang upon a myrtle spray as gayly as on his native hawthorn or apple-spray bough in Westmoreland or Calvados.

All these and many more she watched as they came, singly, or in bands, according to their habits, upon the chilly wind that blew from their native North countries.

In the moorland ponds and the marsh rivulets there were the persecuted coots all the year round, the water-hens too in their demure garb of olive-brown and gray, and their brilliant relative the beautiful porphyrion, showing the sapphires and the rubies of his feathers in all seasons, amidst the white vapors of a wintry dawn as amidst the gold of the pond-marigolds in midsummer; and over all the land, all seasons through, the red-legged partridges ran under the cistus and rosemary they best love, and the cushats, though their voices were mute, stayed at home and braved the autumn rains and winter sea-fogs that stretched to the mountain's foot.

All these innocent and most lovely creatures had cruel foes; cruel-est foe of all the pitiless snarer or sportsman who had no better aim in his own miserable life than to slaughter these lives that were so much lovelier than his own.

But the moors are vast, and vast the virgin meadows of the scythe, and vast the labyrinths of forests and of undergrowth stretching at the mountain's foot. There was many a lagoon where never other voices than the birds' were heard; there was many a league of woodland where the thorns of the firebush and the sloe and the tangle of matted vegetation made impenetrable barriers to the greed of trappers.

When the boats came at night with the lanterns to daze and be-wilder the roosting wild ducks, and the cowardly showers of shot fell like hail on the unresisting myriads, Musa could do nothing; she could only listen with throbbing heart and clinching hands and laugh aloud in derision to think that men called the hill-fox a robber and the falcon a bird of prey. But when she found the nets stretched across the pools and the *paratoio* set on the turf, and the setters of these had gone away for the night, fearing the deadly vapors of the soil, then she, seeing these fell things at twilight, and not being afraid, would wait and go without sleep, and when the night was fully down, and the invaders of the birds' kingdom had gone to some distant knot of houses on the hill-side or the shore, or to some shepherd's hut, she would work her hardest at the snares, pulling up the stakes from the ground, drag-ging the huge nets out of the water, hacking down with her hatchet the poles, and destroying all she could destroy of those treacherous engines.

If the men had ever suspected her, if they had ever returned before dawn and come upon her at her work of demolition, they would have shot her in all probability, as they would have shot the poor birds, and with no more scruple or remorse after it. She knew that very well; but her love of the soft wild things of lagoon and woodland was stronger than self-love, and the bold blood that filled her veins was warm with pleasure as she strained at the wood or the cordage of the great traps closing in the mouths of streams or drawn round the sleeping-places of the unconscious palmipedes.

It was not often that she had the chance of saving her feathered friends, for not very often did the snarers leave their prey; but whenever the power came in her way she made use of it, and whenever she saw ill-looking fellows, strangers, or natives, coming in upon the territory which she regarded as the birds' and beasts' and hers alone, she followed them unseen, creeping under the heather of the uplands and the cane-brakes of the swamps, to watch their choice of place, and foil their efforts if she could.

To a snarer of birds she would have had no more mercy than he would have had to her if he had known what she was about; and she had almost as much scorn for the so-called sportsmen, hiding among the reeds to take the bright porphyrion unawares, or steering their boat through water strewn with a thousand dead and dying coots.

Her watching of the sea- and land-birds, and her care over them, made the absorbing interest of her lonely life. Her wants were so few that they were soon provided for, and almost all the day long she could pass in the open air: like Borrow, she did not fear "nature's clean bath, the kindly rain." When she went home dripping with water, she changed her clothes, lighted a wood fire, and was none the worse. Leone shook himself, and slept after the rain, and so did she.

In that free life she grew still taller and still stronger, slender and supple, and fit model for a young Artemis, had any sculptor been there to copy the fine and graceful lines of her limbs in the modelling-clay that comes from Tiber.

She, like the flittermouse, passed the winter there as tranquil as though beside Joconda's hearth; nay, more tranquil, for in her old home the constraint of severe habits, the enforced household labors, and the squalor and the sickness of the people round had been irksome and painful to her. Here she was sole possessor of her painted chambers, and without had the wide moors and the blue sea to roam over as she would.

Even the sea was kind to her; for one night, when there was a great storm and she sat beside her fire in the warrior's sepulchre, Leone howling by the kennel tomb where the Etruscan dog-ashes lay, there was a barque wrecked a mile or so down the coast; and when the weather cleared on the third day—for the white squalls of violent wind and rain upon these waters usually last three days—she went down to the beach to see the sea, that was sobbing still like a child after vain passion, and, washed up upon the driftwood and the glass-wrack of the rocks, she found a little boat, bruised, but still service-able,—doubtless belonging to the lost brig that had foundered with all hands off the dark, grim peaks of Monte Argentaro.

It was flotsam and jetsam, and she took it as a sea-gift.

It was light and shapely, and its two oars were in it. She dumbly thanked God for it: having a real boat,—for what she had made for herself was but an awkward and unseaworthy tub,—she felt as though wings had grown upon her shoulders. The sea seemed to be all her own, as it had seemed to the Tyrrhene pirates three thousand years before to be theirs and none others'.

She was as thankful as a dog: she dragged her treasure up over the rocks out of the wet sand in which it was bedded keel downward, and hid it in a little aperture she knew of in the cliffs within a few yards of the water.

With this boat for her use when she would, she felt strong and free as any osprey. It was another means of livelihood also: she could make a net, and catch a fish, as well as any man of the sea-hamlets; in the hill-villages they never tasted fish, their few folk were too far off and too lazy by far to drag their limbs a dozen miles down to the beach at any time, and the shore-folk were too indolent and too feeble to go to them. But she, who was neither idle nor weak, determined to carry fish to the hovels of the plains and hills if she were ever pressed for hunger, and get their bread and goat's flesh in return. So she said to herself as she hauled up the boat over the stones, though she would not take the lives of the fish if she could help it. And she felt satisfied, having her future thus provided for; it seemed to her as if she could live thus so easily all her days.

With the winter she clothed herself in the warm, thick, woollen clothes made of lamb's wool that Joconda had woven for her; and at night, when rain, like the rain of the tropics, poured on the sandstone rock that made her roof, and was sweeping in sheets of water over Maremma from mountain to sea, she spun at her wheel, as Tanaquil had done before her, by the low light of one oil wick burning in the lofty candelabra whose like had charmed the delicate and lofty taste of Sappho's Hellas.

Sometimes a snow-storm would sweep over the moors and the sea; sometimes the broad lagoon, formed where the marsh-waters joined the salt pools in the sand, was one mass of boiling, wind-lashed, turgid, yellow froth; sometimes thunder rolled and blue light-ning flamed above the bare peaks and crags of the easterly mountains, and a darkness that could be felt descended at noontide on Maremma as on the land of the plagues; sometimes, rarest of all, there was the film of frost on all the moors, and the terns and smews had to tap with their bills at a sheet of ice on their tarns and streams, and fancied themselves back in their own Greenland or Siberia.

But rough weather, and wet weather, were the portion rather of autumn than of winter, and for the most part the sun shone above the Arctic birds that had come southward for shelter, and upon the child of Saturnino gathering the fallen wood off the moor or driving her lit-tle boat through surf and spray. The winter-time was short,—shorter than counted by the solstice,—for by the turn of the new year the corn was springing and covering, like a thin green cloud, all the vast plains to the north; and on the yet vaster grass-lands, where no foot of a ploughman or hand of a mower was ever known, under the gauze veil of the rime forest, the bulbs of the wild crocus and the wild nar-cissus began to feel their trustful way upward through the earth, like little children timid in the dark yet confident because they think that God is near.

Then, in those still, starlit nights, cleared by the magic wand of the frost till all the lustrous sky seemed alive with throbbing light, Musa would leave her hearth and lamp and go up into the air, and stand and look at the silent procession of those distant worlds of which none had ever told her anything.

She had no conception what they were. She knew that fisher-men and mariners steered by them all night long, and that was all she knew.

The gorgeous constellation of Perseus hung above the sea, and over the weird peaks of Elba the great star Aldebaran burned; the Golden Plough was driven on its fiery way down the northeastern heavens; above the great south moors, far down in the purple night, where Rome was, there flamed Orion, and straight above her head, in the zenith, Auriga shone, holding in his hand Zeta and Eta, the dreaded storm-bringers of the Greeks. To her they had neither name nor message, yet she would stand and gaze at them for hours. Surely they could not burn there only that ships might steer?

Her only idea of them was inspired by the songs of the Maremmano people, which call on Hespera to help their loves as on a living spirit, and hymn the star that has an angel by its side, a young angel—"*un' angiolin*"—attending it always on its path through the shining heavens; a graceful fancy, which took root as a fact in her belief, so that she would gravely gaze upward for hours, trying to see the winged servitors of the constellations; and sometimes she grew angry with them, thinking, "There are so many angels, cannot they warn the tartane off the shoals? cannot they stoop and let a light shine on the sea when their stars are covered and the boats go aground in the dark?"

The planets and the stars were as great a perplexity to her as the birds, and much less consolation.

Every one knows (or at least every one who takes thought of these things, which, perhaps, is a small minority) that to see birds in their own homes is difficult. The nest of the blackhead is made so like in hue to the thorn-bush it rests on, the nest of the cisticola is woven so wisely among the rushes of the water-side, the flight is so swift, the vigilance is so great, the feathers are so often like the brown of the bark or the gray-green of the sedges, that even the quickest eye may see but little of them, and even the gold of the oriole and the blue of the magnificent roller may escape detection in the shadows of the woods. But with tenderness for them and patience they may be traced in their daily ways and wanderings, and few lives repay attention to them so delightfully as do the lives of the birds. She was herself so much a native of the woods, she was as motionless as the kingfisher himself beside a stream, she was as solitary and as wary of men as the woodpecker; she was heedful never to disturb a nest or startle a callow brood; and as her recompense she grew as acquainted and familiar with the winged tribes as was ever Audubon or Naumann. She had not their knowledge, indeed, but she had more than their love. When the naturalist fires on a sanderling or a bunting, he may be a man of science and culture, but he is no lover of birds.

Musa knew very few even of the common names of either the flowers or the birds; of their names in men's books she knew not one; but she knew the look and the season of every blossom that blew, and she knew the haunts and the habits of every one of the singers, and the divers, and the many creatures that made populous the wastes around her, and at night could tell by the manner of their flight whether the barn-owl or the Athene Noctua went past her, whether the wild-duck was going through the shadows, or the night-loving plover.

She knew the Northern birds went away with the first warm wind of February; she had every year since she could remember seen the gulls and gannets and storm-swallows, and all their congeners, take their flight due north, never to return until winter returned too.

She missed the timid and yet bold creatures of the Pole, after which the people of Santa Tarsilla had named her; and she missed the little red birds of the North, with their tiny, sweet song, piping when the full melody of the nightingale was mute.

But whilst the sky was full of storm-clouds and the sea of froth and foam, and the snow was still half-way down the sides of the black Argentaro rocks, and wholly clothed the Apennines, she was cheered by the glad exuberant chatter of the dauntless starling.

Then, as the year grew a little older, and the blackthorn of the brakes grew white with blossom before the leaf, and the green silent wolds that enwrapped the dead cities and the dead nations were rosy and purple and lilac with the springing of the anemones,—then, though the little robin no more showed his red waistcoat under the myrtle scrub, in the stead of him and his came back the truants, the birds which, by the law laid down by naturalists, could claim the country as a home, since it was there they made their nests.

Why some went, some stayed, was a strange, unending perplexity to Musa; and a perplexity indeed it is.

Why does the blue thrush stay on the same spot all the year long and all the years he lives? and why does his brother the stone-thrush go off on autumnal equinoctials as far as the White Nile? Why, indeed? The birds can laugh at science: their secrets none shall know.

Musa sorely missed her friends of winter, but the budding of the crocus and the daffodil brought her many others in their stead, and soon she grew reconciled to the new-comers and knew their looks and haunts and ways as well as those of their predecessors. With earliest break of the year the red buzzard came, so much more cowardly and cruel than his cousin the python-slayer, to watch all the summer long warily amidst the water-stars and the pond plantain, to seize some unwary moor-hen, or snatch a coot away as she brought the rushes together to begin a home.

All the moist ground that stretched for leagues on leagues south-ward, ground that trembled with water as human eyes will do with unshed tears, was covered with little feathered people who loved the marsh and pool and found health and nourishment where men found death.

There the sedge-thrush hung his nest upon a bulrush, lining it with cobwebs and with shred rosemary as softly as a lady sleeps on down; there the bearded titmouse would slumber upon a reed, covering tenderly with his wing the female he loved so well; the pewits, and the finches, and the chats, and the cricket singers, and the grasshopper warblers, and all the multitudes of *oscines*,[1] fluttered and flirted, and darted and dived, and made the lonely wastes mirthful and peopled. The fisher-heron, as timid and solitary as any that the Thebaïd knew, walked by choice rather beside the brackish pools where fresh and salt water met, or along the white line of the rippling surfs, eyes downward and head bent, meditative, melancholy, and absorbed. The sheldrake shared his taste for those saline pools,—where the salt club-marsh and the pungent sea-rush throve, which have defied and made the despair of all engineering skill from the days of the Etruscans; and Musa grew well acquainted with him on the soaked sand where the many streams of her moorland trickled together and formed, with the in-running sea, a broad, shining, reedy mere,—the breeding-place of many a noxious vapor, but the delight of her and of the birds.

When the asphodel was all golden and white over the green deserts of Southern Maremma, and she left the sea-shore for the inland charm of fresh-born vegetation, and the undergrowth was like snow with the laurestinus flowers, and the thyme and the basil began to be dewy and fragrant underneath her feet, she found the fieldfares that had come from Nubian sands, and the tiny fly-catcher that was putting on his ruby coat for springtime and for courting, and the song-sparrow busy building his high nest in some solitary pine and lining it solidly with bark-fibre or with fish-scales, and the bush-singer hanging his upon a branch of thorn or under close leaves of myrtle, and the red-breasted shrike darting on butterflies and locusts as the falcons on the herons, and the bee-eater falling through the bright air on his prey, and the green woodpecker drilling a citadel for himself in the stem of a dwarf cork-tree, and the hoopoes patiently following the buffaloes' slow march, and the blue nut-thatch holding his seed beneath his claw

---

[1] Song birds.

as a dog holds a bone under his foot, and his cousins the *sittæ* of the rosy tails descending tree-trunks head foremost, and the wood-lark making music from a tuft of rosemary or broom, clearer and sweeter than the love-songs of any lute; and with these countless others, too many to name the half of, and Philomel herself forever pouring her heart out in rapture, as she does all day long and all night long from the first Lenten lily to the last midsummer rose.

All these together made such a jocund company upon these unknown and silent wastes that it was the saddest pity that Milton and Shakespeare and Shelley could not awake and come and hear. Oftentimes in such a place I long for them and wonder as the children wonder of the flowers that die with summer,—where are they gone?

She had the heaven-born faculty of observation of the poets, and she had that instinct of delight in natural beauty which made Linnæus fall on his knees before the English gorse and thank God for having made so beautiful a thing. This child of the foolish and sensual Serapia and of the murderer Mastarna was a poet at heart; in another land, and under other circumstances, the world might have heard of her and have hearkened as eagerly to her as the people of Santa Tarsilla had listened to her singing. Had study and wise companionship been given to her, she might have found utterance for all the thoughts and the fancies, the dreams and the affections, that thronged on her amidst the woods and on the sea, but left her dumb and moved to a mute joy, keen almost to pain.

In a freer and a gladder day than hers, in time of Urbinan or Florentine or Venetian greatness, she might have forced her own way up to light and learning, and made the heaven of some great soul, and been crowned with the golden laurel on the Capitol.

As it was, her sympathies and her imaginings spent themselves in solitary song as she made the old strings of the lute throb in low cadence where she sat solitary by her hearth on the rock floor of the grave; and out of doors her eyes filled and her lips laughed when she wandered through the leafy land and found the warbler's nest hung upon the reeds, or the first branching asphodel in flower. She could not have told why these things made her happy, why she could watch for half a day untired the little wren building where the gladwyn blossomed on the water's edge. It was only human life that hurt her, embittered her, and filled her with hatred of it.

As she walked one golden noon by the Sasso Scritto, clothed with its myrtle and thyme and its quaint cacti with their purple heads of fruit, the shining sea beside her, and above her the bold arbutus-covered heights, with the little bells of the sheep sounding on their sides, she saw a large fish, radiant as a gem, with eyes like rubies. Some men had it; a hook was in its golden gills, and they had tied its tail to the hook so that it could not stir, and they had put it in a pail of water that it might not die too quickly,—ere they could sell it. A little farther on she saw a large green-and-gold snake, one of the most harmless of all earth's creatures, that only asked to creep into the sunshine, to sleep in its hole in the rock, to live out its short, innocent life under the honey smell of the rosemary: the same men stoned it to death, heaping the pebbles and broken sandstone on it, and it perished slowly in long agony, being large and tenacious of life. Yet a little farther on, again, she saw a big square trap of netting, with a blinded chaffinch as decoy. The trap was full of birds, some fifty or sixty of them; all kinds of birds, from the plain brown minstrel, beloved of the poets, to the merry and amber-winged oriole, from the dark gray or russet-bodied fly-catcher and whinchat to the glossy and handsome jay, cheated and caught as he was going back to the North; they had been trapped, and would be strung on a string and sold for a copper coin the dozen; and of many of them the wings or the legs were broken and the eyes were already dim. The men who had taken them were seated on the thymy turf, grinning like apes, with pipes in their mouths and a flask of wine between their knees.

She passed on, helpless.

She thought of words that Joconda had once quoted to her, words which said that men were made in God's likeness!

In the loneliness and meditation of her life the pity of her nature deepened, and her scorn of cowardice grew still stronger. She was brave, self-reliant, and tender to all those creatures whom the human race, because it understands not their language, chooses to call dumb. Of the human beast she had not fear, but a great mistrust.

The short winter, the enchanting spring-tide, came and went, and none had traced her to her hiding-place; the solitudes around had kept her harmless secret as they kept the mysteries of the buried multitudes. The only creature she ever spoke to was little Zeffirino; and he did not tell of her because he loved her herb soup, her pullets' eggs, her store of bilberries, her skill at finding edible mushrooms; and she let him come and nibble when he would, squatting like a little faun upon the floor of the tomb, and holding some platter or bowl of the dead Lucumo tight in his brown hands.

CHAPTER XI.

DURING this second summer that she passed upon the moors, early in a May morning, when she was out on the waters, having the old dog with her in the boat, there was a vessel standing off the shore,—a rare sight there, for, though many sailing-ships and steamers passed in the offing, no one of them ever came close in, unless it were a tartana coasting, much less cast anchor anywhere nearer than Civita Vecchia one way or Livorno the other.

This vessel, however, a comely barque of Sicilian rig, a brig of some hundred tons, had paused in her course for her crew to fish, as in the clear water a shoal of tunny had been seen, and the nets had been thrown in amidst it. The men hailed her in her boat, and asked her some questions as to the soundings and the coast; for there was a fog on the horizon, a white fog like a silver veil, and they thought it meant wind and water both, and they were strangers.

She answered them willingly, for she thought well of all sailors; and their skipper, a young fellow and handsome, whose first voyage it was on these seas, as he was of Palermo and had always traded east-ward, pulled himself out to her in his long-boat and threw into her little skiff some oranges and other fruit. As they were from a sailor, she took them, and let him see her white shell-like teeth in a smile like sunshine in a storm. When she pulled her boat to shore, he pulled his too inland; and when she stepped through the shallow water and the sands, he stepped beside her.

He was very handsome, with a glowing, sun-warmed beauty, like one of his own Sicilian fruits. He was but twenty-three years of age; his heart was warm, and his head was hot. He said to her,—

"Maiden, where I come from the land is beautiful as the sea is; the shores laugh; the hills are rich as a mother's breasts for her first-born; men and women live on fruit and wine and song and love; yet not in my own Sicilia did ever I see so handsome a maiden as art thou!"

And this he said in his own soft amatory Sicilian tongue, which is like the flow of honey from the lip of a ewer of gold.

She looked straight at him and frowned a little.

"I took your fruit, friend, because you gave me it with good friend-liness: if you clog it with lies, I will fling it in the waves."

The Sicilian stared at her hard with his brown starry eyes; then he laughed all over his face.

"Lies? I said never a truer word. But if it displease you so much, the wiser are you. Tell me, who are you? Nay, do tell me, I pray of you."

"I am no one," said Musa, curtly. "They call me the Musoncella and the Velia. Go you back to your ship, and leave me to go home."

"Where is your home?"

"On the moors; miles inland."

"May I visit you there?"

"No."

She was silent a moment. Then he spoke again with fire and force:

"I am a stranger, and you answer me rightly. But listen to me one little minute. Nay, I am an honest man. I am Daniello the son of Febo, of the house of Villamagna. I have been a seaman all my days, and now I command the brig yonder, and own part of her too, my fair Ausili-atrice; as good a brig as there sails on the high seas, trading with fruit as far as the misty, cold Scottish coasts. That is all. But it is enough. I would not change with princes. I am my own master; and yonder, in my island, I have withal to keep a wife in comfort. Now, look you, if you will be that wife I will be a happy man. What say you?"

He was only the rough skipper of a coaster that made the chief profits of her voyages for her merchant owners, not for him. But he was a Sicilian; he had fire in his veins, fancy in his brain, passions in his heart; he had been born under the flame and snow of the mighty Etna, and he had been lulled to his sleep from infancy with the sound of the waters that wash the Golden Shell.

He was a sailor; a son of rude Sicilian mariners; but love had stricken him through the eyes, even as it struck great Dante, gallant Ariosto, and grave Petrarca.

For in this land this sudden birth of love is still a truth; a fact, like the gold in the lily's heart or the red in the pomegranate's flower.

She stared at him, half enraged, half amazed. Then she shrugged her shoulders with a gesture of scorn and scepticism.

"Go back and say that to your Sicilian maidens. You remind me well that I have spoken too long to a stranger."

Then she shook his fruits down on to the sands and turned her back on him and began to walk homeward with the dog, who had been in her boat beside her. The sailor was stung and wounded, yet he approved her. He stepped quickly on too, and kept pace with her a moment.

"As Gesù lives, I speak in seriousness, and swear you honest love. One flash of your eyes to mine was enough; that is how we love in Sicilia. My eyes to your heart say nothing, alas! alas! But this I swear to you, O cruel one and unjust! I pass by here in four months' time with my cargo from the Scotch shores. Here I will land, and, if you will meet me, I will say the same again, and you shall go back with me to my isle, and we will build you a nest in the fig-tree and the cactus-hedge of my own shore. There is my hand on it, as I am Daniello, son of Febo, of the house of Villamagna."

He stood before her on the lonely beach, and held out his hand: he looked eager and passionate, and youthful and handsome as a young sea-god.

But he failed to touch her.

Her eyes laughed with incredulous scorn.

"In four months,—we will see," she said, with the same incredulity in her accent as in her glance.

"In four months you shall see," said the sailor, with suppressed fury and pain. "Oh, maiden, with whom have you dwelt, that you have a heart like a stone to a man?"

"What matters it?" she said, with a shrug of her shoulders once more.

Her soul was dumb and blind as yet; she could not understand: she thought him mad, or in joke.

"It will matter to you also, some day," said the Sicilian skipper.

"Will you promise to be here on the beach this day four months?" he pursued. "Come what winds and tides there may, here will I be."

"Not I," she answered him: "if you want to see me, then you may find me. But you will not."

"I will find you," he said passionately: "you have said they call you a sea-bird and the Musoncella."

But ere he spoke she had taken to flight, going over the moist, red, moss-eaten earth as the wary lapwing skims it when the nets are spread in his sight. He could have followed her, for he was young and fleet, but a sense of awe and of timidity withheld him. He looked after her a little while, then he went back to his good brig.

It made no impression on Musa; her senses were unawakened, like the sting of the bee that lies undeveloped in the alveolus; and her emotions were more quickly moved to anger than to pity. She ran on like a young ostrich who hears the negroes after it, and felt no safety till she had plunged once more into the friendly twilight of her home.

No thought of the future troubled her.

If the charcoal-burners never drove her out, or the shepherds never found her refuge and maltreated her, she feared nothing. It seemed to her that she would live on for hundreds of years so in that calm unending solitude, in that dreamful quiet place.

Meanwhile, that morning, Zirlo, lying on the wild thyme and grass, was accosted by two strangers who were wandering over the moors on a vain quest for an Etruscan city which was marked on old maps as lying to the south of San Lionardo.

These persons looked down on to the little faun-like figure of the shaggy child and his upraised pretty face, and said to him, "My little man, can you tell us of any buried tombs, or any great old walls, known hereabouts?"

Zirlo rose up on his rosy feet and put his hand up against his eyes as if he were dazzled by the sun, and he answered at once and sturdily, "No; I never heard of any such thing."

"Try and think again. Look at this. It strengthens memory marvellously. If you can lead us to any such old places under the ground this shall be yours."

This was a broad silver coin,—a whole scudo in solid silver! Zirlo felt as if he were giddy.

"There is no such place," he stammered; but his accent was unsteady and his eyes fastened on the silver bit glancing in the sun-rays.

"There is such," said the stranger, with insistence, "and I think you know it very well; and if you will bring us to it this scudo shall be yours. Come, my little lad, you will earn it cheaply."

Zirlo grew red, grew pale, shuffled his feet on the turf, trembled, longed, feared, denied, then longed again.

"You will not hurt her if I show you?" he said, wistfully.
The strangers laughed.

"What should we hurt? We are only travellers, artists, archæologists. We will do no harm, little man; we will only give you that money and as much again if you lead us aright."

Zirlo was silent in an agony of hesitation.

"Is it a cave you want," he stammered, "with coffins, and painted walls, and pipkins strewn about?"

"Yes, yes," they said, eagerly: "you know where to lead us. Come, go on, and we will follow you. Your goats can come to no danger here in this solitude. Why are you doubting about such a simple thing?"

Zeffirino grew very white; his hands clinched nervously together, his teeth chattered as with cold; he was afraid of his own perfidy and of her vengeance. But the silver scudo!—it tempted him as the "Dio del Oro"[1] tempts alike in desolate country places and in crowded cities. What would it not buy! The boy, whose stomach was never full, and whose appetite was always keen, shook with the intensity of his longing.

"And the place is as much mine as it is hers," he thought, with a sophism that came to him by nature.

Yet she had trusted him, and she had threatened him. Between his desire and his dread the little fellow was like one torn in twain by wild horses.

"I dare not!" he said, at last, with a piteous sobbing and shivering.

"You are afraid of the place?" said his tempters, who were all the more eager to see it. "Well, money can buy courage as well as it can buy bread, or a pretence of it at any rate. Come, little man, and if you show us a true Etruscan tomb you shall have two scudi. There!"

Zirlo's hands fell to his side.

He gave a little gasp, as though yielding up in sheer desperation his soul to the evil spirit.

"I will take you," he muttered, between his little pearly teeth, and then he grew very cold, as cold as though it were mid-winter: and he looked scared over his shoulder, fearful of seeing the friend he was about to betray.

"That is well," said his unconscious corrupters, and they sent the little figure on before them across the brown solitudes of the autumnal moor.

---

[1] "God of Gold."

Zeffirino walked as if he were dizzy and faint, and for a moment the blue belt of the sky spun round him in circles.

He heard the strangers talking one to another in a strange tongue, and he heard all those words as though they were spoken in a dream, and his heart kept beating against his sides, and he kept saying to himself, "If she should have come back?"

Still he walked on steadily for a space of two miles and more, always across the great green and purple moorland, and skirting the flowering marshes where the waters ran, and so coming out on to that wild growth of marucca and arbutus and myrtle scrub which hid from the light of the sun the graves of the Etruscans and of old Joconda.

There he stopped and cleared away the branches and grasses which she was so careful to pull together over the entrance, and he laid bare to the view of the two strangers the first steps of the stone staircase.

"It is down there. Now give me!" he said, stretching out his little feverish hand, which had all its fingers clutching and moving greedily like a miserly old man's.

The stranger who had always addressed him put two scudi in his palm with a sense of astonishment and distaste.

"Who would think that the money-lust lived even here in a baby goatherd!" he said, as Zirlo took to his heels and, with his little fist closed on the silver, tore headlong backward through the bryonies to the place where his flock was grazing.

"The dead whom we seek had that passion, and it is the only human passion that is immortal," said his companion. "You were too quick to pay the greedy little imp: who knows whether he has cheated us or not? This may be but a fox's earth."

"Foxes have no stairs, and we can soon see for ourselves," said the other, and he descended into the aperture and felt his way down the steps, and at the foot of them stood still in surprise at the tomb that was Musa's home.

It was a grand tomb, he saw, Etruscan beyond doubt, and more perfect than most of these graves are when once the light of day and the eyes of curious mortality have fallen on them and found them out beneath their veil of myrtle and of bay leaves.

The stone biers, the stone chairs, the black pottery, the niche for the dog, the various paintings, all were Etruscan beyond question; but on the earthen floor there were the sticks and ashes of a spent fire; in the platter and one of the cups there were milk and bread and wild fruits; in a corner there were a spinning-wheel and a mandoline.

"Some one must live here," they said to each other, and understood why the child had been so afraid to bring them to it.

"This is a coffin of to-day!" cried one of them, who had penetrated into the third chamber, where old Joconda lay.

"Some one lives here, sleeps and eats here, and here buries his dead," said his companion. "A woman it must be, for here are female clothes and the distaff."

"It is strange," replied the other. "But it is a grand tomb, and finely preserved. Let us make sketches while we can."

And they sat down and spread out the colors they carried with them, for they were both artists, and one was a scholar. The latter sketched the proportions of the chambers of death, and copied the strange figures of the dancing women, of the winged boys, of the lotus-flowers. The other made a drawing of the spinning-wheel and the mandoline and the blackberry boughs that were thrown, full of fruit, across an Etruscan dish, while a bronze lamp stood on the floor beside a bowl full of yellow marsh-lilies.

The one would serve for some grand cartoon of an Etruscan marriage-feast or burial-banquet. The other would serve for some minute *genre* picture.

When Musa returned from her headlong flight across the country, she saw at the first glance that her careful screen of brushwood had been disturbed. Supposing that Zirlo had so stirred it by his usual boisterous entrance, she descended the steps, thinking there to find her playmate. But Leone growled and looked at her for some word of command, and she saw instead of the child the two strangers, who were intent on examining the paintings of the walls. She had no conception of what the men were like: it was enough for her that they were human creatures, violators of her sanctuary and of the dead.

She advanced to them with all her face dark as the summer skies in tempest, and her eyes flashing like lightning.

"How dare you? How dare you?" she cried, with intense passion. "All this is mine and *theirs*. You profane it! you blaspheme! Out of it! Out of it! or I will set the dog upon you!"

The two men stared at her, confused, and almost doubting whether she were mortal, so sudden was her descent into the twilight of the cave, so burning and furious were her eyes and words.

"Pardon us," said one, with hesitation. "Is this Etruscan tomb your care in any way? We did not know. We sought for a sepulchre that is marked on ancient maps. A little boy, a little goatherd, brought us here. If we offend——"

She turned very pale.

"A goatherd! Zirlo?"

"How should I know his name?" said the stranger. "A little, long-haired, bare-legged fellow. I am grieved if you are distressed; but how were we to know?"

"Zirlo! Zirlo!" she said again, with a bitter wondering sadness in the words that touched her listeners, though they could not understand its cause, and thought she was but jealous of the custody of the tombs and of the silver scudi.

"If," began one of them, holding out a French gold piece; but his very breath was caught and stopped by the girl's imperious gesture.

"Get you gone, or I shall hurt you!" she said, as she motioned to the stairs. "This is my house, my home, my temple, my grave, my all! The boy betrayed me. He is vile. Get you gone!"

"She is mad," they murmured to each other, awed by her anger, which they could not comprehend, and dazzled by her beauty.

"Get you gone, or the dog shall tear you!" she said, with a passion that was the more intense because restrained. "The place is mine. I am here with my dead. Get you gone!"

"Let us go," said the men to each other; and they did go, slowly, and looking back at her, and doubting still whether she were mortal, and, if mortal, mad.

"Mad, surely!" they said to each other, and one of them added,—

"It is best to humor her. But we will go back again. She is beautiful. It must be she who owns the spinning-wheel and the guitar."

Left to herself, she sat quite still, and hot tears gushed into her eyes.

"Zirlo! Zirlo!" she repeated. "And I loved him!"

There is no knife that cuts so sharply, and with such poisoned blade, as treachery.

Time went over her head uncounted. She sat there, lost in the intense pain that consumed her at this her first taste of the bitter-sweet apple of human confidence and friendship.

She had trusted him, and he had betrayed her.

It seemed to her that fire ought to descend from the skies and smite him, and burn up his little, weak, false, worthless life. She did not know that if this vengeance overtook human falsehood the skies would be forever as a scroll in flames.

She sat there a long time, motionless. Then she was seized with a deadly fear. Had they come for Joconda's body?

She went into the third chamber, and there she found the wooden coffin untouched, the flowers she had laid there undisturbed, and the lamp burning steadily.

She left it, and ascended the stairs, and looked over the moors.

The day was dying down, and the grand red glory of the west blinded her for a moment as she looked on it from the gloom of the tombs. There are no sunsets more gorgeous than those on the sea of the Maremma, and their pomp of gold and purple is a mockery of kings.

This day the gold was burning behind a transparent cloud of dusky blue, and the scarlet, soft, yet intense as the color of pomegranate-flowers, glowed above it and melted into the azure of the still shining skies. The moorlands were dark and hushed; the sea was the hue of the zenith.

She looked, and her eyes filled.

Then, far off, very far off, she saw a little dark figure, black against the ruby and the gold. All her rage sprang back into her heart, and she ground her teeth like a wolf. She wound her short and narrow skirt about her limbs, and with bare feet and bare shoulders leaped across the grass and ran like a grayhound.

He was half a mile off. In his babyish cunning he thought that if he were near at hand with his goats she would think him innocent. Seeing her, across the moorland, coming towards him, swift and silent as the wind, his cunning deserted him, and his fear alone mastered him. He fled.

She gained on him nearer and nearer. No fawn of those wild meadows was swifter on her feet than she; she ran as the Greek girls ran of old in the arena, in the spring-time of their lives and of the year.

The dark elastic turf, the springing wood-moss, rebounded from her touch; she sprang through the sunset glow of the air as the doe springs.

The boy, leaden-footed with terror, and not fully braced as she was to the movement of his limbs, tumbled forward rather than ran, and in his blind and palsied terror gained no ground, but stumbled round and round in a circle.

With every moment she drew nearer to him. He thought he felt her hands amidst his hair, her breath against his cheek, her steel upon his throat. He put the silver coins that were the price of his treachery between his teeth, and his teeth chattered so that he scarce could keep their hold upon the treasure for which he had lost his own soul and her trust and love. He ran on and on, falling forward in his terror, and plunging into watery grasses, slimy, and sinking under him. The glow faded, the sun had sunk to light the nether world. It was night; still he ran on and on, and she ran in his wake. At last, as the moon rose above the distant hills, she reached him, and he fell prone under her grasp.

She stood over him, and to his terrified eyes she seemed to grow in stature and dilate until she touched the stars.

"You betrayed my shelter!" she said, again, and her hands fell on his shoulders and she swayed him to and fro till the glittering vault of the night seemed to rock about him.

"Oh, miserable!" she cried to him; and the deep intense scorn of her voice seemed to roll like the notes of an organ over the solitary land. "You betrayed me for silver pieces as Judas betrayed his Lord! Do you know that I could kill you, you mean and wretched thing?—you so small and so light, and I as strong as the buffalo? Do you know that I can dash out your brains on these stones, and hurl you dead into the sea? And wherefore should I not, you vile and faithless worm, viler than the adder and the newt?"

As she spoke, she swung him backwards and forwards, and he was dumb and blind with horror; his eyes gazed up into the sky, but saw nothing.

He believed she would take his life.

"I trusted you, I trusted you!" she said to him; and it seemed to him as if her grasp were closing at his throat and pressing the breath and the air and the life out of it.

An unutterable terror kept him mute and motionless; the whiteness of the moonlight shone on his ghastly little face, and its abject fear stung her to disgust, that made her rage seem too high an honor to so cowardly a thing.

She threw him off her some distance, so that he fell heavily on the turf.

"You are a traitor!" she said; and her voice rang loud through the night. "I will not hurt you. You are too vile. But come never in my sight. Breathe never the air I breathe. If you were dying, never would I lift a finger of mine to save you. I trusted you, you base, false, foolish, trembling thing, and you lost my trust for a silver coin! Oh, you fool! oh, you fool!"

Then little Zirlo, lying where she had flung him, saw her for a moment, seeming to him to touch the stars and gather all their brilliancy about her hair and shoulders and luminous fire-flashing eyes, and the night appeared to snatch her up into itself, and a great darkness fell between them, and he was all alone.

Musa, convulsed with passion that was still but half spent, went slowly away from the spot through the luminous air, and retraced her steps until once more she sat in the shadow of those solemn chambers which now were hers no more, but opened to the world of men.

A shudder of rage shook her from head to foot; then she bowed her head down upon her knees, and wept bitterly.

She had been betrayed.

Kinder than treachery is the knife that severs the cord of life.

It was her home, this kindly temple of the dead, this sanctuary of the lonely moors that sheltered her and Joconda.

It was her home, and stood in the stead to her of all those ties and defences which surround the lives of other female creatures. Here she had been safe, her only visitants the timid hare, the friendly goat, the winter-burrowing lizard, and the night-birds that love gloom and silence.

Now all that sweet calm sense of security was gone forever. Strangers any day might come and disturb her and the dead in their tacit amity, and drive her, as they would drive the scops-owl from his hole in a tree, from the refuge of the tombs. She knew nowhere else to go in all the world; she had no other home, no other friends.

The child knew that, and yet he had sold her for silver!

As she sat in the darkness of these chambers, where the moon-rays could not come, she wondered that she had not killed him. What had held her hand?

Not fear, of a surety, nor pity; some awful sense of unutterable strength and scorn, set high above herself and him as the stars were, which had come upon her as she had gazed up into the brilliancy of the shining summer heavens.

CHAPTER XII.

ON the following morning she was sitting outside the tombs, plaiting the *biodo*,[1] with her mind still darkened and her spirits still troubled by the treachery of Zeffirino. Her rage had been like a styptic, and in a measure had cauterized the pain she felt, but it was sorrow as much as wrath that filled her heart this morning; she had been fond of the child and had trusted him, and he had sold for silver her secret, her peace, her safety,—since all security for her depended, as she knew well, on no one being aware of the existence of the sepulchres.

It was, therefore, with heavy and anxious thoughts that she plaited on at her rushes in the early day, whilst the bees buzzed about the yellow-flowered coronilla, and the jewel-like snakes crept harmlessly under the emerald leaves of the wake-robin.

Her worst fears took definite shape as between her and the glory of the morning rays, pouring down over the mountains behind her, there came a human figure.

His back was to the sun, and she could not discern his features, but there was that about him which made her sure it was one of those to whom Zirlo had sold her,—the one who had spoken most to her.

Her first instinct was of flight, as it is that of all other moorland creatures at sight of an invader of their solitudes. Her next was a bolder one: she rose, thrust her plaiting down on the ground, and went forward to meet him. Her eyes blazed as they had done the night before; her teeth were set.

"How dare you to come hither again?" she shouted across the heather and the holy thorn, the coronilla and broom, that parted him from her. "How dare you? I forbade you. This land belongs to me. Get you gone, or I will force you to repent of it."

The stranger paused humbly and looked at her over the golden flowers of the coronilla and the broom.

"May I speak one word to you?" he said, gently.

The man who drew near her was about thirty years old; he was

---

[1] *Scirpus paludosus.* [Ouida's note.]

tall and strongly made; his face was delicate and full of thought; it had not much beauty, except that which was due to the luminance of expression, and the color and largeness, of his clear blue eyes. It was a physiognomy strange to her, for it was entirely Northern.

He came on as quickly as the prickly shrubs, and the creepers that laced them together, would allow him to do. He was looking at her with an expression of keen interest, and she stood awaiting him with knitted brows and dark suspicious glances, ankle-deep in cinquefoil and sainfoin.

"Are you not she whom the shore people call the Velia and the Musoncella?"

"Yes," she answered, angrily: "what is that to you?"

"It is much," he said, gently, being as fearful of her taking flight ere she could hear him as the bird-catcher is of alarming the lapwing when it is turning its crested head in innocent curiosity to the nets he spreads. "It is much. I will tell you who I am: I am the grandson of Joachim Sanctis."

All the rage and the imperious scorn went out of her face; she was amazed and awed.

"You are of *her* people!" she said, under her breath: then, with the lapwing's caution, she drew back her momentarily awakened sympathies.

"Maybe you only lie," she said, with impatience. "Any one on the shore knows that I lived with Joconda. It is very easy to say this; and you crept into my house yesterday while I was away, as a fox creeps into the moor-hen's nest when she is absent."

"I am no fox, indeed," he said, with a faint smile, "and I mean you nothing but friendliness. Here is Joconda's letter, written to Joachim, who has been dead five-and-thirty years and more, when I was not born myself."

Across the morning light and the amber blossoms she glanced at the letter which the public letter-writer had penned in ceremonious and very flowery language; but she did not take it.

"I knew nothing about the letter," she said, suspiciously. "And how did you come to have it? It was not written to you."

"No; it was written to my grandfather and his brother. Both are dead. All are dead of her generation. There is a bailiff in the farm-house she knew. The letter went to the priest down at Cogne, and he sent it on to me. But I was in Asia, and never received it till this spring, when I returned from the East; and when, as I landed at Naples, I got it, I resolved to come and see you and Joconda. At Santa Tarsilla I heard of her death, and of you no one could tell me anything. I have roamed about your Maremma to look for you. Yesterday, a friend who travelled with me wanted to find out these tombs, and when I saw you I felt sure that you were the 'Musa' of Joconda's letter, only I would not speak before the other man. I slept up at a wretched place, San Lionardo, and at sunrise came to see you. That is all. I do not know why you should doubt me."

She was silent, unconvinced, yet a little touched by his words and troubled at the thought that one of her dead friend's blood should be living and standing before her.

"Why did you look for me?" she said, curtly.

"The letter asked Joachim to befriend you if she died: I thought I ought to do what he would have done."

"That was kind."

"If it were, I have more than my reward."

The flattery passed by her unseen, making no more imprint than the dew as it rolls off a cabbage-leaf.

"I do not see why you should care," she said, at length; meaning what she said.

"But I did care," he said, with some anger. He did not add, "because Joconda said that you were beautiful, and alone, and I love all beautiful things, and I pity all lonely ones."

She stood silent, looking at him, musing.

"Come to her," she said, abruptly and yet with a great tenderness in her voice; and she motioned him to follow her into the chamber where the coffin of poplar-wood lay in the twilight of mother earth.

She knelt down by it and kissed the rough wood.

"Dear and good friend," she murmured, "canst thou not hear? Thy people forgot thee so long, but at last they have repented and remembered."

Then, kneeling still, she prayed in Latin, as she had been taught, to the God who was to her a vast, unknown, incomprehensible Spirit brooding on the face of the waters and smiling with the sunbeams of the morning.

Maurice Sanctis felt his eyes grow moist, and he bent his knee beside her: though for prayer and paternoster he had the easy scorn of a modern student, yet for the old faith that moved the simple hearts of the women of his family he kept a reverent indulgence.

When Musa rose, her face had grown tender, and had lost the suspicion and the impatience with which she had received him. He seized that moment of softer feeling to draw from her some account of how she lived there, and why, and of how her early years had passed in Joconda's house.

She told him, simply and frankly, having nothing to conceal, and unconscious of how her narrative made her short history stand before his mind's eye in as bold and pure and heroic lines as those of a Parthenaic frieze. What added to his interest was his own knowledge of the blood of Saturnino that ran in her veins, her parentage having been written by Joconda's scribe on a separate page that he had not offered to her. From the dragon had come forth, not indeed a dove, but a white-winged curlew, strong alike on sea and moor.

"But how is her coffin here?" he asked, with surprise, after long silence.

She told him how she had brought it there.

He listened with emotion.

"You are as faithful as a dog," he said: "it is not Southern, such constancy."

She did not understand: she knew nothing of any divisions and races of men.

"Do you not think she would have wished to be with me?" she said, anxiously.

"I am sure that she would. Who of us all cares to lie alone in the black earth with the worms? You loved her much, it seems?"

"She was good, and I was too thankless. I know it now; now it is of no use."

"My poor child! We all feel that when we have lost what served us. When my father lay dead before me I seemed to myself to have been a very brute, living all for my own aims and pleasures in Paris, not giving a thought to the old man by the lake, who would fain have had me live all my life where I could look upon Mont Blanc; and very likely I shall go and live there ere I die. When you are mountain-born you use cities, you do not love them."

"Is Paris a city?" she asked.

"The city of cities."

"Where is it? Is it far from here?"

"Will you come with me and see it?"

He spoke half in jest, half in earnest. She took the question literally, without it seeming strange to her.

"I would never go where roofs lie close together," she said: "how can the people bear it? always breathing others' breath instead of the honey-smell of the flowers."

"It is a false taste; like choosing wine rather than water. So you are wedded to your Maremmano moors?"

"I love Maremma," she answered him, slowly; for she had never been called on to analyze and express what she felt. Then she added,—

"Where is that other gone who was with you?"

"He is gone back to Genoa, to go to Vienna, where he lives. Did he please you, that you ask?"

"Please me! I am only afraid that he may come back, or tell others of these tombs. I wish that you did not know of them."

"Why?"

"Because it is the solitude that I care for, and if people know of them, travellers will come and look; they do wherever there are *buche delle fate;* and if the shepherds find it out they will drive me away and stable themselves in my stead; it would be much better for a shepherd than his hut, because in storms and very cold nights he could drive his flock in with him."

Sanctis gazed at her in amazement.

"But—but you do not mean that you think in all seriousness of staying here all your life long?"

"That is what I hope to do."

"Good God! Have you no other dream for your future?"

Musa knitted her brows angrily.

"What better can there be? I have all I want. I can maintain myself very well. I am in the midst of the birds, and of the beasts. There is the air in my mouth, the wind on my face, whenever I choose. I am content. In summer-time it is too hot perhaps, and they say the steam of the marshes is bad to breathe, though never has it hurt me; but to live here is good, so good! I do not know what cities may be like, but I know that I will never go to one. Men and women make me angry, cruel, wicked; I never am with them that they do not; they are so mean, they are so cowardly, they are so greedy. But here I am content, and I think, wherever she is, she is content with me."

Maurice Sanctis was silent; he was moved by that intense and reverent remembrance of the dead woman; he was bewildered at this creature's absolute ignorance of her own physical charm, and of the passions and the hopes that agitate humanity and illuminate for youth its visions of love. He was loath to disturb her repose. Besides, he saw that he would speak to her in an unknown tongue; he saw that she was a child entirely in thought and feeling.

The early hours of the morning grew warmer, and the noon chimes swung drowsily in many a belfry in little villages upon the shore and on the plains; Sanctis remained there in the shadow of the burial-place, breaking his fast with her oaten bread, and drinking the spring water from the ivory-handled *ryhton*[1] that had served the funeral feasts of the dead Lucumo.

Musa had resumed her plaiting of the *biodo*, and was all the while longing for him to be gone. He was sacred to her, but he was not welcome; and all the while, also, the treachery of the little curly cherub-faced Zirlo was heavy at her heart.

He had sold her for a silver piece!

As she plaited she had a rebellious and unwilling look, as if the stranger held her captive instead of being but a visitor there, a guest sharing her bread. She was vaguely distrustful of him; his hands were so white, his linen so fine.

"Joconda was poor," she said abruptly; "you are not a poor man."

"No, I am not. Anton, the son of Joachim,—named after his brother Anton,—went to live in Geneva, and owned small craft upon the lake. He throve, and earned bigger boats, and built them for himself, and at last became owner of lake-steamers, and made much money. He was a simple hard-living man to the last, and saved all the money he made. I am his only son: I inherited all he had years since. I myself am a painter of pictures, and live in Paris. Men call me famous, but I do not think I am worth as much as were Anton and Joachim. Now," he continued, almost solemnly, "will you not come with me? My dear, do not be afraid: you will be sacred to me beyond everything. I will take you to sisters of mine, who live upon our lake in such a green wooded place; in spring it is a bower of apple and pear blossom and

---

[1] An Etruscan drinking flask.

rosy chestnut flowers. I swear by that good dead woman, whom her kin forsook and you have cherished, that we will be tenderness itself to you, and make your life a fairy-story. Now, answer me, you will come? I do not ask you to come to a city; you will come to mountains grander than yours, and to wider waters and healthier winds."

"All these words are very well," said Musa, with scorn; "but why did you all let her live and die alone?"

"It was wrong," said Sanctis; "but mine was not the blame, nor was it my father's. Joachim and Anton had hated and opposed her marriage, and in later times resented her silence. For want of a word lives often drift apart."

"Was not a Maremmano mariner as good as a cow-keeper in Savoy?" said Musa, with continuous contempt.

"It was the antagonism of races; our people came from Glarus, and were of a Teuton stock," said Sanctis; and then he remembered that he was talking in an unknown tongue to his companion. He added quickly, "I am very sorry that we let her live so. But to me she was only a vague name, she belonged to such a distant time: even my grandfather Joachim I never saw."

She was mute. She was angered with his intrusion on her solitude, and she was resentful of that long neglect under which Joconda had lived through so hard a life to pass away in so lonely a death.

If he had been a shepherd, or a herdsman, or a rude sailor, he might have awakened her sympathies; but there was about him the atmosphere, as it were, of another world than hers,—a sort of look of ease, of culture, of success, of all things which were beyond her comprehension, yet which alienated her.

He could not prevail on her to listen, nor on himself to give up so easily what the dead woman's letter had entreated her brethren to do. He stayed a few days at Telamone, at the wretched little wine-house which was all the accommodation it could afford, and hired a little felucca and sailed along the coast to the Sasso Scritto, and thence walked inland to the tombs. This displeased her, and she made him feel it, though she left many a harsh word unuttered because he was of Joconda's kindred. He meekly asked her permission to finish his sketches of the sepulchres, and she gave it reluctantly, suspicious of a stranger's entrance in those solitudes.

Oftenest when he arrived there to go on with his careful drawings of the walls, he found the place silent and empty; she was away, gone over the moors which she knew so well, and in whose mazes of vegetation it was hopeless for him to follow her. She avoided him; he was alien to her, he was outside the pale of her sympathies; she had more friendship for a sheldrake plunging and splashing among the pond-lilies, for a porcupine or a hedgehog creeping on its careful excursions under the giant fennel. She vaguely felt, as the gipsy feels it in the stranger who accosts him, that he desired to take her away from all this freedom.

She did not know the world he came from, but she hated it without knowing it; a world where the roofs were close together, and the birds were in cages, and the free air of heaven was feared; that was what she thought it, and she was afraid lest he should in any way compel her to go to it.

She did not think he would betray her, because he had Joconda's clear blue eyes; but she did not breathe freely where he was: it seemed to her that he wanted to take her as the bird-snarers took the poor stream-swallows, to carry them into cities and sell them, to have a thread tied about their foot for house-diversion.

Once or twice he met her upon the shore, and she gave him a curt word or two, and pushed her boat out into the water and sculled herself out of sight. He was unwilling to alarm or to scare her by too close pursuit, and he began to feel that his journey here would be fruitless. He was a man of honest purpose and clear conscience; he was incapable of wronging even by a wish a child bequeathed to the mercy of his people by a dead woman, but he began to grow dissatisfied and angry with his failure. He had obtained some rare drawings of an unmutilated tomb of Etruria; and this was the sole result that seemed likely to accrue to him from the waste of a midsummer month.

The air, too, which gives "distemper if not death" to the stranger, began to work its evil way on him. He began to lose strength, to feel chilly, to have a touch of fever; the burning suns on the rank soil began to pour their poison into his Northern blood. She met him on the twelfth day of his stay at Telamone as she came home towards sunset with wild strawberries and blackberries as her afternoon's gleaning.

She looked at him and smiled a little. "Maremma makes you ill," she said, with unconcealed contentment: "you are very unwise to stay in it. The sun is always angry with strangers. Why do you not go away?"

"Dear, you know very well why I stay," said Sanctis, gently and with humility. "I cannot bear to leave you here, all alone, in so utter a solitude, in so wild a life."

She frowned impatiently.

"That is not for you to think about: myself I would not live elsewhere. It is foolish of you to stay on at Telamone. You may stay twelve weeks, twelve months, twelve years, and you will not make me live in any other way than I do. You will only lose your own health."

"You will lose yours. All the people are sickly——"

"They are sickly chiefly because they are dirty. The heats never hurt me; I bathe twice a day. But strangers are always ill here. If they wait too long, they die."

"Do you wish that I should die?"

"No; I do not. That is why I tell you to go away while it is time. If you stay much longer, the fever will get in your blood, in your bones, it will be like fire inside you, and your limbs will feel to you no better than the dry empty canes in autumn. The fever has never touched me, but I have seen it often; and then there is the ague that comes with it, and you shiver as if you were up to your throat in snow, though the air is like the blast of an oven round you. It will be a pity if you wait for that. You will never be the same man again after it, even if you do throw it off in time."

"But why are you so well here?"

"I do not know. Why are the roebucks well, and the boars, and the pretty hares? I belong to the soil; you are a stranger."

She belonged to the soil; she was one of those Etruscan Mastarna who had dwelt on the slopes of the Apennines for so many generations. He thought, as he looked at her, should he tell her that she was the daughter of Saturnino, would he make any change in her? Would it render her more willing to come away from a land soaked with the blood of her father's prey? No; he thought she would only cling more closely there if she learned that one of her race was in chains upon these shores; and she was so calm, so bold, so innocent, so proud, he had not the heart to say to her, "The man who stole your gold is the man who gave you your life."

He let her go home with her summer fruits, and himself returned to dreary and unhealthy Telamone.

He had the hand of a painter, but he had the heart of a mountaineer. What he loved best were the rush of ice-fed waters, the stillness of the great glaciers, the rarefied air of the peaks and domes that towered above the earth-hiding clouds. This sea-coast in summer was loathsome to him, even whilst his eyes saw and his soul acknowledged the lovely light on its amethystine hills, the transparent wonder of its distances, the rose and the gold of its daybreak.

The enervating atmosphere seemed to steal the strength from his sinews like Delilah; the squalor and the sickness in the clustered hovels that were called a town made him weary and depressed; he grew ill, as Musa had told him that he would do; he began angrily to feel that it was of no use to lose his time and his powers only to force on an un-willing ear what was unwelcome, only to try and offer safety and ease to one who scorned the one and could not understand the other.

It seemed to him that it was his duty to compel this lonely child to accept the succor and the asylum whose benefit she could not com-prehend; but then duty could only be done by means that would be base. He must resort to that betrayal of her which would seem to her most vile. He must state what he knew of her to the civic authorities of Grosseto; he must set at work against her the machineries of that law against which Saturnino's life had been one long revolt. He must publish to her and every one that story of her birth which the rude tenderness of Joconda had so carefully concealed. The law would have to take her for him as the trappers took the field-birds, and when that was done he could show no right to her; Joconda's letter would be nothing before the law, and the Musoncella would be only to them the love-child of a galley-slave, to be thrust into some public institute at best, and forced into some social groove without regard to how that pressure hurt or drove her desperate. Very possibly the law would only treat her as a nomad, as a vagabond, and he himself could have no standing-point of legal right from which to oblige her to receive his benefits.

What could he do? It was a difficulty which perplexed and began to sadden him. This creature, who seemed to him so beautiful, so fearless, and so redundant of animated life that she appeared a very in-carnation of Artemis, was happy as she now was, innocent as the wild doe of her own oak-glades, and bold enough to defend her innocence were it menaced. Would not interference with her do more harm than good? He knew the danger that accompanies meddlers, and he was of too modest a temper to be sure of his own wisdom. He had no hold on her; that he felt. He might as well have tried to make the wild doe sit by his side.

He knew the force of hereditary instincts, the strange and subtile influence of descent. He knew that though the soul of the Tzigane is full of music, and full of music his hands and his feet, if you try to teach him the science of sound and make him play from written notes he is dumb; his very soul dies in him. So he felt that with her it would be impossible to take her from the melody of the woods and the waters, to set her down amidst conventional life.

True, in this land the pastoral life has been more general and more honored than in any other; the shepherd still lives under his conical red-thatched hut, the cattle-keeper still camps out amidst his bullocks and his horses on the thyme-sweet plains; their lives are much the same as those of the peasants of old who looked for the Pleiades as the bringers of spring, and saw in the great constellation of the North oxen drawing the corn-wains of the gods across the sky. True, Maremma was so lonely, so wide, so virgin in its water-fed greenery, so severed by its season of disease from all the moving world, that such a life here was less strange than it would have been elsewhere, and the northern mountaineer in the hill-side woods and the shepherd from the north on the rich grass-lands were nomads as utterly as ever were their forefathers in days when Pan and Faunus were the gods of the forest and pasture.

They would have understood well enough that the tombs made a dwelling-place, and that any one with eye and ear trained to the sights and sounds of the moors and the woods could without much hardship find enough from them to hold body and soul together. On the lonely mountain-sides of Italy many still live as simply as San Francesco did upon Aldernice; their only bread what the wild oats give, their only esculent the fungi that grow about the roots of the holm-oaks, their only wine the spring that bubbles up among the water-cress.

But to Maurice Sanctis, fresh from the world of civilization and culture, with its infinite multiplication of needs and desires, it appeared terrible for a woman who was scarcely more than a child to dwell thus, to be alone in the winter nights, to face the privations of the winter weather, to be dependent on her own strength of limb and surety of eye for all her maintenance, to have neither dream nor desire of any other life than this, which was no higher than the deer's in the moorlands, the flamingo's in the willowy swamps.

Had she been dissatisfied and restless and ashamed, he could have moved her easily to some ambition, some curiosity; but before this absolute tranquillity of content, this fierce repudiation of any possible better thing, he was helpless. It was the content of the pastoral Greek, the content of the Bedouin Arab. It was a kingdom in itself, and a kingdom not easily invaded or impaired. It was like the invisible line drawn by the magician: no step could pass it, no adamant could oppose a barrier as strong. She had aroused a strong pity within him, and had a seduction for him in that classic and nomadic charm which hung about her as its fragrance clings to the dried herb and the mown grass.

He would willingly, without a single selfish motive or ignoble thought, have done for her at any cost any service; but since she only saw in the outstretched hand of friendship the grasp of the jailer, he knew not what to do.

"I am near my end: save the child from the sins she has inherited, from the loneliness in which I leave her," Joconda had written to her brothers; and their descendant was almost morbidly anxious to fulfil her prayer. When he had received that letter sent by a dead woman to his father's father, his imagination had been stirred by the few words that spoke with a yearning fear of the storm-bird on the Southern sea-shore.

He was a man rich in most of the blessings of life, and whose name was already illustrious; love of the arts lent their beauty to his days, and wherever he went men welcomed him.

He was a man often lonely amidst troops of friends, and a man to whom the thought of duty was not irksome but readily welcome. It had seemed to him so simple a thing to give a home among his kindred to a child who was all alone on earth. Pity and a chivalrous charity had been at work in him, but he found himself before a young Artemis who would have nothing at his hands, an Atalanta whom no golden apple would tempt.

It was midsummer, and the miasma of the country began, as she had said, to steal the health out of his face and the marrow out of his bones. It was time also for him to be beside the high Biscayan waves on the west coast of France, where he had promised to paint the frescoes of a great gallery in a friend's Breton castle.

Thinking, alone, in the hot nights as the sails of the tartane grew silvery under the moon, and the lights of the fishing-boats glimmered in the deep blue of the night, he came to the conclusion with a sigh that his greatest, his only possible, kindness was to leave her to her-self.

The conviction wounded his conscience and hurt his self-love, of which, however, he had less than most people; but to do otherwise he must be harsh and treacherous. He could not bring himself to be either; it seemed to him that she was the last of the hamadryads,[1] and he could not bring himself to be the one who should snatch her from her mossy couch and canopy of leaves to drag her into that fictitious need, that artificial custom, and that always in a measure vulgar strife of human life in modern days.

Her manner of existence was like nothing else now on earth; it was like that of a young priestess of Fauna or of Pales in the Golden Age. He could not forcibly disturb it, any more than he, of a humane and a poetic nature, could have plucked out of the reeds the little blue warblers' nest in the season of their love and in the spring-time of the year. Would she have come willingly, willingly would he have run all risks of misconstruction and ridicule from his fellows to do her loyal service in any way she chose. But he could not use against her the pricks and bands of that civil law of whose very name she knew noth-ing,—a law always cruel in all lands to the homeless wanderer and to the offspring of a criminal.

The law would not see, as he saw, the innocence and beauty of that woodland life, of that tender fidelity to dead Joconda, of that se-rene independence of the help of man. She would seem to the law no more than any one of the hill-foxes that burrowed under the centaury and cinquefoil of some fern-grown bank.

With daybreak on the fifteenth morning of his fruitless stay at sorrowful Telamone he went to speak to her, if he could, for the last time. He had the good fortune to find her as she was returning to the tombs with a load of freshly-cut chair-maker's rush put on the back of the mule. Her hands were quick and clever at the plaiting of the reeds, and wove rude matting and baskets with care and skill. She did not know how she should be able to sell them now that she had no more the assistance of Zirlo; but she continued to make them, and meant, when she had made enough to fill a boat, to sail with them to some

---

[1] Wood nymphs who inhabited trees and forests.

place on the coast where she was not known, and barter them herself for shoes, and flax, and other necessary things. Of clothing and linen she had still a good store, for Joconda had laid by much of the cloth she wove, and the stout hand-woven stuff was tough and lasted long even in the wear and tear of Musa's open-air life.

She saw Sanctis approach with a frown on her straight brows and no greeting on her lips. He wearied her; he importuned her; he rendered her angry and impatient.

Her life was good in her own sight; she could not see why he should want to interfere with it.

On this last day he argued with her almost passionately for a man so calm of temper. He offered her that alpine farm facing the Grand Paradis where the girlhood of Joconda had been spent. He told her if any thought of cities and of cultured life appalled her she should have nothing of either; she should dwell there, under the glaciers, as free as any chamois, and since she had so proud and resolute a spirit she should owe him nothing, but maintain herself by her spinning or by any other work she chose. Only, if she would but come thither she would be safe; she would be no longer alone, she would be with good women, and the last wishes of Joconda would be fulfilled.

But Musa only laughed, deep down in her starry blue-black eyes.

"A Sicilian asked me the other day to go to his island," she answered him; "and he was a sailor, and he had a fast-sailing brig; and if there be a thing that I would care to have it is a vessel of any sort. But I said to him what I will say to you: I will not go from Maremma."

"And how did he ask you to go with him?"

"Oh, he said he would marry me," said Musa, indifferently. "He owned the ship, and she was a fast and a good one; but I would not go."

"A sailor is seldom to be trusted in such invitations," said Sanctis, with some irritation. "He makes them in most ports. What I offer you, my poor child, is very different: you should go to good women, to peace and safety and comfort, to knowledge and light and the grace of life. You are as beautiful as a young goddess, but you are as wild and untamed as a kestrel. What I want to do is what Joconda would have wished to have done for you. My dear, is it possible you mistrust me?"

"I neither trust nor mistrust you," said Musa, a little angrily. "I do not think about it, because I do not want anything that you offer me. I shall not leave Maremma."

Sanctis was silent and baffled. He had no means by which to control or coerce, and it began to seem impossible to persuade her.

The Northern mind was in him, all artist though he was; order, security, education, protection, seemed to him the very breath of life to any female creature; the liberty, the loneliness, the indifference to the future, the ways of living like any bird or beast of the moors, which were so good in Musa's eyes, were intolerable to him. He sympathized with her passion for her strange dwelling-place as little as the Hollander can sympathize with the Bedouin.

He was a great painter, but his creations were cold, clear, classic, faultless, full of intellect; and even in the color and movement of Parisian life the influences of the stiff, serene, precise routine of the Swiss home of his boyhood had never entirely left him.

Musa, with her lovely face and her noble regard, had fascinated him, and a pity, so intense as to be pain, had moved him for the child of Saturnino, whose birth-history he knew, though she did not. But his pity was impatiently rejected, and a certain anger began to grow up in him.

"Why should I trouble about her?" he thought; "she has wild blood in her: doubtless a wild life suits her; and doubtless, too, to take her to that tranquil home on the Lake of Geneva would be to loose a tornado in a greenhouse; and yet it is horrible that she should be left here to go to ruin, body and soul, as she must do."

So he urged her again and again. It seemed his duty, and it was also his desire; he was a man of noble temperament, he had no sinister thought; he meant to do for her what Joconda would have wished done,—more, if possible. She seemed so young and so intelligent that he thought there would be little difficulty to make of her a grand and thoughtful woman, although he knew that it is hard to tame the nightingale that has had a single year in the woods,—so hard that it dies under the effort.

With all the eloquence that sincere longing to succeed could inspire in him, he used every argument he could think of to shake her resolution and induce her to trust herself to another land and to another life. But it was utterly in vain.

Musa heard him more or less patiently, but his persuasions passed over her head as if they were thistle-down flying on a breeze.

"Go and see if you can drive a gray-lag goose[1] into your poul-try-byre," she said once, with a little low laugh: "do you think you can? You know nothing of wild birds' ways? More pity. Well, I will tell you. The wild goose will very likely walk and fly with your tame ones when they are out on the open grass-lands; perhaps he will even go with them part of their road home; but never will you get him to enter with them. Never. When he sees a house-wall he gets up upon his wings and goes away upon the air."

He saw that he had no effect upon her, took no more hold on her than the water takes upon the glossy laurel-leaf or the plumes of the coot.

"Let her stay!" he thought, angrily; "she will go away with the Sicilian sailor, no doubt, sooner or later; she will be happier so than amidst culture and repose."

His heart revolted from leaving her here all alone in the twilight of the sepulchres and upon the wildness and vastness of the moors. But he saw that if he pressed her more she would very likely say noth-ing, but go and hide; that if he remained in the Maremma to return and urge her afresh she would very likely on the morrow be flown, as the hunted snipe flies to new willows and to strange waters, thinking its familiar pool deceived it. He felt that if she did not distrust him she had no friendliness for him.

She had brought him the clear spring water in the graceful rhy-ton, and tendered it to him with a pile of wood strawberries and a loaf of her own oaten bread, because she had nothing else to give; but he felt that the hospitality was for the sake of dead Joconda, and her tolerance of his presence due to the same cause.

"Since you cared for Joconda, you should have some kindliness for me," he said.

"You do not recall her to me, though I believe what you say," she answered him. "She was so poor, so sad of heart."

"I am neither, thank heaven," said Sanctis. "But it is no merit of mine: my father amassed wealth as I have told you, and I am able to walk in the sunshine and give my years to art."

"That is no fault," said Musa. "But yet one does not care for it."

---

[1] The *anser cinereus*, which migrates here in winter; not, of course, the *chens hyperboreus*. [Ouida's note]. Her ornithological definitions are not totally correct. *Anser anser* is a grey-lag goose; *chen hyperboreus* is a greater-snow goose.

"I never knew any one who was well off," she added, after a while. "It does not seem right: why should you not work as every one does in Maremma?"

"I work in my own way."

"To do what you like,—that is not work."

"You are very stern and harsh," he said, with a smile, as he looked at her Antinoüs-like face, which it seemed to him the lotus-flowers of love and dreamful ease should crown. "We must not quarrel, for Joconda's sake."

"No."

"Is there nothing I can do for you?"

"There is one thing, but you will not like me to say it, perhaps."

"Yes, say it. Whatever it may be, I will do it."

"I should be glad if you would go away: that is what would please me."

He was silent and chagrined.

"In this brief time have I made myself so offensive?" he exclaimed bitterly.

"Oh, no," said Musa, a little eagerly, for she did not wish to pain him. "I have no dislike to you; you are one of her people: that is enough for me, But I shall be glad if you will go. In the first place, it teases me to talk to you. Your Italian is not what we use in Maremma; it may be better, I dare say, but it is not ours. And then, if you go on living anywhere near and come to see me here, somebody on the moors will be certain to observe it, and then they will find out these tombs, and, as I have said to you, the shepherds will come."

It was so long a speech for her that she drew a deep breath of fatigue after making it. She did not wish to be harsh to Joconda's relative, but she intensely desired him to be gone from Maremma.

Sanctis was mortified and discomfited. She had taken a strong hold on his imagination, also on his pity. She was like nothing he had ever seen, and he could get no hold in return upon her mind. It was closed to him. He was sure that she would never give him a remembrance if he did as she wished, and left Maremma.

"But to leave you thus now, once I have known you," he said, almost timidly, "that hurts me and troubles me. You are content in it, but indeed it is not a life for a woman."

Musa laughed a little, low in her throat.

"It is a life for *me*, just as it is a life for the moor-hen and the stream-swallow."

"But it is dangerous————"

"Not for me. I can hide as the mole does, and I can fight as the mole can. I am never without my knife."

The fierce fire of Saturnino's eyes glowed for a moment in hers; her nostrils dilated, her lips smiled, her breath came quickly, there was blood in her veins that was warm as wine at the vision of conflict.

"Oh, I do not doubt your courage," said Sanctis, and paused, hesitating how he could awaken this savage innocence to a sense of its own true peril. He felt a momentary shudder go over him at the glance that her eyes gave; he seemed to see the panther in her, as the Greek sailors saw it in the young god Dionysus when he leaped and rent the garland from the mast.

"If I could but persuade you," he said, with the timidity she was quick to hear in his voice.

"But you cannot," she said, rudely. "Do not make me angry; I do not wish to part with you in anger, for Joconda's sake. But you would never persuade me if you stayed a thousand years: you would only drive me away up into the hills; for if I were not alone here, this place would be nothing to me. If it be true that you wish to please me—go."

His face flushed; a deep discomfiture and mortification filled him as he heard. He tore a leaf out of his note-book, wrote on it, and laid it down beside her.

"That is where I live," he said to her; "if ever you want me, send there; I will be here as soon as steam can bring me."

"Why should I want you?" said Musa, with unconscious cruelty of wonder. "I thank you for your thought of me; but I need nothing."

"You may, some day."

She shook her head.

"What I cannot get myself I go without. The sun will be soon setting. You will lose your way on the moors, if you do not set out at once."

"You are hard of heart, Musa."

"I am the Musoncella," she said, with a little smile.

"Will you not say a kinder word at parting? I came out of good will."

"Of that I am sure. God speed you!"

Then she turned away from him, and began to walk back towards the tombs.

He looked after her, while the clematis vitalba, that made a thick screen all around the place as it clung to the shrubs and trees, enclosed her in its starry veil and shut her from his view.

"The virgin's bower," he thought, as the peasant's name for the parasite of the woods came on his mind. "May she be safe in it!" But his fears were with her, though his anger would fain have extinguished them.

"She is only a savage, wild creature, as the *dondola* of her moorland is," he said to himself, as he walked through the blossoming ling which the slanting sun-rays made into "a path of gold." But he could not persuade himself that she was only this; he could not banish from his sight the face that was fit for the young Cleopatra's: he could not forgive himself for having missed the way to fulfil Joconda's wishes. Yet his conscience was blameless.

The fault was not his.

She was a pomegranate-flower blooming in the wilderness; a paradise-bird captive in a cellar. He felt a fool, and guilty, because he had been unable to gather the flower, and too weak to persuade the bird that liberty and light were without.

After him Musa did not look back.

She descended into her shadowy home and called the old dog to her.

"Oh, Leone, how good it is to be alone!" she said, with a smile on her mouth; then the smile faded and the darkness of wrath and of scorn came upon her face.

"The little asp that bit me by betrayal!" she said, bitterly, between her teeth.

For never would she feel quite safe again. She was always on the watch for some strange face, some strange step; and the loss of little Zirlo and the sense of his treachery weighed on her. It was her first experience of the human curse.

The little, chattering, good-humored, selfish boy had been welcome to her at all times. They had blended their young voices together in many a lay of sea and shore; they had been mirthful about nothing, as it is the privilege of childhood to be. Zirlo, trotting to and fro between the mountains and the moors, had been the one note of gayety, the one touch of affection, which had allied her with that common humanity which she often hated, oftener despised and always pitied.

CHAPTER XIII.

A FORTNIGHT or a little more after that curt farewell to Maurice Sanctis when she was out cutting osiers far away from the tombs, the mule was stolen. When she came home, to fetch him to carry the osiers for her, he was missing from the stable she had made for him in the tombs with a cosey litter of moss and ling and a plentiful ration of wild oats and grass. He was missing; and she knew in a moment that he had been stolen. He could not have slipped his halter and opened the stone doors himself.

"It is Zirlo!" she said, between her tight-shut lips. It could be no other than Zirlo.

She went out and saw the wet sand marked with the fresh impress of two little naked feet and the four hoofs of the mule. She tracked them till nightfall over the moors and through the shrubs, but night soon fell over the land and then she could see nothing. She returned, and could not sleep, thinking of the poor old animal gone to unknown misery in hard toil and strange hands.

She remained wide awake, listening to the delicious song of the nightingales that came from every knot of thyme and clump of rosemary, crossed discordantly now and again by the croak of the snipe, the mourning of the owl, the scream of the coot seized by the fox.

At dawn she looked for the tracks again, but they were effaced by the dew.

With full daybreak she went across the country to San Lionardo, where it stood naked and white upon its low spur of the Apennines. She had never been there, but she ran all risks rather than not see Zirlo and find the mule. It was three hours' walk, and most of it was climbing work; but she reached there as the sun, that had long been up over the Umbrian pastures and Adrian shores of the east, first reached the dreary little hamlet hidden in the rocks. She asked for the house of Zeffirino the *pastorino*,[1] and went straight to it. It was a foul-smelling place, reeking of garlic and stable-filth; she saw the father of Zeffirino, who was eating an onion and throwing young boughs into a manger for cows.

---

[1] Shepherd boy.

"Zirlo has stolen my mule," she said, abruptly. "I am come to you to have it back."

"You are a bold one, whoever you are," said the man. "Why do you think he has robbed you?"

"Because the mule is gone, and he alone knew where I kept it; and because he is a false and wicked creature, and did me a treachery but a few days ago: and I spared him then, and I was foolish———"

"Oh, ho!" said the man, "my little lad has told me about you; you are a gypsy, and a witch, and worse, and you live in the bowels of the earth, and some fine night we will come and smoke you out. As for your spavined beast, I know naught of it; and Zeffirino is gone away to Bolsena to his mother's folk, who are fishers there, for he was afraid for his life to remain where you could get at him———"

"Then he has taken the mule to Bolsena!"

"No, no; your mule be burnt! My little lad went away with a good *sensale*———"

"To whom he has sold it!" she cried, beside herself with powerless rage.

The man's face turned red, but he only swore at her.

"If you say more about that, I will say something to you," he said, savagely. "Who stole the gold out of the tombs? The tombs were ours as much as yours."

"I stole nothing," said Musa; "but your little liar has robbed me of my mule, and you know it very well, and you have the *sensale's* silver in your house now, and you are all of you wicked and accursed; and sooner would I that you had cut off my right arm than that you had taken that poor beast to misery in its old age———"

She felt a sob choke her as she spoke, thinking of the patient beast that she had known and cared for all her life, and of the baseness and the vileness with which the child she had trusted had rewarded her trust.

She knew her own impotence. She could prove nothing, and she was full sure that Zirlo and the dealer were far away,—no doubt in some direction the most opposite to the great lake, since this wretch had named Bolsena. She was too proud and too strong to protest when she was powerless to avenge. She turned away and went down the steep street of San Lionardo, roughly paven with rough granite of the mountain.

"We will come and smoke you out some night, as we do the foxes," yelled the father of Zeffirino after her, and muttered to his cow and his pipe, "They say there were bags full of the Austrian's gold florins in those caves. Zirlo was sure there were none left, else a knife across her throat———"

Happily for her and for himself, he was a very lazy man, and munched on at his big onion without going after her to try the persuasion of his knife.

Musa scarcely saw the mountain-side as she descended it for the mist of passionate sorrow that blinded her eyes. The menace to herself passed her ear unheeded: what she grieved for, what she saw in her thoughts, was the poor old mule plodding far away over cruel, stony roads, with no one to give him a draught of water or pull for him a handful of grass,—taken in his old age to the torture-loads of the Carrara marbles, or to the hard labor of the *bindolo* or water-crank, or to those brutal taskmasters the charcoal-burners, who compel their beasts to sleep standing, and kick them up if they dare to lie down, and drive them night and day with the black loads from the forests in long pitiless journeys over stone and sand to the gates of cities.

Poor old Cecco! Never more would he have his fragrant couch of heather, and browse off the sweet shoots of the honeysuckle, and stand at will, knee-deep in the pools, among the green water-plantain. Never more would she rest her cheek against his shaggy neck, and say in his long, soft, furry ear, "You and I, we do not forget Joconda?"

Those who live in the great world or the world of haste and toil may think it a very little thing to lose an old mule to an unknown and almost certainly cruel fate. But to this child, in her loneliness, it was a loss more cruel than words can easily tell. He was the only thing left to her of her old life, and he was gone away into misery.

She searched far and wide over the land for many days, and dropped her usual caution to ask questions of the few men she met; but Zeffirino had been too cunning for her. He and the mule were far away,—the animal, in a dealer's hands, being sold at Massa, and the little traitor safe with his mother's brother, who lived not on Bolsena water, but at the foundries at Follonica. So Zirlo dropped out of her life, and the solitude which she had told Sanctis was so dear to her closed in upon her yet more completely.

She was not alarmed by the threats of Zeffirino's father, for she knew there was now nothing in the tombs to which his kind would attach value; but she was afraid lest others hearing of the tombs would drive her out of them, and often in the night she awoke and listened, hearing the call of the bittern, or the cry of the hare seized by a boot-ed-eagle. She was not afraid, but she was troubled.

Another and a yet greater sorrow also fell upon her at that time. Leone was killed.

To the woods one afternoon two of the smiths of Follonica came with their guns to shoot what they might of the furred and feathered owners of the soil. It was against the law at this season, but there was no one to enforce the law; it would need legions of mounted guards to scour Maremma and enforce obedience. No one sees, no one cares; the shot beasts and the trapped birds are carried through the very gates of the towns, and the law is a dead letter.

She had been at one work or another all the morning, and was tired. In a mossy dell some mile or two distant from the sepulchres—a green shady place, pranked with the blue and the rose-colored lychnis and the wild convolvulus and the clematis both white and purple—she sat down to rest a little while among the mosses, and the warmth and the drowsy air overcame her, and her eyelids dropped, and her limbs stretched themselves out at ease, and she fell fast asleep. There was many a danger there of asps that might creep from under the boulders of tufa, and of vipers that might steal from under the great leaves of the *pandi serpe*; even the booted-eagle, who passes his summers in the Apennines, might sail across the sky and espy her and do battle with her, as she had once seen him do it with a grand-duke till both of them fell dead together. But of these risks she seldom thought, and Leone lay at her feet and watched her quiet breathing.

As she so slept, there came near the two smiths from Follonica, and they caught sight of her, and, being warm with wine they had car-ried with them, they burst through the net-work of greenery and were about to put rough hands on her in her unconscious slumber, when the dog, who had seen them approach without a sound, but with his lips curled back from his teeth and the hair of his shoulders bristling, sprang upon them with a leap of such sudden force that he sent one of them staggering backwards till he fell, and pinned the other at the throat.

The one he held with his powerful teeth he shook like a rat to and fro; the man could do nothing; but the other, who had fallen, and whose fowling-piece had been unloaded, tottered to his feet, rammed a charge down the muzzle of the gun, and fired. At the sound of the shot, Musa, awaking, sprang to her feet; but it was too late to save her friend; shot through the head, Leone dropped like a stone and fell dead. Ere her startled eyes were fully awake, her knife was out of her girdle, and the cowards fled for their lives as they saw its blade flash in the air. She flew on in their wake, but they dived and dipped beneath the thick oak scrub; she lost them as the gaze-hound loses its quarry. She threw herself beside the body of the dog, and the green earth and the blue sky seemed to her to grow red as if soaked in his blood.

He had been her playfellow and her protector for so many years. At night she had slept safely, knowing him near; from infancy, when her baby hand had closed on his white curls, he had been her comrade, her companion, her keeper, and of later years in her sorrows and her solitude he had given her all the tender and comprehensive sympathy which the dog so willingly gives, so rarely receives.

And now his life was gone out in her defence; never again would his frank brown eyes seek sunshine in her smile.

He lay stone-dead in a pool of his own blood that crimsoned the white bells of the bindweed; and his murderers had escaped and were lost forever in the wide waste of Maremma. She could not weep, she could not cry out: she took his poor shattered head in her hands and kissed it. If she could have avenged him with her own life, she would have given it. She cursed her foolish hour of sleep.

She sat there beside him till the day waned and the deep blue shadows of evening began to lengthen over the wold.

Then she raised his great body in her arms and put him over her shoulders as she would have carried a child, and began slowly and with effort thus burdened to make her sad way homeward.

The weight was great; the mile of moorland seemed like ten. She went with bent back and limbs that trembled as if all in a moment she had grown very old; but she did not relinquish her task. He had done more for her. She would not leave him in the woods for the fox and the pole-cat and the carrion birds to find.

It was long past nightfall when she reached her refuge; her clothes were soaked through with blood, his weight had chilled, stiffened, numbed her; but she brought him home.

The next day she made his grave under the rosemary and the myrtle; and now on earth she was utterly alone.

The summer passed on. Sanctis did not return, and she gave him no thought. The wild flowers ceased to bloom; the torrid heats descended on the earth; under the passing rain-storms the hot soil seethed and smoked; the Serpent-bearer gleamed nightly in the south-east, and from Perseus shooting-stars fell across the heavens. The height of summer here is the weird, the oppressive, the ghastly season of the year; rarely has the sunset beauty, the red rayless ball too often lends but a dull hectic to the sun and sky. The chanting tree-frogs are happy, and all the snakes and the heat-loving lizards; nothing else is.

The panting fox hangs his tongue out even as he lies in his cool damp earth; the porcupine sleeps supine; the birds doze, songless; the hare is hot even in her leafy form lined with the milkwort; there is not a breath even among the sedges, that rustle so readily at the least air; the very water is sickly and lukewarm, even under the moon, when the snipes are bathing and questing.

When the rains come, as they do often here, they scarcely bring any coolness; they only serve to distil the dangerous miasma from the ground.

For the first time in her life, the season affected Musa: she was not ill in any way, but she felt tired and oppressed. Treachery is like the fever of these lands; its injury may be shaken off and its poison defied, yet where it has once entered no life is ever quite the same again. Zirlo was only a little, selfish, cunning, merciless child; but he had stabbed her to the quick.

Never once did she regret her refusal to Maurice Sanctis. He had been so unlike all she had ever known, what he offered was so unintel-ligible to her, his relationship to Joconda seemed to her so like a fable, so unreal, so intangible, that he had left no impress on her mind.

When she thought of him at all, it was with a contemptuous im-patience and wonder, such as she had felt at Daniello Villamagna.

But the sailor was nearer to her, more comprehensible; she would have liked to own the good brig if she could have done so without his owning her.

The Sicilian she laughed at, but in a measure understood; Maurice Sanctis she understood not at all.

Meantime, in a great château of the western provinces, Sanctis himself pursued his work on vast blank wall-spaces, which he had promised to make bloom as the rose with frescos of the old sweet story of Eros and Psyche.

To every true artist there is no such true delight as fresco, no method which gives so entirely the sense of the power of instantaneous creation. Surely, also, art has never been so great since the panel and the canvas supplanted the wide wall-surface, so eloquent in its barrenness to those who can see with the eye of the mind, as Raffaelle saw when he went through the Stanze that he was called to decorate, dreaming of the School of Athens. Sanctis would not have been unworthy to unloose the sandals of the Angel of Urbino.

He worshipped Art and followed it with humble and perfect reverence.

If there were too great an austerity, too chill a calm, in his creations, as in Flandrin's, and Lauren's, and Overbeck's, they were absolutely pure, entirely noble.

Under his touch now his Eros became too entirely the incarnation of spiritual love, his Psyche too entirely the embodiment of the soul; but the myth lost none of its grace and gained a holiness not its own under his treatment.

But, for the first time, his heart was not in the work of his hand, and he had not his usual interest in his creations. He had his usual fine thought, delicate touch, subtle meaning in what grew beneath the sweep of his brush, but forever between him and the fresco came the remembrance of the Musoncella of Maremma.

As he drew the gold curls and fair face of his Psyche, he saw always the dark and brilliant face of that daughter of the Etruscan Mastarna. As he painted the Greek portico, the cool *atrium*, the dark green of orange and myrtle touching white marble, he saw only the red glow of the tufa soil, the amethyst and sapphire of the mountains, the dusk of the silent tombs, the lustre of the eyes of the offspring of Saturnino.

He knew her origin; his knowledge let him trace the possible current of Oriental blood that had most likely been unmingled with any foreign stream in all the generations who had borne the name of Mastarna and dwelt upon the site of the ancient Saturnia. Her passionate instinct of attachment to the Tyrrhene nation might come from transmitted influences that for three thousand years and more, under the shadow of the Apennines, had been strong in a race that had changed neither its dwelling-place nor its habits.

It was a fantastic idea, but it took hold of the mind of the artist, which was more dreamy and enthusiastic than he knew. He saw the voluptuous Lydian of the days of Asian supremacy look from under those level brows and full eyelids of Saturnino Mastarna's child.

The memory of her pursued him and unnerved him; he was an-

gered against her. His reason told him that it was best for his peace to
see no more of a life which, brought into his own in any way, would
be as the wind and the lightning-flash of the tempest are in serene pale
April skies; yet, think as he would, he could not shake off a sense of
cowardice and wrong-doing in leaving undone the task that Joconda
had asked her brothers to do. He could not, whether in the historic
silence of the old Armorican castle or in the mirthful and crowded
streets of Paris, forget for any length of time that solitary figure as he
saw it stand amidst the amber of the coronilla and the broom.

She was so strong, so fearless, so fierce, so lonely, dwelling there
amidst the graves of her perished nation; she was beautiful as a hawk
is, poised on a bough of oak and looking with bold and brilliant eye
down the shaft of the golden sunbeam. She had that grace, that
strength, that untamed dignity and daring, which the free things of
forest and crag alone possess. The memory of her haunted Sanctis,
whose life, all artist though he was, had been chill, orderly, calm, cultured, with little passion in it, and on it the yoke of an early training
whose precision could never be wholly abandoned, for strong are the
bonds of birth and habit.

He was a man of genius, and by custom a Parisian; but there was
much in him of the calm and simple mountaineer, of the patient and
prudent Alpine peasant. His work, his mind, his modes of life, were
those of a famous painter who was also a rich man and could build for
himself a house that was a temple of art; but his nature remained that
which had been Anton's and Joachim's before him.

He loved order, method, cleanliness in morals, serenity in the
manner of his days; his paintings erred in almost too great an abun-
dance of limpidity, of mathematical exactitude, of faultless perspec-
tive; they were so perfect that they seemed a reproach to a hurrying
and careless world that loves *brio* and celerity. Never in all his life had
a thought that was unwelcome and poisonous been harbored by him
for more than a moment: his clear and calm mind had been always
able to repel it.

But the desire to return to that strange, unhealthy, luxuriant,
mournful land where Musa dwelt grew upon him, and although he
resisted he could not banish it. And he smarted with a sense of cowardice, remembering that he had allowed her to drive him from it.

"Doubtless the Sicilian lover is with her," he said again and again
himself, as he worked on at the great frescos.

And yet he could not fancy her with any lover; he could not think of those superb lips as tremulous with any tenderness or warmed with any kiss. It seemed to him that she could never live in any other way than so, alone with her Etruscan dead.

To living humanity she was the Musoncella.

He worked at the frescos summer and autumn, and was never content with them, and went back to Paris, where his house was the envy of his fellows. There he shut himself in during those chilly autumn days when the leaves were flying in scarlet squadrons down the asphalte without, and painted that which haunted him.

He portrayed her just as he had seen her in the hot transparent morning, with the gold of the coronilla and the broom behind her, and the turquoise blue of the sky beyond. He gave the picture that strength, that liberty, that untamable spirit, that freshness of open-air life, and that repose of solitude which were in her. His friends came and saw it in progress, and called it Maia and Atargatis,[1] and many another classic name, and said that it would be the grandest and most luminous thing that he had ever created. But one day he was struck with a sudden unreasoning sense of utter hatred to it; he drew a great branch of bistre over the damask rose of the mouth, the Oriental sombreness and mystery of the eyes, and set it with its face to the gray wall, and locked his studio and went away.

CHAPTER XIV.

MEANWHILE, in Maremma, as the August heats lay heavy on the land, fate was at work for Musa,—the fate which comes to all, and sometimes, like the prophet of old, blesses and curses in the same breath.

One day she went out on the water; the sea was as hot as the land was, but still she was glad to bathe in it, to swim against it, to pull her boat through it, to watch its lovely colors, here the hue of a pigeon's breast, there deeply, darkly blue as the indigo-berries of the laurestinus when they purpled the moors in autumn. There was a slight southerly wind, and it filled the little lateen sail that she had contrived, by much hard work with axe and mallet, to fix up in her

---

[1] Maia was the eldest of the seven Pleiades; Atargatis was the Syrian goddess, referred to as the fish goddess.

treasure-trove of a boat. She had made the mast from a young pine, and had woven and stitched the canvas herself. In the pleasure of her sail, she went far and stayed late: it was evening when she went down the steps of the tombs.

As she descended, she saw in the twilight of her home a lonely figure sitting crouched before the embers of the fire. Her heart beat wildly, not with fear, but with rage. Who had dared to violate her sanctuary? And with her wrath there mingled apprehension: if shepherd or forester found out this safe shelter, would they ever leave to her sole ownership of it?

She looked through the boughs down into the gloom. She could not see the face of the stranger: his head was bowed on his hands, and his whole frame crouched up like that of a stray and shivering dog.

She took the long knife she always wore in her girdle and went down the steps; at the slight sound she made the intruder looked up as she had seen startled animals look, sprang to his feet, and, before she could stop him, had prostrated himself at hers.

"I claim your shelter," he said, and he kissed her rough woollen skirts. "I am an innocent man, hunted and miserable. Save me!"

Musa stood over him with her grave luminous face full of sudden compassion. Her hand still held the long knife, but she showed neither doubt nor fear of him.

"Who are you?" she said simply.

"I was a prisoner on Gorgona; I escaped with Saturnino; we parted company in the storm that overtook us. I saw him again when he was hiding a few days later: he had doubled like a fox. He described this place to me and bade me make for it. I am wounded—and tired—and—forgive me."

A great faintness came over him as he spoke; his lips turned blue, his heart seemed to cease to beat, and he sank downwards on the earthen floor. A wound in his shoulder had burst out bleeding afresh.

Musa threw her knife on the ground; she busied herself with such restoratives as she knew, and with a firm hand bound up the gunshot wound while he still lay insensible. Then she forced a little wine that Joconda had kept as a cordial between his lips, and bathed his head and face with cold water.

After a little he regained consciousness, but only languidly, and he did not fully awake to the remembrance of what had passed.

"You are good; you are good; that cools me," he murmured, as the water fell on him. He was in a feverish sort of trance; his skin was burning, and his breath was short and quick.

She was absorbed in her efforts to help him; she did not notice that he was a man young, and wonderfully handsome, with the beauty of the Greek ideal,—beauty which not exposure, or imprisonment, or shame, or terror, or privation, or the ghastly horrors of the galleys had had any power to destroy, though they had wasted, darkened, and dimmed it, as dust and ill usage obscure the soil-less glory and fine lines of the marble god. Of all this she saw nothing, thought nothing; it was enough for her that he was hunted and in fear, like the beasts and the birds of the Maremma.

She tended him as she would have taken care of a stricken deer or a maimed hawk. Saturnino's name said nothing to her. She thought of him only as a thief who had robbed the dead; but even as she had aided and pitied him, so she did this man. There was in her blood a fierce hatred of law and oppression, a keen sympathy with all that was driven and persecuted.

After a while the stranger became more awake to where he was, and recovered, as the wine flowed down into his chilled, bruised, weary body, sight and speech and sense. She had piled dead wood on the hearth, and he was still stretched where he had first dropped before it. The night was cold, though the days were scorching, and the heat of the fire was welcome to his limbs, numbed with long fatigue and exposure in woods and marshes where he had disputed the acorns with the boars and the squirrels.

"You will not give me up?" he said, with a timid appeal in his great dark eyes.

Musa, standing above him, in her strength and her health, smiled with little scorn. "Why do you come to me if you think so?"

"Saturnino said you had been good to him, and that the place was a sure refuge."

He did not say that Saturnino had also said to him,—

"If the maiden be squeamish, or be like to be treacherous, you can easily rid yourself of her: a fawn's neck is soon slit."

"He was vile himself," she said, hastily, with sternness in her eyes. "What think you he did? He stole the gold cups and platters,—*theirs*. I was glad when I learned he was taken."

"Can you be so cruel?" said the refugee, with a little look of wonder and fear.

"I do not see that I am cruel," said Musa. "He was a traitor and a thief. If I let you stay, will the place be sacred to you?"

"You and it, that I swear."

"Stay, then," said Musa, with calm unconcern.

It did not occur to her that he was a man, and young; her innocence was too grand a thing for that.

"You did not do the crime they took you for?" she asked him, with a long, grave look into his face.

"No; that also I swear. I was guiltless as you."

She felt that his answer was the truth.

"What was the crime?"

"I was accused of the murder of my mistress."

"Ah!"—she drew a deep breath; it did not seem to her anything very strange: the knife was a common cure of faithlessness in Maremma.

"She was false?" she added.

"Not false to me. Nor slain by me. God in heaven hears me! Never."

"Very well. I believe," she said, simply. "You can tell me more when you will. Now you are unwell,—tired and feverish. I will make you a bed of leaves—there is nothing else—in the farther chamber, and you had best go to it."

"Can you sleep among these tombs?" he cried, and glanced around the sepulchres with awe.

"The dead do not hurt us," said Musa, with a grave tenderness. "They have but gone before where soon we go."

The young man shuddered a little. Life had been glorious to him, and was still sweet and precious.

It needs a pure soul to love the dead.

She left him, and made a bed of moss and leaves in the innermost chamber of the tombs; she filled one of the black vases with the thin wine she used herself, and put it with some bread beside the bed; she lit a little wick in a little oil in one of the Etruscan lamps, and set it in the place; she went to the spring that welled through the passage beyond, and filled a big copper vessel with it for a bath.

"That is all I can do," she thought, intent on her preparations as Nausicaa for her hero from the sea.[1]

It was a pleasure to have some one to serve and to defend.

"Can you walk to the spot?" she said to him. "If not, lean on me: I am strong."

"I think I can walk," he said, embarrassed somewhat because she was not so; and he rose and dragged himself feebly into the third chamber.

"I am so tired," he muttered. "I think I should let the carabineers take me now as easily as a stunned hare."

"The carabineers will not come here," said Musa. "Do not think of them. Sleep, and if you want any aid give a shout, and I shall hear."

"You are good to me," murmured the stranger, with a little confusion, looking at her as she stood with the light of her own lamp shed on her dark level brows, her lustrous eyes, her upthrown masses of bronze-hued hair, and the form that was clad in the white lambs'-wool as the fauns and nymphs of old may have been clad in Tempe and Arcadia when through the gladness of the woods the winds of winter rustled.

"I will say of you as the angel Gabriel said of Madonna Lisa," he said, with a little smile, "that you are the fairest thing that ever was seen in Mondo or Maremma."

"Oh, not I," said Musa, with a little displeasure. "When the rose and crimson flamingoes come like a cloud red with the sun's setting, they are much more beautiful than I. Do the angels ever remember Maremma? I think not. Who could tell you they did? Good-night to you; good repose."

Then she went across the other chambers, crossing herself as she passed the coffin of Joconda, and in time laid herself down on her own bed as calmly as though no human intruder had disturbed her solitude.

Only, every now and then she kept awaking with a start, and, sitting up on her rough couch, listened with ears as eager and sure as the deer's to hear whether any sound on the night's silence was like the tramp of the soldiers of the State. She was afraid for him; she was not afraid of him.

---

[1] In *The Odyssey* Nausicaa finds the shipwrecked Odysseus on the shore and takes him to her father, King Alcinous.

True, once before she had sheltered a galley-slave, and he had robbed her; but she felt no distrust now. When this man had said, "I am innocent," there had been truth in his voice; and she had sympathy with him as she had with the large-eyed deer, with the rose-red phenopteræ, with the timid hare and the brave boar, and with all the man-hunted things of the marsh and the moor.

The blood of an outlaw was in her.

She was up whilst the sun was still unseen, and only a geranium color, lovely and wondrous as that of the flamingo's wings, was spreading over the darkness of the Maremma. She looked into his chamber; the lamp was spent, but he was sleeping. She could see the outline of his head and shoulders resting on the homely linen she had spread above the leaves.

She went softly back again, went out, and plunged into the tarn and bathed, then clothed herself and set about the preparation of such humble meal as she could make with water and with bread and with the sweet herbs of the moors. It had always done very well for her, but she doubted whether it would suffice for him. She looked for some eggs from her fowls, and she was pleased that she could find three.

Then she took up the silver-framed mirror of burnished steel that had been buried there with some regal or noble woman, and that now served her to give her back a dim reflection of her own face, and combed and brushed her short rich hair till it shone like dusky gold that the fires have burnished and reddened. For the first time in her life she looked at the great eyes that surveyed her from the mirror, and said to herself, "Is it true that I am good to look at? Joconda said so once or twice, but then she loved me."

She had never heard of Boccaccio, but a drop of the old potent Florentine philtres[1] that Boccaccio used had touched her lips.

For the first time she looked with interest on the face that the Etruscan mirror reflected, and wondered if indeed it were handsome.

She did not know that her head was like that of Carlo's angel, and her body like one of the beautiful, lissome, strong, and harmonious figures that are still left to us in Greek marble.

As she looked down on the mirror when she lay with her chin resting on her hands and her elbows leaning in the thick wild thyme,

---

[1] Love potions.

a scorpion, black and hideous, ran out of the herbs and passed across the steel face of the mirror which was engraven with the figures of the Tyndarides, dear to Etruria as to Rome.

She started as the ugly dangerous insect passed over her own reflection. She rose to her feet and left the steel flatterer lying among the dews on the ground. The scorpion remained upon its silver framework.

"Do you come to tell me that to think of my face is a sin?" she said to the beast,—"a sin as ugly and as poisonous as you?"

Joconda had always told her so; but the soul of her vigorous and brilliant youth insensibly rebelled against these austere negations of the flesh. Nature told her to rejoice in herself as the Hellenic anthologists told the beautiful boy and the virgin who stripped for the race.

The soul of the Greek lives oftentimes in the Italian, though it lives benighted and struggling in bonds and unconscious of itself.

She left the mirror still lying on the grass and went within. She took some food in one of the earthen jars and went towards his chamber.

"Are you arisen?" she called, softly.

He answered her feebly:

"I cannot rise; my limbs seem made of stone. I fear the chills have got into my very bones; I am in great pain———"

She went forward to his side.

"Our marshes will do that sometimes," she said, with a soft pity in her eyes, like that which came there when she saw a hunted bird or beast and could not save it. "I have seen that malady: it is as though your whole body were frozen; but if you have not much fever it may pass. I have brought some good food: eat it."

She held the earthen *holkion*[1] and a wooden spoon towards him, and he took a little of her broth and said that it was good, and then took more.

With the momentarily revived forces that came to him after the food, he drew a quick breath from aching lungs, and with many a pause from weakness, and many an involuntary shudder from cruel memories, he told her how he had first come thither from Gorgona.

"Saturnino and I escaped together, and one other man, who, poor

---

[1] An Etruscan vase for drinking.

wretch, was shot as he leaped from the wall. We had planned it long before we could find the occasion to take that mad plunge into the sea. We swam and swam, and at last fortune favored us in a wondrous way, we came on a drifting boat, the boat, I suppose, of some wrecked tartana: she was of Mediterranean build. In that we rowed, and sculled ourselves warily all night long, and gained the coast, and hid all day long under the rocks off Romito. There is a wild thicket of rosemary there: it served to hide us. At nightfall we took to the sea again. The idea of Saturnino was to get ashore somewhere near either the Albegna's or the Fiora's mouth, and so in time creep home to his old lair by Monte Labbro. We pulled all day long; we were half dead of hunger and thirst; we had drunk at a spring near Romito, and for food we had a bit of black Gorgona bread, but we had finished that at dawn. We rowed on, keeping some way off the shore, hoping against hope that if the coast-guard or the carabineers saw us they would see in us two fishermen and nothing more. The heat was frightful; the sea looked still enough and glassy and oily, but there was a heavy swell underneath that made the pulling hard. I know not how many miles we rowed that day, but they must have been many. We rowed on all that day, and caught some fish and ate it raw, and chewed the sea-weed, and were nearly mad. At night we stole on land; thirst drove us: it was a wild place, and we found fresh water and some wild fruit. At daybreak, after sleeping like drunkards, we went to sea again and pulled along the coast: we saw the mounted soldiers riding along the Tombolo in the bay of Populonia. They were looking for us,—that is certain. At three o'clock, or thereabouts as nearly as we could tell by the sun, an awful storm burst over us. It was quite sudden, or seemed so: it was rainless and horrible. The waves rose like walls; the wind drove us like a whip in some giant's hand; great clouds of foam on the sea, and of dust on the land, obscured the shore and the horizon. We were thrown to and fro like a cockle-shell; the noise of the wind all the while like rushing cataracts. The sky was livid with lightning, the thunder pealed like the cannon of vast armies. Our little skiff overturned; we could not right her, we were thrown headlong into the hissing water. She was flung about a few moments, and then dashed like a plaything far out of our reach. We were in the deep sea, faint for want of food and almost weary to insensibility. How I gained the shore I cannot tell. But I did. Saturnino I never saw. Later I heard that———"

"I saved him!" said Musa, who had held her breath and listened with parted lips.

"Yes, I know———"

"Yes," she proceeded, unheeding, "I plucked him out of the sea, and I hid him here, and he paid me by stealing the gold of the tombs."

"He told me that. We met up in the mountains, up under the Labbro; he had made me acquainted with all the haunts and hiding-places of the hills. We had endured unutterable misery, both of us. To me women had been kind: they are always so to a man in misfortune" (in his thought he said, rather, to one who is young and well-looking). "We were but a few days together; he told me of the gold out of the tomb, and I blamed him hotly, and we came to fierce words; he went down to the Orbitellano to sell that gold, though I told him to attempt it would be his own undoing; and I went up to his old favorite lair on the Rocca del Giulio, where it is cold as winter even in the canicular heats. You will understand, of course, that all this time we moved with the greatest caution, and only at night, like the bats and the owls. Well, in the Orbitellano he was taken, as I heard, but I heard it long afterwards, and I remained awaiting him up at the Giulio. There were some stone cabins there, very wretched ones, where his band had dwelt, and there were still remnants of their booty and of the things they used. There was even a child's toy in ivory of Indian workmanship,—taken, I suppose, when they plundered a train or stopped a travelling-carriage. It seemed strange to see it, that frail toy in such a solitude. Well, there I passed the autumn and the winter: I lived miserably, that is of course. I picked up the pine cones and cut the brush-wood; and there were old friends of Mastarna's down at a hovel that is called a hostelry in the hamlet of Saturnia, and for his sake and for love of outwitting the law, for they were all smugglers, if not worse, they sent me up coarse food once in eight days and took down the fuel. So I lived. It was hardly better than Gorgona, except there was the sense of a relative freedom and the sight of the clouds that lay beneath one of a morning, and, when they cleared at noon, showed so glorious an expanse of wood, and moor, and cliff, and sea, far down, so far down!—One saw as the eagle sees. But I was forever on the watch, and scarce dared, even in the bitter days and nights of winter on the mountains, light a fire, though timber was so plentiful and near, lest any glow of flame or any curl of smoke should tell my hunters I was hiding there. Then I heard from the men of Saturnia that Saturnino had been captured afresh and had been for months in the prisons of Orbitello. That hurt me greatly, for though I knew he was but a brute and stained with many crimes of blood-guiltiness, yet there was a force and a rough generosity in him which allured one."

"It was generous to steal the gold!"

"No, it was mean; but what would you? He had been a robber all his life, and he was at that moment desperate, starving, homeless, besides, it was only *roba delle tombe*[1] to him."

"That is what is so vile! The dead could not defend it, or strike him down."

"I know, I know. But, my dear, wild and lawless men who go to the galleys come out of them devils. I myself, who had long habits of education and social observance behind me, I was little better than any, for when I had been for six months in that accursed place, when hunger and thirst tortured me I could have killed or robbed like Saturnino. What we call our soul is only in safety so long as our body feeds! He took your gold, and that was bad, and to wrong your trust was worse; but he has paid for both sins heavily. He will not get away again from his torture. Well, when I heard he had been shot down, but taken alive, I lost heart and hope: he had seemed my only friend. The time went by most miserably, until, one daybreak, I saw down amidst the cork woods the glitter of the musketry of soldiers. Whether one of the men at Saturnia had betrayed me or not I cannot tell, but it was certain the soldiery were out after me. In the stillness of dawn I could hear their heavy tread, and their weapons breaking the branches as they passed. They were hundreds of feet down below me. I packed a little bread up, and took a dagger I had found in those huts—the dagger you see, a three-edged old dagger of Florence,—and then I fled for my life again, and hid in the holes of the rocks with the other hunted beasts of the hills. That was in April last; I knew the month because the ashes were in blossom and made the woods below look as if a snow-storm had fallen on them. It is of no use going over all I suffered,—suffering of starvation, of exhaustion, of cold, of heat, of rheumatism, of cramp, of wet, of darkness, of perpetual terror. Ah! do not think me a coward! I have been palsied with fear: I am still!"

---

[1] Spoils of the tombs.

He gazed at her with dilated eyes, with straining ears, with panting breath, with shivering flesh; his danger was ever present. Even now the muskets of the soldiers might be glancing in the moonlight among the Christ's thorn above the sepulchres.

Musa was alarmed at his look.

"You are unwell," she said, gently. "Do not talk any more, and be not afraid. Here no one will come; you are safe!"

"Safe!" he echoed, with so poignant a despair that it struck her heart with cold as if his three-edged dagger of Florence had pierced it. "No; I can never more be safe on earth, though I wander as long as Ahasuerus.[1] There is nothing more to tell; you can guess what my life has been,—hiding and creeping away through all this green land, forever afraid of every sound, of every breeze, of every leaf! I came down here without knowing I was near you, and then by certain landmarks that I saw I recognized the place of the tombs that Mastarna had described to me, and I resolved to throw myself upon your mercy, and in your absence I crept down the steps. I was very faint; I had eaten nothing but berries for several days, and I have an open wound on my shoulder. A month or more ago the soldiers were near enough to me to fire at me, and they hit me; though it is but a flesh-wound it does not close, and it is painful. I have lain out many nights on your moors, and men used to say that it was death to do that. I have doubled like the fox; the soldiers believe me gone to the hills again; but any hour they may find out and come."

He shuddered; his eyes closed, his head fell back upon his rude pillow of dried grasses. So much speech had exhausted his enfeebled spirit and frame.

"I shall be very ill," he said, wearily. "You had better turn me out whilst I can crawl away from you."

"I will care for you till the illness passes," she answered.

"It were better to call the carabineers," he said, bitterly. "A sick man and a felon,—what can you do with me?"

"I will tend you till you are well," she said, simply, again. "You are quite safe here. No one, except a little goat-boy and two strangers who

---

[1] The Wandering Jew. According to legend, Ahasuerus mocked and mistreated Christ before his crucifixion. As punishment, he was condemned to walk the earth for eternity.

are far away, even know of these tombs. It is true there is little food for you, but there will be enough to keep you from hunger."

"But why should you do all this for me?"

"Because you have no one else to help you."

"That is very noble of you!"

"Why that? I have no one either. Leone, whom I loved, is dead."

"Leone? What was he?"

"He was a dog."

"Is that all you have had to love?"

"I had a woman: she was very old. She died in the summer of last year."

"You loved her very much, I think, by the sound of your voice: there are tears in it."

"She was very good."

"Tell me, what is your name?"

"I am called Musa. And yours?"

"I am Luitbrand d'Este."

"That is a very long, fine name. It is not of Maremma: at least, I think not."

"No, it is not; it is of the North, of the Lombard plains, where the snow lies long in winter-time, and the rivers rage and outspread themselves till the land is drowned, and men and their cattle and their cities are drowned too."

"You should not speak any more. You are weak. I will go and get a brazier and light you a fire, and I will make you some herb-tea that will be good for your pain. Lie and sleep if you can. It is such a fair day without. It is a pity you cannot see it."

"I should not dare to look out into the light if I could rise. You forget that I am a hunted beast."

"That is why I trouble myself for you," she answered. "I would always save the boars if I could. They kill nothing; they only eat roots and berries, and men hunt them wickedly. Of course they fight when they are pressed; so did you. Now lie still and sleep, and I will light a fire."

She had burned some fallen wood in the summer into charcoal, and made of that the *brace*,[1] which was the only form of fire known in

---

[1] Coal

Santa Tarsilla. She filled a big vessel with this,—a metal *lebes*[1] that had served in Etruscan times to hold the wines of a funeral feast. Once lighted, the slow warmth of the smouldering embers soon spread itself through the place, though it had no power to cure the chills and shivering of the sick man.

She did for him what she had seen Joconda do for those thus afflicted; and the grand sunshine and storm of autumnal days passed over the moors and mountains, and the *libeccio*[2] blew the sea into a field of foam, a steam of mist, and for the first time she kept no count of the change on the face of nature, but in the twilight of the Etruscan tombs watched the waning of strength, the flickering of breath, the half-unconscious torture of a human frame.

For days together she never left the sepulchre.

She waited on his lassitude, his heats, his chills, his shuddering pains, all the long hours through, doing what she could do to alleviate his ills; and at night, when she lit the little bronze lamp, she was alone with a man delirious and who seemed to her on the point of death. She never felt that temptation, which a coward would have felt, to leave him to his fate and rush away from this misery and danger into safety where the dwelling of men and the meeting of roofs would give it. She prayed passionately for him. That was all she did. She never had heard of physicians; there was not one at Santa Tarsilla. If such a person were needed he had to be sought from Orbitello, and no one dreamt of doing that once in ten years, though the surgeon of the Orbitellano was considered the parish doctor of the whole district. There was hardly any one in the villages in summer, and the few that were there in winter cured themselves with nostrums or with simples,[3] and, if they could not cure, lay down meekly like suffering animals, called the priest, and died. Therefore of medical help or service she had no idea, and, if she had known of it, could not have left the sick man to seek it. And Zirlo had been a traitor; she could no more call to him across the moorlands and see his little brown face peer through the brushwoods in answer.

She was utterly alone with this hunted creature who seemed at

---

[1] A cauldron.
[2] South-west wind.
[3] Nostrums are untested medicines—quack remedies; simples are medicines obtained from plants.

once frozen and on fire, and of whom she knew nothing. It never occurred to her to be afraid or to summon other help. Distrust of others was an instinct in the child of Saturnino, and the loneliness of her life with Joconda had made independence of human sympathy and aid her second nature.

If she had wished it, moreover, she knew that she would have called for help in vain. Of the sickly timid souls of Santa Tarsilla, not one would have ventured here, and of the rude, scattered herdsmen and husbandmen of Maremma she knew nothing, and they had their toil, which was their all, to fill their time.

So she remained alone beside the nearly dying man.

But as fear paralyzes the feeble, so it nerves the courageous: she was brave, and she did not let her fear conquer her compassion. And she was afraid of the strangers coming as Sanctis had come, afraid of the greed of the laborers on the moors and the hills if it were known that there was something here strange and worth seeing; and if such as these came, then after them would come the guards. These thoughts kept her anxious and awake all through that long night: she sat by the sick man's bed on the stone chair sculptured there for the dead Etrurians to occupy, and listened to his disjointed, wandering speech, and watched the oil flame flicker in the lamp that had been fashioned by hands lifeless three thousand years before.

She knew his malady to be that deadly scourge of the soil, called the *perniciosa*,[1]—that terrible fever which seems to have joined hands with frost and fire. Twice the fatal fit came on him,—the ceaseless shivering and trembling, the blue pinched cold, the bloodless icy collapse of the whole tortured body. The third seizure would mean death, she knew. Raging heat, as though his flesh were melting in a furnace, followed, and held him in its power for many days, but the cold fit returned not, and she began to hope that life would be stronger than the marsh-poison.

What the fugitive said in his stupor told her nothing of him.

When he was sensible, he complained of thirst and racking pain; when he was delirious, he thought that the carabineers were on him, and he struggled with them and shouted aloud. Sometimes he mur-

---

[1] Malaria.

mured passionate love words and called with yearning endearment on the name of Aloysia.

"How could they think he killed her, since he loves her so?" thought Musa, as she heard.

For fifteen months he had been wandering, pursued, hidden amidst hill-forests or by the sea in caves, holding his life in his hand, more wretched than a hunted stag or fox, waking from every hour of jaded sleep with the memory that his foes were seeking him and might be behind each rock, each tree, each tuft of marucca. Now that he had dropped thus into exhaustion, his harassed brain could not escape the horrid terrors of his haunted past.

Once she had seen a trapped flamingo struggle in the gin, writhing its flower-like body and its flame-like throat, and beating its crimson wings in madness and terror, till it died: he made her think of the Egyptian bird.

It was a fear so natural which pursued him even into the stupor of insensibility that it seemed not craven, but merely human, as is the fear of men in shipwreck.

She soothed him as well as she knew how, with wet moss upon his head, and water ever to his reach. To her, used as she was to the open air and the open sea, there could have been no greater deprivation than to remain cooped up under the vault of stone all through the brilliant days of the late summer. Yet she stayed down in the tombs for this stranger's sake, only going out for such time as it was absolutely necessary to take for the finding of simples and of food. She missed the help of Zeffirino sorely; and without him the little gains she had made were lost to her, at least were lost until she could be free to carry what she sold herself to the hill-villages, and this she would be afraid to do, lest it should lead to discovery not of her refuge alone, but of the fugitive she harbored there.

She wanted many things for this terrible sickness with which she alone fought; but she could get none of them. She could not bring herself to leave him in his great peril for so long a time as it would take to go to Santa Tarsilla or Telamone; and, even if she had left him, her appearance in those places to which she had been so long lost would have provoked comment, wonder, and possibly pursuit, and, with pursuit, the sight of one for whom to be seen by human eyes would mean a lifetime spent at the galleys. So she had to do as she could with the narrow means within her reach; and whilst the fever

lasted the demands of the sick man on her were not great. The water
from the nearest spring, a drink she made from the bilberries on the
moor, a little broth of herbs thickened with beaten egg, such as she
had seen Joconda make for sick people,—these were all he wanted,
and often more than she could force through his scorched lips, drawn
back from his teeth in the convulsions of alternate heat and cold. The
terrible nausea of his disease made even the spring-water taste bad
and bitter to him, though in his devouring thirst he drank of it almost
unceasingly, as if he had been shipwrecked on some bare rock without
a drop to cool his mouth save such as rained from the clouds upon
him.

But, if he should recover, when he should recover, she said always
to herself, she knew very well that his hunger in convalescence would
equal his long fasting now; that he would want meat, wine, many
things that she would never be able to procure; and the thought of this
kept her harassed and anxious, and blinded her eyes to the autumnal
colors on the moors and woods, and made her heedless of the departure of her songsters from the myrtle coverts and the jungle of cistus
and bay.

When the call of the striginæ echoed over the marshes, or the
night-heron's croak thrilled hoarsely through the dark, they startled
her now. She took them for the shout of soldiery or the boom of powder.

As she watched his fever, and scanned the moors for him, so, as
a child, she had watched the fluctuations of life in a storm-swallow
with a broken wing that she had taken off the waves after a boatman
had shot it. Often the bird had seemed lifeless, with blind eyes and
dulled plumage, and she had been sure that it was dead. Then she had
warmed it in her bosom, and it had recovered. She had kept it all winter, and then the wing had grown whole once more. On Easter-day it
had flown off her shoulder over the sea, a speck of silver and bronze
in the sunshine, which she had watched with big tears in eyes that had
never been so dimmed before.

As she had watched the bird then, so she watched now the struggle between life and death in the body of this doomed and hunted
man.

When he was restless and could not sleep at all through the nights
that seemed long as centuries, she took her mandoline and sang to
soothe him such sonnets as she had sung to the shore-people at Santa

Tarsilla. The mellow, tender thrilling of the old *chitarra* chimed in softly with her voice, which in its youth and its clearness was as melodious as the spring and autumn song of the woodlark, which chants ever, as the old French quatrain has it, "Adieu, adieu, adieu!"

Once above ground a shepherd went by over the turf, not witting of all that lay below; and he heard that sweet lullaby beneath his feet thrilling through the earth, and was so terrified that he ran headlong, leaving his flock behind him, and told for many a day in his own Pistoiese mountain-home on winter nights that in Maremma the dead people sang below the soil, in the very heart and core of the round globe.

So, slowly, by one care and another of hers, her sick man rallied, and cast off little by little the weight of disease, and stretched out his thin transparent hands for more food than she found it easy to supply to him.

Slowly, as the September days grew shorter and the winter solstice came nearer, his resurrection began in the shadow of the Etruscan grave.

Towards daybreak at the close of the fifth week of his sojourn there, his fever grew lower; a quieter sleep came on his heavy eyelids, his limbs shivered less; he got some rest. She left him to let the fowls out into the air. The sun was once more coming up behind the dark edge of the moors. She scanned them with beating heart lest she should see any new-comer on them. Dread woke up with every dawn for her now; her old simple peace was gone forever,—the peace that she had shared with the kid that cropped the pasture, with the arum that was curled within its green spathe.

She was thankful beyond words because at last some hope had come for him. Yet a deep sorrow took possession of her soul as she realized the burden bound upon her; tears rose in her eyes and veiled the carnation of the morning skies. She did not reason on it, but she felt that vast irreparable loss which no treasures of the world, or passions, or joys, can adequately pay,—the loss of youth's unconsciousness.

Never again could she go light-hearted to the shore to wade amidst the sea-things, glad as they; never again would she come back over the brown moor in the hush of evening, content because a meal of chestnuts or a few wild figs had been her day's sufficient gleaning.

The unconscious life—the life that is content with itself from sunrise until sunset from the mere sense of living, from the sheer sweet strength and health of the body that is fleet as the roe and tireless as the swallow—was gone forever; and in its stead were the unrest, the bitterness, the pangs, the ecstasies, of human affections.

CHAPTER XV.

HE was young and by nature strong, and his constitution conquered the insidious poison that had entered his blood from the vaporous marshes in the August heats. The unbroken silence, the cold water, the salutary herbs, all served to contribute to his victory over the fever-fiend of Maremma, and little by little he grew sensible of other things than those deadly chills, those waves of lava-heat, which turn by turn had filled his entire consciousness so long. Then he saw that a woman all alone had done this great service for him, and hidden him from his pursuers, and kept vigil by him through many weary days and nights.

The days passed. Health very slowly returned to him. He was but five-and-twenty years old, and the clinging to life was strong in him. Little by little, as time wore on, the light came back into his great brown eyes; the blood coursed smoothly beneath the delicate olive of his skin; the traces of fatigue and privation effaced themselves; a sense of safety and of tranquillity came on him. In the strange twilight of this home made with the dead the world seemed very far away. Sometimes it seemed to him as if he were himself dead, and buried there, and dreaming in his tomb. Only she was here too, this girl who waited on him as serenely as a boy, who had neither bashfulness nor boldness, who was without fear as she was without knowledge.

"How can I thank you? What can I say to you?" he muttered, as he became awake to the large debt he owed a stranger.

"I would have done the same for a stag or a boar that had been hunted and hurt," she answered him, a little roughly; for she was unused to talk of what she felt, and she was ashamed to be told she had done well.

He was too weak and too drowsy to say more.

A great catastrophe had shaken all his previous life to pieces and plunged it into utter darkness. It seemed to him as if he had awakened in some other planet than the familiar earth.

But he was too feeble to reflect long or to ask more. She made him think of those immortals of whom he had read in Greek and Latin and in marbles,—they who moved through earth compassionate, yet aloof from love. As she stood before him in the gloom, clothed in her tunic of white wool, and with the birds of night about her, he thought of Persephone, of Nausicaa, of the nymphs looking on whom a man grew mad,—of all old-world tales of beings who were on earth, not of it.

Yet it was humble cares she had for him. She made his fire, she made his bread, she made his soup; she wove linen for him; she sought far and wide for roots and berries and mushrooms such as he could eat. Sometimes she went down to the sea and netted fish for him; at night, by the solitary lamp, she spun and sewed diligently to replace the garments of his prison that he wore.

She did the simplest and the humblest things for him, but she did them as of yore they were done in Tempe, in Ilion, in Thessaly, in days when the Sun-god herded and ploughed for Admetus.

And all the while never once did it seem to cross her thoughts that she was a girl and he was a man.

He was weary, worn, full of care and fear; his senses were all absorbed in the one incessant carking anxiety lest his refuge should be found out, and his body, with a dead soul in it, killed by despair, dragged back to the hell of the galleys. As his ear was always strained for the least sound that should tell of his pursuers, so his whole nature and existence seemed to him bound up in that one terror of pursuit,— the terror of the deer as he lies in the fern-brake, of the she-wolf as she hides with her cubs.

All other human instincts were momentarily suspended in him; all his being was absorbed into this one intense, overwhelming dread of his hunters and his doom.

"If I but once get free," he thought, "never, so help me God, will I hunt to death any poor forest thing again!"

But how was he to get free? This was not freedom, this hiding amidst tombs and darkness. It was a shelter, and as sure a one as earth could offer him, but it was a prison too. Often he thought of the sea, but the sea was guarded yet more closely than the mountains. He had passed the whole of one ghastly day floating on it, with the sun beating on his face and head, and an agony of thirst and an agony of exhaustion making the blue water terrible as Procrustes' bed.[1] He dared not trust himself to it again.

Sunstroke, the jaws of a shark, the paralysis of cramp, death by thirst,—any one of these might be his fate if he sought the sea. He would not dare to land anywhere; he would have to swim on and on and on: escape that way was hopeless.

These two passions—the passion of dread, and the passion of desire to escape—were too strong in him to let any other emotion move him. He dwelt on in this Etruscan solitude with this beautiful handmaiden beside him, and he only thought of her with vague doubt.

"Is it true that she will not betray me?" he wondered. "If they give her gold, will she not lead them hither?"

As he recovered he grew more and more suspicious of her. Yet, had he known it, she watched for him as the stork watches sleepless on tower or tree-top by its wounded mate.

What she feared most was Zirlo. He had sold her secret, and he would, if he could, sell this fugitive: of that she was sure. Every hour her eyes searched the thickets and the hollows for the form of the faithless little goatherd; but she never saw him. He had been too terrified to venture near the tombs.

From Zirlo she was safe. But it was now autumn: shepherds, hunters, travellers, came at times across the moors. Any moment the white cone of the wood smoke might be seen by some passer-by; any moment some one might ask her what she did there under the thick marucca scrub.

She was forever alarmed and on the watch, like the wild partridges that sleep in their circle, back to back, ready for instantaneous flight at any second.

The very shadows cast across the plains by moving clouds made her heart throb more quickly. When the long dark line of a string of animals or wagons crawled across the horizon, small in the distance as a line of ants, she held her breath in terror lest it should draw near. The long horns of her old familiar friends the buffaloes seemed to her fancy like the weapons of the carabineers, and when a shot cracked

---

[1] In Greek mythology Procrustes was a bandit who had an iron bed. He invited every passerby to lie on it. He either stretched his guests to fit the bed or chopped off their legs or heads if they were too long.

in a far-off swamp full of water-fowl, her pity and her fear were no longer only for the winged dwellers of Maremma.

It was near the season of the year which she had dreaded for herself. She dreaded it a thousand times more keenly now.

Why was it not the windless, vaporous, silent summer, when all the land was empty, and the great heat lay on it like a pall, covering all the motionless mute figures of the drowsy, sweating cattle and colts dropped down beside some reedy drinking-place,—the only multitudes that peopled the great plains of that Etruria which now was dumb as they?

"If it were but the summer!" she thought. If it were but the summer there would be no cause to fear, no need to scan the sky-line and gaze apprehensive through the leaves.

It was once more the month of October, and the time had again come when the Maremma awoke to motion and noise of men. Already the snow upon the Apennines' crests looked like battlements of ivory round about the citadel of God; already axes were ringing, and tree trunks were falling, on the wooded hill-sides, shots were cracking over the still lagoons, and birds began to fly with shrill screams from bush and brake. In the distant plains the plough-oxen were moving, white and slow, in long and level lines over the rich, moist red earth; amidst the herds of buffalo the rude *buttero*[1] was riding to capture the young bull calves of the year. Countless flocks of sheep and goats came down from the far mountains and chestnut forests of the north, and wended their way across the grass-lands, the shepherd, and his women and children and dogs, dragging their tired limbs in their wake through the pale lilac of the blossoming meadow-mint. On the sea-shore the torpid villages were stirring under the autumnal winds as moles bestir themselves from slumber at the sounds of spring-time; tartanes were loading in the weedy, slimy ports, little lateen craft were home-coming or fitting-out, and striped sails were shaking merrily in the rough *libeccio*.

The days passed, and the weeks grew into months, and he became able to leave his bed of leaves, and help himself and pull himself, leaning against the wall of the tombs, over the floor of rock. He did not dare to see the light of day; even from his deliverer he was inclined

---

[1] Horse-riding shepherd, common in Maremma and in Tuscany.

to hide himself as much as it was possible to do; he was shy and suspicious, like a long-hunted animal that fears even the hand that feeds
it, and cannot get over the fear that its friend's hand hides a knife. His
brain was weakened like his body by long fasting and suffering; when
he could think calmly he was ashamed of his own fears.

Meanwhile, she was sorely troubled by the simple question of
his presence there, more troubled than she would even acknowledge
to herself. Not because he was a man, and young and hunted down;
not because she would be taken and punished by the law for harbor-
ing him if the law found him; not for any of these reasons, but because she could not tell how she could maintain him nor how long
she could keep his being there unknown. She herself wanted so little;
a few berries, a little grain, a little fruit, and, like the birds, she was
satisfied: when she had an egg and a cup of milk she had a banquet.
But how to keep this stranger, now exhausted by the most enfeebling
of all maladies, and who, each day recovering more, would need more
nourishment,—this was a terrible problem. Yet it never occurred to
her to leave him, as she could so easily have done, and go up to the
hill-villages, where her spinning and her rush-plaiting would have kept
her very well throughout the winter-time, when all busy hands are
welcome. She never thought once of deserting him. All at once a duty
seemed to her to have sprung out of the earth for her as the orchid
sprang out of the rank grass of the moors, to glow on the dulness of
her solitary life as the *nupha lutea*[1] gleamed, a cup of virgin gold, upon
the stagnant pools.

She knew what he wanted, and would want more and more,—
good red wine and animal flesh, to give him back the strength of which
the insidious marsh fever had robbed him, emptying his veins of their
blood and health and pouring into them instead its own poison. The
nausea of the ghastly malady remained with him after the fever had
ceased to consume him as though fire were turning his bones to ashes,
as the flame of the woodsmen scorches up the strong green wood of
cork-oak and ilex into black sticks and shreds of charcoal. Nothing
tasted to him welcome or good: it was the sickness of his own palate,
that would have found disgust in nectar, and wormwood in the honey
of the moorland thyme-fed bee.

---

[1] Yellow waterlily.

But she did not know that this was but the inevitable result of the blood-poisoning he had suffered; she thought it was because she had only water for him to drink, only such poor simple food to give to him; and she was distressed, beyond any power of her own to express the infinite sorrow she felt, at her own poverty, her own incapacity to help him better. All this time she never asked him one question as to himself.

Instinctive in her, as his courage is in the boar, and his gladness in the nightingale, was the sense of the sanctity of a fugitive and a guest, and of the shame that would lie in taking advantage of power to force confidence. She longed very greatly to know his history, to learn what woman had brought him to such a pass, but no word of inquiry or hint of one ever passed her lips. He had said that he was guiltless, and she had said that she believed him: this was enough.

She waited for him of his own free will to tell her more. He did not do so: apathy, and the selfishness of extreme feebleness and misery, kept him mute, and indifferent, and absorbed in his own past.

An extreme lassitude and impatience came over him turn by turn; his long malady and his terrible privations had unnerved and paralyzed him. Great tears would gather in his eyes and roll down his cheeks. He was heart-sick and bruised, body and soul; and there was no opiate in her pharmacy of simples that could give him rest from his own thoughts. Terror was always with him; and he never escaped from it even in his disturbed and heavy sleep.

As he recovered his strength, this life became irksome and almost unendurable; these darksome chambers of the dead seemed almost as abhorrent to him as the prison-cell of Gorgona. There was no change from one morn to another; only when the sun had set did he dare to come to the door of the tomb, and breathe the air, and cast a hurried glance, the glance of the hunted creature, over the silent and lonesome plains. All that made this silence musical, this loneliness lovely, to her, he did not see. When he saw the nocturnal plover winging his slow flight over the marsh, he only envied its power of motion; when he heard the great boar pushing its heavy body through the brakes of bay, he only fancied it was the tramp of some pursuing force.

The terror of that life was on him: he had been condemned to thirty years of the chain and the cell. If he were taken, the sentence would not be lessened; all his manhood would go away in agony, as the captive lion's does. When he should be set free, he would be old, gray-headed, miserable beyond compare; a childless and friendless outcast, to whom the unfamiliar world would be full of unknown faces, strange voices, alien ways, who would feel in his hideous loneliness that the galleys had been home.

"Take me back!" said the man who was let out of prison when he was seventy years old: to him the trodden bricks, the bare stone walls, the warder's round, the very chains and bars, were all he had of home.

With a passion that was almost madness, Este longed to escape from the possibility of capture, as strength returned into his limbs and blood and brought with it all the natural longings and revolt of manhood. He had his dagger close within his bosom: thus, if no other way, he would be free. Musa was right. But death was terrible to him, even while less terrible than the galleys.

To the sensuous and glad temperament of the Italian, death must ever seem horrible and cruel,—a blank darkness that closes in and ends all things. The love of death, morbid and gloomy, which comes upon the Northern is the choice of a man who knows not how to live; who knows not the delight of love and light; who has dwelt in mist and in cold, and never has seen the red rose of a woman's mouth, or of a Southern dawn, or of a pomegranate-flower glowing in the sun.

It is only to those who have never lived that death ever can seem beautiful.

To Este, who had been happy when his mistress kissed him, when his boat floated over the fields of reeds, when the moon came up over the meadows and the waters, and the throb of a lute beat on the soft air like the sigh of Aphrodite herself,—to Este, the tomb and the galleys were alike a yawning void, in which he would sink and perish. The dread of them—a natural dread like that of the Greeks of old—weighed on him and made his sight blind, his ears deaf, his soul insensible.

Scarcely cared he whether it were a youth or a maiden who waited on him with those tall slender limbs, those short curling locks, those grand pitiful eyes.

To get out, to get away, to flee hard and fast over plain and sea, and put all the width of the earth between him and his prison,—that was his one thirst, his one dream, his one craze.

He thought only of escape. Meanwhile she thought only of him. She was like the maidens of old to whom a god has descended.

For herself she had had no fear; but now fear filled all her days with timidity alien to her temper that made every rustle of a fox amidst the withered canes, every call of a heron across the marshes, terrible.

"What would you do if they took me?" he asked her once.

"They should not take us alive," she said; and he did not notice how she had identified his fate with her own.

That day she cleaned and burnished and gave a sharper edge to his dagger and to the long slender stiletto that she always wore inside her girdle.

"It is all we have," she said, sorrowfully, thinking of the rifles of the hunter and the carbines of the guards.

Este shuddered.

He recalled the ghastly struggle of unarmed men with full-armed foes, the horrors of that night of insurrection when blood had run like water, and the flash of musketry had blazed through the darkness, and alone he and Saturnino had dropped into the sea, stunned by the blow that water can give a falling man, and long pursued by the roar of the guns of the fort booming dully through the night.

She did not know what such scenes were, but he knew, and he sickened at the memory of them; his nature had made him for languor, rest, and love, not combat; and he knew that when men wish to die they never can.

One day a thought struck her that if she could sell her collection of herbs she could get money, and so get food for him. Joconda never would sell herbs: she gave all away. She had said that God's afflicted were not there for her to make pence out of, and thus to Musa it had always seemed impossible to turn her simples into coin. But now she thought it would be honest dealing,—no shame in it, and no robbery. She was glad she had gathered and dried so many plants in the hot autumn weather.

It was a grand day outside, such days as deck October weather with a glory of color and of luminance that make all other months of the year seem pale. It was such a day as made her always seek the open air from dawn to dark, beside the sea, or in the brakes and thickets where the wild boar hid.

She determined that she would go to Telamone and try and sell all she had, and bring him back some wine and better food. She was alarmed to see that he remained so weak. It seemed to her so unnatural that a man should lie all day long listless and dumb with despair, and no more able to move than the pine-tree that the foresters slash down with their hatchets.

She was alarmed, too, because food there was none, save a little of the oaten bread which she could eat but he could not. Unless she could buy flour she could get nothing better. Of fish he was weary, and to go out and fish took her as long as it would take to go to the little sea-town. She had a large stock of herbs of all kinds, sweet and bitter,—some medicinal, some for kitchen uses. Joconda had taught her all their various properties, and in the autumn of the previous year she had gathered a great store, and dried them and kept them carefully. They were the only things she had to sell,—they, and some score of baskets and mats that she had not given to Zeffirino.

She went, and told him for whom she slaved that she must be absent some hours. She was going to Telamone.

He was lying on one of the stone couches, in that prostration and silence which had been habitual with him since he had crept off his bed of fever.

He lifted his languid lids, and looked at her with suspicion.

"Why should you go?" he said, angrily.

"There is nothing to eat in the place," she answered him, gently. "You want food and you want wine, and I am going to get them both. I will be quick."

"How long will you be?"

"I must be several hours. We are on the moors here: the nearest place is far."

"They may take me while you are gone."

"There is no fear of that. I will cover the entrance so that a polecat would not find its way down."

"That may not prevent———How do you go?"

"I will walk over to Telamone. It will be nearer so. I had thought of the boat, but it will be nearer across the land."

He looked at her, and let her go in silence.

He was ashamed and afraid to tell her that he doubted her. Even his dazed mind could see that there was no treachery in those clear fearless eyes. Yet all the time she was absent he would doubt her,— strain his ear at every sound, and whet his dagger, the only weapon he had.

She put her herbs in a great frail basket, took the few articles she had made with the reeds and the canes, swung them across her back, and stepped out for the shore.

It was a grand autumnal morning, steeped in the color and the moisture of late autumn.

The grass was embrowned with the red-brown feathers of the graceful *sanguinella*[1] and the fairy-like sprays of the *tremolino*,[2] and every moss-grown nook was painted delicately with the exquisite color of the tender cyclamen-flowers hanging over the moist autumnal earth, leafless, and looking like rose-tinted shells. The golden stars of the dandelions were gleaming everywhere, and above the blossoms of the ivy swarms of wild bees were humming in ecstasy; but in the water-places the reeds and canes were growing ragged and broken, the nuphar and the nymphæa leaves were getting yellow and torn, and here and there a leaf fluttered from the silver-poplar trees.

To walk against the wind, to feel the wet grass under her feet, to smell the fresh scent of the sods as a troop of young horses galloped past her, scattering the earth with their unshod hoofs in merry scampers, unconscious of the cruel fate—of the whip, and the curb, and the shafts, and the brutal mastery—that waited for them in the future: all these sights and sounds of nature were such delights that the pressure of anxiety which weighed upon her for the sake of the man she protected was lifted off her as she went; and her young body, and the heart that beat in it, both felt light as thistledown.

She saluted all her friends and familiars. She saw the first flight of herons of the year sailing towards the Ciminian range; she saw a goose alight, jaded after long journeying, and settle, as if with a sigh of content, in a fringe of the red reeds; she espied some grasshopper warblers in the sedges, and she saw a water-rail, arrived before his female, look around him, calling, and wearing his little mind out with seeking her high and low upon the waters of his favored pool, she all the while most likely flying steadily and faithfully towards him, but afar off where he could not see her, and where, perhaps, a shot would lay her low and widow his tender constancy.

All these, and many another welcome and well-known comrade, she saw as she struck across the moors and thickets, and the black

---

[1] *Panicum ciliare* [Ouida's note].

[2] *Briza maxima* [Ouida's note]. Large quaking grass, an annual grass with rattle-like seed heads that dangle from delicate stems.

heads of the buffaloes pushed themselves up above the red-berried bryony, and the wild swine began to sniff for the first acorns of the scarlet-oak, and the beautiful buck fled across the sunlight, made timid in his innocence because man has so much of the devil and spares nothing.

She was so glad to see them all again.

It seemed to her ages since she had been free to run and loiter at choice amidst these green solitudes. But she could only give them a glance and a smile; she was bound, or she thought so, to be no longer away from the tombs than she could help. Her voluntary loyalty to the man she sheltered was like a chain upon her foot that was fleet as the roebuck's and had been as free.

She walked on rapidly, and sorely tempted to turn aside into many a leafy defile she knew of, where the hill-hare made its form, to pause beside many a sedge-rimmed shallow where the sultan-hen was splashing. But she resisted the longing to revisit all those beloved haunts that she shared with the winged and the four-footed peoples. She held on straight across the narrow dangerous paths that intersected the marshes, and the cattle-tracks that led through the mazes of underwood, and after some hours of incessant motion she saw the cattle on its headland that marked Telamone. Another hour brought her to its desolate beach, where the ruins of many a Roman villa divide the sand with the stunted aloes and the glazier's weed.

It is a dreary, dirty, miserable place, though in other ages it was decked with the snowy marbles of patrician palaces, and bore, on its then deep waters, the gilded pleasure-galleys of the great Romans.

Here she tried in vain to sell what she had brought: the few people were too poor to be willing to spend a bronze coin, even on field medicines which they knew were good. They recognized her in Telamone, and asked her where she had been all this while. She pointed vaguely eastward and told them she had found work to do over yonder, and she only now wished to sell her herbs because she wanted a little money to spend at the autumnal fairs. This they thought so natural that the Telamone women were willing to help her. They told her of a pharmacy in Orbitello where her simples would be willingly bought, and one of the old men, called Febo, who had his felucca lying off the dirty, shallow port, where once Marius landed with his thousand men, said to her,—

"You used to be a good one on a deck; I want to go to the Orbitel-lano: if you take the tiller, I will carry you there."

"That is kind of you," she said, gratefully.

"Nay, nay, you will give me something when you have sold your stuff," said he. "The wind will serve us: we shall fly. You know the water hereabouts: you will not run us aground?"

"Not I," she answered, as she sprang on deck.

The little felucca did fly: these butterfly-like boats are the lightest and the swiftest in the world. A strong wind was blowing from the northeast and made the little sail swell out as if it were a soap-bubble being blown by the children of Glaucus in play.

"I shall be so late home," she thought, with a pang, as the blue wa-ter raced past the sides of the boat, and the sandy shore, and the red tufa hills, and the white vapors rising from the morass, and the stately line of the receding mountains, all drifted by her as they went. Her eyes filled as she saw the old stone house where she had dwelt with Joconda standing against the crumbling quay of Santa Tarsilla, whose stones were fewer every year as the rains soaked them, and the weeds dragged them down, and the stormy water sapped their base.

"Andrea is always alive?" she asked of the old man with her.

He chuckled, "Ay, ay, always. We old blasted sea-pines are hard to kill; all the sap has been run out of us, but we hold fast on the sand. I am eighty years old, and Andreino he must be going on for a hun-dred, but we are alive, we can suck our pipe-stems still; and there were two youngsters from the Lucchese just come down here who died last week like flies, just of our air and our smoking soil. You die early, or never, here."

She did not answer him. The words sent a chill through her blood: she thought of the man at home. He was young and of the blood of the North; the fever had eaten all the life out of him, and it was still very possible that he never would rally entirely, but would sink away out of apathy into death, as slowly and as surely as the sea was sinking away from the shore and leaving disease and desolation where once the coral had grown and the dianthus spread its pale pink plumes.

The old sailor mumbled and chattered on of the seaboard as he had remembered it, and the time when he had known the great works begun in 1829 for the drying up of the Castiglione lagoon (once so fair and harmless a lake that we know from Cicero rich men coveted an island on it), and chuckled to himself over his prediction that the *bon-*

ificamento[1] that was still going on would be only so much squandering of money and labor, and that the salt and fresh water would always manage to meet, all engineers notwithstanding, and that they would repent ever having meddled with the ways of God and the course of the Ombrone, and that he for his part should be glad to see the houses of the Pescaja sink down into the swamp, for he liked not such meddling with the shape of the earth and the run of the rivers; and he expected heaven's vengeance yet.

Musa listened inattentively, though his views were her own, for she too hated "the meddling" with the streams and the waves, the dikes and the locks that shut out the sea, the drainage that killed the little fish and the reeds and the brilliant marsh flora, and the men who would fain make a dry place, and build a factory, or a foundry, where the bulrushes now nodded to their own reflection in the water and the birds from the North found food and shelter.

Almost as quickly as a storm-gull could have flown there, the felucca sailed over the ten odd miles that part Telamone from Monte Argentaro, and, drawing so little water, ran easily in over the sandy bottom and through the submerged fields of algæ into the *stagno*,[2] and lay to underneath the huge block of the Pelasgic sea-wall.

Then ruin seemed to menace her, for she was stopped on landing by the customs-takers, and toll and fee were imperiously demanded for her bundles of herbs and her frail baskets, and she had not a single coin upon her! She had not one in the world, indeed, for Zeffirino had always paid her by barter for whatever he sold for her, and had brought her food or oil or flax or wool, and never any money. As a great favor and goodness, the guards at last, after debating and scolding half an hour, agreed to take two of her baskets in lieu of the number of centimes that she ought to have paid to the State.

"Eh, Musoncella," said old Febo, tugging her sleeve as they landed, and pointing to a proclamation pasted on the water-walls, "can you read that? I cannot. They say there is money to be made. You who are always roaming, you may come across that man they want."

She looked where he pointed, and went up to the big printed letters and spelled them out slowly, not being skilful in reading.

---

[1] Drainage.
[2] Pond.

Her heart beat fast; her eyes seemed to grow for the moment blind.

The State offered a large reward in money to any one who should aid in the discovery and apprehension of the Count Luitbrand d'Este, escaped from the prisons of Gorgona fifteen months before.

The proclamation had been pasted up, and torn down, or defaced, and put up again, some hundred times since the summer night when the galley-slaves had dropped off the rocks into the deep water and swum for their lives, with the musket-balls raining around them and hissing in the sea.

The people of the Orbitellano had more sympathy with the fugitives than with the authorities, and thought that the young man was hardly dealt with: "Poor lad! It was only a love-murder," they said, pityingly. "After all, if you are jealous and stab your *dama*,[1] you do what is but natural. Does not the stork kill the faithless mate? So they say."

She read it; but she had self-control enough to let no emotion betray her: side by side with strong passions in her went strong self-command and power of silence.

"I should think," she said, indifferently, turning to Febo, "that they might be pretty sure that the marshes have killed this poor youth. What will you do, Febo, if they should take to offering rewards for whoever will tell of contraband goods run ashore to Maremma?"

She smiled slowly as she said it, and the old man winced.

"Hold your tongue," he said, angrily, "and with these *doganiere*[2]— burn them!—so near! Are you mad? Come, let us go and find your pharmacy."

She was free to go into the town, which to her seemed a large bewildering place, enclosed as it was between its stone fortifications and its sea-walls. She had never been there before, and she had the true mountain and moorland instincts of distrust and hatred for all places where men dwelt in numbers, cooped up in stone or brick compartments, and shut out by tiles and timber from the sight of the sky.

The men began to stare at her and make admiring jests; she pulled farther over her head the woollen hood which Joconda had always enjoined on her to cover herself with if she went amidst a crowd; and,

---

[1] Dame (lover).
[2] Customs officers.

laden with her goods, she set to work to find out the pharmacy, and did find it in time, though with trouble.

It was a little, dark, vaulted place, made out of no one knew what old ruin of Roman work.

She knocked and went in boldly, and found an old chemist, who was the leech of half the Orbitellano, and far more trusted by the people than the youth with many greater accredited qualifications who was set by the municipal rule to cure their ills as parish doctor and surgeon.

The chemist was a wise and kindly person, curing chiefly by those herbs which modern medicine neglects, to ransack nature for minerals and poisons. He was liberal, and could afford to be so, for he had a large following in the maritime population, and when the haul was large after the night's fishing those men were open-handed. He was pleased to see so rare and large a store of the most useful plants, and said so honestly, and questioned her where she found them, and asked her how much she wanted for them.

"I want quinine, not money," she answered him; "but if you can give me money too, I shall be glad; I have none, and I want to get wine as well."

"You have some one sick? A father? A brother?"

"I have some one who has been sick," she answered, curtly. "But he is only weak now. But it is such weakness!—it is like death."

"He has had the fever?"

"Yes. Quinine is what he should have, is it not? You would know."

"Quinine and pure wine. I will give you both for your herbs; and as for those baskets, I dare say my wife will take them."

He called his wife, and she haggled more than he liked over the baskets, but at last consented to buy the lot. Frail baskets are much in favor here, and are used by women marketing, by masons and carpenters for their tools, by anybody who has to carry anything and can carry it with most ease thus.

The wife gave her a handful of bronze pence for the lot, and knew she could sell them again for as many silver ones. The chemist put up quinine in two large phials, and three flasks of pure Campagna wine.

"That is strong and good red Lacrima," he said to her. "That will pour life into your sick man as the sunbeams pour color into the green fruit. As for the quinine—you can read?—then give it him as I have written on the phials, and if that do not cure him, nothing will, but our Maremma will take him to herself as she takes so many. Can you carry those flasks? See, sling them together so; and when you have other simples to sell, bring them to me. They are God's own medicines."

She thanked him and went out: at the door he slipped a little money in her hand.

"You were not paid enough for your baskets, my dear; and get your sick man some meat with that."

"I will bring you the rarest plants in all Maremma," she said, with a tremor in her voice, "and you shall pay me nothing at all for them. You are good."

Ashamed of her emotion, she ran away up the little dark twisting street.

At the end of it, the old owner of the felucca was waiting.

"You will give me something now," he said: "you have done well."

"I will pay you when we are back at Telamone," she said, knowing her people.

"Oh, no, indeed," said the old fellow, angrily: "that will not do at all. In the first place I am not going back. My son lives here, and we go harpooning to-night. You must pay me now."

"I have no right to pay you. You were coming, and you said I might steer. And how shall I get back without the felucca? You will let me have the felucca at least? I can manage her all alone quite well."

"Eh, eh, Musoncella!" grinned the old man, "you will not pay for the voyage here, and you think I shall trust you with my boat? I go out in her to-night myself; that is why I came. Pay me now, or I will make it worse for you; and if I call a guard, then I shall know where you really live, for it is my belief———"

"What will content you?" she said, in desperation, feeling her cheeks grow cold with fear.

"Pay him nothing," said a voice behind her, and, turning, she saw the face of Daniello Villamagna, the Sicilian skipper. "Pay him nothing, and let him stay here with his cockle-shell. The 'Ausiliatrice' will land you where you will."

"Oh, I was only joking," said the old sailor, for he knew the skipper of the "Ausiliatrice," and knew his tongue was hot and his knife not very slow to back up what his tongue spoke, and he had no wish to come in collision with this son of the lava of Etna.

Musa looked from one to the other doubtfully. She was sorry to see Daniello Villamagna there.

"You will let me have your boat," she said, in a low tone, imploringly, to the man of Telamone. "Pray let me have it. It will be quite safe with me, and I will give you silver for its use."

"Oh, no; that I cannot anyhow," said the man; "I go out to-night; I have promised my son."

"My brig is off the *stagno;* she cannot come in, there is no draught for her. But if you will come out to her she shall land you where you choose," said the Sicilian.

"I can hire a boat on the *stagno*," said Musa, and she turned away from them both and began to make her way back to the port, pausing at a butcher's stall to buy some sound fresh meat, as the chemist had bidden her do.

The Sicilian sailor followed her; he looked amidst the yellow faces and the yellow sands of Orbitello like a native of some other planet; his warm brown cheeks, his brilliant eyes, his elasticity of step, his rapid movements, were all the signs of a perfect health and a dauntless manhood; a scarlet cap upon his black curls, and a scarlet kerchief at his shapely throat, caught the sunshine as he went. His glance was full of triumph and gladness.

"Eh, Musoncella!" he murmured. "You see I kept my word. I am back in four months. I was coming to you."

She felt the great dread tighten at her heart.

"How should you come to me?" she said, with assumed indifference. "You cannot tell where to find me."

"I should soon find you; there are not two like you on these shores. Have you ever thought of what I said to you?"

"No. Why should I think of it?"

"I have thought of nothing else night and day. I love you!———"

"That is nonsense! I can be nothing to you. Why will you walk through the streets with me? I dislike it."

"You never remembered me, never once?"

"Why should I?"

"Ah, Musoncella! The old man called you aright."

She smiled superbly.

"They have always called me that."

"But if you would listen," he pursued, the passionate blood flushing his clear brown skin, "I am no poor, sickly, dawdling Maremmano, and my brig—she is as good a barque as the high seas hold. And Sicily is beautiful, and at home we laugh and sing and dance all day; and my people are merry and good, and we are well enough off to deny ourselves nothing in reason. And in Sicily the men are strong, and the maidens gay. You would be happy there. I love you! I have seen nothing but your face; it was always between me and the great tumbling Biscay breakers, and the thick white fogs of that Scottish coast, where once nearly we foundered and went to pieces, for the fog there is like a wall, and the very light-ship is hidden in it——ah, you do not listen; you do not care. Yet, heaven is my witness, if you will, I will prove my love in every honest way before men and the saints, and I will take you back with me to Sicily and be more proud than if my hold were filled with gold and silver. And if you doubt what I say and what I am, you can ask the syndic of this very town, for he has known me and my people many years, since my father traded here——"

Musa only tried to move faster before him.

"You are mad, I think," she said, angrily. She thought he was. A man to talk thus who had only seen her once before for five minutes, on a summer morning, upon the sands!

In vain he urged, in vain he pleaded: he could make no impression upon her as he walked beside her, pouring out his full heart in words as the nightingale pours his in song. He was vehemently in earnest; he cared nothing for who she might be, or whence she came: he wanted her, this strong and fearless and beautiful creature! What a mother she would be for sea-born children cradled by the winds and waves!

He might as well have spoken to a figure of bronze for aught that she was moved by it. She scarcely heard him; she was thinking every moment of the fugitive hidden in the tombs of the rocks: was he safe? did he want for anything in her absence? might faintness overcome him, and, without succor, pass into the endless swoon of death? if he were well, was he wondering why she was so long? was he doubting her? would the old man of Telamone talk of her and cause her refuge to be found? All these anxieties were torturing her: what cared she for a foolish, fire-tongued Sicilian who doubtless said all those fine phrases to somebody in every port at which the "Ausiliatrice" touched?

Soon they had threaded the dirty streets and come out upon the harbor. It was a busy day; fishermen by the hundred sat on the sea-walls, or swarmed on the narrow tongues of land that join Argentaro with the mainland; the harpooning of the night was to be on a large scale, shoals of fish had been seen, and, less welcome, several large sharks. The men were telling long and grim shark-stories one to another; the fishing fleet was all ready and anchored, but the fishing had to wait for the dark of the moonless night.

One part of the sea-wall had been recently washed down during a tempest: those huge blocks of Pelasgic or Tyrrhene architecture have seen the storms of years when Alexander was yet unborn and Christ and Cæsar names unknown. Three thousand years and more the sea has raged at them in its furies of autumn and of winter, but it has only been able to displace, never been able to destroy them.

At these vast blocks, which tax the strength of yoked oxen, a gang of galley-slaves was working, the overseer near them with his whip, as though they were wild beasts of an arena and he their tamer. One of them, a Hercules in build, and burnt black with the sun on all his naked limbs and throat, looked up and saw her and knew her.

It was Saturnino. He had not yet been moved from Orbitello since his capture there.

She looked at the great black figure of the man with a pity that quenched the scorn she had always felt for the baseness of his theft. She knew his story,—the great Saturnino, as the country-side still called him! And he was working there as elephants do in timber-gangs, old before his time, calcined with sun and powder, bent, but massive still, with angry, sullen, bloodshot eyes gleaming like a lion's out from his black bent brows.

She pitied him, and that pity came back like dew on her own heart. Almost she loved this cruel, savage, brute-like creature, stained with so much blood, burdened with so many crimes. Had he not sent her Este?

That memory made her eyes soft as they dwelt on him: he saw their softness, and deep down in his fierce, ravenous, sullen heart he was glad.

"Does she know I robbed her tomb?" he thought: galley-slaves hear nothing.

On an instinct of pity she paused beside him a moment.

He had taken the gold of the tomb, and he was for that accursed, and he had betrayed and wronged her shelter of him, and when she had heard of his capture she had been ferocious in her triumph. Yet now that she saw him she was sorry,—sorry as she felt for the great boar when she saw him plunge through the rushes bleeding and torn, with the hounds at his flanks and the steam of his panting lungs coming like smoke from his red tongue. She longed to say a syllable to tell him that his companion in flight was safe with her, but she dared not, lest others should overhear.

She nevertheless paused by him one moment and slipped one of the silver coins the chemist had given her into his hand.

"Yes; I know," she murmured, answering the guilty interrogation of his eyes. "You robbed the dead. That was worse than robbing me. But I think they would forgive—now."

Something in the tone of her voice brought to him the echo of a voice that he had loved,—the voice of Serapia.

He put her coin between his teeth in silence. Then, as he looked up and saw her standing in the full daylight, with bare head and throat, something in her aspect and her features stirred memory in his brain.

He seemed to see his own face in the innocence of its adolescence as it had looked back at him mirrored in some hill-side pool in that season of his boyhood when no blood was on his hands, no price was on his head.

A thrill of remembrance, a throb of wonder, stirred the sluggish apathy into which his ferocious passions had sunk under the drugs of monotony, inactivity, and despair.

He had become half madman, half brute, the dullest, most savage, most hopeless unit of all that hopeless world to which he now belonged. But for that one moment humanity stirred in him,—he was a man once more.

He remembered the little child that he had left under the stone-pines on the crags above the Fiora torrents.

He sprang forward; he cried out: the whip of the overseer lashed him back into the ranks, the guards hustled him with oaths into silence.

Musa passed on, going she knew not where.

Daniello Villamagna looked hard at her.

"You did not turn your face from that hound," he said, jealously.

"He is a hound chained, and so to be pitied," she answered him.

"He was the robber of Santa Fiora."

"I know."

Her face was sad and anxious: she was thinking of him who had been sent to her by Saturnino.

Out in the deeper water beyond the Argentaro rocks the Sicilian brig was at anchor,—a trim vessel still, though she had been buffeted about in the mists and storms off the Isle of Arran. Daniello pointed to her where she lay rocking gently on the wondrous blue of the Archipelago.

"If you will come out to her," he said, softly, and more timidly than he had spoken before, "I swear on the good faith of a sailor to put you ashore where you will, and to speak no word whilst you are on my deck of what you do not choose to hear."

"I can hire a boat," said Musa, and she turned and tried to bargain with a ragged lad who had an old punt there beneath the wall. But the youth would not be hired or bribed; there was the night-spearing to be seen and shared; no man or boy would leave Orbitello with that prospect of delight in store for the evening as soon as the slender crescent of the young moon should have vanished.

"You will get no boat here," said Daniello. "Not one of them will stir this afternoon. Since you are distrustful of the 'Ausiliatrice,' hear this: yonder is my own boat, with which I pulled from the ship here; there are some of my crew about; you could not row that boat yourself, but I will send the best man I have with you wherever you want to go."

She was silent.

"I will not come with you myself," he added, "since you flout and hate me so. But remember what I have said, and I shall see you and say it again."

She was still silent; she could not bear to owe him a service, but there was something in this generosity of his action which touched her as all his amatory eloquence had had no power to do. She could not endure to use his boat, yet unless she did so she could never reach home that night, and what would Este think of her? What might not happen to him alone, and feeble, and without food?

As she hesitated, the Sicilian shouted to a sailor on the little isthmus of sand,—his own boatswain, a man of years and one to be trusted. The boatswain ran to his call, and Daniello whispered to him. A long slim boat was soon aground against the sand.

"That will take you where you wish to go," he said, and his large black eyes gazed on her with a reproach that dimmed their fire and light.

She looked at him with a certain shame.

"I am thankful to you," she said, simply. "But give me your word first that when I land your sailor shall not follow me."

"Sailors are not spies," said the Sicilian, with a haughty anger. "No; I take no unfair means. But we shall meet again. It is written."

"Farewell," she said to him, and she sprang into the boat and took the tiller-cords.

For herself she would not have done it. For herself she would rather have run all the certain dangers of night upon the moors than have incurred this debt to the man whose frank fair passion seemed to her an intolerable offence. But, left to herself, she knew she could never reach Telamone, much less the sepulchres, that night; already the sun was slanting towards the sea, already the glowing amber of his afternoon beams was falling like molten gold upon the many colored sails of the numerous fishing-craft that lay close in to shore upon the salt-water lagoon, and farther out under the shadow of the twin-peaked rocks.

The boatswain pulled with long and steady stroke against the nor'-wester that was blowing still. It was Ave Maria when she reached Telamone. The boatswain carried out his orders strictly, and when he ran her into the harbor never asked her a word, but turned his boat's head with a cheery "good-night," and sculled himself back again towards the south.

It was Ave Maria, and in another moment would be night. She got through the little town as quickly as she could, holding the precious medicine closer in her bosom, for quinine was coveted there like the very elixir of life. She had eight or nine miles of moor and hill and woodland and marsh before her still; but she was not afraid, once in her own country as she called it. Of the less known lands around Telamone she was less confident. She had her knife slipped, safe and secret, in her garter, and a bold heart in her breast; she walked on without pausing, through the damp warm night, full of vapor, only just rustled by the wind from the north, which, though it was strong and high upon the sea, had little power over the low and close-woven foliage. She met nothing worse, however, than a mounted buffalo-driver, who swore at her because the lantern she had lit to save herself from straying into the swamps had frightened the horse he rode; and all her furred and feathered friends of the season who like to hunt and travel by night, the grand-dukes and the scops, were out, of course, and all the various races of the snipe tribe were busy after mollusks or mice, larvæ or frogs, according to their size and prowess; the moor-fox was stealing through the osiers to where the moor-hen slept, and the first wild ducks of the year flew by against the slender moon. Once a great dark bird sailed over her head so near that she could almost have touched him: it was a booted-eagle going from his summer haunts on Monte Amiato to his Asian or African eyrie on Himalaya or on Atlas.

Save these, she met nothing.

Men do not care to be out on the Maremma lowlands after sunset: every pretty brown tarn reflecting clouds and stars may be a poison-bowl of noxious gases; every will-o'-the-wisp that dances over the hairy sundew and the vernal sandwort may be a torch that leads on to the grave.

She met no creature to do her harm, and knew her country so well that she did not lose her way or miss the unsteady bridge that oftentimes the rough tussocks of grass alone offered as passage-way across some marsh that was like a soaking sponge. It was midnight, she thought, by the skies, when she reached the tombs and knocked aloud at the stone doors, and called, with a tired but happy voice, "Open! it is I!"

CHAPTER XVI.

ALL this day and evening Este had passed in the alternate stupor and agitation of great fear. Against his judgment, against his manliness, he could not conquer the idea that she had gone to give him up to the law. He was very feeble; the simple fare that kept her in health had no power to restore the lost strength to his muscles or vivify his impoverished blood. He had nothing to do the whole day long; the gloom of the sepulchres, from which he dared not stir, oppressed him like a nightmare. His weak pulse beat fast with terror as he said in his soul, "She has gone to tell them. She will never come back. She will only send the soldiers."

When he heard her voice, he could have screamed for gladness. When he saw her enter with the flasks of wine on her shoulders, he laughed for very joy and kissed her feet for shame.

"I have brought the quinine and the good wine," she said to him, joyfully, yet with a tinge of reproachfulness in her voice. "Why did you doubt me? I do not tell lies."

"Forgive me! Hunted creatures doubt their own shadows. You sold the herbs well, then?"

"Ah, yes! so well, and to a kind old man who promised me that these would soon give you back your strength."

"You never told him of me?"

"I did not tell him of you, of course; only that some one had had the marsh-fever and could not get health again. I had to go to Orbitello; that is what has made me so late."

"What can I say to you? How can I repay you?"

"Ah! I want nothing but to see you well. You have suffered so long and so much."

"Yes, I have suffered. But I do not see why you should care," he said, using the same words that she had spoken to Maurice Sanctis.

She said nothing, but poured him out some of the rich red wine, which he drank eagerly.

"It is like drinking sunbeams," he said, with the first smile that had dawned on his wasted features. "Tell me, how could you get to Orbitello?"

"Febo, a fisherman of Telamone, took me there."

"But he will suspect?————"

"Nothing: he is stupid, and, if he did, he knows that I know he smuggles goods from Sardinia: he will hold his tongue about me."

"There are many smugglers on the coast?"

"There are few people, but all the men that there are do smuggle,—from the islands chiefly, to escape the customs dues. Why not? Do you know that when a Tuscan laborer comes back from working in Sardinia they make him pay duty on his Sardinian wooden shoes?"

He was silent: he was pondering whether one of those smugglers would take him across to France. But he had no money to offer as a bribe, and the crime of which he had been accused was one for which any country would surrender him up to undergo his sentence in his own land.

"You are very good to me," he said, with emotion, as he saw her rake together the embers of the fire and begin to prepare his evening meal.

"I do not know that," said Musa, and turned on him her luminous eyes that were like those of Carlo's divine messengers. "I am sorry for you, and you have no one else."

For the first time, the glance of her eyes startled him into perception of her as a young girl.

"Are you not afraid to come and go like this,—alone?"

"I have my knife," she said, curtly; then, tired as she was, she turned away to light wood for a fire, and put the meat she had brought into water, making graceful this homely work by her own simplicity and grace, as women did in days of old, when great Demeter herself thought household cares no shame.

He sat by the blazing wood and cones of pine and watched her,— for the first time sensible of her beauty, for the first time also grateful for all she did for him.

It was she who gathered the wood and the fir-apples; it was she who cut the dry heather to keep for fuel; it was she who fished, who span, who worked in all ways, who brought heavy loads upon her shoulders and shared her refuge with him, disdaining any personal fear or harm. It seemed to him that he ought to rise and go out into the daylight among men at all peril rather than bring risk and toil upon a woman—a girl—thus.

She appeared to divine his thoughts, for she spoke to him across the stone chamber of the Lucumo.

"I do not know that it is safe for you to be in this first room. I heard to-day in Orbitello that there is a reward up for you, and they say soldiers have come anew to the fort at Santa Tarsilla; there never have been any there in my remembrance."

He shivered a little.

"A reward? You saw it?"

"Yes, for you: it describes you. And Febo said to me, 'If you see yon poor soul on your moorlands, there are gold and silver to be made.'"

"And what did you answer him?"

"I told him he knew I was no trapper of birds or beasts. I thought it best to tell you this, because you must hide more carefully; the inner rooms are best. They call you in that printing on the walls Count d'Este. You did not call yourself so?"

"Men call me so," he said, wearily, "or did so until I became a mere number among slaves."

"That is a title, is it not?"

"A title, barren as the honorable names written under the paintings of these tombs! We were a branch of the Este of Ferrara, the great Este,—the mightiest lords there were ever, save the Gonzaga and the Montefeltro. That is of no good now. All we have is a damp, ruined palace in Mantua, a few breadths of water-meadows; beyond Bergamo there is a little city on a rock—men come to it for its arts and architecture—that once was ours. Now we do not own a brick within its walls, and it is only remembered by travellers now and then because its houses are Bramante's and Sansovino's and its altars are Giovanni Bellini's. We are almost as dead, almost as forgotten, as your Etruscans here."

"You know who they were?" she said, under her breath, as she spoke of her lost people. "Tell me of them. When first I entered here, there was a king in golden armor, and with a golden helmet, lying there, just there; and as the light touched him the gold melted, and he fled———"

"They were a great people, and they perished," he answered her: "their clay vases survive, but they are gone, obliterated, passed into nothingness. Now and then men find a wall of huge stones; a gateway hard and black as iron; a sepulchre full of gold and pottery. Then they say, these were Etruscan. But when that is said, it is but a word: we know but little."

"They were greater than the men that live now," she said, with a solemn tenderness.

"Perhaps. Why think you so?"

"Because they were not afraid of their dead; they built them beautiful houses and gave them beautiful things. Now, men are afraid or ashamed, or they have no remembrance. Their dead are huddled away in dust or mud as though they were hateful or sinful. That is what I think so cowardly, so thankless. If they will not bear the sight of death, it were better to let great ships go slowly out, far out to sea, and give the sea their dead."

"Great ships whose freights should be death? Yes; the thought is fine. Would you mantle them with black, like the homeward-coming vessels of Theseus? They should be the sailing ships of old, with 'canvas stately in the wind,' and their masts twined with myrtle Greeklike."

"Tell me more of them," she said, softly, motioning with her hand to the painted shapes upon the walls dimly glimmering into color here and there as the lamp-light touched them.

"There is so little! My own Mantua was once theirs, named from their Mantus, that grim god of the land of shades,—you see him yonder: we Latins called him Pluto. With other names, their deities and ours were all the same."

"But was Christ among them?"

"No, dear: Christ was not born of a woman until this nation had been beaten, captured, absorbed, trodden under the iron heel of Rome. Christianity is a thing of yesterday: it looks beside Etruscan creeds as this year's bulrush beside the holm oak of the hills."

"And where are those earlier gods?"

"Around us still: they are the unknown forces, the unalterable fates, that rule us then as now. What matter whether I called you Luna, or Cupa, or Hera, or Juno, or Musa; you would be yourself always, and always beautiful, as your marsh-lilies are that glow in gold upon the swamp."

For the first time in all her seventeen years of life her face grew warm with a quick blush.

"I am not handsome," she said, quickly. "They call me Musoncella, the ugly face, always on the shore. If you want what is handsome, you should see Giano's Mariannina: she has hair like the scales of the gold and red mullet."

"I do not want Giano's Mariannina!" he said, with a soft intonation that escaped her.

"Well, she would be of no use here," she answered him literally. "She thinks of nothing all day but 'gilding' her hair in the sun and getting bits of coral."

Then she devoted her care to the meat broth she was setting on the wood fire in a bronze rhyton. His heavy eyes watched her as she bent over the ruddy gleam from the crackling heather.

"You must be tired," he said, with sudden perception of his own selfishness. "Go and rest, my dear; pray go. I can wait very well for the broth until morning."

"Oh, no. You shall have it as soon as the fire will stew it. I am not greatly tired. You know I am made of strong stuff, and I rested in the boats."

He did not urge her more.

As she sat by the fire she took some of her oaten bread, and some water, and made her supper of them, sitting beside the burning wood that sent out resinous odors as it burned.

"I ought to tell you why I am accused of this crime and condemned for it," he said, abruptly, after long silence. "You ought to know,—you who do so much for me on trust. You have a right to hear why they hunt me down as a murderer."

"Do not tell it if it hurt you," said Musa, as he paused. She saw that he shrank from telling the tale.

"Yes; you have a right to know. After all, it was ruin to me, but it is not much of a story: a tale-teller with his guitar on a vintage-night would soon make a better one. I loved a woman. She lived in Mantua. So did I, too. For her sake I lost three whole years,—three years of the best of my life. And, yet, what is gain except love, and what better than joy can we have? A pomegranate is ripe but once. And I,—my pomegranate is rotten for evermore! We lived in Mantua. It is a strange, sad place. It was great and gay enough once. Grander pomp than Mantua's there was never known in Italy. Felix Mantua!—and now it is all decaying, mouldering, sinking, fading; it is silent as death; the mists, the waters, the empty palaces, the walls that the marshes are eating little by little every day, the grass and the moss and the wild birds' nests on the roofs, on the temples, on the bridges,—all is desolate in Mantua now. Yet is it beautiful in its loneliness, when the sunrise comes over the seas of reeds, and the towers and the arches are reflected in the pools and streams; and yet again at night, when the moon is high and the lagoons are as sheets of silver, and the shadows come and go over the bulrushes, and Sant' Andrea lifts itself against the stars. Yes: then it is still Mantova la Gloriosa."

His voice dropped; the tears came into his closing eyes, as though he looked on the dead face of a familiar friend.

He felt the homesickness of the exile, of the wanderer who knows not where to lay his head.

The glory was gone from the city.

Its greatness was but as a ghost that glided through its deserted streets calling in vain on dead men to arise.

The rough red sail of the fishing-boat was alone on the waters once crowded with the silken sails of gilded galleys; the toad croaked and the stork made her nest where the lords of Gonzaga had gone forth to meet their brides of Este or of Medici; Virgil, Alboin, great Karl, Otho, Petrarca, Ariosto, had passed by here over this world of waters and become no more than dreams; and the vapors and the dust together had stolen the smile from Giulio's Psyche and the light from Mantegna's arabesques. On the vast walls the grass grew, and in the palaces of princes the winds wandered and the beggars slept. All was still, disarmed, lonely, forgotten, left to a silence like the silence of the endless night of death. Yet it was dear to him, this sad and stately city, waiting for the slow death of an unpitied and lingering decay.

It was dear to him from habit, from birth, from memory, from affinity, as the reeds of its stagnant waters were dear to the sedge-warbler that hung its slender nest on the stem of a rush. A price was set on his head; and never more, he thought, would he see the sunshine in ripples of gold come over the gray lagoons.

With an effort he took up his tale.

"We dwelt in Mantua. She was another man's wife. It is a common story. She was—nay, I cannot tell you what she was. Gather a lily in its whiteness and steep it in the sunset, and you will see something like her. She was of noble blood; the people always called her Donna Aloysia, as though she were a prince's daughter. She was poor,—every one is poor there,—but when she sat at her barred casement, with her mandoline leaning idle against her breast, she was a wife for Gonzaga's self; and her lord was an old, wizen, dull, and pitiful wretch—a judge of one of the petty courts there. So we loved each other. When the night fell, I rowed beneath her tower windows; if she were alone, there was a knot of flowers at the bars, and a lamp behind them: if all were dark, I stole away and hid among the reeds. So three years went by: you do not seem to understand! We were happy; we would have had nothing otherwise. All the stillness, and the gloom, and the hush of the close streets, and the noiseless pathways of the waters, all seemed made to make our lives the sweeter and the closer-knit.—You do not seem to understand: you have never loved any one?"

"Only Joconda."

"Joconda! I speak to you, then, in an unknown tongue. We were happy. Three summers went by. One night in August I rowed under her wall. The lamp was in the window behind the knot of jessamine and datura. The cord hung down from the bars: I tied my boat, and moored it as usual. As usual I swung myself up the rope, and entered her room by loosening one bar of the grating, which we had filed through long before. Whenever I shut my eyes, in thought or sleep, I see the pale, wide waters, the waving reeds, the white light of the full moon; I hear the hooting of the mosquito-clouds, the lap of the water on the wall, the great bells of the city which tolled midnight. I smell the scent of the creamy daturas and the jessamine flower as I brushed them down in my haste and my joy. They are always with me,—always. When I lie in my grave I think they will be with me there. The room was light with the light of the moon. I saw her lying on the bed asleep,—the great old bed with its velvet baldacchino[1] and its gilded angels,—but she had no kiss for me, no look, no murmur of delight. She was still, quite still, and on her breast, under a cluster of white flowers, there was a deep, dark gap, and a stream of blood was running slowly—oh, so slowly!—over the linen on to the marble floor. For, you see, she was dead. There was a three-edged dagger on the couch; a dagger of mine. I took it up. I understood. Jealousy had killed her and had used my weapon; jealousy has killed its thousands and its tens of thousands. At that moment men seized me. I know nothing more. When I came back to any sight or sense I was in prison, charged with the assassination of my mistress, Donna Aloysia di Albano."

He ceased, and buried his face upon his hands. Musa listened, her eyes dilated with wonder, fear, and awe, her color changing with unspoken sympathy, that was at once too timid and too strong for words.

"Who had killed her?" she asked, at last.

"Her husband. Of that I am as sure as that the sun hangs in the heavens. He had a double vengeance so. I could but deny: I had no proof of innocence. Adultery with her was proven on me, and he, a man versed for many years in all the crafts of law, easily worsted me, delirious with the misery of her loss as I was then. Some furious words that I had been overheard to speak to her at a masked *fête* a few nights before, because she smiled more than I chose upon a youngster, were brought against me. My family were poor and proud, and ill liked in Lombardy. They condemned me as guilty of her murder, and sentenced me to the galleys for thirty years. Thirty years! That is my tale. Well, no doubt in a way I murdered her, for she was slaughtered through our love."

He was silent again; his head was sunk upon his arms; he had forgotten all except those nights in Mantua.

She was silent too. She was troubled by the ghastly story. Passion and death seemed to pass by her like the scorch of fire, like the chill of a grave.

"Does that old wicked man still live?" she asked.

---

[1] A canopy of silk and gold brocade (usually carried in church processions or placed over an altar or throne).

"No doubt. He had his vengeance. After love it is the sweetest thing on earth. I know not how I came to touch the dagger, the foul thing, but being thus found with it in my hand was proof enough for the dolts who were my jury. Besides, old Piero di Albano was a man of weight in our poor ruined city, and I was an idler and a titled beggar. So he had his way. He laid her in her grave with a black cruel hole in her beautiful breast, and he sent me out among felons, to parch my life away like a dog chained in the sun, without a drop of water near, who looks up at the hot brazen skies till he is mad. Whilst I was in my cell, a written paper, unsigned, was brought to me, which told me she had been as faithless to me as to her lord. It might be so; I know not. Or it might be but her husband's lie. This I know,—love is a sorcerer's poison: It burns the brain to ashes, and shrivels the soul up in its heat, till it is no more than the cast coat of the tree-cricket."

CHAPTER XVII.

When Daniello Villamagna saw his boat go out of the lagoon of Orbitello bearing her with it, he looked after it as long as he could see its path over the water, that was growing lilac and purple under the after-glow of the west. Then he retraced his steps slowly towards the town. The galley-slaves were still at work; the labor at the sea-wall was urgent, and they would be kept at it by lantern-light. There were a score of them. They were all there until the State should have decided whether to send them to inland or island prisons, or to the mines, or to public labors on the coast.

Daniello looked curiously at the one amidst them to whom she had spoken. Saturnino Mastarna looked in turn at him, with a hungry, longing look.

"You know her?" he muttered, very low, as the sailor passed him.

Daniello, eager to catch a hint or a sign, with his quick, ardent Southern mind, murmured back to him,—

"What is she to you? tell me."

"I am her father," answered the galley-slave; and he bent his shoulders to the rope-yoke with which he and five of his comrades were doing oxen's work in moving with cords the great blocks of the fresh stone that was being fitted into the Pelasgic wall.

To the Sicilian, the red sunset skies and the shallow waters of the lagoon seemed to circle round him: he felt as if the high black rocks of Argentaro had fallen upon him.

The men of Sicily in general do not think a brigand a criminal: the calling to them seems a fair and a brave one. To take to the hills is, in their sight, natural enough, and honorable, since it needs a sure eye, a firm hand, a steady foot, and a bold spirit. But Daniello Villamagna came of an old seafaring stock, who had been always most loyal and honest mariners. He and his did not look with the common Sicilian sympathy on the *malandrini*[1]. They did not abhor their crimes, indeed, as Northern nations or people of the cities might do. They believed a man might be a mountain-robber, yet have heaven's grace touch him all the same. Still, no one of them had ever had dealings with or friendship for the brigands that undermine public security all over Sicily, as the scolytus[2] will do the trunk of a beach-tree; and to him Saturnino of Santa Fiora was a sinner who merited his chains.

That this great brute, with the dark hair on his naked breast like a wild beast, and his cavernous, cruel eyes that glowed like a wild beast's in the dark, should claim her, his Musoncella,—his scarcely-known, tenderly-adored, proud, self-willed, silent, haughty daughter of the moors and sea,—seemed to him so incredible that he leaned there against the broken wall staring straight before him, and wondering if he were awake, and, if awake, were in his senses.

The deeds of Saturnino were not of his generation, but he had heard tell of them; they had reached even to his own Sicilian shores, where the Sicilian mountain-chiefs had been jealous of the Achilles-like valor and the countless ghastly acts which had marked the blood-stained rule of the Maremmano hero.

He knew that Saturnino had made no more account of the life of a man than a fisher of those shores made of the life of a fish. His blood ran cold as he stood there in the glow from the carmine color of the west. He tried by every method he could to approach and speak again to the galley-slave, but in vain. Saturnino was kept at work amidst others, close under the eye of the overseer. Vigilance was redoubled as the shadows of evening drew near and the lamps were lit on the mole.

The men worked there till ten at night, and then were called off

---

[1] Naughty (i.e., criminals).
[2] Bark beetles.

to their prisons, while the sea grew alive with the boats for the spearing, and a myriad of little golden lights sparkled on the water as the fireflies do on the land, and the whole seafaring population of the coast, from ten miles up and down, strained, and leaped, and cursed, and laughed, and wrangled, and shouted, as the shoal of fish was murdered.

All the uproar, and the mirth, and the quarrels, and the triumphs, failed to divert the young skipper from his thoughts. He pulled out alone to his good brig, and spent the night on his own deck, astonished and perplexed.

With morning he tried again to get an instant's speech with Saturnino.

In vain he spent his day by the sea-wall, watching the labors of the gang. It was sunset again before he could seize a moment when the overseer was occupied and Mastarna had been allowed to pause in his ox-like toil. Then he said quickly, in a whisper,—

"Are you truly her father?"

"She has the face of the woman I loved most: she has the face of Serapia," answered the galley-slave. "When I was taken first, I gave her to a woman of Santa Tarsilla. I see she knows naught of me. Last year she saved and sheltered me; but then I scarce looked at her. I was half drowned, and mad with hunger. I took the gold toys out of the place she hid me in. I would rather she should never know————"

"Why do you tell me, then?"

"Because, by your eyes as you walked beside her, I saw that you loved her; and for her sake, perhaps, you will free me."

"Free you!"

Daniello stared at him in amaze, forgetting how absolutely the one single longing to escape filled all the thoughts and ate up all the soul of this mountain-eagle who was caged by the hot sea-shore.

The heart of Saturnino had thrilled with a sudden memory of tenderness as he had seen the girl in whom he had recognized Serapia's daughter; but far stronger and more absorbing in him was his own thirst for deliverance. It was almost the only instinct left in him, and the few weeks that he had been free on his own hills in the summer before—all wretched, hungry, filled with fear and compelled to concealment, though they were—had been so sweet to him that night and day since he had been captured afresh he had meditated escape,—schemed for it, lived for it, scarcely felt the heat of the sun or the cold of the wind, the aching of his old wounds or the lash of the overseer's whip, for thinking every moment, could he get away?

He would have torn himself from his trap as the eagle does, leaving its foot wrenched off behind it. The thirst for the liberty of the hills was like a madness on him.

To his jailers and his companions in misery he never spoke. If he could have slain them all and so escaped, he would have done it.

"She is beautiful, and her mother was noble," he muttered. "The woman who took her was a good woman. There was love in your eyes as you looked at her; one gives the world for that: I have not forgotten. Will you help me to get free for her sake?"

"You would torment her———"

"No; I might have called to the jailers yesterday, and if I had said to them, 'Yonder child is of my blood,' they would have let me speak to her. But I would not. I stole her gold toys; I would rather she should never know. You are a sailor, you have a ship; if you can get me away, take me to Sardinia. There are Mastarna men there, kindred of mine. They, too, live by the mountains; they would make me welcome———"

The overseer turned and resumed his walk near them.

Saturnino lapsed into the sullen silence he had preserved since his capture.

"I will see you again," murmured the Sicilian, and for prudence' sake he left the sea-wall and went towards the town to summon those of his sailors who were drinking and domino-playing at the wine-houses.

To do what the galley-slave asked him might be utter ruin and disgrace to him: it might cost him his ship, and his liberty, and his good name. If he helped the captive to cheat the law, the law would most likely find out his complicity and fling him in turn into its prisons; and he knew well that Saturnino Mastarna had been a murderer, not once, but many times, that his crimes against the law were dark and numberless, that he was still a wild beast ready to tear even the hand that aided him.

Yet it hurt him to leave the man there in his hourly torment, in his hopeless misery; and who could tell, if he were left thus, growing more and more brutish and desperate every day, that he might not in sheer despair call upon his daughter to drink his cup of bitterness with him? Or, if he escaped by himself, might he not seek her out and compel her to shelter him afresh, and bury her youth forever underneath the weight of his own secrecy and guilt? If it were possible to rescue him, would it not be well done for her sake?

He was generous, and he took little thought, and the memory of Musa was with him, potent and intoxicating as the fumes of strong wine; her coldness, her scorn, her strength, enhanced her beauty of person to him. The dangerous race she sprang from gave her a mystery and a magic the more. To the Northern mind and worldly knowledge of Sanctis this lineage had seemed the most terrible of all inheritance. But to the Sicilian it made her look the lovelier; as Persephone looked to her lover when the darkness of the shades was about her instead of the flowering fields.

That in her veins ran the bold, fierce blood of the Mastarna of the Apennine rocks was but a reason the more for him to long to bear her away on the deck of his own good brig, and dwell with her under the dark-green orange-groves beside his own blue sea, and make her the happy mother of dauntless children who would ride the waves like the dolphin and nautilus.

CHAPTER XVIII.

Este's had been the usual tranquil, amorous, unoccupied life of young Italian men in old Italian cities that are away from the common track of travel: a life of sleepy calm, of often harmless dalliance, that usually has its story told from birth to death within the circle of the old town walls. Why not? Men used to be greater when they lived only on one spot, and more content. Unhappily, now, the greatness and the content are gone, because that which used to be repose too often is now but apathy, languor, rust.

He had studied under monks in an ecclesiastical college, ancient and solemn in art and architecture, where no boy laughed above his breath, and a Greek chorus was second to a Latin hymn. There he had grown up a beautiful, graceful, pensive lad, in a home straitened by penury and made austere by devotion, but keeping something of the stateliness of grander times.

To drop slowly down the wide lagoons and thread the mazes of the reed thickets was his chief, often his only, occupation; to make his mandoline throb a love-lay under some old sculptured casement, where some fancy of the hour was hiding behind a curtain of frayed velvet or tattered tapestry, was his sole diversion. There was enough to live on; that slender pittance which kept his father and himself in a corner of the dark old palace would be enough for him to live on afterwards. No one spoke to him of action or of ambition; they were unknown words in Mantua; he lived through his years as idly and as thoughtlessly as any one of the dragon-flies above the rushes lived out their summer hour. If he were pensive and serious, it was only because the spirit of the place was on him and the sense of narrow fortunes curbed his youth.

Then, when he was twenty-four, this passion for an old man's young wife came on him with force and sorcery, and changed the whole tenor of his dreaming, sleepy days. He lived thenceforward only for one woman, in all the beguiling mystery of a secret and mutual love.

What he saw now was the beauty of that dead woman. There is no coldness so unchanging, so unyielding, so absolute, as the coldness of one who loves what is lost. Simply, he never saw Musa with any eyes that realized her beauty or her girlhood.

He saw some one who was good to him in his sickness and extremity; that was all. The woman dead in Mantua, with the cruel hole in her breast and the lilies red with her blood, was forever between him and this creature who tended him, fed him, sheltered him, saved him.

He had passed through one of those terrible hours in life which even in the most sensual temperaments burn out for the moment all fires of sense and quick desire in horror. He loved with all his force the woman murdered in Mantua; and yet he knew she was dead, dead, dead,—a putrid thing pushed away under the friable, watery soil. The terror of that, the ghastliness of it, the despair of it, froze the blood in his veins. What was this girl to him?

No more than the empty lamps of the tomb whose lights had been out two thousand years.

CHAPTER XIX.

NAUSICAA, in the safe shelter of her father's halls, had never tended Odysseus with more serenity and purity than the daughter of Saturnino tended his fellow-slave.

The sanctity of the tombs lay on them, the dead were so near; neither profanity nor passion seemed to have any place here in this mysterious twilight alive with the memories of a vanished people. Her innocence was a grand and noble thing, like any one of the large white lilies that rose up from the noxious mud of the marshes,—a cup of ivory wet with the dewdrops of dawn, blossoming fair on fetid waters. And in him the languor of sickness and of despair borrowed unconsciously for a while the liveries of chastity; and he spoke no word, he made no gesture, that would have scared from its virginal calm the soul of this lonely creature, who succored him with so much courage and so much compassion that they awed him with the sense of an eternal, infinite, and overwhelming debt.

It needs a great nature to bear the weight of a great gratitude.

To a great nature it gives wings that bear it up to heaven; a lower nature feels it always as a clog that impatiently is dragged only so long as force compels.

Which nature was Este's he would not have known himself.

At times, indeed, the weight of his debt to the fellow-creature who had sheltered him came upon him with a shock and startled him at its vastness. But commonly he thought no more of it than the cuckoo thinks of debt to the tree-sparrow in whose nest he lies so safely whilst April storms shake off the April blossoms.

All she did for him was done so simply, so wholly as a matter of course, that no mute claim on her part, even of look or gesture, ever recalled to him the fact that she owed him no more duty than she owed to any hill-fox or wounded scops who should have hidden itself in her retreat.

Sometimes he liked to talk to her; it took him in a measure out of himself to tell her those truths or traditions of science or history which to her seemed like tales of magic. Sometimes he liked to hear her sing the mournful sea-songs of the people, though oftener the sound of the mandoline hurt him with an intolerable pain, recalling to him the moonlit nights in Mantua, when his lyric underneath her walls had told his love that his boat was there, casting its shadow on the reedy waters, white with the shining of the moon-beams.

But always she was no more to him than the slave had been to the Lucumo.

Her strength, her courage, her directness of speech, her power of exertion, all made her seem to him rather a youth than a girl. He had loved a woman with soft, idle hands, and languid, inert limbs, no more capable of facing the hurricane or steering through the winter waves than a peacock, in his pomp of purple, is capable of breasting the breeze, or cleaving the breakers, with the gyps-vulture or the storm-swallow.

He had loved one who was as useless as the painted butterfly, as lovely and as idle as the lotus flower floating on its broad green leaves, rocked on the rippling water.

This creature, all strength, and daring, and continual effort, had for the moment, at least, no woman's charm for him as he saw her come home from her day's hard labor, bearing on her shoulders the fagot of sticks or the sheave of bracken, and in her hand the fishing-nets and the sickle or the hatchet. So might have looked any maiden of Tempe or of Calydon; so might have looked Theocritus's love when the Sicilian vales were lilac with the meadow-mint and rent by autumn gales.

As these she had looked to Maurice Sanctis. But Este, though he knew the pastoral poets by heart, did not see her with those eyes. For him her humble daily cares of him obscured her beauty, as in days of old it obscured for mortals the divinity of those gods who came amidst them and drove their ploughshares and sat beside their hearths.

If he had known of Daniello Villamagna, with his face like a Veronese portrait, and his sinewy elastic frame and stately yet supple movements, some pulse of anger might have quickened in him, and with it some smart of sudden appreciation.

But she never spoke of the Sicilian sailor; some vague instinct locked her lips about him, though a little while before she had opened them so carelessly to Maurice Sanctis. So to Este she remained nothing more than a dryad of the lonely woods, who scarcely touched him with any sense of the sex in her; a *genius alba* who ministered to his dire need and saved him from his hunters, but who came and went without exciting one impulse in him to keep her hand in his and say to her, "I am beggared of love: make me once more rich."

So nothing troubled the perilous peace in which she dwelt; and the autumn deepened into winter, and the rain-storms deluged the earth above, and she was still innocent as Nausicaa, he was still sacred to her as Odysseus.

She did not know her own heart.

She did not know why all the ardor of the Sicilian left her hard and scornful; why all the gentleness of Sanctis had left her cold and thankless; and why one languid smile from Este's eyes, one listless word from his month, made her grateful and full of joy.

She was drinking at that fatal fountain which Joconda once had feared that she would drink so deeply from that she would drown. But its waters were clear and harmless at her lips as yet: she could not tell that there was poison in them and bitter after-taste.

She did not even know the name of this fount at which all pilgrims of earth drink soon or late.

She tended him as she had tended the wounded storm-swallow from the Polar seas. She loved him as she had loved that; but passion was still dumb and slumbering in her. Often in youth it lies and dreams like Endymion,[1] and would never wake but for the kiss that startles sleep and changes the dream into desire.

Once awakened, that peaceful rest, careless on the crushed cowslips, can come back no more.

So the months went on, and the days renewed themselves, each like the other, filled to her with bodily exertion that had become delightful because no longer for her own sake alone, and to him with the dull, heavy, stupid pain that men of cultured mind feel when they are barred out from the world of other men and from the face of nature.

He told her all he knew of the Etruscan nation; all (that all so little) which Pliny and Dionysus and Silius Italicus have told; all the old tales that the Etruscans cherished, and he himself had read in dreamy boyish days of drowsy Mantuan summers—the old, old tales of Ulysses and his son; of the Dioscuri, whose images were engraved on the mirror she used; of Diomedes, snatched to the gods upon the Adrian isle, and his companions changed to birds.

He pictured to her the grand and puissant lucomonies that have perished so utterly off the face of the earth that even their records have perished; he pictured to her the people driving their cattle and carrying their corn to the forests dedicated to Feronia, to exchange them with the Umbrians, the Latins, and the Sabines; the white sacred cattle drawing the brazen ploughshare through the moist green soil, to trace the walls of cities to be; the long, prosperous, ease-loving, and luxurious life that was led, through so many centuries, within those

---

[1] Endymion was a handsome shepherd boy, the mortal lover of the goddess Selene. Each night she kissed him to sleep.

cities' walls when raised, doomed to succumb and change and die out, little by little, when the tramp and the clang of the Legions came over the mountains, and the greed of consul and of emperor robbed the land of her marbles of Luini, of her temple-columns, of her bronze and her gold work, of her delicate potteries, of her colossal statues.

The brother of Fabius Maximus,[1] with his slave, disguised as shepherds of Gaul, with javelins and sickles, wending their perilous way through the darkness of the dreaded Ciminian woods, and descending to the rich plains and the stately cities to propose the admittance of that mission from Rome which was ultimately to be the curse of Etruria; the augurs tracing with their wand the lines of separation on the heavens, watching the flight of herons, of storks, of crows, to gather the secrets of the future, taking warning or counsel from the play of lightning on the heads of the spears, worshipping with blood-sacrifice Jupiter Elicius amidst the thunders of the storm; the fifty-oared armed galleys going out from the sunny crowded ports, some up the tawny Tiber, some away to Spina for the tin and amber come overland from the far Scandinavian waters, some by the Ægean coasts to the gorgeous and languid lands of the East, where the Tyrrhene manners were welcomed as brethren and sons; the sunlit towns, now level with the dust, then strong with colossal bastions and ramparts, graceful with temples and with statues, stately with religious feasts and princely banquets; the son of Atys setting sail with his famished Lydians from Smyrna; the Tyrrhene pirates capturing Dionysus, and changed for their sin into water-spouting dolphins; the Persian faith brought with the Persian eagles to the Italiote soil; the great Etruscan confederations gathering in harmony at the temple of Voltumna; the oxen drawing the fair Carrara marbles into the port of Luna, to make the altars of the beloved orchard-god, or the likeness of the Cytharœdus; all these things he pictured to her, and as she followed his words she saw all that they portrayed; she heard the brazen bray of the Lydian trumpets, she saw the purple glow of the Lydian robes; when she went down to the edge of the sea, she thought of the Naviguum of Isis, as the people had gathered for it on those very shores with their torches flaming against the daffodil light of a March morning; when she collected the broken boughs of the sea-pines for fuel, she thought

---

[1] Fabius Maximus was a Roman politician and soldier who served as consul and as dictator.

of the pine laid low in symbol of lost Attis, and borne garlanded with flowers to the shrine of the Mighty Mother.

And when he told her that all this Etruscan and Latin life had been lived long ere the Galilean gathered his disciples from the fishers of the lake-side, and that before this yet again, in long ages ere the Italiote or the Tyrrhene had turned a sod of the soil of Maremma, all these green, wet, shining woodlands and red blossoming grass-lands had been the haunt of the meridional elephant, of the armored rhinoceros, of the terrible machairodus, of the huge hippopotamus, and, later than that, of the mammoth and the lion and the bear, com-ing down over the Alps as the Goths did after them,—then her eager imagination, starved so long, fed itself on all these wonders with en-tranced delight, and he who told her of them seemed to her a magi-cian as marvellous in power as the Etruscan aruspice[1] had seemed to the Etruscan slave.

Of all the tales, what fascinated her the most were these of that prehistoric time when all the Tuscan valleys and plains had been forest and marsh, and grass and water, and the vast quadrupeds had moved with massive measure through the woods that no axe touched, in the twilight that no hearth-fires lit, in the green virgin wastes that had no sound but the tread of their mighty feet, the trumpet of their solemn voices.

Man, when he did at length come amidst them, had been a small and timid and puny creature, glad to profit by the branches the el-ephants broke down, grateful to follow the course of the hippopota-mus along the shores of the brimming rivers, meekly and humbly culling the fruits the great lords of the soil did not need. She wished that she had lived then to have been friends with the huge leaf-eating beasts. She sorrowed for them, driven away little by little off the soil they reigned over as man multiplied and climate changed, until at the last they perished utterly, as ages after them the Etruscan people did in turn.

He told her all these stories, that are written in fragments in ivory letters on the heart of the earth, when he was in the mood to speak, in the long evening-time that now approached, as the winds drove the

---

[1] Fortune teller.

last leaves from the maple and ash, and the dyer-oaks and the downy-oaks grew yellow.

His shallow studies were enough to seem to her ignorance a very ocean of knowledge, in whose depths were wondrous pearls.

When he spoke to her of all these unknown things, her mind, by nature eager, poetic, and aspiring, followed his with breathless attention and delight.

As she watched her round loaves bake in the warm embers, she hearkened to these stories of lands and peoples that she had never heard of; Herodotus and Pliny yielded what to her were tales of absolute truth, and her grave and brooding fancy, starved so long, spread with rapture over these new fields of thought, glad as any bird loosed from a narrow cage. They were all as real and beautiful to her as they were to the Etruscan sacrificing to his garden-god in the red and gold of his autumn orchards, or to the Latin beseeching the smile of the goddess of the myrtle-bough alike upon his vineyards and upon his nuptial joys.

They sat together in the chamber of the Lucumo, the oil burning in the bronze lamps, the wood fire upon the stones, while she wove the basket osiers or spun the hemp; and it beguiled the time to him to recall the things he had read in his college books, and after college in other books that his ecclesiastical masters called heretical and damnable, since they treated of geology and science.

Time was long and dull; he could hardly keep so much count of it as the Etruscans had kept of the years that they marked by nails in their temples.

They were all so precisely similar, so uneventful, so like was the night to the day, here, where he never saw the sun itself, but only some stray thread of it which came down through the bryony and bindweed, some faint reflection of it which shone through the open doorway of the entrance-cell, that all the weeks became confused in his mind into one blurred, gray, colorless mass of time that might have been a century, so long it seemed. He used to think that he would remain here till he became like Carolus Magnus in the depths of the Unterberg, with gray beard grown downward to the stones, and the ages rolling on without awaking him.

His life seemed to him broken in his hands, like a plume of golden-rod or red amaranth snapped off in its full flower and left to wither. To venture forth into the light and air was almost certainly to return to the galleys; to stay on here, though life itself was kept up in him, was to die in all save the actual rotting of the body.

Musa to him was only like a brave boy who had rescued him; he did not feel to her more than the Lucumo (once prince here) might have felt to the faithful slave whose ashes he had placed between his own bones and his dog's.

She was perforce out all the day, getting him such food as she could, or such work as she could glean from the moors; cutting the distaff canes to make them into bundles, seeking for edible roots, bringing in wood blown down in the autumn winds, or the dry brake to make a couch for herself, netting or spearing fish for his evening meal, searching for and gathering those medicinal herbs which she relied on as the chief means of making money enough to buy quinine and wine. Unless she went out he must starve, and so perforce she left him in these dark and stormy autumn days alone with his passionate regrets, his almost sullen despair.

If he could but have gone with her, and labored beside her, he would have regained strength and tone.

The cumulus clouds hurrying in vast masses before the west wind; the often angry sea lashed by the north blasts into a smoking field of foam and mist in which the barques were lost as caravans of the desert are lost in the simoom; the beauty of the green, wet, shining earth, with pool and estuary brimming from the copious rains and thronged with the flocks of arctic birds; the glory of shadow and color, and sunbeams glowing through the steam of rain, and dark hill-sides swept by the mists and echoing back the thunder,—all these, which to her were so beautiful, might have taken some hold also upon his mind, and freed him from the brooding dread and desire which consumed him like a disease of vital parts.

But the outer air could never touch him save at rare short times when, fearfully, he stole to the entrance and looked up at the brambles and branches crossing one another, and envied the brown wings of the pilgrim-falcon wheeling against the wind, the silver-gray triangle of the storks travelling across the sky.

Air is the king of physicians: he who stands often with nothing between him and the open heavens will gain from them health both moral and physical. But he could not do this, and there was nothing to arouse him from the morbid dejection into which he fell with scarce an effort. The struggle had been too long for him, and these tombs at their best were but a naked prison.

Walls hung with storied tapestries, couches rich with old embroideries, a woman's ringed hand among his curls, a mellow warmth scented with the orange-flower and the carnation blooming in gardens green and old, love-murmurs, low laughter, pensive fancies, "sad only for wantonness,"[1]—these were what suited him, as they suit the soft Italian night.

She was, meanwhile, always troubled more or less by what is called a vulgar care: she found it difficult to get such food as this man, still weak and weary, could be induced to eat. The bread she made from her summer-garnered store of wild oats was hard and indifferent; there was no longer Zeffirino to bring any change of diet in ewes' milk or maize flour for polenta; the crust with spring-water and wild berries, which had been enough for her strong health and unpampered appetite, was nothing to tempt the nausea and the languor of a still feeble convalescent. She knew how to do what Joconda had done. If she had had them, she could have prepared the goats' ham, the curd cheese, the broth, with wine in it, of savory herbs; but except the herbs she had none of the materials needful for these things; and even for sake of Este she could not bring herself to snare the birds, her dear friends, her cherished playmates, beloved by her before she had seen his face.

This life of the wild moorlands and woodlands had been all-sufficient for her in her simple needs; but the more complicated wants of a man once used to gentle life, and now worn with long languor and weakness, found it utterly barren and empty.

It was a blessing to her that it was autumn, that many a rough fruit and edible fungus could be gathered off the moors, and that the teeming sea was still so near that she could draw from it fish succulent and various. Still, food was hard to obtain, and obtained hardly, by the sheer strength of her arm and sureness of her eye; and when afar off on the sky-line she saw the great corn-wains passing black against the sun, laden with the wheat that in all time has made Maremma the granary of Rome, she looked at them with longing hungry eyes, as

---

[1] This quotation is probably from Shakespeare's *The Life and Death of King John*, IV. i.: "as sad as night, / only for wantonness."

her father had looked from his lair upon the rich men traversing the vale below.

True, she did not know that there were such things as riches any-where; the life of wealth, of luxury, was invisible to her; every one around her lived on roughly-made polenta, a sea or a fresh-water fish, a mussel, or an onion. This was all they tasted for relish or for rarity. All the opulence and ease of the world were hidden from her by the stretching sea, the solitude of the moors, the noxious and uninhabit-able marsh. But she knew that there was a region where all the grain went, all the cut grass, the burned wood, the felled pines,—a fairer, happier region, which rejoiced in all that left Maremma poor, and where sickness was not in the soil, nor fever always in the sunbeams.

Those immense plains which the men from the mountains ploughed and sowed in autumn, in summer were golden oceans of grain, reaped ere midsummer was passed. And not a bearded head of it all could she have! The rebellion that had been the passion of her father's life rose up in her,—the unreasoning rebellion of those who only know that they have nothing.

Had not her honesty been natural to her as her courage, and braced by the Piedmontese woman's stern repeated lessons, it would have broken down now under her longing to serve this man, and her wondering rage at the inequalities of fate.

"These might fetch money," Este said once to her, taking up a *fibula*[1] of gold and a necklace of amber which had escaped the raven-ous greed of Saturnino.

"They are *theirs*," she said, quickly and sternly, and took them out of his hand and laid them down reverently. He smiled faintly.

"Oh, do not think I would rob you like Saturnino. But these things belong to you by right of discovery, and they are no good to the dead."

She shook her head.

"That may be. But I would sooner seize some one by the throat and rifle his pockets than I would rob those who sleep and are si-lent."

"I cannot quarrel with you for that," said Este. "Theodoric was less scrupulous than you. He ordered the plunder of the graves, and the moderns followed him."

---

[1] Fibulæ were ornamental jewels that had the shape and function of a safety pin. They were used to decorate clothes.

"Who was Theodoric?"[1]

"Never mind: I like your instinct better than his greed. It is a right one. They give to the galleys a poor wretch who opens a tomb made yesterday to seek for treasure; and the nobles and the students who plunder the Etruscans and carry their toys of death off into cabinets and glass cases are applauded. Life is very unjust: most crimes are sanctioned in some form or other when they take grand names."

"I could not steal from them, even for you," she answered him, without noticing his subtler argument.

Even for him she would not have touched those golden *fibulæ*, those golden grasshoppers that the dead had carried with them to the earth and trusted to it as the wild partridge trusts her nest.

Even when she used the vessels of bronze and pottery, and looked at her own face in the steel mirror of the Tyndarides, she was afraid she did an irreligious thing,—an ungenerous thing, since the dead could not avenge an insult. Though these tombs had been heaped with gold, the child of Saturnino would have touched none of it.

Having nothing else of her own, she gave Este the uttermost of her strength and patience; she labored late and early, she hunted for edible fungi, she netted fish,—a cruelty she loathed,—she worked hard at the rush-plaiting and the spinning to have something to take in to Telamone or Orbitello with which to purchase the wine he needed. She raked up the pine-cones, she cut the ling and broom; she carried in the dry wood she collected from under the trees; she kept the sepulchres as clean and sweet as any sea-shell with the cleanly ways that Joconda had made a second nature to her in her childhood. She worked arduously and willingly in all ways, and this very devotion to him obscured her beauty to him: sometimes he was ingrate enough to murmur angrily because she left him so much alone.

She was only his servant to him; he did not see his ministering angel in her. He did not see that glory as of a young goddess which was about her buoyant feet and her close-curled head for the eyes of Maurice Sanctis and of the Sicilian mariner.

To them she was so proud; to him she was so humble.

When he threw her a soft word or two of thanks, she was repaid a thousandfold; when at nightfall she sat at her spinning, and he told her

---

[1] Theodoric the Great (c. 454-526) was the King of the Ostrogoths and conqueror of Italy.

old-world stories of all that Maremma had seen since the mammoth pulled down the foliage of its esculus-oaks, she was so happy that her thoughts never travelled past that glad immediate hour.

She knew nothing of her own danger.

The only fear that ever quickened her pulse was when in the hush of night she heard the call of the bittern booming over the marshes, or the loud rush of the wild ducks' wings through the air, and trembled lest the sound should be the coming of armed men to break into her sanctuary.

Now and then a quiver of sharper alarm ran through them both, when she saw any figure of shepherd or hunter on the horizon, when the mounted *buttero* crashed through the thickets chasing a broodmare or a bull-buffalo, when the shots sounded from the marshes or the estuaries, or the boar with the hound on his flanks burst through the evergreen brakes.

But these alarms were few and far between. Maremma is wide, and the tombs of the Lucumo were fenced about with many prickly outworks of all the *ruscus*[1] tribe, and the holy-thorn, and the box-holly, which horses could not face and that hunters had to hack with their knives. Usually the days were perfectly still, with no sound in them save such as the birds made, or the foals as they whinnied and capered, or the wild hogs as they grunted for joy over a new fall of acorns.

She saw day by day the color of health return to Este's face, and strength to his listless limbs; the potent medicine of the Orbitellano leech had restored the tone and the nerve to a constitution naturally good, though never vigorous. His physical beauty grew with each week that his lost health and force came back to him. His eyes ceased to have beneath them the dark sunken circle of weakness and pain; his skin had the delicate brown of his youth in lieu of the pallor that had been like the hue of worn ivory; his limbs lost their emaciation, and regained their symmetry of proportion and ease of movement. When he stood at nightfall for a few wary moments at the entrance of the tombs, to draw a few timid breaths of air, and the white light of the moon fell full upon his upraised face, it was beautiful as the Vatican Hermes' is, as some human faces are here still in this land of the Apollo and the Antinoüs.

----

[1] A shrub with stiff pointed stems.

They were both in their youth; they had each that physical beauty which is still, despite all the efforts of the soul and mind, the one sure sorcery that earth still knows. They were together in the solitudes of the marshes and forests, in the gloom under the myrtle and the heath; but they had never as yet touched each other's lips, or found their solace on each other's breast.

Of love she knew nothing, even while she loved unconsciously; and he, for a while, still only saw the dead face of his mistress lying in the pale lamp-light under the great golden canopy of the Gonzaga's bed.

While it is winter, the porphyrion sails down the willowy streams beside the sultan-hen that is to be his love, and sees her not, and stays not her passage upon the water or through the air: she does not live as yet to him. But when the breath of the spring brings the catkins from the willows, and the violets amidst the wood-moss on the banks, then he awakes and beholds her; and then the stream reflects but her shape for him, and the rushes are full of the melody of his love-call. It was still winter with Este,—a bitter winter of discontent; and he had no eyes for this water-bird that swam with him through the icy current of his adversity.

To break the frozen flood that imprisoned him was his only thought.

Had he been asked, he would have answered that his heart was dead, like last year's violets, and his passions with it.

"If only you could come out with me!" she said, often, with a sigh, to him, since to her greatest and most cruel of all losses was it to be debarred the feel of the wind as it blew, the sight of the cloud-shadows as they sailed over the moors and meadows.

"Nevermore shall I see the sun and smell the heather," he said, wearily. "It is hardly worth while to live on—thus."

Yet it was not the heather and the sun that he missed the most, or would the first have sought. His heaven had not lain, like hers, in the sense of the broad sky, in the feel of the elastic moss, in the simple joys of motion and vision and the gladness of bright weather. What he longed for were amorous secrecy, forbidden delights, the silent ways of an old city that he knew, the warm loveliness of a woman who had leaned from her casement to draw him the sooner upward to her arms.

Nature was nothing to him, and to him said nothing. What he longed for with intolerable weariness was once more himself to live.

At his age men cling to life tenaciously, and death appalls at all ages the Latin temperament. Yet even he at times felt tempted to make an end of this dull, torpid, aimless existence, maintained at such difficulty and in such hardship,—the life of a hawk, half starved, in an iron cage. Often when she was away he looked at the Florentine dagger, or thought of the deep pools of this wilderness, where none but the moor-hens and mallards would see a human life come to its last rest amidst the reeds.

But he was young, and so against all reason hope remained with him, and made endurance possible.

It was November weather, brilliant and luminous, with noons warm as summer, and gorgeous sunsets, and cold misty dawns that heralded bright days. The woods were in all their pomp; the poplars yellow as guinea-gold; the ashes, in their wondrous mingling of fawn-color and purple and brown and crimson, the most glorious of all autumn foliage; the oaks resisted change sternly for a while, and then transformed themselves suddenly into masses of amber and of bronze; the bays were black with fruit; the pines were knobbed with ripe cones; the maple was a glow of scarlet; the osmunda and the hart's tongue were like great flames of fire, on the ground. The huge white clouds that wise men call cirri-cumuli swept grandly over the blue sky, and gathered in masses westward as the sun went down. The air was strong and full of exhilaration; the pungent odors of the wood-smoke rolled down the mountain-sides. Last of all the flowers, the pretty canary-colored dragon's-mouth was in blossom in all green places. It was a season in which, despite the added perils that came with it, only to breathe and move seemed joy enough to Musa, the earth and air around her were so gorgeous, so clear, so radiant, so healthful.

CHAPTER XX.

ONE day she went out fishing as soon as the mountains grew red with the uprising of the sun. When she came ashore the morning was still young; the water had been very cold, the air was stormy with a west wind, far away where Sardinia lay unseen in the south, mists were hurrying up in great armies; here the sun still shone, and the dazzle of golden light and the play of deep-blue shadows cast from the wind-tossed clouds were very beautiful upon land and sea.

The Sasso Scritto was all purple and green with the flowering rosemary that covered its marble-veined sandstone; the rock-pigeons were wheeling and meeting above it and across it, foreseeing a change in the sunshiny weather; some kittiwakes had arrived and were float-ing away to the estuary; a Dutch dogger with square sail was passing in the distance, and a little fleet of feluccas, graceful as the kittiwakes, were running merrily under the west wind towards the Cape of Troja.

Musa, in haste to return, put the rope of her boat over her shoul-ders and began to pull it over the sand to that hole in the rocks where she was wont to hide it. As she bent her head and shoulders forward to make the first effort at hauling it from the fringe of the waves, she heard the sound of oars in the water behind her. Always afraid of being watched, and above all afraid when she had her boat, lest any should see and steal it as soon as her back was turned, she let the rope fall from her shoulders and looked towards the sea.

In another moment, another boat's keel ground upon the sand and stones, and from it Maurice Sanctis leaped, and stood before her among the southern wood and sea-rush. For a moment they were both mute,—he from hesitation, she from fear and anger commin-gled. By the Sasso Scritto no human foot but her own fell on that solitary shore from one year to another. It was a bad place for landing, and its ill repute for this among the fishermen had long kept it untrou-bled for her and the blue-rocks and the rock-martins.

She had never dreaded disturbance there. She stood with wide-opened angry eyes staring on him, the rope slipping through her hand, the sea-water running from her kilted skirt and shining feet, the west wind blowing the dusky gold of her curls, her cheeks warm with exertion and the cold sea-air till they glowed like the damask of the autumn rose.

"Why did you come back?" she said, with a sombre wrath in her voice. "I told you to go away; I told you to stay away."

"I could not obey you," said Sanctis, gently. "I have been away five months and more. I strove against the wish to return, since I knew that I should be unwelcome to you. But at last the thought of you all alone now that winter is so nigh overcame my resolution. I could not

stay on in ease and mirth and luxury in Paris and think of you in the
wild weather dependent on chance for bread."

He looked at her wistfully. She seemed to him more lovely than
before, and more than ever sternly and fiercely hostile to him.

In truth, she was not thinking of him at all, except in the sense
of a fresh and terrible danger. How could she keep him out of the
tombs? How could she prevent his finding Este there? It was of that
alone she was thinking as she continued to gaze at him, her eyes full
of anger and alarm.

"Do not look at me with so much fear and hatred," he said, patiently, "I can wish you nothing but good. There is the memory of
Joconda between us. Can it not be in some little measure a peace-
maker?"

Her eyes softened at the name he invoked, but she was too deeply
disturbed for her to be won over by his words.

"I do not know why you should trouble yourself as to me," she
said, with a sullenness that was the outcome of extreme dread. "I told
you in the summer-time I have all I want. I am happy. But I do not like
to be hunted like this. Go back to your own country, and leave me
alone in mine."

"You are alone still?" he asked: he was thinking of the Sicilian
sailor.

Her face grew troubled, and the rose of her cheeks spread over
her brow and throat. She had never lied in her life. She must needs
lie now. It was the shame of that which made her blush so hotly; but
Sanctis only saw in the sudden flush of color an answer to his question made in such wise that there was nothing else left to learn. Yet he
could not repress an impatient word.

"It is the Sicilian?" he said, quickly.

She laughed angrily.

"You remember the Sicilian? No: he is gone as he came. I tell you
I want no one. If I did, what would that be to you? I do not know why
you torment me. I loved Joconda, but, I told you before, you have
nothing of her. You are rich and she was poor; your people forgot her
all her life long, and I do not see why you should think of her now. As
for me, I am well and I need nothing; but do not hunt me: it makes me
wicked."

"I do not hunt you," said Sanctis, distressed and perplexed. "Why
should you think of such a thing? I would be your friend if you would

let me, and I cannot understand why I should seem to you an enemy. It is impossible that I can be that. You are set against me, but that is no fault of mine. I have met you by mere accident. I came here to go over the moors to your sepulchre. I intended nothing but what was open and simple. I landed at Orbitello this morning————"

The color faded as quickly out of her face as it had come there. A great dread froze her very heart. How could she keep him from the tombs? His patient gentleness with his unchanging resolve alarmed her much more than any fiery menaces or reproaches of Daniello Villamagna's would have done. It gave her the impression of being something she could neither bend nor break. This Northern persistence gave her the sense of being meshed in by it as the fish were in the web of the nets.

She did not know what to say to him, nor how to rid herself of his importunity.

"You see I do not want for anything," she said, at last. "You see I am strong and well. Go back to your own land and leave me in mine. I told you in the summer you cannot drive a gray-lag goose by force to the poultry-byre."

"Will you not let me come with you?"

"No: if the people, any one of them, see you here again, they will talk of me and find out where I dwell. I told you so in the summer. You are a stranger, you are a signore; it looks odd to see you here."

"I will come to you there————"

Her heart beat loud; a great terror which she concealed was upon her.

"It will be ungenerous if you do," she said, coldly. "I should never have been found by you if Zirlo had not betrayed me. Do not be as mean as he. When I see where a moor hen has made her nest, I never go near; I will even walk miles out of the way sooner than disturb her. Why do you not feel that for me?"

"Is it a nest that you have made there?" said Sanctis, with an irritation that he would have been ill able to explain to himself. "You were all alone with your dead in the summer."

"The dead are better friends than the living."

"You escape my question."

"I do not see why you should question me. Let me go: that is all I wish to do."

"You are free to go, of course. But if you forbid me to follow you, will you meet me here once at the least?"

"What can you have to say? If it be what you said in the summer, you know that it is of no use to say it all again. I shall not come."

"Let me put your boat up for you, at the least," said Sanctis, controlling whatever impatience he felt, and having faith that patience soon or late prevailed with all women. "Your shore-folks must be very honest people that they have never stolen it from you."

"It is not because they are honest, but because they are afraid of the Sasso Scritto. It has a bad name. There are sunken rocks and quaking sands about it. I know where they are, but they are always dangerous."

As she spoke, she drew the rope over her shoulders and began to pull her boat upward.

Seeing that she was obdurate, Sanctis went behind the boat and pushed it and lifted it through the stones and the sand and the sea-grasses that choked the way.

"I have put it up every day that I have used it without help," said Musa, angrily.

But he did not desist, and with the aid of his strength the little skiff was soon safe beyond the water-mark of the rocks in a cleft that glittered with marbles golden and white, and gleams of porphyry and agate. Then she took out of it the little fish she had captured, and turned her head to Sanctis.

"If really you do not hunt me, do not come with me. If you try to follow me, I will run: you know I am swifter than you. I can go as fast as the bunting when I choose."

"Will you meet me here once for Joconda's sake?—I will not ask you for myself."

"Very well," she said, reluctantly. "It is folly. But I will come, if nothing else will content you. I will, be here to-morrow at this hour."

"Not this evening?"

"No; to-morrow. Keep your word, and do not follow me. It makes me feel as the buck feels when the dogs are after him. I am very sorry that you have come from your own country, for it is loss of time, and to you I seem thankless and rude, no doubt. Look up yonder at those rock-martins. What is the best thing you can do for them? It is to leave them alone. I am like them: I have my house in the rocks. I do not want to go away to other air, as the nightingales go, and the lories."

"But in those sepulchres, under the earth————"

"The kingfisher's house is under the earth, and he would not thank you to pull him out of it. I will come here to-morrow,—for Joconda's sake. Farewell to-day."

With the little glittering fish in her hand, and the sea-wet wool of her clothes clinging to her limbs, she turned away and began to climb the face of the cliff as rapidly and as easily as a woodpecker climbs a tree.

She went so quickly and with such sure feet that the bluish-gray of her kirtle was soon lost among the bluish-gray of the rosemary. The sun-rays and the shadows played about her head, and the rock-doves who knew her so well flew in circles round her path; soon she had climbed to where the little rain-clouds floated across the upper portion of the cliff, and there the vapor of them took her to itself as if she were indeed the goddess of the golden bow and hidden in a cloud.

Sanctis stood baffled and troubled, looking up at the face of the cliff and watching the blue-rocks whirling under the shadows and the martins swaying under the force of the wind as they flew. He could not tell what to think. An irresistible desire to try once more to persuade her, to see once more this sad green land she loved, had driven him here on an impulse altogether against his judgment. A vague jealousy stirred in him, thinking of that hot blush that had come upon her face. Had any found the mystical secret of influence that escaped himself? Had any more akin to her learned the way to tame and move her? It did not seem possible; she was still so bold, so dauntless, so grave, so innocent. Surely Love had not passed by there?

His heart set itself on winning this halcyon from its subterranean home,—on bringing this flame-winged flamingo from the loneliness of the marsh and the estuary into the world of men.

It was no wise wish, nor was it one easy of fulfilment, but in its very unwisdom and difficulty it dominated him with the same persistence of possession as that with which the desire of her beauty haunted the Sicilian mariner. He did not try to follow her: she had touched his pride when she had called the attempt ungenerous. But he stood motionless, and followed her in thought over the head of the cliff and along that green winter country which stretched between the shore and the tomb of the Lucumo.

Sudden splashes of white rain and the breaking of the clouds

massed southward into storm aroused him. Under the heavy down-
pour from the skies and against the wind he made his tedious way
back to desolate Telamone.

Musa ran home as fast as the little felucca fleet was scudding before the wind to the Trojan cape. Este was looking impatiently upward through the shrubs that screened the entrance.

"How long you have been!" he said, with a little accent of reproach that was almost querulous.

"I will make haste now," she said, humbly, and, without waiting
to change her skirt, still heavy with sea- and rain-water, she began at
once to make a charcoal fire in the bronze which served her for that
purpose.

"I wish you had not to be so constantly away," said Este, as he
watched her at her work. "It is very lonely here. There is not even a
dog."

"What can I do?" she answered him. "You must have food, so
must I. It does not grow on these rocks."

"I know, I know! And I am so useless!"

She was silent as she fanned the charcoal with her breath. She was
wondering whether she had better tell him of the new danger to him
that might arise if Maurice Sanctis should come thither.

But silence was so habitual with her that she doubted the wisdom of any departure from it. Of what use to torment him with a
new dread? She trusted to her own powers of repelling her undesired
friend in so resolute a manner that Sanctis would abandon his at-
tempts to force his companionship and assistance on her. She knew
that he would not come there all that day: amidst her suspicion of
him as so unlike anything she had ever known, her instinct made her
unconsciously do justice to the loyalty of his nature.

"What is a place they call Paris?" she said suddenly to Este, as she
watched his fish roast in the heat from the charcoal.

"It is a great French city," Este answered her. "I was never there. It
is all light and noise and mirth, they say; it is carnival with them all the
year round. They are very great in comedy and spectacle; they are half
Greek and half Harlequin. What made you think of Paris? I would
sooner you saw Mantua, with its water-meadows and it long lines of
reeds, and its dying frescoes, and all the ghosts of the Gonzaga. What
could make you think of Paris? The sea-gulls could not talk to you of it."

"I met a stranger on the shore; he said he was of Paris."

"A stranger? A young man?"

"He is not old."

"Have you seen him before?"

"Yes,—in the summer before you came here. Then he went away, and now he is here again; and you will be very careful, because in the summer he made paintings of these tombs, and it may be that he will come back to do the same."

Then she took the fish from the embers, and served them with a tempting grace on some green leaves on one of the red and black dishes of the Etruscan ware. She took none of them herself; she ate her rough oaten bread with good appetite, whilst she gave a roll of wheaten flour to Este and a draught of wine in the silver *skyphos*.[1]

"I thought you always hid yourself from all eyes," said Este, with some anger, as he looked suddenly at her. "You must have stayed to converse with this man, since you know whence he came."

"I had talked to him in the summer-time. He means no harm; only he must not see you, though I do not think he would speak; do not come so near the entrance as you were to-day."

Este was silent. A new sense stirred in him that was almost a jealous anger. When she was away all through the long hours he had never thought of her as seeing or being seen by any human creature; he knew she hid herself from the shepherd, from the hunter, from the cattle-keeper, from the charcoal-burner, and he had thought these were the only men that ever passed over the moors or came down to the marshes, and that these were scattered and met with but rarely. All in a moment, as he heard her speak of meeting a stranger on the shore, he became suddenly alive to that great personal beauty in her which his mind had languidly acknowledged but his pulse had never quickened to before.

This stranger had been here in the summer and had come again!

All at once he realized that here, growing unnoticed by him in the twilight in the heart of the rocks, was a wild flower that men of science would envy him,—an orchid of the swamps, an amaryllis of the woods, that they would covet for hothouse and hortus siccus in the cities of the world.

"Why do you go out so long and so often?" he said, angrily. "You

---

[1] A drinking cup.

are too young, you are too handsome: you cannot wander as the hare does and the polecat from morn to eve."

She laughed a little.

"I must, or what food should we have? The danger is not for me: it is for you. If any one comes down into these tombs you must hide yourself, and you are not careful enough when I am away."

"Stay, then. Do not go. We can live on bread."

"I can. You cannot."

"I would sooner die of hunger than that you should meet with other men and talk with them and let them see the glory of your eyes." He spoke rather with petulance than with passion. Musa colored a little.

"I did not suppose you cared," she said, and then was silent, not understanding entirely why he was displeased and why his displeasure gave her joy.

"Of course I care! You are all I have!" he said, impetuously, and then paused. He was not sure that he did care; only he was sure that he did not choose for men from the North to meet her on the shore and tell her stories of Paris.

Musa put down some of her bread uneaten, and rose and went towards the stone chamber where Joconda's coffin was, and where he would no more have dared to enter than he would have dared to draw a knife across her throat as Saturnino once had bidden him do if she were troublesome or squeamish.

"I must change my clothes," she said to him, as she moved away. "It rained very hard as I came back; and the rain gives ague, they say, though never yet has it hurt me."

"Stay! have my words frightened you?"

"No. Why should they?"

"Then you care nothing for me!"

"I think you talk idly."

She spoke gravely, with the shadow of some reproach for the first time upon her face.

"Oh, you care,—as saints care for sinners, as wood-nymphs cared for mortals! What is that?"

She might have said to him, "It is your life, at least;" but she answered nothing. She took her hand from the hold of his fingers, and alike without haste and without hesitation passed into the chamber where the dead body of Joconda still gave her its defence, as the sense of holiness in a consecrated place protects the jewels and the silver of an altar from bold hands and covetous eyes.

All that day they spoke little to each other. At daybreak she rose to keep her tryst by the Sasso Scritto. When she crossed the entrance-place, Este stood before the stairs.

"You go to meet that Northern stranger?" he asked.

She looked him straight in the eyes. "Yes: if I do not go, he will come here."

"Let him come. You shall not stir from here."

For a moment her eyes flashed fire. "You could not prevent me if I put out my strength," she said, quietly. "I promised to see him there to prevent him from coming here. If I do not go, I tell you he will come: he will feel that I have not kept faith with him."

"I wish that he should feel that. If you do so, I will go over to Orbitello and give myself up to the law."

"That is madness."

"I swear that I will surrender myself if you meet this man."

He spoke now with both a petulance and a passion that carried truth with them. For the moment he meant what he said; for the moment nothing on earth seemed of any import to him except to keep her there.

She grew pale, and her dauntless temper did not rise in revolt.

"You will make me break my word!" she said, with a wistfulness of appeal in her voice.

"Yes; I will make you break it, or I will keep mine and give myself to the galleys."

"I will not go," she said, with a humility of obedience utterly alien to her nature. "I will not go. But it is folly; and I am afraid that harm will come of it."

"Let come what will," said Este, with a glow of triumph on the pale olive of his cheeks.

He said no more to her, nor she to him.

She occupied herself in the common cares of that cleanliness and order which Joconda had taught her, and with which she kept her strange dwelling-place as heedfully as though it were a palace. She made her bread; she drew fresh water; she prepared a meal of mushrooms and herb broth; then she took her spinning-wheel and sat at it without lifting her eyes from the distaff.

Without, the rain was still falling heavily; the wind was high.

There was no sound on the moors except the rushing of swollen rivulets and the sough of the bay and the arbutus boughs blowing and rustling together; the woodland animals were in their forms, their lairs, their earths; the birds were all tucked away under the leafless willows or the thick ilex-oak foliage.

The rain fell all the day.

She spun on and on; he wove the osiers, as he had learned to do to while away the tedium of the long uncounted hours. Ever and again he watched her with eyes that saw her as though they rested on her for the first time.

It seemed to him that he had been blind. He saw her now as Sanctis saw her,—a creature half divine from strength and innocence united, and with all the fragrance of the woods and all the freshness of the dawn and of the dew about her, and with the mystery of the forest night and the silence of sleeping nature part of her as they were of the nymphs, on whom no mortal looked without madness befalling him, or death.

Disease and weakness and the carking pain of continual apprehension had kept him dull, sightless, half dead; now he was roused and saw, and his dead love drifted away from him and went to join the many ghosts that walk at midnight down the dim ways of Mantua, once the Glorious.

Yet still he knew that he had loved his lady there as he would not have strength or faith in him ever to love again.

CHAPTER XXI.

On the shore, in the wild, wet morning, Maurice Sanctis waited for her in vain.

He was too hardy a mountaineer by birth to heed rainy weather; he sat or stood beside her boat in the cleft in the rocks, and patiently counted the hours as they went by. There was nothing to be seen on sea or land; the one was all mist and wind, the other was obscured by the driving sheets of rain. When noon had gone, he gave up all hope of seeing her that day; he knew she did not fear bad weather, yet he thought it was possible the ink-black skies might have deterred her from coming so far as the Sasso Scritto. "She will be here to-morrow," he said to himself, and went back to the wretchedness of Telamone.

With all the pleasures and successes of the cultured world ready to his hand, he, whose every hour could be rich in creation and ambition, stayed on by choice in the squalor and poverty of a sickly fishing-village,—his days empty, his mind barren, his art neglected, and the world forgotten.

"I am a fool," he said to himself, but the folly grew with him. He had set his heart on saving her from this wild and solitary life, which was endurable only as long as youth and health should last, but even then was hourly filled with a thousand sources of peril and possible evil.

He grew uneasy. It was unlike her nature to fail in what she had promised; she was too grave to be capricious, too tenacious to be deterred by any obstacle or accident from doing what she had said she would do. He saw she had not come there in his absence, for she had not used the little boat, which remained always high and dry upon the shelf of rock, the oars and the fishing-gear lying inside it. For her to be so many days away from the sea, he felt that something unforeseen and serious must have occurred. Any day, a wild boar might turn on her; a false step take her from the narrow path of safety into the slimy slow death of the black bog; the fever that she never feared might yet overtake her, or the lawless fierce men from the mountains find out her dwelling-place under the marucca and myrtle. The soil of Maremma was treacherous as Iago,[1] and, though she made no count of it, her days were full of danger as the timid snipe's for whom the fox waits in the brushwood, and the muzzle of the gun slips through the reeds, and the hawk watches above in the air, the dog steals through the fennel and brancursine. She in her courage and ignorance hardly ever thought of these perils, and trusted to the earth and to the water as a child to its progenitors. But Sanctis, who had thought of them almost unceasingly ever since he had first seen her face, was tormented now by his own imagination.

The people of the coast wondered to see him there, but they supposed he was one of those foreigners who to them seemed half-witted, who endured privations, and penetrated trackless swamps, and asked innumerable questions, in the effort to find buried stones and marbles under the vegetation of Maremma.

---

[1] The villain in Shakespeare's *Othello*.

He spent money willingly and gave no trouble, and understood their boating and their fishing; he had not been unwelcome to them in the summer-time, and he paid largely for the little vessel that he hired and sailed himself.

He went to the Sasso Scritto on three fine mornings when the weather had cleared into the buoyant and transparent brilliancy usual in winter; but Musa did not come. He had thoughts of going on to Orbitello and there obtaining permission of the authorities to see the man who had once been the terror of all travellers and the idol of all Maremma.

He was curious to know and study something of that wild nature whose love of liberty and impatience of control and custom were inherited by her. He took blame to himself that he had not done so in the summer, that he had allowed her intolerance towards him to drive him so soon away from her shores.

He promised himself that with the morrow he would repair his fault. But when that day he reached Telamone, the people of the little town were talking of an event that had happened that night in Orbitello.

Listening to their chatter on the beach, where the aloes pricked through the sand, he heard that Saturnino of Santa Fiora, as the people still called him, had escaped a second time. As they had worked at night on the sea-wall, he had leaped at one bound into the waves, as he had done off the island of Gorgona. The night had been dark from heavy clouds; in the fitful light from the lamps and lanterns he had been lost to sight; though bullets had ploughed the waters and boats been sent out in all directions, he had never been seen again. Sharks were about, and it was guessed that he had met his fate in their jaws.

It was said that one of the jailers, who was a native of the Monte Labbro country, had favored the prisoner by intentional lack of vigilance; but no one suspected of any "complicity with him" the Sicilian brig that had been beating about up and down the coast for some weeks, waiting for a southeasterly wind to bear her back merrily to Messina,—a wind which rose that night.

The few folks of Telamone, loitering out there among the aloes and the sand and the loose stones, once more recalled the long-past time when Saturnino Mastarna had been the hero of every tale that was told on tartana-decks in a calm, or on land in the hot windless weather.

Sanctis listened to their rambling disjointed talk, and gathered the facts out of the loose, redundant words, and a light of comprehension broke in upon him. Saturnino was at large once more; he felt sure that it was in the tombs that he was sheltered. He did not for a moment believe that either the sharks or the sea had killed him: he made no doubt for an instant that her father's presence was her secret, and his danger her anxiety. He grew angry against himself for ever having suspected otherwise, for ever having attributed to that fearless life of hers the passions and the weakness of an amorous secrecy. His heart grew lighter; and he felt that he could not leave her land.

He waited patiently a whole week, willing to have her come of her own accord, if it were possible, rather than rouse her susceptible apprehensions of him as of one who haunted her.

He spent all his time under the great wall of the Sasso Scritto, while the turf leaped up among the rosemary and the waves ran in between the branches of the now leafless rock-rose.

Great ships passed in the offing, their canvas swelling in the wind; yawls and brigs and the tartane of the coast went to and fro in the fresh weather, dipping and showing their copper under the rolling of the seas; now and then a little felucca with her single sail stood off the shore while her men were fishing or out from the bay of Follonica a whole lateen fleet came crowding when the news was told of a shoal of *ragni* or *rombe*[1] seen at sunrise. He waited patiently, with the sea and its vessels before his eyes, and the big white clouds floating above the head of the Sasso Scritto.

But not a soul came there.

Even his patience, which was long, began to give way under the stress of time.

He might wait forever on this shore. He began to think that he was under the sway of Circe,[2] and that these fables after all were not so far from truth.

Then his fears took a more prosaic path, and he began to be alarmed lest any accident of asp-bite or marsh-miasma, of too rash trust to the chill waters of the pools and streams should have befallen

---

[1] Turbot or sea bass.
[2] In *The Odyssey* Circe was an enchantress who detained Odysseus and his crew for a year on her island.

the child of Glaucus,[1] that she came not to the sea, to which he knew her face had turned ever so faithfully, as the face of the sunflower to the west at evening. At last, on the morning of the eighth day, he climbed the cliffs and began to walk across the evergreen water-threaded land above, where the little slender pipes of the robins were sounding under the berry-laden boughs of the bay.

Wild as the country was, and dangerous with bog that moss and couch-grass hid from sight, he remembered by certain landmarks of the tree and tufa-mound and the look of the distant mountains how to find his way back to the tomb of the Lucumo. "She cannot blame me if I go there now," he thought: "she has failed me." His heart burned within him with as much anger and alarm as ever she had felt at his presence. His natural calmness forsook him. He had come in good faith for good offices, and he had been met with indignity.

There was not a disloyal thought in him, and she dealt with him as if he were the hunter and snarer she had called him.

"She shall do me justice ere I go, if I must leave her to her fate," he thought, as he walked on over the soaked turf and cut his way through the *pungente*[2] and the prickly pettygree. His step flushed woodcocks, the partridge flew before him up from her tuft of rosemary, the coots fluttered and splashed as he passed their pools, a pilgrim-falcon sailed by holding a rat in its talons. He was a mountaineer, a hunter on his own Alps, but he never noticed these creatures now. Even, artist though he was, the beauty of the scarlet balls hanging among the glossy leaves of the arbutus, of the red earth glowing under the morning sun, of the brimming streamlets coursing through the grass, of the flocks of white Northern divers settled on the estuaries, of the azure and emerald wings of the kingfisher and the porphyrion flashing amidst the gray net-work of leafless willows,—even these, and all the untellable wonder of color woven there in the shadow and the sunshine as on a web of green and gold, of scarlet and purple, escaped his sight that day.

All he saw were sombre eyes, the color of summer skies at midnight, looking at him with mistrust and disdain, and a mouth, red

---

[1] Glaucus was a mythological fisherman who ate a magical herb. It made him immortal, but it also gave him fins and caused his legs to transform into a fish's tail. He then lived forever in the sea—a Greek sea god.

[2] Prickling, stinging shrubbery.

as the red arbutus-fruit, saying to him, "Though you ask me forever, never will I come."

The way seemed long to him, and his progress slow. Though Musa ran from there to the shore almost as quickly as the hare could do, it was because she knew her way at its shortest, and sprang over the bogs by a leap from tussock to tussock, and over the streams by shallow places that she and the fox alone had found. To him the path was tedious and entangled, and it was past noonday when he at last saw the blasted oak which marked the place of the tombs.

Whilst it was still some distance from him, he saw Musa herself coming across the moor. She had been gathering mushrooms and collecting wood; she had a bundle of dry boughs poised on her head. She walked easily and erect under the burden of it; some amber leaves which were still on the branches hung down and touched her shoulder.

There was nothing in her of the toil that is sorrow and poverty,— of toil as Millet has painted it and modern eyes seen it. Hers was the old, glad, rural, health-giving, open-air labor of the Italiote *pastarella*,[1] of the Greek girl treading with feet winged by youth the honey-scented herbs and the wild ivy of Mount Ida.

The world has lost the secret of making labor a joy; but Nature has given it to a few. Where the maidens dance the *saltarello*[2] under the deep Sardinian forests, and the honey and the grapes are gathered beneath the snowy sides of Etna, and the oxen walk up to their loins in flowing grass where the long aisles of pines grow down the Adrian shore, this wood-magic is known still of the old, sweet, simple charm of the pastoral life.

Some wistful thought of the sort crossed the mind of Sanctis as he saw her approach. After all, what was it he wanted to force on her? Constraint for freedom, formality for fawn-like ease, the breath of crowds for the flower-fragrance of the fields, the midnight oil of anxious study or of feverish pleasure for the gracious night of a slumbering earth fresh with dews, unvexed with noise, stirred only at dawn by whisperings of birds.

For a moment all he had to offer looked poor and trivial. She had

---

[1] A young shepherdess.
[2] A lively dance with jumps and hops.

found the charm that escaped the hands of men when they slew Pan
and drowned his cries in whirr of wheels and scream of steam.

The courage of Maurice Sanctis went out of him as she drew
nigh, the golden leaves touching her lightly-breathing breast. Plato's
self could have found no plea to urge the hamadryad to leave her
groves, the maid to forsake her fountain. At first she had not seen him,
for there was a screen of carob boughs and withered bracken between
himself and her. When she did perceive that he was there, a great and,
it appeared to him, utterly inconsistent and disproportionate trouble
and anger came together into her speaking eyes.

She stopped short; she did not speak.

He approached her, and said, with his usual gentleness,—

"I was afraid some ill had happened to you. It was not like you to
break your word."

"I could not come," she said, with some hesitation. "I thought
you would understand when you did not see me, and that you would
go away."

"I asked you to hear me once, for Joconda's sake."

"I could not come," she repeated, impatiently; "and I do not want
to hear. I told you so."

"I know you do not," he said, with regret; "and I can fancy that
you are reluctant to leave your woodland life. It is free and has a beauty of its own; but it needs perpetual youth and a certainty of health
that are not given to our poor humanity."

"I shall be young a long time," said Musa, with her grave smile;
and she drew a deep breath with the conscious strength of perfect
powers of life rejoicing in themselves.

"Yes; no doubt to you it seems that you have a kingdom there
that you can never lose. But it will go away from you as it goes from
all; and water and wind and weather bring its loss early. Do you never
think of a future?"

"No," she answered, curtly. A shudder went over her for a moment. What might the future bring? Could Este always be saved from
his pursuers? Would the time come when all her care and thought and
vigilance and sacrifice would be unavailing to shelter him?

"But Joconda would have bidden you think," he urged to her. "She
herself thought for you, or she would not have written to us. I know
that the life you have made for yourself, all alone as you have been, is
full of courage and strength, and has much nobility of purpose and of

independence in it; and I can understand that it seems more delightful to you than any other, because of your wise love of the open air and the beasts and the birds. But, dear, it is winter even here; and if sickness should overtake you your solitude would become very terrible. I want you to think a little of that. You have no friends, you have no home, you have no one to look to in any need; and there are dangers for a creature that is as beautiful as you are when she is so near womanhood."

He paused, not knowing well how to put his meaning into words that her pride would hear patiently or her innocence understand.

"I have no one who has a right to say a word to me," said Musa, angrily. "If that is what you mean, you say truly; and you should know by that to hold your peace and not to importune me."

"I do not wish to importune you," said Sanctis in his turn, a little moved from his long patience; "but the wishes of the dead are sacred,—to me at the least. A woman, now dead, wrote to her brothers on your behalf, and I am their representative. As I have their name and their fortune, so I have their duties. I should be unworthy of them if I refused to accept the last as well as the first. You are too young to know what perils you run, what a frightful future you prepare for yourself. If you will not hear me willingly, I must try what aid the law will give me. Before the law you are an outcast, and it would deprive you of independence, it would regard your dwelling-place as nothing better than the owl's hole or the fox's earth; it would certainly compel you to accept some other asylum. If I go to the authorities of Orbitello———"

He paused in words which he was using as his last resource without fully knowing what they meant, or how far they would lead him; for Musa, as she stood before him, suddenly changed from a listening, angry child into a pythoness, a lioness, a very incarnation of every shape of rage that the earth has ever seen upon it. She snatched from her girdle her long two-edged knife; she cast down her brambles and branches from her head; she leaped to within an inch of him and flashed the steel before his eyes. All the savage blood of the Mastarna of Saturnia leaped up in her, like a naphtha flame from the soil.

"Unless you swear to me that you will never breathe a word of my name or of my dwelling, I will kill you where you stand," she said, as her eyes flashed their sombre fires into his; and her voice was not loud, but low and deep, like the lioness's voice of menace. Her whole frame seemed alive with rage, as a tree, lightning-struck, is alive with the electric fluid; but it was a rage that would strike as it threatened, not a rage that would die of its own violence.

So intense a surprise seized him that he for the moment could say nothing, and did not move. They gazed into each other's faces.

"Will you swear it?" she said, her voice still low, but as fierce as a snake's hissing. "If you will not, you shall not leave this place alive. You are a man and strong; but you are unarmed, and I can kill you."

She kept her eyes fixed on him, and her hand clinched on the stiletto. She had no fear nor any sense of sin; all conscience and all judgment were drowned in the flood of one passionate instinct,—to save Este.

For herself she would not have so spoken. But for him she was ready to do the thing she threatened. Why would this meddler come unasked and undesired and thrust himself before her in these green glades that were all her own? She turned on him as the boar turns on his pursuers.

He did not move. For a moment he thought of wresting the knife from her; then he knew her strength and her tenacity; the manhood in him recoiled from a struggle with a woman who was scarce more than a child.

"I think you would kill me if you wished to do it," he said, gently, and with the sadness that he felt. "I am stronger than you, but you are like the lightning of the skies; you would find your way to cut the cord of my life somehow. But I am not an utter coward, my dear; and I cannot promise or swear you anything under a threat. Put the point of your knife against my heart if you like, but listen to me for a moment."

Musa gripped her stiletto the tighter, but she did not move it nearer to him.

She understood what he meant, that he could not say what she wished under a menace. All courageous instincts found their echo in her.

"You must say that you will speak of me to no living soul," she said, slowly, "or I cannot let you go alive out of these woods. It is not that I want to hurt you, but that if you will not be silent any other way I must silence you so: that is all."

"And you would do it," he said, for he did not for a moment underrate the unblenching determination that was in her, nor the ferocity of the wild blood in her when once aroused. "But hearken one moment."

"I will not. You wish to betray me. That is vile. I will have no more words."

"Betray is a bitter thing to say. I am no traitor. I meant only that since you throw yourself away, and all your future, in a barren and a dangerous life, I should do no more than my duty if I sought the aid of the law, which would protect you in your own despite, and to which you would in time grow grateful."

"That is betrayal. I have told you that rather than you should live to do it——"

Her eyes were full of fire; her breath came and went through her clinched teeth; an agony of fear made her ferocious; her hand, as it closed on the handle of the stiletto, trembled with passion; all the mercilessness of Saturnino was up and alive in her.

She longed to strike down this man who menaced her secret and her treasure.

Had he not been kindred to Joconda, she would have struck, without giving him a choice.

"Do not *make* me kill you!" she muttered behind her shut teeth.

He disregarded her words. He said, abruptly,—

"Tell me one thing: you are not alone now?"

She was silent.

"Is that why you menace me?"

"What is that to you?"

"You say always, What is it to me! Well, it is much; more than you know, or would understand if you did know. I think you are the loveliest creature upon earth, and your ferocity does not disgust me. It becomes you; and it is natural, being what you are. I want to take you out of all your ignorance, your peril, your barbaric liberties, and make of you the noble woman that you might become. I have no other motive. I would neither wrong you nor the dead; and you are so young; but if you be not alone, if there be another——"

"It is nothing to you," said Musa, with passion and with desperation. "It is nothing to you what I am or what I have."

"You are not alone any longer," he said, with his gaze trying to penetrate hers.

"Why should you say so?"

"Because you care too little for yourself, and are too generous to wish to kill me if it were only yourself who was disturbed by my interference."

He kept his eyes fixed on her as he spoke: what he thought was that she sheltered Saturnino. She did not change color or give any sign of the intense agitation that was in her.

"Very well, then; think so," she said, between her shut teeth. "Think anything you please; but leave me to myself."

"I cannot promise that. I should feel a coward if I did. I cannot leave you to yourself, for you are your own worst enemy,"

She was silent; she was thinking sternly and unflinchingly, as her father had often thought of his foes, how she was to be rid of this man who would be Este's ruin. All life had been sacred to her in the birds and the beasts around her; but now it seemed to her that she would have no choice but to take his, since he would persist and rush upon his doom. She had been frank with him and rude; she had warned him, she had refused him, she had done all she could to turn him aside from what appeared to her his persecution of her, and he would not be persuaded. There seemed no choice for her but to turn on him as the boar was forced to turn on those who drove him from the shelter of his bed of bracken and his screen of oaks.

He had menaced her with the law, and what would the law on herself mean but the discovery, the seizure, the eternal misery of the one for whom she was giving all her own life without counting it as sacrifice?

"Will you let me come with you to the tombs?" said Sanctis, with entreaty in his voice. "Beside Joconda's coffin I do not think you would be at war with me like this. I could make you understand———"

"I understand well enough. You want to give me up to the law, though I have done no ill. And I have said that you shall never do it."

"Will you let me go home with you one moment?"

"No. I will never take you there again."

"Because you are no longer alone?"

"You have threatened to betray me. That is reason enough."

Her eyes never ceased to keep their lioness-like watch on him; her hand never relaxed its hold upon the stiletto. He was of Joconda's kindred: that was the only thought that made her pause, and give him one more chance.

"You must promise me, swear to me," she said, passionately, "or you will make me kill you. I cannot let you go to bring the law you boast of as your helper. If first of all Zirlo had not betrayed me to you, you would never have had the power to betray me again yourself. I am not unjust to you; if you are a traitor you deserve a traitor's death, and I would give it to you,—yes, though I tracked you for twenty years over one-half the earth."

He looked at her with perplexity and admiration. He had lived all his years in the midst of cultured and controlled communities, where the passions were tamed and the inborn ferocity of the human animal was scarcely visible; he had been reared among pious and reserved people, and his manhood had been spent amidst men whose minds were steeped in light and art, and who had little of the natural brute left in them. This intensity of purpose, this readiness for fierce action if by no other means its ends could be attained, this constancy in vengeance which would wait through half a lifetime rather than forego punishment,—these, the qualities of an earlier time, of a simpler and freer world than his, fascinated him by their force and their absolute unlikeness to anything in his own life. The sense of impotence that she had felt before his Northern calmness and tenacity now fell on him before her more spontaneous and more violent nature: he felt that he might as well have tried to change the course of volcanic lava as endeavor to sway or alter her or ever make her regard him as a friend.

He looked at her, and through his mind passed many images and memories to which she had so much likeness. She belonged to the soil; she was one with it; she had its fierce suns and its fierce storms in her nature. Here on this coast, where the Dea Syria had been worshipped with madness and mutilation, where Cybele had been adored with flame and sacrifice, where earlier yet Mantus and Orcus had been propitiated with the palpitating hearts of scarce-dead victims, and the tempest and the hurricane had been charged with the dread messages of the gods, here she alone seemed to live, the last echo and shadow of those vanished years, of those forgotten religions, of those changed or perished races.

To him she seemed less a living soul of his own time than some young priestess of Isis, some vision in which Lydia and Latium both lived, eternally young, preserved in the secrecy of these forests, without change, whilst all the rest of earth grew old.

What could he say to her?

How could he hope to alter her?

Who could ever have wooed Pan from his thymy nest, and Glaucus from his cool sea-depths? and who should win her from their woods and waters that she alone enjoyed now that Glaucus and Pan were dead?

He felt himself powerless and humbled, as the artificial world is always before the strength and the simplicity of the sylvan life that has none of its necessities.

A sigh escaped him. She was dearer to him than he knew, and he felt that he could no more hold her than he could have held the fires of Vesuvius in his hand. He knew that he could no more bind and influence her than the shepherds and the mariners of old could capture Pan and Glaucus.

"Well," he said, slowly, at the last, "I will not seek to force your secrets, and I will even dare to seem a coward to you. It may be the truer courage, and perhaps one day it is as such that you will see it. I promise you that I will not seek alien aid or bring the law you abhor to my assistance. So much I will promise you, though I do not see why you should trust my word, since you mistrust myself."

"I thought no one ever broke their promise," said Musa: in such good faith the woman of Savoy had reared her.

"Well; think so. I do not; and you may trust me. I will speak to no one of you, or of the sepulchres that shelter you. But at the same time I do not promise you to renounce all effort to change you by my own persuasion if we meet in the neutral solitudes of these moors or on the shore. I do not promise yet to go away."

"I cannot send you away," she said, with the dusky fire of her eyes still luminous. "But you will not come to me?"

"No; since I am unwelcome."

She slipped her stiletto back into its hiding-place, and stooped and replaced the boughs and brambles on her head.

"That is enough," she said. "But it will be better that you should go: me you will never see."

"You cannot prevent my seeing you abroad?"

She smiled a little at his stupidity.

"You will no more see me than you can see the dwarf-heron when he makes himself into the likeness of a dead stump and sits, all gray and brown, among the sedges. You do not know the wisdom of the woods."

Before the last word had reached his ear she was away, and was soon lost to sight beyond a dense wall of arbutus and mastic.

She knew the wisdom of the woods herself as well as the bittern or the great plover knows it. Sanctis retraced his steps with a heavy heart, seeing nothing in the blue pale light of the wintry day but her face as it had been raised to his while her hand had played with the steel. He was discouraged and discomfited, and a sense of painful defeat and mortification was upon him: she had threatened his life, and he had yielded to her. He was a man of courage enough to bear to look a coward if it were needful to do so, yet it hurt him as he went away to think that no doubt as she was going through the leafless woodlands and the green bay thicket she was thinking of him with contempt, perhaps with laughter. But his nature was calm and very patient. He knew that he had been unwise to use the menace of the law to her, and that her menace of the knife had been but her natural reply. He promised himself to do better, to speak more tranquilly when next he sued her; for her threat that he should never see her had passed by his ear unheeded.

That she was not alone he believed, but since he had heard of the second escape of Saturnino Mastarna he had felt little doubt but that her father had sought her out in the tombs and claimed her shelter by making himself known to her. He did not think her savage pride and her stern self-dependence compatible with any other secret.

She, who to Este was gentle and soft as the cushat to her mate, by him had been always seen untamable and shy and fierce as any one of the dwarf-herons that she defied him to discover by the pools.

On the mountain-side above San Lionardo, set well above the miasma and rain-mists of the marshes, there was an old castellated place, called Præstanella, half villa and half fortress, which from the ninth to the thirteenth century had been a mighty stronghold, changing hands often in the internecine wars that ravaged the Massa Maritima. Later on it had been less of a fortress and had taken some of the characteristics of a mountain-villa, having terraced gardens made before its machicolated walls and hundreds of acres of wood behind and around it. It now belonged to a noble family who had many such places. It was neglected and half dismantled. No one cared to come to it; stewards ate in its tapestried halls and peasants made pig-sties of its long vaulted corridors.

Maurice Sanctis had wandered over it in the first days that he had

stayed in Maremma: the glory of its views, the intensity of its loneliness, and its war-scarred towers and weed-grown terraces pleased
him. Money was nothing to him; his father Anton had left him very
rich, and he had simple tastes that cost him little. He thought to himself now that he would buy this place: the price was a mere trifle,
hardly more than the value of the pine woods about its bastions. It
was melancholy, and had been stripped of all its carvings, marbles,
and tapestries long before; but the magnificence of its landscape and
the solidity of its walls nothing but an earthquake could destroy.

That night he went to Grosseto and there saw the notary who
had been charged with its sale for twenty years and more. To the rich
an easy path is soon made. He was promised that in a week or two at
the uttermost this old fortress on the Apennines should be made over
to him with all formality and security, a true eagle's nest set up on
high, and from its heights commanding all the deep green vales, and
the asphodel meadows, and the reedy marshes, where of old Etrurian
and Italiote, Roman and Goth, mercenary of Bourbon and soldier of
Borgia, free-lance of Florence and horseman of Massa, had turn by
turn made the earth a field of death.

CHAPTER XXII.

IT was now near the turn of the new year, and the earth was green as
an emerald, though it was midwinter, with the forests of holm-oak
and pine, and the dense growth of laurel, of box, of bear-berry, of
alaternus, of pyracantha.

In the late afternoon, as darkness closed in without, she and Este
sat in the larger chamber of the Lucumo's bier.

The fire burned; the lamp was lighted; she sat once again at her
spinning, whilst he was modelling clay that she had brought for him
from the bed of the Ombrone. He had that facile skill in the arts which
is the gift, and often, also, the curse, of his countrymen, since it is too
readily skilled at imitation to be often capable of original creation.
It passed the weary hours for him to mould the clay with his hands
and such rude instruments as he had been able to fashion out of the
bronze Etruscan *spillæ* and knives found in the tombs. He thought,
too, that the time might come when she would be able to sell them

for a trifle in some town; and he would thus be able to bring his quota to their maintenance.

He had modelled, in the gray river-earth, flowers and fruits and oak-leaves, all forest things she brought him; the Typhon, and the Chimæra, and the lotus-lilies of the walls around him; but, oftenest of all, the head of Musa. Sometimes he made her with the lotus on her brow, like that Braschi Antinoüs she resembled; sometimes he set the sacred hawk of Egypt upon her head, as it had been set upon Cleopatra's; sometimes he took her in her own simplicity, with no wreath but her own curls, and her woollen gown still cut like the tunics of Della Robbia's choristers, drawn close up around her slender, rounded throat; and often, as he did so, the features and the eyes of the woman murdered in Mantua would come before him, and sometimes the bust changed despite his own will, and had a likeness in it to his dead love that he would fain have blurred out and could not; and then again, also, there would be, do what he could, a reproach in the eyes and a sternness in the mouth which so annoyed him that he would dash the earth out of all shape, and leave it in a heap upon the stone floor of the tomb.

To her, all these things that he did seemed marvellous and exquisite. To be able to take a lump of mud from the stream, and make it fair, in the likeness of flower or bird or human face, seemed to her a power and possession as wonderful as his knowledge of the past of perished nations. It was the first time she had been ever touched by the sorcery of the arts,—the true magicians.

She would look at the likeness of herself with a grave smile; she was proud to be like that. Then she would turn her eyes away.

"Joconda always bade me think nothing of how I was made," she said once.

Este always heard her speak of Joconda with impatience.

"I told you the first day I saw you," he said to her, "that one could say of you what the angel Gabriel in Boccaccio's story, says to Madonna Lisa."

"I do remember," said Musa, with a sudden flush upon her face. "But the very day, when I looked in the steel mirror because you had said so, a scorpion ran across the mirror; and I believe that Joconda sent it,—to remind me."

"You keep her memory about you like a knotted cord of penitence!"

"No, no," said Musa, softly; "like a little bit of sweet basil, that keeps away the evil eye."

Este heard with no sympathy.

Without distinctly knowing it himself, it was just that "bit of sweet basil" that he desired to pluck out of her hold,—which held him aloof from her, and surrounded her with an invisible defence.

It was that sweet basil set against her breast which made her so unlike his dead love in Mantua, whose beauty had dropped to his wooing as the ripe nectarine drops at a touch off the sunny south wall.

It was but five or six o'clock; accurate time they could only keep by listening for the Ave Maria bells, morning and evening, from the monasteries on the mountain-side and the village churches down the distant shore. The stone doors of the Lucumo's chamber were shut close, but there was no lock or bar, from their inability to make either, and in the stead of those they relied on their quick ears and their unceasing apprehension of approach.

But in this early evening hour, as the freshly-lighted heather and pine cones crackled and blazed, and the coldness and the gloom of the wintry night closed in upon the country above them, suddenly she lifted her head and met his eyes fixed on her in angry and suspicious contemplation. She conquered her habit of silence, so long fostered by Joconda, and spoke to him.

"Perhaps it is better you should know: he who comes from Paris, and who wished me to meet him that other day, is a son of Joconda's nephew, Anton Sanctis. They were poor, but he is rich."

Then she went on to tell him, in her terse and simple diction, of the coming of Maurice Sanctis, through the letter of Joconda's dictation written by the public scrivener in Grosseto.

Este heard without response, his hands all the while shaping the clay; the lids drooped over his pensive eyes.

A confusion of anger, dismay, and jealous apprehension made him hear with disordered mind; he kept thinking only, "She will go; sooner or later, she will go."

He had heard enough of Paris to know that it is to all women who have the chance of it an irresistible paradise and perdition,—a phosphorescent whirlpool in which all their barques swim giddily and go down, one in a thousand escaping.

For a moment he saw her in his fancy taken there, as a wild forest animal is taken to the light and noise and glitter of the circus. What would not an artist make of that beauty that was at once Greek and Lydian, at once classic and Oriental, at once so vivid and serene? What would she be like, with jewels on her smooth transparent skin where the blood mounted so readily beneath the golden brown, with her great eyes wide opened, astonished at the world? Would he set pearls about her throat, and a red amaryllis at her breast, and take her there where all the multitudes of rich and idle life could see her, in some great circle of some dazzling amphitheatre?

All in a moment he saw her as she would look,—Penthesilea in chains of gold; the nymphæa alba of the forest waters in a hot-house; the pilgrim-falcon hooded and jessed with silk for sport.

"If he be rich, why should you not go where he asks?" he said, without raising his eyes from their work.

The question hurt her, though in her own simplicity and integrity of purpose she saw no insult in it.

"I would never leave Maremma," she said, as she had said to Sanctis.

"Never is a word; you are a woman. Your 'never' will be as long as a summer day,—no longer. Maremma is accursed, your home is but a tomb; you will go———"

"I shall not go," she answered, while melancholy and impatience came upon her face. Did he understand her so little? Did he so little believe?

She clung to her own old land as the firefly clings to its field of corn, knowing of, and wishing for, no other share of earth.

"Is he rich,—rich indeed?" he asked again.

"What is it to me?" she answered. "He says so. He must be, no doubt, for he does no work, merely makes pictures, such as they put over the altars in Santa Tarsilla and Telamone. Let us say no more of him. I only told you because I thought it best that you should know."

"You will think more of him," said Este, with sullen insistence. "He will tell you of Paris till you will want to go; you will learn to forget Maremma, and to forget me."

"You speak foolishly. Even the birds do not forget; year after year they build in the same place. Am I less worthy than they?"

"He will talk to you till he makes you go," persisted Este; "and why should you not? You are not made to stay by me in the twilight, here, forever. I am but a felon, and this is but a grave. Elsewhere there are worlds full of light, of sound, of stir, of color; you will go to them and look at them with your mysterious eyes that have all the night in them,—the night that means silence, and dreams, and love,—and they will not understand you, because you come from the depths of the forest and are not as they are; but they will adore you, they will crown you, they will flatter you, till you will no more remember Maremma than you think now of the sand that clung to your feet yesterday as you came from the sea————"

"I shall never go; therefore shall I never forget," she said, simply, unmoved by the visions that were framed in his words.

She was sorry he understood so little; he seemed to her to speak foolishly and thanklessly.

"Have I once failed him?" she thought. "Have I once tired, that he thinks me so poor a thing?"

"Why should you not go?" he said, obstinately. "Why should you stay?"

"Why does the snipe stay in her reeds, and the mountain-dove cling to her rock?"

He was silent awhile. Then he rose and pushed the clay aside, and came nearer to her.

"The snipe has her mate, and the rock-dove too," he said, with a soft murmur of his voice. "But you—you do not love me, though you befriend me so."

A troubled look came into her eyes, and she left off her spinning.

"You love the woman in Mantua," she said, almost sternly; this Mantuan memory hurt her, although love was in no way distinct to her, and although when she used its name she still understood little of its passion.

"Yes," said Este, with a quick sigh and shudder. "But that past is past. She cost me dear. Her memory is only terrible————"

"Is that love?" said Musa, with a scornful smile upon her mouth. It seemed to her very poor.

"It was ours," he answered. "We had a summer night; then tempest. The storm wrecked us. Oh, I loved her,—yes. For months I never looked at you; do you not remember? Now that I look, now that I see, you bid me be blind."

"I do not understand," she said, troubled and confused. "If you loved her, that was forever. Just because she is dead, is that a reason to change? Why should you look at me? I serve you. I do what I can; you are safe with me; that is all you want, since liberty you cannot have."

"No; liberty and I have said farewell. My life must pass in a prison, here or elsewhere. But you may make the prison so fair that I shall deem it one no longer. You serve me, yes; but do more, love me. In a way you do, I know; but it is not that way which will content me. You are not a dog, nor a servant, like those two whose ashes lie in the entrance there. You must give me more than dogs and slaves can give, faithful and tender though they be. Oh, my dear, love is given us to make a sunshine in this gloomy place. The mountain-doves you talk of do not dwell apart———"

He glided to her feet and sat there, and drew the distaff away from her and gazed at her with caressing eyes that subdued her and poured trouble into her heart.

"We are happy as we are," she murmured. "Do not look so! No; you are not happy: I forgot. But I thought it was always for Donna Aloysia you sorrowed———"

"Let the dead be. We live!" said Este, with sudden passion, as his arms enclosed her and his face drooped towards her breast.

But she, with a sudden movement of alarm and anger that were rather at herself than at him, thrust him away, and rose with abrupt rapidity.

"You hurt me," she said, feverishly, and with the first personal fear that she had ever known. "Oh, I have been so happy!———"

The tears rushed into her eyes. She did not know what ailed her. Some great impending loss seemed to hang over her.

"Dear, there is more happiness than that," he murmured. "You have known but the daybreak: I will lead you to the noon. Are you afraid of *me*?"

His hand stole towards her, his eyes magnetized her, his lips approached her.

For the first time she shrank from him.

"Let me go; let me think," she said, faintly.

Neither of them heard a step come over the moist ground above, and descend the steps, and pass the entrance-chamber. Before either had been warned by the slightest sound, one of the rock doors was thrust open, and through its aperture there came Maurice Sanctis.

They sprang to their feet, and the hand of each went quick as thought to the haft of a knife; but before they could move, or even think, he cried, quickly,—

"Wait! I come in warning. Men from the hills, from San Lionardo, mean to visit you to-night. They have a fancy that gold is hidden in the tomb. I overheard them: so I came."

He was out of breath from the haste he had made; the night-dews clung about him. His eyes, even as he spoke, were staring in blank amaze upon Este.

Este himself stood erect, white to the lips with overpowering fear; but as he met the gaze of another man, the old chivalric blood that ran in his veins compelled him to conquer fear, and with dignity, even amidst his terror of discovery, and with a patrician's grace, he put Musa aside as she sprang towards the stranger, and himself advanced a step.

"I am Count Luitbrand d'Este," he said, simply. "If you be my enemy, you can give me up: I am a runaway felon."

There was silence between them for a moment; the grasp of his hand on her wrist held Musa motionless, and her hatred and her anguish alone spoke to the other through her eyes.

"Count Luitbrand d'Este," said Maurice Sanctis, at length, with a voice that he had hard pains to control, for his heart was beating in tumult against his ribs, "I know nothing of you: I am not a hunter of men. I heard what I said awhile ago on the hills; the men will come here after Ave Maria————"

"Go out," said Musa to Este. "Hide under the shrubs till I call you: I will wait and give them welcome."

She did not even look at Sanctis; she heard the words of warning, thinking of Este, taking their sense by instinct, but without attention to their speaker.

"I will not leave you. Can you think me so poor a creature?" he answered; the presence of another man stung the dulled spirit in him into life.

"What of me?" she cried, with agony of entreaty. "I will show them that there is no gold; then they will go. But if they see you——"

"Go, both of you," said Sanctis, sternly. "Since you dwell here together go together: I will stay and receive these men. When I have dismissed them you can return; I, too, shall be gone."

"Why should you do this? Why should you think of us?" said Este.

"I do not think of you. I do not know you. I came to warn her, to save her from insult and violence, for when the men find there is no gold they will be brutal. She will have told you of me: I am the grandson of the brother of Joconda——"

"You are generous," said Este.

There was a tone in the words that drew fire from the calm eyes of Sanctis as steel does from the flint-stone.

"It does not matter what I am," he said, with effort keeping his patience. "What matters now is the loss of a moment. These hill-men come on a devil's errand in hope to get man's godhead. Let them find me here alone. They will find with me dogs that bite."

He showed the steel of his pistols that he wore in a belt about his waist.

She broke from Este, and came up to Sanctis, and gazed at him with passionate, imploring, searching eyes that tried to read his inmost soul.

"You will not betray him?" she said, under her breath. "Now you know why I said that I must kill you if you told!"

Sanctis drew away from her.

"I am not a spy of the State," he said, coldly. "You may be satisfied of that."

She looked at him in silence.

She did not doubt him, yet she was afraid.

A secret once disclosed is like a bird once loosed: who can say where it may go?

"Go, and take him with you," added Sanctis, with a certain harshness in his tone. "I shall not betray him; but these men, once they see him, will."

"We had better stay," urged Este. "We have both daggers; we can do something——"

"There must be nothing of that sort," said Sanctis, with cold indifference. "If blood were shed, the hue and cry would be out over the country and the guards here. The men will go when I speak to them."

"It must be the father of Zirlo!" said Musa, between her teeth. "I will wait; but go, go, go: if the men of San Lionardo see you, the carabineers of Telamone will be here to-night."

Sanctis laid a hand on her shoulder with an imperious gesture.

"Go out into the dark and hide,—you and your friend: you have 'the wisdom of the woods,' you say; use it. When I sound this whistle three times, it will be safe for you to return. Go; or you will have the men down on you—and him."

A quick shudder of cold, like an ague, passed over her as he spoke of Este's danger. She dropped her head on her breast and drew Este towards the inner chambers with both hands.

"He is right," she said. "Come, O my love! Come!"

Even in that moment of supreme peril and fear, the eyes of Este shone with a great triumph.

He glanced at Sanctis; then went.

CHAPTER XXIII.

SANCTIS, left alone in the chamber of the Lucumo, heard the sound of their retreating steps as they passed across the other cells and began to ascend the rocks without.

Then he sat down on the stone bier where the Etruscan prince had lain in his golden armor, and placed his pistols beside him.

He had received so great a shock that it seemed to him as if the very pulse of his life had stopped; but he was quite calm, and he listened for the sounds without with the fine ear that was his mountaineer's heritage.

As he had walked down through the woods that afternoon from Præstanella, he had overheard a scheme discussed between the father of Zeffirino and two charcoal-burners of the oak forests below San Lionardo. Their plan was to come, some dozen in force, and plunder the tombs, and treat the dweller there better or worse, according as she yielded to them or resisted.

"She will resist," Zeffirino's father had said with a laugh, "and then—well, there are dead there already; and who will know?"

Then the minds of the men had inflamed themselves with mad hopes of uncountable treasure and unearthly beauty.

"They do say she is the daughter of Lucifero," they muttered one to another.

So much he had heard, passing by unseen in his gray clothes among the gray tangle of leafless branches and tall-growing rosemary.

He sat still and waited for them, and rested his eyes whilst he did so on the clay busts that wore the likeness of Musa.

"He has been here long," he thought.

With his eye trained to perceive beauty in the lowliest flower, the most fleeting phase of nature, he had rendered instant justice to the personal beauty of Este, to his supple panther-like grace, to his patrician air, to his face that was such as Lionardo might have seen in a vision of Adonaïs.

He understood everything now.

He smiled once, bitterly.

"Poor Joconda!" he thought: "of what use was it to stretch a dead hand from the grave?"

Then he remembered that Joconda's body was lying there, within a few feet of him.

The remembrance subdued the sardonic bitterness which was coupled with his pain.

He sat still there, and time went on, and the evening deepened into night.

He needed to ask no question.

He had seen the printed notice all along the coast, offering the government reward for the apprehension of Luitbrand d'Este. One glance at Este's face and hers had told him all he had to know.

He guessed the whole story, and he understood why she had guarded her secret so fiercely and had threatened his own life under her terror of the law.

He remembered when he had passed through Italy two years before, when on his way eastward, pausing in Ferrara, and Brescia, and Mantua, and staying longer in the latter city on account of a trial then in course of hearing in the court of justice, which had interested him by its passionate and romantic history: it had been the trial of the young Count d'Este, accused of the assassination of his mistress. Sanctis had gone with the rest of the town to the hearing of the long and tedious examination of witnesses and of accused.

It had been a warm day in early autumn, three months after the night of the murder; Mantua had looked beautiful in her golden mantle of sunshine and silver veil of mist; there was a white, light fog on the water-meadows and the lakes, and under it the willows waved and the tall reeds rustled, whilst the dark towers, the forked battlements, the vast Lombard walls, seemed to float on it like sombre vessels on a foamy sea.

He remembered the country-people flocking in over the bridge,

the bells ringing, the red sails drifting by, the townsfolk gathering together in the covered arcades and talking with angry rancor against the
dead woman's lover. He remembered sitting in the hush and gloom
of the judgment-hall, and furtively sketching the head of the prisoner
because of its extreme and typical beauty. He remembered how at the
time he had thought this accused man guiltless, and wondered that
the tribunal did not sooner suspect the miserly, malicious, and subtle
meaning of the husband's face. He remembered listening to the tragic
tale that seemed so well to suit those sombre, feudal streets, those
melancholy waters, seeing the three-edged dagger passed from hand
to hand, hearing how the woman had been found dead in her beauty,
on her old golden and crimson bed, with the lilies on her breast, and
looking at the attitude of the prisoner,—in which the judges saw remorse and guilt, and he could only see the unutterable horror of a
bereaved lover to whom the world was stripped and naked.

He had stayed but two days in Mantua, but those two days had
left an impression on him like that left by reading at the fall of night
of some ghastly poem of the Middle Ages. He had thought then that
they had condemned an innocent man, as the judge gave his sentence of the galleys for life; and the scene had often come back to his
thoughts.

The vaulted audience-chamber; the strong light pouring in
through high grated windows; the pillars of many-colored marbles;
the frescoed roof; the country-people massed together in the public
place, with faces that were like paintings by Mantegna or Masaccio;
the slender supple form of the accused drooping like a bruised lily
between the upright figures of two carabineers; the judge leaning
down over his high desk in black robes and black square cap, like some
Venetian lawgiver of Veronese or of Titian; and beyond, through the
open casement, the silvery, watery, sun-swept landscape that was still
the same as when Romeo came, banished, to Mantua:—all these had
remained impressed upon his mind by the tragedy which there came
to its close as a lover, passionate as Romeo and yet more unfortunate,
was condemned to the galleys for his life.

"They have ill judged a guiltless man," he had said to himself as he
had left the court with a sense of pain before injustice done, and gone
with heart saddened by a stranger's fate into the misty air, along the
shining water where the Mills of the Twelve Apostles were churning
the great dam into froth, as they had done through seven centuries,

since first, with reverent care, the builder had set the apostle statues there that they might bless the grinding of the corn.

Sitting now in the silence of the tomb, Sanctis recalled that day, when, towards the setting of the sun, he had strolled there by the water-wheels of the twelve disciples, and allowed the fate of an unknown man, declared a criminal by impartial judges, to cloud over for him the radiance of evening on the willowy Serraglio and chase away his peaceful thoughts of Virgil. He remembered how the country-people had come out by the bridge and glided away in their boats, and talked of the murder of Donna Aloysia and the sentence of Luitbrand d'Este; and how they had, one and all of them, said, going back over the lake-water or along the reed-fringed roads to their farm-houses, that there could be no manner of doubt about it, the lover had been moonstruck and mad with jealousy, and his dagger had found its way to her breast. They had not blamed him much; but they never doubted his guilt; and the foreigner alone, standing by the mill gateway, and seeing the golden sun go down beyond the farthermost fields of reeds that grew blood-red as the waters grew, at that hour thought to himself and said, half aloud,—

"Poor Romeo! he is guiltless, even though the dagger were his——"

And a prior, black-robed, with broad looped-up black hat, who was also watching the sunset, breviary in hand, had smiles and said, "Nay, Romeo, banished to us, had no blood on his hand; but this Romeo of our city, has. Mantua will be not rid of Luitbrand d'Este."

Then he again, in obstinacy and against all the priest's better knowledge as a Mantuan, had insisted and said, "The man is innocent."

And the sun had gone down as he had spoken, and the priest had smiled,—a smile cold as a dagger's blade,—perhaps recalling sins confessed to him of love that had changed to hate, of fierce delight ending in as fierce a death-blow. Mantua in her day has seen so much alike of love and hate.

"The man is innocent," he had said insisting, whilst the carmine light had glowed on the lagoons and bridges, and on the Lombard walls, and Gothic gables, and high bell-towers, and ducal palaces, and feudal fortresses of the city in whose street Crichton[1] fell before the hired steel of bravoes.

"The man is innocent," he had said that night in Mantua; and now once more he had looked upon him, and his innocence seemed no longer to him clear as then.

The priest, no doubt, he mused now, knew better than he, a prior of Mantua as he was, and able to judge aright the lover of Donna Aloysia. To live here, sheltering himself by ruin to the one who aided him; to live here, defended by a girl's love, maintained by a girl's labors:—was this not as guilty a thing as to have struck the dagger through the lilies at that Mantuan woman's breast? And baser, perhaps, because less bold than it.

To Sanctis it seemed so, at the least, in this first hour of overwhelming surprise, of extreme bitterness, of intense disappointment and chagrin. To him the savage purity of her life had been sacred; he had believed in it undoubtingly. To him she had been a vestal, a dryad, Penthesilea, Maia, Britomart, everything strong, pure, heroic, virginal, steeped in innocence as the flowers were steeped in the penetrating force of the sunlight, clothed in the impenetrable armor of an absolute ignorance of evil. He had called her Una in his own thoughts as he had gone away from her through the aisles of the evergreen-oaks.[2]

And now——

It hurt him like a personal shame, it wounded him as if in his own honor, to find her here in the heart of the earth, side by side with the lover of that murdered Mantuan woman whom angrily to himself he called the hero of a tawdry tragedy.

He remembered that in Mantua that day he had thought the accused prisoner innocent, but now it seemed to him that he must have been in error, and the judge and the priest been right. He was a man

---

[1] James Crichton (the Admirable Crichton) was killed in Mantua in 1588. He became tutor to the dissolute young prince, Vincenzo Gonzago, who was apparently resentful and jealous of his teacher. He and a group of his rowdy, masked friends ambushed Crichton. The actual killer was alleged to be Gonzago.

[2] Vestal Virgins were priestesses of Vesta (Roman goddess of hearth fire). They had to maintain their chastity or face a frightening death; Dryads were female spirits of nature who presided over the groves and forests; Maia, the eldest daughter of the Pleades was the goddess of spring and rebirth; In Edmund Spenser's *The Fairie Queene*, Britomart is a virginal female warrior who represents chastity, and Una, chaste and pure, represents the singleness of the true religion.

of noble temper and usually just judgment; but, unconsciously, the finding of Este there had made the Mantuan tale stand out before him in new color, in strange guiltiness, blood-red as the sunset he had watched over the westward lake.

Nevertheless, guilty or guiltless, he had promised to save him. He had to do so, even whilst at that very hour, no doubt, this other Lombard Romeo was hiding with her hand in his, her breath upon his cheek, in the darkness of the wooded glades and the hushed mystery of the moorland night.

He moved into one of the inner cells all the traces of her residence there, the lute, the candelabra, the handsomer bronze vessels, the look of which might tempt the San Lionardo men to plunder; then, with the lamp burning but the fire extinguished, he sat down. By his watch, two hours went by; then, listening intently, he heard a sound of several feet moving amidst the grass above him.

They were near.

He sat in the same position, but he took a revolver in each hand, ready cocked, and fixed his eyes on the stone doorway.

The steps came, heavy and trampling, down the few steps into the entrance-place.

There were some dozen men in all, black-browed fierce-eyed men of the mountains, for the most part charcoal-burners: the father of Zeffirino was in the rear; he carried the only lantern amidst them; they were all armed with daggers or knives, two or three had axes and pick-axes.

They expected in the *buche delle Fate* to find more gold than all the Emperors of Rome had owned.

Sanctis watched them, without moving; they did not see him as they hustled and trampled through the entrance, already jealous of one another, hot with greed, burning with wicked passions, yelling aloud for the girl and the treasure.

When they stumbled, like fierce, stupid cattle, into the chamber of the Lucumo, Sanctis rose, and levelled his aim at them.

"Halt there," he said to them. "The first that advances is a dead man."

They hung together in a throng; they did not approach. They stared in bewildered awe at the steel tubes of the pistols and at the calm, stern eyes of this unknown man.

"What do you want?" he asked them.

They for a moment did not speak; then the father of Zeffirino, who was the ringleader and promoter of their foray, cursed heaven and earth, and cried aloud,—

"We want the gold; there is gold here; it belongs to us of right; we are the men of the soil. She is a witch, a devil, and the child of devils; she struck my own boy till almost he died under her hand. We want the gold she has found; we will let her go if she give us the gold——"

Sanctis kept his eyes fastened on them, and he saw the whole dusky, restless mass of them writhe and cringe under his gaze and the death-dealing tubes of his weapons.

"You are wicked men," he said, sternly; "and you may thank God and me that you are spared to-night adding the blackest crimes of earth to your souls. I know all you came to do. I know the names of you all. There is no gold here; there is nothing of any value here whatever. There are dead men's skulls, if you be bold enough to look on them. Constantino, father of Zeffirino, you lie; and you have brought your friends on a fool's errand. Go back as you came; and swear by the Madonna and the Holy Spirit never to return."

His calm voice, which had so much menace in it, awed them not less than the slim steel of his arms, beside which their knives seemed weapons so poor and slow. They were astounded and affrighted. They began to mutter against Constantino who had brought them thither, and to turn on him with gnashing teeth.

"If you do not take the oath, it will be worse for you," pursued Sanctis, as he saw the impression he had made. "I have bought all the lands above San Lionardo: you are all men of my ground and my forest. If I say how you have come hither to-night, the law will lay hold of you and not let you go lightly. Gold there is none here. Had any found it, would they be such fools as not to bear it away? Learned men care for these tombs, but there is nothing in them for those who are ignorant. I treat you more peaceably than you merit. Come, take the oath I bid you, while my patience lasts."

"It was Constantino!" they muttered, with one voice; and they cursed him.

"If there is no gold, there is the girl," he shrieked, in self-defence. "Where is she?"

"She is not here," said Sanctis. "And if she were she should be sacred to you as your cross, or I would kill every one of you like flies. She has those who can defend her from afar, and whom you had better fear in the future. Come, I have seen enough of you: take the oath that I tell you, or I may lose my patience. I have your lives in my hand."

They were men, ferocious enough if crossed, with all an animal's instincts without an animal's innocence; they were brutal in their lonely lives, where it was so hard for the law to reach them. They had come primed for any and every crime that the hidden sepulchres would cover, and they had mad dreams of riches that should make them free from need to labor all their lives to come. But they were so amazed, so discomfited, so cowed by the stern serenity of this Northern stranger and the cruel gleam of his merciless weapons that they hustled one another uneasily to and fro, and gnashed their teeth against their misleader and deceiver; and unwillingly, yet with one voice, they swore never again to molest the tomb.

Their hungry eyes, roving over the chamber, saw its nakedness, its emptiness. The half-worked clay told no tale to them.

They felt a mortal terror of this fair-faced, cold-eyed man risen up there against them in the midst of this place of the dead. The father of Zeffirino muttered that he had meant nothing,—only to share the gold honestly.

"Go all of you," said Sanctis, surprised at his own facile victory. "Since you repent, I too will forget. But if you transgress again, then you will find my memory is long and my bullets reach far."

"We will go," muttered the charcoal-burners, feeling still a shivering cold, as of those steel barrels pressed against their brows; and they began to trample backwards, hustling against one another in their mortification and confusion, and looking with strained, dazzled eyes forever at the levelled pistols.

He heard them make their slow way out, and heard them when they reached the air fall into furious recrimination and loud reproaches one of the other, while the voice of Zeffirino's father rose shrieking in their midst.

He went up the stone stair himself, and sent a shot up into the starry heavens.

"Be off in silence," he called to them, "or you will have more of these messages."

In the fitful shadows of the night, lit only by the stars, he saw the whole troop of them seem to melt away and be swallowed up in the great void of the darkness.

The last thing he heard was a shriek from Zeffirino's father and a curse.

Then the night once more was peaceable, with no other sound in it than the wings of the water-hen splashing in the pools, and the feet of the rodents scurrying through the brushwood.

He laid his ear to the ground to hearken to the retreating tread of his discomfited antagonists; but he heard nothing save the rustle and the murmur of insects and cheiroptera. There was no fear of the return of the San Lionardo men, for their souls were white-livered though their appetites were fierce, and they had been scared and palsied with awe of this man who had known their secret thoughts and waited for them in the place of the dead.

Sanctis listened for half an hour or more for any echo of their returning steps, but there was nothing near save the bats wheeling through the gloom, and the wood-rats running fast and noiseless through the grass.

Then he descended into the tomb, laid his pistols down upon the Lucumo's bier, and blew a dog-whistle three times. It pierced the stillness of the night air with a shrill blast.

CHAPTER XXIV.

WHEN the two who had hidden without returned with timidity and wonder to their resting-place, they found it empty. He was no longer there; he had left them his weapons. They stood a moment, silent, from the reaction of a horrible fear and an overwhelming sense of wonder, gratitude, and rejoicing.

Then the glance of Este lighted on the slender tools of death, and he took them up and examined them with tenderness and delight.

"He has left these for us!" he cried to her. "Look! he must love you very much."

"It is for Joconda's sake," she answered him: her face was gray with a terror that she would never have felt for herself alone. The horror of the past hours clung to her as the spider's web clings to the hand that has touched it. A sense of cowardice and of something shameful was upon her; she could not have explained what she felt. It hurt her that all the courage, all the sacrifice of self, all the risk and peril, should have been allotted to Sanctis, not to her.

It was a great debt that would forever hang like a stone about her neck; she could never again be free to menace him, to brave him, to insult him if she chose, and drive him away with the scourge of her words.

He had saved Este and herself.

"He has done us a very noble service," said Este, as he still feasted his eyes on the pistols; "and he has done us a still greater by leaving these. Now we need never be taken—alive. He is a generous man. You must think so?"

"No doubt he is generous," she answered, slowly; then with sudden violence she turned on him: "Will he stay here, think you, or go away?"

"How can I tell?"

"I think he will go, now that he has seen you."

"You have told him nothing?"

"How could I tell him? He might have betrayed you."

"No; he would never do that. I wish we knew whether he would go; he loves you———"

"I do not think so. Why should he? It is for Joconda that he does these things. I hope he will go; now that he has saved us, I can say nothing to him that I used to say."

"You have been harsh to him?"

"Yes; because he wearied me. He wanted me to go to his own land, to another life. I told you all that: it troubled me and I was harsh. The other day I told him I would kill him; I had my knife out against his heart, and I would have done it. Yes, he is generous, but I do not like such debt as this laid on me. One cannot breathe under it. When I see him again, what can I say? I shall never be free; he has saved you; how can I pay him for that, if I live a thousand years?"

"All the payment he would wish, you would not give; and if you would, I should not let you give it. Oh, my dear, you are very blind. Men love you———"

"I do not want love," said Musa, with the sternness he so seldom saw in her. "You do not understand: he has done this to-night because it was right to do it, because he is generous, as you say; and the other day I would have killed him!———"

"Because it is myself you love," murmured Este, as his hand laid down the pistols and stole up about her throat.

She shook him off a little roughly.

"Yes, I love you," she said, with an infinite meaning in the simple words. "I love you. You are all I have, and I have saved you, and I would give my life for yours."

"That is love. Yet you are so cold————"

"Cold? I? I think not; but do not touch me: it was *so* you touched the woman dead in Mantua. It angers me————"

She was about to say "it frightens me," but the strong courage inherent in her shrank from the acknowledgment of any fear. When he would have insisted, she still put him away from her, with more sternness than he had ever seen.

"We have escaped with our lives to-night," she said, with reproach and awe in her voice. "Think not of me: pray to God."

Then she loosened his hand off her once more, and went to where the coffin of Joconda lay, and kneeled down there and murmured her thanksgiving.

He stood by the Lucumo's bier and did not venture to follow her.

Neither did he dare to put up any prayer.

CHAPTER XXV.

Two days later in the year Sanctis stood alone in the great central hall of the old fortress of which he had become lord.

The shadows of the early winter morning were gray and sombre; a pale sunshine coming through them faintly touched a gigantic caryatide in Carrara marble at his side. In that splendid age when the prince and the noble, sheathing their swords in moments of repose, turned to the arts alike for pleasure and for glory, the lords of Massa had summoned painters of Florence to decorate and ennoble this place that was now forgotten and going to decay on the solitary mountain-side, as so many other palaces and castles fade and fall, all over Italy, burying their stories with them.

The colors were dim on the vast vault of the ceiling; the gilding of the friezes was covered with webs of dust; the marbles of the columns and the statues were stained and broken; but there was a grandeur in the place that gained rather than lost from that invasion of time, that dimness of age. He had purchased, but he was about to leave it, and he knew that most likely he would never return.

His heart was sick within him.

He had been beaten and baffled.

It seemed to him that the good and evil genius in which the Etruscan, like the Asiatic, had believed, had striven together for the soul of her, and the holier spirit had lost.

He could do nothing more. She had chosen this man, and must abide with him since that was her choice. Now more than ever it was impossible to invoke the aid of the law, since to let in one ray of light upon that myrtle-hidden necropolis would be to deliver her companion to his jailers. There she must stay and drift to whatever misery she might: the burden she had bound upon her shoulders none could lift off from them against her will.

He stood in the hall of this ancient place of Præstanella, which he had bought with a faint but pleasant hope which he had never cared wholly to analyze; and his heart was heavy as he said to himself that there was no more for him to do than to turn his face forever from this "sun-bright waste,"[1] which would haunt him, he thought, through all the remaining years of his life.

His eyes rested, without his knowing well what they saw, on the wild landscape beyond the columns of the loggia,—on the slope of the olive-covered mountain bathed in morning vapor that drifted down, and spread like a lake, over all the wooded valleys and level pastures far away below. As he looked, he saw a figure coming up the hill-side, with the white mists all about it,—a figure which always looked to him like the very divinity of the woods, which always seemed to him to have a forest fragrance and a wild doe's grace.

She came steadily upward, clothed in her garment of lambs'-wool, with a white cloth folded on her head as a *ciociara*[2] wears it on the mountain-ways that lie about Soracte.

He saw her for a while, mounting slowly but surely under the olive boughs; then he lost her from sight for a time where the rough road wound away under the outer bastions of the old fortress; then in a little while, which seemed very long to him standing wondering and

---

[1] From "The Maremma" in George Dennis's *The Cities and Cemeteries of Etruria* (1848): "The green Maremma—/A sun-bright waste of beauty—yet an air/Of brooding sadness o'er the scene is shed."

[2] A woman from a region in southern Italy.

expectant there, she came unannounced through the farthest circle of the long open arcade that opened from the loggia.

She came towards him in silence, without embarrassment, without hesitation.

Himself, he neither moved nor spoke.

A great anger and a great yearning wrestled together in his heart, and held him silent.

"I wished to thank you," she said simply, as she came and stood before him.

He was mute.

"I thought I ought to thank you for all you did," she said again. "I heard that you were here, so I came."

"It is a long way to come for so little," he said, his strong emotion seeking a refuge in a commonplace truism.

"That is nothing to me," she said. "I wished to thank you. You were brave and kind; you were very generous: I had been rude and thankless."

"Do not talk of that: I did nothing."

"You did much. And you left your pistols."

"They may be of use."

"It was good of you; and I am grateful."

He had not looked at her since she had first entered; he did not look at her now: many words sprang to his lips, but he did not wish to utter them.

"You know I am not ungrateful," she said, wistfully. "That is all I came to say. You were bold and generous, and we seemed cravens. It was hard, but you understood: it was not for myself I would have hidden."

"I know," said Sanctis, quickly. "I have never under-valued your courage."

"That is all I came to say. You will go away now, will you not?"

"Yes; I go away,—at once."

"And this place?"

"This place will not be more forsaken than it has been. It is mine, but most likely I shall never look on it again. Child, why could you not trust me? Could you think I should have betrayed your friend?"

"How could I tell? And his secret was not mine to give away."

Sanctis was silent; he had not yet looked at her face; her presence hurt him. He wronged her; he thought her bold and without the natural shame of her womanhood.

She had no shame, because she was as yet as innocent as a forest-doe.

"Do you want anything of me?" he said, abruptly.

She looked at him in some surprise.

"No: I only wanted to say that. I could not bear to seem thankless and a coward. I am sorry, too, that I was harsh and rude, since you have been so brave and have saved him."

The face of Sanctis darkened.

"I should not have lifted my hand to save him; I did what I did for you. How can you harbor him? how can you care for him? He is a felon."

"He is innocent. He never killed her."

He did not reply. The scene in the judgment-hall of Mantua rose up before his eyes.

Watching him, she grew angry at his looks and at his silence.

"You believe he is innocent? You must; you shall. It was her husband killed her. He loved her: he would not have hurt a hair of her head."

"I was present at his trial," said Sanctis, coldly. "Mantua believed him guilty."

"Mantua might; you could not? You are a painter of men's faces: look in his."

He was silent a moment. Then the justice of his nature conquered him: he remembered that when the man was nothing to him he had believed firmly in the innocence of this most unhappy lover. Had he not said to the priest on the bridge of the Argine, "Poor Romeo! he is guiltless." Should he say less to her? Should he affect to see the stain of blood because the accused was hateful to him?

"I did believe him innocent," he said, at length, with effort. "Few others did; but I believed so, though the dagger was his own with which the woman was murdered. He has told you that?"

"Yes: it was one he had left in her chamber after a masked spectacle. He is innocent."

Sanctis said nothing.

"I will go now," said Musa. "I came to thank you. I do thank you from my heart; I never will forget. We shall not meet any more. Farewell."

He turned suddenly, and for the first time looked full at her: his eyes were dim, and his face was pale and very troubled.

"Oh, child, what can I say to you?" he murmured. "If you would only have listened in the summer; now it is too late. Have you thought what it is that you do?"

"Do not speak of me. It is of no use."

"I fear it is of no use; yet even now, dear, I would always befriend you; I would serve you in any way. You cared for Joconda: think of her a little. If you would still put your trust in me, you might still be saved for a better life than this one,—hiding in the heart of the earth with a condemned felon as your companion. Nay, we will say he is condemned unjustly. His city does not think so. Once discovered, he must suffer his sentence; and you, as the one who has hidden him and braved the law for him, will be condemned as well."

"Oh, I know," she answered, quietly: "they will punish me with him,——now."

Her words were quiet, but in her eyes there shone gladness and exultation.

A revulsion of feeling came over him as he heard. He thought her devotion hardihood; he thought her loyalty audacity.

"They would punish you, no doubt," he answered, more coldly than he had spoken before. "And sooner or later they will find you: the moors and the woodlands are wide and lonely, but some time the eye of the law will find him out in your cave. The peril of last night will renew itself when I am not there. He may kill you and himself, perhaps, but there will be no other way of escape."

"That will be as it must be: men have hidden all their life, I think, in Maremma. There are many stories——"

"I do not wish to say what hurts you; we will not speak of him; but listen,—for yourself. This man is dear to you,—dear, no doubt, through his beauty and his misfortunes,—but what future will he give you, with what misery does he not dower you? Leave him to me. I will busy myself with his safety; I will share his risk; I will be to him as a brother, if you will leave him and go where women can care for you, where your youth may blossom unblighted, where you may be safe and happy without any sort of fear. For me, if you will, I will swear never to see you, if only you will let me place you out of the reach of harm. What can your life be as the mate of a felon hidden in a hole in the earth? You do not seem to understand what you have become; but think once of all I say for sake of the dead woman who loved you."

The words were wrung out of him almost despite himself. All the night long he had told himself that it was too late,—that she chose her own fate and by it must abide. All the night long he had argued with himself that there was no other course for him than to set his face northward and banish her from his thoughts forever. She was no longer lovely to him in body or mind; she seemed to him to have the gloom and taint of that Mantuan murder on her, and of the sin and shame of Saturnino. She was to him a Britomart, stripped and bound; a Penthesilea who was but her lover's slave and did not blush to be that humbled thing. All his fancy and his faith which had grown about, and rooted themselves in, her had withered when she had put her hand in Este's and led him out into the night of the moorland. He could not tell that Este's lips had never touched her own; he could not tell that the "bit of sweet basil" of a dead woman's prayers had been as a magic girdle of defence about her. He could not tell. They dwelt there together, and he had heard her say, "Come; O my love, come!"

He had meant never to look upon her face again; he had thought of her as of a creature quite as lost and dead as the Mantuan woman was, in her grave beside the reedy waters. Yet an irresistible longing to snatch her away, to send her out into light, peace, safety, to save her from the touch of the hands that had the fetters of the galleys on them, rose up in him stronger than himself, and made him speak words which he knew were as vain as ever had been the call of Este on his murdered love.

She heard him without any movement, and she answered him without emotion. She did not understand that in his sight she had lost all her Una's innocence, all her holiness and purity of power.

"I will never be angered against you," she said, simply, "because you saved us, and were good. But to speak to me so is foolish. It is of no use. I would not leave a fox that needed me as he needs me, and you could never be his friend: there is no love between you. The hole in the earth is all the home I want: we are happy in it. If the soldiers come to take us, then we can die. That is not so terrible."

Then she turned, with a long look at him,—a look of reproach,— and began to walk down the long arched corridor, open to the air, which led out to the woods.

Sanctis put his hand up a moment to his throat as if he were choked. A certain emotion of disgust at what seemed to him her lack of natural shame mingled in him with veneration for her fidelity, with passionate pain at her rejection.

"Wait one moment," he said, in broken tones. "Will you say one thing to him? Say it from me. I am a rich man, as I have told you, and gold can do most things: it is the only magician. Go, and say to him from me that I will compass his escape in some way; I will hire a vessel and a crew, and carry him in safety away in the darkness of the night (it will be possible on these lonely shores), if he will trust himself to me. Are you loyal enough to serve him so? to tell him this? It will be your own separation from him: it is only fair to warn you of that. Are you generous enough to take my message?"

She grew very pale.

She covered her eyes a moment, and was mute.

"I do it for you, not for him," continued Sanctis. "I should care nothing if he died to-morrow; but I will do my best to aid him to escape if he will trust himself to me,—that I swear to you. Will you go and tell him so?"

She was still silent; so was he.

"It will be possible if money enough be spent on it; and I will grudge nothing," he added, after a long pause. "If he attribute to me base motives, he must do so. I do not care for his judgment. If he will come, I will aid him in every way that he may wish."

"You would take him to your own land?"

"Yes."

She said nothing more for a while; she rested against the marble column, with her hand before her eyes still. Then suddenly she looked up; she was as pale as the white marble by which she leaned.

"I will go and tell him," she said, simply. "It is for him to choose."

Without more words she turned and began to traverse the loggia. At some little distance she looked back and spoke:

"The way is long: I cannot be here till to-morrow," she said, as she paused.

"Will you not have a mule, a horse? Will you not rest and eat?"

"No: I will be here to-morrow."

Then she went.

CHAPTER XXVI.

"Where have you been?" said Este, with anger and with doubt, when she returned as the afternoon shadows grew into the gloom of evening, and the Ave Maria was tolled or rung by all the belfries along the hills or coast.

"I have been to see him," said Musa, wearily. "We had one of us to thank him, and you could not. I set out before dawn. It is a long way. Let me rest but a little, and I will tell you all."

She went into her own chamber, made fast the stone door, bathed her face, changed her clothes heavy with dew, and sat awhile in the solitude, thinking.

What she was called upon to do cost her all her courage.

When she had summoned up her strength, and rested a little her tired limbs, she approached Este. He did not look up from the clay he worked on by the light of the oil-wick. He was angered, irritated, suspicious.

She went to him and rested her hands on the slab of nenfro.

"I could not bear that he should think us thankless, so I went. He bade me give you a message from him. If you will, he is ready to buy or to hire a ship, and carry you over the sea. If you like, you can go. That is what he told me to tell you."

Este started violently and let fall the tool with which he worked.

He rose to his feet and breathed quickly.

"He—a stranger—would do this for me? Are you jesting? It is impossible!———"

"No; it is true," she said, in the same measured, low, grave voice in which she had spoken the other words. "He will do all that, if you wish him. I am to go back and tell him what you answer to-morrow. He says that with gold all things can be done."

"*That* is true," said Este, bitterly. "But why should he do this for me? Why?"

"I do not know. Because he is generous, or because———"

She hesitated: she remembered that Sanctis had said he would do this for her sake.

A sudden light of fell suspicion flashed on Este. His eyes lit up with it as a dark night is lit up by blue fire.

"And the price?" he said, between his teeth.

"The price?"

She did not understand him.

"Do you not see? Are you so simple? He will aid me to escape because he will thus sever me from you. He is your lover, or would be so. You are the price that he will claim for freeing me."

A dark-red flush came over her face.

"I do not think it is so," she said, firmly. "He is a generous man; he is not a traitor. He will save you if you choose."

For the first moment his natural impulse had been one of rapturous acceptance of his liberty, of passionate ecstasy at the mere thought of feeling the winds of heaven upon him and beholding the width of the sea before his eyes.

Then in another moment that rapture passed, to be succeeded by the memory that he who offered him this possibility of escape was a stranger and an enemy,—an enemy because a lover of Musa; one from whose hands he could not and would not take a benefit. A darker suspicion also came upon him. Was not this only the Northerner's scheme to sever him and her? Was it not prompted by jealousy rather than by generosity?

He stood silent, with these irresolute thoughts chasing one another in tumult through his mind.

He felt that he ought to leave her, to take away from her the burden of his useless existence, to lighten her of the weight and the peril of his concealment there; and yet all the manhood and nobility of descent that were in him told him that it would be but a greater meanness to use the money and the assistance of a man who loved her, and buy his own liberty by the tacit surrender and barter of herself.

The baser motive which Sanctis had known he would attribute to the message seemed the only one which could possibly move a stranger to offer him a boon so immense, to incur a risk so weighty; and the quick suspicion that lies in wait in every Italian nature, forever watchful and sleepless, suggested to him darker reasons, crueller hopes, that might spur on this foreigner to share his danger and propose his flight. For the crime of which he had been accused, and for which he had been consigned to the galleys, any other nation would give him up, any other civilized country would be compelled by the laws of extradition to deliver him over to his own land to undergo his sentence.

After the first moments of involuntary gratitude and hope, he saw nothing in the message of Maurice Sanctis but an intricate and acute scheme to remove him forever from Musa and consign him, with more or less directness, ultimately to the prisons whence he had escaped.

"Your friend forgets," he said bitterly to her, as all these thoughts coursed through his brain, "or maybe rather he remembers apposite-ly, that I have been accused of and condemned for murder. That is a crime to which nowhere any land is lenient. Go where I would, I must hide myself in secrecy and shame, or be given up, the first time I walked abroad, to my own judges. He is a man who knows the world. He must know this very well. He would take me over the sea, indeed; but on the shores whether of France, or Spain, or Greece, I should be assailed by the law and seized as soon as recognized. I am like your poor playfellows the birds: if I escaped from the nets of my own land, it would be but to fall into the traps set on a foreign coast. They have hung this crime like a millstone about my neck, and in whatever wa-ters I may try to swim it will always drown me, like a doomed dog. He talks of saving me!—he cannot do it so long as this charge, this sentence of me as an assassin, clings to me; and the law has fastened it and locked it on me, and the world thinks the law cannot err! Except on some desert island like to Crusoe's,[1] I can never be safe; I can never be sure that any night the hand of the law may not rouse me up from my sleep and shake me awake to my misery like the wretched hunted rat I am!"

"I do not think he knew that. Or at least he believed, I think, that he could protect you some way. He is not false."

"Why are you concerned to praise him?"

"To praise or to blame, I try and say the thing I see. I do believe he spoke in honesty. If I had not believed that, I would not have brought the message to you."

"Cannot you see his aim?"

"To save you! I can see no other."

"Who so blind as those who will not see! He would do this thing, even if he did do it honestly, for the sheer sake of severing you from me. I know I injure you, I hurt you; I know I have no right to let the burden of my fate lie on you. Perhaps long ago I should have gone out into the light, and called the soldiers, sooner than bring this peril and

---

[1] A reference to Daniel Defoe's *Robinson Crusoe*.

trouble upon you. No doubt I have been a coward. No hunted man is brave————"

"Do not think of that. You know—you know————" Her voice failed her; it was not easy to her to find words for what she felt.

"I know!—I know all your goodness to me, though of late you have been hard and cold——"

"No, no,—never to you!"

"Yes. You are the Musoncella even to me. That is because you do not love me! Listen. This is the most cruel dilemma you could place me in: I must do what is base, either going with him or remaining by you. Why did you bring me his message? Why did you put me in this strait? A man in my circumstances is like a bird with a broken wing: strive as he may, he cannot rise. You have but brought me a torture the more. Take his arms back to him; I will owe him nothing. He sent me this offer only that he might make me feel the impotent thing I am. Whether I owe my bread and my shelter to you or to him, either way I am a beggar and ashamed!"

She heard him with infinite distress.

She could not follow the sudden changes of his thoughts; she did not see the injustice of his upbraiding; she was only stirred to contrition at her own share in this message which it had cost her so much to bear to him. She was overwhelmed with grief that she had seemed to put before him her own service, her own danger, for a single instant.

His rapid facile speech and his more subtle and cultured reasonings always bewildered her and left her at a disadvantage before him; and she who had never feared any living creature did fear him with the tremulous and exquisite timidity of all great love.

"If, indeed," he continued, with passionate emphasis, "it is you who would have me go to be rid of me————"

"I!————"

Her eyes spoke all the rest.

"And I would never go,—with his help or by his means. He loves you. There is no more doubt of that than of the earth's turning. I am a felon, that is true; but once I was a free man and a noble, once I was Luitbrand d'Este. I am not so low or so base yet as to give *you* up in barter for my freedom, or to owe an hour's liberty to one who envies me your love."

Musa shrank away, the hot color burned in her face; she was astonished, bewildered, confused.

"I am sure there is no thought of me," she said, with effort. "I am sure he does not think of me in that way. He would save you because he is a good man; but if you do not choose to go—"

A smile lightened all her face, her mouth trembled, her heart heaved.

"I did tell you truthfully," she murmured, "because it was yours to judge. But it was hard to do it—ah! very hard."

He looked at her with a quick glance.

"Why will you always say you do not love me?" he cried, with a little laugh of gladness and of triumph,—the first laugh that had left his lips since his mistress had died in Mantua.

A shadow came back over her face.

"I never said it," she answered him. "Only I cannot be what she was to you. She is still there. What is death, that it should give us leave to be unfaithful? The dead are but gone before———"

"You need not think of her!" he answered, angrily. "She would not have troubled her soul for you unless she had killed you as her lord killed her!"

She was silent. Her instincts were all true, but to reason on them was beyond her.

"I am tired," she said, at length. "I am very tired. I want to rest and sleep. In the morning I must go up to the mountains and tell him that you stay: am I to take his weapons?"

"Yes. Tell him I will accept no gift from a man who loves you."

"He does not love me. Nor can I tell him that."

"Take them back to him, though they are the most precious things on earth. He shall not despise me more than he does already, and I will owe him nothing. Tell him that whenever, if ever, I am sure you do not love me, then I will rid you of the burden of me without his help. That will be easy enough. Gorgona is on the sea yonder, and death is at hand in every lagoon and pool."

A shudder went over her.

"You know well that I love you," she said, gravely; then, without more words, she went into her chamber.

CHAPTER XXVII.

WITH the dawn she rose, after a long dreamless night's rest, and went out towards the mountains. She put the pistols in her girdle: no thought of disobedience to him ever passed through her mind.

The dawn was red and very cold, the geranium hue of the sky glowing through the whiteness of mist as it had done the previous day: nothing is more beautiful than these winter dawns, so rosy, so luminous, yet so vaporous, with the morning star shining clear and lustrous in the red of the easterly heavens, and the clouds drifting like smoke along the faces of the hills. All is so still, all is so calm; here and there out of the mists rises a belfry, or a tower, or a group of pines; all the rest of the earth is hidden in vapor, which, as the sun rises higher and the day-star is lost to sight, gradually disperses and by noon has cleared away.

In these mists she walked and climbed, her lambs'-wool clothes about her close, her heart light and her step swift.

At the foot of the mountain she saw a figure standing beside a great gnarled olive, many centuries old. It was the figure of Sanctis, who had come down so far and waited for her. As she drew near he read the answer of Este on her face.

"He has refused?" he said, ere she could speak.

"Yes. He says that you forget he is accused of a crime for which he would be nowhere more safe than he is here, since in any land they would surrender him. He bade me thank you and bring you back your pistols. He cannot keep a gift he has no power to return in kind."

Sanctis said nothing.

He understood that Este had misconstrued his motive and suspected his good faith, and he had expected that it would be so. He was not surprised; only the man seemed to him a coward and of poor spirit.

She said no more. She stood still, awaiting some expression of his anger or his regret, but he made none.

"He has doubted me: he is unwise," he said, coldly, at last. "I would have done well by him. There is nothing more to say."

"You will take the pistols?"

"Nay, keep them yourself. The time may come that you will want them."

"I cannot keep them. It would vex him. He said that you would despise him————"

Over the face of Sanctis went a passing look of unutterable scorn.

"I do," he said, curtly: "one little thing more or less can make no difference. Keep the pistols. That ever he has burdened you with need of them is what I despise."

"Since you insult him, I cannot keep them."

She laid them on the grass beside him.

He took no notice: he was in no mood to think of trifles.

"You, so brave, can you care for a coward?" he said, abruptly. "I thought like went to like. Your boar of the forests does not mate with the shrinking doe."

"He is not a coward. It is you who are unjust. He is guiltless, and he is hunted. Even the boar flies from the dogs."

"He little deserves your faithfulness. Why will you not leave him?"

"I would not leave a fox that had trusted me in such a strait. I told you so."

"It was not you who brought it on him, and, were he a man indeed, he would walk straight up to the gates of a guard-house rather than he would bring on you the peril, the secrecy, and the shamefulness he does bring now."

"Those are only words. You said all that yesterday. I will go back. I only came to give you his answer."

He did not ask her whether she had given his message truthfully. Este might and did doubt her often; he never did so. He understood her nature as Este never could do though he should live beside her till age came to them both.

"Come up to the house with me a moment," he said, at last. "I wish to write a word to him; and you need rest and food."

"I will not eat your bread. You speak ill of him; you call him a coward."

"And you? Can you say he is not?"

Her face crimsoned with a more painful shame than she would have felt at any fault or folly cast to her own share.

"He is hunted," she said, sadly, "and he has been accused of crime whilst he is guiltless. Who would be brave that must needs fly and hide and fear every breath of the wind that blows? The heron and the hawk are both brave, yet they flee away."

"Come up to the house," he said to her, seeing that all speech was useless. They went up the steep grass path under the gnarled boughs of the old olive-trees, and left the pistols lying on the turf.

"Eat and rest," he said to her, as they reached the marble court and corridor. He had wine and food ready for her, but she refused both.

"I brought some bread with me, and I drank at a spring; that is all I want," she said, and was steady in her refusal. He was a friend to her, but he was a foe to Este. She would not break bread under his roof. She had the old barbaric honor and resentment in her.

He went to a table where an inkstand stood, as he had signed at it a few days before the deeds that made him master of the castle and the lands of Præstanella. He dipped a pen in the ink, then, pausing, turned and looked at her.

"You are resolved to share his fate?" he said, abruptly. "You will not change in that?"

Her eyes looked at his fully and fearlessly.

"Have I not said, if he were but a fox I would not leave him, since he has trusted me?"

"And since he loves you!"

She was silent. She did not choose to speak of that to him.

"Such love!" said Sanctis, with an impetuosity not natural to him, and a passion of scorn for which all words were too poor and small. "Have you never thought that it is your life you give away almost before it has begun? For you are so young; and this disgrace you take on you will last so long, so long,—last till you lie in your grave, however old you be when death comes to you. Why should you give yourself to him? Why should you not be honestly loved in open day? Why should you taint yourself with guilt that is not yours? Who will look at you after years past in the solitude of those caves with a felon? Who will ever believe in your innocence, if innocent you still be? You shut the doors of fate upon yourself. You turn your life of your own will into stone. Nature has made you glorious gifts, and you throw them all away like rotting leaves. Think not that I speak for myself. I am nothing to you. I know I never touch a fibre of your heart or fancy. In all likelihood you will never see my face again. I speak for you; it is for you I sorrow. Better would it be for you to love a man dead in his coffin, than to love one whom at any hour the law may snatch from you and send to fret his years away in the horror of the prisons. When the law takes him it will never yield him up to you; it will never let you rest your eyes on him one moment; it will take him and keep him. Through his misfortune or his guilt, he belongs to the law. He is not even a free man. All he can bring you, all he has brought to you, are a cruel burden, a shameful secrecy. Why should you give him this fidelity? He can give you nothing but disgrace———"

He paused, suddenly conscious of the futility of any such reasoning, of the utter uselessness of attempting to make her remember her own safety or her own welfare.

"I thought you were proud," he added, abruptly; "I used to call you 'icy flame,'[1] as Shelley called the moon. Are you not too proud to live thus,—*you?*"

She had listened peaceably, with no sign of either emotion or anger except in the drawing closer together of her straight dark eyebrows, that looked as though a brush of ink had finely drawn them.

Even now she did not fully gather all his meaning, which his heart failed him to cast at her in coarse words.

"I do not think of myself, and you need not," she said, simply. "While he needs me, never will I leave him. If ever he do not need me, then will I never trouble him. I wish to go. Will you let me go now?"

He glanced at her, and ground his teeth together with a short, sharp sigh.

What was the use of words?

They would stir her no more than the spray of the sea stirred in a thousand years the stones of the colossal walls of the Pelasgians along the coast.

He turned away his face, and leaned his arms for a moment on the marble table where the manuscripts and documents were, and rested his head upon them. He was struggling with himself to repress what it rose to his lips to utter. He was tempted for the moment to the cruelty that would have said to her, "You are the daughter of Saturnino Mastarna."

Soon he recovered his self-control, and his resolve was taken. He

---

[1] From *Epipsychidion*: "'That wandering shrine of soft yet icy flame / Which ever is transformed, yet still the same, / And warms not but illumines. . . . '"

drew a sheet of paper that lay on a table near, wrote a few lines upon it, folded the paper and sealed it.

"Give that to him," he said to her.

"You need not have closed it," she said, with a little scorn. "I should not have read it; it is not for me."

The stern teaching of Joconda, blending with the wayward honor that she inherited from a race whose boast it had ever been that they never broke a promise though they often dealt a death-blow, had made her grow up in an integrity of good faith that was neither of her sex nor of her country.

"Give it to him," said Sanctis.

Then he leaned against one of the columns of the corridor; his face was ashy pale and his breath came and went heavily; he looked away from her out over the landscape, that was still half covered with billowy clouds that did not break and were transfixed with sunbeams as with golden lances.

"I will give it him," she answered. "Farewell."

He did not reply.

He leaned motionless against the marble pillar and covered his eyes with his hand. She went down the corridor with swift elastic tread, and disappeared beyond the farther archway amidst the gray foliage of the old olive-trees that covered the hill-side. There were twelve long miles down the mountains and over the meadows and the moors to the tombs; but she was sure of foot and used to fatigue. She went as lightly and as easily most of the way as the fawns did or the kids. When she grew very tired towards the close, she spurred on her aching feet with the thought of Este. He was alone; he was unhappy, perhaps alarmed, at her absence.

She had the folded paper safe; she never thought once of looking at it.

Even so, Saturnino, oftentimes a monster and a murderer, had once, without looking at it, carried a bag of gold ducats from a dying traveller to a woman in a distant city. The traveller had trusted the robber, and had said, "It is all I have, and she whom I love, without me will be penniless."

CHAPTER XXVIII.

WHEN she brought to Este the written lines, he read them in silence. They said,—

"I will give up my life to the endeavor to prove your innocence, in which, at your trial at Mantua, I, almost alone, believed. If I be successful, I will only ask one thing of you: when you are free, do not forget your debt to her, and justify her in the eyes of all men." The paper was signed in full: "Maurice Anton Sanctis."

Este read it twice; then burnt it.

"Does it anger you?" she asked.

"No. I do not understand————"

It embarrassed him: he could not comprehend. Why should this man, who loved her, seek to do him service? The greater nature, with its finer impulses, escaped him; he felt baffled and humiliated; he groped in the dark of dim conjecture after possible motives which he conjured up one moment to reject the next. Thinking long, again and again, over the words written to him, he ended in disbelieving them. Vague suspicion was easier and more natural than belief in instincts entirely unselfish and pure of origin.

"Is he truly gone?" he said, looking at her with eyes that doubted her.

"Gone? I do not know. He said that he was going. It does not matter: he will not come to us."

"You know that he loves you?"

"No; that is not love; he does not speak as the Sicilian did————"

Jealousy darted from the dreamful gaze of Este: it is a hooded snake that always lies beneath the amorous smile of all Italian eyes.

"There is another?" he said, with a quick breath of rage and of suspicion.

She was vexed with herself that she had spoken without thought.

"It was only a sailor who wished me to go with him and live on an island that he calls Sicily," she said, with a troubled confusion in her thoughts. "I told him I would never go; that it was folly. He will not come back again."

"And I thought no eyes ever beheld you!" he cried, with amazed anger. "I thought you hid unseen in the reeds and the woods like the moor-hen. Are there hunters for you as for her? Is the Maremma one great net? You should not listen. Why do you listen? If you loved me, you would be blind and deaf. That is love; that only. In all the sounds of the earth only to hear one voice——"

She looked at him. She did not speak, but in her humid sombre eyes there was such infinite love, passing all power of words, that he in turn was dumb.

His jealous petulance sank to silence, abashed before that mute eloquence of a single glance. The momentary fever of his roused senses was stilled and chilled by the immensity of sacrifice and heroism which that one look recalled to him.

"Ah, forgive me!" he murmured, with instant contrition; and emotion, which for the time was true and profound, brought quick tears into his eyes as he stooped towards her and leaned his lips upon her shining curls.

She drew herself from him with the same fear which at his touch, before, had stirred and trembled in her dauntless nature; a fear, vague, unintelligible to her, oppressive, cruel.

"Why are you so afraid?" he murmured. "Since we love each other——"

She put him away almost angrily. Her eyes had perplexity and terror in them.

"I do not know why we should talk of it. I have loved you,—always, I suppose. I have only thought of you, only of you, since that first night I found you in the tombs. But you,—you have loved her. That cannot change. If you were dead I should but love you more."

He shuddered as she spoke: the ghost of that woman slain in Mantua, with the lilies on her breast, seemed to him to glide in between this living love and him.

"I think you would but love me better," he murmured, with some sense in himself of shallowness, of littleness, of guilt. "But I am not like you; I am not great or strong in any way, and she,—well, she *is* dead, and she has brought on me a living death, and in my misery you alone can give me any joy. Dear, men are not faithful so: why will you speak of her? The grave has her; her lord has heaped up marble over her; she is nothing, nothing, as the fruit is that rots and drops away. Why will you put her ever between yourself and me? We live, you and I; we are all alone, and the earth is above us, and we have nothing to do with it; we are alone, and we love each other——"

His eyes poured their beseeching passion into hers, his hands held her, his lips approached her; but once more she put him away from her with a look upon her face that he had never seen there.

"Ah, yes, I love you," she said, very low, and her voice seemed to him to have the very melody of the nightingale's in it, so infinite a caress did it give with these three words. "But we were happy: why did you speak?—it was better as we were. Do not touch me; it is ungenerous: let me alone; let us live as we have done. Never will I forsake you; but never must you make me ashamed."

Then she withdrew herself quickly from him, and went to the place where Joconda's coffin lay, even as she had done the night before. She shut to the stone doors, and threw herself upon her knees, and prayed passionately. He dared not follow her.

He remained in the gloom of the Lucumo's chamber, alone with his thoughts.

Before his vision stretched the pale, cold body of his murdered mistress, with the moon-beams finding out the death-wound in her breast. Her voice that was forever silent seemed to rise and cry at his ear,—

"Our hours of joy cost me my life; and already hast thou forgotten?"

Already he had forgotten; rather had done worse than forget,— had upbraided and cursed her memory because of the fate that through her had befallen him; had done his very uttermost to thrust away from him remembrance of one in whom for three long years he had seen his heaven, his arbiter, his treasure, his supreme destiny.

A vague sense of shame stole on him. Did he love this other now, he who in the moonlit luminous Mantuan nights had sworn his love eternal as the stars?

Was this new-born passion love indeed? Or was it not the mere pulsation of reviving senses, the mere covetousness of a thing born only of the knowledge that others coveted it?

For months she had been beside him, and been no more to him than a generous boy who should have so defended and labored for him would have been. For months he had seen her and heard her, and let her go and come, with no perception of her sex or of her youth, because his eyes were tired and his heart was sick.

But all at once he saw, and his dulled desires leaped from their ashes into fire, because other men also saw, other men also desired.

But for them he would still have let her go by him the unnoticed Nausicaa of his bitter Odyssey.

CHAPTER XXIX.

THE winter heliotrope blossomed in the grass and the black hellebore
bore its flowers as the year was born; the nights had frosts that melted
with the sunrise, and were splendid with the winter lustre of the constellations; out of sight on all the great ploughed plains the corn was
again as high as a man's hand; on the hills at dark the fires of the charcoal-burners flamed with every fall of eve. It was the time she always
feared,—the time when the sound of a foot on the grass made her
hide, when all Maremma was given up to the northern laborers, when
the animals panted and trembled with terror, and the wild birds flew
in panic from the waters. She had always hated and dreaded the winter that brought aliens to the land and death to the forest creatures.

Now she feared it with unceasing alarm. Any day the father of
Zirlo might speak to a man from the mountains, and a shepherd with
his travel-worn Lucchese sheep might tear the bryony from the en-
trance-stairs, and oust her, and find the hunted fugitive, and claim
the gold at Orbitello. Any day, any hour, she knew very well that this
might betide them; and often all the night through she listened outside the tombs, her heart standing still with fear as the wild ducks
flew by screaming hoarsely, or the greater owls beat the air with their
broad wings, or the fox crept homeward through the rustling of the
withered brake, a moor-hen or a coot in his mouth.

The great Church feasts of winter followed on one another.
Through the frosty air of the nights the bells of many a distant hamlet
came sonorous though faint to their ear, ringing in the first masses of
the morn. On such feasts she had been used to go up to the old dark
church with Joconda and ask a blessing on the year; but it seemed to
her now that she asked such blessing better, kneeling down where the
walls of the thick-growing bay enclosed her, and the turtle-dove and
the partridge and the friendly blackbird flitted by her as she prayed to
heaven in her vague trustfulness which was rather hope than faith.

"Keep him safely!" was the perpetual burden of her prayer.

"Yet what is the use?" she would think, wistfully, as she rose from
her knees and heard some distant report of a gun breaking the frosted

stillness of the early morning. "God cannot care. He lets the birds be netted, and the little gentle hare be torn with shot. They are his creatures as much as we, and he gives them over to make the wicked sport of men."

No one cared: the terrible, barren, acrid truth, that science trumpets abroad as though it were some new-found joy, touched her ignorance with its desolating despair. No one cared. Life was only sustained by death. The harmless and lovely children of the air and of the moor were given over, year after year, century after century, to the bestial play and the ferocious appetites of men. The wondrous beauty of the earth renewed itself only to be the scene of endless suffering, of interminable torture. The human tyrant, without pity, greedy as a child, more brutal than the tiger in his cruelty, had all his way upon the innocent races to which he begrudged a tuft of reeds, a palm's breadth of moss or sand. The slaughter, the misery, the injustice, renewed themselves as the greenness of the world did. No one cared. There was no voice upon the blood-stained waters. There was no rebuke from the offended heavens. To all prayer or pain there was eternal silence as the sole reply.

CHAPTER XXX.

THE words of Sanctis haunted her.

Any day, he had said, any day, the law might come and snatch him from her and take him where never should she look on his face again. She had always known this; but spoken by him it took shape and substance as it had never done before. When she went into Telamone with her work and sold it to return with meat and wine, she saw indeed that the paper pasted on the wall by the State concerning his escape had rotted away under rainy weather and had not this time been replaced. Perhaps, she thought, the law had forgotten him. The law, no doubt, had as many in its hold as the bird-catchers had songsters in their nets.

Yet she dared not hope that; he said that it was impossible he could be pardoned,—that his sentence, deemed a just one by his native city, was one that all other nations also would deem just. Any day, any soldier who sauntered down the grass-grown moles, any day, any carabineer riding along the solitary shores, might hear some story from a shepherd, or a hunter, or a charcoal-burner, that might awaken suspicion and bring mounted troopers over the moors and the gleam of gun-barrels among the thickets of brier-rose and myrtle.

He, too, grew more irritable at his fate. What Sanctis had written to him, although he disbelieved it utterly, yet had aroused in him a faint hope, a faint sense of some possible eventual deliverance which made in the present his restlessness greater, his captivity almost more unbearable. One man had believed him innocent of the crime laid to him. Might he not find other men who believed also?

To Este it had always seemed so incredible that they had suspected him; that they had overlooked the wrongs received at his hands by the jealous husband; that they had been so readily deceived by the affected grief of her lord and by the marble mausoleum that he had built to her.

"Why should I have killed her? She loved me always. Him she betrayed for me," he had said again and again to his counsel in Mantua. But none would see it so; even his counsel, affecting to believe, had doubted, and had seen a young lover's jealousy, rather than an aged husband's vengeance, in that wound by the three-edged dagger.

He could not now credit the promise of the stranger to strive for a justice to him which his native city had denied to him; yet the mere fancy of it moved him to a fitful longing and despair that were as a fever to him. One man believed him: that was so much!

As the oil lamp burning at night upon the slab of nenfro only made blacker the dense gloom all around, so this promise, which he disbelieved in, yet shed a ray of hope against hope upon him which only made the darkness and emptiness of his imprisoned life seem worse to him.

Silence and constraint, too, parted him from Musa. Anger on his side and fear on hers made a wall between them.

The words that had been said could not be unsaid. The magic syllable had been spoken which broke up for evermore their simple and innocent good-fellowship.

He had learned that other men found her fair; she had learned that he also could thus regard her. He was angered at what seemed to him her coldness and her obstinacy; she was troubled at his persistence and his irritation. The frank, familiar intercourse of the past was over forever; constraint and irritability came into their communion;

silence and timidity grew up like a barrier between them, builded by invisible hands.

A kind of reverence came to him for this daring and sinless nature, which was so unlike his own: vaguely he feared her as in another way she feared him. Sometimes, when he watched her from the entrance-way come across the moors with the sunbeams about her head and the shadows about her feet, old classic fancies came to him as they had come to Sanctis, and she seemed to him like a young Immortal for whom a mortal love were too fleeting and profane.

But this mood lasted but a brief space with him: there soon rose up in him the lower impulses, the less noble instincts. She was beautiful as any forest creature, all grace and vigor and harmonious movement, could be; and she had said that she loved him, and yet he had not even touched her cheek with his.

A sombre anger brooded perpetually in him. He ceased to remember all he owed to her; he was absorbed in the sense of all that she denied him.

"I ask for bread, and you give me a stone," he said bitterly to her one day, in that tone which always hurt her, confused her, and filled her with a dumb pain like that of an animal punished cruelly for no fault of which it is conscious. Sometimes, in her vague terror of this potent influence which stole the strength out of her nature and the peace out of her heart, she almost longed to leave him, to run away into shelter and solitude as she had fled from the hunters and the shepherds.

But it would have been a cowardice, and in her sight therefore a crime.

Without her, what would become of him? How could he, who durst not venture into the light of day, who durst scarce creep out at night for a breath of air, maintain himself by seeking from the woods and moors what she sought for him? Without her he must starve, sink into absolute wretchedness, die most likely like a hunted beast walled up in a cave. Without her, the only link that held him among living men would be broken, the only kind of maintenance and of repose possible to his fate would be snatched from him. She had said, and said truly, to Sanctis that she would not leave in such a strait a fox that had trusted her. How much less could she ever leave this man, whose life was so dear to her,—as all things do become dear to us that we purchase at the risk of our own lives!

He, meanwhile, thought her cold, not choosing to understand the conflict in her of her innate independence, courage, and innocence with the new and subtle and merciless passion which had invaded and dominated all her nature. In his experience, women drank in love as flowers drink the dews and sunbeams: he did not choose to acknowledge that here was a stronger nature than his own, or any he had ever known, which could not bend and accept the yoke of passion and obedience without instinctive revolt against its own subjugation.

"You do not love me!" was all he would say, and even whilst he cast the reproach against her he knew very well that not *thus* would any of his light-won loves have served him and defended him; not thus would Donna Aloysia have dwelt content in the twilight of the sepulchres and the gloom of his own fate.

He was thankless, unjust, exacting, tyrannical, as love oftenest is; and his love was but the mere froth and fume of jealousy and sensual covetousness, and so lacked all higher aim or element, lacked all palliative of tenderness.

All the pure gold of his nature had been burned out of him under the captivity and torment he had suffered; little but the dross remained. Men in the Thebaïd might gather strength and purity and spirituality from the desert-silence; but to him the endless lonely hours, the dull heavy hopelessness, the carking sense of perpetual danger, were on his nature like a block of stone upon turf: all grew barren under the continuous pressure and the exclusion of all light and dew.

And in this misery of his there was only one joy near him possible to him, and that she withdrew out of his reach and denied him. He began to think her cruel, as he called her. All that she did for him, all that she endured for him, all that she refused for his sake, grew as nothing. She would not let him take away that "bit of sweet basil" which was on her breast.

Yet he had conscience enough in him to know that he was thankless and sought to repay good with ill; he had the pride in him that is born of gentle blood; he hesitated to overcome by surprise, or solicitation, the resistance that he met with when he spoke of love.

She grew greater in his sight, holier, at once more woman-like and more divine. Her reserve, her proud timidity, her superb innocence, gave her a power over him she had not had before. When she was absent he missed her, not only as a man misses his dog, but as a lover misses what is the breath of life to him. And her absence was

longer and more frequent than even her daily work had before neces-
sitated. She was oftentimes no further away than the nearest group
of trees, watching as she worked for any sound or sight of danger to
him; but to him, shut in the gloom of the tombs, she was as utterly
away when only a few yards distant as when out upon the sea or in
some sea-shore town. Never dare he rise and go and scan the horizon
to watch her coming. She was absent; that was all he knew. He, too,
though he had read nothing of the poet drowned down northward by
Lerici, began to find her "icy flame."

The love of her, at first mere jealous fuming, began at once to
chill and to consume him.

"Why are you so cruel?" he muttered once, as he stayed her as she
passed by him. She had some yellow crocuses in her hands: she was
going to put them in a vase of water before Joconda's coffin.

"Are those in the fields already?" he said, touching them. "Is it
another year, then?"

"Yes. Do you forget? I told you February had come."

"Did you? What is it to me? Here, all months are alike. Shipwrecked men lose count of time."

He held her hand with the crocuses in it still within his own, his
fingers on her wrist.

"If you loved me, then I would count the sunsets!" he murmured.

A blush went over her face: she was silent. With her other hand
she loosened his fingers.

"Why are you so harsh?" he said, angrily. "We who are so poor,
we might be rich in love. Why are you so cold?"

"You promised that I should be sacred to you," she said, with a
timid protest, scarcely daring to recall to him the first hours of his
asylum there, lest in so doing she should seem to make of his shelter
a debt.

"What is more sacred than what we love?" he murmured, with
the music in his voice which stole all the strength out of her and lulled
to drowsy gladness all her vague unrest.

Then with a sudden pang of memory she said to him,—

"And *who* is it that you love? Not me. If you were free to-morrow,
would you stay, of your own will?"

He was silent.

"We would go away together," he said, after a pause,—"go away as the swallows you watch for go. Ah! why do you speak of the impossible?"

"If you did love me indeed," she said, wistfully and gravely, "this place would be to you more than all the palaces of earth. If they offered me a palace such as you tell me of I would not go to it: we met here."

He sighed with impatience and regret.

So once had been dear to him the grass-grown streets, the reed-filled waters, the melancholy ways, of ruined Mantua, because there at evening-time, when the white gnats came in clouds about the old bronze *fanali*,[1] by the lamp-light, behind a grated casement, he had seen one woman's face.

That had been love, even though it were dead now, killed with the same dagger-thrust which had killed her.

"You are free to walk abroad," he said, with vexed impatience. "Were you a prisoner as I have been, and as I am, you would know that one curses one's prison, and would curse it though its walls were alabaster and its bars were gold. I am not thankless to these tombs, but they *are* tombs; and in them I am buried, alive, as the Etruscans were buried, dead. Do ever you think of the future? I do, when I dare, and it would soon make me mad if I thought long. Shall we live here together, you and I, till we are old?—here, in the twilight, like two bats? Shall we never breathe without fear? shall we never hear an owl hoot without dread? Shall we see the seasons come and go, and never count the years by more than that? Shall I hear the sheep scamper above my head, and forever envy them that they can trot at will among the thyme? Shall I watch age come upon your face, and you watch it come upon mine, and have no other record of time than the white hairs that come upon our heads? Shall we grow stupid or desperate, you and I, in all those years? Shall we lose our wits, living like this, shut away from all the world? Will the day come when we shall curse each other as I have lived to curse Aloysia?———"

His passionate utterance broke down; the dread and horror of his own visions overcame him; his eyes grew fixed and glazed, as if he saw painted on the walls the shadow of those ghastly endless years to come.

---

[1] Light.

She said nothing.

Pain seemed to ache through her heart as if some hard hand closed on and bruised it. If he had loved her indeed, the rocky prison would have smiled to him with heaven's sunshine; the world of men would have been as naught; the years would have been blent in one long dream without awaking once. Herself she would have asked no better thing than this,—to live thus always, hidden from human sight, undivided by any envious claim, alone in the soft twilight of this un-disputed home, together, until age or death should find them both and they would rest forever here, with the myrtle blossoms dropping on the rock above, and the wild-birds calling under the wild olive. She thought that even dead she would hear the murmur of the cushat and the wood-lark's hymn.

He saw the softness come into her face, the sigh come upon her lips.

"Why will you not give me love at least?" he cried. "We should snatch some joy at least from fate!"

He had that skill which always made her feel that she herself had erred.

Was she wrong to shrink away when he spoke thus? Was he not so unhappy that she ought to give him any peace she could? Ought she not to put her arms about his throat and kiss him on the eyes?

She doubted; she wondered; she was dissatisfied and ashamed at herself.

Did he call her cold,—she in whose veins the blood was lava?

Cold! Who would do for him what she would do? who would give her life for him as she would give it, fighting for him as the stork and the eagle fight for their nest in the air?

"So long ago, when I was but a child," she said, timidly, "Joconda made me promise—I did not know well what she meant—that no man's hand should touch me without the blessing of God upon it. Now I do know: you and I cannot go up to any house of God in the open day as others can do when they will; and I must keep my word to her: she is not living to release me."

He looked at her askance in surprise, chagrin, annoyance, and perplexity.

Must these dead souls, so still and helpless, with the lids of their coffins shut down on them, come thus perpetually, one or another, betwixt himself and her? And could she think that, were he free to

walk abroad in open day, it was the way to the house of God that his
steps would turn with her?

A sombre irritation rose up in him.

Could he never pluck it out, this "bit of sweet basil" that was her
superstition and defence?

"You do not love me," he said, with a great chillness in his voice
that sank on her heart like ice. "Love does not reason so. It sees no
past, because it knows it never lived before. Such ignorant vows wom-
en have taken in all ages, and in all ages have broken them for men.
You cling to yours because you do not love me. Call the Sicilian back,
or Sanctis. They can go out in daylight where you will."

The injustice was so keenly cruel, so brutal in its very quietude,
that it seemed to her to cut her very heart in two as with a knife. With
the subtle adroit skill of unscrupulous argument, he turned her truthfulness and her simplicity against her, and made her feel as though in
some way she had sinned to him.

"I want nothing with them; I have sent them away," she said,
whilst the emotion she repressed made the veins of her throat swell
with the sob she checked lest it should weary him. "Why cannot we
live as we have lived? We were so happy so; now you are always angered, always reproaching me. How can you doubt me? Since that
midsummer night you came here, I have had no other thought than
you."

"Those are words," said Este, with impatience. "Kiss me once,
and I will believe———"

The color came up over her throat and cheeks and brow; a tremor
went over her.

"I promised her, and she is dead," she said, wistfully, while her
voice was low and grave.

He flung himself away from her in wayward wrath.

"You place an old dead hag before me, and you dare to say you
love me!" he cried, with a child's petulance and a man's furious injustice.

"You hurt me!" she murmured, with an unconscious cry of pain.
He bruised her, wounded her, stung her, bewildered her, tortured her;
and yet she did not turn on him. She only vaguely felt that she had
been to blame, and that he was too harsh in punishment and hurt
her.

Este did not answer.

He did not even look at her; he picked up his rude modelling-tools and set a mass of the river-clay on the slab of nenfro where he usually worked.

She watched him awhile, in wistful silence, as a dog chastised watches its master. Receiving no word, no sign, no glance, she took her bill-hook from its corner and a coil of cord, and went out into the air to go into the thickets and cut heath and broom for firing.

"Which of your lovers waits for you on the moors to-day?" he cried to her with bitterness and irritation.

"Lovers I have none," she said, as she paused in the entrance-place and looked back at him. "You I love with all my soul; but you do not understand."

"Nor you," he said, with wrath. "You think a living man can be loved as you love a swathed mummy in her coffin. You have lived in these stone graves till you are as cold as they. You think the blood in one's veins is water———"

A sigh quivered all through her; the hot blush came on her face again, half in shame and half in anger.

"It may be that I am cold," she said, with some bitterness. "They call me the Musoncella."

He let her go without more effort to detain her. She went out amidst the wild olive and myrtle and arbutus, and worked hard in the clear winter air, as the bittern sent his loud love-call over the water of the pool, and the brown partridge flitted from under the rosemary.

As she cut the withered shrubs and made them up in bundles, the tears she would not shed before him fell upon the bill-hook and the heath, and dimmed for her all the purple shadows of the moors and the sapphire heights of the enclosing mountains.

Where the bittern was calling near at hand, there was a broad sheet of water set within a frame of olive and willow and sedge,—a shining steel-gray lagoon, reflecting on its bosom the shapes of the clouds and the blue of the heavens. In this pond the *bos butor*[1] stood sending his long deep call to his mate, stooping his head down into the water and spouting its spray into the air as he uttered his continuous music. The female listened with closed eyes and body gently swaying above the yellow reeds, lulled to delight by the sonorous chant that

---

[1] A bittern.

he was intoning, in her honor and for her wooing, over these solitary shallows.

The strange sound came to the human creature, to whom love was so perplexed and bitter-sweet a thing; she rested from her work with her hand upon her hip and the dry heath about her; she looked along the gray screen of the willow and olive bough, and saw the wild bird of the marshes and his mate yet unwon.

They were happy together there amidst the glancing water and the winter boughs. Love was the law of life, the gift and glory of all nature. Why not for her? Why not?

She knew so little of it.

She scarcely yet understood what she felt herself, and still less what he felt. To her innocence his anger was unintelligible; to her ignorance their life as it had been seemed so sweet that she could not comprehend why it only filled him with dissatisfaction and discontent. Herself, she would have asked no better than to live on so until death should find them out together.

Tenderness had awakened in her long before passion. For many a month it was as a devoted sister that she loved him; and only slowly and at intervals did the deeper, hotter springs of life stir in her: besides, there was always on her, like the cold and heavy hand of a dead thing, the memory of what he had loved in Mantua.

To the concentrated and intense nature which so many hours of solitude and so much silent unuttered thought had made even graver and more passionate than it was by instinct, it seemed impossible that a woman he had adored should have passed out of his life because death had taken her. The terrible might and melancholy of that story, which had thrilled on her ear the first night she heard it told, and sunk into her very heart as she had listened, weighed on her still. He might forget; she could not.

That dagger-stroke in Mantua seemed to her to unite him with that dead woman in indissoluble union.

She did not know that tragedies drift out of the memories of men as wrecked ships sink from sight under a rising tide; she did not know that "violent delights have violent endings,"[1] and that passion is not always love, nor even love always remembrance. She did not know

---

[1] From Shakespeare's *Romeo and Juliet*. II.vi.: "Violent delights have violent ends."

that over a man's soul the sirocco of the senses blows madly for a day, and then often dies down and leaves but dust behind it.

CHAPTER XXXI.

THE day following she said to him,—

"There is no more flour and there is no more wine: I must go to Telamone. I have a roll of cloth that I have spun to sell. Shall I go to-day?"

He looked at her in doubt.

"Do you go to meet the Sicilian sailor?" he said, bitterly, and was ashamed of himself as he did so.

"That is not fair to say to me," she answered him, patiently. "Though I did meet him, what would it matter? I have no eyes that see him. Wherever I go it is you who go with me. You know that."

"I know I am not worthy of your answer," he said, with instant repentance.

"It is but the truth," she said, simply. "As for the sailor, I think he is far away by this time. Shall I go to Telamone to-day?"

"Do as you wish: you are wiser than I."

"I must take the boat if I go; I cannot carry the cloth all the way by land. Pray, pray be prudent. Do not burn a fire by day, the smoke might be seen; it passes upward through that hole in the rock: I saw it myself yesterday. If a shepherd saw, he might come."

"Put the fire out, if it trouble you."

"Without it you are cold, I know; down here it is cold, though above the sun is so hot. Ah, that you could but see the light."

"I see it through your eyes as blind men do by eyes they love."

She was silent; she busied herself in getting ready the strong linen cloth she had spun in the winter, and in getting ready also the simple meal that he would require in her absence. For herself a crust of bread taken with her was enough.

"The first nightingales sang last night," she said. "Did you hear them?"

"No: do you know what I hear when I sleep or lie awake at night? I hear your voice always, saying cruel things."

She colored, and did not answer him.

Was she cruel?—and to him?

It was early day; the sun had but just come over the mountains; there was a loud piping and trilling of birds above-ground among the myrtle and olive.

She was ready to go; she had the cloth rolled in a bale, which she would carry on her shoulder. She looked at him wistfully; a great longing came over her to drop down at his feet and bury her face upon his knees and cry out to him, "I am thy servant, thy dog, thy love!"

But she was haunted by the memory of the dead Mantuan woman, and by the remembered words of Joconda: she restrained the passion of tenderness that welled up in her as the moment of her own departure drew nigh. She placed before him all that he might need during the day, and without meeting his eyes said to him, "Farewell for a little while. Be careful, oh, I pray you! Be careful."

"Why should I take any care?" he said, bitterly. "If we are forever to live thus, Gorgona will be less pain to me than where you are."

She gave a quick sigh, and without answer took up the bale of homespun cloth and mounted the steps of the entrance.

When she parted the boughs and emerged into the open air, the glory of a dazzling morning was sparkling all around her on the brimming waters and the dewy earth.

A hare was peacefully nibbling at the grass; a jay was swaying on a bough and meditating his own homeward flight; farther away in the distance, against the light, there was a pretty group of a mare and two foals; down in the dark green rosemary-bushes at her feet a pair of green grosbeaks, hardly to be told from the shrub, were pecking in play at each other.

"If only he could come into the air!" she thought, with passionate pain.

Of what use are the most loving eyes of others to the blind shut in the impenetrable darkness of his own calamity?

She could do for him what the sister, or wife, or daughter does for the blind man,—she could watch for peril for him, bring him food, labor that he should live,—but she could not lead him from the gloom up into the light, she could not make him rejoice in the green world that was renewing its youth.

An impulse of longing to look on him once more made her retrace her steps, and made her kneel, leaning down to look through that cleft in the rock roof of the tomb which she had made in the earliest days of her occupation of the tombs, that by its orifice the smoke of her wood fire might escape. Through the fissure she saw straight down into the chamber where she had first found the golden warrior on his bier. She saw Este as he sat in the stone chair once sculptured there for visitants to the dead. His body was bent, his arms lay outstretched on the table of nenfro that held his modelling-tools, his head was bowed down on them; his whole attitude expressed the unnerved, weary, hopeless dejection of a man to whom life was valueless.

The sight of him thus smote her as if with a blow. He called her cruel: was she in truth cruel? Was she cruel as one who denies water to a chained dog, air to a caged eagle? Did she indeed give him a stone when he craved bread?

A vague, heavy sense of wrong done by her to him went with her over the broad moors and meadows, and along the shining sands of the shores.

She got her boat out and pushed it into the water and loosened her little sail.

The wind was favorable to her, and the boat danced buoyantly on its southward way. But her heart was heavy as lead.

When the swell of the Sasso Scritto rose up between her and her moors, she felt as if she had bidden him farewell forever.

For once she had no eyes for the gannets gathering above the sea for their northward flight, for the rock-martins flying along the face of the cliff, for the sandpipers tripping among the samphire of the shore, for the curlews screaming above the estuary.

She had told him the truth.

She only saw him wherever she went.

No one would buy her cloth at any reasonable price at Telamone: she knew what she ought to get for it, and was unwilling to sell it for too little. Most of the people there were poor, and the few who were not so were mean. She saw nothing to do but to try at Orbitello. The wind was all in her favor, and the sea, though boisterous, was no stormier than pleased her, sea-gull as she had been called so long.

The boat beneath her, as it rose and sank and leaped the crests of this wave and of that, was to her as the horse is to the fearless rider. The sea was so familiar to her, she was at home upon it as any one of the storm-swallows after which they had named her in her babyhood.

The red and green of the tufa land, the deep shadows of the pine woods, the pale aloe-dotted shores, the distant mountains amethyst and purple as the mists cleared from them, flew by her rapidly, a belt of seething, wind-blown, sunny water flashing and heaving between herself and them.

At Orbitello she could sell her linen, not over well, but at a fairly decent price.

She rested a little, ate her bread, and bought for a small bronze coin a plateful of cooked rice; then she purchased the wine and the flour she needed at home, and put the rest of the money she had earned safely away in the breast of her tunic.

There did not remain much, for wine was dear in vineless Maremma. She paid a visit of gratitude to the old chemist, and took him a basket of rare mushrooms, and told him that when the time came to gather herbs she would not forget her promise.

"You have a face that remembers," said the old man, pleased.

"How can any one forget?" said Musa. It was that which seemed to her strange. Neither benefit nor wrong would have been ever written in sand with her. Though he had been dying before her, never would she have forgiven Zirlo.

"Did the sick man recover?" the old chemist asked.

"Yes; it was your cordials that saved him. That is why I came now to thank you."

"And does he marry you, this spring-time?" said the old man, with good-humored pleasantry.

"Ah, no!" cried Musa, quickly, with a color deep as the dark winter rose on her face.

She went out of his pharmacy without bidding him good-day. The thoughtless question had gone like a knife into her heart.

That was what Joconda had meant when she had made her swear on her Madonnina.

Laden with the flasks of wine and oil and the little sack of flour, she took her way to the quay, and as she went almost ran against an old lean man with a pipe in his mouth.

"Eh, la Velia!" stammered Andreino, in sad fright.

"Is it you?" said Musa, with contempt in her voice. "Did they not tear you to pieces among them, squabbling for the money in the pitcher?"

"Ay, ay, almost they did, the greedy souls," said Andreino, quaking. "And where have you been all this while? You know I always loved you. I did hear that you were in service somewhere upon the mountains; but I said to them, 'So handsome a wench, and so handy with a boat, have the coaster-lads no eyes————'"

"I have found a home and work yonder," said Musa, cutting short his compliments, with a sign of her head as she spoke towards the westward. "As for you, I do not forget that you used to lend me your boat when I was a child. But you were weak and miserable when those women raged————"

"Oh, my dear, my wife was among them: if you had come quietly to us instead of dashing that pitcher down and wasting all that fair money————"

"Oh, you would have loved me as long as the money had lasted," said Musa, with curt sarcasm. "So would any one of them: you are not alone there."

"But you have got money now?" he said, with an envious glance at the flasks she carried.

"These are not for myself," she answered. "And how goes on the smuggling? Has the coast-guard never yet found out that closet of yours behind the olive wood Pietà?"

"Oh, now, my sweet child, be quiet!" began the old man, trembling. "There are guards and soldiers all about, and never did I do you any harm, but lent you my boat and gave you pretty shells, and would have welcomed you always."

"You are safe with me, Andreino, and your secrets, too," she said, with a little laugh, as she bade him good-morrow and went down towards the quay. He would let her alone, she thought, now that he knew she could bite.

The old man hobbled after her and touched her on the arm. "You were always running about over all the wild places," he said, timidly. "Did ever you see that young man the law is looking for always? The placards have been down a long time,—the rains made havoc with them,—but no doubt you will have read them, and there is a pretty penny to be made that way, and if you should have ever seen him————"

"There is a pretty penny to be made, too, by telling how tobacco is run in at Santa Tarsilla," she answered him, calmly. "I am no informer, you know that: do not you begin to be one in your old age. If the young man escaped the fever of the marshes, surely men may let him live in peace wherever he be,—such peace as he can have with a price upon his head."

"Who is your lover that has been ill?" murmured Andreino, in wheedling insinuating tones, as though he were caressing her. It was the merest guess with him, made in shrewd cunning.

His eyes, keen still to mark such things though he was nigh ninety years old, saw the blood go away from the peach-like cheek that the sun and the air had kissed all her years through. Her very heart seemed to stand still in her terror. But she had courage and presence of mind: she looked the old rogue full in the eyes.

"If a lover I have, what is that to you? We do not ask you for bit or sup, Andreino. You used to know me well. Remember how I bit the hand of the man that struck my dog. My dog is dead, but my blood is alive."

She looked at him all the while full and sternly in the face, and the old man was frightened.

"I meant but a jest," he mumbled. "For sure you are the same as you were, with your terrible eyes and your terrible tongue; but your friend you know I always was and always will be, my dear."

"That is well," said Musa, carelessly, hiding the apprehension that sickened her as she thought of the hand of the law held out with the blood-money, and the greedy hand of this old man stretched out to take it. If Andreino ever knew, the law would know also before the day was an hour older.

She left him and gained her boat and put her purchases in it, and let fly the little sail. Andreino stood watching by the sea-wall. To give him a false scent, she steered southwestward for a mile or two, with the black peaks of the Argentaro between her and home. Then, when she was distant enough for none to be able to tell hers from the many other similar boats that were out on the sea that day, she tacked and put her little vessel about and repassed the rocks of Orbitello, standing herself well out to windward, so that from the mole of the town her sail looked no bigger than a white speck against heavy leaden-colored clouds that were drifting up slowly under the pressure of a strong cold wind.

But to put about thus, and place that square mile and more of heaving water between Orbitello and herself, had taken several hours; the day was advancing, and the sun was low, as she came once more on the northerly tack and began to steer to the northeast. She was too good a sailor not to guess the meaning in the whistle of the wind and the steely hue of the great banks of clouds that rose higher and higher over the face of the sky. Far away, where the Atlantic races through the Straits of Gibraltar and the waves of Biscay lash the Spanish coast, a sea-storm was raging already, and coursing like a greyhound to reach and overtake the blue Ligurian waters.

Even if she had not known what soon would come by the look of the sky and the feel of the waves, she would have known it by the way in which the big ships in the offing spread every stitch of canvas in the effort to make a port before the tempest should be upon them, and the way in which the little lateen craft came running in from every point of the compass, fishermen knowing that "the devil would take the hindmost."[1]

Her own boat flew like a curlew, for the change in the wind favored her, but, though it sprang from wave to wave and was as buoyant as any cork, Musa knew her own danger very well. Her boat was but as a nautilus-shell that would soon be tossed and whirled in a typhoon. To reach her own shore would be hard; to land might prove impossible. She reproached herself bitterly that she had not read more wisely the look of the skies at daybreak; but even wary and weatherwise fishermen make such mistakes at times, and have the blackness of the tempest and the howling hurricane down on them, and their vessel keel upward in the boiling surf, ere they can cry out one single prayer to the Mother of mariners.

Sometimes, she knew, out of a score of feluccas that went out at sunrise blithe and busy as a swarm of swallows, five or six only would come home to the mole next morning. The hungry *libeccio* would have swallowed up the rest.

The storm was not yet down, but made itself felt in the chill of the air, in the force of the gusts, which fell like blows, in the swirl and surge of the waves, in sunshine so blue, now yellowish-white and leaden-gray. The little boat still flew, elastic and easy, before the wind, rocking and reeling often, but always righting herself, even though drenched again and again with water. Musa was wet through; the shrill wind whistled among her curls and blew them upright; it was all she could do to keep her place, and cling to the tiller to keep the boat's head due north.

The hours she had lost going about to hide her destination from

---

[1] From "The Great Metropolis" by A. H. Clough.

Andreino had brought her into the very press and peril of the wild
weather that had come upon sea and land. But for that she would have
been home by now. She could scarcely keep in a bitter cry, all useless
as was such lament, thinking of him at home watching for her, wondering, doubting perhaps, alone with the bitterness of his own heart
all through the weary day.

The sun had long been covered by the dense western clouds, and
she could not well guess the hour, but it began to grow very dark,
and big rain-drops began to fall. She could hardly tell her course; all
before, behind, on every side, was fog and spray and gloom.

She thought with a continual agony, "What will he do if I should
drown?"

She knew it was very likely that she would drown, alone, out at
sea on such an evening in a little open boat. She had seen the cruel-
ties of the sea in all their shapes from her babyhood. She had seen
many a drowned man washed up on the sand, swollen, eyeless, half
eaten by the sharks. She knew the great fish that waited down there
underneath the waves, to give an added horror to death. She knew all
the ghastliness of death in the deep sea. But it was not of herself she
thought, but of him. He had no one in all the world but herself: what
would become of him if the sea killed her?

All the while as this one thought kept place in her mind, to the
exclusion of all others, she did all that it was possible to do to save the
boat and herself. Once she was washed fairly out of the boat, but she
clung to it with both hands, and climbed over its wet side, and went on
again in the trough of the trembling waves. The flasks of wine and oil
and the sack of flour had been washed over also, and were lost. Even
in that moment of mortal jeopardy she felt a pang the more to think
he would not have those things he so sorely needed.

What headway she was making, whether she was close in-shore
or out at sea, she could not tell: all was black as night around her. Now
and then the lightning flashed, now and then she could see the whiteness of the hissing water; now and then the wind lulled, and she could
hear the minute-guns of some ship in distress firing far away behind
her. There is many a coral reef and many a sunken rock along the sea-
shore of Maremma.

"Are the angels all dead that tend the stars?" she thought, in the
vague fancy that the songs of the "angiolin" had imbued her with;
and then she set her teeth and clung on for dear life again. No one in

heaven cared. It was with her as when the moor-hen was shot on the waters, as when the woodlark was trapped in the net. No one cared. There was no "angiolin" besides the stars!

She was now almost numb with cold. The water drenched her, rain and salt water both poured over her, and the night had grown bitterly cold. She supposed it was night; she could not tell. She put off her heavy shoes, and made her clothes as light as she could, knowing that at any moment she might have to float and swim for her life. She kept her hold as well as she could on the tiller, and kept the boat as far as she could guess due north.

The sea seemed like some great caldron that boiled and seethed. The roar and the shriek of the winds were incessant. The rain seemed to strike like whips. The little boat was well built and sea-worthy, and kept afloat where a heavier vessel would at once have filled and sunk. But she knew very well that every moment might be her last, and a great cold had crept into her very blood. She began to grow giddy and to feel deaf, the noise of the winds was so loud, the swirl of the water was so riotous. She began to be bewildered and dull; and she kept saying, ever and ever and ever aloud, "What will he do if I drown? What will he do?"

That was her only distinct thought. All the rest, without and within, was darkness, utter darkness, in which she was thrown hither and thither and buffeted by the winds and the waves. At last one great wave took her and threw her over the boat's side. She flung up her hands in vain; the boat was no more there; the weight of the leaping billow dashed her on her back, and the salt foam poured between her lips.

"What will he do?" she thought. "What will he do?"

That was her last conscious moment.

The sea closed over her, and she knew no more.

CHAPTER XXXII.

WHEN she unclosed her eyes from out of the trance of death, she lay upon the stone floor of the tomb before the wood fire.

Este knelt beside her; her hands were in his, his breath was on her cheek.

"What has happened?" she said, stupidly, then suddenly remembered.

"The oil and the wine are lost!" she cried, then grew drowsy and stupid again as the warmth from the burning wood stole over her and rejoiced all her cramped and frozen body.

"What matters that?" he murmured over her. "You are saved; you live."

She smiled dreamily: her eyelids had dropped again. She was but half awake. It was so pleasant to lie there, at home, with the glow of the fire spreading over all her wet numb limbs, and the sense of his hands on hers, of his voice on her ear.

Her head rested on a log of wood covered with a goatskin; her damp curls began to grow crisp, and the gold in them shone in the light of the blazing wood; her face was pale as marble; her slender feet lay bare and white upon the other goatskins he had spread beneath her; she was more lovely so in her helplessness than she had ever seemed to him in all the plenitude of her strength and health.

He murmured tender and passionate words over her; he kissed her curls and her hands and her feet; it had been those kisses which had awakened her.

Now, as she lay half dreaming, half smiling, only half conscious yet, he drew back from her a little; he was afraid to alarm her; life in her had seemed for a time so still that he had thought her dead. She had had no more motion, no more breath in her, than a broken lily thrown down on the grass.

But Glaucus had only played with this his favorite child: he had not killed her. She lay still for many minutes; now and again her eyes looked for a moment up at the familiar shadows of the tomb and then closed with the dreamful pleasure of a child that lies half asleep and hears sweet music.

"I was afraid," she murmured once, "I was so afraid,—for you!"

Then she lay still and seemed again to dream; her eyes closed, her lips parted with a faint glad smile.

The tears fell from the eyes of Este.

After a while she raised herself quite suddenly, and a look of alarm and of fuller comprehension came upon her face.

"I was drowning," she said, aloud. "I was thrown out of the boat and drowning. What has happened? I was coming back, and the storm broke. The wine and the oil were lost. I am sure that I swam, and the water threw me down and buried me. How am I here? Who helped me?"

"Do not ask that?" said he, tenderly. "It is enough that you *are* here. Be still; forget."

She raised herself higher and leaned on the skins with one elbow, and so sat half erect and fastened her gaze on him.

"Tell me, tell me; I want to know! I am not mad? I have not dreamt it, have I? I was drowning; oh, yes, I was drowning: is it long ago? Who brought me home? Is the boat safe?"

"I brought you home, dear."

"You! Tell me about it; tell me quick! I do not think I am mad. I am sure there was a storm; I am sure I went underneath the sea, down—down—down. The water was in my mouth and in my ears. I have not dreamt it. Where is the boat?"

"Be quiet; try to be calmer, and I will tell you. Yes, you went out in the boat to-day, and there has been a storm, a terrible storm. It is not over yet, but you are safe here."

"Yes?" She listened as a child listens to a tale, her eyes dilated, her lips parted, leaning still on one arm upon the goatskins before the fire. She was quite warm now; the color had returned to her face, her curls were scarcely wet, and lay heavy and soft over her brows.

"Yes, you are safe here," he answered her, afraid that her consciousness was still dim and her thoughts still vague, and speaking in the simplest and the clearest words he could, that they might find their way to her brain without startling her. "You are home and with me; we are both safe. When the storm came I sat here till I could bear to hear it no longer, knowing that you were out upon the sea. I do not know the time—it may have been at Ave Maria or later—that the horror of the thought grew too great for me to sit here and endure it. I was in safety, warm beside the hearth that you had made for me, and you were there alone in the dark on the waters. I got up and I went out. I could see nothing for the rain, I could hear nothing for the wind; I could only tell that out at sea the night was terrible. I lighted your lantern, and I walked on and on, on and on, making for the shore as well as I could guess. You had told me certain landmarks, and by the lantern light I could avoid the bogs and the trunks of the tress. Still I think I must have been a long time getting to the shore. It seemed to me the whole night, perhaps it might be less than an hour; I cannot say. I could hear a minute-gun far away over the waters; and I knew you were out at sea, unless by heaven's mercy you had had some warning of the storm and had stayed in harbor. But I thought, whatever the weather was, you would be trying to come back to me. I was sure that you were in the boat in that awful darkness. I walked and walked; there was not a star to guide me; all above and below was black as ink. I could only hear the rushing of the wind, the crashing of the boughs. Once a herd of cattle and horses tore past me, mad no doubt with fright: they almost trampled me down among them. I saw no other living thing. I forgot that I was a hunted felon: I only remembered you. I felt the wind was from the southwest, and so walking against it I hoped to come to the beach at last. If I had known the country as well as you, I should have had no fear. As it was, I knew I might walk the whole night yet never find the sea. But all at once I felt my feet wet. I stooped and tasted the water: it was salt. The roar of the wind was so loud that I had missed the sound of the sea, but the sea it was. By the lantern light I could see the foam on a breaking wave. Now I was there I seemed no nearer you. I had no boat; I could do nothing; my sight could not pierce the darkness by a yard's length. You might be drowning, I knew, within a foot of me, and I helpless, knowing nothing of it. On Gorgona I saw many storms, but none so dark as this. I wandered miserably up and down, to and fro, on that stretch of sand. The sea had rolled up, I think, much higher than it rises in fair weather. I could not tell what to do; only I could not go home, thinking you were lost in that hissing, boiling, howling blackness, that seemed to have swallowed up both earth and sky. The soldiers might have taken me if there had been any there: I do not think I should have known they touched me. Going along the shore, to and fro, like a lost dog, with the great wall of those waves you love beside me, and the water rolling with a sound like thunder, I touched something with my foot. It was you! You were lying there in the wet sand, with the foam of the surf all about you. How you came there I cannot tell. The sea loved you because you never feared it, and so saved you, I suppose. I suppose the breakers had nursed you like a child, and thrown you gently at last upon the lap of the shore. You were quite insensible, but your heart was beating. I carried you here. I missed my way twice or thrice, and the way was long. But at last we came home. That is all. Ah, dear, do not say I do not love you ever again."

She had heard him in perfect silence, her eyes wide open, her lips parted, pushing back her hair with her hand, and seeming to hang upon each accent of his voice.

When his words ceased, she gave a startled cry that was half a sob.

"You did that for me?" she said, in a wondering whisper. "You ran that risk—for me?"

He stooped and kissed her.

With a sigh and a smile in one breath, she threw her arms about his throat.

CHAPTER XXXIII.

ALL the earth was rejoicing with the thrill of the spring.

The song-birds were returning, and through the hush of morning and of evening the merry song of the starling and the sweet piping of the woodlark stirred the woods. In all green moss-grown places violets were blossoming and the tender fronds of new ferns uncurling; along the sides of all the runlets of water the first primroses were budding, and all along the sandy shores the squills and the sea-daffodils were beginning to appear. The nights began to grow melodious, the first nightingales arriving with their love-chants; and all the daylight seemed full of flitting wings and amorous trills, till even the sombre rosemary trembled with their mirth and their pleasure; the lowly tussocks of dog-grass and the lofty ilex and robur oaks were alike the home of their innocent passions, and down the shadowy waters, between the solitary brakes and thickets, the water-birds sailed before each other's eyes in their pomp of courtship and coquetry of wooing.

All living things loved one another,—from the partridges that tripped together through the thyme to the little warblers sounding the first notes of their return amidst the sedges of the pools.

And the human lovers were also happy, and even in the shadows of the sepulchres their hearts thrilled in unison with the joy of the awakening year.

Now and then love triumphs over circumstances, and nature is a stronger thing than all the laws of men.

CHAPTER XXXIV.

AWAY in Mantua the weather was still chill and cheerless, the waters were still yellow with the snows of winter that melted into mud, the sun that warmed the green Maremma land and set a nest under every tussock of grass, and covered with blossoms every inch of the rich red soil, did not as yet shine on the melancholy city in the midst of the Northern plains. White fogs drifted up over the surface of the lakes, and keen winds came over the Venetian Alps and sighed down the deserted arcades and through the lonely palaces.

At evening-time a man would walk always the same way out westward by the Argine del Mulino, and would watch the sun go down in the west where Maremma lay far away beside the sea, and would say to himself, as he looked, "What does the sun see in that green land?"

The people of Mantua only knew him as a stranger, one of the many travelling painters who were lured there by the sad charm of the pale waters reflecting the domes and towers and walls, and the arches of the bridges, and the tall belfries whose metal tongues called but to mass, and never more to war. He was silent, reserved; they thought him poor; he passed his days drawing the austere palaces, the ruined fortresses, the many stories told in stone; sometimes he took a boat and passed long hours out on the lagoons still gray and windblown with the lingering winter's breath. No one noticed him; he was but a painter like so many; out in the world he might be famous, but here in Mantua he was unknown and disregarded.

Mantua slept like a magician enchanted by his own spells, whilst the grass grew long on the roofs and the battlements, and the works of gorgeous Giulio faded and dropped to dust in the palaces above the waters or down beneath the blue acacia shadows.

The stranger attracted no notice as he came and went among the market-people and the fishermen; they did not observe that he was constantly watching the dark figure of Don Pietro di Albano as it emerged from the vast arched ways of the palace on the Lago di Mezzo, or returned from the law courts in the mist of the frost-touched evenings. Don Pietro had raised a mound of fair marble to his wife, and paid daily for masses for her soul, said in the noble church of Sant' Andrea, and went about among his fellow-citizens still in the garb of woe and with a long face, mourning for his young spouse.

But Sanctis never saw his shadow lengthen on the moss-grown stones but what he said to himself, "This is the assassin."

How to prove it? That was the problem which perplexed him and baffled him, and which he turned over and over in his thoughts every evening-time that he walked out by the mills of the Twelve Apostles, and looked across the water to the sombre front of the great iron-bound Gothic palace, where in the summers that were gone Donna Aloysia had leaned from her casement to watch her lover's boat glide towards her in the moonlight.

"Do you still believe in Romeo?" said with a smile the Abbate he had spoken to on the evening after the trial, recognizing him once as they paced side by side over the draw-bridge.

"I believe him to have been guiltless of that crime," Sanctis answered, gravely.

"Mantua condemned him, and Mantua knew him," said the Abbate: "you did not."

Sanctis was silent.

"And the husband?" he said, abruptly. "What has Mantua to say of him?"

"A pious man," said the priest, "and a forgiving one. Donna Aloysia was notoriously unfaithful, yet he has built her a fair tomb all of marble, and with a silver ever-burning lamp above it; and every day—every day, mark you!—masses are said for her soul at his cost in Sant' Andrea."

"No doubt a most holy man," said his hearer, assenting, and leaned over the parapet and looked at the sun setting in crimson glory beyond the leagues of bulrushes and the gray placid waters.

"Why should I try to do him this good?" he thought. "Mantua knew him, and Mantua condemned him; and if ever I should be able to prove his innocence, how will he use his liberty? Will he be faithful to her once he ceases to need her? Will he justify her before the world when the world is once more open to him? I doubt; I doubt. Perhaps I shall be able to force him to it; but of what value is extorted honor, is compelled love? I doubt; I doubt. He has no real love for her. He is a wayward, weary child, and she is the only plaything that lies near his hand, the only blossom to be plucked within his reach. That is all; and she—she gives life and eternity, body and soul; she only breathes through his breath, she only sees through his eyes, she only lives by him. That is love. Nothing else is. And if I should set him free to-morrow, what would he do? Forget? I think so. Here his dead love was slain, his passion was closed in death; and he has forgotten that. Once free, he will forget this too. He will leave Maremma behind him and remember it no more than he will remember the marsh-lilies that bloomed there last year."

That he knew; but he had promised to give his life to Este's service. He could not draw back, once having pledged his honor to the task.

He watched the sun sink away over the pale, leafless Lombard plains, and sink out of sight amidst the golden mists of the coming night. The rays from the set sun were still red in the heavens, and, falling on the many casements of the dark palace where Donna Aloysia's beauty had once been like a gorgeous flower blooming in a dungeon, turned all the glass behind the iron bars to flame-like radiance, and made the melancholy waters washing the walls glow for the moment like a stream of opals and rubies.

"I will keep faith with him," Sanctis said to himself, as he leaned and watched the sombre pile. "Maybe he will feel his debt to me and so keep faith with her."

CHAPTER XXXV.

THE fair commencement of the spring spread into fuller glory; the air grew full of the scent of narcissus and woodruff; the gladwyn and the iris, purple and azure, blossomed beside every pool and runlet of water; in the woods the flowering ashes were white as new-fallen snow, the sombre ilex glades grew light with their young leafage, the bird-cherry and the fragrant cherry were in bloom, and the goats cropped once more the tender leaves of cistus and of myrtle.

In the great unmeasured meadows the grass grew already breast-high; the buffaloes and the roebucks wandered through seas of flower-foam; the honeysuckle garlanded the straight pine-stems, and the cerulean clusters of the mouse-ear and the deep green fans of the nymphæa began to spread themselves between the sky and the little merry fish and the ever-chanting frogs that filled with noise the silence of the pools and streams. All the earth was running over with foliage and blossoms and young new-born things, as the week-old fawns slept beneath the acanthus shade, and the colts gambolled on the velvet softness of the mossy glades, and the pretty little foxes ran out of their earths in the moss-covered sandstone, and the yet prettier leverets stole in their mother's wake across a bed of hyacinths blue as the sky.

The cuckoo called from the leafy heights of the esculus-oaks, and all night long the nightingale told the rosemary that she had seen nothing sweeter than itself in Egypt or in Palestine; for it is the rosemary rather than the rose that Philomel loves best.

Sometimes when Musa came up from the shadow of the tombs into all that abounding light, that universal fragrance, that immense sense of life and loveliness, in which she could almost hear the green earth growing, she would stretch out her arms in love of it all and gratitude, and cry out aloud to the sunlit solitude,—

"I, too, am happy! I, too, live!"

Every pulse of life in her rejoiced with rejoicing nature. She envied no more the water-birds sailing all day beside their nests; she no more wondered why the woodlark sang praise, praise, praise, and nothing but praise, to the Creator of all.

The joy of a strong nature is as cloudless as its suffering is desolate.

He loved her; at least he loved her enough to have that power over her which steals all the strength away from the woman it rules, and closes her eyes in a trance.

He loved her; and when she went out away from him into the golden air, all her life seemed to sing its joy within her; she could have laughed aloud and have danced with the fawns in the pastures.

Even he was startled at the change and radiance that came upon her beauty; her eyes seemed to have imprisoned the sunbeams in their depths; her lips seemed to have ever on them that sigh of love which is happier than all smiles; when he embraced her it seemed to him that he touched an Immortal.

"You are glorious as a young goddess," he had murmured to her once; "and I—I am but a hunted felon, afraid to meet the light."

Then she had laid her arms upon his shoulders, and raised her beautiful mouth to his.

"You are my love! my love!" she had answered him; and in the brief whisper there had been such eloquence of passion as he thought no poet's words or musician's melody had ever yet been able to give to sound.

It is often said that the strong cannot love the weak, the high-tempered courage cannot cling to the coward; yet it is rather the strong who alone can love the weak, who can have the patience, the pity, the abiding tenderness to bear with feebleness, so unlike itself; it is rather the high courage that can stoop, and, full of infinite compassion, feel that where others despise it can defend, and comprehend what has been made in its own unlikeness.

Moreover, love is forever unreasoning, and the deepest and most passionate love is that which survives the death of esteem.

Friendship needs to be rooted in respect, but love can live upon itself alone, rootless like the orchid. Love is born of a glance, a touch, a murmur, a caress: esteem cannot beget it, nor lack of esteem slay it. *Questi che mai da me nonfia diviso*,[1] shall be forever its consolation amidst hell. One life alone is beloved, is beautiful, is needful, is desired,—one life alone out of all the millions of earth. Though it fall, err, betray, be mocked of others and forsaken by itself, what does that matter?—that cannot alter love. The more it is injured by itself, derided of men, abandoned of God, the more will love still see that it has need of it, and to the faithless will be faithful.

When she took the flowers of the woods and put them before Joconda's coffin, as she never forgot to do, she said always, as she knelt a moment there,—

"Dear friend, where you are you understand: he loves me, and we are happy, and you, you will forgive?"

It seemed to her that the dead must see as God saw, with whom they were.

Her daily life was the same as it had been before. There could be but little remission of her labors, since nothing but her strength and her effort stood between them both and death by hunger. She passed many hours of the day in her usual work; the boat had been flung up on the shore by the Sasso Scritto not injured too much for her to repair it. She continued to fish, to spin, to hew and carry wood, to plait the *biodo*, and to cut the heath; only he would never have her go more into the towns and villages, and so they lived as best they could on the wild oats of the last year, on the roots of the earth, and the eggs of

---

[1] Dante's *Inferno*, Canto V: This one, who never from me shall be divided.

the plover and water-hens, and when she took those she was always heedful to leave one or two in each nest.

"I could make nothing unhappy *now*," she said to herself; and only for his sake—never for her own—would she ever have robbed the birds even thus far.

Her daily labors remained the same, but it seemed to her as if she had the strength of those Immortals he told her she resembled. She felt as though she trod on air, as though she drank the sunbeams and they gave her force like wine; she felt no sense of fatigue; she might have had wings at her ankles and nectar in her veins. She was so happy, with that perfect happiness which only comes where the world cannot enter, and the free nature has lifted itself to the light, knowing nothing of and caring nothing for the bonds of custom and of prejudice with which men have paralyzed and cramped themselves, calling the lower the higher law.

She was as innocent as the doe was in the brakes, knowing no will but its forest lord's. Her pride had melted into willing submission as the night's frost of the Maremma dissolved before the kiss of the sunrays at morning.

"It is not as though he were free as other men are": she said in her communion with the memory of Joconda. "I am all he has. Even you would never have bidden me leave him."

CHAPTER XXXVI.

FOR a space, for a few weeks, a few months, the physical beauty of her and her absolute devotion moved Este to some emotion that was nearly love, and so in its momentary empire possessed him and consoled him. But it took no real hold upon him, had no real power to absorb him and reconcile him to his fate; nay, his very infidelity to his dead mistress made him remember her with renewed tenderness. With his heart beating against Musa's he would think bitterly, "Why cannot I love as I once loved? Why does all her beauty leave me cold? Why cannot I know again that old sweet madness? Alas! alas! with her—my dead queen—should I have cared whether a prison or a palace held her, should I have known where we were, so long as we were left together?"

That was all dead in him.

He knew it. Vainly he strove to call alight the fire that had died down in him; vainly he sought to persuade himself that sensual covetousness was the same thing as passion, and chill desire sweet as adoration. Like those kings of the East, who slay living slaves to warm their own frozen veins, he had thought by sacrifice of her to make himself drunk once more with that intoxication of the soul and senses in which the despair of his hopeless fate could be forgotten. But his heart beat but dully; he could give but a poor, short-lived, languid gratitude to this hard-won love which merited such endless recompense. Sometimes, when he bowed his head down on Musa's breast, the bitter tears would rise under his closed eyelids, as he would think, "If only *she* lived again! if only once more my lips could touch her!" And he knew that she was a dead thing there in Mantua, a thing rotted out of all likeness of itself, in her grave under the marble pile in Sant' Andrea!

She longed to have delicate apparel that she might seem the fairer before him; she was tempted to set the golden grasshopper upon her bosom that she might look the lovelier to him; she would put flowers at her throat; she would take the sweet smell of the broken bay-leaves on her hands; she would say to the sunbeams that could not enter the tomb, "Oh, come in with me, that my hair may have your light!" and she would cry to the birds among the blossoming trees, "Oh, tell me your secrets, that I may sing to him a song that will never tire him."

For her songs tired him; that she saw. He was always tired, he who could not see the face of the sun, who dared not walk across a rood of turf, who had no range but these narrow stone chambers that he paced with restless feet, as the caged lions pace their den.

He was the world to her; if she had been in the crowds of a city she would have seen but his face amidst the multitudes. In the twilight of the tombs his smile made for her a light more lovely than the morning glory of the skies; she could have lived so through years, through centuries, content.

But he,—his caprice crowned, his victory assured,—he began once more to weary of the long and empty days, to sigh for the ways of the world and the voices of men, to fret his soul in that dull dejection which had been roused and dissipated for a little time under the eagerness of jealousy, the excitation of failure.

"It is no fault of yours, dear," he said once, wearily: "you do all you can. But I am a prisoner here. Though you console, you cannot change my fate. I have read of a bird, a great vulture, who lived in his cage, but his wings grew paralyzed and hung helpless. I am like the bird. I am half paralyzed. I am scarce a living man."

Then, when he saw the great tears start into her eyes and her face grow pale, he repented, and kissed her, and drew the close-curling bronze of her hair to his breast.

"Nay, I *do* live, through you. I am an ingrate to lament. Forgive me, and forget it!"

But his lament echoed in her heart, and remained in his. It was the one shadow across the sunlit path of perfect joy down which her feet were going, careless of their goal. He was not free; and without freedom the sweetest fruit has a bitter taste, the clearest water has an acrid flavor.

He was not free; and she who had had power for a while to make him oblivious of his doom soon lost that power, through no fault of her own, but merely through the seldom-varying laws of reaction that govern the man in his passion as the child with his toy.

She had made her boat sea-worthy again, and hung a cluster of pine-cones at its bow, because Este had told her that they were the symbol of Etruscan Nethlans, the god of the deep sea.

"He brought me back to you," she said, thinking of that night of peril, and, like a child as she still was in some things, she thought to please and to propitiate the sea-king by thus hanging his emblem at her bows.

But the boat she could use little; he did not choose she should go far afield, and her love of wandering was tamed and stilled, her world was narrowed to one human life; she was like the nightingale that came so far, from Persian rose-fields and from Syrian cedar groves, and was content—so content!—to sit all the day long, all the spring through, in one little nest on one low bough, amidst the ploughman's spikenard and the blue borage and the prickly safety of the field ononis.

As the birds rested, so did she, and lost her wish to roam hither and thither over the far meadows stretching to the south and the dense woodlands leading to the Ciminian Hills.

If he could have gone with her, indeed, then, with her hand in his, gladly would her steps have passed through the wood-spurge and the trefoil and the plumy grasses whilst the blessing of the spring was upon all the land. But, since he could not, dearer to her than the sunlight was the twilight of the tombs. She, to whom air was at once the nectar and the necessity of life, gave up the green and golden days without a sigh, except a sigh that he was unable to behold the radiance and smell the fragrance of them.

She was abroad for the inevitable work needful for their maintenance, but no more did she linger amidst the parnassus-grass by the pools to watch the water-birds, no more did she lie for hours on the soft wood-moss to watch the clouds move by and change. The sylvan life, the impersonal life, was over for evermore, and she deemed her loss her gain. But, since he durst not trust himself to the daylight, she stayed beside him, and let the starry squills uncurl along the shore, and the tulips spread a scarlet carpet through the meadows, and the royal asphodel uplift its sceptre to the sun, unseen by her eyes, that loved them with the poet's love.

But he could not go out into the light of day, he could not venture forth when his hunters might at every step fall on him: never a syllable escaped her of regret for that which was impossible. The world was so far from her; she knew not of it; she was a law to herself, and her whole duty seemed to her set forth in one simple word,—perhaps the noblest word in human language,—fidelity. When life is cast on solitary places, filled with high passion, and aloof from men, the laws that are needful to curb the multitudes, but yet are poor conventional foolish things, though needful, sink back into their true signification and lose their fictitious awe.

He and she were as utterly alone as the first human lovers in the allegory of Eden: as in Eden, the only sin that could come nigh them would be unfaithfulness.

She lost her dread of losing him.

It seemed to her that no one could ever reach and hurt him, prayed for as he was daily, hourly, with all her soul sent up in prayer, even in those very moments when she felt most fear that there was no mercy anywhere to hear her more than the hunted doe's and the trapped redbreast's cries were heard. He was guiltless of the crime they accused him of; she was too young to doubt that innocence was a buckler holy and impenetrable, a defence such as the gatherer of the dove-orchid is thought to hold against all foes of flesh or spirit.

It seemed to her that they might live thus together, in these solemn shadows, in these twilit chambers, where nothing came of the world above save some stray beam of the sun, some echo of a bird's carol, some scent of the woodruff or the sweet herbs blossoming above. She seldom thought of the future—who does that is happy in the present?—but whenever she did so she seemed to see a long vista of the years to come, lengthening away in golden haze as the sea-shore did, winding to the south, till it was lost in soft suffused light: she seemed to see them always. All she asked of fate was to be forever together thus, till age or death should find them, and lay them gently down, folded in each other's arms, still in the place of their refuge where men would never behold them, but only the wandering wind would sometimes bring the flower's message to them, and sometimes a ray of the sun would come and kiss them where they slumbered.

She could not divine the intolerable impatience that tormented him, the unutterable nausea of life that at times overcame him, so that even she only seemed to him a part of the burden of his days, a portion of the weariness that weighed him down.

He to her was as the daybreak, as the morning, as the smile of the earth in the spring-time, as the rainbow that breaks through the darkness, as the star that guides the mariner into harbor; but to him she was at best but what the humble flower growing in the stones at his feet was to the prisoner. Above her, behind her, beyond her, forever between him and her, there was the passion of his longing to escape, there was the vision of the world he had lost.

At times, almost he could have cried aloud to her, "Better to have let me die in the cane-brakes of the marshes than have kept me alive to live thus!"

Childlike, he had thought that, could he but break down a blossom that hung out of his reach, he would amuse himself with it all the year through, and forget how long time was, and cheat his dreary destiny by oblivion of it. But, like the child, having reached and culled the blossom, he cared little to play with it; almost he looked with regret at what his sport had done; almost he wished it once more out of reach, that he might once more long for it.

In their loves men often are but children,—and captious children, too.

Who thwarts them rules them best.

The time went on, like a long golden ribbon slowly unwound.

The world was transfigured to her. Now and then the fables of heaven cannot match the ecstasies of earth; only so soon they perish, so soon they pass.

He was not content; that was the only shadow on her path. He was restless, weary often, often impatient of the restraint, the tedium, the emptiness, of all his days.

If she could see his face and feel his touch, all the world could have added nothing to her joy; but with him it was otherwise. His short-lived passion, violent for the time, burnt itself quickly out. "One cannot make love forever," he thought, with a man's captious ingratitude. What he wanted was to walk among the cities of men, to go whither he would, to hear the laughter of the streets, to move and roam, and like and hate, and change and choose, and lead the life that others led,—in a word, to be free.

His captivity was like an eternal night forever about him. For others the sun shone and the world turned, but he ate his heart out here; and the gloom of his destiny was so great that it even stole from him all warmth out of her cheek, all delight out of her caress, and made her seem to him but a portion of the interminable weariness that enveloped him.

She was beautiful always, and to him most tender; and the humility of a proud nature has in it a homage the most sincere and the most exquisite in flattery that human nature holds. Yet she could never more than half console him; she could never so content him that he did not envy the brown-winged scops as it flew out at evening to wing its way over moor and marsh.

A chained creature grows cruel because of its own endless fret and pain.

He hid this from her as much as he could, conscious with shame of the ingratitude he could not control; and she was less quick to perceive it than she was to note other emotions in him, because her eyes were blinded with the celestial beauty of a love that asked for itself nothing more from earth or heaven than this life it had.

What to her were privation, alarm, toil, solitude, danger, hunger even, so long as she could hear his voice or feel his touch? They were no more than the rain-drops that fall on the leaves around are to the swallow nestled by her mate in the little warm house beneath the coping of the wall.

So time slipped away; and each week, each month, brought more strength and patience and infinite adoration to her love for him, and brought more fatigue, more irritation, more despondency at his fate, to him.

This long hot summer, with its damp air, its bursts of tropical rain, its sultry perilous vapors, seemed like one tedious day to him, yet a day that would never end, but was reeled off from the wheel of destiny in horrible, perpetual, unchanging sequence.

All the thrones of the world might have been offered her, and all the anathemas of all its various religions hurled at her, and she would never have left his side in that lonely chamber of shadows. But he?——

The greatness of her nature escaped him. The beauty of her sacrifice did not touch him to more than a passing emotion.

He did not see that here was a soul on which his own might rise to any heights,—that here was a love which could become to him as the "white genius" of the Etrurian myth.

He failed to comprehend the magnitude of her gifts to him. The reason was simple: he never really loved her.

Happily for her, she was not learned enough in passion's vagaries to perceive that.

To her it seemed forever wonderful that he looked for her return as the shades of evening fell with longing eyes, that he found any loveliness in her, that he forgot his dead mistress for her sake.

She was nothing in her own sight.

She was proud in some ways, but she was utterly humble in others.

She was but a moorland thing in her own sight, no higher than the loosestrife or the woodspurge was, just fed with sun and dew, and born out of the soil where she took root.

If she were, indeed, fair to see as he and the others said, it was only, like the flowers, by the grace of nature and the smile of heaven. Her character was molded on too grand lines for any vanity to find place to lurk in it, and that selfishness which is the safeguard and armor of all average women was also absent from her.

"You love me as angels might love!" he said once to her, roused to some momentary sense of wonder, recognition, gratitude.

Sometimes she seemed to him like some grand young angel leaning down over his weakness, and sometimes at this he was angered.

Sometimes that ineffable tenderness, so inexhaustible, so divine, that was in her for him oppressed and daunted him. It seemed to lay a burden on his life, on his conscience.

If she had but been as other women are, captious, changeful, impatient, uncertain, he would not have felt this vague fear of her which seldom left him, blindly subject to him though she was. Her patience was so perfect, her love was so intense, that at times he felt humbled and unworthy before her, and would cry to her angrily. "Why make a god of me? I have brought you nothing but woe. Chafe me, deride me, upbraid me, then perhaps I shall love you always: men are made so."

Those bitter words hurt her without her understanding them.

Her tongue could not have framed a rough word to him. The harmless cunning of feminine wiles was as far away from her as the fret of cities was distant from her calm green woodlands and her solitary shores. As soon could a Greek marble of Electra have stooped to coquetry as she.

"If you would but offend me that I might quarrel with you," he said once, half in jest. She smiled because he did, but she did not comprehend.

Ah! the fair hours! he thought, when in Mantua he and his love had quarrelled almost to rupture, and black jealousy had been there to sting to life the waning passions, and the burning rage of mutual reproach had melted into the amorous delight of reconciliation, and the gall-apple bitten through had made sweeter the honey of delight.

Unholy memories, base gladness, this he knew, yet he sighed for them.

These grand eyes of Musa, these lips that were always mute unless they spoke in blessing, made him feel feeble, ungenerous, unworthy. Her very silence on it made his debt the greater,—too great: it weighed love down.

CHAPTER XXXVII.

THE spring waned and grew summer, the plains of corn became yellow and ruddy, and the bearded grain fell to the hundreds of sickles reaping there, as to thousands of scythes the high grass had dropped in the May-time. The flocks and the herds wended their way to the cool mountains; the days were long and glowed with heat. The old summer silence, the old summer solitude, were come again; the crickets laughed in all the grass and all the trees, and she was happy because the land was lonely, left to him and her, shared only by the blithe birds and the innocent beasts.

She began to lose the fear of his arrest. As the calm days and weeks glided by they brought by their tranquil recurrence a sense of safety with them. The season of peril had passed, and the sun now put a zone of torrid heat and dazzling light about their refuge, and the fever-mists that to others were terror were to her as a welcome wall risen up between them and mankind.

The long, deep, unbroken stillness of the Maremma day was sweet to her in this midsummer time, when even the lusty, full-throated merle was tired of song, and, except the hum of insect life and the mirth of the tree-frogs, there was no sound at all throughout the land from sunrise until sunset. Into the tomb of the Lucumo the heat of the upper air could not penetrate greatly: there was a drowsy warmth in it, no more. Whilst even the moor-hen was hot among the mat-grass, and even the eagle flew with languid wing over the olive woods of the hills, in the Etruscan grave it was cool and twilight always.

Once she went to the shore to gather mussels and take home for him; they would cook in the wood-ashes, and he would tell her the while of Petronius, of Apulius, of Lucullus, of all that luxurious life of Rome, of Greater Greece, and of the *otiosa Neapolis*.[1]

She took off her shoes and kilted her skirt, and waded almost knee-deep in the shallow sea-water, while the shore beside her was fragrant with the rosemary and the southern-wood, and the sea-pinks were blowing like little puffs of rosy cloud, and a kingfisher, all azure and emerald in the sun, did not fly away at her approach, but went on with his own fishing and meditations.

She gathered her harvest of the sea, and found a few oysters, too, in among the rocks and the sea-fennel. The water was blue as the kingfisher's breast; a sweet west wind was stirring it; in the clear air Elba stood forth like a giant's castle in tales of magic; above-head the rock-doves and the rock-martins were wheeling and soaring among the golden motes of the sunbeams.

It was early and all was still. There was not even a sail on the horizon.

She waded on to the sand, out of the water, and leaned to rest

---

[1] An Epode about Naples by Horace.

against a great boulder of ruddy tufa, putting her creel down beside her.

She wore one of those straw hats shaped like the *petasus*[1] of Hermes, which still, with the shepherd's crook and the shepherd's reed pipe, and the water-jar balanced on the women's heads, and the attitudes of the half-nude, symmetrical, and supple limbs, recall the statues of Phidias and of Cleomenes to the student as he wanders here, wherever the lands are lonely and the goats crop the wild thyme.

With one hand resting on the rock behind her, and her feet tightly crossed and glistening with the yellow sand and the sea-water, she looked out over the broad blue heaving plain of light, and thought with grateful heart of that terrible night when the sea had devoured her and released her.

How dark it had been that night! "Dark with the thoughts of the Lord," as a Russian poet has said of the night on the steppes of Ukraine. She had died and come to life again. She had descended into the grave of the deep waters, and been delivered by the hand that she loved. Her heart swelled with emotion and was thankful as she looked through the sunlight on the sea which had been thus merciful.

How the black wall of water had risen and towered above her! how the foam of it had hissed, and boiled, and seethed! How impenetrable had been the cruel starless skies! how deep and how hoarse the thunder of the storm!

She remembered it, and recalled it with a thrill of awful pleasure, as a child that has been lost, lying safely in his little bed at home, will recall the terrors of the unknown roads and unknown faces that scared him on his way.

Absorbed in those memories, she did not hear a boat approach through the water and ground on the sand, as that of Sanctis had done in the winter noon.

Before she had heard any sound about her, Daniello Villamagna had come beside her.

He looked, as the phrase of a *stornello*[2] runs, "as handsome as an almond-tree in flower." He was as tall and lithe as a young poplar. He

---

[1] A flat felt hat with a broad round brim.

[2] Stornellos are poems which were popular among Tuscan peasants. The first line always refers to a flower.

seemed to have all the force and the freedom of the high seas in his movements and his glance.

It was eight months since she had left him standing by the sea-wall by the salt lagoon of Orbitello. Since then he had made another voyage,—this time to the surly Flemish coast, to the gray cloudy Scheldt, carrying his rich amber and green Sicilian fruit through the snow-storms and the north winds of the great waves that Scandinavia and Iceland sent rolling in to the Low-Country shores.

He was paler and thinner than before, but his eyes were bright and full of eagerness.

"I have found you once more!" he cried to her. "Ah! do not move, do not go away: you hurt me. Why will you mistrust me?"

All the softness had gone out of her face, and all the light had gone, too, as soon as she had seen him. He was nothing to her but another danger, another difficulty, another trouble the more.

"I do not mistrust you," she said, remembering how he had lent her his boat and bade his boatswain not follow her. "I think you are a loyal man: sailors are always loyal. But I am sorry that you do not forget me and cease to come after me, for though you should so come for twenty years, never shall I say you are welcome."

Pain and anger both swept over his handsome face, as a cloud sweeps over a landscape.

"I have been seeking you many days," he said, "to and fro, up and down the coast. I came back from the Flemish seas last month. It was bad weather for the most part; the snow-storms were many. Sometimes the rigging of my brig was hung with icicles. The winter is long in those parts, as long as the summer with us. I think they never see a sunbeam, save such as the oranges we take them have caught on their rinds of gold. You do not listen. I could tell you many things that would divert you, but you will not listen. Well, only hear me say this: I took the memory of you with me all the way over those cold seas. When my men shivered in the frost, I said to myself, 'It is not so cold as were her unkind words.' I have not looked a woman in the eyes since last I saw you yonder by the *stagno*. Nay, that I swear——"

"Look at whom you will," said Musa, angrily, "only look not at me——"

He pursued his discourse, unheeding her displeasure, though it struck him hardly.

"If you had been with me, the life would have pleased you; it is good. It is good to go and see those poor muffled wretches who scarce ever feel the sun and move like ghosts about beneath their fogs, and then to come back to see our own shores, where all the sunshine is, and where the very moon makes us a second day, and where the lutes sound half the night, and the olive grows down to the sea, and in winter all the air is full of the smell of the orange-flower and of the coltsfoot in the grass."

She gave an impatient movement as he paused, but he pursued the thread of his own thoughts aloud.

"If you had only come! It is at you only that I look. Though I have not seen your face seven long months, it has been with me always. Out of the gray and yellow fog you seemed to beckon me. Oh, yes! I know well you never do, you never even wish to see me. But I—I love you so well it seems to me that some time or another I must bring you to care a little. I am not much myself, though women have smiled on me before now; but the ship is a good ship, and will cradle you safely on the waves; and you love the sea; and down on my Sicilian shore I would make you a nest, as the lory makes his among the orange-trees, and your nest should be all among the white orange- and lemon-flowers, and overhang the waves so that you should be able to see the coral and the fish of the deep water, just leaning from your balcony. When I heard the church-bells ringing inland as I went along the black, wintry, bitter coast, it was for you I prayed. I took my good ship into her dock, and then I came back here to find you. Why will you not say something gentler? To love you is no offence."

"You have seen me twice!"

"When I had seen you once it was enough: I love you, and I was not afraid———"

He was thinking of the fierce Mastarna blood which he knew ran in her veins; he was thinking, "Though I knew that she would live to plunge a knife into my breast, yet would I make her mine,—if I could, if I could."

She heard him with pain and with anger. Her whole nature had softened and changed under the influence of a great passion as bronze melts under the flames. She was more able to feel sorrow for him than she had been before in the unthinking hardness of her ignorance of love. But she was still offended, troubled, and perplexed.

She was silent awhile, watching the motionless body of the kingfisher glancing like a jewel in the sun. The sailor watched her as she stood erect on the edge of the waves.

"Where do you live?" he said, abruptly.

"That will I never tell you."

He thought to himself, Should he tell her of Saturnino? Should he tell her whence she took her grand luminous eyes, her passion for freedom, her strength of body and spirit?

But how should she believe him if he did?

How should he persuade her that he spoke the truth? And how much it would wound her, humble her, make her ashamed, to know herself the daughter of that galley-slave, that mountain-thief, that murderer, whom she had abhorred whilst she had pitied him! He dared not: she would but hate himself the more.

He said to her only, "Do you remember that day by the *stagno*, when you were sorry to see the brigand of Santa Fiora working like an ox in a yoke?"

"Yes; I remember that. He got away, they said, and was eaten by the sharks."

"He got away, but he lives still. I myself,—I made his escape possible. He threw himself from the sea-wall and swam; I picked him up; in the darkness no one saw my boat. I carried him across to Sardinia, where men of his blood live in the forests and on the hills. I did it for you, because you pitied him."

"You did a brave thing," she said, and almost she smiled at him, and his heart was glad.

"I did it for you," he said, and hesitated. Should he tell her?

"He was a bad man," she answered. "He was a murderer and a thief many times. But chained there I felt sorry for him, though he did betray me and steal the gold."

"What gold?" said the mariner, quickly.

"Gold that was trusted to me," she said, remembering how nearly she had betrayed herself.

"The gold of the Etruscan grave?" he said.

The blood went out of her lips with fear.

"How did you know of that?" she asked, with terror at her heart.

"Saturnino himself told me. He told me that you showed him a place in the earth,—a *buca delle fate*,—and that there were gold toys there, and armor, and he stole them, and they led to his own undoing."

"As he merited," she said, between her lips. She breathed again at ease, remembering that Saturnino had not known she lived there.

"Did ever he speak to you of one who escaped with him," she asked, desiring to know the worst,—"a noble, sentenced for murder, for whom reward is offered?"

"No: he never spoke of him. Why?"

"There would be money to be made if you knew where he was," she said, with the subtlety of her race, which ran side by side with their bold passions.

"I am not a blood-hound to track him," said Daniello Villamagna, with contempt. "No, I know naught of him, and would not use my knowledge if I did. Nor would you, I think?"

"They offer money," said Musa, with feigned avarice; "but I, too, am not a spy."

"If you love money, look at this," said the sailor, deceived by her apparent greed.

He brought out from the breast of his shirt a little case, and in the case was a necklace made of that fine gold, *lavorato a sfoglia*,[1] for which Sicilian goldsmiths are still famous as they were in the old Greek days.

She looked at it with a smile.

"It is pretty. You will give it to your *dama!*"[2]

"I brought it for you," he said, with the timidity of true love making his voice tremble and his brown hand shake.

"For me! Ah, I am not like Saturnino of Santa Fiora. I care nothing for trinkets. Go you back with it to your island and give it there to some one who will smile at you. As for me, I have no time to idle with you: I am going home———"

"You will not take it?"

"Certainly I will not."

He threw the case, with the necklace in it, by a sweep of his arm far out into the sea.

The kingfisher, startled at the splash, rose and took wing regretfully.

---

[1] *Sfoglia* is a type of pasta; literally, this means "worked into the shape of pasta noodles." Ouida may have meant *foglia*, "gold foil."

[2] Dame or Madame (i.e., girlfriend).

"The sea has enough treasure without yours," said Musa, with indifference. "You scared the bird————"

For the first time he lost patience, and a fierce oath escaped him.

"You have no more heart than a stone," he said, bitterly, as Este once had said it.

She did not answer, but took up her creel with the mussels and oysters in it.

"Where do you live?" he said, abruptly.

"That I shall not tell you."

That she dwelt in the tombs never occurred to his thoughts. Saturnino had spoken of the place as a hole in the earth, and he himself had only guessed that from containing gold toys it was some Etruscan burial-place. He had heard of such.

"You will not tell me?" he said, in his teeth. "Then I will find out for myself."

She did not reply; she thought how the kingfisher blinds and baffles men to where his underground home is made: surely she could do as much as the birds did. Yet a great dread was at her heart: it would be hard to rid herself of this persistent wooer.

At last a thought struck her, and she looked him full in the face.

"What can it matter to you where I live? Leave me in peace. You should be too proud to come where you are undesired. As for the other things that you say, thus much I will tell you: I dwell with one I love. All the rest of the world may die—for me."

There was no color on her face as she spoke, and no tremor in her voice: she looked him full in the eyes, calmly and coldly; there was sternness and repose in her look. So might Fate itself have spoken.

He grew as pale as though she had struck him a blow which he could not return.

He drew back a step or two, and gazed at her with pain which would have been pathetic to her if she had had any sight or thought to give to him.

"All the rest of the world may die—for me."

The words seemed to go through him and slay every hope and fancy in him, then and for evermore, they were so entirely the expression of a passion that was only so tranquil because it was so absolute. All in a moment he felt broken, bruised, grown old. His youth all at once seemed to slip away from him, never to return.

"Is that so?" he said, at last. "Then truly have I nothing to do here.

I thought your heart white marble, on which no hand had writ any name; and why, I thought, why not write mine? but to you, no doubt, I look mad."

Then, with those halting words, so inadequate and feeble to utter what he felt, he reached with a stride his little boat, and launched it, and plunged his oars into the water.

The jutting wall of the Sasso Scritto in another moment or two hid him from sight.

He was gone over the silent pathway of the sea; while the gold of his necklace hung five fathoms down upon a branch of coral, among the gliding incurious fish and the strange foliage of the deep-water weeds.

Neither to the trinket nor to him did she give a regret. She lifted the creel of mussels on her shoulder, and stepped out with wet feet and lightened heart over the sand homeward.

CHAPTER XXXVIII.

IN the gray river-clay that she brought for Este with arduous toil from the bed of the Ombrone River, he had made in the twilight of his sombre and solitary workroom a full-sized statue of her. He had a facile talent, and here, where it was his only solace, his sole pursuit, he had achieved a certain greatness of conception, and freedom and grace were both in the work of his hand. When she came in that day, he stopped her with a gesture. "Ah, how like you are to my image of you!" he said, with pleasure in his own creation.

In his statue he had made her with nude feet and arms, fresh come from the sea, with the bronze *aryballos*[1] poised upon her head, as he had seen her stand a hundred times before him. On the rough clay of the base he had scratched Glauca as her name. His work was both graceful and noble: it had truth to nature and a beautiful youthfulness in it. He who had only idled now and then with clay in the Lombard studios of friendly students was both amazed and proud that he could now call so much life out of the gray earth that the Ombrone washed daily towards the sea.

---

[1] A small flask used to hold perfumes or oils.

"Is it like me, indeed?" she said, for the twentieth time, as she looked timidly at it. "I see my bare feet, and the ribbon-weed in the sand, and the bronze jar; but all the rest,—can it be like me?"

And he told her for the twentieth time,—

"It is like you, if gray clay can be like a living flower."

She looked at it doubtingly, unable to believe in any flattery so sweet as this. Then she said to him,—

"You will be glad to know that Saturnino Mastarna has got safe away from Orbitello; he has crossed over to Sardinia; it is an island, you know, a big one; we can see it very far away, like a cloud, and the flamingoes come from there, they say."

"Who told you?"

"A man upon the shore."

A certain sensitiveness—rather for him than for the lover she had rejected—made her shrink from saying that a man who was free to woo her had spoken to her of love that day. She was afraid to rouse his jealousy.

Este ceased to look at the statue; his face grew overcast, he sighed with impatience.

"That brute, cursed with a thousand crimes, can get free! And I—I shall rot away my whole life here in a hole in the rocks, and hear the feet of men go by above in the grass! And there is no blood on *my* hands?"

She looked at him in awe and pain.

"I thought you would be glad, for his sake," she said, wistfully, and then added, with a quiver of exceeding tenderness in her voice, "For me, I wish all his crimes forgiven him: he sent you here."

That exquisite softness of meaning and of accent passed by him; he was envying the freed man his flight across the sea to that mysterious isle, where, safe in the darkness of immemorial forests, the wild beasts still live in peace.

"He can go, and the flamingoes, and the swallows, and the falcons," he said, bitterly; "only I must stay! How did he get away?"

"The boat of a friend took him; he sprang from the sea-wall in the dark, as the gang left off their night-work."

"I should have been better there than here; then I too might have taken that leap."

"And I?" said the eyes of Musa; but her voice said nothing.

Was it of this he was always thinking? To escape, to get away, to go elsewhere? Was this home, that was as dear to her as its hole in the rock to the cliff-pigeon, only to him but a prison the more?

"If you had never seen me, it would have been well for you," he said, with a sudden sense of self-reproach.

"When you are content, it *is* well with me,—so well!" she said, softly.

The very tenderness of the answer galled him: he passed it over. "Saturnino did not mean you well," he said, bitterly. "He said to me, 'A fawn's throat is soon slit.'"

"That was only because he has been a bad man, and cruel all his years, and his knife always ready. He knew well that you would not hurt me."

"Have I not hurt you? Heaven pardon me!" he murmured, and he kissed her.

Sometimes he seemed in his own sight what men would have called him,—a base coward.

"You hurt me when I think you wish yourself away," she said, timidly, under her breath; and he said to her in answer,—

"Nay, not away from you, but free to go out into the light, free to feel the wind on my face and hear the stir of the world once more. Ah, dear! if they had opened his cage door for that vulture that I told you of, I think he would have found strength, even in his paralyzed wings, to rise and go."

"Perhaps," she said, simply, and said no more.

But that night, in her sleep, she sobbed bitterly, and she dreamed that she watched a flock of flamingoes, as she had watched one many a time, going westward, rose-red against the blue sky, and she thought that their wings were so ruddy of hue because they had been dipped in her own heart's blood, and she grew fainter and fainter the farther they flew, and when they were lost to sight in the cold haze of the sun, then her life went from her and she sank down and died.

CHAPTER XXXIX.

In Mantua that night, an old man sat writing in a large dark chamber in an ancient house looking on the Lago di Mezzo and having its foundations sunk deep down among the reeds and osiers and the shifting sands. There was no sound but such as came from the hoarse chorus

of the frogs that thronged the lake, and now and then a bittern's call
or an owl's hoot.

In the city, now dark with the gloom of a moonless midnight, the
white marble of a mausoleum, with a lamp burning ever before it, was
shut away behind the stately doors of the noble church of Sant' Andrea; and the tomb, with its guardian angels, was raised to the memory
of his wife, who had died young whilst he was old; and that which he
wrote at the black leather-covered table, by the light of oil-wicks burning feebly, was his own confession that he had killed her with a dagger
which her lover had left in her chamber in carnival time.

A pale-faced foreigner had haunted his steps for weeks and
months, had traced all his past years almost hour by hour, had pieced
together a million fragments of infinitesimal evidence, fine as dust,
that together made a tale written on granite, had found out old servants, and made them speak in secrecy under their oath, and, when the
proof was so complete and overwhelming that no denial of or escape
from it was possible, had come straight to the worthy judge of the
civil court whom Mantua reverenced, and had said to him four words,
only:

"You were the murderer."

With the eye of a trained man of the law, the masked assassin
knew at a glance that there was no loophole of escape for him; that
this pale stranger, come he knew not whence, and working to what
end he could not tell, had pulled down all his careful fabric of fraud
and falsehood and hemmed him in between two stone walls of evidence.

He confessed, seeing in that act some paltry chance of life and
public pity, and wrote out his confession and signed it, clearing from
all guilt the name of the Count Luitbrand d'Este, and setting forth
how he himself, with his own hand, had slain his wife and falsely accused her lover of the crime.

When on the morrow the confession was in the hands of justice,
and the miserable body of Piero di Albano was conveyed to the prisons of the city, the task of Maurice Sanctis was over, the gift that he
would bear to Este was complete. Greater gift than this of freedom
can no man carry to another.

"I myself will tell him," he thought, on the eve of that memorable
day when the people of Mantua gathered about the marble tomb of
Donna Aloysia, and talked in the narrow contrade of the city of this

strange tragedy which had come in fresh guise to their mouths to help them pass the long, hot, empty hours.

But that night Mantua, as though jealous that a stranger from beyond the snowy mountains on the Lombard frontier should have come there to seize its secrets from out of its dark old palaces, that have seen so many crimes and kept so many mysteries untold,—Mantua, as though angered against him, poured into his throat the poison of her subtle vapors, of her fever-mists, that lurk forever amidst her long fields of reeds and her pale-gleaming water-meadows.

That night he fell ill.

With morning he had almost lost consciousness. The people where he lodged, being frightened, called in Italian leeches, who, true to their school, drew blood from the body that needed all its strength, and then did little else. Without them his constitution might have done battle with the disease and conquered it, but, bled to utter weakness, he had no force left in him to resist the destroying power of that fatal and insidious venom.

By the part he had taken in the detection and accusation of Donna Aloysia's husband, Mantua had learned his name and his place in art and fame; but wiser science was too late summoned: he died on the fifth night, before even his own people could come to him from over the mountains.

His window was open to the wide waters, to the bulrush-thickets, to the slow-gliding Mincio that had given him his death: at this last hour, some sense returned to him, and he strove in agony to speak, gasping for breath the while.

"I want—I want—to bequeath her Præstanella," he muttered. "He may be faithless; and she has no one else———"

That was all they heard, and those who heard could make nothing of the words.

Who shall say what torture the paralyzed soul in him knew, as he strove in vain for power to speak, for strength to make a sign?

But the utter blank of death soon fell upon him, and he perished miserably, with only hirelings and strangers about him, as the midnight hours were tolled from the belfries, and the moon-rays slanting across the water fell through the casement of what had once been Donna Aloysia's chamber, and gleamed on the old gold of the baldacchino above the empty bed.

CHAPTER XL.

THE summer passed on and entered the sign of the lion once again, and more than a year had gone since that night when she had come down the steps of the tombs and found a nameless fugitive seated by her hearth. All the summer, since he had forbidden her going into the towns to sell her work, they had had but little food. It was the season of the year when the woods yielded the least, when it was hardest without going far afield to get enough to make even a slender meal. The wild oats indeed she had cut and threshed and kept; but it is unpalatable, and yields but little nutrition, and ill sustains the strength of a man.

Her old carking care came back on her; she saw that he grew paler again and thinner, and a terror seized her lest again the miasma of the land should take hold of him in his weakness. So strong was this fear, so vivid were her memories of that awful fever-fiend with which he had wrestled, half dead, so long, that she passionately besought him to grant her leave to go and sell her store of work and bring him back food and wine.

He himself began to see that they could not long continue to live thus, and let an unwilling assent be wrung from him; and, after all, he cared less.

She had a lovely face, but he had looked on it so long that he knew its every line by heart, and thought he could have molded it in clay with his eyes shut.

She was always there; that was her only fault to him. But perhaps it was the most fatal fault of all.

Therefore he let her go on this errand without objection, and bade her take with her a few of the trifles he had modelled: he fancied they might bring in a few pence.

She could not bear to leave him for a day, but she knew not what else to do. There was no one she could seek aid from within reach, nor could she have trusted any living creature with the secret that was his life.

She could not see him waste away for the bare need of food, and she was well aware how the fever-mists that rose at sunset from every morass and every stream seized on empty viscera and impoverished blood.

She clung about his throat, and kissed him with tender passion; then she went.

She had lost her buoyant vigor of movement; she had felt unwell the last few weeks, and did not know what ailed her; but she summoned her courage and her strength, walked to the coast, and there set sail in her little boat, that had the pine bough at its prow. The morning was fine and calm; the sea was blue, and so were the skies; there was no chance of foul weather. It would have been nearer to have crossed the country on foot to Telamone; but she did not feel as strong as usual, and the linen she had spun and the matting she had made were heavy to carry.

The sea was quiet; there was wind enough to fill her little sail, and what there was favored her. Under the easy motion of the boat, with the play of air and light around, she recovered her natural spirit; she sat and steered, and now and then thrust an oar in the water, that was all. She wanted to make all the haste she could; she longed to be at home again, carrying home good food and the red wine that is man's strength.

She sailed in over the sea-weed and the sand of the choked-up bay of Telamone under the shadow of its castle on the rock. She moored her boat hastily and went into the sorry place to try her fortune. The townspeople, such a few as they were, would buy nothing; but there chanced to be there a peddler who had known her as a child in the house of Joconda. He was one of those who bring goods and news together from the outer world into Maremma, and round whose packs the housewives and the gossips gather eagerly.

He was a jovial man, and not more unjust than trade makes all traders, great and small. He bought all she had of spun linen at a fair price, and being a man who knew the bigger towns and their tastes and went about with his merry eyes open, he discerned at a glance the talent and grace of the clay images, and bought them also and shut them in his wooden brass-bound box. Then he persuaded a huckster of the coast to take her matting too, and altogether made her passing rich.

"Nay, I knew Joconda forty years," he said, "and a good soul she was, though silent as a clapperless bell, but good and sturdy and honest, and hospitable always if she had but a crust."

Then, being a chattering man, a bell with more clapper to it than was needful, he would ask her many questions, all of which embarrassed her to answer. She replied at random, vaguely, longing to get away, and buy what she had come for, and set sail again. But the peddler was not easily denied, and chattered on; and then out of a dirty lane came Andreino, who had pulled himself over in his old punt from Santa Tarsilla to speak *sub rosâ*[1] of some tobacco he had received contraband from fishers of the French coast, and which he was willing to sell, as he usually sold such good consignments, to the parish priest of Telamone.

Andreino would be chatted with as well, and listened to, and was curious, and hard to pacify, as he hobbled by her side to the edge of the shallow anchorage.

Had she come by the sea? Was she living as far off as the foundries, then? No? Under the mountains? Then why come by sea? She looked grand and proud; a little pale, but quite a woman now. Had she no wooers? Was she still the Musoncella? Well, time would cure her of that. And then the sly old man looked at her sideways, and said, with a low chuckle,—

"And the youth that was sick, my dear? Do you make the *muso*[2] to him too? Eh—eh? I fancy not! Well, pluck your cherries while they are ripe: the cherry-time soon passes."

The only answer she gave him was the hot blush that came over all her face, and he chuckled the more.

Then all at once he said to her,—

"There is a fine piece of news put up all down the coast. But no doubt, my dear, you have seen it; though in that cherry-time I talked of most of you are blind. But if you do know that stray dog, you may get the reward."

"A stray dog?" she repeated. She was ready to help any dog, for sake of dead Leone.

"A dog that will pay well," said the old man, with a grin. "You can read; I have only heard tell of it: look, it is up on the tower there."

The south wall of the old martello tower in which the coast-guard had of yore been located had a large white placard on it, covered with printed letters that were only confused lines and dots of black from where Andreino was sitting. It was but a step to the wall, and she went up to the printed proclamation.

---

[1] In secret.

[2] Literally it means muzzle. He is referring to her cold nature.

What she read, written there, was the declaration of the pardon of the State to an innocent man, in the common formula of the law.

The published words stated that one Count Luitbrand d'Este had been cleared of the imputed crime of blood-guiltiness by the dying confession, made in Mantua, of Ser Piero di Albano, who had acknowledged himself to have been the assassin of his wife, Donna Aloysia Gorgias, and who had further declared that he had planned and carried out the assassination in such wise that the accusation of it should fall upon his wife's lover, and be vengeance of their adultery.

It proceeded to declare that whereas, by due confession before judges of the real murderer, Piero di Albano had declared himself the assassin of his wife, therefore he who had been accused of and punished for the crime of Donna Aloysia's murder was now declared innocent and free of law; and whosoever might have seen him living, or heard of him dead, was bidden under penalty to report their knowledge to the State.

The print said, further, that a large reward would be paid to whosoever should either give information of the whereabouts of the Count d'Este, escaped from the isle of Gorgona two years before, or proof of his death, if it had been known to take place.

She read this, standing in the sunshine, with the blank wall before her, and about her the buzz of the people's voices.

She read it, seeing each word in a black haze which seemed to veil the sun that shone all around so vividly, and yet for her was darkened.

She read it once again slowly, as unlearned people read, her eyes following the black lines one by one. Then that blackness seemed to spread and spread like a dark cloud before her, and blot out the day.

She stood gazing stupidly at the white sheet fastened up there upon the old, red, peeling, heat-cracked bricks.

Then the sea and the earth seemed to heave and rise up before her, as they do in an earthquake, and a great darkness came down, as from heaven, over her eyes.

The world was gained for him; but he was lost for her. "He will go away!"

CHAPTER XLI.

THAT was the one thought standing out from the blackness that seemed to have fallen over her like a veil flung by some unseen hand.

Then, quick as a snake darts out of its hole in the ground, another thought crossed and supplanted that one. She remembered that unless she told him he would never know.

Not a soul but herself and Maurice Sanctis knew that he lived. Not a tongue save theirs could tell of his hiding-place. Not a living-creature would he ever dare to accost; no human eyes would ever behold him.

With the instinctive concealment of her race which is in the Latin nature side by side with so much fire and fury, she turned from the wall with no evidence of any emotion on her face or in her voice.

"The law makes blunders, and people suffer them," she said, simply.

Andreino shrugged his shoulders despairingly.

"They say the law is never wrong," he answered; "but were I that young man, I would have some one's blood for being shut up and chained and all for naught. If he be living anywhere, methinks he will find out his unjust judge and kill him."

"Perhaps," said Musa; but she did not hear his words; they were like the burr of the water running in and out of the old stone piers, where some men were busy setting their lobster-pots in the shallows.

Her head was throbbing quickly; all before her eyes seemed blood-red; at her ear there was a sound like some one whispering, "Why should he know? why should he know?"

When he knew, he would go away.

With the profound humility which is the characteristic of all great love, she knew at once that he would go; she never doubted for a moment that she would have no power to hold him.

She did not reason on it, or frame it in any conscious formula, but her reason told her that he would go, once learning he was free.

Yet she bade Andreino a good-day in a steady voice, threw her packages into the boat, and set sail homeward.

The old man looked after the little vessel as it went over the waves, dipping and righting itself with pretty ease.

"Her lover cannot be that missing youth of Mantua," he thought, "or never would she have taken it so quietly. A great reward, and a *damo*[1] with a title to his name! Nay, nay, such good luck would have turned her head. She used to be in heaven when one but gave her a silly flower or a shell."

The boat went over the sea homeward.

It was now high noon.

The sea sparkled, blue as woodland pimpernels, and ran merrily from under her bows.

She was hardly conscious of anything she did; she steered straight by sheer force of habit, not seeing either the sky or the water, either the pale white coast or the dusky belt of the pines that divided the beach from the hills.

When the boat was beneath the Sasso Scritto, she ran it ashore, left it lying on the sand with the wine and the food in it forgotten, and took her course over the familiar moor and marsh and grass-land lying steaming in the sun.

Gray and opal hues were cast over the land by passing clouds; where some herds were crossing it, a cloud of dust rose, dusky and curled like smoke.

She traversed the well-known ways. The sky and the earth were whirling round her. Her feet moved without her knowing it. Her body seemed one great pulse, beating, beating, beating.

She never thought of his innocence being made known: had she not always known it? What she thought of only was, As soon as he is told, he will go. Need he ever be told?

She held him as one holds a bird in the hollow of the hand.

If she never unclosed her hand, he would never go.

He need never be told: she said so to herself as she walked: never, never.

If her mouth were shut, no other could speak. He was hers, as the dead are the earth's.

She could keep him close here, hers only, hers absolutely. Was he not hers, purchased by all that she could give, won from the very edge of death, wrestled for long with sickness and pain, and possessed and adored?

But for her he had been ere now a lifeless creature, fallen under some tangle of mastic, some bush of marucca, eaten by the hogs

---

[1] A lover.

of the brake and the marsh, picked bare to the bone by the birds of Maremma; no more than any rotting lizard or carcass of a buffalo dead of draught.

She was but a wild creature of the moors herself, with something noble in her instincts, born there as in a dog's, and with something of strength and faithfulness taught her by Joconda.

Her first impulses were of passion and of possession.

He was hers here in the shadowy caverns of the earth. Why should she lose him to the world of light, that unknown world where she had neither place nor part?

His water-city that he loved, the women leaning from their lattices, with the pearls braided in their hair, the hum of strange towns, the stir and strife of streets, the laughter and the music, the learning and the love, the jocund comedy and bitter tragedy that jostle each other on the stage of life,—why should these become her rivals? She could not contend with them; they were to her known only through his words; they were mere phrases to her, but she feared them.

She vaguely pictured, beyond the opaline horizon of her plains, brilliant and shadowy hosts, dream-cities, golden gates of ivory palaces, faces of women lovely as the opening blossoms of the lily and the rose. Why should she yield him up to these?

She walked across the width of white sunshine shining on the dust, and said in her heart, "I will never tell; I will never tell."

She was not conscious of any treachery in her resolve: she had only the barbarian's instinct to hold and keep.

They were so happy; so it seemed to her. She would have wanted nothing more all her life long than to live on in that solitude, and spin, and weave, and hunt, and fish, and bake bread, all for him, enough repaid by a caress, a murmur, even a mere glance.

It seemed to her as if iron were bound about her ankles; the placid, drowsy amber light seemed like a wall of steel between herself and him. Without knowing what she feared, she was afraid to look upon his face with this secret withheld in her breast.

They had always met each other as simply, as naturally, as two blossoms that blow together in the summer breeze, as two children that run to meet and play. But now already there seemed a dark cloud between his eyes and hers. The shadow of the thing she knew, and would not tell, went before her, and would stand like a ghost from the grave between his life and her own.

She walked with dull step and heavily throbbing heart over the sunburnt earth. The many miles seemed like a rood, yet they cost treble the time to traverse that ever they had cost her before.

The old joy with which she had always seen the brown swell of the uplands, the blasted stem of the big cork-tree, was all gone. She was afraid to see them now, the burden of this knowledge being shut up in her breast.

It was high noon when she did see them at last; two hours later and more than she had reckoned to be at home.

The heat was very great; it was a heat as if the fires, burning in the woods and on the mountains, had coursed down in streams of flame and licked up all the beauty of the earth as prairie-fires do.

It was only the scorch from the blaze of the sun at his zenith, but it was terrible; the very toads were panting, sunk downward in the lowest deeps of the pools. The buffaloes and the boars buried themselves low in beds of canes and cotton-grass; the birds were all still; only the tree-frog shouted in the shrubs, and the snake lay basking and happy on the sand.

The wild mares and their foals could scarce drag one hoof after another; but she was insensible to the sun-rays, that darted at her like arrows red-hot, and lapped her with tongues of flame, and lay on all the land around her like a plague.

She thought only of this secret she carried in her brain. Would he whom she loved not read it in her eyes?

She would never tell him.

That fierce tenacity which was in her blood, as it had been in Saturnino's, fastened on to the one resolve and clung to it.

For the time all that was passionate, violent, fierce, selfish, held their sway, and all she thought of was to hold and keep him, as the child in the cruelty of his possession holds the poor bird it loves until it dies strangled in his embrace.

For the time she did not even realize that what she would do was base. She only remembered that he was hers, that if the world took him he would be hers no more.

Yet, though she was not fully conscious of the treachery she meditated, all the speed and gladness with which hitherto she had always flown homeward to him had gone from her heart and from her feet.

She went on more slowly than her wont across the grass; an unwillingness to look upon his face had taken the fleetness from her steps. Without her consciousness of it, this secret which she would keep, this wrong that she meant to do, was already a barrier between herself and him. When she had drawn quite near the myrtle brake above the tomb, she stopped and sat down upon a hillock of earth; and for the first time in all her life she trembled. If he should read what she had seen upon her face!

With a desperate hand she pushed away the brambles and went down into their place of refuge.

Even here in the heart of the soil the heat had penetrated. The air even underground was heavy and warm, and with little power in it to refresh the panting lungs of man or beast.

In the outer chamber, where the most air came, Este was lying asleep.

He was cast down for coolness on the stone bier where once she had seen the king lie in his armor of gold. He looked like a dead man. He was very pale, his chest scarcely heaved as he breathed, his lips were close shut, his long lashes rested on his wasted cheeks.

The loose shirt he wore fell off his breast and showed the emaciated bones and the feeble yet feverish beating of his heart. In his noonday sleep he looked exhausted, hopeless, heart-broken.

Suddenly, as if it were written in letters of fire above his head, she saw the truth,—that what was her home was but his prison, that what was her heaven was but at best a living death to him.

Without awaking him, she went away and climbed again into the upper air; and there, where the marucca and myrtle made a shadow above the tombs, she sat down on a block of palomberie, stunned and dumb.

At sight of him she had known the baseness of the thing that she would do.

She saw herself as guilty, as cruel, as vile as he who betrayed with a kiss, and whose memory has come down through all the ages as the traitor of all traitors.[1]

---

[1] Judas Iscariot, who betrayed Christ for thirty pieces of silver.

CHAPTER XLII.

SHE sat in the hot air and felt neither heat nor fatigue, though she had walked nigh twenty miles since daybreak. An adder crawled by her under the dry grass, and she saw it not. She was struggling with herself, with all her ignorance, her strong instincts, her absorbing passions, her unutterable love for this the only living thing she cared for out of all the universe.

Had he been left to her, all the nations of the earth might have perished in droves like oxen that die of pest and drought, and she would have looked on indifferent.

She sat here, in the silence and the sultriness of the day, like a statue of bronze set upon the dry and cracking ground.

She was quite motionless; the folded linen on her head kept off her face the vertical rays of the sun, but they fell unfelt on all her crouched form, on her closed hands that were resting on her drawn-up knees, and on her tired feet, past which the adder slid unseen.

She had no knowledge, no experience, but she had imagination.

Imagination showed her the world that waited for him outside that girdle of the moors that held her fast. The vision was in no way like the real world, but it was lovelier, richer, fuller,—such a world as haunts poets in the dreams of a summer's night, crowded with shapes divine and clothed in light.

Here he was hers, but there——

She had no hope, no illusions.

She never thought once that he would say to her, Come also; she never doubted that he would take his freedom as the polar bird had done, spreading its wings without once looking back.

Whether she stayed there moments or hours she knew not: the great heat falling upon her seemed to numb her as if it were a rain of ice. Her eyes grew strained and bloodshot, her veins swelled and grew dark, her mouth was parched as with great thirst. Still she never moved, she was unconscious of physical suffering, she was saying always to herself, "He will go! he will go!"

The most terrible, the most cruel temptation that any human soul could ever know assailed her.

Almost she felt as if the priestly fables were true,—as if the Power of Evil in bodily shape stood over her in the burning heat, with vast black wings outstretched above her head.

"Oh, dear God, help me!" she cried aloud, in utter agony. All that was violent, imperious, and sinful in her sided with the mighty passion she bore her lover, and urged her to bury forever this secret, which would put an end to all her joy and give him to the world. All that was noble, tender, and full of the impulse of self-sacrifice in her heart told her that to be false to him, to deceive him, to destroy his life that it might slowly consume itself within her arms, would be as base as though she killed him sleeping.

The darkness and the light strove for the mastery over her. She was like one torn in pieces by ravenous beasts that rent her asunder.

The sun was going towards the west, but was still high in the heavens, whose cloudless space looked gray beside the deep and sparkling azure of the sea, when to her ear there came a low faint sound; it was the voice that she loved, calling to her, timidly and with caution, from below the nightshade and acanthus foliage.

He wondered, and was afraid, at her long absence.

The sound pierced her apathy, and roused her, as a child's cry does its mother after birth.

She rose to her feet.

Her bright clear skin was pallid and dull; her throat was dry; her brain was hot, and beating in her skull.

She looked once over the yellowed moors and up to the cloudless skies, as a beast that is hunted to the death will do, seeking for pity, finding none.

She drew her belt close about her loins, as though she went to combat, then plunged without pause into the twilight of the tombs.

Ere he could speak, she cried to him, hoarsely, with her parching tongue out of her swollen throat,—

"They have set you free! Go yonder, read it."

He looked at her, and trembled violently.

He stood just within the entrance of the sepulchre; and, as she spoke, such a change came over all his face as comes to a dead man galvanized into sudden life. His lips, his eyes, his whole frame, seemed suddenly to grow instinct with life and light and wonder and rapture and radiance. He caught hold of her with both hands.

"What? what?" he said, with tremulous force. "What do you say to me? Tell me again—quick, quick!"

It seemed to her as if all his life would go out of him in that passion of hope; as if he would dissolve into the air and vanish, as the Etruscan king had done.

He vibrated from head to foot with passionate desire.

She could not bear to look at him or feel his hand upon her.

"It is true," she muttered, hoarsely, as she shook herself loose. "Go and see it for yourself. The old man has confessed. They look for you: you are free."

Then she glided out of his hold entirely, and went away into the darkness of the inner chambers.

CHAPTER XLIII.

HE stood mute and motionless awhile. Then, as the truth was borne in on him, tears gushed from his eyes like rain, and he laughed long and laughed loud, as madmen do.

He never doubted her.

He sprang up the stone steps, and leaped into the open air,—into that light of day which he had been forbidden to see so long.

To stand erect there, to look over the plains, to breathe, and move, and gaze, and stretch his arms out to the infinite spaces of the sea and sky,—this alone was so intense a joy that he felt mad with it.

Never again to hide with the snake and the fox; never again to tremble as his shadow went beside him on the sand; never to waste the sunlit hours hidden in the bowels of the earth; never to be afraid of every leaf that stirred, of every bird that flew, of every moonbeam that fell across his path!—he laughed and sobbed with the ecstasy of his release.

"O God, thou hast not forgotten!" he cried, in that rapture of freedom.

All the old childish faiths that had been taught to him by dim old altars in stately Mantuan churches came back to his memory and heart.

On the barren rock of Gorgona he had cursed and blasphemed the Creator and creation of a world that was hell; he had been without hope; he had derided all the faiths of his youth as illusions woven by devils to make the disappointment of man the more bitter.

But now, in the sweetness of his liberty, all the old happy beliefs rushed back to him; he saw deity in the smile of the seas, in the light upon the plains.

He was free!

He laughed again, as children do in utter gladness, the great tears coursing down his cheeks.

Man had remembered him, and God!

He was so happy.

Only through his heart one sharp pang shot, as though a dagger pierced it.

They could give him back his freedom and his youth, but never more could life be given back to that dead woman slain in the season of her youth by the waters of Mantua.

CHAPTER XLIV.

AFTER a while, when some calm had in a measure succeeded to that intoxication of wonder and of thanksgiving, he went within and called to her.

Her voice answered him from the innermost chamber, where was the coffin of Joconda.

"I am tired," she said, gently: "let me rest."

"But tell me, tell me once more," he urged, with nervous eagerness: "this is true? Beyond doubt? What is it you have seen?"

"What I said. It is printed on the walls. Take the boat and go. You will see and hear what I have said."

"You are sure it is no snare?"

"I am quite sure. Let me rest a little."

Her voice was weak and broken.

He had no ear to notice that.

He thought only that she was sure,—sure,—sure. Then it was no dream. He was indeed free.

She was then standing within a foot of him in the gray gloom of the tomb that had been his home so long; but she was no more living for him. What were alive were the throngs of men in the cities, were the laughter of women and their dances, were the ways of the world, and its gladness, and its dreams, and its passions, and its strife: all that he had been a stranger to so long; all that the youth in him sighed for, imprisoned here in the night of the grave.

He was not more ungrateful than the storm-bird had been; only in him, as in that, there moved the irresistible instincts of movement, the longing to spread wings to the air and go. And in that tumult of emotion and aspiration and remembrance and desire, she who gave him his liberty was forgotten, as she had been forgotten by the bird. It was natural, and she understood it. She had not looked for any other thing. Only she said once more, "I am tired."

She was tired, no doubt, going all those roads over the hot earth to get him bread; but he did not think of it. The whole world had changed for him; life smiled at him once more.

Oh, the joy, only to sit unmolested in the public square, and see the careless crowd go by, and feel the sun and wind upon his cheek!

That she was tired he had no leisure to remember. All the memories of his past were thronging about him like brothers and sisters giving welcome from long absence.

His heart was in that silent town among the shadowy waters, where he had drifted on his oars under the swell of the deep brazen bells of Ave Maria, and where he had seen the glisten of the lilies in the moonbeams when Death had slept with his mistress.

She was tired, no doubt; but all at once she fell back to nothing in his life; she vanished from it as a plucked rose that drops to pieces goes silently away out of a careless hand.

"My dear, come forth and speak to me," he said, with a sound of joy in his voice such as she had never heard in it even when he had first said, "You love me!"

"Wait a little," she answered him; and in a few moments she came out to him, thankful that the light of the tombs was so feeble.

He caught her hands.

"Oh, tell me, tell me again, it is true indeed? Tell me all they say."

She answered him in a strange measured voice, as though she recited a lesson:

"They offer five thousand lire to whosoever can tell where you are. Perhaps your people put it there. It said that the old man has confessed himself guilty of his wife's murder, and that the State pardons you because you are innocent; that I do not understand———"

"It is the common formula when the law has been at fault and condemned the wrong person," he said, quickly, a joyous agitation still trembling in him. "Yes, yes, no doubt my poor mother offers the reward. What she has suffered! You are sure you read it all?"

"Quite sure."

He did not observe her, or he would have seen that the calm she had by such effort attained was strained almost to bursting.

She stood a little away from him, her head was bent, her hands were clasped in each other.

Once she thought, perhaps now that he was free to go where he listed he would remember the promise she had given Joconda, the promise she had broken for him, and would say, "Shall we go up to the house of God together?"

A vague expectancy, too faint and too unformed to be a hope, came to her now and then. But the great humility and resignation of her love for him made her doubt whether he would even remember her, once having back his liberty and the world, and not one syllable escaped her lips to recall either his duty or his debt to him.

"I think I am mad," he said, with a gay, unsteady laugh. "I feel as if I had drunk new wine; the place goes round with me! Ah, to be free, to be free———"

"*She* will not rise again to welcome you," she said, in a low and bitter voice.

For the first time she felt a throb of pity for the woman whose memory she had abhorred: they were alike forgotten.

"Hush! you are cruel," he said, angrily. "Do you think I did not remember? I would give my liberty up now—now—to make her living once more!"

There was a vibration of true passion in the words; the woman dead in Mantua was dearer to him still than she who had given him a love surpassing human love in its sacrifice and its effort.

She was silent.

He stood silent also, unconscious that he was cruel as men mostly are.

They rarely wound because they wish to wound, but because they do not remember, do not understand, do not measure the pain with which women love them.

"Might I go and read that, think you?" he said, suddenly. "It may be best to lose no moment of time in showing them I live,—some impostor may cozen them,—if you will not feel me unkind. Oh, heavens! if you knew—if you only knew—how I long to walk out among men in the bright broad day once more!"

"Go; go at once," she said to him, still with that strange faintness and constraint in her voice, which he did not notice. "The boat is there; you can find the shore without me: I am—tired."

"I will go, then, and I will return by nightfall, by midnight at the latest. Ah, dear, forgive me if I speak like a drunken man: I feel drunk,—drunk with joy! Sweet one, kiss me, and farewell; farewell for a few hours! Love, you have been to me what no living man could merit in any living woman! Often have I felt ashamed——"

"Hush!" said Musa, and she strove to smile. It might be that never more would she behold him; she would not let him hear one accent of reproach as her farewell.

He took her tenderly in his arms and kissed her tenderly, feeling indeed that all the life he had to live on earth could never be long enough to repay to her all that she had given to him, all that she had done for him here in these twilit chambers of the Etruscan dead. He kissed her again, and yet again, then went.

He ascended a second time into the light and air, and walked a few steps across the ground.

It was so strange, so beautiful, so delicious, this mere sense of utter liberty,—to stand and move erect in the sunshine of the declining day, without danger, without terror, without being forced to scan the farthest distance lest any living soul should be in sight. Almost insensibly he moved onward and onward, and it seemed to him as if the dry turf were velvet and the hot air a caress from heaven.

Across the moor he saw the azure glisten of the sea: the boat was there.

Insensibly he walked onward, his feet elastic as the deer's that goes to drink at the forest spring at daybreak.

The sun was now near its setting.

Maremma saw that western pomp and splendor in its uttermost perfection, its low shores shelving to the sea that rolls away to Spain and Africa. All colors of all jewels known to men glowed there, where the great beams shot upward, like archangels' spears. A storm afar off, beyond the headlands of Sardinia, gave majesty and magnificence to the hour. Low down, southward, dark purples and crimsons strove together, and a beam of lightning ever and again flashed zigzag athwart them. But these were distant, and did not disturb the golden serenity, the rose-like radiance, of the immediate west, where the sun hung still high above the waters, one white sail and one brown crossing each other full in the effulgence of its rays.

He had not beheld the sun since, tortured with heat and thirst, he had drifted face upwards, hopeless, and seeing no escape from the galleys save in such death as he would find sinking to those depths below him, where the shark and the octopus waited for drowned men.

It allured him with sweet unconquerable attraction.

He went softly, almost insensibly, on and on, over the sand and the grass, his head held high, his eyes happy, his breath coming quickly and gladly, like the sighs of love that is content.

The sea was there; the world was beyond; men would welcome him back in their midst.

A vague sense of shame, of duty, of ingratitude, drew him backward like an unwelcome hand; but it had not strength to detain him.

"I will come to her; I will send for her," he said to himself; and he continued to walk on and on, through the luminous warm air, towards the shining of the blue waters through the red-brown stems of the pines.

He was so happy; he could not stay to look behind. He longed for the voices of the world, for the hum and the laughter of the streets, for the sound and the sense of living, for the dark old houses leaning above the silvery shallows of Mantuan waters, while the lute throbbed below and the human heart beat above!

Away there, north and south, and east and west, the earth was alive with the mirth and the music and the triumphs and the passions of men.

He forgot that there were pain and privation and struggle and sorrow there also; he only remembered the world as an orchard of fruit and of flowers, fair to behold and to taste, full of sunshine eternal, and musical with tireless song. That winter came there, and sickness, and grief, and death, he had forgotten.

The boat was on the edge of the sea, tied by a rope to a pine-tree, and with the oars of it lying on the beach.

"I will come back to her," he thought, and he pushed the little skiff through the loose yellow sand to the surf.

For a moment it ploughed the soil, sullenly grating on the pebbles as it went; in another moment it floated buoyant and borne up by the water.

He sprang over its side, and plunged the blades of the oars in the sea.

The breeze that comes a thousand miles in a breath blew a scent of orange flowers from the woods high above in the north.

His nostrils drew in with delight the sweet familiar scent; his lips laughed; his heart rose; he set the head of his boat northward, and rode straight for where the orange-trees grew, and ran down to the sea and kissed it.

CHAPTER XLV.

FOUR days and nights went by, and he did not return. To her it seemed as if the whole green and peopled world was dead.

A great despair fell on her, numbing, deadening, destroying all her life as paralysis falls upon the body and enchains it. No tears came to her eyes; no sound came to her lips. She was like a creature suddenly struck dumb.

She crouched in a corner of the inner chamber by Joconda's coffin, and stayed there as a frightened animal, whose spirit is all gone out in terror, crouches in a corner, refusing in the stupidity of its fear even to take what would keep life in it.

Four days and nights went by, and she crept up into the air, and sat half the hot hours through under the tall tree-heaths: looking, looking, looking across those sunburnt levels over which he had passed away to the unknown world. For all that seemed left to her of him, it might have been but a dream that ever she had found him there, seated beside the embers of her fire on that August eve.

She was not surprised that he had gone. She had never thought that he would stay, once knowing.

He had gone; she did not reproach him; she did not even wonder. She would have wondered if he had stayed.

She had known very well that when she had told him he was free she had drawn the knife across the throat of her living joy and killed it forever.

She did not reason on it, or protest against her doom; it seemed to her inevitable as that when the sun rose darkness fled. The instinctive fatalism, the strange passivity, that are in the Southern temper, and succeed its gusts of passion, its heat of rage or love, made her accept her abandonment as a thing not to be questioned, to be borne as any visitation of nature is borne by the earth, though it trembles and changes as the earthquake destroys or the flood effaces it.

Thought seemed dead in her, dead with all other forms of life.

He was gone, he was hers no more: this was all that she knew.

Her soul was dark and empty, like the spent lamp and the dry cup that he had need of no longer.

The light of the world burned now for him, and he could drink from the springs of the world's pleasure-places. He did not want these sad and humble things of hers. She rebelled no more than the earthen vessel and the bronze lamp rebelled because they lay untouched.

CHAPTER XLVI.

ON the fifth morning there came across the moors the shadows of a man and of a mule. Standing, looking with tearless, aching eyes along those sunburnt levels over which he had gone, her heart gave a leap of rapture and her face grew warm with blood as she saw a human figure through the haze of heat. He had come back!

Soon that joy, too exquisite to live longer than a breath, was broken roughly. It was a stranger who stood beside the laden mule: his face and figure were unknown to her. She dropped back into her attitude of crouching hopeless apathy. What was any peddler or other traveller across the plains to her?

The mule came on and was led beside the trunk of the cork-tree, and the man who led it called aloud to her, "Is it you who live beneath the ground here? If it be you indeed, I have a letter————"

At that word she leaped to her feet, changed in an instant, as the dry wood is changed when the rosy flame catches it.

"Is he well?" she cried. "The letter! the letter! Give me, quick!"

"The Count d'Este, my master, is well and in Mantua," the man answered. "He sent me here with these; he bade me get a mule at a town on the shore; he bade me see you myself and take him all tidings————"

"The letter! the letter!" she cried, with her hands outstretched.

He gave it to her.

"Oh, dear God! what a blessed thing it is that I can read!" she thought, as she seized it, herself transformed, her cheeks the color of the wild rose that burns with midsummer on a hundred hills and vales, all her whole face instinct with life and rapture and gratitude and wonder,—wonder that he had remembered, he who never in any moment of her life was absent from her memory.

"Wait without," she said to him, and hurried down the stone steps of the tombs.

She could not bear that a stranger's eyes should see her happiness.

It was hard for her to read written words, she had seen so few.

But love aided her; she read it, trembling in every limb.

It was not long.

It gave her tender names and words; it begged forgiveness that he had been unable to return; he had been compelled to leave at once for Mantua; there he had learned that no good thing comes alone, that not only had the law freed him, but that he had inherited the vast property and the palace in Rome of a distant relative on his mother's side from whom he had never expected aught. This heritage took him to Rome at once, where henceforth he would spend much time: soon he would come to her or send for her.

"What can I say to you? I owe you so great a debt, it weighs me down," he wrote, in conclusion. "Think me not heartless that I fled. Nay, dear, it is only that liberty is so rapturous a joy, it makes one mad, when for so long one has been thirsty for it. I send you a few things that women care for,—mere nothings, indeed, but they will remind you of me. Soon I will come to you or send for you. I took your boat with me and lost it, but you will need it no more, for you must leave that wretched life you lead at once. Go where you will, and tell my messenger where I shall find you. Love me always."

And as he had written those words he had thought,—

"Will she be forever on my life? I owe her so much, but—but— what shall I do with her in the world? She is but a beautiful barbarian, and she will never understand, and she will be forever like a chain about my feet. And all I want is to forget,—to forget!"

She read the letter once,—twice,—thrice. Inside it was a roll of bank-notes bearing the cipher of a large sum.

If he had killed her she would have kissed his hand as it took her life; and it would have hurt her less.

There was on the slab of nenfro near her paper and a pencil which she had bought for him long before, that he might make drawings for the clay he molded.

She could write very ill, in the large, straggling, ill-shaped letters which were all she had been taught.

She wrote thus, with much labor, on a sheet of the sketching paper: "I am well. I want nothing. I am yours always; there is no need to say it. I send you back all the things you send, because I wish not for gifts and have no need of money. I shall be always here. Think not of me save when you desire."

Then she signed it *tua eterna devota*[1], and put it up in a packet with the bank-notes. His letter she thrust into her bosom.

She went up into the light; the messenger, who was an old servant of the house in Mantua, thought, as he saw the change in her face, "Was the letter cruel? Why did he not come himself?"

He had undone his burden, which was one of the great Italian nuptial caskets, velvet-studded and metal-bound. He had spread out upon the grass some of its contents. They were things of great delicacy and value,—strings of pearls, fine raiment, Eastern stuffs, jewels. At them she scarcely glanced.

"Put them all up," she said to the messenger, "and take them back to him, and give him this letter. I do not want anything: if he ask you, say I am quite well."

The servant went back faithfully to Mantua, and faithfully delivered the great casket and the poor, ill-written, humble, yet proud words.

Este was deeply angered.

The words failed to touch his heart, because they stung his conscience.

"Will she ask all my life?" he thought.

But she asked nothing. And the heroism of her silence, as of her sacrifice, awed him, oppressed him, humiliated him.

---

[1] Your eternally devoted one.

CHAPTER XLVII.

THE autumn came and passed, and soon the green moist winter returned to Maremma.

The rose-winged flamingoes and the snow-white birds of the North came over the sea: her lover returned not with them.

But the knowledge of a great consolation was come to her, and she bore the anguish of her lonely, empty, cruel hours with endurance, since when the March hyacinths and asphodels should open to the light she would hold a human blossom to her breast.

She labored hard in this winter-time, knowing that the season would soon come when she could work no more.

Some instinct led her to make friends with a woman at this time, the only woman she had ever been near since Joconda died,—a hard-featured, sunburnt, toil-bent creature, prematurely old from a hard toil, who every year came down with her husband and children, and flocks of sheep and goats, all the way by the roads on foot, from the chestnut woods above San Marcello to the green pastures of Maremma. There are many do the same: it is a laborious life, always beaten about by wind and weather, but the hill-shepherds and herdsmen and their families are used to it, and cling to it as gypsies do. In summer they are up in their own northern hills from hazel-time until the chestnuts drop, and that return consoles them and sustains them.

This woman she saw once, washing linen by beating it with stones in a little stream; Musa gave her some bread she carried, and spoke to her; the shepherd and the ewes and rams were farther off, upon the moors. The woman was not curious or intrusive; the hard life she had led had blown and scorched and chilled and drenched her with rains till she was scarcely higher as an animal than her own mother-sheep, who wanted nothing but to nibble and browse and hear their lambs bleat and lie safe at night.

She was stupid as a stone; but she was not unkind or unfaithful. She kept the secret of the tombs even from her own man, and took a dull liking to this beautiful woodland solitary so unlike herself, who gave her food and helped her to beat her rags in the water, and who looked to her so grand, so fearless, so young, so fair, and yet had the burden of women on her and was all alone.

"Never saw I anything like her on these pastures or above on our own hills," she thought often, and had a dim, superstitious fear of her, and obeyed her without hesitation, and deemed herself paid abundantly by a basket full of fungi or of arbutus-fruit for her children, who were growing up as the lambs and the kids do, tumbling with them on the pastures.

Hers had been but a sorry life; all winter passed on the lonely moist meadows of Maremma, all summer spent in hard work upon the corn-lands on the mountain-sides or in the olive and the chestnut forests up above, where the snow lay on the highest rocks in June. It had made her dull, indifferent, always tired; but, being an open-air creature, she was faithful.

She stayed beside Musa in the beaming days of earliest spring, when the daffodils' trumpets of gold were blowing in all the grass, and the poet's narcissus was shining in every shady place, and the eyes that loved them could not rejoice in them, but were closed in the blindness and languor of pain.

The child of Este was born with the daffodils; but he only breathed a few short days after his birth, and died, softly and painlessly, as the daffodils did when they had bloomed their little hour.

The woman of the Apennines was frightened, because for many hours she could not take his small dead body from Musa's hold. When at last his mother could be made to understand that dead indeed he was, despair seized on her, long convulsions succeeded to her passionate weeping.

If he had lived—if his little feet had run over the grasses to her, if she had heard his first laugh at the first flower; if she had seen Este's eyes smile again in his, and heard the voice of Este in his broken babyish murmurs; if she had taught him to look with tender eyes at the little wren in her hole and the brown coot on her water-side nest; if she had carried him on her shoulder to her morning work upon the moors, and borne him homeward with her as the evening bells rang from the far hills and shores;—if he had lived, she would have loved her lover in him.

For him she would have worked day and night as she had done for Este; she would have kept him fresh as the rose, fair to see as the white birds from the north; she would have carried him in her strong young arms, she would have taught him love as the nightingale teaches its song to its offspring; she would have prayed for him, tended him, cherished him, made him lovely in all ways, and then perhaps one day she would have taken courage and led him by the hand up to his father's side, and said through him, "Love, who has ever loved as I?"

But he was dead,—dead as the faded narcissus shrunk away beneath the leaves. All that could never be,—never, never.

He was dead like the child Itys,[1] for whom his mother mourns through all the ages with every summer eve.

CHAPTER XLVIII.

THE shepherd's wife went back to the mountains with her flock as the days of the spring lengthened into midsummer, and the warm winds came from the south and blew among the ruddy wheat and the browned hay-grasses.

Musa was once again utterly alone; alone with a grave the more,— a little grave, small almost as if a bird were buried there, that she had made herself with laborious effort in the rocky floor and lined with rosemary as the sedge-thrush lines its nest.

This was all that was left to her of her love.

But her lover lived still, though her eyes could not behold him and his heart called no more to hers: he lived in that great unknown world which had stolen and absorbed him; and therefore the courage of her life came back to her after a time.

Some day he might remember.

Some day he might have need of her.

So she lived on, and the warmth of the year grew into full summer, and the field-flowers perished, as her little child had done, under the unbearable light of the sun.

A strange silence seemed to her to have fallen on all the world, although around her in truth the silent moors were still musical with many a nightingale, and many a cushat cried its happy call from pine to pine, and across the far edge of the great plains there went many a band of reapers, come down from the mountains to lay the tall wheat low, many of them going by singing, with lutes strumming in front of them, and dogs about their feet, and wild magnolia-flowers from old

---

[1] In Greek mythology Procene murdered her son Itys and served his flesh to her husband.

forsaken gardens slung with the wine-gourds and swinging at their waist.

But they were too far off to be more than distant dark lines against the sky, and could their songs have reached her she would have been deaf to them, as she was to the nightingales thrilling through the night in those last melodies that would cease as the fire-flies would die with the fall of the wheat.

Yet in this intense stillness and desolation in which she dwelt it never came into her thoughts to seek out Este, never at any time. She could not go to him without seeming to say, "Have you forgotten,— you my debtor in so much?"

She could not go to him without bringing both a rebuke and a reproach before her. If he forgot, he must forget. All she could do was to live on and wait; some time he might remember.

This seemed to her neither heroism nor sacrifice, but simple necessity.

If he had passed by her in a crowd, she would have kissed the stones his steps had touched, but she would not have spoken, since to speak would have been to say to him, "You are thankless."

Her love was her religion.

Fools may say what they will; there is none holier.

She lived on without joy, but not wholly without hope.

The long, slow-footed days seemed very long; the cloudy heat, the rainless wind, seemed wearisome and sad. She labored enough, just enough, to meet her barest wants; no more.

She no more watched the stars, the plants, the birds, the streams and shallows with the blue butterflies at play upon their surface.

Her youth seemed to have died in her with the little child, her eyes seemed forever to be darkened with tears that never fell.

As each hour went by, she thought, "Where is he? who beholds him? who watches for his step?" When night fell, she prayed that in his dreams he might once dream of her, and so remember once.

Did he fear her reproaches, that he did not come? Ah! how little he knew!——

CHAPTER XLIX.

As she sat at the entrance of the tombs on the day of the vigil of St. John, watching—always watching—for the shadow she never saw, the step she never heard, there crept slowly over the pathless turf two large white bullocks yoked together.

There also was a group of men, seven in all, who led the oxen, and the ox-wagon bore loads of masons' implements and cordage, and empty sacks and baskets.

She did not notice them, except dully to wonder what they came to do there, and to be thankful that they had not come a year earlier, when he had hidden in the earth under their feet.

They crept on straight over the moor, and towards the hidden burial-place.

The foremost of them, who was a sullen-looking, aged man, advanced from the rest a little, and approached her.

"It is you who live below there?" he cried, roughly. She was mute.

The old man was the steward of that absent Neapolitan prince who owned the house at Santa Tarsilla which had been occupied by Joconda for so many years,—the steward who at her sudden death had made pretence of a year's rent being due, and under that pretext sold her chattels.

To him there had gone a man of San Lionardo, leading with him his little son, and the two together had told him how on those moors which had been for a thousand years a portion of the fief of the Altamonte princes there had been found *buche delle fate* by a girl, who had stolen the treasure possibly, and made of the tombs her home. The little boy, who was no other than Zeffirino, deposed gravely to having seen mountains of gold and jewels under the earth. In this country vengeance may doze and wait, but does not die.

The imagination and avarice of the steward were inflamed to fever-heat. There had of late been discoveries of tombs near Cære to the south, in which had been found vases of great worth, and quantities of armor, shields, crowns, toys, and ornaments of gold, all of which had been sold for large prices to foreign States for their museums. The steward readily believed the little lad's tale, which was confirmed by a *buttero* of his own, who said that when he had ridden near the blasted suber-oak one twilight time he had seen a maiden with a bronze amphora on her head going down for water at a spring that rose near there.

Musa knew him at a glance, and he knew her.

He came to her and spoke roughly:

"You wicked wench, you stole Joconda's mule away from me. I have not forgotten that. Ever since then I meant to track you when I had time, and at last I come upon you. You are an evil one!"

"It is you who are evil," she said, coldly. "Joconda had paid her rent beforehand, on the first day of August, and you accused her falsely, and sold her goods out of despite, under pretext of a debt. You are a bad man. It is a pity that the prince, your master, does not know how bad you are."

"Oh, ho, vermin!" cried the steward, frantic with rage. "That is the tongue you dare to use to me, is it? Spawn of the devil you always were, and the pity is that the days are gone by when one could have had you burned as the devil's daughter. Pray you, now, do you know whose ground this is?"

She gave a gesture of negation, of indifference, of ignorance. She had never thought of the ground as any one's property: it belonged to God and his dead. The moor was free to all, so she thought. These great green silent lands seemed too vast, too mute, too solemn, to be parcelled out amidst the legal claims of men. Who claimed the sea? Who would, went on it, gleaned from it, was fed by it, lulled by it, devoured by it when it was in haste and rage. As the sea was free to all, so she had always believed was the plain.

"Well, this land is the prince's, my master's," said the man, with great unction and vicious wrath united. "If we had known that you had harbored here, out you would have gone, long, long ago. And indeed it would go hard with you now did my master choose to have the law on you, for who knows what treasures you may not have made away with; but he is merciful, and so am I, and therefore we do not mean to hurt you; only, out you go."

She heard but dully. Only a few months earlier, and she would have fought for her refuge and her rights to it as a tigress may fight for her den; but now the spring of her life was broken; her courage was not gone, but was deadened; her whole spirit was sunk in hopeless apathy. Yet a great terror fell upon her. Without this home she would be desolate as the house-martin who sees the wall that held his nest crumble into dust. For so long she had lived there, for so long each moment of the day had been given to some thought that centred in these familiar tombs. They had been hers, so entirely hers, borrowed in all humility and gratitude direct from the dead who were with God. Without them she would be not only homeless, but exiled from all she knew, from all she loved. No palace, had they given her one, would have been as dear to her as these hallowed chambers, shared with the lizard and the bat.

"There was gold in these tombs," he said to her.

She answered him, coldly,—

"Yes, there was when I saw them first."

"And you have stolen it?"

"I never steal: I leave that to you to do at your lord's expense. The gold was stolen by a galley-slave, one you have heard of, Saturnino Mastarna. It can do him no harm to say so, for he has escaped."

He believed nothing that she said. He was certain that the gold was either in the tombs or safe hidden underneath the soil.

"If you will tell me honestly where the treasure is, I will not give you up to justice," he said, thinking so to possess a secret which without her might escape him forever.

"I cannot tell you what I do not know," she answered him. "Ask Saturnino Mastarna, if you can find him."

"You are a cursed jade!" said the old man, with the *rabbia*[1] seizing him, and called her many worse names still. Musa turned her back on him, and stood awaiting his next act. She would not show him what she felt, but her heart was beating to suffocation with fear lest she should be hunted from her home.

"The tombs are my lord's. They are of value, they are full of treasure, they are my master's," he kept repeating now. "Go you down into them, and get your chattels,—that I will let you do, but nothing more,—and waste no time about it, for we are about to clear the entrance and take all the old work there may be there back with us. These are the orders we have had. But I see very well that you have robbed us of all that there was good in it. You look aghast, and you are dumb."

She was so: she was like the poor hare on the moor who could not

---

[1] Rage; anger.

understand why she was grudged her form of grass, that caused no loss to any living thing, yet was the whole world to her.

"I have stolen nothing," she said, once more. "I found these sepulchres. They are not your lord's nor mine, but belong to the dead. I have done no hurt there. It is all I have of home."

"She is but an impudent jade living thus, in the bowels of the soil, and with a paramour, I make no doubt," said the angry steward. "Men, get you to work: we can waste no more time. If there be sculptures, we are to hew them off; and that is a long business. Get to work and look for this vixen's earth."

In an earlier time she would have plunged a knife into the first hand that had touched those sepulchres, but now she was mute and motionless. The greater loss that she had endured made this loss almost light to her. Only she knew not where to lay her head if she was driven out, and every stone was dear to her—"dear as remembered kisses after death."[1]

When the first blow of the axe fell on the shrubs around, the sound roused her: she leaped into their midst with her old force and fire.

"You shall not touch them!" she cried, passionately, as she wrenched the first axe away. "They are not yours, nor mine, nor any one's. You shall not touch them. They belong to God."

The men laughed. They were, together, stronger than she was. They seized her and tied her wrists with a cord, and then bound her ankles with one, and cast her aside upon the soft sand under the shrubs as they would have cast a troublesome dog or goat.

They were not cruel, but they thought her a strange wild creature, and they were desirous to get their work over and lie in the shade and drink their wine, and sleep the noontide sleep that Italians love.

Their steward eyed her with a more evil glance. He had long sucked all the best juices out of his lord's properties himself; he was bitterly chagrined that he had missed such treasure-trove as Etruscan tombs unopened yield: he made no doubt that she had stolen all the gold.

He had ridden over this moor in spring twelve months before. Why, he thought, had not his horse's hoofs broken through the crum-

---

[1] From Alfred, Lord Tennyson's "Tears, Idle Tears."

bling sandstone, the thick soft moss, and shown him this kingdom of the dead? He was angry at his own negligence, and hated her, since she, he never doubted, had rifled all the place and now they would find nothing; so he grumbled to his peasants who were at work with spade and hatchet, being ignorant of where the entrance was.

She, bound as they had bound her, lay upon the sward and watched them, mute.

"If you will spare our labor and tell us where the entrance is, we will set you free," they said to her; but she did not unclose her lips.

The calm under torment that the Southerner shares with the Oriental had come upon her. She was dumb as the dead within. Only her great eyes looked on, wide open and full of anguish.

Soon the laborers lighted on the entrance-place with a shout, and she saw her sanctuary was discovered. She heard the blows of mallet and axe; she heard the grind of chisel and pickaxe. They were hewing out a wider space by which to enter. Then they lighted on the open portico of the *cellula janitoris*.[1]

Writhing in her bonds, she called to them in anguish, "You must not enter; you must not, you shall not; my little child lies there!"

She cried the same thing over and over again a hundred times, struggling and twisting madly in her captivity.

The old man heard, and put but one meaning on her words.

"She has killed her child and hidden it here!" he thought, and searched for the place of burial, and soon saw that recently the rock of the floor had been broken up.

There was a bronze Etruscan lamp burning where the stone had been cut through, and a little handful of honeysuckle was in an earthen *mastos* standing by: the "mother of the woods" is the flower that braves longest of all the summer heats.

"Is that her remorse?" thought the bitter-hearted old man, as he bade his men tear up the pieces of broken rock.

Soon they found the small body of the little child, wrapped, needfully, in linen and lying in the buds of rosemary. There was a gold Madonnina buried with it. There were no marks of violence upon it, and some property of the air or rock, not uncommon in this soil, had

---

[1] A small room for a servant or porter.

preserved the little corpse from all corruption and made it look like a pale waxen image.

Even the hard hearts and dull souls of the men were moved to some emotion as they looked on it, lying dead upon its bed of withered rosemary.

"She never harmed it," they murmured to one another; but their director grew angry and bade them be silent.

"You are idiots," he said to them. "She killed it and hid it here. If she had not killed it, would she have denied it honest Christian burial?"

Angry and disappointed, and inflamed with baffled cupidity, the old man roamed from chamber to chamber, making no count of the paintings of the walls, and of the slender grace of the bronze lamps, being too ignorant to know their value in their arts, and being greedy for the yellow glitter of the metal that he loved. All the traces of her occupation of the place infuriated him more and more, for he saw in each assurance that she had dwelt there long enough to rifle and to rob. He called out to his men to clear the rubbish away, and was the first to fling with his own hand on the ground the black and red earthen vessels that he despised as valueless.

Lying where they had placed her under the sharp foliage of the marucca, she saw the violation of the sepulchres that were sacred to her alike for the living and the dead.

All the black earthenware of the tombs they furiously broke upon the ground, until, of it all, there only remained a pile of shattered potsherds; the metal lamps they threw upon the cart, these would serve to help light their kitchens; all her own simple things they threw down in a heap, and the old man snapped across his knees the keys of the old tortoise-shell lute.

It seemed to her as if every sound fell on her breast, on her brain.

The men were angry because, entering, they found no metalwork of value, no platters, or vases, or cups, or chains, or bracelets of the virgin gold of Etruria, such as were yielded in such rich harvest by the famous necropoles of Palestrina, of Cervetri, of the Monterozzi.

They were bitterly irritated, the steward most so of all, he having been sure to make a fine gleaning there, a tithe of which he would have given to his master, who knew nothing of this day's work, though his name was used so glibly.

It was yet very early.

The old man sat in the shade of the tomb and drank the clear red wine that she had bought for Este, and cast his cunning eyes about in search for some gold or silver or amber that might be hidden in the sand, or lost in the dark where the bats clung. He saw none: all the gold-work that had ever been there had been taken by Saturnino, and, finding none, despite all his pains and diligence, he grew more and more suspicious; he had had visions of such wealth within these graves as that which was found by the Prince of Canino,[1]—wealth of which he could give his owner a discreet portion, and with the rest of which he would swell that ever-growing hoard which was the sweetest sight his twinkling eyes ever dwelt on as he was wont to feast on it by oil light, when his doors were bolted and barred with locks three hundred years old, in his old gray house set down amidst the marshes and the salt lagoons.

Discovering at length the *fibula* and the few ornaments which Saturnino had overlooked, and which she had once refused to sell even for Este's sake, the sight of these only inflamed his cupidity the more, and made him the surer that there had been some vast treasure seized and sold by her; and this conviction so tormented and enraged him that with his own hands he would have strangled her had it not been that he was timid where the law stepped in, and knew he should be punished for doing such rough justice on her.

His gaze roving thus, sullen and eager to discover more, fell at last on the coffin of Joconda, with the black cross rudely painted on it, where it rested in the twilight behind the stone bier of that Etruscan knight who once had been sole lord there.

His shrewd sense saw at once that this was a thing of yesterday, that no Etruscan dead were slumbering in that long, rough, shapeless box of unplaned pine wood. His cunning little soul, steeped all its days in chicaneries, and usuries, and efforts to outwit his lord and to grind down his people, fell all at once on the darkest and the foulest meaning that this strange sight could bear.

Some murder had been done here, hidden away with the dust and ashes of two thousand years,—done by this girl, no doubt.

So he believed, and his small soul leaped up in gladness.

---

[1] Lucien Bonaparte, Prince of Canino and Napoleon's brother, discovered a number of important Etruscan tombs in the late 1820s and early 1830s.

It would be hard to punish her for the missing gold-work, for there was no proof there ever had been such in these graves, though morally he was sure of it; but for these dead bodies hidden away, justice could be easily summoned. He shook a little, for he was a timid man, and to be thus in company with the dead was ghastly to him, and he called aloud to his men to leave off hewing at the stone lion and come look here.

Between them they got the coffin of Joconda open, and, shuddering and muttering paternosters, they uncovered the poor, withered, lifeless frame of her that was untouched by corruption as yet, being so shrivelled and fleshless with old age, and further preserved by the dry aromatic air of the painted chamber.

"It is a woman. It is Joconda Romanilla!" he said, gasping; and his men shrank together awed and frightened, and shut the coffin down and stood staring.

A thrust of the knife in a brawl, a shot on a lonesome hill, and fierce vengeance deftly worked out,—these they were well used to in Maremma, and they saw no great harm in them. But this body, torn from Christian burial and sanctified ground, and shoved away with these Etruscan mummies, seemed to them a ghastly horror; for had not the girl taken all the gold?

Meanwhile, outside in the sunshine, Musa lay with bound limbs, strained ears, and aching eyes, powerless to move, not knowing what they did, judging only of their violence by the broken lute and the heap of broken Etruscan ware that were thrown out beside her on the sand.

"It is God's mercy he is gone," she thought; that was her chief remembrance.

Yet all her life ached in her as if it were snapped asunder like the lute; she was like the bird who sees rough hands tear down and scatter on the winds the nest that it cost him such anxious care to build and that he guarded so jealously whilst he sang his love-song underneath the leaves. Like the bird, she had offended none, making her home as silently and meekly as he did where the wild bay grew and the woodspurge crept with the moss. She had asked nothing of the world more than the bird does; yet they could not let her be.

She heard the blows of the mallet on the marble cease, and all was still. She wondered dully what they were doing now,—dully, for pain had numbed her, and the worst that could have come to her seemed already done.

The men, within, held council.

Some were jocose and jested broadly: she was a handsome creature, they said; the old steward was blind to such charms, the chills of age and avarice made him insensible to such a plea; he was angry that the gold was gone, he only longed to punish her, to see her hurt.

She had sold all the jewelry, of that he felt sure, or had buried it somewhere on the moors, to get it when she chose.

And this dead woman's body,—if it were not the cover of some crime, why should such a corpse be hidden here thus?

No; he was resolute; to justice she should go, away to Orbitello. They would take the dead body in its deal box with them, and the corpse of the little child wrapped in its linen, and let the judges see. He persuaded himself and them that he was acting from pure rectitude and horror of crime; in truth, he would never have cared though a hundred corpses had rotted there, if he had found the gold vases, the gold platters, the gold chains. Aloud he said that those who would desecrate a sepulchre would do any other sin: such were best dealt with and put aside by law. He washed his hands of it.

So he went out into the sunny air, and bade his men lift her, bound as she was, upon the ox-cart, which was done.

But, although bound, she revolted so fiercely at their touch that they were frightened and hung back.

"What have I done?" she cried to them.

"Waste no words on her," said the steward. "She shall answer before the judges."

"I have done no harm," she said, as she wrenched her ankles free by violent effort and stood before them, her hands still tied behind her back. "I knew not that those tombs had any owner. They belong to the dead. I did the dead no harm. They were not afraid of me, nor I of them. Why do you touch me? Why do you bind me? I have done no evil. It is you who insult the grave. It is you who break their laws and rob——"

"Where is the gold that was there?" shrieked the old steward, stung into accusation. "Where is the gold, you wanton? And where is your lover that you screened there? Who was the father of your child?"

She was silent.

They took her silence for guilt; she seemed to them to be overwhelmed with her own crime thus brought before her. Her great luminous eyes stared at them with a terrible, unutterable sadness that they were frightened at and took for guilt.

"To justice with her," said the old man, cruelly. "Heave her in the cart, men: she has the *mal'occhio.*"[1]

She was heaved into the cart by the ropes that tied her limbs; her feet hung over the rail, her head and body were on the hard wood: she was used as they used a young heifer.

They thought her something unnatural and unearthly; they dreaded the evil eye; they had no mercy; and their director hovered round her, tightening a rope with unction, or knotting her hair upon a nail, in vengeance for that gold he had not found. It hurt her more when they touched her bare feet, or when their rough movements unloosened the linen off her breast.

All her beauty was Este's; for these to look on it was treachery to him.

To her own fate she was almost callous. He had gone, and she was driven from the place where he had been, and where every stone, every leaf, every grain of sand, seemed to speak to her of him: it was indifferent to her what else befell her. If they broke her on the wheel as they did the saints of old, she would not suffer more than she had done when she had heard his footsteps go away so willingly, so lightly, over the scorched turf.

The oxen moved on, the ponderous wheels turned, the springless wagon rolled upon its road.

The old man and one other came with her; the rest of the men stayed to guard the tomb and hew out the sculptures in the rock.

The way they went was not towards Santa Tarsilla, but southward to the marshes which, where the moor sloped to the south, replaced it and made all the earth like a sponge, now white with cotton-grass and billowy water-reeds.

Turning her burning eyes from side to side, she saw the places she had roamed over and hunted for cactus-fruit and the wild prickly pear and the blue bilberries of the thickets. She saw the little pools where she had splashed and bathed; the fringes of cane where reluctant she

---

[1] Evil eye.

had searched for the eggs of the fluttering water-hen; she saw the broad blue sky above her head; a green ibis on its voyage was the only cloud upon it; it flew high above her, straight above her, and winged its wise way eastward to the lands of sunrise. She envied it.

She lay face upward on the bottom of the wagon, her hands tied so that she could not brush away the gnat or fly. The sun beat on her, the insects tormented her, mosquitoes fastened on her feet as they hung over the rail.

The men took no notice of her; they jolted on as they would have done with a bound calf or a shot doe behind them.

As long as she could, she looked for the pine-trees that grew by the sea, for the great branches of the cork-tree that spread themselves above the place of the tombs. When she could behold these no longer, tears of blood came into her eyes; the sky and the moor and the air grew crimson to her.

The oxen crept on, pulling against their rings of iron, groaning against their heavy yokes; they licked their lips with parched tongues, they sobbed now and then like beaten children when the goad struck them.

The wagon rolled on, over the burned moorland, to the marshes where the earth was still wet and the stagnant waters were green as the broad leaves of the nenuphars. Here all was treeless, level, vaporous; the black buffalo wading content in the ooze, the butor sitting motionless in the swamp; here and there came gladiolus flowers, rising like red plumes; everywhere there was a sea of reed-grass and rushes murmurous with clouds of insects,—a watery desert where disease walked abroad alike by noonday and by night.

A narrow road, often raised on piles, crossed the morass, and oftentimes a false step of the oxen to right or left would have plunged the wagon into the bog on either side that was hidden under the rank vegetation of grass and rushes. This single road traversed the marshes, and united the moorland with the great fields of grain that lay beyond, square leagues of corn stretching far as the eyes could reach from sea to mountains, and now brown and bending to the sickle.

Before they entered on these great corn-lands where harvest was ending, mirthfully, despite the pestilence that rode on every sunbeam, the men stayed their tired and beaten oxen, who, footsore and with the water falling from their eyes, would, pressed longer, have dropped down to rise no more.

Then, and then only, they bethought them to look at their burden,—as they would have looked at the heifer to see that she did not
die before the butcher's mallet should strike her.

They found her unconscious, and breathing heavily: the sun had
struck her and made her, for the hour, insensible to all her pain.

"She is a jade, but we must not kill her, or they will call us to account," said the old steward to his man.

So they halted there for her sake as well as for that of the oxen,
and laid her down upon the ground, and tried what rough surgery
they knew to call back the senses that the sun had slain.

The illness in a few hours passed off her, and she regained the
consciousness of her unutterable misery.

CHAPTER L.

THE old man, not to be diverted from his vengeance and his purpose,
rested with her that night at his own farm-house on the edge of the
great corn-lands, and in the morning began his journey afresh with
other oxen, and took her to the sad sea town of Orbitello, where the
people die of the heat like flies of poisoned meat, and the salt crystals
on the shore are all its wealth.

The seizure of her was not legal, and he had no legal power to
make it; but such trifles as legality could easily be ignored by the steward of a grand prince who was absent, and had half the Orbitellano in
his keeping. When he left the inland tracks and entered on the long
line of darksome pine wood that by land connects Telamone and Orbitello, he for form's sake made the matter known to a brigadier of
carabineers who was his friend, and, to have all matters right in form,
his friend sent two mounted guards, with their carbines slung beside
them and their cutlasses at their side, to go beside the ox-cart into the
town and give the captive up to the prison authorities.

Thence they went on again under the pines by the side of the blue
glancing sea, and she lay, almost senseless, on the straw at the bottom
of the wagon.

They met old Andreino on the coast. He held up his hands and
cried aloud,—

"Dear Lord! Did I not always know that she would meet her end
like that. The saints be praised she did not get my sweet Nandino!"

At Orbitello they threw her into prison after hearing how she had hidden a dead body in the closed Etruscan tomb.

She did not understand of what they accused her. She thought vaguely that they missed the gold things stolen by Saturnino, and that they attributed the theft to her. But it was not clear to her; neither could she comprehend why they should blame her for having buried her little child and brought the body of Joconda there. She had done no harm; she could not see why they should seek to punish her. But the spirit with which a few months earlier she would have laughed them to scorn and cut her way free of them, if needs be with her knife, was gone out of her. He was lost to her, and her child was dead: little else mattered.

She was kept in that prison a month, awaiting such time as they should see fit to remove and to try her for this crime. The air grew very hot; the town was like a sick-ward in a hospital, the miasma crept up at sunset every night from the swamps around, and found out the people sitting on the sea-walls, or in the streets at dominoes, or lying panting and naked on their beds.

She was shut in her little cell; she who had all the day long roamed moor and shore, and plunged in the sea, and led the life of a woodland beast or of a silver-plumaged guillemot.

The cell had a square window, with four transverse iron bars; it was very narrow, but through it she could see the sea, the only familiar friend she had. She thought in after days that it was this sight of the sea which alone kept her alive in those terrible weeks. She could see a hand's-breadth of its blue jewel-like surface leaping, and seeming to laugh, and every now and then a felucca sail would sweep across the narrow field of her vision, or the wing of a gull would flit by, and these familiar things kept sense in her, and saved her from insanity.

If she had had only the four whitewashed walls, she would have gone mad.

Presently they put with her a prostitute,—a woman abandoned and loathsome, who was there on a charge of having murdered a youth in a brawl. She was a creature of foul and filthy tongue, and she tried her uttermost to hurt what she saw was a pure soul; but Musa shut her ears and her lips, and looked at the sea; and the obscenity passed by her without harming her. She was beyond that woman's reach.

This great love which absorbed her was like an ivory wall built up between the world and her.

All the while, day and night, she was thinking, If he should go back? if he should go back and find the tomb empty, and her place vacant? Would he think her faithless? would he think she had tired so soon?

This doubt was such agony to her that at times it conquered her reason, and she would shake the bars that divided her from sea and sky, and cry aloud to the gulls and ships to take her message to him, to tell him where she was mewed up against her will, torn away from her moors and her beach and her innocent liberties of wind and sunshine.

The next day but one they led her out to be examined. She regained her self-control, and was quite calm, though very pale.

"I have done nothing wrong," she said to her guards: "wherefore should I be afraid?"

They set her before her judge, the Pretore of the court there, a lawyer in black gown and cap. He was startled by her look, by her solemn luminous eyes, the repose of her attitude, the contempt upon her beautiful mouth.

"She is no criminal," he thought, and called for the deposition of the testimony against her.

Then the steward, who gave his name and that of his lord, made his declaration of all that he had seen and done; of the dead bodies he had found there, and of the uses to which she had put the Etruscan tomb. He could not accuse her of theft as well, but he said that a shepherd boy, whom he could produce, had known her and seen gold there in an earlier time, whereas he had only found a gold *fibula* and a gold grasshopper or two.

When he had sworn all that, his men were called, and described on oath their entrance and examination of the tombs, and their discovery of the body of the little child and of the woman's coffin. The steward then added his own witness that the body of the woman was beyond doubt that of one Joconda Romanilla, who had been a tenant of his master's at Santa Tarsilla, and had died three years before.

This was the case against her.

The young judge, who had felt prepossessed in her favor, looked grave and stern: on the use of the tomb as a dwelling-place he would have been inclined to look leniently; but for the concealment of the dead bodies he could see no plea: nothing could extenuate such an act, so hostile to every prejudice of a Christian land, even if no darker bloodguiltiness were involved in it.

The accusation ended, he addressed her, and asked her for her own explanation of her acts.

It was at all times difficult to her to find many words to explain her thoughts, and in this strange place, before these cruel unfamiliar faces, without a friend beside her, her heart was sick, her brain was dizzy, her eyes swam. Nevertheless she strove to be calm and to answer them. She could not bear that the listening crowd should think her afraid or guilty.

"I buried my little child with me," she said, simply, while the hot tears swelled up in her eyes and throat, "because I wished to have him near me always. How can you think I hurt him? I would have given my life for his, of course. As for Joconda, they thrust her away in a hole in the sand, and I went for her because it seemed thankless to leave her all alone in the rain and the wind; she had been most good to me, and I loved her. I did not think I did any harm; I do not think that I did do any. I have nothing else to say. I found the tombs; I did not know I might not use them; I have maintained myself honestly in them, I owe no one anything."

Then she ceased to speak, and stood without indifference, but without anxiety, with a tranquil and haughty simplicity and repose.

The judge was perplexed.

"How long did the child live?" he asked.

"Only seven days."

"Of what did he die?"

"I cannot tell: he faded as the flowers do when the sun is too hot."

"Why did you not give him Christian burial?"

Her old scorn flashed in fire from her eyes.

"Christian burial?—to pay a stranger to dig a hole, and mumble something, and then to go away and forget?"

"It is the law of the land."

"The law is cruel, and foolish, and blind," she said, coldly, thinking of how in Mantua the law had condemned an innocent man and honored and praised the murderer.

"The law is sacred and omnipotent, as you will find," said the judge, in rising anger. "Who was your lover?"

Over the pallor of her face the color mounted fast, then faded.

"That I will never tell you."

"The law shall compel you to speak."

"That the law cannot do," she said, with a calm disdain. Had not Læna bitten through her tongue rather than speak of him she loved? So also could she. Este had told her the old Greek story.

The judge was angered, irritated, and bewildered. He knew not what to do. He could not think her guilty, yet he could not, in face of the offended majesty of the law he represented, declare her guiltless and refuse the steward of Prince Altamonte his right to demand a trial.

He closed the examination hurriedly, and remanded her to prison, there to await her fate. There was no one to tell her that perhaps she might successfully ask to be left free until the time of trial, and, indeed, such a request would probably have been refused in view of the guilt of which she was accused.

But that night the judge said to his subpretore, "Never did I see innocence if I did not see it there; and she would go to the scaffold, if we sent her thither, mute."

In the populace, on the contrary, there were furious wrath against her, and readiness to condemn her to the worst chastisement had they had her fate in their hands. She was only the Musoncella, and she had offended all the dearest superstitions. What was she, to deride the consecrated ditch in which they all hoped to lie, when it came to their turn, made snug till the day of doom, and made safe for that by their priests' mumbled rites?

They said among themselves that they would warrant she had the *mal'occhio* and that this lover whom she would not name had been the foul fiend himself. Had they had their way they would have given her short shrive.

Meanwhile, the guards took her back to her prison-cell.

Then she understood what Este had felt,—why she had been powerless to console or to content him so long as the sense of captivity was upon him, so long as he could no more go whither he listed.

Now, it was at this time the close of midsummer, and the law courts throughout Maremma would be closed until autumn by reason of the unhealthiness of the hot season, so that there she would remain until they opened again, and might die of the malaria of the town for aught that any one knew or cared. An accused is always two-thirds of a criminal in the eyes of the law, which always looks through magnifying glasses. The steward went his way, the judge and the lawyers went theirs. No one cared whether she lived or died, and the hot winds came and blew the *stagno* into pestilential vapors, and the white piles of the salt glared in the sun, and the heavy livid heat settled down on all the shore, and disease walked abroad with every fall of evening dew.

They shut her in her cell, and the sole solace she had was that she was left alone in it. But it went hard with her to keep her reason,—not to let go her hold on life and sense. She to whom it had been torture only to see the birds imprisoned in the nets, to whom the open air had been as breath from the very lips of a merciful God, to whom the lowliest weed had had beauty and the lowliest beast had been a comrade; who had never missed the setting of the sun and the rising of it; who had watched the passage of the round moon through the illumined clouds with the deep delight that poets know; to whom the forest or the moorland day had been one hymn of praise to nature; and who, amidst her deepest sorrow, had found that consolation in the solitudes of the wolds which Nature keeps for those who love her perfectly,—to her, a prison-cell was every hour such misery as those know who, buried in haste, awake from their swoon to find the oak of the coffin, the stone of the vault, forever between them and the living world.

The only thing that saved her from madness was that small square space in the wall through whose bars she could see a hand's-breadth of the sky and water and smell the salt glad scent of the sea.

The only thing that made her cling stubbornly to life was the faint hope, shut in silence in her own breast, that Este might hear, and come.

CHAPTER LI.

ONE day they told her a friend asked to see her. All the dying courage sprang up in her, and the passion of longing made her face rosy as the day-dawn. It was he!

She leaped on her feet and ran to the grated door, and put out both her hands, and cried with laughter and with tears in strange abandonment and delirium for her grave nature.

"Oh, my love! oh, my love! you have remembered———"

The words died on her lips, the blood seemed to ebb away from her heart and brain, she turned sick and cold.

It was not Este; it was the Sicilian mariner. It was Daniello Villamagna.

He stood on the threshold of her cell, and the tears were coursing down his cheeks; he was very pale, and he was silent; words came to his throat, but seemed to choke him and were mute.

She shrank back in unspeakable revulsion of feeling; the blood seemed to turn to ice in her veins under the disappointment.

She sat down and turned her face from him.

The action smote him to the quick and unloosed his tongue.

"Let me help you! Let me help you!" he said, piteously, and could think of nothing more or better to say.

She shook her head in sign of refusal.

Help her! How could he help her? How could heaven itself help her, since her lover had forgotten, and her child was dead?

"If I had only known! If I had only known!" he said, stupidly. "Oh, the beast—the fool——"

She turned her face towards him, and looked up from under her lowering brows.

"Go away," she said, sternly, and in a low, steady voice. "I do not want you. I did not send for you. I told you I never should for twenty years. Go! go!"

Almost weeping as women do, he came nearer to her.

"I cannot go!" he said, passionately. "Oh, I know you do not care. I know I cannot comfort you, but something I may do. I am better than no one, though I am only a rude foolish seaman. Do not think I will talk of myself, of anything I feel; I only want to speak of you, I only want to defend you against these devils——"

"If they would only let me go back——"

The one great longing that was in her heart escaped her despite herself. If only they would let her go back! She wanted nothing more from the mercy of men.

"They must let you go back!" he said, vehemently. "They must! they shall! What harm have you done, poor innocent?"

"I have done none," she said, wearily. "But they do not believe that. As if I would have hurt his child!"

The infinite tenderness that was in her voice stung cruelly the man who heard her. But he controlled his own pain; he only said, gently,—

"You could hurt nothing. You loved all the little birds and the poor hunted beasts,—oh, my dear! oh, my dear!"

His strength failed him, and a low sob quivered in his strong throat.

The horror of it, and the pity of it, conquered his fiery temper and broke down his bold spirit into utter weakness.

She was silent.

His sorrow did not touch her any more than his passion had ever done. She had no place in her thoughts left for him.

"And where is he?" muttered the sailor. "Where is he, the white-livered coward, the false faithless wretch you loved? Where is he? May the curse———"

She sprang to her feet, and looked at him with the fire of other days in her eyes.

"Do not dare to speak of him! What is it to you? You are a stranger to me. Get you gone! get you gone!"

"But he has been false to you!"

"What is that to you? You are not my brother. You are a strange seaman, of whom I know nothing, of whom I wish never to know aught. Go your way, and leave me to mine,—whatever it be."

Then, exhausted by the momentary violence, she sat down once more in the same attitude, leaning her head wearily against the wall of the cell. He could not see her face.

"I only wish to serve you, if I can," he said, humbly, and trembling as no danger of the deep seas had ever made him tremble.

"You cannot," she said, with her face still hidden from him. "But go, go. It hurts me to speak and to be spoken to: I am best alone."

He lingered, torn in two by his grief and his love for her. It had been wild love, born of a glance, of a word, of a glimpse of dark eyes, of a summer morning that shed its light on a beautiful face that had been fixed on his heart for evermore; but it was faithful love, ready to do and to dare all things.

He only hesitated here because he knew not what to do.

"I will go, since you wish it," he said, at last. "But I shall be always in Orbitello, and I will do what I can. I think they must soon set you free. You have harmed no one. You have offended the law, perhaps, but so innocently, and no law of God or nature, but only the trumpery vexatious rule of man. I am sure soon they must set you free; but if they do not, bars have been sawn through ere now, and stouter ones than these, and there is the sea at hand; and—and I want you to believe, if I should help you to escape, if there should be no other means, never, never will I presume on any service I may have done to you. Once free, you shall never see me again. I am not a cur, I would never plead to you by what I might have done————"

His eyes were glistening, his voice was feeble with haste and emotion and eagerness to assure her that no self-seeking thoughts or selfish hopes were stirring him; the strength of love that was in his soul lifted him out of common egotistic passion; he in truth forgot himself in her.

She did not answer; she scarcely heard him; after he had spoken she thought over his words but dully, and with little faith in them. To escape,—yes, that would be blessed indeed; but she did not wish to owe him anything. She thought Este would sooner choose that she should suffer here than become free by the aid of any hand not his.

The love of the Sicilian, even in its simplicity, honesty, and generosity, had always struck a chord of anger in her. She had always wondered if she had been too familiar with a stranger that morning on the sands, that he had thus been led to fasten his fancy on her.

He waited a little while in hope that she might answer him, that the hint of escape might at the least rouse some flutter of the old bold spirit in her. But he waited in vain. She was ready, indeed, to escape by any means of her own, in any way, at any hour of the night or day, but she did not accept his help. It seemed to her, without her reasoning out her instinct, that to take any benefit from any man was in a measure to be false to Este.

He waited with beating heart and longing ear; but she said nothing.

"It is best to see what one can do, without, with all these brutes," he thought, and turned to go.

"You will know I am always ready," he said, softly; and then the jailer repeated his summons, and the door unclosed, and he passed through it and was gone.

She did not even look up once.

Daniello Villamagna went out of the gloomy place into the intense light of the noonday that was shining on the salt lagoon till it glistened like a mirror of steel.

His shrewd sense told him that his first care should be to find a good advocate; his next, as he had little faith in those land-sharks who live by the adversity of other men, was to study all ways and means by which, in case of any condemnation of her, her rescue might be compassed.

These two things he did, and put all his soul and his might into them, and praised heaven that he had made enough gains out of his latest voyage to be able to throw money about in her cause without much prudence.

All the hot listless day in the dull sea-town he spent his whole time in pondering over that which he might do, and to the advocate he had hired he said again and again, "Let her think the judge has appointed you: if she knew I had spoken to you, she would be angered: she is very proud, pray let her never know."

And when the man of law pressed for his reasons in having this great anxiety for her, he answered once for all, "I have seen her but thrice,—out of doors, by the edge of the sea,—and she thinks nothing of me, and never will think anything; but she is as innocent as the rock-doves yonder, and I love her well, though never, I tell you,—oh, never!—shall I be more to her than yon weeds that grow in the *stagno*."

There was that accent of passionate truth in him which carries conviction to its hearers whenever it can obtain a hearing.

He was well known along all the sea-board of Maremma: even her accusers began to think better of her since the dauntless sailor of Palermo loved her.

As the people of the Orbitellano sat about by the sea-wall, and spread out their nets to dry in the sun, they began to say, after all, her story might be true: why not? And the tide of opinion turned in her favor.

All through the hottest weather he stayed there, and was thankful that he had leisure and time to serve her.

Once in each two weeks they let him see her in the presence of the guards or jailer; and he persuaded her to speak a little, very little, enough to give him some clue by which to do something for her. The name of Este, of course, she never spoke. They might have kept her there all the years of her life, but she would never have disclosed it.

He only saw her thus in cruel fleeting moments which wrung his inmost soul, but he stayed on, glad to be able to feel himself her only friend, glad to be able to watch for hours together the little grated window of her cell.

He and the advocate he employed, and on whom he spent all the gains of his latest voyages, hunted the Apennines for the shepherd's wife of whom Musa spoke once, when the lawyer retained by Daniello Villamagna asked her if there was no one who could testify that her little child had died of a new-born child's mere feebleness. Musa knew only that the woman was called Pomfilia, and that her husband's name was Nerone, and on that slender help they had to rely, and did at length trace the shepherd and his family from Maremma up to those chestnut woods on the sides of Monte where their summer home was made.

They also called on the priest of Santa Tarsilla, who, although when he heard of the coffin of Joconda having been taken away without his sexton even missing it was deeply incensed and terrified, yet was too tender-hearted a man to refuse his testimony that the girl reared by Joconda Romanilla, in his parish, had been always of innocent life, and of noble if strange and wayward temper.

Who she was by birth he could not tell. That secret had died with his predecessor.

Daniello knew, but he shut it in his own heart as she shut her lover's name.

The hot months went by, and she lived through them in her misery as the caged lark lives beating his breast against his bars. The greatest terror to her was that of which she never spoke,—lest Este should return to the tombs in her absence, and, angered at what would seem her faithlessness, go without knowing the truth.

On the other hand, there was always the faint hope in her that he might hear, and come to Orbitello.

The months passed, and the law court opened earlier than the custom of it was, because there was a great case of fraud, in which public names were involved, for which it was desirable to clear the way by getting through all trials of lesser interest.

By persuasion and some free use of his good money, Daniello's advocate procured the early hearing of her case whilst it was still warm, radiant October weather.

The woman Pomfilia came down from the mountains, and when Musa was allowed to see her once, the sight of a familiar face did her some little good. It did not occur to her to ask how, or by whom, the shepherd's wife had been summoned; her thoughts were too absorbed, her mind was too much distraught.

Yet she had no fear of any sentence they might pass on her.

"I did no harm," was all that ever she said.

Her old pride, her old courage, her old antagonism to the tyranny of law, gave her strength to hold it at arm's length still. Her father's spirit awoke in her.

They might capture, they should not subdue her, they should not humiliate her.

There were other days in the stifling, thronged audience-chamber; other long discourses, now from this speaker, now from that; other terrible weary hours filled with the buzz of tongues, the stench of the crowd, the wordy vaporings of petty pompous people. She was brought in and set in their midst, and she understood nothing of it,—no more than the trapped hawk understands why he is caught in the cruel wires.

It all went past her ear like a confused noise without sense or meaning.

She vaguely comprehended that some one whom she did not know was pleading in her favor and trying to set her free.

But she was always thinking, "In Mantua they condemned him, all innocent as he was: men pleaded in his favor, too, he said, but they condemned him: so will they me."

She had no hope that they would understand her and let her go.

The woman Pomfilia gave simple, staightforward testimony as to exceeding love she had borne the little child, and the despair its death had caused her. The woman added that she herself did not know that it was wrong to have said nothing and made the little grave there: had the child lived it would have been carried up to San Lionardo and baptized there. That she knew would have been done.

The evidence of the woman, timid before the law, but honest, went far with the judge and with the listening audience of seafaring folk and peasants.

Then they brought forth the little traitor Zeffirino, who grew white and shook as with a palsy when he looked across the hall and saw her face.

"Thou also!" said the scorn and sorrow of her grand calm eyes.

When he recovered a little from that trepidation of terror, he swore glibly enough that on the first day when she had taken him down into the tombs there had been much gold, much,—it lay in heaps and heaps, so he affirmed; and when he had returned thither the next day by himself,—not meaning to touch it, oh, no! only to look if it were safe,—he saw none there, none at all; it must have been carried away in the night. He declared that she had the *mal'occhio*, and that she had threatened his life because he took two travellers to see the *buche delle fate*, and that he had gone to dwell at Populonia because he went in perpetual peril from her vengeance. He told his tale very convincingly, and with pretty childish innocence of bearing.

When he had quite ended, her voice rang out like a clarion in defiance of him, of her accusers, of her judges, of all the listening people.

"You are a miserable little traitor," she said to him. "I sheltered you from the storm; I fed you often; I was attached to you; I dealt honestly and well with you always; and you betrayed my sanctuary for two silver pieces. You are the son of Iscariot, go! For the gold, you know well that the galley-slave Saturnino Mastarna robbed the dead and took it. It was his own undoing here in the Orbitellano. You know that. You are a son of Iscariot; you stole my old mule in his days of weakness to sell him away into misery. You are vile as a viper that stings the hand that has spared its life. Go! Away from my sight, go!"

He slunk away between the guards; and there was that in her glance, in her voice, in her attitude, which thrilled the hearts of the people, which before were steeled against her.

These days in the public court were terrible to her.

She had dwelt in her moorland solitudes till she was shy of every human glance, till every sound, save the dreamy sounds of the hills and woods, was harsh and jarring to her. As the arum-leaves lie hidden in the shadow of deep dells, so had she been shrouded underneath the greenness of the earth.

Torn from her shelter, and dragged into the crude light of noon, with hundreds of hard eager eyes fastened upon her, and the buzz and bray of human voices deafening her ears, she was bewildered as an animal is, dragged from his jungle or his desert into the glare and hooting crowds of a menagerie to make the sport of fools. The natural courage in her, and that instinctive dignity, so common in classic ages and so little seen in ours, made her hide all the alarm she suffered; but she suffered all the more that she stood there like any statue made of bronze, and never winced, and let her eyes rest in cold disdain upon the faces of her accusers and her judge.

She had said the truth once.

She opened her lips no more.

The Pretore at length, after long preamble, and an examination lasting three days, censured her in a long discourse with severity, but pronounced her free, the accusation being dismissed as non-proven.

She heard the sentence of deliverance without any movement of gratitude or joy. Her proud serenity of repose remained unbroken.

"Why not have found me guiltless before you punished me with these long frightful months?" she thought; but aloud she said only, "I may go back—now?"

That was the one desire panting, like a netted bird, at her heart.

CHAPTER LII.

WHEN a little while later the formalities were fulfilled, and she was allowed to leave her prison, homeless, friendless, penniless, but free, she understood why Este had gone,—why love had become nothing to him beside that ecstasy of liberty.

She was free once more.

The hot light whirled round her in giddy circles, her limbs were weakened by long and harsh captivity, she was feeble and faint, but she was almost once more happy. The earth was her own once more, and somewhere on the earth was her lover.

"If only they had left me that little grave!" she thought.

On the threshold of the prison there met her an old shrivelled man,—the steward, her accuser.

He muttered quickly, in some shame,—

"My dear, I am sorry; I had too much zeal; go back to the sepulchres if you will; go back; and the little child is buried in God's ground, buried beside Joconda, do not be afraid."

Then he hurried away, being in great fear of her.

For Daniello Villamagna had said to him, "If you will not disturb her in those tombs she loves, I will rent them of you at a hundred scudi by the year, and your lord need never know."

They had brought her out by the white salt-covered shore; and she stood still a moment, drinking in the autumnal air, all her soul and mind and body absorbed in one unspoken prayer, praising heaven that she was free.

Everything was feverish, pallid, weary with that ghastly weariness of great heat which makes the ice-floe and the north wind seem in desire as paradise; the heat which blanches and enfeebles and fevers and wastes all in one; the heat in which flowers and birds wither and pant, and children droop as the tall stems of the sunflowers do; the heat in which all the beauty goes out of the land, and the trees grow gray, and the skies are ash-color.

In all that pallor and whiteness of the sickly town and the low-lying shore and the feeble people, the figure of Musa stood out with the grace and the rich color of some crown-imperial lily growing out of sand, straight as a young palm, luminous, golden, distinct.

She had not a friend in the world, nor any roof to cover her, nor even a coin to buy bread.

But she was not troubled by that; she was absorbed in thinking, "How can I get back?" They might tell her, how they would, not to go there: this was her one thought. How would he find her elsewhere? And was not his memory there with every remembered hour of joy? The temptation came to her to go and seek him, but she thrust it away. She said to herself, "I must not remind him of his debt."

Nay, though she died of longing to look upon his face, she would never do that.

A hag came up and hissed in her ear that with such a face and such a form as hers money was to be had thick as the salt upon the sands, and Musa turned on her her great troubled eyes, half in wonder, half in scorn, and the woman shrunk away.

It was afternoon. Though close on autumn, the sultriness of summer had not abated there. The air was still thick with mosquitoes. The sails of the boats out at sea hung like painted sails of wood. Some men were killing a half-dead shark; his eyes rolled in horrible futile agony; they were cutting the live flesh off his spine.

Pale shores stretched on either side, pale mountains slid away into heat-mists in the distance. She knew the danger of the marshes. She did not wish to die: who does that loves? Whilst the earth feels the steps of the feet we adore, to live is beautiful; whilst the eyes that we love unclose to the day, the sunrise that wakens them still smiles at us.

She shrank from any thought of death, since death would be

eternal silence, endless separation; and she knew that to sleep on the swamps was death as sure as to drown in the deep sea. Yet the swamps stretched between her and the moorland tombs.

She stood irresolute upon the shining shore: the old hag looked longingly at her, but dared not speak again. Something in the grand innocence of those troubled eyes awed and frightened her.

"Will you not even take my boat?" said the voice of Daniello near her, as he came from under the shadow of the sea-wall, and stood in her path, submissive, timid, with bared head as before an empress.

"You are all alone," he said, feebly and stupidly, not knowing well what he did say.

"Have I so many friends?" she said, curtly. "Nay, do not think I want any. Now they have set me free, I need nothing."

"But you will not go on foot, all that long way to your own moors?"

"Will I not? It is so long since I have felt the ground under my feet, I could walk on, and on, and on, I think, all day, all night———"

"You fancy so, because it is beautiful to you to be free. That I understand. But you are not as strong as you were a year ago. You are weaker than you know. You may faint by the way, and if you sleep out, you know that sleep after sunset means death where you go. Will you not let me take you in my boat? Or, if you choose the inland road, may I not find a mule-cart for you, an ox-wagon? There are plenty in the Orbitellano."

"You mean kindly," she said, with her mind made up and beyond any pressure or inclination from without. "But I need nothing but the freedom of my feet. It is months since I saw a tuft of grass. That is pleasure enough."

"Where are you going?"

"I am going home."

"To those tombs?"

"Where else?"

He was silent. He dared not say to her, "There is a home in Sicily."

He dared not. He would almost as soon have dared to strike her a blow.

"The old man said just now he would not drive me out again," she added: "I think he was sorry that he had been cruel."

"I hope he was," said Villamagna, simply. "But oh, my dear, that is no place for you,—a hole fit only for the fox, and the bat, and the owl. Will you not think a little before you return to it?"

A smile flitted over her face,—pale as a moonbeam, but of ineffable tenderness.

"It is dearer to me than if it were a palace. I would never live elsewhere. You have been good to me, that I see; but let me go now, and do not follow me."

He looked at her with infinite longing; but he drew out of her path and left her to go onward unmolested and unquestioned. In the amorous impetuosity of his nature, a finer and a rarer feeling had come since her misfortunes had made her sacred to him. He had done her some service, so his lips were sealed, as were hers to Este. He could not say to her, "This you owe to me," without becoming a base hound in his own sight.

"After all, I have done so little," he thought. "But more she would not take."

She would never know that he had done anything; in all likelihood she would never have enough sympathy for, or remembrance of, him to guess the share that he had had in her release. But he thought it was best so. If she had known, she might have been humbled, angered, troubled. She might have even been afraid to go back to that solitude which was all she knew of safety, all she cared for as home.

And other thoughts thronged on him. He had been born amidst the forests that deck the seaward side of Etna, and the fires of the mountain were in his blood and in his soul. He had been always taught from childhood that a just vengeance was a holy thing,—that women might sit down and weep, but that men should scorch their tears up with a dagger's flash and the smoke of blood justly shed.

All these days he had been saying always to himself, "Who is the coward that has left her alone? Who is the beast that has forsaken her?" and, thinking and thinking thus perpetually of one thing, he had come slowly to put together this and that, and to divine that her lover had been the companion of Saturnino, the man of late set free by the same law which had condemned him.

But he was not sure.

No tortures would have forced the lips of Musa to speak Este's name.

They might have done with her what they would. She had the temper of Greek Læna in her. She would never have spoken.

He let her go away from him along the sad sea-shore with the strewn weeds steaming in the torrid sun; then with a few long steps he overtook her and spoke in her ear.

"It was Count d'Este that you loved?"

She turned her head with a quick, frightened anger, but in the warmth that mounted over the pallor of her face, in the look of her dilating eyes, he knew the truth.

She could not lie, she would not speak: with that one swift glance over her shoulder, she shook him off, and hastened on. He had been answered.

He let her go once more onward and northward towards the moors, alone.

He stood motionless, looking after her as long as she was in sight.

When a curve in the land took her from his eyes, he gave a deep short sigh, he muttered a deadly oath; then he retraced his steps and went back to the harbor, where, in the shallow salt water, the lateen craft in which he had come hither was lying moored, the sun on its one white sail. In another moment he had leaped into the boat and cast her loose.

There was wind blowing, a hot wind straight from the east, and full of sand. He set the boat's head towards far Sardinia, lying hidden in the pallid clouds of heat.

She had escaped the horror of years of an imprisoned life only through him; but that she did not know, and he would not have her told of it.

"She would be angry with me," he thought, in his humility,—the humility which is the sign of all great love. He knew, besides, how intolerable it would be to her to learn that he had spent money in her defence which she could never hope to be able to repay to him.

A little way out of the town, as she reached the shade of the pine woods that lined the shore, the woman Pomfilia overtook her.

"Let me go with you," she cried. "You are not well enough to go alone; let me go with you. My husband and the sheep are on the moors: I could go by the boats, but I would rather walk with you."

"You are kind to think of it," said Musa; "but I would sooner be alone."

"Ah, you have had a rude time," sighed the shepherd's wife, "and never might I have heard of it but for that good Sicilian skipper who came up upon my hills at home and hunted me out and brought me here in time."

"Did he do that?"

She colored with pain and vexation: she could not bear to think she owed so much to him.

"Ay, that did he," said the woman of the Apennines. "To my thinking, but for him those brutes would have caged you for half your life and more. It would be well if you could care for him: he has a good heart, and loves the ground you tread on. I know not what the other one is, nor where; but for sure he left you alone in your trouble and your adversity, and merits nothing."

She paused, frightened at the look of the eyes which silenced her without any need of speech.

"Go you by the boats," Musa said, curtly. "For me be not afraid: I know my way home. I thank you for all you have done, and when you want shelter or food come to me. But, if ever you dare speak to me of the Sicilian again, I will not see you ever any more."

The shepherd's wife shrank away humbly, and went back to the sea-wall, where boats were always coming and going.

Musa went on under the pines.

She could not have borne the fret and jar of the woman's well-meant condolence and sympathy. She could not have borne the sound of any human voice,—save one.

All she could bear to hear was the breathing of the wind among the trees, the lap of the sea-water on the beach. All human words only lacerated and hurt her, be they gentle as they might.

She had been sorely wounded. The insult of her captivity was bitter to a nature which had inherited all her father's pride, and something of her father's arrogance, with a sensitive reserve that her lonely life had fostered till she shrank like the mimosa from any human touch.

She needed to be alone,—alone with the shadows, and the leaves, and the wide waters, and the green wet plain, and all the things that told her she was free.

She found her way back as the hunted hare escaping travels footsore to its form among the saintfoin and the spurge.

She was very tired. She was often faint; she had not a coin upon her; she slept the night out under a little hut of brake and ling made for a goatherd and deserted by him when the heats had come.

She was feeble now; her glorious perfection of health and strength had gone from her, and the symmetrical limbs that had never known ache or pain were now languid, and felt broken as she dragged them over the great silent moorlands.

But the hope of her return sustained her, as it sustains the beaten panting fox, or the stockdove with shot in its little aching body that yet flies on to die, if it can, in its own familiar place.

Her one thought, her one terror, was, if he should have been there,—if he should have found her absent, would he think her so soon faithless and tired? Would he have gone away in anger and doubt?

That thought of him, and the longing in her to be alone once more,—to be by her own hearth and within the walls that held her memories of him,—kept up her fainting spirit, kept erect her trembling limbs.

With unutterable joy she at last entered on the wild woodlands, where a rising of the soil let her look away eastward over the sea of foliage and search with yearning eyes for the landmarks by which she would know from afar the place of the graves of the Lucumo.

When she saw them at last, and the great suber-oak rose up above its fellows to her sight, then indeed she knew that she was home once more.

She dropped on her knees and praised God.

CHAPTER LIII.

In the gloom of the great cork forests of Sardinia Daniello Villamagna found Saturnino Mastarna. They spoke together long in the leafy solitudes of the mountain-side beside the camp-fire lit by the Mastarna men.

In these primeval woods, in these wild untrodden recesses of the almost barbaric isle, the galley-slave was safer than kings are on their thrones. He was once more happy; he sent at pleasure a ball from his rifle down the azure depths of the air; he drank deep and drank often; he had a long fine dagger in his belt; he had danger, plunder, bloodshed, the three things that made up daily bread that he had pined for and hungered for as the first food of life; he felt once more to have hold on his manhood which they had done all they knew to chain down and cudgel out of him. He could lean against the ledge of granite and look down through three thousand feet of air and foliage on to the blue sea below, and lift his gun to his shoulder and deal death to whatever distant thing he saw: that was to live once more.

The Sicilian said to him,—

"Either you or I——"

And he made answer,—

"The Mastarna cure their own wounds."

For the first time in all his lawless and outlawed life, a duty, that he deemed the one sacred, supreme duty of life, rose up before him and claimed him. To pity he might have been deaf; to shame, indifferent; to the wrath of earth or heaven, callous; to the cry of woman or child, adamant; but when vengeance called aloud to him, he dared not refuse to answer. It was the only invocation before which the men of the blood of the Etruscan Mastarna never ventured to be deaf or to dally on their road.

CHAPTER LIV.

THE tombs were no longer what they had been when by means of cleanliness, orderliness, and her own sense of beauty she had contrived to make them into the likeness of a home. The vases and bowls and jars had been for the most part broken in pieces by the rabid fury of the disappointed steward, the sculptured Chimæra and Typhon had been hewn from the walls, the best of the bronze utensils and candelabra had been taken, and the statue that Este had made of her had been carried away by the old man in his greed, who, ignorant of all those matters, had imagined it a work of Greek or Roman art. Her mandoline had been thrown down and broken, her spinning-wheel had been treated in the same way; the whole place, had been defaced, mutilated, profaned. She found her bed and bedding, and other things of household use, and all her clothes and linen there; for the bribes of Daniello Villamagna had been at work here also to secure to her the humble necessaries of human life.

She began her existence once more in this lonely abode, sadly content to be once more where all her memories of joy had been garnered, and where her lover, if he looked for her ever, would surely come. She took up the thread of her days where it had been broken, but it was no longer the same.

There was no more the body of the little child beside her: no more did the coffin of Joconda seem to bring a quiet blessing on the place.

And there were no more for her the joys of a light foot and a glad heart, of a happy ignorance of evil, of a simple self-taught philosophy which was content with finding daily bread and living like the birds of the air, careless of to-morrow, trustful of nature. All these were gone forever.

Love had passed by there.

They had let her come back.

For so much she was thankful. She clung to her home under ground as the stormy petrel clings to hers.

Without it she would have strayed, miserably and helplessly, as the rooks do for a while when their elm-trees are felled and their nests destroyed. After a while the rooks go and make their home elsewhere, but she could never have done that: here alone was memory close about her, here alone had love been with her.

She began her life again with something of her old intrepidity and infinite relief in the peaceful sense of silence round her. She had not a penny in the world; she had only her two hands with which to maintain herself. There was some store of oats and other things which had escaped the notice of the men and were safe from the quest of rats in an old coffer which she had brought there on the mule's back long before on the day after Joconda's burial. There was also a little store of rice, beans, coffee, and some wine, which had been put there by the Sicilian when he had persuaded the old steward to allow her the use of the tombs. There was enough to live on for some few weeks; she looked no further. She would resume her old habits of work little by little, and so maintain herself.

The consolation of the fresh air, of the sight of the green autumnal earth, of the sounds of fluttering wings and rustling feet of forest creatures, revived the soul in her, gave her back hope and health.

Surely some day he would come.

That was all she thought of: she sat hour after hour looking over the wolds, hoping against hope for a step that never came.

The golden autumnal days went by, beautiful, full of the fragrance of falling leaves, and of the music of the woodlark, and the chaffinch, and the song-sparrow, and the little robins come from the high hills or from foreign lands.

With every dawn that rose she thought, "Perhaps he will come to-day." With every nightfall she thought, "Perhaps to-morrow."

It was more than a year since Este had sent his messenger to her with his gifts which she had repulsed, and that letter which she had torn in a thousand pieces when the men of Prince Altamonte had invaded her sanctuary, lest any should take it perforce from her and read it and cause Este trouble.

A whole year and more had passed by, and she had heard nothing of him, he had given no sign that he remembered her.

True, where he was, amidst his new pleasures and his new riches, her memory passed over him again and again, a score of times each day, with a sharp reproach in it, and he said always to himself, "To-morrow I will go—next week I will go," and let the days and the weeks slip away into the abyss of the past.

But she could not tell that. She could only know that he had forgotten. She tried to believe it was but natural and no cruelty. She was young, and she still clung to hope. To-morrow he would come.

One day in early November weather—the grand, buoyant, sunlit weather that comes in this season in these lands, with wondrous pomp of sunsets and lovely noontides warm as midsummer, and a delicious stir and freshness in all the sweet-smelling air—she was sitting at the entrance of the sepulchre, when a figure did appear in the transparent light of early day, and came onward across the grass-lands, and she rose and regarded him with dilated eyes, knowing him even though he wore the garb of a Campagna shepherd.

The great, gaunt, sunburnt figure of the shepherd came between her and the sunlight. He looked old; his hair was white, and white were his shaggy eyebrows, from under which his sombre cavernous eyes looked out in a savage pain, like those of a great animal struck by a bullet. He wore a broad hat and clothes of goatskin, and bore in his hand the crozier-shaped crook.

He paused before her, leaving some yards of earth between herself and him. He seemed afraid to approach her. She at a glance knew him again.

"You are Saturnino Mastarna," she said, and her voice had neither pity nor scorn in it, but a weary calmness of indifference. Nothing mattered to her.

"I am Saturnino Mastarna," he answered, mechanically, whilst his eyes rested on her, and he said to himself, "Yes, it is she; Serapia's child,—my child. She has Serapia's face and mine, blended together, as when we stooped over a stream the water blent in one our two reflections; and all the life and the fire are gone out of her, and it is he who has done that."

"You are Saturnino Mastarna," she said, again. "What do you do here? Will they not take you if they see you?"

"They shall not see me: I know how to hide. They watch for me in Sardinia. I have been there with mountain-men of Mastarna blood. I got away on a good ship: a Sicilian who loves you pitied me."

She was silent; it was nothing to her. She only wished that he would go away. It was not fear that she felt for him, but apathy,—the apathy of a mind which has but one thought, of a heart which has one emotion.

Then she remembered that this man had once sent her Este: her eyes softened.

"Come inside," she said to him: "I will give you bread and a little wine that is there: you will be safer within. Come."

He followed her. He took the food and the drink, but remained standing. His eyes followed her with a pathetic yearning. He was saying always to himself, "She is mine, she is Serapia's; and all she knows of me is that I stole her gold, and sent to her the coward who has killed her heart in her before she has seen a score of years on earth."

She served him with the little she possessed, then seated herself with those fatigued movements which now nearly always replaced her once vigorous and agile animation.

He leaned against the stone wall where the dancing-boys and the lotus-flowers were painted, and rested his gaze on her timidly, as a dog looks that loves and is yet afraid of a blow from the hand he would caress.

"You sheltered Este?" he said, suddenly.

The little color that there was in her face faded out of it utterly.

"I did," she answered, coldly.

"You fed him, you tended him, you succored him, you loved him, you gave him all you had to give; and when they set him free he left you and forgot you: is it not so?"

She lifted her face; it was as cold as marble, and as stern.

"When I blame him, then may you. Leave his name alone."

"I sent him to you,—I!"

"It is for that I bid you break my bread," she said, with so great and exquisite a tenderness melting the coldness of her voice that it thrilled even the savage and brutalized soul of Saturnino.

He said nothing; he was thinking of that night of flight when, under the snows of Monte Labbro, lying beneath the tangle of ruscus and arbutus where the Fiora water ran between the rocks, he had said to his companion of the galleys—

"To that tomb there comes a maiden with grand eyes like two stars. She will let you shelter there, and will not speak, I think; but if you fear her speaking—well, a fawn's neck is soon slit."

Why had not his tongue rotted with cancer in his mouth ere ever it had spoken those words?

"I sent him to you! I sent him to you!" he muttered; and he could not comprehend why she—his daughter and Serapia's—did not leap up in rage and curse him. There had been but one answer from the Mastarna to what was faithless. And she, she bade him welcome because he had sent this man to her!

He did not understand. He looked down on her with his angry and bloodshot eyes; furious imprecations rose to his lips, but something in the look of her held him mute; he was afraid to say the thing he thought.

Should he tell her what he was to her?

Should he claim her by that tie of parentage?

Should he say to her, "I, who stole your gold, I, who have a hundred murders on my soul, I, whose name the Maremma has shuddered at and gloried in, I am your father?"

He had been a selfish tyrant always,—a brute, with little thought but for his own passions, his own greeds, his own revenge; seldom, since his earliest years, had he felt any single unselfish or generous impulse such as had moved him when he had found the grandson of Joconda sleeping in the snow; and the accursed life of the galleys, that scorches up every well-spring of feeling and withers up every slender shoot of better instincts, had made him a devil rather than a man.

But now a movement of generosity, of self-sacrifice, stirred in him.

Better, he thought, better and kinder to leave her in ignorance forever; better not to lean the weight of his own immeasurable guilt, of his own unutterable past, upon her. She had burden enough already.

It was the first instinct of any nobility, of any self-denial, that had

ever moved him since the hour that Joconda had held up her stoup of
wine to his mouth in the cathedral square of Grosseto.

He longed to fall down before her, to cry aloud to her, to say to
her, "Pity me, if you cannot love me; your mother loved me once!"

His heart, so long denied all natural affections, so long without
any kind of tenderness given or received, so long barren as the rock in
the midst of the salt water on which he had been caged, grew thirsty
with longing to slake itself at these simple springs of natural love at
which the poorest can drink and for a while feel rich.

He had been a fierce and cruel creature, often following his instincts as the tiger and the vulture followed theirs; but he had not been
without fine impulses here and there, and he had been capable of love.

All his soul looked on her now out of his deep wild eyes. The
words rushed to his lips that would tell her the truth,—words which
never again could be effaced. Almost he had cast himself down before
her and cried to her, "I stole your gold, I sent your lover here, I have a
thousand crimes upon my head, I am steeped in human blood; but I
am yours, and you are mine: take me, hide me, pardon me, pity me!"

But something stronger than himself, more powerful even than
this hunger for compassion and affection which possessed him, held
him mute.

He had done her harm enough: why should he do her more injury?

The dead woman of Savoy had kept his secret faithfully: should
he do less?

He, who never had stayed his tongue in cursing, or held his hand
back from a blow, choked down the passionate desire in him and said
to himself, "Nay; why should she know?"

Why should she know?

Why should he lay his burden of foul sins upon the back of this
his lamb? It seemed to him that if he told her he would do the cruell-
est thing ever done in all his years of cruelty. He, who had hurled a
traitor over the rocks like a mere bough of dead wood, and drawn his
steel without a pause across the throats of harmless captives, dared
not do this one last selfishness.

He would take his life in his hand, he thought, and go out and
wander alone, and leave her in ignorance. He would avenge her: that
was all he had to do with her.

She, forgetful of him, sat on the stone seat, her head drooping, her hands crossed on her knee.

He looked at her, and said to himself that this one good deed he would do ere he died: he would keep silence; he would not speak in weakness and self-pity; as a woman would have spoken.

He would avenge her; and life might blossom afresh for her. When the summer is young, if the spikenard and the balm are mown down with the grass, they send forth new blooms from the bleeding roots. So he thought.

He leaned against the stone of the wall, and forgot that he was an outlaw and a hunted felon. He only remembered that he was her father, and Este's judge.

He saw the face of her lover as it had been with him in the twilight of the woods, in the scorch of the sunlight on the sea, a beautiful, proud, pensive face, like one of Signorelli's angels; and he stretched his hands out, his sinewy hands, with their grip of steel, that had done to death so many, and in fancy he clinched the slender fair throat that had uttered false words, and made the mouth that had kissed her open wide in the ghastly smile of suffocation, and choked the flickering breath into silence.

A cry of horror from her at his look roused him from his trance.

"What do you see? What do you think of?" she said, as she rose in terror. "There is no one here who would injure you. I am alone; all alone."

"Yes; you are alone," said Saturnino, with a strange look, as he withdrew his mind with painful effort from the vision that had absorbed him. She was alone,—she who had loved her lover as few women love on earth.

He gathered himself together with a heavy sigh, such as might burst from the aching heart of a lion that lay dying on the desert sands with the vultures waiting above-head in the light.

He shook his rough clothes, and felt for his long knife safe within his bosom.

Then he stood before her a moment and looked at her; he did not speak.

"You will hurt no one?" she said, touched to a vague anxiety at his aspect.

"I will never hurt you," he answered her, with a tenderness deep as her own when she breathed Este's name.

"Lay your hand on my forehead one moment," he said, a little later, "and wish me my sins forgiven."

He stooped to her as he spoke.

She hesitated a brief while; then she made the sign of the cross on his brow, and rested her hand on it an instant as he had asked.

"I wish you well," she said, softly, "I wish you well on earth, and after death may God be merciful to you. I bless you, for you sent me him!"

Saturnino rose erect, with a curse: his face lost in one moment its fleeting gentleness, and grew black as a night in tempest.

"Do I owe your touch to his memory?" he said, savagely, through his ground teeth.

Then he gazed at her once more, furiously, longingly, thirstily, and without other words turned his face from her and went out into the open day.

Once he looked back.

Already she had forgotten both his presence and his departure.

She was seated on the low stone chair, thoughtful, passive; her hands were lying on her knee; her eyes rested upon the ground; her whole body seemed to listen for a step that never came; her whole soul was absorbed in remembrance.

He looked one instant, and yet another, and another, and yet another still: his gaze, he knew, would never rest on her again.

Then he drew his long slim dagger from its sheath and let the sun-rays play on it; it was an old friend, a loyal comrade: he had no other upon earth.

Then he took his way across the marshes and the moorlands, go-ing southward, where Rome lay.

CHAPTER LV.

As he passed away over the moss-grown earth, and she sat there in the shadow of the Lucumo's chamber, some sudden perception of his words, some sudden sense of the menace which had been in them, came to her, breaking through her absorbed mind as the glare of a torch burns through a dull gray fog.

Whilst he was with her, the full purport of what he had said had not dawned on her; she had dully wondered why this man, a stranger, an outlaw, should think of her in any way; but now, in his absence, certain of his muttered disconnected words came back on her recollection. A great dread suddenly seized her; surely danger menaced Este. Perhaps, she thought, this man was mad, perhaps his long-accumulated crimes, and his many years of captivity, had made him lose his reason; but, mad or sane, remembering how he had looked, how he had spoken, she began to doubt, she began bitterly to lament that she had blessed him and wished his sins forgiven him. Assassination had been no more to him than the slitting of the kid's throat is to the butcher; human life had never been of more account to him than the grass of the field as it drops is to the mower; he, like Etruscan Tarquin, had held men of no greater sanctity than the poppies growing with the corn.

There had been cruel hate in him when he had spoken of Este: why had she not seen that before? why had she let him go away? An agony of fear came on her,—the worst of all fear to bear, because it was so vague.

Instinct rather than any reasoning made her feel that the return of Saturnino meant some peril, if not the greatest, to her lost lover.

Some sinister motive must have brought the outlaw from those dark Sardinian glades where he was safe from arrest unless the State sent soldiery swarming through the forests and over the mountains in greater numbers than it would ever spare for the mere sake of capturing a galley-slave; and her instinct told her that no motive would be ever so grave, no magnet ever so powerful, to the brigand of Santa Fiora as vengeance,—such vengeance as can only quench its thirst in blood, such vengeance as on the soil of the Italiote has ever been held as justice and as holiness.

She could not tell what root his desire of vengeance sprang from; whether it were some fancied wrong long brooded over, some smouldering fire of antagonism, which had burst into flame in envy at Este's liberty; or whether it were some fantastic sense of amends owing from him to her because through him Este had first come to the shelter of the tombs; she had heard in days of her childhood the stories that were told in Maremma of the impulses of capricious honor, of uncertain generosity, which had at times broken through the ferocity and selfishness of his natural temper. Which of these might be the motive that ruled him she could not tell; but such instinct as makes the dog scent danger for his master whilst yet nothing is seen or heard,

made her tremble for the one whom she loved, whom she had so long
sheltered and defended that to save him from his enemies was still
second nature to her.

In an instant the thought that Este still might need her poured
new life into her limbs, awakened the old bold spirit in her that had
sunk into the apathy of sorrow, and revived in her alike the courage
and the subtlety which had so often served him when he had been a
hunted criminal with a price set on his head. She knew at once what
she would do, what she must do.

In open dispute she could never hope to vanquish or disarm Saturnino Mastarna; by betrayal of him she could never stoop to arrest
his steps, she would sooner have killed him; she knew that what she
had to do was to watch him, and if he let Este alone, then would she
in turn leave him alone. She knew that she might suspect him falsely,
but that if his soul were bent on guilt no words of hers would turn
him from it; whilst, on the other hand, if he had no such thought, to
gall him by suggestion and accusation of it might sting into crime a
temper which had always found in crime the fiercest joy and most lasting desire of life.

She wasted not one moment, but took her course with that swift
decision which had often served her in good stead. In Este's service
she recovered the elasticity, the force, the energy, the physical animation, which since he had left her had gone out of her as utterly as its
color and palm-like grace go out of a dianthus that has been plucked
from its place in the rocks beneath the sea and cast down to perish on
the sand.

She took some bread, some maize, and a gourd of water, took
that three-edged poniard of Florence which Este had found in the
brigand's lair by Santa Fiora and left behind him here, took one little
silver piece that had remained in the old coffer with the corn, and,
closing the stone doors of the tombs behind her, went out on the
track of Saturnino.

To her skilled eye, used to trace such slender signs, the marks of
his footsteps were visible on the wet mossy ground he had traversed.
She followed them; they went always southward, straight ahead to
that golden horizon where Rome lay, sixty miles or more beyond the
moors, out of sight, sunk down in the sunlit ocean of the air.

Her heart stood still as that southward direction of his steps
brought confirmation of that sudden fear which had dawned on her

as though its light were shed from heaven. But it was not for the first time that terror gave her fresh courage, as the spur wrenches fresh effort from the sinking horse. To baffle and disarm this man would need all her prudence and all her boldness, that she knew; and almost her terror was effaced by the sense of returning happiness which came to her with the thought of once more shielding Este from any danger.

She walked on and on, cautiously though quickly, stooping every now and then to verify the traces of Saturnino's passage through the woodland. There was but one path practicable southward; and she knew that he would not dare to show himself on the main road, the once Consular and Imperial highway that ran far nearer the sea than did this mule-track over the moors and meadows, which was only in use by the charcoal-burners, the herdsmen, the foresters, and the hunters, and which now mounted over tufa or sandstone rocks, now delved down into wooded hollows, and now was interrupted by brawling streams descending from the hills. She had walked perhaps three miles from her own abode, when a rise in the ground let her look far ahead, and in the bright light, dark against the sunny sky, still holding on straight towards the south, she saw the tall gaunt figure she pursued. He was moving quickly, still clad in the goatskin clothes which shepherds wear, and still carrying the crozier shaped crook and the wallet on his back.

She had him in sight; she breathed more freely; now there was nothing to do but to keep upon his track and go wherever he went, unseen by him. It would be difficult, and it would be dangerous; but her spirit was not lightly daunted, once aroused.

She felt for the dagger in her girdle as he had felt for his; it was the only sure friend that either of them trusted. She drew the breezy autumn air more deeply into her lungs, that she might get strength from it as men do from draughts of wine. She walked on, keeping in his path as surely as his shadow did, watching with untiring eyes every movement that he made,—now losing him perforce from sight as the ground he traversed sank beneath the bushes, regaining sight of him as he emerged from the scrub of myrtle, of oak, or of olive, and climbed some rugged steep over which the bridle-path ran.

She marvelled that he dared be out thus in open daylight; but he trusted to his disguise in part, and in part to the fact that the State believed him in Sardinia, and hunted him no more, letting sleeping dogs lie as the proverb bade them do. In truth, they were not unwilling that he should thus escape; his name had once been like a trumpet-call to all Maremma, and they were content that he should get away and trouble the law no more. He had suffered sixteen years of the galleys; to all the populace that seemed punishment enough,—too much, in truth, for a bold, open-handed son of the soil who had taken to the hills as other men took to the ploughshare or the forge. He knew that that popular sympathy would everywhere be with him, timid, yet strong enough to make the law sometimes willingly blind. Relying on it, and on the solitariness of the Maremma wilds, he walked boldly on towards his goal, and she, unseen by him, followed step for step.

Would aught save crime have had the power to lure him from the safe secrecy of the Sardinian forests?

She thought not.

She remembered the gleam in his great black eyes when he had spoken Este's name, the steel-like gleam of an unquenchable hatred.

Happily for her, he only moved by day, and this by reason that the nights were moonless, and the half-covered mule-tracks which he alone durst follow could not be found, even by his knowledge of the country, after dark. So at night sleep did refresh her, even though it were fitful, startled, and roofless. The owls flew by her, and the polecat glided past, and the bats and the rodents stirred the air and the grass, and the wild ducks rushed by on the chill northern winds, but these were all old friends and comrades; she was afraid of no creatures of the earth or sky. She slept on a pile of fallen leaves, in the hollow of a tree, on the leeward side of a rock, anywhere that gave her momentary rest and let her see from some safe shelter Saturnino arise and go forth as the dawn came.

For three days she kept him in sight often enough to be able to follow in his track. For three nights, when he crept within some hut that he had made for as a shelter, she wrapped herself in her woollen mantle, and rested among the leaves hard by, and slept fitfully the deep dreamless sleep of great bodily fatigue.

It was late in autumn; it was not certain death to pass the night abroad, as it was in summer seasons. Cool winds from the north had swept away the noxious gases of the canicular heats; there were damp and cold to dread, but the malaria had in a great measure gone with the past summer. Moreover, her nerves were at that tension, her mind was in that overwrought anxiety, in which women, through all ages of the world, have performed miracles and passed through physical dangers of all kinds without physical harm.

There was the dread lest at any moment he should see her and take her for a spy upon him, and slit her throat with his knife as he had once bidden Este do. There was the dread lest at any moment, from the inequalities of the ground and the impossibility of drawing near to him, he should escape her sight and go whither she could not follow him. When sleep conquered her despite herself, and pressed her heavy eyelids downwards, she awoke with the apprehension of his having gone away from his resting-place during the night whilst she slept. If she once fairly lost him from view, she might, she knew, never come on his track again; and now that she had left the territory that was familiar to her, and crossed the Fiora water, and come upon lands that were utterly strange to her, she might, if she lost sight of him, lose her own way hopelessly and perish of hunger on the waste.

He, she saw, turned aside at times into the huts of shepherds or of the ploughmen come to till the corn-lands, and there no doubt ate, and paid for what he ate with Sardinian pence, and no doubt told them he was a shepherd, too, going towards the Campagna to rejoin his flocks. But she had only the loaf of bread and the handful of maize she had brought with her; they would last her, eaten sparingly, four or five days, but after that she would have nothing except the one little silver piece, and she began to be afraid lest her strength should fail her ere she knew whither he went.

Between sunrise and sunset he covered from fifteen to twenty miles, and she did the same. Two years before, such walking as this would have been mere sport to her; but now she was no longer as strong as she had been, her splendid vitality had been rudely shaken, and her limbs began to tremble as she moved, and she began at times to stumble and recover herself with effort. Still she kept onwards, and was scarcely sensible of anything she felt, from the passion of anxiety that possessed her. She could not but believe some wicked purpose sent this murderer on this strange pilgrimage on foot to Rome.

Of the land he knew every rood. In all the province there was not a mule-track he had not followed, not a cluster of hovels he had not visited in those many years of vigil and of violence when his lair had been made by the snows of Monte Labbro, and his gallant person had been pointed out with pride at the feasts of the mountain-villages, and even in the-market-places of Grosseto, of Massa, and of Volterra.

He was at home here in these woodlands, on these moorlands, as any dog-fox that had burrowed there from the time he had been a cub. The map of all this wild country was clear in his brain, and all that the prisons had done to him had not made one memory fainter of all that labyrinth of foliage, all that desert of green pasture, all those untrodden hillsides, all those barren moors silent as Sahara.

As a child he had run through them barefoot, light-hearted as the scampering goats; as a man he had ridden over them, trodden through them, hidden there, fought there, there loved and hated, and there called with one shrill whistle a score of his men from bush and brier. Until the iron heel of that great jailer Death should stamp his brain out into nothingness he would remember every wind of the dizzy path up the face of the rocks, every spring that coursed through the moss and the ling, every hole to hide in where the wild olive grew with the holy-thorn above the white travertine or the yellow sandstone.

So he dreamt not of descending to the sea-shore, but held on his way inland, whilst the Apennines that had given him shelter so long behind their ramparts of stone cast their wide purple shadows over the plain.

And behind him, unseen, followed the tall, slender figure of Musa, with the sun shining on her pale stern face and in her luminous eyes; as if the God he had outraged so long had bidden a young angel, an *angiolin*, come down from its watch amidst the moving worlds of heaven to follow in the footsteps of this one blood-stained, brutal human creature.

He, knowing nothing, pursued his way, whilst the noonday light and the afternoon shades in turn came across his path. Rome was still fifty miles away, if one.

Her greatest fear was lest he should descend to the sea, and take the seaway south: if he did that, it would be impossible to follow him or to know whither he went; even if her boat had not been taken, she could not have gone back for it in time to overtake any craft in which he might sail.

But he did not go down towards the shore. He was indeed afraid of the coast, where at every hamlet there was some rural guard, some watchmen of the shore, or some soldiers quartered at one of those martello towers which dot the shore at intervals.

Every rood of the soil that she trod was full of Etruscan memories, but that she knew not.

Here had been Vulci and Toscania; here had been Tarquinii and its vast necropolis; here had been Cære and the Centum Cellæ; the melancholy Marta flowing through immense and silent meadows to the sea, the low sombre hills that rose and fell in monotonous sequence, and now revealed the belfries of Corneto, and now the blue waters by what had once been Graviscæ, whilst on the eastward they rose higher and higher and met the dark-gray wall of the mighty Ciminian, half hidden in stormy clouds: all, all, had been Etruria Maritima, and beneath the mastic and the locust-tree, beneath the matgrass of the moors and the salt-rush of the marsh, there were cities, and palaces, and ramparts, and labyrinths, and necropoles, with their buried treasures that never more would see the light of day.

But she knew nothing of this.

She only saw a sad wild country that was unknown to her, vegetation that grew scantier and sicklier at each step, green swamps that had a familiar look, and moorlands that looked endless and had no living creature anywhere upon them save the meek and melancholy buffalo, and the wild mares and colts that here and there swept like a hurrying wind over the brown grass-lands.

Rome, too, said nothing to her.

The name that alike the poet and the scholar, the devotee and the agnostic, can never hear without emotion, to her had no meaning save as a place where her lover dwelt. In her childhood she had heard speak of Rome as of the city of the Holy Father, and had had vague fancies of it as of a great white throne set upon the everlasting hills, with walls of ivory and gates of gold, and all the angels as its ministers, and on it forever a light like that of sunrise.

That had been her vision of it as a child.

Now she knew it was what men called a city,—a place terrible to her as of meeting roofs and brawling crowds,—a place where he lived, and, living, forgot Maremma.

"Is it far, so very far, to Rome?" she wondered, with a sinking heart and tired feet.

Saturnino had still chosen the inland instead of the seaward way; he still feared those watch-towers of the coast, the soldiery who were perpetually on vigil to seize the smugglers from the isles.

In lieu of descending to follow the Via Aurelia where it wound down a few miles off the coast, by Santa Maranella and Santa Severa and mediæval Palo, and the volcanic soil and the steep ravines by Cervetri, where the long avenues of cliff-sepulchres are all that remain to show the site of Cære, and gaining so the mouth of Tiber to ascend the stream in any boat that he might find by Fiumicino, he still struck across the country by cattle-tracks known alone to himself and wild men like him, and chose to leave the Maccarese morasses untrodden in his rear, and had followed the course of the Arrone River as far as the high cliffs up by forsaken Galera.

At this deserted rock-village he slept that night, the fifth night of his pilgrimage, and she, still unseen by him, climbed also in the twilight of the early autumn night, and there rested also, as a hill-hare worn out with travel might have done.

He, all unconscious that she was near, slept soundly with rude stones for his bed.

In his days of pride his range had sometimes swept as far as those wood-clothed cliffs that rise about the lake of Bracciano, the Lacus Sabatinus of the Romans. In that time he had been well known in all this country-side, and the wayside wine-house farther away on the stream of the Due Fossi had once been proud to entertain the lordly brigand from the Apennine hills when it had seemed good to him to sweep down on travellers too curious and too incautious, coming out by the Via Flaminia to see Veii or Scrofano or the classic baths of Apollo's Vicarello.

Ere the light of daybreak had come over the green mountain of Rocca Romana in the east, he rose this night from his rough couch of stones, and broke his fast on dried goat's-flesh and a draught from his flask of wine, and then began to descend the hills, using greater prudence and more wariness now that he neared Rome.

Musa, who had been yet earlier awake, had bathed her face and feet in the Arrone, and was watching to see him stir, herself screened amidst the brushwood.

It was a fair morning, golden and light.

Over the Campagna away southward there were white mists that hovered longest where the Tiber rolled, but eastward on these rocks the woods were all alight with sunbeams, and the glancing streams ran sparkling through grasses, starred with dragon-flower and cyclamen, and shaded with heavy boughs of beech and chestnut.

Even in the strained, vague terror which filled her mind to the exclusion of any other emotion, a sense of the beauty of this morning smote her, and her eyes involuntarily dwelt upon the scene around her.

Before her, some sixteen miles away, there was a dome that lifted itself from the circling mists and the green shadows of a great plain,— a dome that looked blue as a hyacinth, ethereal as a shadow itself, against the clearness of the morning skies. The plain was the Roman Campagna, and the dome was the dome of San Pietro.

She did not know it, but dimly she divined it. Something of that ineffable thrill which comes to all who thus behold it moved her even in her ignorance.

"Yonder must be Rome," she thought, and knelt a moment on the grass, forgetting Saturnino.

The moment passed, she sprang to her feet again, remembering her errand,—alert, lithe, agile, wary even in her fatigue as any forest animal that watches for the hunters to spring away at the first sound it hears.

Saturnino went down the cliffs, and passed the Arrone by a ford, and, giving La Storta a wide berth to his right, kept clear of the post-road and passed by a path across the downs to Isola Farnese. He walked slowly now, being himself fatigued; she followed over the turf, a gray gliding figure, little noticeable, for the hood of her woollen mantle was drawn over her head. On these open fields she feared that he might turn his head and at a glance recognize her.

He did not ascend the cliff to Isola, but passed on beneath it, still keeping clear of the highway.

The "Troy of Italy" lay behind them on its bare ground; but of this she knew nothing. Beyond that were the dark heights where the waters of Tivoli fall, and the snow-line of the Sabine range; in front stretched the Campagna, broken here into narrow ravines, and with scattered groves of trees, whose golden leafage caught the sunshine of the early day as the morning broadened behind the frozen summit of the Leonessa and over the once sacred oaks of Eleusinian Musino.

To her they were but such long heaving mountain-lines, such hills, with barren sides and wooded summits, such downs and moors, with the yellow dragon's-mouth, the amethyst-hued cyclamen, in their grass, as she had had always about her in autumn in Maremma. Even the tumuli and the tombs that often marked the way were familiar features in her home landscape. But that blue dome in the blue air afar

off, that bell-flower that seemed to hang downwards from the floating clouds, that was new, strange, marvellous; that seemed to call her
forward towards it, that seemed to say to her, "Hasten, hasten! here is
the city of God."

Only before her, between her and it, went the form of Saturnino,
like the shadow of death.

When they left the glens and broken ground, and came out on the
level turf of the Campagna nearer Rome, she was afraid that he would
turn and see her. But he did not. He was walking a little lamely now,
but with a dogged persistence, as if the thoughts with which he was
accompanied would not let him delay or rest.

He knew very well that now he was going with open eyes straight
into the jaws of danger, and his dread of capture was much greater
than his dread of death. He knew that at any moment a question put
to him, a suspicion caused to any guard or soldier, might fling him
back into the hands of the State. Away in the wild country he had
been comparatively secure; but here, where perforce he must mingle
with other men, and perforce pass the guarded barriers, he knew that
at any moment the law might fall on him and claim him. But he went
on all the same, feeling every now and then for his dagger, which was
hidden beneath his goatskin breeches.

A body of mounted carabineers chanced to ride past, their horses'
hoofs cutting deep into the wet Campagna turf; he turned quickly
aside and hid himself behind a mound of tufa.

Turning, he saw her, but he saw in her only a peasant-girl coming
with her head hooded against the keen winds that were blowing up
from the mouth of Tiber away in the west.

When the mounted patrol had trotted by and were lost to sight
beyond a fringe of alders on the Valca's curve, he did not even think to
look for her, a mere woman of the Campagna, as he thought, coming
to the city as so many come.

He was absorbed in one terrible purpose, in one mission which
was the only shape of duty that had ever guided his steps: its preoc-
cupation obscured in him his usual wariness of eye and brain.

By this time it was afternoon, for he was footsore and walked
slowly, and the ground was for the most part rough and heavy, and
often encumbered with thorns and brambles and stones half sunken
in the turf.

They met few living things; now and then an ox-cart came along the deep ruts in the turf; a bird-catcher spread his nets to snare the greenfinch and the goldfinch in the red-berried bryony; a mountain-lad went by playing on his pipes a melancholy hymn; a shepherd lay asleep amidst his nibbling flock, whilst his dog watched. That was all.

They were now treading on what was once the Via Cassia, and they pursued it some little way; but in lieu of going on by it to the Ponte Malle, Saturnino crossed the green turf by paths he knew, and at length entered on a broad, crowded public road, which once had been the great Flaminian Way. He deemed it less perilous to pass through the gates with other men than to endeavor to enter the city secretly by any suspected means.

Her heart tightened as she saw him take the road.

It would be far more difficult to follow him in any highway or any street than it had been upon the downs and moors, where the clear air showed every figure on them as far as the human eye could reach in vision. Once in a street, a momentarily-gathering crowd, the passage of a wagon, the twist of any unknown passage, the barrier of a group of people, any unforeseen trifle, might take him from her sight, never, perhaps, to be found again in this great city, which appalled her, as she drew nigh it, with its ever-spreading walls and roofs, and palaces and cupolas and towers, and dusky piles of red-brown travertine, and gigantic churches that seemed to surge colossal, from a petrified sea of stone.

Fear took the place of that exaltation which had sustained her sinking limbs so far,—the nameless fear which comes on all free forest things when they are driven to approach a city.

She, like them, was bold so long as the width of the green grass-lands, of the heath-grown moors, was around her,—as long as she possessed the lovely light of the unobscured skies, the wholesome wine of the strong wind, the fresh fragrance of the dewy soil.

But as she drew nigh this wilderness of stone, of brick, of marble, of iron, she saw no more the purple flower of the great dome: she only saw a labyrinth of men's making in which she would wander miserably, finding not her lover, and losing her hold upon his assassin.

A greater terror than that which she had felt in the prisons and judgment-chamber of Orbitello fell upon her. If she could not find Este, if she lost sight of this man bent on his destruction, what could she do? How could she warn him whom she would have given every drop of her life-blood to save?

The autumn day was drawing to a close; the splendor of sunset in November was beginning to lend its deeper gold, its darker blue, to the western heavens; the bells of Rome were rocking and beating on the air.

With that frost of fear on her heart, she followed Saturnino as he passed through the wine-carts, the hay-wagons, the horses, the mules, the brawling men, the shouting children, about the gates of the Porta del Popolo. He had thrown his wallet aside when he had left Galera; he had nothing on him that the custom-guards could ask to examine. He passed them unnoticed,—a tall, sinewy, black-browed, brown-cheeked shepherd, like so many that came down from the mountains with their goats and asses, to go the round of the streets at daybreak.

She passed also,—a slender, youthful figure, clad in homely home-spun clothes.

She was in Rome.

She had walked sixty miles in five days.

She looked neither to right nor left.

She only watched the figure of Saturnino, towering a full head above the throngs through which his long stride passed.

Once only he paused: it was to go into a wine-shop, and, under cover of drinking, ask the way to the palace that Este had inherited,—the palace once of a Pope's mistress, a grand and gorgeous place, standing with its sculptured walls on a small piazza, dark and old, across the water on Trastevere. It had a wooded garden sloping to the Tiber, as the Farnesina had. So they told him in the wine-shop, making clear to him the way that he should take.

His back was to the entrance-door as he drank, and paid, and spoke. She leaned against the lintel, and listened, and heard.

She had believed all along that he came thither to kill Este: she heard without surprise the question that gave her confirmation of all she feared. What reason moved him, she wondered dully, while the pulse of her life beat in her as if every vein would burst.

She shrank back into the shadow of the wall as he came out. His face was dark with drink and passion; his lips were set. His eyes had a red fury in them, as an angered mastiff's have when he is about to spring.

Almost she was tempted to leap on him and drive her dagger through him.

To save or serve Este any crime would have seemed to her holiness.

But she knew that beside him she was as a reed beside an oak,— that if her first blow failed to strike home, he would turn in his rage and stab or strangle her: then who would warn Este if she died?

She dared not touch him, lest she should fail and no living thing be left betwixt her lover and him.

She continued to follow him, going through the strange ways of the wondrous city with no more sight of them than if she had been blind.

The noise of the streets, the confusion and babble, and sounds of moving horses, of soldiers' trumpets, of shouting charlatans, of rapidly-revolving wheels, all went by her unheard.

Her fear of the city was lost in a yet intenser fear. Had its streets been a furnace, she would have plunged into its flames.

Saturnino left the noisier and gayer streets to pass into the dark steep lanes that encompass the Pantheon and lead the way to Tiber. It seemed to her as if these miry, crooked, gloomy ways would never end: their rough uneven pavements, their battered darkling house-walls, their stench, and the cries that filled them from the brazen lungs of the populace thronging through them, made them seem to her like the passage-ways of hell. Yet she scarcely felt the flints under her feet, the foul smell in the air, the uproar on her ear; she was almost as sightless, almost as deaf, as a hunted dog that runs straight on, hearing and seeing naught, made mad with terror.

Only mad she was not: the great love in her burned too clearly, like a strong light in a lamp of alabaster, and her courage made her calm.

Saturnino passed through the ancient ways that dive down through the heart of the city to the river-side. He crossed the Tiber by the bridge of Sant' Angelo. The sun had now set; a crimson hue was upon all the scene; the river rippled in lines of gold, the pine-trees were black against the glow, the angel on Hadrian's tomb lifted a flashing sword into the light.

Even in that moment the beauty of the evening upon Tiber forced some perception of itself upon her. He never paused nor saw. He entered Trastevere.

Its streets and lanes were dark. Lamps were burning, and the glisten of fountains showed white through the gloom.

The great bells were tolling, for on the morrow it was the feast of St. Elizabeth. The air seemed to palpitate visibly with their rocking sounds. There were many monks and priests in the streets, their white or their black robes flitting by beneath the shadow of high walls overtopped with orange-trees and cypress and here and there a palm. The people came out of their dim arched doorways, from under their iron lamps, with mass-books in their hands or long rosaries of olive-beads. From some church or monastery whose portals stood open there came a low subdued chorus of Gregorian chants swelling softly out over the evening air.

Saturnino neither noted nor paused for any of these things. He, a man of religion always, had for once no heed to the call of vespers, no salutation for the lighted altars. He pressed through the priesthood and the populace alike in haste and with feverish steps.

He still walked lamely, but he went fast, stopping in his course only to ask once or twice his way to the palace of the Count d'Este.

Once a brown-eyed Trasteverina with red laughing mouth heard him ask that, and smiled.

"A handsome youth, and open-handed," she said: "he lives yonder where you see the statues on the roof. He led a mirthful life last winter, but he did not forget the poor. He was away all summer at some pleasure, I suppose; now he is back again. Yes, he is there; he is not alone, he is never alone; he is a gay gentleman, and handsome as a camellia-tree in Carnival."

Saturnino said nothing: he slid his hand within his clothes to feel his dagger-hilt.

Musa was not near enough to hear the woman's words. She saw him change the direction of his steps, and she saw a dark grand pile, with a vast doorway, Gothic statues of saints along its roof, that stood at the farther end of a narrow piazza, great trees of the gardens behind it making a black cloud against the evening sky. Then for a moment her eyes grew dim, her brain grew dizzy: she felt that she was near Este.

And if she could not save him! if she had chosen a foolish, useless way! she had erred when she had been afraid to strike her knife into his enemy's breast lest the blow should fail from any feebleness of her hand!

This was all she thought of. That her lover had forgotten her she never remembered: a great love is an unchanging pardon. Strained to the uttermost, it will not fail or faint; it will endure all things.

She quickened her steps, and, trusting to the deep shadows that fell from the house-walls of the piazza, crept close upward to him, so close that stretchout her hand she could have touched him.

He, knowing nothing still, went on across the pavement of the narrow square. No one noticed him; shepherds came in oftentimes from the Campagna on the vigil of holy feasts, and he, they saw, was from the downs and moors, with his rude goatskin clothes, his wild dark hair, his pastoral staff, his leather-girt strong loins.

The oaken iron-studded doors of the palace stood wide open; there was a keeper of them; clad in red and gold, like all such servitors of Roman princes, but he had crossed the piazza for a moment, and was quenching his thirst at a canteen, where some of the Swiss guard of the adjacent Vatican were lolling and drinking in his company, their yellow and red uniforms and the steel glitter of their halberds making a glow of color under an old bronze swinging lamp.

She gave the men-at-arms a swift glance, and felt glad that they were so near: if she failed they would be there to hear.

She crept up closely towards Saturnino, so closely that she walked in his very shadow. Her footfall was noiseless. He did not know that he was followed,—that he had thus been followed all across the wastes of the Maremma.

He passed without a moment's pause through the doorway; whenever he had struck a death-blow, he had always struck quickly as the eagle does.

Within, there was a vast and lofty hall, austere with sculpture, its floor mosaic, its ceiling frescoed; a staircase of immense width, made of marble, stretched upward between walls of marble; silver lamps swung from above and lighted it dully. It was deserted and silent: all the footmen dozed, in Roman fashion, in the antechambers before the great apartments up above where the first flight of the great stairs ended, and where, in a great arch within the wall, a statue of St. Michael stood, colossal, with white wings outspread and spear uplifted.

Saturnino crossed the hall and mounted one by one the steps of marble.

Once he looked back to be sure that no one saw him there. She shrank against the pillars of the balustrade, and her gray clothes were so like the shadows on her that she escaped his sight.

All around the landing-place there were large doors, black doors touched with faded gilding; there were oil lamps burning; their pale light fell on the marble of St. Michael, with the fiend conquered at his feet.

By hazard Saturnino flung open the nearest door to him, and thrust back the curtain of gilded leather that hung behind it. The chamber within was an antechamber, spacious, but well warmed by a bronze brazier in its centre: here several lackeys in liveries of purple and white were lounging at their ease in idleness.

Some stared, some started up at sight of the strange figure of this Campagna shepherd, as he looked to them, standing on the threshold, with one hand putting back the gilded Cordovan leather of the curtain.

He called to them in a loud voice: "Go, tell your master I am here,—I, Saturnino Mastarna. Say that I bid him for old friendship's sake come out for a word with me."

There was something in his tone, something in his look, which awed into silence the arrogant and impudent words with which they were always ready to greet and turn away one of the populace: to them, all Roman youngsters as they were, the name that was still a sacred name to the Maremma said nothing, but they were impressed and cowed by the rude majesty, the lordly, haughty command, of this strange man, who spoke to them as though he were an emperor.

They whispered among each other in hesitation and vague alarm. He stood on the threshold waiting and impatient, his great dark eyes glowing with flame beneath his bent and stormy brows.

"Go," he said again to them, "go: your master and I kept company for two long years, until we sawed each other's chains asunder. Go: I am Saturnino Mastarna."

Two of them slunk away upon his errand, the others waited about alarmed.

Behind the leathern curtain Musa stood, within a hand's-breadth of her father. Her heart beat so loudly against her breast that she thought he must hear it and would turn and see her there. Her whole being was strung to tension, all the blood had gone out of her face, tongues of flame seemed to dart through her eyes, her lips grew dry and parched. In the agony of her watching fear she almost forgot that her sight would soon see Este. If she failed to save him!—this was her one consuming thought.

It seemed to her hours that she stood there, on the threshold of the vestibule, waiting, whilst the idle lackeys loitered within, looking at this strange unbidden guest with stupid curiosity and amaze. She heard a clock striking the seventh hour of the night; she saw the hand of Saturnino steal within his belt of leather, and knew that he was fingering the dagger hidden there.

The doors at the upper end of the long frescoed chamber unclosed; Este came through them, the light from the swinging lamps fell on his classic face. He looked surprised, disturbed; he came across the floor with a rapid step, and motioned back his eager lackeys.

"Are you prudent?" he said, in a low tone. "I have not forgotten; I will befriend you; but what———"

Saturnino cut his words asunder.

"This!" he said; and swift as the lightning flash above his mountain-lair his dagger flashed in the air.

Ere it could strike she had thrown herself on him, and with the strength of a young lioness had torn the steel out of his grip, and forced him, staggering like a drunken man, against the marble columns of the door-way.

"You!" cried Este; and all his debt, and all his sins of oblivion and ingratitude, came back upon him like a rain of curses and held him dumb and paralyzed.

"I would not have come," she murmured, careless that the blood was streaming from the hand with which she had seized the dagger and still clinched it close, "I would not have come,—oh, never, never,—but he meant to kill you, and I have followed him all the way, all the way."

Then she dropped senseless on the marble floor at his feet.

Saturnino stood silent, leaning against the columns of the door.

The veins of his throat and his forehead were black and swollen, his dark face was crimson, the blood was surging in his temples and in his brain: he only saw a crimson reeling mist that circled round and round him. The servants seized him, and he felt them not: he saw nothing, he knew nothing; only one memory remained with him.

"She was the child of Serapia," he muttered, "and you—you—you—you will escape me!"

He strove to wrench himself free from the grasp of the men who

held him; he strove blindly, madly, to get away and throw himself on
Este; but he could see nothing, he could hear nothing, for the rush of
blood in his brain. The darkness over him grew denser and blacker,
the sense of suffocation grew worse, he thought the hands of a hundred men were at his throat; then, like the carcass of a slaughtered
bull, his body slipped from those who had seized him, and he fell face
forward on the floor.

He breathed a few times with labor, but his brain was already
dead: so the trunk and the limbs were dead also, and his unquiet soul
was still. The silver image that Joconda had given to him still hung
about his throat.

So he perished, unpitied, unassoilzied, and they let him lie like
carrion, and like carrion be carted to the streets. The law he had forever hated and warred against vanquished him at the last, and cast
him with scorn like a dead rat into a pit, nameless and unmourned.

When she returned to any consciousness and sense of sight or
hearing, she was alone with Este: he knelt beside her as he had knelt
by her on that night of storm when he had found her on the shore
beneath the Sasso Scritto.

"Forgive me! forgive me!"—that was all he could think of to say.

He loathed his sins, and he abhorred himself.

Little by little she recovered breath and power and remembrance:
she had only swooned from long fatigue and terror and the effort
made to save him.

For a while she lay quite still, letting the deep delight of his touch,
his voice, his presence, steep all her being in unutterable, dream-like
ecstasy.

Then all in a moment she remembered.

"My love! my love!" she murmured, and smiled, and leaned her
head against his breast, and was at peace at last.

He kissed her again and again and again, and in that moment
loved her and said only the same words, "Forgive me! forgive me!"
and then was still and leaned his lips upon her hair in silence.

For a while she rested so,—so motionless he might have thought
her dead but for the close-clinging pressure of her unwounded hand
on his.

She lay as in a trance,—a trance of more than mortal joy.

All in a moment she drew herself from him.

"Saturnino," she murmured,—"where is he?"

"He is gone, dear. Never mind him," he answered her. He could not bear to tell her that this man was dead.

"Gone?—gone where? He may come back. He may try to kill you. He hates you: I cannot tell why———"

She had started from his hold, and was trembling with terror. Este shuddered with his own memories.

He had understood the dying words of Saturnino; he had understood that this poor dead brute had been her father.

"He is gone where he will harm no one any more," he said to her, with tears in his own eyes. "He is dead, dear. He had a rush of blood over the brain that killed him. Let us leave him to God."

"Is he dead?" she said; but it moved her little. He had been nothing to her, this outlawed man, who first had stolen her gold and last had striven to slay the only life she loved. She had pitied him because men had hunted him; that was all.

Suddenly she raised herself and looked in Este's eyes, and a great wave of hot color went over all her face.

"My child died," she murmured, timidly, as if afraid he would rebuke her.

"Yours!—mine!"

A great pang of remorse went through him. Had she suffered thus, he knowing nothing, living in pleasure and in oblivion?

"Ours," she said, softly, under her breath. "He lived a few little days. I did all I could."

Her eyes closed, and large tears rolled slowly off her lashes and fell upon his hand. He kissed them as they fell: a poignant repentance made him ready to curse himself, though she would never curse him.

"I would not have come," she said, suddenly: "you know that? you are sure of that? Only I knew he wished to hurt you, and I could warn you no other way. Oh, love! oh, my dear love! you do believe me? Never, never would I have come to remind you of—of———"

"Of my debt," he murmured. "Ah, I believe! You are the most generous and the most pure of living souls, and I am the most base."

"No, no," she said, softly, "I am nothing. It was natural you should forget. You have the world now; you have no need of me. Never, never would I have come for any lesser thing than this,—to save you."

"How do you live?" he said, with his voice broken and hoarse.

He was ashamed,—greatly ashamed.

"I live as we did," she said, simply, and thought she would not tell him of all her sufferings, lest he should hear in them a reproach.

"In the tombs? In those tombs still?"

"Where else?" she said, in wonder that he should ask.

"When I drink from what you called the *skyphos* that you drank out of," she added, simply, "it seems almost as if you kissed me still———"

He leaned his face upon her breast to hide his shame.

"What ever was I, that you should adore me thus?" he cried. "Nothing to you but a bringer of burden and shame."

"I love you," she murmured, with her old trouble at finding any words large enough to tell the great emotions that swelled her heart. Who that loves can ever find them?

She loved him, indeed, and he———

A passionate remorse was on him. Why had he been faithless, treacherous, more thankless than a cur that bit what fed it? Nay, he thought, no beast but what was human could ever have been ingrate thus.

Suddenly she freed herself from his embrace, and raised herself erect upon her couch.

"I will go now," she said, all her soul in her eyes as they dwelt on his. "I have saved you, I have seen you: night and day I will thank God. I will go now; I am not tired. I shall be always there, and if you wish for me ever, you will call me. But that will not be———"

Her eyes were full of large tears which did not fall. She put her arms about his throat and kissed him, as though he lay dying and was leaving her for evermore.

"My love—my love—my love!" she murmured.

Then she rose; her face was very pale, her head swam, her limbs trembled still, her hand was wounded and wrapped in linen and throbbed and ached, but she was ready to go.

He should not think that she had come to call him back to any memory of his debt or of her sacrifice.

The old heroic light shone in her eyes, the old high courage rose in her heart. She would go back and live in solitude and silence, and if he wished for her he knew the way over the wild thyme and the dewy wood-moss to the moors. She would be always there.

Perhaps some day, when the world had tired him, or strength had failed him, he would remember.

Este caught her hands.

"You must not go!" he cried, passionately. "You must never go! What do you think me? Could ever we part now? If I had known———"

Then he was silent: a cruel knowledge was in his mind, a cruel dilemma beset him: he remembered other ties, other passions. She loved him as no other did, indeed, but he———

The tapestry at the farther wall of the great painted chamber in which they were alone wavered and moved; a hand pushed it with petulance aside; from the gloom behind it there came a woman as white as the swan's throat is, with hair that was about her like a golden nimbus, a collar of old jewels set in silver at her throat. She moved with calm, slow, undulating grace; she wore some soft and shining texture, white, too, with lights and shadows in it as the swan's whiteness has; she had a knot of crimson roses at her breast.

She had cruel eyes. She had a beautiful mouth, that laughed as children's do. She came forward and looked, smiling, at Este.

She was but a base, venal, wanton thing enough, who had but one love, gold; but the world had taught her all its sorcery, and she had its grace, its skill, its power. She was the Venus Pandemos which in all time has triumphed.

She put her hand upon his shoulder, and laughed a little, noiselessly.

She glanced at the poor, gray, dust-stained, travel-tired form that she saw there.

"He is mine," she said, with a smile. "Was he yours once? Well, why have you let him go?"

He shivered under the hold of the courtesan, but he said nothing. His head drooped; he was ashamed,—bitterly ashamed.

He envied that dead carrion which lay in the lower chamber of his palace. He, at least, living, had been a man.

Musa stood mute, her eyes fastened on this beautiful soulless white and golden thing that held him there.

Then all at once she understood.

With one cry she turned and fled.

When he shook off his sorceress, and followed her down his great marble stairs into the darkness of the night, she was gone,—lost to him in the wilderness of Rome.

Then perhaps, at last, he loved her.

CHAPTER LVI.

On the sixth day from that she reached her home. She knew not how she reached it,—knew no more than does the hunted beast, that runs panting, sinking, almost dying, at each step, and yet runs on to die at home. She had no consciousness of what she did: her hand bled, her brain turned, her feet stumbled, yet she kept on, with only that one instinct of the stricken doe left in her, to reach her home and die there.

She lost all beauty, all youth, all likeness of herself. She crept on with the torpid movement of old age: in her heart she carried its despair.

Everywhere around her, in the buoyant clouds, in the mountain-snows, in the greenness of the land, in the light and lustre of the sunbeams, she saw only one thing,—the face of the woman who had robbed her,—of the woman who was by his side, with the noiseless laugh on her mouth and the glisten of the old gems at her throat.

That was all she saw.

The few men who met her in the fields and on the moors were frightened at her look, and thought her mad, and hurried from her path.

For six days and nights she wandered, now running, now creeping, now dropping and lying like a stone, now gathering herself up and going onward as a deer does that carries a mortal wound with him through the brake and the stream, over the hill and the heath.

Sometimes she slept.

Sometimes all night she lay with eyes wide open to the stars, staring, wondering where God was.

On the seventh morning she came home.

There were redbreasts singing amidst the myrtle. She went down into the tombs. They were very cold: the ashes of the spent fire were on the stones.

In the ivory *skyphos* he had always used there was water: she drank it thirstily. She kissed the rim his lips had used to touch. She kneeled down and said a Latin prayer. "If God care," she thought,—and wondered dully.

The little timid song of the mountain-birds came into the stillness of the tombs.

She did not hear it: she only heard Este's voice.

She took from her girdle the three-edged dagger that he had once worn near his heart night and day; she set it upright in the spot where the little child had lain upon its bed of rosemary, forcing the hilt down into a crevice in the rock floor of the chamber of the Lucumo.

Then she threw herself forward on the upright blade, which sank straight through breast and bone.

When the messengers of her lover came thither a day later, having sought her in the city and on the downs and hills in vain, she lay as though asleep, face downward, her head upon her arm.

He made her grave there, and buried with her half his life.

But men forget,—and he forgot.

In time the wild olive, and the myrtle, and the evergreen alaternus grew closer and closer around the entrance of the Etruscan grave, and at last wove so impenetrable a veil between it and the light that even the wild birds and the hunted hare seeking a refuge could not enter there.

It defended her in death as it had sheltered her in life; and the woodlark sang above amidst the woodspurge, and the balm and the spikenard and the wild rose grew over the place of the tomb.

THE END.

APPENDIX: CONTEMPORARY REVIEWS OF THE NOVEL

"Novels of the Week." *The Athenæum*. 1 April 1882: 410.
In Maremma. By Ouida. 2 vols. (Chatto and Windus).

Ouida's last novel, 'A Village Commune,' led her readers to hope that she was improving a little. It was full of absurdities no doubt, but as far as we remember it was decent. Almost to the end of the second volume we had hopes that 'In Maremma' was going to show a further advance. It was certainly dull, and sentimental with a false sentiment, besides having apparently been compiled with the aid of popular treatises, not thoroughly digested on Etruscan tombs and on the natural history of the district in which the scene is laid, together with the never-failing Lemprière. Also there was apparent once or twice a disposition "to trench more than needs on the nauseous" in reference to the physical changes which follow death. Still, on the whole this story, too, was so far decent. The heroine, in whom the author seems to have had inklings of a rather noble nature, that make the ultimate development of the story more repulsive, is an untaught girl, daughter, though she knows it not, of a famous brigand. Brought up by a good old woman in a village of the Sienese Maremma, she goes at her foster-mother's death to take up her abode in an old Etruscan tomb which she has accidentally discovered in her solitary rambles. This is literally the whole business of the first volume. It is eked out with sentimental regrets over the brigand (who is compared favourably with what the author is pleased to call the Barabbi of commerce), and with the doubtful natural history and antiquarianism before mentioned. We call them doubtful because, though the author may give the Latin names (with more or less approximation to correct spelling) of plants and birds or talk learnedly about Lucumonies and Jupiter Elicius, not forgetting, as in private duty bound, the god of the gardens, it is not possible to regard her as a safe guide or original observer so long as she calls a bird of which the prevailing colour is black "the silver-plumaged guillemot," and turns the "fatidica Manto" of Virgil into "Mantus, that grim god of the land of shades." Such as it is, however, this sort of stuff is harmless, but it cannot last for ever. In the middle of the second volume the hero turns up. He is an escaped convict, a comrade of the regretted Saturnino, who by the way, has himself run away and been saved from the sea by his own daughter. The noble robber, after carrying off the gold ornaments from the tomb, informs his "pal" of the hiding-place generously hinting that "a fawn's throat is soon slit." But Count Luitbrand d'Este (such a likely name for a modern Italian!), for he is no murderer, albeit sentenced for a murder which the author says he had not committed, but only a profligate and selfish scoundrel. So in course of time, taking advantage, as far as the reader can make out, of a moment when the poor girl, having been wrecked in her boat, is temporarily weak both in mind and body, he repays her care of him as might be expected. When his innocence of the crime for which he was sentenced is, much to the reader's regret, made clear—chiefly through the exertions of a man who would have honourably loved the girl whom the count has ruined—Este, it needs hardly be said, deserts her. After various mishaps, she follows him to Rome, just in time to save him from the dagger of the brigand her father (for once to be used in a good cause); and when she finds that he is consorting with another woman, she goes back to her tomb and commits suicide. Such is the brief outline of a tale which few readers, we think, will lay down without an unpleasant taste in their mouths. There are cruelty and lust enough in it to satisfy one of Juvenal's ladies. It is ridiculous to pretend that this kind of thing is what is called holding up the mirror to vice; rather it is a picture of the world seen through the distorting medium of a distempered imagination, which either has ceased, or affects to have ceased, to believe in an essential difference between right and wrong, or in the ultimate ascendancy of the better side of human nature.

"In Maremma," by the Author of "Moths."
Chicago Daily Tribune, 29 April 1882: 9

We doubt much whether "Ouida's" prolific pen has ever given to the world a better proof of its unrivalled facility in the delineation of Italian life and Italian character than in this volume, fresh from Lippincott's press and the latest addition to Mme. de [Ramé's] writings. "In Maremma" is a thrilling, heart-moving story, comparatively free from the faults so conspicuous in many of this writer's other works, and not devoted to a wholesale uncovering of vice in order to contrast it with virtue. If it is not a book fitted for the shelves of a Sunday-school library, neither is it a volume devoted to insulting morality. It is written in a different vein from "Moths" or "Strathmore." None but a strong heart can read the pathetic tale of Musa's life without feeling the most intense sympathy for this child of nature chosen as the heroine. If in the end she falls, she herself makes prompt retribution. "Ouida" is a brilliant novelist. She understands thoroughly how to play upon the chords of the human heart. She moves to tears, rouses the fire of indignation, turns to ridicule at will. And in this volume she is at her best. "In Maremma" is an entertaining novel. Its scenes and characters are taken from life, and the reader who turns the first few pages will regret that the book should end when and as it does. It is to a certain extent sensational and in tone not altogether wholesome. But it is so far an advance toward a higher plane of morality on the part of this writer that it is justly entitled to words of praise. Brilliant and talented "Ouida" always has been. That her pen has too often been dipped in immorality and made to serve a bad cause is a matter of regret.

"Recent Novels", *The Times* (London), 14 April 14 1882: 3

"In Maremma" is the most powerful novel that "Ouida" has lately written; nor is there anything in it to which the fastidious moralist need take exception, although an unsophisticated maiden whose innocence is childlike is betrayed into a connexion unsanctified by the Church. The faults of the story are that the most exciting and dramatic of the situations are chiefly in the opening chapters; that, consequently, the interest inclines to flag as we get involved in a love affair which drags rather languidly; and that the description of the Maremma scenery with frequent iteration becomes monotonous and almost wearisome. But in the first volume, and in the first freshness of their novelty, these eloquent descriptions are as impressive as they are sombre. We are introduced through the succession of seasons to that fever-stricken country, which is given over through half the year to death, and through the whole of it to desolation, though nature is often most treacherously beautiful. We might have dispensed with much of "Ouida's" parade of botanical learning; yet we can forgive it for her admirably spirited painting. We look across the Maremma, when the long-brooding storm has burst, with "the white straight rain, the slanting wind-blown showers, the blackness of hurrying, storm-charged cloud, the strange yellow light that made the leaves look like foliage cast in copper and the skies like a vault of brass, the ominous shriek and hiss of the wind that made the slow buffaloes gallop fast with fear, and filled the air with the hurrying wings of passing birds." We see the lonely heroine, become a keen, practical naturalist, through her sympathy with all the wild creatures about her, watching the passages, the arrival and departure of the migrants; seeing that "triangle of silvery grey" overhead as the storks took their flight from Northern Europe to Africa; or half sadly welcoming the descents of the plovers or the cranes that would tempt the mercenary bird-snarers to risk the malaria.

The story of this solitary heroine is a strange one, yet not very unnatural even in this 19th century, considering her circumstances and surroundings. [A long plot summary follows.] We do not know that we can say anything more strongly in favour of the story than that it has awakened in us a lively desire to revisit solitudes which we have always associated with sport and gloom, more especially now that heroes as Saturnino Mastarna are no longer to be met with save in the pages of novels.